# *American Empire:*
# *The Victorious*
# *Opposition*

# HARRY TURTLEDOVE

AMERICAN EMPIRE:
## THE VICTORIOUS OPPOSITION

BALLANTINE BOOKS
NEW YORK

A Del Rey® Book
Published by The Random House Publishing Group

ISBN 0-345-44423-X
Manufactured in the United States of America

**Manicheism,** *n.,* The ancient Persian doctrine of an incessant warfare between Good and Evil. When Good gave up the fight the Persians joined the victorious Opposition.
—Ambrose Bierce, *The Devil's Dictionary*

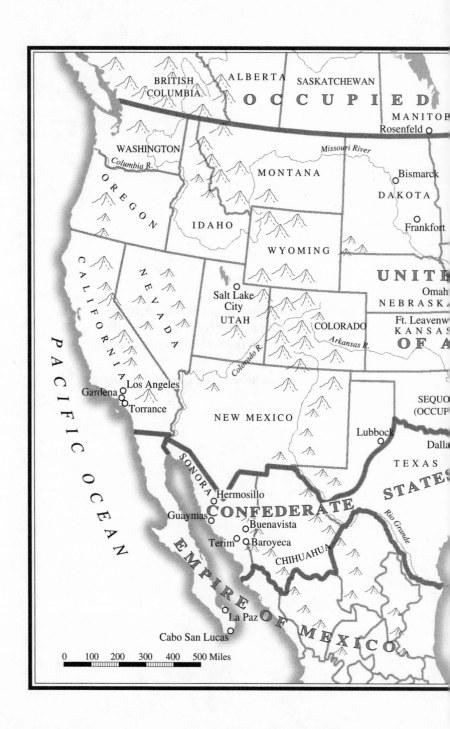

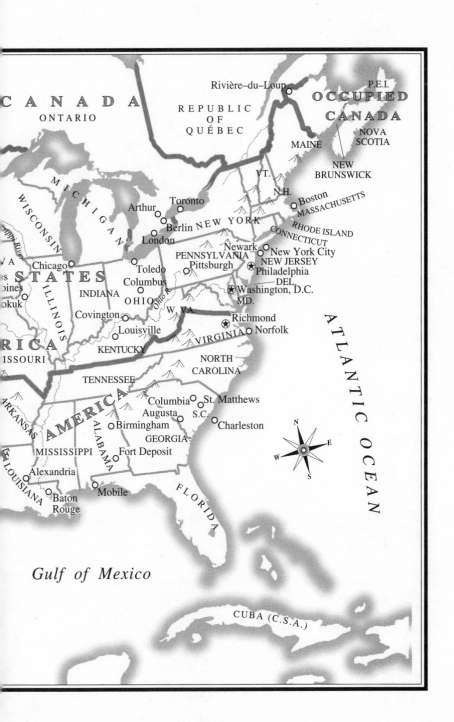

# *American Empire: The Victorious Opposition*

# I

Clarence Potter walked through the streets of Charleston, South Carolina, like a man caught in a city occupied by the enemy. That was exactly how he felt. It was March 5, 1934—a Monday. The day before, Jake Featherston of the Freedom Party had taken the oath of office as president of the Confederate States of America.

"I've known that son of a bitch was a son of a bitch longer than anybody," Potter muttered. He was a tall, well-made man in his late forties, whose spectacles made him look milder than he really was. Behind those lenses—these days, to his disgust, bifocals—his gray eyes were hard and cold and watchful.

He'd first met Featherston when they both served in the Army of Northern Virginia, himself as an intelligence officer and the future president of the CSA as an artillery sergeant in the First Richmond Howitzers. He'd seen even then that Featherston was an angry, embittered man.

Jake had had plenty to be bitter about, too; his service rated promotion to officer's rank, but he hadn't got it. He'd been right in saying his superior, Captain Jeb Stuart III, had had a Negro body servant who was also a Red rebel. After the revolt broke out, Stuart had let himself be killed in battle rather than face a court-martial for protecting the black man. His father, General Jeb Stuart, Jr., was a power in the War Department. He'd made sure Featherston never saw a promotion for the rest of the war.

*You got your revenge on him,* Potter thought, *and now he's getting his—on the whole country.*

He turned the corner onto Montague Street, a boulevard of expensive shops. A lot of them had flags flying to celebrate yesterday's inauguration. Most of those that did flew not only the Stars and Bars but also the Freedom Party flag, a Confederate battle flag with colors reversed: a star-belted red St. Andrew's cross on a blue field. Few people wanted to risk the Party's wrath. Freedom Party stalwarts had broken plenty of heads in their fifteen-year drive to power. What would they do now that they had it?

The fellow who ran Donovan's Luggage—presumably Donovan—was finding out the hard way. He stood on the sidewalk, arguing with a couple of beefy young men in white shirts and butternut trousers: Party stalwarts, sure enough.

"What's the matter with you, you sack of shit?" one of them yelled. "Don't you love your country?"

"I can show how I love it any way I please," Donovan answered. That took guts, since he was small and skinny and close to sixty, and faced two men half his age, each carrying a long, stout bludgeon.

One of them brandished his club. "You don't show it the right way, we'll knock your teeth down your stinking throat."

A gray-uniformed policeman strolled up the street. "Officer!" the man from the luggage shop called, holding out his hands in appeal.

But he got no help from the cop. The fellow wore an enamelwork Party flag pin on his left lapel. He nodded to the stalwarts, said, "Freedom!" and went on his way.

"You see, you dumb bastard?" said the stalwart with the upraised club. "This is how things are. You better go along, or you'll be real sorry. Now, are you gonna buy yourself a flag and put it up, or are you gonna be real sorry?"

Clarence Potter trotted across Montague Street, dodging past a couple of Fords from the United States and a Confederate-built Birmingham. "Why don't you boys pick on somebody your own size?" he said pleasantly, stowing his glasses in the inside pocket of his tweed jacket. He'd had a couple of pairs broken in brawls before the election. He didn't want to lose another.

The stalwarts stared as if he'd flown down from Mars. Finally, one of them said, "Why don't you keep your nose out of other people's business, buddy? You won't get it busted that way."

In normal times, in civilized times, a swarm of people would have gathered to back Potter against the ruffians. But they were ruffians whose party had just won the election. He stood alone with Donovan. Other men on the street hurried by with heads down and eyes averted. Whatever happened, they wanted no part of it.

When Potter showed no sign of disappearing, the second ruffian raised his club, too. "All right, asshole, you asked for it, and I'm gonna give it to you," he said.

He and his friend were bruisers. Potter didn't doubt they were brave enough. During the presidential campaign, they'd have tangled with tougher foes than an aging man who ran a luggage store. But they knew only what bruisers knew. They weren't old enough to have fought in the war.

He had. He'd learned from experts. Without warning, without tipping off what he was going to do by glance or waste motion, he lashed out and kicked the closer one in the crotch. The other one shouted and swung his bludgeon. It hissed over Potter's head. He hit the stalwart in the pit of the stomach. Wind knocked out of him, the man folded up like his friend. The only difference was, he clutched a different part of himself.

Potter didn't believe in wasting a fair fight on Freedom Party men. They wouldn't have done it for him. He kicked each of them in the face. One still had a little fight left, and tried to grab his leg. He stomped on the fellow's hand. Finger bones crunched under his sole. The stalwart howled like a wolf. Potter kicked him in the face again, for good measure.

Then he picked up his fedora, which had fallen off in the fight, and put it back on his head. He took his spectacles out of the inside pocket. The world regained sharp edges when he set them on his nose again.

He tipped the fedora to Donovan, who stared at him out of enormous eyes. "You ought to sweep this garbage into the gutter," he said, pointing to the Freedom Party men. The one he'd kicked twice lay still. His nose would never be the same. The other one writhed and moaned and held on to himself in a way that would have been obscene if it weren't so obviously filled with pain.

"Who the dickens are you?" Donovan had to try twice before any words came out.

"You don't need to know that." Serving in Intelligence had taught Potter not to say more than he had to. You never could tell when opening your big mouth would come back to haunt you. Working as a private investigator, which he'd done since the war, only drove the lesson home.

"But . . ." The older man still gaped. "You handled them punks like they was nothing."

"They *are* nothing, the worst kind of nothing." Potter touched the brim of his hat again. "See you." He walked off at a brisk pace. That cop was liable to come back. Even if he didn't, more stalwarts might come along. A lot of them carried pistols. Potter had one, too, but he didn't want anything to do with a shootout. You couldn't hope to outsmart a bullet.

He turned several corners in quick succession, going right or left at random. After five minutes or so, he decided he was out of trouble and slowed down to look around and see where he was. Going a few blocks had taken him several rungs down the social ladder. This was a neighborhood of saloons and secondhand shops, of grocery stores with torn screen doors and blocks of flats that had been nice places back around the turn of the century.

It was also a neighborhood where Freedom Party flags flew without urging or coercion from anybody. This was the sort of neighborhood stalwarts came from; the Party offered them an escape from the despair and uselessness that might otherwise eat their lives. It was, in Clarence Potter's considered opinion, a neighborhood full of damn fools.

He left in a hurry, making his way east toward the harbor. He was supposed to meet a police detective there; the fellow had news about warehouse pilferage he would pass on—for a price. Potter had also fed him a thing or two over the years; such balances, useful to both sides, had a way of evening out.

"Clarence!" The shout made Potter stop and turn back.

"Jack Delamotte!" he exclaimed in pleasure all the greater for being so unexpected. "How are you? I haven't seen you in years. I wondered if you were dead. What have you been doing with yourself?"

Delamotte hurried up the street toward him, his hand outstretched and a broad smile on his face. He was a big, blond, good-looking man of about Potter's age. His belly was bigger now, and his hair grayer and thinner at the temples than it had been when he and Potter hung around together. "Not too much," he answered. "I'm in the textile business these days. Got married six years ago—no, seven now. Betsy and I have a boy and a girl. How about you?"

"Still single," Potter said with a shrug. "Still poking my nose into other people's affairs—sometimes literally. I don't change a whole lot. If you're . . ." His voice trailed off. Delamotte wore a handsome checked suit. On his left lapel, a Freedom Party pin shone in the sunlight. "I didn't expect you of all people to go over to the other side, Jack. You used to cuss out Jake Featherston just as much as I did."

"If you don't bend with the breeze, it'll break you." Delamotte shrugged, too. "They've been coming up for a long time, and now they're in. Shall I pretend the Whigs won the election?" He snorted. "Not likely!"

Put that way, it sounded reasonable enough. Potter said, "I just saw a couple of Freedom Party stalwarts getting ready to beat up a shopkeeper because he didn't want to fly their flag. How do you like that?" He kept quiet about what he'd done to the stalwarts.

"Can't make an omelette without breaking eggs," Delamotte answered. "I really do think they'll put us back on our feet. Nobody else will. . . . Where are you going? I want to get your address, talk about old times."

"I'm in the phone book," said Potter, who wasn't. "Sorry, Jack. I'm late." He hurried away, hoping Delamotte wouldn't trot after him. To his vast relief, the other man didn't. Clarence wanted to puke. His friend—no, his former friend—no doubt thought of himself as a practical man. Potter thought of him, and of all the other "practical" men sucking up to Featherston's pals now that they were in power, as a pack of sons of bitches.

He met the detective in a harborside saloon where sailors with a dozen different accents got drunk as fast as they could. Caldwell Tubbs was a roly-poly little man with the coldest black eyes Potter had ever seen. "Jesus Christ, I shouldn't even be here," he said when Potter sat down on a stool beside him. "I can't tell you nothin'. Worth my ass if I do."

He'd sung that song before. Potter showed him some brown banknotes—cautiously, so nobody else saw them. "I can be persuasive," he murmured, as if trying to seduce a pretty girl and not an ugly cop.

But Tubbs shook his head. "Not even for that."

"What?" Now Potter was genuinely astonished. "Why not, goddammit?"

"On account of it's worth my badge if I even get caught talkin' to you, that's why. This is good-bye, buddy, and I mean it. You try to get hold of me from now on, I never heard of you. You're on a list, Potter, and it's the shit list. I were you, I'd cut my throat now, save everybody else the trouble." He jammed his hat back onto his bald head and waddled out of the saloon.

Clarence Potter stared after him. He knew the Freedom Party knew how hard he'd fought it, and for how long. And he knew the Party was taking its revenge on opponents. But he'd never expected it to be so fast, or so thorough. He ordered a whiskey, wondering how he'd crack that pilferage case now.


After a lifetime of living in Toledo, Chester Martin remained disbelieving despite several months in Los Angeles. It wasn't just the weather, though that helped a lot. He and Rita had gone through a winter without snow. They'd gone through a winter where they hardly ever needed anything heavier than a sweater, and where they'd stayed in shirtsleeves half the time.

But that was only part of it. Toledo was what it was. It had been what it was for all of Chester's forty-odd years, and for fifteen or twenty years before that. It would go right on being the same old thing, too.

Not Los Angeles. This place was in a constant process of *becoming*. Before the war, it hadn't been anything much. But a new aqueduct and the rise of motion pictures and a good port had brought people flooding in. The people who worked in the cinema and at the port and in the factories the aqueduct permitted needed places to live and people to sell them things. More people came in to build them houses and sell them groceries and autos and bookcases and washing machines. Then *they* needed . . .

Chester had to walk close to half a mile to get to the nearest trolley stop. He didn't like that, though it was less inconvenient here than it would have been in a Toledo blizzard. He could see why things worked as they did, though. Los Angeles *sprawled* in a way no Eastern city did. The trolley grid had to be either coarse or enormously expensive. Nobody seemed willing to pay for a tight grid, so people made do with a coarse one.

A mockingbird sang up in a palm tree. Martin blew a smoke ring at it. It flew away, white wing bars flashing. A jay on a rooftop jeered. It wasn't a blue jay like the ones he'd always known; it had no crest, and its feathers were a paler blue. People called the birds scrub jays. They were as curious and clever as any jays he'd known back East. A hummingbird with a bright red head hung in midair, scolding the jay: *chip-chip-chip.* Hummingbirds lived here all year round. If that didn't make a place seem tropical, what did?

Hurrying on toward the trolley stop, Martin ground out the cigarette with his shoe. A motion caught from the corner of his eye made him turn his head and look back over his shoulder. A man in filthy, shabby clothes had darted out from a doorway to cadge the butt. Things might be better here than they were a lot of places, but that didn't make them perfect, or even very good.

Some of the eight or ten people waiting at the trolley stop were going to work. Some were looking for work. Chester didn't know how he could tell who was who, but he thought he could. A couple, like him, carried tool chests. The others? Something in the way they stood, something in their eyes . . . He knew how an unemployed man stood. He'd spent months out of work after the steel mill let him go, and he was one of the lucky ones. More than a few people had been looking for a job since 1929.

The trolley clanged up. It was painted a sunny yellow, unlike the dull green ones he'd ridden in Toledo. By the way they looked, they might almost have been Army issue. Not this one. When you got on an L.A. trolley, you felt you were going in style. His nickel and two pennies rattled into the fare box. "Transfer, please," he said, and the trolleyman gave him a long, narrow strip of paper with printing on it. He stuck it in the breast pocket of his overalls.

He rode the trolley south down Central to Mahan Avenue, then used the transfer to board another for the trip west to a suburb called Gardena. Like a lot of Los Angeles suburbs, it was half a farming town. Fig orchards and plots of strawberries and the inevitable orange trees alternated with blocks of houses. He got off at Western, then went south to 147th Street on shank's mare.

Houses were going up there, in what had been a fig orchard. The fig trees had been knocked down in a tearing hurry. Chester suspected more than a few of them would come up again, and their roots would get into pipes and keep plumbers away from soup kitchens for years to come. That wasn't his worry. Getting the houses up was.

He waved to his foreman. "Morning, Mordechai."

"Morning, Chester." The foreman waved back. It was an odd wave; he'd lost a couple of fingers from his right hand in a childhood farm accident. But he could do more with tools with three fingers than most men could with five. He'd spent years in the Navy before returning to the civilian world. He had to be close to sixty now, but he had the vigor of a much younger man.

"Hey, Joe. Morning, Fred. What's up, José? How are you, Virgil?" Martin nodded to the other builders, who were just getting started on the day's work.

"How's it going, Chester?" Fred said, and then, "Look out—here comes Dushan. Get busy quick, so he can't suck you into a card game."

"What do you say, Dushan?" Chester called.

Dushan nodded back. "How you is?" he said in throatily accented English. He came from some Slavic corner of the Austro-Hungarian Empire; his last name consisted almost entirely of consonants. And Fred's warning was the straight goods. Dushan made only a so-so builder (he liked the sauce more than he might have, and didn't bother keeping it a secret), but what he couldn't persuade a deck of cards to do, nobody could. Chester would have bet he picked up more money gambling than he did with a hammer and saw and screwdriver.

"Come on, boys. Enough jibber-jabber," Mordechai said. "Time to earn what they pay us."

He wasn't the kind of foreman who sat on his hind end drinking coffee and yelling at people who did stuff he didn't like. He worked as hard as any of the men he bossed—probably harder. If you couldn't work for Mordechai, you probably couldn't work for anybody.

Nailing rafters to the ridgepole, Chester turned to José, who was doing the same thing on the other side. "You know what Mordechai reminds me of?" he said.

"Tell me," José said. His English was only a little better than Dushan's. He'd been born in Baja California, down in the Empire of Mexico, and had come north looking for work sometime in the 1920s.

Chester didn't know whether he'd bothered with legal formalities. Either way, he'd managed to keep eating after things fell apart in '29.

"You fight in the war?" Martin asked him.

"Oh, *sí*," he answered, and laughed a little. "Not on the same side as you, I don't think."

"Doesn't matter, not for this. Had to be the same on both sides. If you had a good lieutenant or captain, one who said, 'Follow me!'—hell, you could do damn near anything. If you had the other kind . . ." Martin jabbed his right thumb down toward the ground. "Mordechai's like one of those good officers. He works like a son of a bitch himself, and you don't want to let him down."

The other builder thought about that for a little while, then nodded. *"Es verdad,"* he said, and then, "You right." He laughed again. "And now we talk, and we don't do no work."

"Nobody works *all* the damn time," Chester said, but he started driving nails again. It wasn't just that he didn't want to let Mordechai down. He didn't want to get in trouble, either. Plenty of men wanted the job he had. He was every bit as much a part of the urban proletariat here as he had been at the steel mill back in Toledo.

After a couple of nails went in, he shook his head. He was more a part of the proletariat here than he had been in Toledo. The steel mill was a union shop; he'd been part of the bloody strikes after the war that made it one. No such thing as a construction union here. If the bosses didn't like anything about you, you were history. Ancient history.

*We ought to do something about that,* he thought, and suddenly regretted voting Democratic instead of Socialist in the last election. He held the next nail to the board, tapped it two or three times to seat it firmly, and drove it home. Another election was coming up in a little more than six months. He could always go back to the Socialists.

Rita had packed him a ham sandwich, some homemade oatmeal cookies, and an apple in his dinner pail. Sure as hell, Dushan riffled a deck of cards at lunch. Sure as hell, he found some suckers to play against him. Chester shook his head when Dushan looked his way. He knew when he was fighting out of his weight. Two lessons had been plenty for him. If he'd had any real sense, one should have done the job.

"Back to it," Mordechai said after a precise half hour. Again, he was the first one going up a ladder.

At the end of the day, all the workers from the whole tract lined up to get their pay in cash. A fellow with a .45 stood behind the paymaster's table to discourage redistribution of the wealth. The paymaster handed Chester four heavy silver dollars. They gave his overalls a nice, solid weight when he stuck them in his pocket. Cartwheels were in much more common use out here than they had been back East.

He walked to the trolley stop, paid his fare and collected a transfer, and made the return trip to the little house he and Rita were renting east of downtown. The neighborhood was full of Eastern European Jews, with a few Mexicans like José for leavening.

On his way back to the house, a skinny fellow about his age wearing an old green-gray Army trenchcoat coming apart at the seams held out a dirty hand and said, "Spare a dime, pal?"

Chester had rarely done that before losing his own job in Toledo. Now he understood how the other half lived. And, now that he was working again, he had dimes in his pocket he could actually spare. "Here you go, buddy," he said, and gave the skinny man one. "You know carpentry? They're hiring builders down in Gardena."

"I can drive a nail. I can saw a board," the other fellow answered.

"I couldn't do much more than that when I started," Martin answered.

"Maybe I'll get down there," the skinny man said.

"Good luck." Chester went on his way. He'd keep his eye open the next couple of days, see if this fellow showed up and tried to land a job. If he didn't, Martin was damned if he'd give him another handout. Plenty of people were down on their luck, yes. But if you didn't *try* to get back on your feet, you were holding yourself down, too.

"Hello, sweetheart!" Chester called. "What smells good?"

"Pot roast," Rita answered. She came out of the kitchen to give him a kiss. She was a pretty brunette—prettier these days, Chester thought, because she'd quit bobbing her hair and let it grow out—who carried a few extra pounds around the hips. She went on, "Sure is good to be able to afford meat more often."

"I know." Chester put a hand in his pocket. The silver dollars and his other change clanked sweetly. "We'll be able to send my father another money order before long." Stephen Douglas Martin had lent Chester and Rita the money to come to California, even though he'd lost his job at the steel mill, too. Chester was paying him back a little at a time. It wasn't a patch on all the help his father had given him when he was out of work, but it was what he could do.

"One day at a time," Rita said, and Chester nodded.

"**R**ichmond!" the conductor bawled as the train pulled into the station. "All out for Richmond! Capital of the Confederate States of America, and next home of the Olympic Games! *Richmond!*"

Anne Colleton grabbed a carpetbag and a small light suitcase from the rack above the seats. She was set for the three days she expected to be here. Once upon a time, she'd traveled in style, with enough luggage to keep an army in clothes (provided it wanted to wear the latest Paris styles) and with a couple of colored maids to keep everything straight.

No more, not after one of those colored maids had come unpleasantly close to murdering her on the Marshlands plantation. These days, with Marshlands still a ruin down by St. Matthews, South Carolina, Anne traveled alone.

*On the train, and through life,* she thought. Aloud, the way she said, "Excuse me," couldn't mean anything but, *Get the hell out of my way.* That would have done well enough for her motto. She was a tall, blond woman with a man's determined stride. If any gray streaked the yellow— she was, after all, nearer fifty than forty—the peroxide bottle didn't let it show. She looked younger than her years, but not enough to suit her. In her twenties, even in her thirties, she'd been strikingly beautiful, and made the most of it. Now *handsome* would have fit her better, except she despised that word when applied to a woman.

"Excuse me," she said again, and all but walked up the back of a man who, by his clothes, was a drummer who hadn't drummed up much lately. He turned and gave her a dirty look. The answering frozen contempt she aimed like an arrow from her blue eyes made him look away in a hurry, muttering to himself and shaking his head.

Most of the passengers had to go back to the baggage car to reclaim their suitcases. Anne had all her chattels with her. She hurried out of the station to the cab stand in front of it. "Ford's Hotel," she told the driver whose auto, a Birmingham with a dented left fender, was first in line at the stand.

"Yes, ma'am," he said, touching a finger to the patent-leather brim of his peaked cap. "Let me put your bags in the trunk, and we'll go."

Ford's Hotel was a great white pile of a building, just across Capitol Street from Capitol Square. Anne tried to figure out how many times she'd stayed there. She couldn't; she only knew the number was large. "Afternoon, ma'am," said the colored doorman. He wore a uniform gaudier and more magnificent than any the War Department issued.

Anne checked in, went to her room, and unpacked. She went downstairs and had an early supper—Virginia ham and applesauce and fried potatoes, with pecan pie for dessert—then returned to her room, read a novel till she got sleepy (it wasn't very good, so she got sleepy fast), and went to bed. It was earlier than she would have fallen asleep back home. That meant she woke up at half past five the next morning. She was annoyed, but not too annoyed: it gave her a chance to bathe and to get her hair the way she wanted it before going down to breakfast.

After breakfast, she went to the lobby, picked up one of the papers on a table, and settled down to read it. She hadn't been reading long before a man in what was almost but not quite Confederate uniform strode in. Anne put down the newspaper and got to her feet.

"Miss Colleton?" asked the man in the butternut uniform.

She nodded. "That's right."

"Freedom!" the man said, and then, "Come with me, please."

When they went out the door, the doorman—a different Negro from the one who'd been there the day before, but wearing identical fancy dress—flinched away from the Freedom Party man in the plain tan outfit. The Party man, smiling a little, led Anne to a waiting motorcar. He almost forgot to hold the door open for her, but remembered at the last minute. Then he slid in behind the wheel and drove off.

The Gray House—U.S. papers still sometimes called it the Confederate White House—lay near the top of Shockoe Hill, north and east of Capitol Square. The grounds were full of men in butternut uniforms or white shirts and butternut trousers: Freedom Party guards and stalwarts. Anne supposed there were also some official Confederate guards, but she didn't see any.

"This here's Miss Colleton," her driver said when they went inside.

A receptionist—male, uniformed—checked her name off a list. "She's scheduled to see the president at nine. Why don't you take her straight to the waiting room? It's only half an hour."

"Right," the Freedom Party guard said. "Come this way, ma'am."

"I know the way to the waiting room. I've been here before." Anne wished she didn't have to try to impress a man of no particular importance. She also wished that, since she had tried to impress him, she would have succeeded. But his dour shrug said he didn't care whether she'd lived here up till day before yesterday. Freedom Party men could be daunting in their singlemindedness.

She had the room outside the president's office to herself. *Too bad,* she thought; she'd met some interesting people there. A few minutes before nine, the door to the office opened. A skinny little Jewish-looking fellow came out. Jake Featherston's voice pursued him: "You'll make sure we get that story out our way, right, Saul?"

"Of course, Mr. Feath—uh, Mr. President," the man answered. "We'll take care of it. Don't you worry about a thing."

"With you in charge, I don't," Featherston answered.

The man tipped his straw hat to Anne as he walked out. "Go on in," he told her. "You're next."

"Thanks," Anne said, and did. Seeing Jake Featherston behind a desk that had had only Whigs sitting at it up till now was a jolt. She stuck out her hand, man-fashion. "Congratulations, Mr. President."

Featherston shook hands with her, a single brisk pump, enough to show he had strength he wasn't using. "Thank you kindly, Miss Colleton," he answered. Almost everyone in the CSA knew his voice from the wireless and newsreels. It packed extra punch in person, even with just a handful of words. He pointed to a chair. "Sit down. Make yourself at home."

Anne did sit, and crossed her ankles. Her figure was still trim. Featherston's eyes went to her legs, but only for a moment. He wasn't a skirt-chaser. He'd chased power instead of women. Now he had it. Along with the rest of the country, she wondered what he'd do with it.

"I expect you want to know why I asked you to come up here," he said, a lopsided grin on his long, rawboned face. He wasn't handsome, not in any ordinary sense of the word, but the fire burning inside him showed plainly enough. If he'd wanted women, he could have had droves of them.

Anne nodded. "I do, yes. But I'll find out, won't I? I don't think you'll send me back to South Carolina without telling me."

"Nope. Matter of fact, I don't intend to send you back to South Carolina at all," Featherston said.

"What . . . do you intend to do with me, then?" Anne almost said, to me. Once upon a time, she'd imagined she could control him, dominate him, serve as a puppet master while he danced to her tune. A lot of people had made the same mistake: a small consolation, but the only one she had. Now he was the one who held the strings, who held all the strings in the Confederate States. Anne hated moving to any will but her own. She hated it, but she saw no way around it.

She tried not to show the nasty little stab of fear that shot through her. She'd abandoned the Freedom Party once, when its hopes were at a low ebb. If Jake Featherston wanted revenge, he could take it.

His smile got wider, which meant she hadn't hidden that nasty little stab well enough. He did take revenge. He took it on everyone who he thought had ever wronged him. He took pride and pleasure in taking it, too. But, after he let her sweat for a few seconds, what he said was, *"Parlez-vous français?"*

*"Oui. Certainement,"* Anne answered automatically, even though, by the way Featherston pronounced the words, he didn't speak French himself. She returned to English to ask, "Why do you want to know that?"

"How would you like to take a trip to gay Paree?" Featherston asked in return. No, he didn't speak French at all. She hadn't thought he did. He wasn't an educated man. Shrewd? Yes. Clever? Oh, yes. Educated? No.

"Paris? I hate the idea," Anne said crisply.

Featherston's gingery eyebrows leaped. That wasn't the answer he'd expected. Then he realized she was joking. He barked laughter. "Cute," he said. "Cute as hell. Now tell me straight—will you go to Paris for me? I've got a job that needs doing, and you're the one I can think of who's best suited to do it."

"Tell me what it is," she said. "And tell me why. You're not naming me ambassador to the court of King Charles XI, I gather."

"No, I'm not doing that. You'll go as a private citizen. But I'd rather trust you with a dicker than the damned striped-pants diplomats at the embassy there. They're nothing but a pack of Whigs, and they want me to fall on my ass. You know what's good for the country, and you know what's good for the Party, too."

"I . . . see." Anne nodded again, slowly and thoughtfully. "You want me to start sounding out *Action Française* about an alliance, then?"

She saw she'd surprised him again. Then he laughed once more. "I already knew you were smart," he said. "Don't know why I ought to jump when you go and show me. Yeah, that's pretty much what I've got in mind. *Alliance* likely goes too far. *Working arrangement* is more what I figure we can do. Probably all the froggies can do, too. They've got to worry about the Kaiser same way as we've got to worry about the USA."

"I won't be bringing back a treaty or anything of the sort, will I?" Anne said. "This is all unofficial?"

"Unofficial as can be," Featherston agreed. "There's a time to shout and yell and carry on, and there's a time to keep quiet. This here is one of those last times. No point to getting the United States all hot and bothered, not as far as I can tell. So will you take care of this for me?"

Anne nodded. "Yes. I'd be glad to. I haven't been to Europe since before the war, and I'd love to go again. And this has one more advantage for you, doesn't it?"

"What's that?" the president asked.

"Why, it gets me out of the country for a while," Anne answered.

"Yes. I don't mind that. I'm not ashamed to admit it to you, either," Jake Featherston said. "I will be damned if I know what to make of you, or what I ought to do about you." Again, he sounded as if he meant, *what I ought to do to you.* "If you can do something that's useful to the country, and do it where you can't get into much mischief, that works out fine for me. Works out fine for both of us, as a matter of fact."

Again, Anne read between the lines: *if you're on the other side of the*

*Atlantic, I don't have to wonder about whether I ought to dispose of you.* "Fair enough," she said. All things considered, going into what wasn't quite exile was as much as she could have hoped for. One thing Featherston had never learned was how to forgive.

Colonel Irving Morrell watched from the turret of the experimental model as barrels chewed hell out of the Kansas prairie. Fortunately, Fort Leavenworth had a lot of prairie on its grounds to chew up. Once upon a time, it had occurred to Morrell that the traveling forts might find it useful to make their own smoke: that way, enemy gunners would have a harder time spotting them. When they traveled over dry ground, though, barrels kicked up enough dust to make the question of smoke moot.

Most of these barrels were the slow, lumbering brutes that had finally forced breakthroughs in the Confederate lines during the Great War. They moved at not much above a walking pace, they had a crew of eighteen, they had cannon at the front rather than inside a revolving turret, the bellowing engines were in the same compartment as the crew—and they had other disadvantages as well. The only advantage they had was that they existed. Crews could learn how to handle a barrel by getting inside them.

The experimental model had been a world-beater when Morrell designed it early in the 1920s. Rotating turret, separate engine compartment, wireless set, reduced crew . . . In 1922, no other barrel in the world touched this design.

But it wasn't 1922 any more. The design was a dozen years older now. So was Irving Morrell. He didn't show his years very much. He was still lean and strong in his early forties, and his close-cropped, light brown hair held only a few threads of gray. If his face was lined and tanned and weathered . . . well, it had been lined and tanned and weathered in the early 1920s, too. Hard service and a love for the outdoors had taken their toll there.

A Model T Ford in military green-gray bounced across the prairie toward the experimental model. One of the soldiers inside the motorcar waved to Morrell. When he waved back, showing he'd seen, the man held up a hand to get him to stop.

He waved again, then ducked down into the turret. "Stop!" he bawled into the speaking tube that led to the driver's seat at the front of the barrel. "Stopping, yes, sir." The answer was tinny but understandable. The barrel clanked to a halt.

"What's up, sir?" Sergeant Michael Pound, the barrel's gunner, was insatiably curious—more than was good for him, Morrell often thought.

His wide face might have been that of a three-year-old seeing his first aeroplane.

"I don't know," Morrell answered. "They've just sent out an auto to stop the maneuvers."

Sergeant Pound's wide shoulders moved up and down in a shrug. "Maybe the powers that be have gone off the deep end. Wouldn't surprise me a bit." Spending his whole adult life in the Army had left him endlessly cynical—not that he didn't seem to have had a good running start beforehand. But then his green-blue eyes widened. "Or do you suppose—?"

That same thought had been in Morrell's mind, too. "It would be sooner than I expected if it is, Sergeant. When was the last time those people up in Pontiac ever turned something out sooner than anyone expected?"

"I'm afraid that's much too good a question, sir." Pound pointed to the hatchway in the top of the commander's cupola. "Pop your head out and see, though, why don't you?" He made *out* sound almost like *oat*, as a Canadian would have; he came from somewhere up near the border. *What used to be the border,* Morrell reminded himself.

No matter what he sounded like, he'd given good advice. Morrell did stand up again in the turret. Any barrel commander worth his salt liked to stick his head out of the machine whenever he could. You could see so much more of the field that way. Of course, everybody on the field could also see you—and shoot at you. During the Great War, Morrell had often been forced back into the hell that was the interior of an old-style barrel by machine-gun fire that would have killed him in moments if he'd kept on looking around.

By the time he did emerge from the experimental model, the old Ford had come up alongside his barrel. The soldier who'd waved to him—a young lieutenant named Walt Cressy—called, "Sir, you might want to take your machine back to the farm."

"Oh? How come?" Morrell asked.

Lieutenant Cressy grinned. "Just because, sir."

That made Morrell grin, too. Maybe they really had been working overtime up in Pontiac. Maybe the combination of war with Japan—not that it was an all-out, no-holds-barred war on either side—and a Democratic administration had got engineers and workers to go at it harder than they were used to doing. "All right, Lieutenant," Morrell said. "I'll do that."

Sergeant Pound whooped with glee when Morrell gave the order to break off from maneuvers and go back to the farm. "It has to be!" he said. "By God, it has to be."

"Nothing *has* to be anything, Sergeant," Morrell said. "If we haven't seen that over the past ten years and more of this business . . ."

That made even Pound nod thoughtfully. Barrels had probably been *the* war-winning weapon during the Great War. After the war, they'd been the weapon most cut by budget trimmers in two successive Socialist administrations. No one had wanted to spend the money to improve them, to give them a chance to be the war-winning weapon of the next war. No one wanted to think there might be another big war. Morrell didn't like contemplating that possibility, either, but not thinking about it wouldn't make it go away.

The experimental model easily outdistanced the leftovers from the Great War, though they carried two truck engines apiece and it had only one. It was made from thin, mild steel, enough to give an idea of how it performed but not enough to stand up to bullets. It had plainly outdone everything else in the arsenal, and by a wide margin, too. For more than ten years, nobody'd given a damn. Now . . .

Now Morrell's heart beat faster. If he was right, if the powers that be were waking up at last . . . Sergeant Michael Pound said, "Maybe seeing Jake Featherston snorting and stomping the ground down in Richmond put the fear of God into some people, too."

"It could be," Morrell said. "I'll tell you something, Sergeant: he sure as hell puts the fear of God into me."

"He's a madman." As usual, everything looked simple to Pound.

"Maybe. If he is, he's a clever one," Morrell said. "And if you put a clever madman in charge of a country that has good reason to hate the United States . . . Well, I don't like the combination."

"If we have to, we'll squash him." Pound was confident, too. Morrell wished he shared that confidence.

Then the experimental model got to the field where the barrels stayed now that they were back in service. Sure enough, a new machine squatted on the track-torn turf. The closer Morrell got, the better it looked. If he'd admired a woman as openly as he ogled that barrel, his wife, Agnes, would have had something sharp to say to him.

He climbed out through the hatch in the cupola and descended from the experimental model before it stopped moving. Sergeant Pound let out a piteous howl from inside the barrel. "Don't eat your heart out, Sergeant," Morrell said. "You can come have a look, too."

He didn't wait for Pound to emerge, though. He hurried over to the new barrel. His leg twinged under him. He'd been shot in the early days of the Great War. He still had a slight limp almost twenty years later. The leg did what he needed, though. If it pained him now and again . . . then it did, that was all.

"Bully," he said softly as he came up to the new barrel. That marked him as an old-fashioned man; people who'd grown up after the Great War commonly said *swell* at such times. He knew exactly what he meant, though. He looked from the new machine to the experimental model and back again. A broad grin found room on his narrow face. It was like seeing a child and the man he had become there side by side.

The experimental model was soft-skinned, thin-skinned. One truck engine powered it, because it wasn't very heavy. The cannon in its turret was a one-pounder, a popgun that couldn't damage anything tougher than a truck.

Here, though, here was the machine of which its predecessor had been the model. Morrell set a hand on its green-gray flank. Armor plate felt no different from mild steel under his palm. He knew the difference was there, though. Up at the bow and on the front of the turret, two inches of hardened steel warded the barrel's vitals. The armor on the sides and back was thinner, but it was there.

A long-barreled two-inch gun jutted from the turret, a machine gun beside it. He knew of no barrel anywhere in the world with a better main armament. The suspension was beefed up. So was the engine at the rear. It was supposed to push this barrel along even faster than the experimental model could do.

Sergeant Pound came up behind him. So did the other crewmen from the experimental model: the loader, the bow machine-gunner, the wireless operator, and the driver. Pound said, "It's quite something, sir. It's a good thing we've got it. It would have been even better if we'd had it ten years ago."

"Yes." Morrell wished the sergeant hadn't pointed that out, no matter how obvious a truth it was. "If we'd built this ten years ago, what would we have now? That's what eats at me."

"I don't blame you a bit, sir," Pound said. "What happened to the barrel program was a shame, a disgrace, and an embarrassment. And if the Japs hadn't gone and embarrassed us, too, it never would have started up again."

"I know." Morrell couldn't wait any more. He climbed up onto the new barrel, opened the hatch at the top of the commander's cupola, and slid down into the turret.

It didn't smell right. He noticed that first. All it smelled of was paint and leather and gasoline: fresh smells, new smells. It might have been a Chevrolet in a showroom. The old machines and the experimental model stank of cordite fumes and sweat, odors Morrell had taken for granted till he found himself in a barrel without them. He sat down in the commander's seat. Before long, this beast would smell the way it was supposed to.

Clankings from up above said somebody else wanted to investigate the new barrel, too. Michael Pound's voice came in through the open hatch: "If you don't get out of the way, I'm going to squash you . . . sir." Morrell moved. Pound slithered down—his stocky frame barely fit through the opening—and settled himself behind the gun. He peered through the sights, then nodded. "Not bad. Not bad at all."

"No, not bad at all," Morrell agreed. "They're going to name the production model after General Custer."

"That's fitting. It's a pity they fiddled around too long to let him see them," Pound said, and Morrell nodded. The gunner asked, "How many are they going to make?"

"I don't know that yet," Morrell answered. "What they think they can afford, I suppose. That's how it usually works." He scowled.

So did Sergeant Pound. "They'd better make lots if they name them after Custer. He believed in great swarms of barrels. Anyone with sense does, of course." Having served with Custer, Morrell knew he'd often been anything but sensible. He also knew Pound meant *anyone who agrees with me* by *anyone with sense*. Even so, he nodded again.


Colonel Abner Dowling opened the *Salt Lake City Bee*. The Army published the paper. It put out what the U.S. authorities occupying Utah wanted the people there to see. As commander of the occupying authorities in Salt Lake City, Dowling knew that did only so much good. The locals got plenty of news the paper didn't print and the town wireless outlets didn't broadcast. Still, if you didn't try to keep a lid on things, what was the point of occupying at all?

On page three was a picture of a very modern-looking barrel—certainly one that seemed ready to blow any number of hulking Great War machines to hell and gone. NEW CUSTER BARREL PUT THROUGH PACES IN KANSAS, the headline read. The story below praised the new model to the skies.

"Custer," Dowling muttered—half prayer, half curse. He'd been Custer's adjutant for a long time—and it had often seemed much longer. Naming a machine intended to smash straight through everything in its path after George Armstrong Custer did seem to fit. Dowling couldn't deny that.

He went through the rest of the paper in a hurry—there wasn't much real news in it, as he had reason to know. Then he pushed his swivel chair back from his desk and strode out of the office. He was a hulking machine himself, and built rather like the desk. Custer had been in the habit of twitting him about his heft. Custer hadn't been skinny himself, but Dowling hadn't lost any weight since they finally forced the old boy into retirement. On the contrary.

*It's good, healthy flesh,* he told himself. Plenty of people had worse vices than getting up from the supper table a little later than they might have. Take Custer, for instance. Dowling's jowls wobbled as he shook his head. He'd escaped Custer more than ten years before, but couldn't get him out of his mind.

*That's how people will remember me a hundred years from now,* he thought, not for the first time. *In biographies of Custer, I'll have half a dozen index entries as his adjutant. Immortality—the tradesman's entrance.*

But that wasn't necessarily so, as he knew too well. People might remember him forever—if Utah blew up in his face. Even back as far as the trouble it caused in the Second Mexican War in the early 1880s, Custer had wanted to lay it waste. Abner Dowling shook his head. *Enough of Custer.*

These days, Dowling had an adjutant of his own, a bright young captain called Isidore Lefkowitz. He looked up from his desk in the outer office as Dowling emerged from his sanctum. "What can I do for you, sir?" he asked, his accent purest New York.

"Mr. Young is due here in ten minutes, isn't that right?" Dowling said.

"Yes, sir, at three o'clock sharp," Lefkowitz replied. "I expect him to be right on time, too. You could set your watch by him."

Dowling's nod also made his chins dance. "Oh, yes." Heber Young was a man of thoroughgoing rectitude. Mischief in his eye, he asked, "How does it feel, Captain, to be a gentile in Utah?"

Captain Lefkowitz rolled his eyes. "I should care what these Mormon *mamzrim* think." He didn't translate the word. Even so, Dowling had no trouble figuring out it was less than complimentary.

He said, "The Mormons are convinced they're persecuted the way Jews used to be in the old days."

"What do you mean, used to be?" Lefkowitz said. "Tsar Michael turned the Black Hundreds loose on us just a couple of years ago. If the peasants and workers go after Jews, they don't have to worry about whether they might have done better throwing out Michael's brother Nicholas and going Red. There are pogroms in the Kingdom of Poland, too."

"People over there use Jews for whipping boys, the same way the Confederates use their Negroes," Dowling said.

Lefkowitz started to answer, stopped, and gave Dowling an odd look. "That's . . . very perceptive, sir," he said, as if Dowling had no business being any such thing. "I never thought I had much in common with a *shvartzer*"—another untranslated word Dowling had little trouble figuring out—"but maybe I was wrong."

Before Dowling could answer, he heard footsteps coming down the hall. A soldier led a tall, handsome man in somber civilian clothes into the outer office. "Here's Heber Young, sir," the man in green-gray said. "He's been searched."

Dowling didn't think Brigham Young's grandson was personally dangerous to him. He didn't think so, but he hadn't rescinded the order that all Mormons be searched before entering U.S. military headquarters. He'd been in the office with General Pershing when the then-commander of occupation forces was assassinated. The sniper had never been caught, either.

Officially, of course, the church of Jesus Christ of Latter-Day Saints remained forbidden in Utah. Officially, Heber Young had no special status whatever. But, as often happened, the official and the real had only a nodding acquaintance with each other. "Come in, Mr. Young," Dowling said, gesturing toward his own office. "Can we get you some lemonade?" He couldn't very well ask a pious (if unofficial) Mormon if he wanted a drink, or even a cup of coffee.

"No, thank you," Young said, accompanying him into the private office. Dowling closed the door behind them. He waved Young to a seat. With a murmured, "Thank you, Colonel," the local sat down.

So did Abner Dowling. "What can I do for you today, Mr. Young?" he inquired. He was always scrupulously polite to the man who headed a church that did not officially exist. Despite half a century of government persecution and almost twenty years of outright suppression, that church still counted for more than anything else in Utah.

"You will remember, Colonel, that I spoke to you this past fall about the possibility of programs that would give work to some of the men here who need it so badly." Young was painfully polite to him, too. The diplomats called this sort of atmosphere "correct," which meant two sides hated each other but neither showed what it was feeling.

"Yes, sir, I do remember," Dowling replied. "And, I trust, you will recall I told you President Hoover disapproved of such programs. The president's views have not changed. That means my hands are tied."

"The problem is worse here than it was last fall," Heber Young said. "Some people grow impatient. Their impatience could prove a problem."

"Are you threatening me with an uprising, Mr. Young?" Dowling didn't shout it. He didn't bluster. He simply asked, as he had asked if Young wanted lemonade.

And the Mormons' unofficial leader shook his head. "Of course not,

Colonel. That would be seditious, and I am loyal to the government of the United States."

Dowling didn't laugh in his face, a measure of the respect he had for him. But he didn't believe that bold assertion, either. "Are you also loyal to the state of Deseret?" he asked.

"How can I be, when there is no state of Deseret?" Young asked calmly. "What happened here during the Great War made that plain."

"A thing may be very plain, and yet people will not want to believe it," Dowling said.

"True," Heber Young agreed. "May I give you an example?"

"Please do," Dowling said, as he was no doubt supposed to.

."Thank you." Yes, Young was nothing if not courteous. "That many people in Utah were not happy with the repression and persecution they received at the hands of the government of the United States must have been obvious to anyone who looked at the matter, and yet the rebellion that broke out here in 1915 seems to have come as a complete and utter shock to that government. If you despise people on account of what they are, can you be surprised when they in turn fail to love you?"

"I was in Kentucky at the time. I was certainly surprised, Mr. Young," Dowling answered. Custer had been more than surprised. He'd been furious. A couple of divisions had been detached from First Army and sent west to deal with the Mormon revolt. That had scotched an offensive he'd planned. The offensive probably would have failed, and certainly would have caused a gruesome casualty list. Of course, fighting the Mormons had caused a gruesome casualty list, too.

Young said, "My grandfather came to Utah to go beyond the reach of the United States. All we ever asked was to be left alone."

"That was Jefferson Davis' war cry, too," Dowling said. "Things are never so simple as slogans make them sound. If you live at the heart of the continent, you cannot pretend that no one will notice you are here. For better or worse, Utah is part of the United States. It will go on being part of the United States. People who live here had better get used to it."

"Then treat us like any other part of the United States," Young said. "Send your soldiers home. Open the borders. Let us practice our religion."

*How many wives did Brigham Young have? Which one of them was your grandmother?* Dowling wondered. Aloud, he said, "Mr. Young, I am a soldier. I do not make policy. I only carry it out. In my opinion, though, your people were well on the way to getting what you ask for . . . until that assassin murdered General Pershing. After your revolt in 1881, after the uprising in 1915, that set back your cause more than I can say."

"I understand as much," Young said. "Do you understand the desperation that made that assassin pick up a rifle?"

"I don't know." Dowling had no interest in understanding the assassin. He suddenly shook his head. That wasn't quite true. Understanding the Mormon might make him easier to catch, and might make other murderers easier to thwart. Dowling doubted that was what Heber Young had in mind.

The Mormon leader said, "The worse the conditions in this state get, the more widespread that desperation becomes. We may see another explosion, Colonel."

"You are in a poor position to threaten me, Mr. Young," Dowling said.

"I am not threatening you. I am trying to warn you," Young said earnestly. "I do not want another uprising. It would be a disaster beyond compare. But if the people of Utah see no hope, what can you expect? They are all too likely to lash out at what they feel to be the cause of their troubles."

"If they do, they will only bring more trouble down on their heads. They had better understand that," Dowling said.

"I think they do understand it," Heber Young replied. "What I wonder about is how much they care. If all choices are bad, the worst one no longer seems so very dreadful. I beg you, Colonel—do what you can to show there are better choices than pointless revolt."

With genuine regret, Dowling said, "You credit me with more power than I have."

"I credit you with goodwill," Young said. "If you can find something to do for us, something you may do for us, I think you will."

"The things you've asked for are not things I may do," Dowling said.

Impasse. They looked at each other in silent near-sympathy. Young got to his feet. So did Dowling. Dowling put out his hand. Young shook it. He also shook his head. And, shaking it, he strode out of Abner Dowling's office without looking back.


"Come on, Mort!" Mary Pomeroy exclaimed, sounding as excitable as her red hair said she ought to be. "Do you want to make us late?"

Her husband laughed. "For one thing, we won't be late. For another thing, your mother will be so glad to see us, she won't care anyhow."

He was right. Mary knew as much, but she didn't care. "Come on!" she said again, tugging at his arm. "We'll all be there at the farm—Ma and Julia and Ken and their children and Beth—that's Ken's ma—"

"I know who Beth Marble is," Mort broke in. "Hasn't she been coming to the diner for years whenever she's in Rosenfeld to buy things?"

"And us," Mary finished, as if he hadn't spoken. "And us." They'd been married less than a year. A lot of the glow was still left on her—left on both of them, which made life much more pleasant. She gave him a playful shove. "Let's go."

"All right. All right. See? I'm not arguing with you." He put on a straw boater—a city fellow's hat, almost too much of a city fellow's hat for a town as small as Rosenfeld, Manitoba—and went downstairs. He carried the picnic basket, though Mary had cooked the food inside. They went downstairs together.

Their apartment stood across the street from the diner Mort ran with his father. Mort's rather elderly Oldsmobile waited at the curb in front of the building. Mary wished he didn't drive an American auto, but there were no Canadian autos, and hadn't been since before the Great War. As he opened the trunk to put the picnic basket inside, a couple of occupiers—U.S. soldiers in green-gray uniforms—went into the diner. They both eyed Mary before the door closed behind them.

She slammed down the trunk lid with needless violence. All she said, though, was, "I wish Pa and Alexander could come to the picnic, too."

"I know, honey," Mort said gently. "I wish they could, too."

The Yanks had shot Alexander McGregor—her older brother—in 1916, claiming he'd been a saboteur. Mary still didn't believe that. Her father, Arthur McGregor, hadn't believed it, either. He'd carried on a one-man bombing campaign against the Americans for years, till a bomb he'd intended for General George Custer blew him up instead.

*One of these days . . .* Mary clamped down on that thought, hard. Smiling, she turned to her husband and said, "Let me drive, please."

"All right." He'd taught her after they got married. Before that, she'd never driven anything but a wagon. Mort grinned. "Try to have a little mercy on the clutch, will you?"

"I'm doing the best I can," Mary said.

"I know you are, sweetie." Her husband handed her the keys.

She *did* clash the gears shifting from first up to second. Before Mort could even wince, she said, "See? You made me nervous." He just shrugged. She drove smoothly the rest of the way out to the farm where she'd grown up. She turned down the lane that led to the farmhouse, stopped alongside of Kenneth Marble's Model T (which made the Olds seem factory-new by comparison), and shut off the motor. "See?" Triumph in her voice, she took the key from the ignition and stuck the key ring in her handbag.

"You did fine," Mort said. "But you put the keys away too soon. We've got to get the hamper out of the trunk."

"Oh." Mary felt foolish. "You're right."

Mort carried it up onto the porch. She remembered how he'd stood there the first time he came to take her out. But then she'd seen him from inside the house, and as a near stranger. Now she stood beside him, and the house in which she'd lived most of her life seemed the strange place.

Her mother opened the door. "Hello, my dear—my dears!" Maude McGregor said, smiling. Mary had got her red hair from her mother; Maude's, these days, was mostly gray. She looked tired, too. But then, what woman on a farm didn't?

Mary knew she'd had no idea how much work she did every day till she went from the farm into Rosenfeld. Keeping an apartment clean and cooking were as nothing beside what she'd done here. With her father and brother dead, she'd worked even harder than most women had to. But in town . . . There, keeping up would have been easy even without electricity. With it, she felt as if she lived in the lap of luxury.

Now, coming back, she might have fallen into the nineteenth century, or maybe even the fifteenth. She shook her head. That last wasn't right. Kerosene lamps gave light here, and her mother cooked on a coal-burning stove. They hadn't had those in the Middle Ages. But water came from a well, and an outhouse added its pungency to the barn's. Mary hadn't needed any time at all to get used to the delights of running water and indoor plumbing.

Even so, she had no trouble saying, "It's so good to be back!" after hugging her mother. She meant it, too. No matter how hard things had been here, the farm was the standard by which she would measure everything else for the rest of her life.

As soon as she stepped inside, two tornadoes hit her, both shouting, "Aunt Mary!" Her sister Julia's son Anthony was five; her daughter Priscilla, three. Mary picked each of them up in turn, which made them squeal. Picking up Anth—that was what they called him, for no reason Mary could make out—made her grunt. He was a big boy, and gave the promise of growing into a big man.

Julia was taller than Mary, and Ken Marble was a good-sized man, though stocky and thick through the chest rather than tall. "Glad to see you," he said gravely. Both he and Julia were quiet people, though their children made up for it. He might have been talking about the weather when he went on, "We've got number three on the way. First part of next year, looks like."

"That's wonderful!" Mary hurried to her sister and squeezed her. Julia looked even more weary than their mother. As a farm wife with two small children, she had every right to look that way. "How do you feel?" Mary asked her.

She shrugged. "Like I'm going to have a baby. I'm sleepy all the time. One day, food will stay down. The next, it won't. When are *you* going to have a baby, Mary?"

People had started asking her that after she'd been married for about two weeks. "I don't know exactly," she answered in a low voice, "but I don't think it'll take real long."

Julia's mother-in-law, Beth Marble, said, "What's the news from in town, kids?" She was a pleasant woman with shoulder-length brown hair going gray, rather flat features, and a wide, friendly smile.

"Tell you what I heard late last night at the diner," Mort said. "There's talk Henry Gibbon's going to sell the general store."

"You didn't even tell me that when you came home!" Mary said indignantly.

Her husband looked shamefaced. "It must've slipped my mind."

Mary wondered if he'd saved the news so it would make a bigger splash at the gather. He liked being the center of attention. It was big—no doubt about that. She said, "Gibbon's general store's been in Rosenfeld for as long as I can remember."

"For as long as I can remember, too, pretty much," her mother said.

"That's likely why he's selling—if he *is* selling, and it's not just talk," Mort said. "He's not a young man any more."

When Mary thought of the storekeeper, she thought of his bald head, and of the white apron he always wore over his chest and the formidable expanse of his belly. But sure enough, the little fringe of hair he had was white these days. "Won't seem the same without him," she said, and everybody nodded. She added, "I hope to heaven a Yank doesn't buy him out. That'd be awful."

More nods. Julia hated the Americans as much as Mary did, though she wasn't so open about it. The Marbles had no reason to love them, either, even if they hadn't suffered so much at U.S. hands. The only Canadians Mary could think of who did love Americans were collaborators, of whom there were altogether too many.

"Let's go take the baskets out to the field and have our picnic," Maude McGregor said, which was not only a good idea but changed the subject.

Sprawled on a blanket under the warm summer sun and gnawing on a fried drumstick, Mary found it easy enough not to think about the Americans. She listened to gossip from town and from the surrounding farms. The Americans did come into that, but only briefly: a farmer's daughter was going to marry a U.S. soldier. It wasn't the first such marriage around Rosenfeld, and probably wouldn't be the last. Mary did her best to pretend it wasn't happening.

Far easier, far more pleasant, to talk about other things. She said, "These deviled eggs you made sure are good, Ma."

Her husband nodded. "Can I get the recipe from you, Mother Mc-Gregor? They beat the ones we fix in the diner all hollow."

"I don't know about that," Maude McGregor said. "If other people use it, it won't be mine any more."

"Of course it will," Mort said. "It'll just let other people enjoy what you were smart enough to figure out."

"He's a smooth talker, isn't he?" Julia murmured. Mary smiled and nodded.

In a low, confidential voice, Mort went on, "I'm not just talking to hear myself talk, Mother McGregor. That recipe's worth money to my father and me. If we were buying it from someone else in the business, we'd probably pay"—he screwed up his face as he figured it out—"oh, fifty dollars, easy."

The farm barely made ends meet for Mary's mother. Mary doubted the Pomeroys would pay anywhere near that much for a recipe—they'd be more likely to swap one of their own—but the diner was doing well, and Mort had a generous heart. After blinking once or twice to make sure he was serious, Maude McGregor said, "When we get back to the house, I'll write it down." Everyone beamed.

When they got back to the house, Mary said, "I'm going out to the barn, Mort, and get us some fresh eggs. I wonder if I remember how to get a hen off the nest."

"You don't need to take the big picnic basket with you, just for some eggs," Mort said.

"It's all right. I've got a smaller one inside," Mary said. That display of feminine logic flummoxed her husband. He shrugged and watched her go, then turned back to her mother, who was putting the deviled-egg recipe on paper.

In the barn, Mary quickly gathered a dozen eggs. She put them, as she'd said she would, in the smaller basket inside the big one, cushioning them with straw. She didn't go back to the house right after that. Instead, she walked over to an old iron-tired wagon wheel that had been lying there since the Great War, maybe even since before it started. The iron, by now, was red and rough with rust. It rasped against her palms—which were softer than they had been—as she shoved the wheel aside.

Mary scraped aside the dirt under it, and lifted a board under the dirt. The board concealed a hole in the ground her father had dug. In it lay his bomb-making tools, the tools the Yanks had never found. She scooped up sticks of dynamite, blasting caps, fuses, crimpers, needle-nosed pliers, and other bits of specialized ironmongery, and put them in the basket.

She was just replacing the wheel over the now-empty hole when her nephew Anthony charged into the barn. "What you doing, Aunt Mary?" he asked.

"I was squashing a spider that had a web under there," she lied smoothly. Anth made a horrible face. She made as if to clop him with the picnic basket. He fled, giggling. She went out to the car and put the bas-. ket in the trunk.

**S**aul Goldman was a fussy little fellow, but good at what he did. "Everything's ready now, Mr. President," he said. "Newsreel photographers, newspaper photographers, and the wireless web connection. By this time tomorrow, everyone in the Confederate States will know you've signed this bill."

"Thanks, Saul," Jake Featherston said with a warm smile, and the little Jew blossomed under the praise. Jake knew Goldman was exaggerating. But he wasn't exaggerating by much. The people who *needed* to know he was signing the bill would hear about it, and that was what mattered.

At a gesture from the communications chief, klieg lights came on in the main office of the Gray House. Featherston smiled at the camera. "Hello, friends," he said into the microphone in front of him. "I'm Jake Featherston. Just like always, I'm here to tell you the truth. And the truth is, this bill I'm signing today is one of the most important laws we've ever made in the Confederate States of America."

He inked a pen and signed on the waiting line. Flashbulbs popped as the photographers did their job. Jake looked up at the newsreel camera again. "We've had too many floods on our big rivers," he said. "The one in 1927 came close to drowning the middle of the country. Enough is enough, I say. We're going to build dams and levees and make sure it doesn't happen again. We'll use the electricity from the dams, too, for factories and for people. We've needed a law like this for years, and now, thanks to the Freedom Party, we've got it."

"Mr. President?" A carefully prompted reporter from a Party paper stuck his hand in the air. "Ask you a question, Mr. President?"

"Go right ahead, Delmer." Featherston was calm, casual, at his ease.

"Thank you, sir," Delmer said. "What about Article One, Section Eight, Part Three of the Constitution, sir? You know, the part that says you can't make internal improvements on rivers unless you aid navigation? Dams don't do that, do they?"

"Well, no, but they do lots of other things the country needs," Jake answered.

"But won't the Supreme Court say this law is unconstitutional?" the reporter asked.

Featherston looked into the cameras as if looking at a target over open sights. He had a long, lean face, a face people remembered if not one conventionally handsome. "Tell you what, Delmer," he said. "If the Supreme Court wants to put splitting hairs ahead of what's good for the country, it can go right ahead. But if it does, I won't be the one who's sorry in the end. Those fools in black robes will be, and you can count on that."

He took no other questions. He'd said everything he had to say. The microphones went off. The bright lights faded. He leaned back in his swivel chair. It creaked. Saul Goldman came back into the room. Before Jake could ask, his head of communications said, "I think that went very well, Mr. President."

"Good." Featherston nodded. "Me, too. Now they know what I think of 'em. Let's see how much nerve they've got."

Ferdinand Koenig walked into the office. The attorney general was one of Featherston's oldest comrades, and as close to a friend as he had these days. "You told 'em, Jake," he said. "Now we find out how smart they are."

"They're a pack of damn fools, Ferd," Jake said scornfully. "You watch. The people who've been running this country *are* damn fools. All we need to do is give 'em the chance to prove it."

Koenig had got to the office faster than Vice President Willy Knight. Knight was tall and blond and good-looking and very much aware of how good-looking he was. He'd headed up the Redemption League till the Freedom Party swallowed it. One look at his face and you could see he still wished things had gone the other way. *Too bad,* Jake thought. Knight wasn't so smart as he thought he was, either. He never would have taken the vice-presidential nomination if he were. The vice president of the Confederate States couldn't even fart till he got permission from the president.

Four months on the job, and Knight still hadn't figured that out. He went right on laboring under the delusion that he amounted to something. "For God's sake, Jake!" he burst out now. "What the hell did you go and rile the Supreme Court for?" A Texas twang filled his voice. "They'll throw out the river bill for sure on account of that, just so as they can get their own back at you."

"Gosh, Willy, do you think so?" Jake sounded concerned. He watched Koenig hide a smile.

Willy Knight, full of himself as usual, never noticed. "Think so? I'm sure of it. You did everything but wave a red cloth in their face."

Featherston shrugged. "It's done now. We'll just have to make the best of it. It may turn out all right."

"How can it?" Knight demanded. "Sure as the sun comes up tomorrow, somebody's gonna sue. You can already hear the Whigs licking their chops, slobbering over the chance to make us look bad. Whatever district court gets the law'll say it's no goddamn good."

"Then we'll take it to the Supreme Court," Ferdinand Koenig said.

"They'll tell you it's unconstitutional, too, just like that reporter fellow said they would," Willy Knight predicted. "They're looking for a chance to pin our ears back. Once they get those black robes on, Supreme Court justices think they're little tin gods. And there's not a Freedom Party man among 'em."

"I'm not too worried, Willy," Jake said. "This here's a popular bill. Not even the Whigs left in Congress voted against it. The country needs it bad. Folks won't be happy if the court tosses it in the ashcan."

"I tell you, those fuckers don't care," the vice president insisted. "Why should they? They're in there for life. . . ." He paused. His blue eyes widened. "Or are you saying they won't live long if they try and smother this bill?"

Featherston shook his head. "I didn't say anything like that. I *won't* say anything like that. We could get away with it if that damn Grady Calkins hadn't shot President Wade goddamn Hampton V. Not now. We don't want to get the name for a pack of lousy murderers." *We've done plenty of murdering on the way up, and we'll do as much more as we have to, but looks count. The Supreme Court justices aren't the right targets for stalwarts. We've got other ways to deal with them.*

"If I were in your shoes, I'd put the fear of God in those sons of bitches," Knight insisted.

Jake Featherston spoke softly, but with unmistakable emphasis: "Willy, you aren't in my shoes. You try and put yourself in my shoes, you're just measuring yourself for a coffin. You got that?"

Knight was not a coward. He'd fought, and fought well, in the trenches during the Great War. But Featherston intimidated him, as Featherston intimidated almost everyone. "Yeah, Jake. Sure, Jake," he mumbled, and left the Confederate president's office in a hurry.

Laughing, Featherston said, "He doesn't get it, Ferd. And he's gonna

be as surprised as a ten-year-old when the magician pulls the rabbit out of
his hat when we give those justices what they deserve."

"The difference is, this way we'll kill 'em dead, and everybody'll
stand up and cheer when we do it," Koenig said. "He doesn't see that." He
hesitated, then asked, "You're sure you want one of our people filing suit
against the law?"

"Hell, yes, as long as nobody can trace him back to us," Jake
answered without hesitation. "Whigs'd take weeks to get around to it, and
I want this to happen just as fast as it can."

"I'll take care of it, long as you know your own mind," the attorney
general said. "You know I've always backed your play. I always will,
too."

"You're a good fellow, Ferd." Featherston meant every word of it.
"Man on the way up needs somebody like you to guard his back. And
once he gets where he's going, he needs somebody like you more than
ever."

"When we started out, they ran the Freedom Party out of a cigar box
in the back of a saloon," Koenig said reminiscently. "Did you ever figure,
back in those days, that we'd end up *here*?" His wave encompassed the
Confederate presidential mansion.

"Hell, yes," Jake replied without hesitation. "That's *why* I joined: to
pay back the bastards who lost us the war—all the bastards: coons and
our own damn generals and the Yankees—and to get to the top so I could.
Didn't you?" He asked it in genuine perplexity. He could judge others
only by what he did himself.

Koenig shrugged broad shoulders. He was beefy fat, with a hard core
of muscle underneath. "Who remembers now? For all I know, I went to
that saloon and not some other place on account of the beer was good
there."

"It was horse piss," Jake said. "I remember that."

"Now that I think back on it, you may be right," Koenig admitted. He
looked around as if he couldn't believe the office where they sat. "But
hell, we were all just a bunch of saloon cranks in those days. Nobody
thought we'd amount to anything."

"*I* did," Featherston said.

His longtime comrade laughed. "You must've been the only one.
Those first few months after the war, a thousand different parties sprang
up, and every goddamn one of 'em said it'd set the Confederate States to
rights."

"Somebody had to have it straight. We did." Jake Featherston had
never lacked for confidence. He'd never doubted. And his confidence had
fed the Party. During the dark years after Calkins gunned down President

Hampton, his confidence had been all that kept the Party alive. *That and the wireless,* he thought. *I figured out the wireless a couple of jumps ahead of the Whigs and the Radical Liberals. They ran after me, but they never caught up. They never will, now.*

"We've got some old bills to pay, you know," he told Koenig. "We've got a lot of old bills to pay, matter of fact. About time we started doing that, don't you think? We've looked meek and mild too long already. That isn't our proper style."

"Had to get this bill through Congress," the attorney general said. "One thing at a time."

"Oh, yes." Featherston nodded. "It's been one thing at a time ever since we didn't quite win in 1921. That's a hell of a long time now. I'm going to be fifty in a few years. I haven't got all the time in the world any more. I want the whole pie, not just slices. I want it, and I'm going to get it."

"Sure thing, Sarge," Ferdinand Koenig said soothingly. "I know who you want to pay back first. I'll start setting it up. By the time we do it, everything'll go just as slick as boiled okra. You can count on that."

"I do. You'd best believe I do," Jake said. "Pretty soon now, we have some things to tell the USA, too. Not quite yet. We've got to put our own house in some kind of order first. But pretty soon."

"First we take care of this other stuff." Koenig was not a fiery man. He never had been. But he kept things straight. Jake needed somebody like that. He was shrewd enough to know it. He nodded. Koenig went on, "Besides, the next step puts the whole country behind us, not just the people who vote our way."

"Yeah." Featherston nodded again. A wolfish grin spread across his face. "Not only that, it'll be a hell of a lot of fun."


Sylvia Enos looked out at the crowd of fishermen and merchant sailors and shopgirls (and probably, in a hall near the wharves, a streetwalker or two—you couldn't always tell by looking). By now, she'd been up on the stump often enough that it didn't terrify her the way it had at first. It was just something she did every other year, when the election campaigns started heating up.

Joe Kennedy went to the microphone to introduce her: "Folks, here's a lady who can tell you just why you'd have to be seventeen different kinds of fool to vote for anybody but a Democrat for Congress—the famous author and patriot, Mrs. Sylvia *Enos!*"

He always laid the introductions on too thick. He didn't do it to impress the crowd. He did it because he wanted to impress Sylvia, impress her enough to get her into bed with him. And there was his own wife sitting in the front row of the crowd. Was she oblivious or simply resigned? She must have seen him chase—must have seen him catch— plenty of other women by now.

"Thank you, Mr. Kennedy." Sylvia took her place behind the microphone. "I do think it's important to reelect Congressman Sanderson in November." With Boston sweltering in August, November was hard to think about. She looked forward to cooler fall weather. "He'll help President Hoover keep the United States strong. We need that. We need it more than ever, with what's going on down in the Confederate States."

Joe Kennedy applauded vigorously. So did his wife. She never showed that anything was wrong between them. The crowd clapped, too. That was what the Democrats needed from Sylvia. That was why, when she finished her speech, he gave her a crisp new fifty-dollar bill, with Teddy Roosevelt's bulldog features and swarm of teeth on one side and a barrel crushing Confederate entrenchments on the other.

"Thank you, Mr. Kennedy," Sylvia said again—she didn't want to bite the hand that fed her.

"My pleasure," he answered. "May I take you out to get a bite to eat now?" He didn't mean a bite with him and his wife. Rose would stay wherever Rose stayed while Joe did as he pleased. And no, supper wasn't all he had in mind.

She wondered what he saw in her. She was in her mid-forties, her brown hair going gray, fine lines not so fine any more, her figure distinctly dumpy. Maybe he didn't believe anybody could say no to him and mean it. Maybe her saying no was what kept him after her. If she ever did give in to him, she was sure he would forget all about her after one encounter.

"No, thanks, Mr. Kennedy," she said now, politely but firmly. "I have to get home." She didn't. With her son newly married and her daughter working, she had less need than ever to go home. But the lie was polite, too. She wanted to make a lot more speeches before Election Day, and she wanted to get paid for each and every one of them.

Kennedy bared his teeth; he seemed to have almost as many as TR. "Maybe another time," he said.

Shrugging, Sylvia got down from the stage. As soon as her back was to him, she let out a long sigh of relief. Every time she got away from Joe Kennedy, she felt like Houdini getting out of the handcuffs in the straitjacket in the tub of water.

She hadn't gone far before another man fell into step with her. "You made a good speech," he said. "You told them what they needed to hear. Then, when you were done, you shut up. Too many people never know when to shut up."

"Ernie!" Sylvia exclaimed. She gave the writer a hug. If Joe Kennedy happened to be watching, too damn bad. "What are you doing back in Boston? Why didn't you let me know you were coming?"

He shrugged. He had broad shoulders, almost a prizefighter's shoulders, and dark, ruggedly handsome features. He looked more like a bouncer, a mean bouncer, than the man who'd put Sylvia's words on paper in *I Sank Roger Kimball.* Considering the wound he'd taken driving an ambulance up in Quebec during the war, he had more right than most men to seem, to be, mean.

When he saw she wouldn't be content with that shrug, he raised one eyebrow in a world-weary way that made him look older than she was for a moment, though he had to be ten years younger. He said, "I am looking for work. Why does anyone go anywhere these days? Maybe I will find something to write about. Maybe I will find something someone will pay me to write about. The first is easy. The second is hard these days."

"Are you hungry?" Sylvia asked. Ernie didn't answer. He had more pride than two or three ordinary men. Pride was a luxury Sylvia had long since decided she couldn't afford. She said, "Come on. I'll buy you supper." Before he could speak, she held up a hand. "I've got the money. Don't worry about that. And I owe you." She found herself talking as he did, in short, choppy sentences. "Not just for the book. You warned me my bank would fail. I got my money out in time."

"Good I could do something," he said, and scowled. He'd wanted her. She'd wanted him, too, the first time she'd really wanted a man since her husband was killed at—after—the end of the Great War. Considering his wound, that surge of desire had been nothing but one more cruel irony.

"Come on," she said again.

Ernie didn't tell her no, a likely measure of how hard up he was. She took him to an oyster house. He ate with a singleminded voracity she hadn't seen since her son was growing into a man.

She put money on the table for both of them. He frowned. "I still hate to have a woman pick up the tab for me."

"It's all right," Sylvia said. "Don't worry about it. It's the least I can do. I told you that already. And I bet I can afford it a lot better than you can."

His pain-filled bark of laughter made people all over the place stare at him. "You are right about that. You must be right about that. I do need to land a writing job. I need to do it right away. If I do not, I will wind up in a Blackfordburgh."

"You could do something else," she said.

"Oh, yes." Ernie nodded. "I could step into the ring and get my block knocked off. I have done that a couple of times. It pays even worse than writing, and it is not so much fun. Or I could carry a hod. I have done that, too. The same objections apply. I am glad to see you doing so well for yourself."

"I've been lucky," Sylvia said. "I feel lucky, seeing you again."

"Me?" Another sour laugh. "Not likely. I have tried to write books that show how things were in the war. People do not want to read them. No one wants to publish them any more. Everyone wants to forget we ever had a war."

"They haven't forgotten down in the Confederate States," Sylvia said.

"Sweet Jesus Christ. I *am* lucky. I have found someone who can see past the end of her nose. Do you know how hard that is to do these days?"

The praise warmed Sylvia. It wasn't smarmy, the way Joe Kennedy's always seemed. Ernie wasn't one to waste his time with false praise. He said what he meant. Sylvia tried to match him: "Jake Featherston hasn't exactly been hiding what he thinks about us."

"No. He is a real son of a bitch, that one, a rattler buzzing in the bushes by the road," Ernie said. "One of these days, we are going to have to settle his hash."

"I say things like that on the stump, and people look at me like I'm crazy," Sylvia said. "Sometimes I start to wonder myself, you know what I mean?"

He leaned forward and, with startling gentleness, let his hand rest softly on hers. "You have more sense than anybody I have seen for a hell of a long time, Sylvia," he said. "If anyone tries to tell you any different, belt the silly bastard right in the chops."

That had to be the oddest romantic speech Sylvia had ever heard. But, where most of the so-called romantic speeches she'd heard either made her want to laugh or made her want to kill the man who was making them, this one filled her with heat. That in itself felt strange and unnatural. She'd known desire only a handful of times since her husband didn't come back from the war.

"Let's go to my flat," she murmured. "My son's married and on his own, and my daughter works the evening shift."

Ernie jerked his hand away as if she were on fire. "Did you forget?" he asked harshly. "I am no good for that. I am no damn good for that at all."

He'd told her the same thing once before. It had balked her then. Now . . . "There are other things we could do. If you wanted to." She looked down at the tabletop. She felt the heat of embarrassment, too. She didn't think she'd ever said anything so risqué.

"I will be damned," Ernie muttered, and then, "You will not be disappointed?"

"Never," she promised.

"Christ," he said again, only this time it sounded more like a prayer than a curse. He got to his feet. "Maybe you are lying to me. Maybe you are lying to yourself. I am asking to get wounded again. I know goddamn well I am. But if you do not change your mind in one hell of a hurry—"

"Not me," Sylvia said, and she got up, too.

Closing the door to the apartment behind them, locking it afterwards, seemed oddly final, oddly irrevocable. Going into the bedroom once she'd done that might almost have been anticlimax. Sylvia wished it could happen without undressing in front of a near stranger. She knew too well she'd never been anything out of the ordinary for looks or for build.

Ernie treated her as if she were, though. By the way he touched her and stroked her and kissed her, she might have been a moving-picture actress, not a fisherman's widow. He did know what to do to please a woman when he was no longer equipped to do one thing in particular. Sylvia rediscovered just how lonely taking care of herself was by comparison.

Only a little at a time did she realize how much courage he'd needed to bare himself for her. His body was hard and well-muscled. His mutilation, though . . . "I'll do what I can," Sylvia said.

"I'll tell you a couple of things that sometimes can help, if you don't mind," Ernie said.

"Why would I mind?" Sylvia said. "This is what we came here for."

He told her. She tried them. George had liked one of them. The other was something new for her. It wouldn't have been high on her list of favorite things to do, but it did seem to help. Ernie growled like some large, fierce cat when he finally succeeded.

"Lord," he said, and bent down to pull a pack of cigarettes from a pocket of the trousers that lay crumpled by the bed. Lighting one, he went on, "There is nothing like that in all the world. Nothing else even comes close. Sometimes I forget, which is a small mercy. Once in a while, everything goes right. That is a large mercy. Thank you, sweetheart." He kissed her. His lips tasted of sweat and tobacco.

"You're welcome," Sylvia said.

"Damn right I am," he told her.

She laughed. Then she said, "Give me a smoke, too, will you?" He did. She leaned close to him to get a light from his. He set a hand companionably on her bare shoulder. She liked the solid feel of him. He would have to go before Mary Jane came home. Scandalizing her daughter wouldn't do. But for now . . . For now, everything was just fine.

\* \* \*

Scipio wasn't a young man. He'd been a little boy when the Confederate States manumitted their slaves in the aftermath of the Second Mexican War. He'd lived in Augusta, Georgia, since not long after the end of the Great War. Everyone here, even Bathsheba, his wife, knew him as Xerxes. For a Negro who'd played a role, however unenthusiastic, in the running of one of the Red republics during the wartime revolt, a new name was a better investment than any he could have made on the bourse.

He'd seen a lot in those mad, hectic weeks before the Congaree Socialist Republic went down in blood and fire. In all the years since, he'd hoped he would never see anything like that again. And, up till now, he never had.

Up till now.

White rioters roared through the Terry, the colored district in Augusta. Some of them shouted, "Freedom!" Some were too drunk to shout anything that made sense. But they weren't too drunk to burn anything that would burn, to steal anything that wasn't nailed down, and to smash any Negroes who tried to stop them.

In the early stages of the riot, what passed for Augusta's black leaders—a double handful of preachers and merchants—had rushed to the police to get help against the hurricane overwhelming their community. Scipio had happened to be looking out the window of his flat when they came back into the Terry. Most of them, by their expressions, might have just scrambled out of a derailed train. A couple looked grim but unsurprised. Scipio would have guessed those men had seen some action of their own in 1915 and 1916.

"What'll they do for us?" somebody shouted from another window.

"Won't do nothin'," one of the leaders answered. "*Nothin'*. Said we deserves every bit of it, an' mo' besides."

After that, a few Negroes had tried to fight back against the rampaging mob. They were outnumbered and outgunned. Dark bodies hung from lamp posts, silhouetted against the roaring, leaping flames.

From behind Scipio, Bathsheba said, "Maybe we ought to run."

He shook his head. "Where we run *to*?" he asked bluntly. "The buckra catch we, we hangs on de lamp posts, too. Dis buildin' don' burn, we don' go nowhere."

He sounded altogether sure of himself. He had that gift, even using the slurred dialect of a Negro from the swamps of the Congaree. Back in the days when he'd been Anne Colleton's butler, she'd also made him learn to talk like an educated white man: *like an educated white man with a poker up his ass,* he thought. He'd seemed even more authoritative then. He hadn't always been right. He knew that, as any man must. But he'd always *sounded* right. That also counted.

Raucous, baying laughter floated up from the street. Along with those never-ending shouts of, "Freedom!" somebody yelled, "Kill the niggers!" In an instant, as if the words crystallized what they'd come into the Terry to do, the rioters took up the cry: "Kill the niggers! Kill the niggers! *Kill the niggers!*"

Scipio turned to his wife. "You still wants to run?"

Biting her lip, she got out the word, "No." She was a mulatto, her skin several shades lighter than his. She was light enough to go paler still; at the moment, she was almost pale enough to pass for white.

"Why they hate us like that, Pa?" Antoinette, their daughter, was nine: a good age for asking awkward questions.

In the Confederate States, few questions were more awkward than that one. And the brute fact was so much taken for granted, few people above the age of nine ever bothered asking why. Scipio answered, "Dey is white an' we is black. Dey don' need no mo'n dat."

With the relentless logic of childhood, his son, Cassius, who was six, turned the response on its head: "If we is black an' they is white, shouldn't we ought to hate them, too?"

He didn't know what to say to that. Bathsheba said, "Yes, but it don't do us no good, sweetheart, on account of they's stronger'n we is."

That *yes* had led directly to the Red uprisings during the Great War. The rest of her sentence had led just as directly to their failure. *What do we do?* Scipio wondered. *What can we do?* He'd wondered that ever since he'd seen his first Freedom Party rally, a small thing at a park here in Augusta. He'd hoped he wouldn't have to worry about it. That hope, like so many others, lay shattered tonight.

"Kill the niggers!" The cry rang out again, louder and fiercer than ever. Screams said the rioters were turning words into deeds, too.

Gunfire rang out from the building across the street from Scipio's: a black man emptying a pistol into the mob. Some of the screams that followed burst from white throats. *Good!* Savage exultation blazed through Scipio. *See how you like it, you sons of bitches! Wasn't keeping us cooped up in this poor, miserable place enough for you?*

But the white men didn't and wouldn't think that way, of course. *Cet animal est méchant. On l'attaque, il se defende.* That was how Voltaire had put it, anyhow. *This animal is treacherous. If it is attacked, it defends itself.* Thanks to Miss Anne (though she'd done it for herself, not for him), Scipio knew Voltaire well. How many of the rioters did? How many had even heard of him?

A fusillade of fire, from pistols, rifles, and what sounded like a machine gun, tore into the building from which the Negro had shot. More than a few bullets slammed into the building in which Scipio and his family lived, too. Then some whites chucked a whiskey bottle full of gasoline with a burning cloth wick into the entryway of the building across the street. The bottle shattered. Fire splashed outward.

The white men whooped and hollered and slapped one another on the back with glee. "Burn, baby, burn!" one of them shouted. Soon they were all yelling it, along with, "Kill the niggers!"

"Xerxes, they gwine burn this here place next," Bathsheba said urgently. "We gots to git out while we still kin."

He wished he could tell her she was wrong. Instead, he nodded. "We gits de chillun. We gits de money. An' we *gits*—out de back way to de alley, on account o' we don' las' a minute if we goes out de front."

Maybe the building wouldn't burn. Maybe the white men rampaging through the Terry would go on to some other crime instead. But if the roominghouse did catch fire, his family was doomed. Better to take their chances on the streets than to try to get out of a building ablaze.

Herding Antoinette and Cassius along in front of them, he and Bathsheba raced toward the stairway. A door flew open on the far side of the hall. "You crazy?" a woman in that flat said. "We safer in here than we is out there."

"Ain't so," Scipio answered. "Dey likely fixin' to burn dis place." The woman's eyes opened so wide, he could see white all around the iris. She slammed the door, but he didn't think she'd stay in there long.

He and his family weren't the only people going down the stairs as fast as they could. Some of the Negroes trying to escape the rooming-house dashed for the front entrance. Maybe they didn't know about the back way. Maybe, in their blind panic, they forgot it. Or maybe they were just stupid. Blacks suffered from that disease no less than whites. Whatever the reason, they paid for their mistake. Gunshots echoed. Screams followed. So did hoarse bellows of triumph from the mob.

*They've just shot down people who never did—never could do—them any harm,* Scipio thought as he scuttled toward the back door. *Why are they so proud of it?* He'd seen blacks exulting over what they meted out to whites during the Red revolt. But that exultation had 250 years of reasons behind it. This? This made no sense at all to him.

Out the door. Down the rickety stairs. Pray no white men prowled the alley. The stinks of rotting garbage and smoke and fear filled Scipio's nostrils. Away, away, away! "Where we run to, Pa?" Antoinette asked as he shoved her on ahead of him.

"Go where it darkest," Scipio answered. "Whatever you does, don' let no buckra see you."

Easy to say. Hard to do. Most nights in the Terry were black as pitch, black as coal, blacker than the residents. The city fathers of Augusta weren't about to waste money on street lighting for Negroes. But the fires burning here, there, everywhere didn't just burn people they trapped. They also helped betray others by showing them as they tried to get away.

Down the alley, into another. Scipio stepped in something nasty. He didn't know what it was, didn't care to find out. As long as he and his family got away, nothing else mattered. Into a side street that would take them to the edge of town, take them out of the center of the storm.

The side street was dark—no fires close by. It looked deserted. But as Scipio and his kin ran up it, a sharp challenge came from up ahead: "Who are you? Answer right this second or you're dead, whoever the hell you are."

Scipio hadn't used his white man's voice since not long after the war ended. He'd sometimes wondered if it still worked. Now it burst from him as if it were his everyday speech: "Go on about your business. None of those damned niggers around here."

Yes, it still held all the punch he'd ever been able to pack into it. "Thank you, sir," said the white man who'd challenged him, and then, "Freedom!"

"Freedom!" Scipio echoed gravely. He dropped back into the dialect of the Congaree to whisper, "Come on!" to Bathsheba and the children. They said not a word. They just hurried up the street. No one shot at them.

Nor did anyone else challenge them before they reached a stand of pine woods on the outskirts of Augusta. Scipio didn't know what he would do come morning. He would worry about that then. For now, he was alive, and likely to stay that way till the sun came up.

"Do Jesus!" All his weariness and strain came out in the two words.

Then Bathsheba asked him the question he'd known she would: "Where you learn to talk dat way? Ain't never heard you talk dat way before."

"Reckoned I better," Scipio said: an answer that was not an answer.

It didn't distract his wife. He'd hoped it would, but hadn't expected it to. Bathsheba said, "I never knew you could talk like that. You didn't jus' pull it out of the air, neither. Ain't nobody could. You been able to talk dat way all along. You got to've been able to talk dat way all along. So where you learn?"

"Long time gone, when I was livin' in South Carolina," he said. That much was true. "Never did like to use it much. Nigger git in bad trouble, he talk like white folks." That was also true.

True or not, it didn't satisfy Bathsheba. "You got more 'splainin' to do than that. What other kind o' strange stuff you gwine come out with all of a sudden?"

"I dunno," he answered. Bathsheba put her hands on her hips. Scipio grimaced. Her curiosity promised to be harder to escape than the race riot still wracking the Terry.

New York City. The Lower East Side. Tall tenements blocking out the sun. Iron fire escapes red with rust. Poor, shabbily dressed people in the crowd, chattering to one another in a mixture of English and Yiddish and Russian and Polish and Romanian. Red Socialist posters on the walls and fences, some of them put up where Democratic posters had been torn down. A soapbox that wasn't even a soapbox but a beer barrel.

Flora Blackford hadn't felt so much at home for years.

She'd been a Socialist agitator in the Fourteenth Ward twenty years before, at the outbreak of the Great War. She'd argued against voting the money for the war. Her party had disagreed. She still wondered whether they'd made a mistake, whether international proletarian solidarity would have been better. She would never know now. What she did know was that the war had cost her brother-in-law his life, that her nephew had become a young man without ever seeing his father, that her brother David had only one leg.

And she knew she couldn't talk about the war today, not to this crowd. She'd represented this district for years before marrying Hosea Blackford, before becoming first the vice president's wife and then the First Lady. Now her husband was a private citizen again, trounced by the Democrats when Wall Street collapsed and dragged everything else down with it. Now she wanted her old seat back, and hoped she could take it from the reactionary who'd held it for the past four years.

She pointed out to the crowd, as she had from a different beer barrel twenty years before. "You voted for Democrats because you thought doing nothing was better than doing something. Do you still think so?"

"No!" they shouted, all except for a few heckling Democrats who yelled, "Yes!"

Hecklers Flora could take in stride. "Herbert Hoover has been president for almost two years now. He's spent all that time sitting on his hands. Are we better off on account of it? Are the lines at the soup kitchens shorter? Are the Hoovervilles any smaller?" She refused to call the shantytowns where down-and-outers lived *Blackfordburghs* after her husband, though everybody else did. "Are there more jobs? Is there less misery? Tell me the truth, comrades!"

"No!" the crowd shouted again. This time, it drowned out the hecklers.

"That's right," Flora said. "No. You know the truth when you hear it. You're not blind. You're not stupid. You've got eyes to see and brains to think with. If you're happy with what the Democrats are doing to the United States, vote for my opponent. If you're not, vote for me. Thank you."

"Hamburger! Hamburger! Hamburger!" They remembered her maiden name well enough to chant it. She took that as a good sign. She'd long since learned, though, that you couldn't tell much from crowds. They came out because they wanted to hear you. They were already on your side. The rest of the voters might not be.

Herman Bruck held up a hand to help her descend from her little platform. "Good speech, Flora," he said. Did he hang on to her hand a little too long? Back in the old days, he'd been sweet on her. He was married himself now, with children of his own. Of course, who could say for sure how much that meant?

"Thank you," she answered.

"My pleasure." He tipped his fedora. As always, he was perfectly turned out, today in a snappy double-breasted gray pinstripe suit with lapels sharp enough to cut yourself on them. "I think you'll win in three weeks."

"I hope so, that's all," Flora said. "We'll find out about how people feel about Hoover—and about Congressman Lipshitz. If I win, I go back to Philadelphia. If I lose . . ." She shrugged. "If I lose, I have to find something else to do with the rest of my life."

"Come back to Party headquarters," Bruck urged. "A lot of the old-timers will be glad to see you, and you're a legend to the people who've come in since you represented this district."

"A legend? *Gottenyu!* I don't want to be a legend," Flora said in real alarm. "A legend is somebody who's forgotten things she needs to know. I want people to think I can do good things for them now, not that I'm somebody who used to do good things for them once upon a time."

"All right." Herman Bruck made a placating gesture. "I should have put it better. I'm sorry. People still want to see you. Can you come?"

"Tomorrow," she answered. "Tell everyone I'm sorry, but I don't think I ought to go over there today. Heaven knows when I'd get home, and I want to go back to the flat and see how Hosea is doing. This cold doesn't seem to want to go away." She hoped she didn't show how worried she was. The difference in their ages hadn't seemed to matter when she married him, but now, while she remained in vigorous middle age, he was heading toward his seventy-fourth birthday. Illnesses he would have shrugged off even a few years before hung on and on. One of these days . . . Flora resolutely refused to think about that.

Bruck nodded. "Sure. Everybody will understand that. Give him our best, then, and we hope we'll see you tomorrow. I'll drive you back to your block of flats."

She eyed him. Would he cause trouble in the auto? No. He had better sense than that. "Thanks," she said again. He hurried off to get the motorcar from a side street. The De Soto bespoke prosperity but not riches.

New York City traffic was even crazier than Flora remembered: more motorcars and trucks on the street, more drivers seeming not to care whether they lived or died. *This in spite of the subways,* she thought, and shuddered. Earlier in the year, she and Hosea and Joshua had been living in Dakota. New York City had five or six times as many people as the big state, and by all appearances had fifty or sixty times as many automobiles.

She let out a sigh of relief at escaping the De Soto. The doorman tipped his cap when she went into the block of flats. The building where she'd lived with her parents and brothers and sisters hadn't boasted a doorman. It hadn't boasted an elevator operator—or an elevator—either. Not having to walk up four flights of stairs whenever she went to the flat was pleasant.

Hosea Blackford greeted her with a sneeze. His nose was red. His face, always bony, had lost more flesh. His white hair lay thin and dry across his skull. This wasn't death's door—little by little, he was getting well—but the way he looked still alarmed her. After another sneeze, he peered at her over the tops of his reading glasses and brandished the *New York Times* like a weapon. "*Another* round of riots down in the Confederate States," he said. "If that's not reactionary madness on the march down there, I've never seen nor heard of it."

"Has anyone protested yet?" Flora asked.

Her husband shook his head. "Not a word. The Confederates are saying it's an internal matter, and our State Department is taking the same line."

She sighed. "We'd sing a different song if the Freedom Party were going after white men and not Negroes. The injustice, the hypocrisy, are so obvious—but nobody seems to care."

"A lot of whites in the Confederate States despise Negroes and come right out and say so," Hosea Blackford said. "A lot of whites in the United States despise Negroes, too. They keep their mouths shut about it, and so they seem tolerant when you look at them alongside the Confederates. They seem tolerant—but they aren't."

"I know. I saw that when we were both still in Congress," Flora said. "It's not just Democrats, either. Too many Socialists wouldn't cross the street to do anything for a black man. I don't know what to do about it. I don't know if we can do anything about it."

Hosea nodded. "Even Lincoln said the War of Secession was about trying to preserve the Union, not about the Negro or about slavery. He couldn't have made anybody march behind his banner if he'd said the other—and even as things were, he failed." He coughed again. "I wish I would have asked him about that when I met him on the train. I wish we would have talked about all kinds of things we never got to touch."

"I know," Flora said. That chance meeting had changed his life. He talked about it often, and ever more so as he got older.

Now he laughed a bitter laugh. "We're two peas in a pod, Lincoln and I: the two biggest failures as president of the United States."

"Don't talk like that!" Flora said.

"Why not? It's the truth. I'm not a blind man, Flora, and I hope I'm not a fool," Hosea Blackford said, words that might have come right from her speech. "I had my chance. I didn't deliver. The voters chose Coolidge instead—and then got Hoover when Cal dropped dead. I don't know what we did to deserve *that*. God must have a nasty sense of humor."

Flora didn't think of God as having a sense of humor at all. She also didn't care to be sidetracked. "We can't just turn our backs on the Negroes in the CSA," she said.

"That's true," Hosea said. "But you'd be a fool if you said so in your next speech, because sure as anything it would make people vote for Lipshitz."

She winced. That was bound to be true, no matter how little she liked it. Turning away from him, she said, "I'd better get to work on that next speech. The election's another day closer."

The speech went as well as such things could. After it was done, she went to the Socialist Party headquarters across the street from the Centre Market and above Fleischmann's kosher butcher shop (now run by the son of the original proprietor). Some of the workers in the headquarters looked implausibly young. Others were implausibly familiar. There sat Maria Tresca, typing away as if the past ten years hadn't happened. She almost certainly spoke better Yiddish than any other Italian woman in New York City. She was also as thoroughgoing a Socialist as anyone in the Party, and had paid a heavy price for holding on to her beliefs: her sister had been killed by police in the Remembrance Day riots of 1915. Flora had been with them when it happened. The bullet could have struck her as easily as Angelina Tresca.

"How does it feel to come back?" Maria asked.

"Coming back here feels wonderful," Flora said, which brought smiles all around. "I hope I can come back to Congress in November. With you people helping me, I'm sure I can." That brought more smiles.

On the night of November 6, she and Hosea and Joshua came back to

Party headquarters to find out if she had won. Her husband was still coughing and sneezing, but he had got better. Her parents were there, too, and her brothers and sisters and their families. Yossel Reisen, her sister Sophie's son, was nineteen years old and six feet tall. In the next election, he'd be able to vote himself. That seemed impossible.

These days, a blaring wireless set brought results faster than telegrams had the last time she'd waited out a Congressional election. The more returns that came in, the better things looked, not just here in the Fourteenth Ward but all across the country. Hoover remained in office, of course, but he would have to deal with a Socialist Congress for the next two years.

At a quarter past eleven, the telephone rang. Herman Bruck answered it. A big grin on his face, he ceremoniously held out the mouthpiece to Flora. "It's Lipshitz," he said.

"Hello, Congressman," Flora said.

"Hello, Congresswoman." The Democrat sounded worn, weary, wounded. "Congratulations on a fine campaign. May you serve the district well."

"Thank you. Thank you very much." Politely, Flora tried to hold excitement from her voice. She was going back to Philadelphia!

The tinny ring of a cheap alarm clock bounced Jefferson Pinkard out of bed. He lurched into the bathroom and took a long leak to get rid of the homebrew he'd poured down the night before. Alabama was a dry state, but a man who wanted a beer or three could find what he was looking for.

Bloodshot eyes stared at Jeff from the mirror over the sink. He was a ruddy, beefy man in his early forties, his light brown hair pulling back at the temples, his chin a forward-thrusting rock whose strong outline extra flesh was starting to obscure. "Do I need a shave?" he asked out loud. He lived alone—he was divorced—and had fallen into the habit of talking to himself.

Deciding he did, he lathered up, then scraped his face with a formidable straight razor. He muttered curses when he nicked himself just under his lower lip. A styptic pencil stopped the bleeding, but stung like fire. He didn't mutter the next set of curses.

When he put on his gray jailer's uniform, the high, stiff collar bit into his neck and made his face redder than ever. After two cups of snarling coffee and three eggs fried harder than he cared for—he'd always been a lousy cook—he left his apartment and started for the Birmingham jail.

Newsboys hawked the *Birmingham Confederate* and the *Register-Herald* at almost every street corner. No matter which paper they waved, they shouted the same thing: "Supreme Court turns thumbs down on damming our rivers! Read all about it!"

"Screw the Supreme Court," Pinkard muttered as he paid five cents for a copy of the *Confederate*. That was the Freedom Party paper in Birmingham. He wouldn't waste his money on the *Register-Herald*. One of these days before too long, he suspected something unfortunate would happen to the building where it was written and printed.

The *Confederate* quoted President Featherston as saying, "Those seven old fools in black robes think they can stop us from doing what the Confederate people elected us to do. This is a slap in the face at every honest, hardworking citizen of our country. If the Supreme Court wants to play politics, they'll find out that floods can wash away more than towns."

"Damn right," Jeff said, and chucked the paper into an ashcan. He didn't know what the president could do about the Supreme Court, but he figured Jake Featherston would come up with something. He always did.

Two cops on the steps of the Birmingham city jail nodded to him as he climbed those steps and went into the building. One of them wore a Party pin on his lapel. The other one, though, was the one who said, "Freedom!"

"Freedom!" Pinkard echoed. He had a Party pin on his lapel, too. Not long after the war ended, he'd heard Jake Featherston speak in a Birmingham park. He'd been a Freedom Party man ever since.

In the jail, he had a desk in a cramped office he shared with several other jailers. The one he was following onto duty looked up from his own desk, where he was filling out some of the nine million forms without which the jail could not have survived a day. "Mornin', Jeff," Stubby Winthrop said. "Freedom!"

"Freedom!" Pinkard said again. "What's new?"

"Not a hell of a lot," Winthrop answered. As his nickname implied, he looked like a fireplug with hairy ears. "Couple-three niggers in the drunk tank, white kid in a cell for stabbing his lady friend when he found out she was this other fella's lady friend, too. Oh, I almost forgot—they finally caught that bastard who's been stealing everything that ain't nailed down on the south side of town."

"Yeah? Swell!" Pinkard said, adding, "About time, goddammit." Like a lot of jailers, he was convinced the police who hunted down criminals couldn't find a skunk if it was spraying their leg. Unlike a lot of men in his line of work, he wasn't shy about saying so. His years at the Sloss Foundry had left him with the strength to back up talk with action if he ever had to. He asked the question Stubby Winthrop hadn't answered: "What about the politicals?"

"Well, of course." Winthrop looked at him as if at an idiot. "They drug in another twelve, fifteen o' them bastards, too." He poked at the papers with a short, blunt finger. "I can tell you exactly how many if you want to know."

"Don't worry about it now," Jeff said. "I can find out myself before I do my morning walk-through—long as the paperwork's there."

"It is, it is," Stubby assured him. "Think I want the warden reaming out my ass on account of messed-up papers? Not likely!"

"Cool down. I didn't mean anything by it. Twelve or fifteen, you say?" Jeff asked. Winthrop nodded. Jeff let out a pleased grunt. "We *are* starting to clean up this town, aren't we?"

"Bet your butt," Winthrop said. "Anybody forgets who won the goddamn election, we teach the fucker a little lesson. Ain't no such thing as a fit night out for Whigs or Radical Republicans, not any more there ain't."

Belonging to a political party other than the Freedom Party wasn't against the law. Pinkard thought it ought to be, but it wasn't. But anybody who raised his voice against the Party regretted it, and in a hurry. Disturbing the peace, resisting arrest, criminal trespass, inciting to riot, and possession of alcoholic beverages were plenty to get a man into jail. And, once he was in, he might be—he probably would be—a long time coming out again. Most judges, like anybody else, knew which side their bread was buttered on and went along with Freedom Party instructions. A couple of holdouts in Birmingham had already suffered mysterious and most deplorable accidents. Their replacements were more cooperative. So were the other judges. A few mysterious and most deplorable accidents could make anybody thoughtful.

Pinkard said, "Hell with me if I know what we're going to do with all these stinking politicals. We've stuffed so many of 'em into cells, we don't hardly have room for real crooks any more."

"Ain't my worry," Stubby said. "And you know somethin' else? There's a fuck of a lot of worse problems to have." Pinkard nodded again. He couldn't very well argue with that. Winthrop went on, "Matter of fact, this whole goddamn jail is your baby for the next eight hours. I'm gonna get outa here, grab myself some shuteye. Freedom!" He headed out the door.

"Freedom!" Jeff called after him. Among Party men—and more and more widely through the CSA these days—the word replaced *hello* and *good-bye*.

The heavy armored door crashed shut behind Stubby Winthrop. Pinkard looked at the clock on the wall. The prisoners would just be getting breakfast. He had time to find out precisely what he needed to know about changes since yesterday before making his first walk-through of the day. He didn't love paperwork, but he did recognize the need for it. He was conscientious about keeping up with it, too, which put him a jump ahead of several of his fellow jailers.

He'd just finished seeing what was what when the door to the office opened. The prisoner who came in had a trustie's green armband on the left sleeve of his striped shirt. "What's up, Mike?" Pinkard asked, frowning; this wasn't a scheduled time for a trustie to show up.

But Mike had an answer for him: "Warden wants to see you, sir, right away." His voice, like those of a lot of trusties, held a particular kind of whine. It put Pinkard in mind of the yelp of a dog that had been kicked too many times.

Whine or not, though, a summons from the warden was like a summons from God. Pinkard did his best not to evade but to delay, saying, "Can't I take my morning walk-through first, anyways?"

"You're a jailer—you can do whatever you please," Mike said, which only proved he'd never been a jailer. Then he added, "But I don't reckon the warden'd be mighty pleased," which proved he had a good idea of how things worked anyhow. Pinkard grunted and decided the walk-through would have to wait.

Warden Ewell McDonald was a heavyset man with a mustache that looked like a gray moth on his upper lip. He was close to retirement age, and didn't much care whose cage he rattled. "Come in, Pinkard," he said, staring at Jeff over the tops of the half-glasses he used for reading.

"What's up, sir?" Jeff asked warily.

"Come in," the warden repeated. "Sit down. You ain't in trouble— swear to God you ain't." Still cautious, Pinkard obeyed. McDonald went on, "That stuff on your record, how you set up that prisoner-of-war camp down in Mexico during their last civil war, that's the straight goods?"

"Hell, yes," Pinkard answered without hesitation. He was telling the truth, too, and knew other Confederate veterans—Freedom Party men— who'd gone down to the Empire of Mexico to fight for Maximilian III against the Yankee-backed republican rebels and could back him up. "Anybody says I didn't, tell me who he is and I'll kill the son of a bitch."

"Keep your shirt on," McDonald said. "I just wanted to make sure, is all. Reason I'm asking is, we've got more politicals in jail these days than you can shake a stick at."

"That's a fact," Jeff agreed. "Stubby and me, we were just talking about that a little while ago, matter of fact."

"It's not just Birmingham, either—it's all over Alabama. All over the country, too, but Alabama's what counts for you and me. We've got to keep those bastards locked up, but they're a big pain in the ass here in town," McDonald said. "So what we've got orders to do is, we've got orders to make a camp out in the country and stow the politicals in it. We save the jail for the real bad guys, you know what I mean?"

Jefferson Pinkard nodded. "Sure do. Sounds like a good idea, anybody wants to know what I think."

McDonald inked an old-fashioned dip pen and wrote something on the sheet of paper in front of him. "Good. I was hoping you were going to say that, on account of I aim to send you out there to help get it rolling. Your rank will be assistant warden. That's good for another forty-five dollars a month in your pocket."

It wasn't the sort of promotion Jeff had expected, but a promotion it definitely was. "Thank you, sir," he said, gathering himself. "You don't mind my asking, though, why me? You got a bunch of guys with more seniority than I have."

"More seniority *in the jail*, yeah," McDonald answered. "But a camp out in the open? That's a different business. Only fellow here who's done anything like that is you. You'll be there from the start, like I said, and you'll have a lot of say about how it goes. We'll get the barbed wire, we'll get the lumber for the barracks, we'll get the ordinary guards, and you help set it up so it works. . . . What's so goddamn funny?"

"Down in Mexico, I had to scrounge every damn thing I used," Pinkard answered. "I cut enough corners to build me a whole new street. You get me everything I need like that, it's almost too easy to stand." He held up his hand. "Not that I'm complaining, mind you." In Mexico, he'd been glad to land that job riding herd on prisoners because it meant nobody was shooting at him any more. He'd never dreamt then how much good it would do him once he came home to the CSA.


Without a doubt, Sam Carsten was the oldest lieutenant, junior grade, on the USS *Remembrance*. That was what he got for being a mustang. He'd spent close to twenty years in the Navy before making officer's rank. No one could tell if he had gray hair, though, not when it had started out platinum blond. He was the next thing to an albino, with blue eyes and transparent pink skin that would sunburn in the light of a candle flame.

The North Pacific in December wasn't a bad place for a man with a complexion like that. Even here, he'd smeared zinc-oxide ointment on his nose and the backs of his hands before coming out onto the ship's flight deck. It wouldn't help much. Nothing ever helped much.

He shifted his weight to the motion of the aeroplane carrier without noticing he was doing it. Most of the crew stood on the deck with him. Only the black gang down in the engine room and the men at the antiaircraft guns weren't drawn up at attention, all in neat ranks, to hear what Captain Stein had to say.

"Gentlemen, it is official at last," the captain said into a microphone that not only amplified his words for the sailors on deck but also carried them to the crewmen still at their posts. "We have received word by wireless from Philadelphia that the United States of America and the Empire of Japan are at peace once more."

Sam kicked at the flight deck. He was standing only a few feet from a big patch in the deck, a patch that repaired the damage a Japanese bomb had done. He couldn't help wondering whether the fight had been worthwhile.

Captain Stein went on, "The terms of the peace are simple. Everything goes back to what the diplomats call the *status quo ante bellum*. That just means the way things were before the shooting started. We don't give anything to the Japs, and they don't give us anything, either."

Behind Carsten, a sailor muttered, "Why'd we fight the goddamn war, then?"

In one way, the answer to that was obvious. The Japanese had been feeding men and money into British Columbia, trying to touch off another Canadian uprising against the USA, and the *Remembrance* had caught them at it. That was when the shooting started. If a torpedo from one of their submersibles hadn't been a dud, the carrier might not have come through it.

In another sense, though, the sailor had a point. The U.S. and Japanese navies had slugged at each other in the Pacific. The Japanese had tried to attack the American Navy base in the Sandwich Islands (more than twenty years ago now, Sam had been in the fleet that took Pearl Harbor away from the British Empire and brought it under U.S. control). Aeroplanes from a couple of their carriers had bombed Los Angeles. All in all, though, Japan had lost more ships than the USA had—or Sam thought so, anyhow.

He'd missed a few words of Stein's speech. The captain was saying, "—at battle stations for the next few days, to make sure this message has also reached ships of the Imperial Japanese Navy. We will continue flying combat air patrol, but we will not fire unless fired upon, or unless attack against the *Remembrance* is clearly intended."

Somewhere out here in the Pacific, a Japanese skipper was probably reading a similar announcement to his crew. *Wonder what the Japs think of it,* went through Carsten's mind. He didn't know what to think of it himself. There was a lingering sense of . . . unfinished business.

"That's the story from Philadelphia," Captain Stein said. "Before I turn you boys loose, I have a few words of my own. Here's what I have to say: we did everything we could to teach the Japs a lesson, and I suppose they did all they could to teach us one. I don't believe anybody learned a hell of a lot. This war is over. My guess is, the fight isn't. From now on, we stay extra alert in these waters, because you never can tell when it's going to boil over again. Remember the surprise attack they used against Spain when they took away the Philippines." He looked out over the crew. So did Carsten. Here and there, heads bobbed up and down as men nodded. Stein's point had got home. Seeing as much, the skipper gave one brisk nod himself. "That's all. Dismissed."

Chattering among themselves, the sailors hurried back to their stations. Sam didn't much want to go to his. His post was in damage control, deep down in the bowels of the ship. He'd done good work there, good enough to win promotion from ensign to j.g. All the same, it wasn't what he wanted to do. He'd come aboard the carrier as a petty officer when she was new because he thought aviation was the coming thing. He'd wanted to serve with the ship's fighting scouts or, that failing, in his old specialty, gunnery.

As often happened, what he wanted and what the Navy wanted were two different beasts. As always happened, what the Navy wanted prevailed. Down into the bowels of the *Remembrance* he went.

Lieutenant Commander Hiram Pottinger, his nominal boss, got to their station at the same time he did, coming down the passageway he was coming up. In fact, Sam knew a lot more about the way damage control worked aboard the *Remembrance* than Pottinger did. His superior, who'd replaced a wounded officer, had spent his whole career up till the past few months in cruisers. Sam, on the other hand, had had two long tours on the carrier. He automatically thought of things like protecting the aeroplanes' fuel supply. Pottinger thought of such things, too, but he took longer to do it. In combat, a few seconds could mean the difference between safety and a fireball.

Quite a few of the sailors in the damage-control party wore the ribbon for the Purple Heart above their left breast pockets. Several of them had won other decorations, too. The *Remembrance* had seen a lot of hard action—and taken more damage than Carsten would have wished.

A rat-faced Irishman named Fitzpatrick asked, "Sir, you really think them goddamn Japs is gonna leave us alone from now on?"

He'd aimed the question at Sam. Instead of answering, Sam looked to Lieutenant Commander Pottinger. The senior officer had first call. That was how things worked. Pottinger said, "Well, I expect we're all right for now."

Several sailors stirred. Carsten didn't much like the answer himself. He didn't and wouldn't trust the Japanese. So far, their trials of strength with the USA had been inconclusive: both in the Great War, where they'd been the only Entente power that hadn't got whipped, and in this latest fight, which had been anything but great.

But then Pottinger went on, "Of course, God only knows how long the quiet will last. The Japs keep bargains for as long as they think it's a good idea, and not thirty seconds longer. The skipper said as much— remember the Philippines."

Sam relaxed. So did the ordinary sailors. Lieutenant Commander Pottinger wasn't altogether naive after all.

Everybody stared at corridors painted in Navy gray, at bulkheads and hatchways, at hoses that shot high-pressure salt water, at the overhead pipes that meant a tall man had to crouch when he ran unless he wanted to bang the top of his head, at bare light bulbs inside steel cages: the world in which they operated. Most of the *Remembrance* lay above them. They might have been moles scurrying through underground tunnels. Every once in a while, a claustrophobe got assigned to damage control. Such men didn't last long. They started feeling the whole weight of the ship pressing down on their heads.

Not without pride, one of the sailors said, "We could do our job in the dark."

"Could, my nuts," Fitzpatrick said. "We've fuckin' well *done* our job in the dark. You don't need to see to know where you're at. The way noise comes back at you, where you bump up against fittings, the smells . . . Difference between us and the rest of the poor sorry bastards on this floating madhouse is, we really know what we're doing."

Almost in unison, the other men from the damage-control party nodded. The fighting had given them a fierce *esprit de corps*. Carsten's head wanted to go up and down, too. And it would have, had he not known that every other unit on the ship was just as proud of itself and just as convinced the *Remembrance* would instantly founder if it didn't do what it was supposed to. Nothing wrong with that. It was good for morale.

Pottinger said, "Here's hoping we don't have to do what we do for a hell of a long time."

More nods. Sam said, "Long as we're hoping, let's hope we head back to Seattle and get some leave."

That drew not only nods but laughter. Pottinger gave Carsten a hard look, but he ended up laughing, too. Sam had always been able to get away with saying things that would have landed someone who said them in a different tone of voice in a lot of trouble. He could smile his way out of bar scenes that usually would have brought out broken bottles.

Seaman Fitzpatrick, on the other hand, was deadly serious. "How long before we need to start worrying about Confederate submersibles again?" he asked.

"We've already worried about Confederate subs," Sam said. "Remember that passage between Florida and Cuba we took on the way to Costa Rica? We didn't spot anything, but God only knows what those bastards had laying for us there."

"That's their own waters, though," Fitzpatrick protested. "That isn't what I meant. What I did mean was, how long before we have to worry about them out here in the Pacific? And out in the Atlantic, too—don't want to leave out the other ocean."

This time, Carsten didn't answer. He looked to Lieutenant Commander Pottinger again. The commander of the damage-control party said, "We've already got Jap subs here in the Pacific, and maybe British boats coming up from Australia and New Zealand toward the Sandwich Islands. We've got British boats and German boats and French ones, too, in the Atlantic. Enough of those sons of bitches running around loose already. What the hell difference do a few Confederate subs make?"

Now he got a laugh. Sam joined it, even though he didn't think Pottinger had been kidding. "Back when I started out in the Navy, all we worried about was surface ships," he said. "Nobody'd ever heard that aeroplanes were dangerous, and submarines were still half toys. Nobody had any idea what they could do. It's a different world nowadays, and that's the truth."

"You betcha," Seaman Fitzpatrick said. "Nobody ever thought of a funny-looking thing called an aeroplane carrier, neither."

"Damage control is damage control," Pottinger said. "Something hurts the ship, we patch it up. That's what we're here for."

Sailors nodded once more. Carsten didn't argue with his superior, not out loud. But it was more complicated than that. Shells did one kind of damage, torpedoes another, and bombs a third. Bombs had the potential to be the most destructive, he thought. Unlike shells and torpedoes, they weren't limited in how much explosive they could carry. And explosive was what delivered the punch. Everything else was just the bus driver to get the cordite to where it did its job.

Sam didn't care for that line of reasoning. If bombs could sink ships so easily, what point to having any surface Navy at all? He'd first wondered about that during the war, when an aeroplane flying out from Argentina had bombed the battleship he was on. The damage was light—the bombs were small—but he thought he'd seen the handwriting on the wall.

Maybe a carrier's aeroplanes could hold off the enemy's. But maybe they couldn't, too. Down in the warm, humid belly of the *Remembrance*, Sam shivered.

**J**onathan Moss was an American. He had a Canadian wife. After studying occupation law, he'd made his living in Berlin, Ontario, by helping Canucks struggling in the toils of what the U.S. Army insisted on calling justice. Without false modesty, he knew he was one of the best in the business.

And what was his reward for doing everything he could to give the Canadians a hand? He stared down at the sheet of paper on his desk. He'd just taken it out of an envelope and unfolded it. In block capitals, it said, YANK SWINE, YOU WILL DIE!

He supposed he ought to turn it over to the occupying authorities. Maybe they could find fingerprints on it and track down whoever had stuck it in the mail. Instead, Moss crumpled up the paper and chucked it into the wastebasket. For one thing, odds were anyone who sent a charming missive of this sort had the elementary common sense to wear gloves while he was doing it. And, for another, taking a crank like this seriously gave him power over you.

During the war, Moss had flown observation aeroplanes and fighting scouts. He'd gone through all three years without getting badly hurt, and ended up an ace. After the real terror of aerial combat, a cowardly little anonymous threat didn't get him very excited.

He methodically went through the rest of his mail. The Bar Association reminded him his dues were payable before December 31. That gave him two and a half weeks. His landlord served notice that, as of next February 1, his office rent would go up five dollars a month. "Happy day," he said.

He opened another nondescript envelope. This one also held a single sheet of paper. Its message, also in untraceable block capitals, was, YOUR WIFE AND LITTLE GIRL WILL DIE, YANK SWINE!

Seeing that, Moss abruptly changed his mind about the letter he'd thrown away. He fished it from the trash can and flattened it out as best he could. The letters in both were about the same size and in about the same style. Moss rummaged for the envelope in which the first threat had come. He set it next to the one he'd just now opened.

"Well, well," he murmured. "Isn't that interesting?" He was no detective with a microscope, but he didn't need to be to see that his address on the two envelopes had been typed with two different machines. Not only that, one U.S. stamp bore a Manitoba overprint, while the other had one from Ontario. The notes, as near as he could see, were identical. The envelopes not only weren't but had been mailed from different provinces. (He checked to see if the postmarks confirmed what the stamps said. They did. One came from Toronto, the other from a town south of Winnipeg.) What did that mean?

Two possibilities occurred to him. One was that somebody didn't like him and had got his brother-in-law or someone of that sort to help show how much. Somebody like that was a pest. The other possibility was that he'd fallen foul of a real organization dedicated to—What? To making *his* life miserable, certainly, and, odds were, to making Canada's American occupiers unhappy *en masse*.

He'd hoped time would reconcile Canada to having lost the Great War. The longer he stayed here, the more naive and forlorn that hope looked. English-speaking Canada had risen once on its own, in the 1920s. More recently, the Empire of Japan had tried to ignite it again. Great Britain wouldn't have minded helping its one-time dominion make the Yanks miserable, either.

With a sigh, Moss put both sheets of paper and both envelopes in a buff manila folder. With a longer, louder sigh, he donned his overcoat, earmuffs, hat, and mittens. Then he closed the door to the law office—as an afterthought, he locked it, too—and left the building for the two-block walk to occupation headquarters in Berlin.

Had he been in a tearing hurry, he could have left off the earmuffs and mittens. It was above zero, and no new snow had fallen since the middle of the night. Moss had grown up around Chicago, a city that knew rugged weather. Even so, his wartime service in Ontario and the years he'd lived here since had taught him some things about cold he'd never learned down in the States.

He saw three new YANKS OUT! graffiti between the building where he worked and the red-brick fortress that housed the occupation authority.

Two shopkeepers were already out getting rid of them. He suspected the third would in short order. Leaving anti-American messages up on your property was an offense punishable by fine. *Occupation Code, Section 227.3,* he thought.

The sentries in front of occupation headquarters jeered at him as he came up the steps: "Look! It's the Canuck from Chicago!" He wasn't in the Army—indeed, most of his practice involved opposing military lawyers—so they didn't bother wasting politeness on him.

"Funny boys," he said, at which they jeered harder than ever. He went on into the building, or started to. Just inside the entrance, a sergeant and a couple of privates stopped him. "They've beefed up security, sir," the sergeant said. "Orders are to pat down all civilians. Sorry, sir." He didn't sound sorry at all.

Moss shed his overcoat and held his arms out wide, as if he were being crucified. After he passed the inspection, he went on to the office of Major Sam Lopat, a prosecutor with whom he'd locked horns more than a few times. "Ah, Mr. Moss," Lopat said. "And what sort of fancy lies have you got waiting for me next time we go at each other?"

"Here." Moss set the manila folder on the major's desk. "Tell me what you think of these."

Lopat raised one eyebrow when Moss failed to come back with a gibe. He raised the other when he saw what the folder held. "Oh," he said in a different tone of voice. "More of these babies."

"*More* of them, you say?" Moss didn't know whether to feel alarmed or relieved. "Other people have got 'em, too?"

"Hell, yes," the military prosecutor answered. "What, did you think you were the only one?" He didn't wait for Moss' reply, but threw back his head and laughed. "You civilian lawyers think you're the most important guys in the world, and nothing is real unless it happens to you. Well, I've got news for you: you aren't the cream in God's coffee."

"And you *are*—" But Jonathan Moss checked himself. He wanted information from Lopat, not a quarrel. "All right, I'm not the only one, you say? Tell me more. Who else has got 'em? Who sends 'em? Have you had any luck catching the bastards? I guess not, or I wouldn't have got these."

"Not as much as we'd like," Lopat said, which was pretty obvious. "We've torn apart the towns where they're postmarked, but not much luck. You can see for yourself—all the Canucks need is a typewriter and a pen, and they could do without the typewriter in a pinch. If it makes you feel better, there's never been a follow-up on one of these. Nobody's got shot or blown up the day after one of these little love notes came."

"I'm not sorry to hear that," Moss admitted. "You didn't say who else got a—love note." He nodded to Lopat, acknowledging the phrase.

"I don't have the whole list. Investigation isn't my department, you know. I go into court once they're caught—and then you do your damnedest to get 'em off the hook." The military prosecutor leered at Moss, who stonily stared back. With a shrug, Lopat went on, "Far as I know, the other people these have come to have all been part of the occupation apparatus one way or another. You're the first outside shyster to get one, or I think you are. Doesn't that make you proud?"

"At least," Moss said dryly, and Lopat laughed. Moss tapped one of the notes with a fingernail. "Prints?"

"We'll check, but the next ones we find'll be the first."

"Yeah, I figured as much. You would have landed on these fellows like a bomb if you knew who they were," Moss said. Lopat nodded. Something else occurred to Moss. "You think this has anything to do with that telephone threat I got last year, where the guy told me not to start my auto or I'd be sorry?"

The military prosecutor frowned. "I'd forgotten about that. I don't know what to tell you. Pretty damn funny, you know? You're the best friend—best American friend—the Canucks have got. You're married to one of theirs, and I know what she thinks of most Yanks, me included. You're the best occupation lawyer between Calgary and Toronto, anyway. Makes sense they'd want to get rid of me. I don't like it, but it makes sense. But why you? Seems to me they ought to put a bounty on anybody who even messes up your hair."

"I've wondered about that, too. Maybe they're angrier at Laura for marrying me than they are at me for marrying her."

"Maybe." But Lopat didn't sound convinced. "In that case, why aren't they trying to blow her up instead of you?"

"*I* don't know," Moss answered. "As long as this isn't too much of a much, though, I won't lose any sleep over it." He redonned his cold-weather gear. "I'll see you in court, Major, and I'll whip you, too."

"Ha!" Lopat said. "You been smoking doped cigarettes, to get so cocky?"

After a few more good-natured insults, Moss left occupation headquarters. By then, a wan sun had come out. His long shadow stretched out to the northwest as he walked back to the building where he practiced.

He'd just set one foot on the steps leading up the sidewalk when the bomb went off behind him. Had he had an infantryman's reflexes, he would have thrown himself flat. Instead, he stood there frozen while glass blew out of windows all around and fell clinking and clattering to the ground like sharp-edged, glittering snowflakes.

Already, a great cloud of black smoke was rising into the sky. Looking over his shoulder, Moss realized it came from the direction of the building he'd just left. He started running, back in the direction from which he'd come. At every step, his shoes crunched on shattered glass. He bumped into a bleeding man running the other way. "Sorry!" they both gasped. Each one kept going.

When Moss rounded the last corner, he came on a scene whose like he hadn't met since the days of the war. Occupation headquarters had had plenty of guards, but someone, somehow, had sneaked a bomb past them. The red brick building had fallen in on itself. Flames shot up from it. Bodies and pieces of bodies lay all around. Moss stepped on an arm that stopped abruptly, halfway between elbow and wrist. It still had on shirt sleeve and wristwatch. Blood dribbled from the end. His stomach lurched.

Here and there, survivors were staggering or pulling themselves out of the building. "My God!" one of them—a woman secretary—said, over and over. "My God! My God!" Maybe she was too stunned to say anything else. Maybe she couldn't find anything else that fit. She cradled a broken arm in her other hand, but hardly seemed to know she was hurt.

A hand sticking out from under bricks opened and closed. Moss dashed over and started clawing at the rubble. The soldier he pulled out was badly battered, but didn't seem to have any broken bones. "God bless you, pal," he said.

Fire engines roared up, sirens screaming. They began playing water on the wreckage. Moss looked for more signs of life under it. As he threw bricks in all directions, he wondered if the people who'd planted this bomb were the same ones who'd written him his notes. If they were, Sam Lopat had been wrong about them—not that he was likely to know that any more.

Down in southern Sonora, winter was the rainy season. Hipolito Rodriguez had planted his fields of corn and beans when the rains started, plowing behind his trusty mule. Now, with 1934 giving way to 1935, he tramped through them hoe in hand, weeding and cultivating. A farmer's work was never done.

These days, he wasn't the only one tramping through the fields. His two older sons, Miguel and Jorge, were big enough to give him real help: one was seventeen, the other sixteen. Before many more years—maybe before many more months—had passed, they would discover women.

Once they found wives, they'd go off and farm on their own. Then Rodriguez would have to work his plot by himself again. No—by then Pedro would be old enough to pitch in. Now he enjoyed the extra help.

When the day's work was done—earlier than it would have been without his sons' help—he stood at the sink working the pump handle to get water to wash the sweat from his round brown face. That done, he dried himself on a towel prickly with embroidery from his wife and his mother-in-law.

"Magdalena, you know I am going into Baroyeca tonight," he said.

His wife sighed but nodded. *"Sí,"* she said. The two of them, Magdalena especially, spoke more Spanish than English. Most Sonorans, especially of their generation, did, even though Sonora and Chihuahua had belonged to the Confederate States ten years longer than either one of them had been alive. Their children, educated in the school in town, used the two languages interchangeably. Schools taught exclusively in English. What the Rodriguezes' children's children would speak was something Hipolito wondered from time to time, but not something he could do anything about.

He said, "There's nothing to worry about now. We have had no trouble holding Freedom Party meetings since *Señor* Featherston won the election."

Magdalena crossed herself. "I pray to God you are right. And I still say you have not told me all you could about these times you were shooting at people."

Since she was right, Rodriguez didn't answer. He ate his supper—beans and cheese wrapped in tortillas—then walked to Baroyeca, about three miles away. He got to town just as the sun was setting.

Baroyeca had never been a big place. A lot of the shops on the main street were shuttered these days, and had been ever since the silver mines in the mountains to the north closed down a few years earlier. If Jaime Diaz's general store ever shut down, Rodriguez didn't know how the town would survive.

Except for the general store and the *Culebra Verde*, the local cantina, Freedom Party headquarters was the only business in Baroyeca that bothered lighting itself up after sundown. The lamps burned kerosene. Electricity had never appeared here. FREEDOM! the sign on the front window said, and below it, in slightly smaller letters, ¡LIBERTAD!

No matter what Rodriguez had told his wife, an armed guard with bandoleers crisscrossing his chest stood in front of the door. He nodded and stood aside to let Rodriguez go in. *"Hola,* Pablo," Rodriguez said. *"¿Todo está bien?"*

"Yes, everything's fine," Pablo Sandoval answered in English.

"Nobody gonna do nothin' to us now." Peeking out from under one of the bandoleers was his Purple Heart ribbon. Like Rodriguez, like most of the men now entering middle age in Baroyeca, he'd gone north to fight for the *Estados Confederados* and against the *Estados Unidos* in the Great War. He'd stayed in the English-speaking part of the CSA for several years before coming home, which went a long way toward explaining why he often used that language.

The Party organizer who'd come down to Baroyeca a few years before, on the other hand, was a native speaker of English but greeted Rodriguez in fluent Spanish: *"Hola, señor. ¿Como está Usted?"*

*"Estoy bien. Gracias, Señor Quinn. ¿Y Usted?"*

"I am also well, thank you," Robert Quinn replied in Spanish. He was and always had been scrupulously polite to the men he'd recruited into the Freedom Party. That in itself set him apart from a lot of English-speaking Confederates, who treated men of Mexican blood as only a short step better than Negroes. Rodriguez hadn't needed long in the Confederate Army to figure out that *greaser* was no term of endearment. Good manners alone had been plenty to gain Quinn several new Party members. *"¡Libertad!"* he added now.

*"¡Libertad!"* Rodriguez echoed. He nodded to his friends as he took a seat. They'd been in combat together, fighting against the dons who didn't want to see the Freedom Party taking over Baroyeca and all of Sonora.

Continuing in his good if accented Spanish, Robert Quinn said, "Gentlemen, I have a couple of announcements to make. First, I am glad I see before me men with many sons. President Featherston is beginning a Freedom Youth Corps for boys fourteen to eighteen years old. They will work where work is needed, and they will learn order and discipline. The Party and the state of Sonora will join together in paying the costs of uniforms. Those will not cost any Party member even one cent."

A pleased buzz ran through the room. Rodriguez's friend, Carlos Ruiz, put up his hand. Quinn nodded to him. He said, *"Señor,* what if boys who come from families where there are no Party members want to join this Freedom Youth Corps?"

"This is a good question, *Señor* Ruiz." Quinn's smile was not altogether pleasant. He said, "In English, we say *johnny-come-latelies* for those who try to jump on the caboose when the train is rolling away. These boys will be able to join, but their families *will* have to pay for the uniforms. This seems only fair, or do you think differently?"

"No, *Señor* Quinn. I like this very much," Ruiz replied. Rodriguez liked it very much, too. For as long as his family had lived in these parts, they'd had to make do with the dirty end of the stick. This time, though, he'd actually backed a winner. Not only that, backing a winner was proving to have its rewards. By the smiles on the faces of the other Freedom Party men, their thoughts were running along the same lines.

"Some of you already know about our next item of business," Quinn said. "You saw, when the *pendejos* who fought for Don Joaquin shot up our headquarters here last year, that we could not rely on the *guardía civil* to keep such troublemakers away from us. The present members of the *guardía civil* have ... resigned. Their replacements will be Freedom Party men."

"*Bueno,*" Rodriguez said. His wasn't the only voice raised in approval, either. Putting Freedom Party men in those places did a couple of things. It made sure the people who enforced the law would do that the way the Party wanted, as for so many years they'd done it the way the local mine owners and big landowners wanted. And, unless Rodriguez missed his guess, it would also make sure several Freedom Party men now down on their luck had jobs that paid enough to live on. Indeed, what point belonging to the winning side if you couldn't reap any benefits from it?

Knowing smiles around the room said he wasn't the only man to have figured that out, either. *It's good to know,* he thought. *One thing you could say about an old* patrón: *when trouble came, he looked out for the men who backed him. Now we see the Freedom Party does the same thing. We can rely on these people. They won't use us and then walk away.*

Underscoring that very point, Robert Quinn said, "Baroyeca is our town now. Sonora is our state. We have to make sure nobody takes them away from us, and we have to show people who haven't joined the Freedom Party yet that they'd be smart if they did."

Several men stirred at that. Carlos Ruiz put their worries into words: "Why do we want all these—what did you call them in English—johnnies-come-lately in the Party? What good are they? They would only be followers. They never fought for the Party. They never shed their blood for it. Who needs them?"

"You will always be special to the Freedom Party," Quinn promised. He tapped the pin he wore in his lapel. "You men who were Party members before President Featherston was inaugurated will be able to wear pins like this one. They will show you followed the Freedom Party before that was the popular thing to do. The others, the latecomers, will have a black border on the pins they wear."

"Not bad," Hipolito Rodriguez murmured. Most of the other Party men nodded. *We deserve to be singled out,* Rodriguez thought. *Carlos is right. We paid our Party dues in blood.*

But Quinn went on, "Still, the Freedom Party has room for more than just us. The Freedom Party is for everyone in the *Estados Confederados.*

Everyone, do you hear me? The Party is here to help all the people. It is here for all the people. And it is here to make sure all the people do all they can to make the *Estados Confederados* a better country, a stronger country. We will need all our strength. All of you who are old enough fought in the war. We were stabbed in the back then. If we ever have to fight again, we will win."

Rodriguez hadn't hated the United States before the Great War. He'd rarely thought about the USA before the war. Down here in southern Sonora, the United States had seemed too far away to worry about. Even Confederate states like Alabama and South Carolina had seemed too far away to worry about.

Things were different now. Men from the United States had spent a couple of years doing their level best to kill him. He knew he'd survived the war at least as much by luck as because he made a good soldier. Then, when the fighting finally ended, the men from the United States had taken away his rifle, as if he and his country had no more right to defend themselves.

Was he supposed to love the USA after that? Not likely!

"We'll all be in step together," Quinn said. "We're marching into the future side by side. One country, one party—all together, on to . . . victory."

One country . . . one party? Not so long ago, in this very room, Carlos had asked what would happen when the Freedom Party lost an election after gaining power. Robert Quinn had thought that was very funny. Hipolito hadn't understood why, not at the time. Now . . . Now maybe he did.

"*¿Hay otro más?*" Quinn asked. Nobody said anything. Quinn nodded briskly—an English-speaker's nod. "All right. If there is no other business, *amigos,* this meeting is adjourned. *Hasta luego.*"

Stars shone down brightly when Rodriguez and the other Freedom Party men left Party headquarters. The wind blew off the mountains to the northeast. It was as chilly a wind as Baroyeca ever knew, though up in Texas during the war Rodriguez had discovered things about winter he'd never wanted to know. He wished he'd brought along a poncho; the walk back to the farm would be less than delightful. Of course, the walking itself would help keep him warm.

Some of the Freedom Party men headed for *La Culebra Verde,* from which light and the sounds of a guitar and raucous singing emerged. "Come on, *amigo,*" Carlos Ruiz called. "One won't hurt you, or even two or three."

"Too much work tomorrow," Rodriguez said. His friends laughed at him. They probably thought that, while a beer or a tequila, or even two or three, wouldn't hurt him, Magdalena would. And, though he had no intention of admitting it to them, they were probably right.

Cincinnatus Driver pulled over to the curb, hopped out of his elderly Ford truck with the motor still running, and trotted to the corner to buy a copy of the *Des Moines Herald-Express* from the deaf-mute selling them there. The fellow tipped his cap and smiled as Cincinnatus gave him a nickel, and smiled wider when the Negro hurried back to the truck without waiting for his change.

He flipped the paper open to the inside pages and read whenever he had to stop for a sign or a traffic cop or one of the red lights that had sprung up like toadstools the past few years. The stories that concerned him most didn't make it to the front page. That was full of the anti-U.S. riots convulsing Houston, the United State carved from west Texas at the end of the Great War. What Cincinnatus wanted to know more about weren't world-shaking events, and they didn't have anything directly to do with Des Moines, either. Sometimes several days would go by without one of the stories that worried him turning up.

Today, though, he found one. The headline—it wasn't a big headline, not on page five—read, PARTY OF 25 NEGROES TURNED BACK AT BORDER. The story told how the blacks—men, women, and children, it said—had tried to cross from Confederate Tennessee into U.S. Kentucky, and how Border Patrol and National Guard units had forced them to go back into the CSA. *They claimed intolerable persecution in their own country,* the reporter wrote, *but, as their entrance into the United States would have been both illegal and undesirable, the officers of the Border Patrol rejected their pleas, as is longstanding U.S. policy.*

He'd made plenty of deliveries to the *Herald-Express.* If he'd had that reporter in front of him, he would have punched the man—a white man, of course—right in the nose. He came down on the clutch so clumsily, he stalled his truck and had to fire it up again. That made him realize how furious he was. He hadn't done anything like that since he was learning how to drive back before the Great War.

But, as he rolled north toward the railroad yards, he realized he shouldn't be mad at the reporter alone. The fellow hadn't done anything but clearly state what U.S. government policy was and always had been. Back when the border between the USA and the CSA ran along the Ohio River, U.S. patrols had shot Negroes who were trying to flee to the United States while they were in the water. The USA had only a handful of blacks, and wanted no more. A lot of people here would have been happier without the ones they already had.

Cincinnatus' laughter had a sour edge. "They was stuck with me and the ones like me, on account of they couldn't no way get Kentucky without us," he said. He was glad to live under U.S. rather than C.S. rule, especially now that the Freedom Party called the shots down in the Confederacy.

The race riots sweeping through the CSA were the main reason Negroes were trying to get out, of course. Jews had run away from Russian pogroms to the USA. Irishmen had escaped famines and English landlords. Germans had fled a failed revolution. Poles and Italians and Frenchmen had done their best to get away from hunger and poverty. They'd all found places in the United States.

Negroes from the Confederate States? Men and women who had desperately urgent reasons to leave their homes, who already spoke English, and who were ready to work like the slaves their parents and grandparents (and some of *them*, as youths) had been? Could they make homes for themselves here?

No.

He supposed he should have been glad U.S. military authorities hadn't chased Negroes south into Confederate territory as they advanced during the war. For a moment, he wondered why they hadn't. But he could see reasons. The Confederates could have got good use from the labor of colored refugees. And if anything could have made Negroes loyal to the CSA, getting thrown out of the USA would have been it. U.S. officials, for a wonder, had been smart enough to figure that out, and so it hadn't happened.

Here were the railroad yards, a warren of tracks and switches and trains and fragments of trains scattered here and there over them, apparently—but not really—at random. A couple of railroad dicks, billy clubs in their hands, pistols on their hips, recognized Cincinnatus and his truck and waved him forward. "Mornin', Lou. Mornin', Steve," he called to them. They waved again. He'd been coming here a long time now.

As he bumped over railroad crossings toward a train, he watched the two dicks in his rear-view mirror. They were chasing a ragged white man who'd been riding the rails and was either switching trains or getting off for good. Cincinnatus would have bet the fellow was bound for somewhere else, probably somewhere out West. Not many folks wanted to stay in Des Moines. Even if this poor bastard had had that in mind, he wouldn't by the time Steve and Lou got through with him.

There stood the conductor, as important a man on a freight train as the supercargo was on a steamboat. Cincinnatus hit the brakes, jumped out of his truck, and ran over to the man with the clipboard in his hand. "Ain't seen you in a while, Mr. Navin," he said, touching the brim of his soft cloth cap. "What you got for me to haul today?"

"Hello, Cincinnatus," Wesley Navin said. Cincinnatus wondered how many conductors came through Des Moines. However many it was, he knew just about all of them. By now, they knew him, too. They knew how reliable he was. Only a handful of them refused to give him business because he was colored. Navin wasn't one of those. He pointed down the train to a couple of boxcars. "How you fixed for blankets and padding? I've got a shipment of flowerpots here, should be enough for this town for about the next hundred years."

"Got me plenty," Cincinnatus answered. "How many stops I got to make on this here run?"

"Let me have a look here. . . ." Navin consulted the all-important clipboard. "Six."

"Where they at?" Cincinnatus asked. The conductor read off the addresses. Cincinnatus spread his hands, pale palms up. "You runnin' me all over creation. I got to ask four dollars. Oughta say five—I might not make it back here to git me another load today."

"Pay you three and a quarter," Navin said.

"My mama didn't raise no fools," Cincinnatus said. "I get my ass over to the riverside. I get honest pay for honest work there."

"You're the blackest damn Jew I ever seen," Navin said. Cincinnatus only grinned; that wasn't the first time people had said such things about him. Still grumbling, the conductor said, "Well, hell, three-fifty. Since it's you."

"Don't do me no favors like that," Cincinnatus told him. "I ain't goin' nowhere till I don't lose money on the way, and you ain't got there yet."

They settled at $3.75. A few years earlier, that wouldn't have been enough to keep Cincinnatus in the black. But he was more efficient now than he had been—and prices on everything had come down since money got so tight.

He loaded what seemed like nine million flowerpots into the back of the Ford, using ratty old blankets to keep one stack from bumping another. Anything he broke, of course, he was stuck with. He winced every time the truck jounced over a pothole. He'd done a little thinking before leaving the railroad yard with the flowerpots. The couple of minutes he spent probably saved him an hour of travel time, for he worked out the best route to take to get to all six nurseries and department stores. That was part of what being efficient was all about.

It let him get back to the railroad yard just past two in the afternoon: plenty of time to get more cargo and deliver it before sundown. With the sun setting as he finished the second load, he drove home, parking the truck in front of his apartment building. When he walked into the apartment, his daughter Amanda was doing homework at the kitchen table, while Elizabeth, his wife, fried ham steaks in a big iron spider on the stove.

Cincinnatus gave Elizabeth a quick kiss, then said, "Where's Achilles at? He in his room?"

She shook her head. She was cooking in the maid's clothes she'd worn to work. "He blew in a little before you got home, stayed just long enough to change his clothes, and then he done blew out again," she said.

"Why'd he bother changin'?" Cincinnatus asked. "What he does, he don't need to." Thanks not least to Cincinnatus' insistence—sometimes delivered with a two-by-four—his son had earned his high-school diploma. Then he'd amazed everyone—including, very likely, himself—by landing a clerk's job at an insurance company. He wasn't likely to work up much of a sweat filing papers or adding up columns of numbers.

But Elizabeth said, "Why you think? He takin' Grace out to the movin' pictures again."

"Oh." Cincinnatus didn't know how to go on from there. Grace Chang lived in the apartment right upstairs from his own. Her father ran a laundry and brewed excellent beer (a very handy talent in a state as thoroughly dry as Iowa). Cincinnatus couldn't deny that Grace was a sweet girl, or that she was a pretty girl. No one at all could deny that she was a Chinese girl.

She'd been going out with Achilles for more than a year now. It made Cincinnatus acutely nervous. These weren't the Confederate States, and Grace wasn't white, but even so. . . . Having the two of them go out together also made Mr. Chang nervous. He liked Achilles well enough—he'd known him since he was a little boy—but there was no denying Achilles wasn't Chinese.

"Ain't nothin' good gonna come o' this," Cincinnatus said heavily.

Elizabeth didn't answer right away. She flipped the ham steaks over with a long-handled spatula. "Never can tell," she said when they were sizzling again. "No, never can tell. Mebbe grandkids come o' this."

"Do Jesus!" Cincinnatus exclaimed. "You reckon he wants to marry her?"

His wife used the spatula on a mess of potatoes frying in a smaller pan. Then she said, "Don't reckon he go with a gal for more'n a year unless he thinkin' 'bout that. Don't reckon she go with him unless she thinkin' 'bout it, too."

"What do we do, he ends up marryin' the Chinaman's daughter?" Cincinnatus asked.

Elizabeth turned more potatoes before answering, "Upstairs right about now, I reckon Mr. Chang sayin' to his missus, 'What we do, they git married?' " Her effort to reproduce a singsong Chinese accent was one of the funnier things Cincinnatus had heard lately.

But that bad accent wasn't the only reason he started laughing. Even though Achilles and Grace had been going out for more than a year, nobody outside their families had said a word to either one of them about their choice of partner. It was as if white Des Moines—the vast majority of the town—couldn't get excited about what either a Negro or a Chinese did, so long as it didn't involve any whites.

Supper was fine. Cincinnatus wanted to stay up and wait for Achilles, but the day he'd put in caught up with him. He went to bed, where he dreamt he was trying to sneak into the USA in his truck so he could take Grace Chang to the moving pictures, but people kept throwing flowerpots at him, so he couldn't get in.

A snore came from behind Achilles' door when Cincinnatus got up. His son didn't have to be at the office till nine o'clock, so he got to sleep late. That meant Cincinnatus had to head out before Achilles got up. It also meant Cincinnatus couldn't talk to him about Grace. He had told Achilles an education would come in handy all sorts of ways. Now, to his chagrin, he discovered just how right he was.

Lucien Galtier got into his motorcar for the drive up to Rivière-du-Loup. The Chevrolet started when Galtier turned the key. One thing any Quebecois with an auto soon learned was the importance of keeping the battery strongly charged in winter—and, up there by the St. Lawrence, winter lasted a long time.

"Here we go," Galtier said. He was a small, trim man who'd just turned sixty. He looked it—a life outdoors had left his skin wrinkled and leathery—but he was still vigorous, his hair no lighter than iron gray. When he drove a wagon up into town, he'd had endless philosophical discussions with the horse. The motorcar made a less satisfying partner for such things than the horse had, but enjoyed certain advantages the beast lacked. No horse yet had ever come with a heater.

The highway was a black asphalt line scribed on the whiteness of fresh snow. By now, with so many years of weathering behind them, the shell holes from the Great War were hard to spy with snow on the ground. Oh, here and there a pockmark gave a clue, but little by little the earth was healing itself.

Healing, however, was not the same as healed. Every so often, the cycle of freeze and thaw brought to the surface long-buried shells, often rotten with corrosion. Demolition experts in the blue-gray uniforms of the Republic of Quebec disposed of most of those. The spring before, though, Henri Beauchamp had found one with his plow while tilling the ground. His son Jean-Marie now had that farm, a couple of miles from

Galtier's, and there hadn't been enough left of poor luckless Henri to bury. Lucien didn't know what to do about that danger. If he didn't plow, he wouldn't eat.

Rivière-du-Loup sat on the bluffs from which the river that gave it its name plunged down into the St. Lawrence. It was a market town, a river port, and a railroad stop. It was the biggest town Galtier had ever seen, except for a few brief visits to Toronto while he was in the Canadian Army more than forty years before. How it measured up in the larger scheme of things he really didn't know. He really didn't care, either. At his age, he wasn't going anywhere else.

On this crisp, chilly Sunday morning, Rivière-du-Loup seemed even larger than it was. Plenty of farm families from the countryside had come in to hear Mass at the Église Saint-Patrice on Rue Lafontaine. As he usually did, Galtier parked on a side street and walked to the church. More and more motorcars clogged Rivière-du-Loup's narrow streets, which had been built before anyone thought of motorcars. On Sunday mornings, a lot of horse-drawn wagons kept them company. Seeing a wagon much like the one he'd driven threw Lucien into a fit of nostalgia.

He came to the church at the same time as his oldest daughter, Nicole; her husband, Dr. Leonard O'Doull; and their son, Lucien, whose size astonished his grandfather every time he saw his namesake. "What is it that you feed this one?" he demanded of the boy's parents.

Leonard O'Doull looked puzzled. "You mean we're supposed to *feed* him?" he said. "I knew we'd been forgetting something." He spoke very good Quebecois French; his American accent and his Parisian accent had both faded in the seventeen years since he'd been married to Nicole.

"How are you, *mon père?*" Nicole asked.

"*Pas pire,*" he answered, which, like the English *not bad*, would do for everything between agony and ecstasy. He'd known his share of agony a few years before, when his wife died. Ecstasy? Getting new grandchildren came as close as anything he was likely to find at his age.

Pointing, Nicole said, "There's Charles," at the same time as her husband said, "There's Georges." Galtier waved to his older and younger sons and their families in turn. His second daughter, Denise, and her husband and children came up as he was greeting his sons. Maybe his other two girls were already in church, or maybe they hadn't come into town this Sunday.

"Come on." Georges, who would always take the bull by the horns, led the way in. "The world had better look out, because here come the Galtiers." He towered over both Lucien and Charles, who took after his father. With Georges in the lead, maybe the world *did* need to look out for the Galtiers.

They weren't the only large clan going into the church. Quebecois ran to lots of children and to close family ties, so plenty of brothers and sisters and cousins paraded in as units for their friends and neighbors to admire. Filling a couple of rows of pews was by no means an unusual accomplishment.

Bishop Guillaume presided over Mass. No breath of scandal attached itself to him, as it had to his predecessor in the see, Bishop Pascal. Pascal had been—no doubt still was—pink and plump and clever. He'd been too quick by half to attach himself to the Americans during the war. Galtier still thought he'd used their influence to get Rivière-du-Loup named an episcopal see—and that he'd done it more for himself than for the town. He'd left the bishopric—and Rivière-du-Loup—in something of a blaze of glory, when his lady friend presented him with twins.

Galtier found it highly unlikely that Bishop Guillaume would ever father twins. He was well up into his sixties, and ugly as a mud fence. He had a wart on his chin and another on his nose; his eyes, pouched below, were those of a mournful hound; his ears made people think of an auto going down the street with its doors open. He was a *good* man. Lucien didn't doubt that a bit. Who would give him the chance to be bad?

He was also a pious man. Lucien didn't doubt that, either, where he'd always wondered about Bishop Pascal—and, evidently, had excellent good reason to wonder. Guillaume preached sermons that were thoughtful, Scriptural, well organized . . . and just a little dull.

After this one, and after receiving Holy Communion, Lucien said, "Sermons are the one thing I miss about Pascal. You'd always get something worth hearing from him. It might not have anything to do with the church, but it was always interesting."

"Pascal's favorite subject was always Pascal," Georges said.

Leonard O'Doull raised an eyebrow. His long, fair face marked him as someone out of the ordinary in this crowd of dark, Gallic Quebecois. "And how is he so different from you, then?" he asked mildly.

Georges' brother and sisters laughed. Lucien chuckled. As for Georges . . . well, nothing fazed Georges. "How is he different from me?" he echoed. "Don't be silly, my dear brother-in-law. *My* favorite subject was never Pascal."

His family, or those among them old enough to understand the joke, groaned in unison. "Someone must have dropped you on your head when you were a baby," Lucien said. "Otherwise, how could you have turned out the way you are?"

"What's this you say?" Georges asked in mock astonishment. "Don't you think I take after you?"

That was absurd enough to draw another round of groans from his kin. Charles, who really did resemble Lucien in temperament as well as looks, said, "You should count yourself lucky Papa didn't take after you—with a hatchet."

Incorrigible Georges did an impersonation of a chicken after it met the hatchet and before it decided it was dead and lay still. He staggered all over the sidewalk, scattering relatives—and a few neighbors—in his wake. He managed to run into Charles twice, which surprised Lucien very little. When they were younger, Charles had dominated his brother till Georges grew too big for him to get away with it any more. Georges had been getting even ever since.

"Come back to my house, everyone," Dr. O'Doull urged, as he did on most Sundays. "We can eat and drink and talk, and the children can take turns getting in trouble."

"So can the grownups," Nicole said, with a sidelong look at Georges.

O'Doull was doing well for himself; he was probably the most popular doctor in Rivière-du-Loup. He had a good-sized house. But it could have been as big as the Fraser Manor—the biggest house in town by a long shot—and still seemed crowded when Galtiers filled it.

Lucien found himself with a glass of whiskey in his hand. He stared at it in mild wonder. He was much more used to drinking beer or locally made applejack that didn't bother with tedious government formalities about taxes. He sipped. He'd had applejack that was stronger; he'd had applejack where, if you breathed towards an open flame after a swig, your lungs would catch fire. He sipped again. "What gives it that flavor?"

"It comes from the charred barrels they use to age the whiskey," his son-in-law answered.

"So we are drinking . . . burnt wood?" Galtier said.

"So we are," Leonard O'Doull agreed. He sipped his own whiskey, with appreciation. "Tasty, *n'est-ce pas?*"

"I don't know." Lucien took another sip. Fire ran down his throat. "It will make a man drunk, *certainement.* But if I have a choice between drinking something that tastes of apples and something that tastes of burnt wood, I know which I would choose most of the time."

"If you want it, I have some real Calvados, not the bootleg hooch you pour down," O'Doull said.

"Maybe later," Galtier replied. "I did tell you, most of the time. For now, for a change, the whiskey is fine." He took another sip. Smacking his lips thoughtfully, he said, "I wonder how people came to savor the taste of burnt wood in the first place."

Dr. O'Doull said, "I don't know for certain, but I can guess. Once you distill whiskey, you have to put it somewhere unless you drink it right away. Where do you put it? In a barrel, especially back in the days before glass was cheap or easy to come by. And sometimes, *peut-être,* it stayed in the barrel long enough to take on the taste of the wood before anyone drank it. If someone decided he liked it when it tasted that way, the flavor would have been easy enough to make on purpose. I don't know this is true, mind you, but I think it makes pretty good sense. And you, *mon beau-père,* what do you think?"

"I think you have reason—it does make good sense. I think you think like a man born of French blood." Galtier could find no higher praise. Most Americans, from what he'd seen, were chronically woolly thinkers. Not his son-in-law. Leonard O'Doull came straight to the point.

He also recognized what a compliment Galtier had paid him. "You do me too much honor," he murmured. Lucien shook his head. "Oh, but you do," Dr. O'Doull insisted. "I am more lucky than I can say to have lived so long among you wonderful Quebecois, who actually—when you feel like it—respect the power of rational thought."

"You phrase that oddly," Lucien said. Maybe the whiskey made him notice fine shades of meaning he might otherwise have missed. "Why would you not live among us for the rest of your days?"

"I would like nothing better," Leonard O'Doull replied. "But a man does not always get what he would like."

"What would keep you from having this?" Galtier asked.

"The state of the world," O'Doull answered sadly. "Nothing here, *mon beau-père.* I love Rivière-du-Loup. I love the people here—and not just you mad Galtiers. But it could be—and I fear it may be—that one day there will again be places that need doctors much, much more than Rivière-du-Loup."

"What do you—?" Lucien Galtier broke off. He knew perfectly well how the American had come to town. He'd been one of the doctors working at the military hospital they'd built during the Great War. Thinking of that, Galtier gulped his whiskey down very fast and held out his glass for a refill.

"**H**urry up with that coffee here!" The Confederate drawl set Nellie Jacobs' teeth on edge. Her coffeehouse had had plenty of Confederate customers ever since the days of the Great War. Even now, with much of northern Virginia annexed to the USA, the border wasn't far to the south. And Confederates were always coming to Washington for one reason or another: occupation during the war, business now.

"I'm coming, sir," she said, and grabbed the pot off the stove. Her hip twinged as she carried the coffeepot to the customer's table. *Sixty soon,* she thought. On long afternoons like this one, she felt the weight of all her years.

"Thank you kindly," he said when she'd poured. She wondered if he would tell her he'd been a regular at the coffeehouse during the war. She didn't recognize him, but how much did that prove? A man could easily lose his hair and gain a belly in twenty years. She wasn't the same as she'd been in 1915, either. Her hair was gray, her long face wrinkled, the flesh under her chin flabby. Men didn't look at her any more, not that way. To her, that was a relief. The Confederate sipped his coffee, then remarked, "Quiet around here."

"Times are hard," Nellie said. If this drummer or whatever he was couldn't see that for himself, he was a bigger fool than she thought— which would have taken some doing.

"Yes, times are hard," he said, and slammed his hand down on the tabletop hard enough to make her jump. Some coffee sloshed out of the cup and into the saucer on which it sat. "So why the . . . dickens aren't you people doing anything about it?"

"Nobody seems to know what *to* do—here or anywhere else." Nellie let a little sharpness come into her voice. "It's not like the collapse only happened in the United States." *You've got troubles of your own, buddy. Don't get too sniffy about ours.*

The Confederate nodded, conceding the point. He lit a cigar. When he did, Nellie took out a cigarette and put it in her mouth. She smoked only when her customers did. He struck another match and lit it for her. As she nodded, too, in thanks, he said, "But you-all don't even look like you're trying up here. Down in *my* country"—his chest swelled with pride till it almost stuck out farther than his gut—"since the Freedom Party took over, we've got jobs for people who were out of work. They're building roads and fences and factories and digging canals and I don't know what all, and pretty soon they'll start taming the rivers that give us so much trouble."

"Wait a minute. Didn't your Supreme Court say you couldn't do that?" Nellie asked. "That's what the papers were talking about a while ago, if I remember right."

"You do," the fellow said. "But didn't you hear President Featherston on the wireless the other day?"

"Can't say that I did," Nellie admitted. "The Confederate States aren't my country." *And a good thing, too,* she thought. But politeness made her ask, "What did he say?"

"I'll tell you what he said, ma'am. What he said was, he said, 'James McReynolds has made his decision, now let him enforce it!' "

The Confederate looked as proud as if he'd defied the Supreme Court in Richmond himself. He went on, "That's what a leader does. He *leads*. And if anybody gets in his way, he knocks the . . . so-and-so for a loop, and goes on and does what needs doing. That's Jake Featherston for you! And people are cheering, too, all the way from Sonora to Virginia."

Nellie was cynical enough to wonder how much people were encouraged to cheer. But that wasn't what really took her by surprise. She said, "You couldn't get away with thumbing your nose at the Supreme Court like that here in the USA."

"Well, ma'am, I'm going to tell you the truth, and the truth is, you can't make an omelette without breaking a few eggs." The Confederate beamed and puffed on his cigar as if he'd come up with a profound and original truth. He continued, "Take the niggers, for instance. We're still settlin' with them, on account of they got uppity beyond their station since they rose up during the war. They got to learn where they belong, and we'll teach 'em, too. You got to go on towards where you're headed no matter what, on account of otherwise you'll never get there."

Although Nellie had no particular use for colored people, she said, "I'm sure I don't know what burning down people's houses has got to do with the Supreme Court."

"Oh, it's all part of the same thing," her customer said earnestly. "That's the truth. It is." He might have been talking about the Holy Ghost. "Whatever you have to do, you go ahead and you *do* that, and you don't let anything stop you. If you think you can be stopped, you're in trouble. But if you *know* you can win, you will."

"I'm not so sure about that," Nellie said. "You people were sure you were going to win the Great War, but you didn't."

"You can say that if you want to," the Confederate answered. "You can say it, but that doesn't make it so. Truth is, we were stabbed in the back. It hadn't been for the niggers risin' up, we would've whipped you-all. Sure as I'm standing here before you, that's the gospel truth. Like I said before, they need paying back for that. Now they're starting to get it. Serves 'em right, if you care about what I think."

Since Nellie didn't, she retreated behind the counter. She hoped this noisy fellow would go away, and she hoped more customers would come in so she'd have an excuse to ignore him. He did eventually get up and leave. He'd put down a dime tip on a bill of half a dollar for a sandwich and coffee, so Nellie forgave him his noise.

Clara, Nellie's daughter, came home from school a few minutes later. Nellie stared at her in bemusement, as she often did. Part of her wondered how Clara had got to be fifteen years old, a high-school freshman with a woman's shape. And part of her simply marveled that Clara was there at all. Nellie had never intended to have a baby by Hal Jacobs. She hadn't always worried about rubbers simply because she'd thought she didn't need to worry about catching, either. That proved wrong. And here was Clara, only a couple of years older than her nephew Armstrong Grimes, the son of Clara's half sister, Edna.

"Hello, dear," Nellie said. "What did you learn today?" She always asked. With little book learning herself, she hoped getting more would mean Clara wouldn't have to work so hard as she had, or have to worry about making some of the mistakes she'd made—and she'd made some humdingers.

"Quadratic equations in algebra." Clara made a horrible face. "Diagramming sentences in English." She made another one. "And in government, how a bill becomes a law." Instead of a grimace, a yawn. Then she brightened. Her face, like Hal's, was rounder than Nellie's, and lit up when she smiled. "And Walter Johansen asked me if I could go to the moving pictures with him this Saturday. Can I, Ma? Please? Wally's so cute."

Nellie's first impulse was to scream, *No! All he wants to do is get your undies down!* As she knew—oh, how she knew!—that was true of most men most of the time. But if she made a big fuss about it, she would just make Clara more eager to taste forbidden fruit. She'd found that out raising Edna, and she also remembered as much from her own stormy journey into womanhood a million years before—that was what it felt like, anyhow.

And so, instead of screaming, she asked, "Which one is Walter? Is he the skinny blond kid with the cowlick?"

"No, Ma." Clara clucked, annoyed her mother couldn't keep her friends straight. "That's Eddie Fullmer. Walter's the football player, the one with the blue, blue eyes and the big dimple in his chin." She sighed.

That sigh did almost make Nellie yell, *No!* By the sound of things, it was a word Clara wouldn't even think about using to Mr. Football Hero. But Nellie made herself think twice. "I suppose you can go with him," she said, "if he brings you straight back here after the film. You have to promise."

"I do! I will! He will! Oh, Ma, you're swell!" Clara did a pirouette. Skirts were long again, for which Nellie thanked heaven. She wouldn't have wanted a girl Clara's age wearing them at the knee or higher, the way they'd been in the 1920s. That was asking for trouble, and girls between fifteen and twenty had an easy enough time finding it without asking. As things were, the skirt swirled out when Clara turned, showing off shapely calves and trim ankles.

*Do I want to be swell?* Nellie had her doubts. "I wish your pa would have seen you so grown-up," she said.

That sobered Clara. "So do I," she said quietly. Hal Jacobs had died a couple of years before, of a rare disease: carcinoma of the lung.

Nellie absently lit a fresh cigarette, and then had to stub it out in a hurry when a customer came in. Clara served him the coffee he ordered. She could handle the coffeehouse at least as well as Nellie, and why not? She'd been helping out here since she was tall enough to see over the top of the stove.

A few minutes after the customer left, Edna walked into the coffee-house. Her son Armstrong accompanied her, which he didn't usually do. Nellie was very fond of Armstrong's father, Merle Grimes: fonder of him than she'd been of any other man she could think of except perhaps Hal. She was positive she liked Edna's husband much more than she'd ever liked Edna's father. If he hadn't got her pregnant, she wouldn't have wanted to see him again, let alone marry him.

Armstrong, on the other hand . . . Yes, he was her grandson. Yes, she loved him on account of that. But he was a handful, no two ways about it, and Nellie was glad he was Edna's chief worry and not her own.

Clara reacted to Armstrong the way a cat reacts to a dog that has just galumphed into its house. They'd never got along, not since the days when baby Armstrong pulled toddler Clara's hair. Now, at thirteen, Armstrong was as tall as she was, and starting to shoot up like a weed.

"Behave yourself," Edna told Armstrong—she did know he was a handful, where some mothers remained curiously blind to such things. "I want to talk to your grandma."

"I didn't do anything," Armstrong said.

"Yet," Clara put in, not quite *sotto* enough *voce*.

"That'll be enough of that, Clara," Nellie said; fair was fair. She gave her attention back to her older daughter. "What's going on, Edna?"

"With me?" Edna Grimes shrugged and pulled out a pack of Raleighs. "Not much. I'm just going along, one day at a time." She lit the cigarette, sucked in smoke, and blew it out. "You can say what you want about the Confederates, Ma, but they make better cigarettes than we do." Nellie nodded; that was true. Her daughter went on, "No, I just want to make sure you're all right."

"I'm fine," Nellie answered, "or I will be if you give me one of those." Edna did, then leaned close so Nellie could get a light from hers. After a couple of drags, Nellie said, "I keep telling you, I'm not an old lady yet." Edna didn't say anything. Nellie knew what that meant. *Not yet. But soon.* She drew on the cigarette again. No matter how smooth the smoke was, it gave scant comfort.

* * *

Jake Featherston turned to Ferdinand Koenig. A nasty gleam of amusement sparkled in the Confederate president's eye. "Think we've let him stew long enough, Ferd?" he asked.

"Should be about right," the attorney general answered. "Twenty minutes in the waiting room is enough to tick him off, but not enough to where it's an out-and-out insult."

"Heh," Jake said. "We've already taken care of that." He thumbed the intercom on his desk. "All right, Lulu. You can let Chief Justice McReynolds come in now."

The door to the president's private office opened. Featherston got only the briefest glimpse of his secretary before James McReynolds swept into the room, slamming the door behind him. He wore his black robes. They added authority to his entrance, but he would have had plenty on his own. Though a few years past seventy, he moved like a much younger man. He'd lost his hair in front, which made his forehead even higher than it would have otherwise. His long face was red with fury.

"Featherston," he said without preamble, "you *are* a son of a bitch."

"Takes one to know one," Jake said equably. "Have a seat."

McReynolds shook his head. "No. I don't even want to be in the same room with you, let alone sit down with you. How dare you, Featherston? How *dare* you?"

With a smile, Koenig said, "I think he's seen the new budget, Mr. President."

"You shut up, you—you stinking Party hack," McReynolds snarled. "I'm here to talk to the head goon. How *dare* you abolish the Supreme Court?"

Before answering, Jake chose a fine Habana from the humidor on his desk. He made a production of clipping the end and lighting the cigar. "You torpedoed my river bill," he said. "No telling how much more trouble you'll make for me down the line. And so . . ." He shrugged. "Goodbye. I don't fool around with people who make trouble for me, Mr. Chief Justice. I kill 'em."

"But you can't get rid of the Supreme Court of the Confederate States just like *that*!" McReynolds snapped his fingers.

"Hell I can't. Just like *that* is right." Jake snapped his fingers, too. Then he turned to Ferdinand Koenig. "Tell him how, Ferd. You've got all the details straight."

Actually, the lawyers who worked under the attorney general were the ones who'd got everything straight. But Koenig could keep things straight once the lawyers had set them out for him—and he had notes to help him along. Glancing down at them, he said, "Here's the first sentence of Article Three of the Confederate Constitution, Mr. Chief Justice. It says—"

"I know what Article Three of the Constitution says, God damn you!" James McReynolds burst out.

Koenig shrugged. He had the whip hand, and he knew it. "I'll quote it anyway, so we keep things straight like the president said. It goes, 'The judicial power of the Confederate States shall be vested in one Supreme Court, and in such inferior courts as the Congress may from time to time ordain and establish.' "

"Yes!" McReynolds stabbed out a furious finger. "And that means you can do whatever you please with or to the district courts, but you have to keep your cotton-pickin' mitts off the Supreme Court."

"No, sir." The attorney general shook his head. Jake Featherston leaned back in his chair and blew a perfect smoke ring, enjoying the show. Koenig went on, "That's not what it means, and I can prove it. There *was* no Supreme Court when the Confederate States started out. None at all. In 1863, just after we finished licking the damnyankees in the War of Secession, Jeff Davis backed a bill setting up a Supreme Court, but it didn't pass. He was wrangling with Congress the way he usually did, and so the CSA didn't get a Supreme Court till"—he checked his notes for the exact date—"till May 27, 1866."

"But we haven't been without one since," James McReynolds insisted. "No one has ever dreamt that we *could* be without one. It's . . . unimaginable, is what it is."

"No it's not, on account of I imagined it." Jake tapped the fine gray ash from his Habana into an ashtray made out of the sawed-off base of a shell casing. "And what I imagine, I do. Ever since I got into the Freedom Party, people have said to me, 'You don't dare do this. You don't dare do that. You don't dare do the other thing.' They're wrong every goddamn time, but they keep saying it. You think you're so high and mighty in your fancy black robe, you can tell me what I can do and what I can't. But you better listen to me. Nobody tells Jake Featherston what to do. *Nobody.* You got that?"

McReynolds stared at him. "We have Congressional elections coming up this fall, Mr. Featherston. The Whigs and the Radical Liberals will make you pay for your high-handedness."

"Think so, do you?" Jake's grin was predatory. He reached into his pocket, pulled out a five-dollar goldpiece, and let it ring sweetly off the desktop. Thomas Jackson's bearded countenance stared up at him. "Here's a Stonewall says we'll have more men in the next Congress than we do in this one."

"You're on." McReynolds leaned forward and thrust out his hand. Featherston took it. For an old man, the Supreme Court justice had a strong grip, and he squeezed as if he wished he could break Featherston's fingers. "The people will know you and your party for what you are."

"Who do you think sent us here to do their business?" Jake answered. "We set out to do it, and then you seven sour bastards wouldn't let us. And now you've got the nerve to blame me and the Freedom Party for what you went and did?"

"That law plainly violated the Constitution," McReynolds said stubbornly. "If you violate it from now on, who's going to stand up to you and call you to account?"

That was the key question. The answer, of course, was *nobody*. Featherston didn't say it. If McReynolds couldn't see it for himself, the president didn't want to point it out to him. No matter how true it was, better to keep it quiet.

"You do see, though, Mr. Chief Justice, what we're doing here is legal as can be?" Ferdinand Koenig said. "You may not like it, but we've got the right to do it."

"You're breaking every precedent this country knows," McReynolds thundered. In the tradition-minded Confederate States, that was an even more serious charge than it might have been in other lands. "You're not politicians at all. You're crooks and pirates, that's what you are."

"We're the folks who won the election, that's what we are. You forgot it, and you're going to pay for it," Jake Featherston said. "And the attorney general asked you a question. I think you'd better answer it."

"And if I don't?" James McReynolds asked.

With no expression at all in his voice, Featherston answered, "Then you're a dead man."

McReynolds started to laugh. Then he took a second look at the president of the Confederate States. The laughter died unborn. The chief justice's face went a blotchy yellow-white. "You mean that," he whispered.

"You bet I do." Featherston had a .45 in his desk drawer. No one around the office would fuss if it went off. And he could always persuade a doctor to say McReynolds had died of heart failure. "Mr. McReynolds, I always mean what I say. Some folks don't want to believe me, but I do. I told you you'd be sorry if you messed with our good laws, and I reckon you are. Now . . . Ferd there asked you a question. He asked if you thought getting rid of you black-robed buzzards was legal. You going to answer him, or do I have to *show* you I mean what I say? It's the last lesson you'll ever get, and you won't have a hell of a lot of time to cipher it out."

The jurist licked his lips. Jake didn't think he was a coward. But how often did a man meet someone who showed in the most matter-of-fact way possible that he would not only kill him but enjoy doing it? Jake smiled in anticipation. Later, he thought that smile, more than anything else, was what broke McReynolds. Spitting out the words, and coming very close to spitting outright, the chief justice of a court going out of business snarled, "Yes, God damn you, it's legal. Technically. It's also a disgrace, and so are both of you."

He stormed from the president's office. As he opened the door, though, he nervously looked back over his shoulder. Was he wondering if Jake would shoot him in the back? *I would if I had to,* Jake thought. Not now, though. Now McReynolds had backed down. No point to killing a man who'd yielded. The ones who wouldn't quit—they were the ones who needed killing.

Koenig said, "Now we find out how much of a stink the Whigs and the Rad Libs kick up about this in the papers and on the wireless."

"Won't be too much. That's what Saul says, and I expect he's right," Featherston answered. "They're like McReynolds—they're starting to see bad things happen to folks who don't go along with us. How many papers and wireless stations have burned down the past few months?"

"Been a few," the attorney general allowed. "Funny how the cops don't have a hell of a lot of luck tracking down the boys who did it." He and Jake both laughed. Koenig raised a forefinger. "They did catch—or they said they caught—those fellows in New Orleans. Too bad for the D.A. down there that the jury wouldn't convict."

"We had to work on that," Jake said. "Harder than we should have, too. That Long who ran for vice president on the Rad Lib ticket, he's a first-class bastard, no two ways about it. Trouble, and nothing else but. If we hadn't beat him to the punch, he'd've made the Whigs sweat himself. Now he reckons he can make us sweat instead."

"Bad mistake," Koenig said thoughtfully. "Might be the last one he ever makes."

"That's something we don't want traced back to us, though," Featherston said. "All the little ones—those are what make people afraid. We can use as many of them as we need. This—this'd be a little too raw just now. We've got to nail the lid down tighter. After the elections things'll be easier—we'll be able to get away with whatever we need. 'Course, I don't suppose we'll need so much then."

"McReynolds thinks we'll lose," the attorney general observed.

They both laughed. Jake couldn't think of the last time he'd heard anything so funny. "That reminds me," he said. "How are we doing with the politicals?"

He already knew, in broad terms. But Ferdinand Koenig was the man with the details. "Jails are filling up all over the country," he answered. "Several states—Alabama, Mississippi, South Carolina, Georgia—have dragged in so many of those fuckers, the jails won't hold 'em any more. They're building camps out in the country for the overflow."

"That's good. That's damn good," Jake said. "We've got a lot of things left to do in this country, and we'll need people for hard work. Nobody's going to say boo if a bunch of prisoners go sweat all day in the hot sun, eh?"

"Not likely." Koenig, who was a big, blocky man, contrived to make himself look not just fat but bonelessly fat. "Render all the lard out of those porky Whig bastards who never did any honest work in their lives."

Featherston nodded emphatically. "You bet. And getting those camps built now'll come in handy, too. We'll have plenty of uses for places like that." He nodded again. "Yes, sir. *Plenty* of uses." He saw a piece of paper sticking out of a pile on his desk, pulled it free, and grinned. "Oh, good. I was afraid I'd lost this one. I'd've felt like a damn fool asking the secretary of agriculture to send me another copy."

"What is it?" Koenig asked.

"Report on the agricultural-machinery construction project," Featherston answered. "Won't be long before we've got tractors and harvesters and combines coming out of our ears. Gives us practice making big motor vehicles, you know?" He and Koenig chuckled again. "Helps farming along, too—don't need near so many people on the land with those machines doing most of the work."

The attorney general smiled a peculiar smile. "Yeah," he said.

**IV**

Colonel Irving Morrell was elbow-deep in the engine compartment of the new barrel when somebody shouted his name. "Hang on for a second," he yelled back without looking up. To Sergeant Michael Pound, he said, "What do you think of this carburetor?"

"Whoever designed it ought to be staked out in the hot sun, with a trail of honey running up to his mouth for the ants to follow," Pound answered at once. "Maybe another honey trail, too—lower down."

"Whew!" Morrell shuddered. "I've got to hand it to you, Sergeant: I may come up with nasty ideas, but you have worse ones."

Someone yelled his name again, adding, "You're ordered to report to the base commandant immediately, Colonel! Immediately!"

That made Morrell look up from what he was doing. It also made him look down at himself—in dismay. He wore a mechanic's green-gray coveralls whose front was liberally smeared and spattered with grease. He'd rolled up the coveralls' sleeves, but that only meant his hands and forearms had got filthy instead. He wiped them on a rag, but that was hardly more than a token effort.

"Can't I clean up a little first?" he asked.

The messenger—a sergeant—shook his head. "Sir, I wouldn't if I were you. When Brigadier General Ballou said *immediately*, he meant it. It's got to do with the mess down in Houston."

Sergeant Pound, who'd kept on guddling inside the engine compartment, poked his head up at that. "You'd better go, sir," he said.

He had no business butting into Morrell's affairs, which didn't mean he was wrong. After the war, the USA had made a United State out of the chunk of Texas they conquered from the CSA. Houston had always been the most reluctant of the United States, even more so than Kentucky, and looked longingly across the border toward the country from which it had been torn. Since the Freedom Party triumphed in the Confederacy, Houston hadn't been reluctant—it had been downright insurrectionary. It had a Freedom Party of its own, which had swept local elections in 1934 and sent a Congressman to Philadelphia. Every day seemed to bring a new riot.

Tossing the rag to the ground, Morrell nodded to the messenger. "Take me to him. If it's got to do with Houston, it won't wait."

Brigadier General Charles Ballou, the commandant at Fort Leavenworth, was a round little man with a round face and an old-fashioned gray Kaiser Bill mustache. Morrell saluted on coming into his office. "Reporting as ordered, sir," he said. "I apologize for the mess I'm in."

"It's all right, Colonel," Ballou said. "I wanted you here as fast as possible, and here you are. I believe you know Brigadier General MacArthur?"

"Yes, sir." Morrell turned to the other officer in the room and saluted once more. "Good to see you again, sir. It's been a while."

"So it has." Daniel MacArthur returned the salute, then sucked in smoke from a cigarette he kept in a long holder. He made an odd contrast to Ballou, for he was very long, very lean, and very craggy. He'd commanded a division under Custer during the war, which was where he and Morrell had come to know each other. He'd had a star on each shoulder even then; he was only a handful of years older than Morrell, and had been the youngest division commander and one of the youngest general officers in the U.S. Army. Since then, perhaps not least because he always said what he thought regardless of consequences, his career hadn't flourished.

Brigadier General Ballou said, "MacArthur has just been assigned as military commandant of Houston."

"That's right." Daniel MacArthur thrust out a granite jaw. "And I want a sizable force of barrels to accompany me there. Nothing like armor, I would say, for discouraging rebels against the United States. Who better than yourself, Colonel, to command such a force?"

His voice had a certain edge to it. He'd tried to break through Confederate lines with infantry and artillery alone. He'd failed, repeatedly. With barrels, Morrell had succeeded. *Does he want me to fail now?* Morrell wondered. But he could answer only one way, and he did: "Sir, I am altogether at your service. I wish I had more modern barrels to place at your disposal, but even the obsolete ones will serve against anything but other barrels."

MacArthur nodded brusquely. He stubbed out the cigarette, then put another one in the holder and lit it. "Just so," he said. "How many barrels and crews can you have ready to board trains and move south by this time three days from now? We are going to put the fear of the Lord and of the United States Army in the state of Houston."

"Yes, sir." Morrell thought for a bit, then said, "Sir, I can have thirty ready in that time. The limit isn't barrels; it's crews. The modern ones need only a third as many men as the old-fashioned machines."

"Thirty will do," MacArthur said. "I'd expected you to say twenty, or perhaps fifteen. Now I expect you to live up to your promise. You may go, Colonel." He'd always had the sweetness and charm of an alligator snapper turtle. But, if you needed someone to bite off a hand, he was the man for the job.

Fuming, Morrell left Brigadier General Ballou's office. Fuming still, he had thirty-two barrels ready to load onto flatcars at the required time. Daniel MacArthur's cigarette and holder twitched in his mouth when he counted the machines. He said not a word.

The trains left on time. People started shooting at them as soon as they passed from Kansas to Sequoyah, which had also belonged to the CSA before the war. Sequoyah had been a Confederate state; it was not a state in the USA. It was occupied territory. The United States did not want it, and the feeling was mutual.

Before long, Morrell put men back in the barrels as the train rattled south and west. They could use the machine guns to shoot back. More shots came their way in the east, where the Five Civilized Tribes had dominated life in Confederate times. The United States weren't soft on Indians, as the Confederate States had been—especially not on Indians who'd looked to Richmond rather than Philadelphia.

But, bad as Sequoyah was, it didn't prepare anybody for Houston. The train was two days late getting into Lubbock because of repeated sabotage to the tracks. Signs screamed out warnings: SABOTEURS WILL BE SHOT WITHOUT TRIAL! "Maybe they can't read here," Sergeant Pound suggested after one long, long delay.

Then they passed a trackside gallows with three bodies dangling from it. One of the bodies had a Confederate battle flag draped over it. That was what Morrell thought at first, anyhow. Then he realized the colors were reversed, which made it a Freedom Party flag, not one from the CSA.

He'd seen plenty of YANKS OUT! graffiti when he was stationed up in Kamloops, British Columbia. Those were as nothing next to the ones he saw as the train slowed to a stop coming into the Lubbock railroad yard. LEAVE US ALONE! was a common favorite. CSA! was quick and easy to write. So were the red-white-red stripes and the blue X's that suggested Confederate flags. LET US GO BACK TO OUR COUNTRY! was long, and so less common; the same held true for HOUSTON WAS A TRAITOR! But the one word seemingly everywhere was FREEDOM!

"Good Lord, sir!" Sergeant Pound said, eyeing the graffiti with much less equanimity than he'd shown rolling past the hanged Houstonians. "What *have* we got ourselves into?"

"Trouble," Morrell answered. That was the only word that came to mind.

"We will advance into downtown Lubbock," Brigadier General MacArthur declared as the barrels came down off their flatcars. "I have declared full martial law in this state. That declaration is now being published in newspapers and broadcast over the wireless. The citizens of Houston are responsible for their own behavior, and have been warned of this. If anyone hinders your progress towards or through the city in any way, shoot to kill. Do not allow yourselves to be endangered. Is that clear?"

No one denied it. Daniel MacArthur climbed up onto the turret of one of the modern barrels (to Morrell's relief, MacArthur didn't choose his). He struck a dramatic pose, saying, *Forward!* without words. The barrels rumbled south, toward central Lubbock.

They couldn't advance at much above a walking pace, because most of them were slow, flatulent leftovers from the Great War. Morrell knew the handful of modern machines could have got there in a third the time. Whether that would have done them any good was another question.

Lubbock didn't look like a town that had seen rioting. It looked like a town that had seen war. Blocks weren't just burnt out. They were shattered, either by artillery fire or bombardment from the air. The twin stenches of sour smoke and old death lingered, now weaker, now stronger, but never absent.

Not many people were on the streets. The eyes of the ones who were . . . In Canada, plenty of people had hated and resented American soldiers for occupying the country. Morrell had thought he was used to it. But, as with the graffiti, what was on the faces of the people here put Canada in the shade. These people didn't just want him gone. They didn't even just want him dead. They wanted him to suffer a long time before he died. If he ever fell into their hands, he would, too.

No sooner had that thought crossed his mind than a shot rang out from an apartment building that hadn't been wrecked. A bullet sparked off the barrel Daniel MacArthur was riding, about a foot from his leg.

At the sound of the shot, all the men and women on the street automatically threw themselves flat. They knew what was coming. And it came. Half a dozen barrels opened fire on that building, the old ones with their side-mounted machine guns, the new with turret cannon and coaxial machine guns. Windows vanished. So did a couple of big stretches of brick wall between the windows as cannon shells struck home. Glass and fragments of brick flew in all directions. People on the street crawled out of the way; they knew better than to get up and expose themselves to the gunfire.

Through it all, Daniel MacArthur never moved a muscle. He had nerve and he had style. Based on what Morrell remembered from the Great War, none of that surprised him. Did MacArthur have brains? Morrell wasn't so sure there.

Only after the front of the apartment building was wrecked did the brigadier general wave the barrels forward once more. *They make a desert and they call it peace,* Morrell thought. But no one fired any more shots before the armored detachment reached its perimeter in the center of town.

Once they got there, MacArthur summoned reporters from the *Gazette* and the *Statesman,* the two local newspapers. He said, "Gentlemen, here is something your readers need to know: if they interfere with the U.S. Army or disobey military authority, they will end up dead. And, having died, they will be buried in the soil of the United States, for they cannot and will not detach this state from this country. All they can do is spill their own blood to no purpose. Take that back to your plants and print it."

They did. The same message went out over the wireless, and in the papers in El Paso and other towns in Houston. Contingents of Morrell's barrels, along with infantrymen and state police, reinforced it. The rioting eased. Morrell was as pleased as he was surprised. Maybe Brigadier General MacArthur was pretty smart after all. Or maybe someone on the other side of the border had decided the rioting *should* ease for the time being. Morrell wished like hell that hadn't occurred to him.

Miguel and Jorge Rodriguez stood side by side in the farmhouse kitchen. They both looked very proud. They wore identical broad-brimmed cloth hats, short-sleeved cotton shirts, sturdy denim shorts, socks, and stout shoes. They also wore identical proud smiles.

Hats, shirts, and shorts were of the light brown color the Confederate Army, for no reason Hipolito Rodriguez had ever been able to understand, called butternut. On the pocket above the left breast of each shirt was sewn a Confederate battle flag with colors reversed: the emblem of the Freedom Party.

"I will miss your work," Rodriguez told his two older sons. "I will miss it, but the country needs it."

"That's right, Father," Jorge said. "And they'll pay us money—not a lot of money, but some—to do the work."

"I'll help you, Father," Pedro—the youngest son—said. He wasn't old enough to join the Freedom Youth Corps yet, and had been sick-jealous of his brothers ever since they did. Being useful on the farm wasn't much consolation, but it was what he had, and he made the most of it.

"I know you will." Rodriguez set a hand on his shoulder. "You're a good boy. All of you are good boys."

"*Sí,*" his wife said. She probably hadn't followed the whole conversation, most of which was in English, but she got that. In Spanish, she went on, "I'll miss you while you are gone." The tears in her eyes spoke a universal language.

"Father was right," Miguel said importantly. "The country *does* need us, so you shouldn't cry. We'll do big things for Sonora, big things for Baroyeca. I hear"—his voice dropped to an excited whisper—"I hear we are going to put in the poles to carry the wires to bring electricity down from Buenavista. Electricity!"

Instead of being impressed, Magdalena Rodriguez was practical: "We already have poles to bring the telegraph. Why not use those?"

Miguel and Jorge looked at each other. Plainly, neither one of them knew the answer. Just as plainly, neither one wanted to admit it. At last, Jorge said, "Because these poles are *special*, Mother." He might not even have noticed switching back to Spanish to talk to Magdalena.

"Come on, boys," Hipolito said. "Let's go into town." His sons had grumbled that they were almost grown men, that they were going off to do men's work, and that they didn't need their father escorting them to Baroyeca. He'd explained he was proud of them and wanted to show them off. He'd also explained he would wallop them if they grumbled any more. They'd stopped.

Before they left, he made sure his own Freedom Party pin was on his shirt. They trooped out of the farmhouse together. Neither the crow that fluttered up from the roof nor the two lizards that scuttled into a hole seemed much impressed. Before long, Rodriguez's sons were less delighted, too. "My feet hurt," Miguel complained. Jorge nodded.

"This happened to me when I went into the Army," Rodriguez said. "Shoes pinch. Up till then, I hadn't worn anything but sandals." He looked down at his feet. He wore sandals now. They were more comfortable than shoes any day. But comfort wasn't always the only question. "For some of what you do, for working in the mountains, sandals won't protect your feet. Good shoes like those will."

"They'll give us blisters," Jorge said. Now Miguel was the one who nodded in agreement.

"For a little while, yes," Rodriguez answered. "Then your feet will toughen up, and you'll be fine." He could afford to say that. His feet weren't the ones suffering.

When they came to Baroyeca—Jorge limping a little and trying not to show it, for his shoes pinched tighter than Miguel's—Rodriguez led them to the town square between the *alcalde*'s house and the church, as he'd been instructed to do. There he found most of the boys in the area, all standing solemnly in ranks that weren't so neat as they should have been. One of the new members of the *guardía civil*, a man who'd been a sergeant during the war, was in charge of them.

"*¡Libertad,* Hipolito!" he called. "These are your boys?"

"My older ones, Felipe," Rodriguez answered. "*¡Libertad!*"

"They'll do fine," Felipe Rojas said. "They won't have too much nonsense to knock out of them. Some of these little brats . . ." He shook his head. "Well, you can guess which ones."

"A lot of them will be ones whose fathers don't belong to the Party," Rodriguez predicted. Felipe Rojas nodded. Rodriguez eyed the youths. He couldn't tell by the uniforms; those were all the same. But the stance gave away who was who a lot of the time, that and whether a boy looked eager or frightened.

The bell in the church struck nine. Rodriguez let out a sigh of relief. He'd been told to get here before the hour. He hadn't realized he'd cut it so close.

A few minutes later, another boy tried to join the ranks in the square. Rojas ran him off, shouting, "You don't deserve to be here! You can't even obey orders about when to come. You're a disgrace to your uniform. Get out! *Get out!*"

"But, *señor*—" protested his father, who was not a Party man.

"No!" Rojas said. "He had his orders. He disobeyed them. You helped, no doubt. But anyone who doesn't understand from the start that the Freedom Youth Corps is about obedience and discipline doesn't deserve to be in it. Get him out of here, and you can go to the devil with him." The boy slunk away, his face a mask of misery. His father followed, hands clenched into impotent fists. He was not the least important man in Baroyeca, but he'd been treated as if he were.

Robert Quinn came into the square, pushing a wheelbarrow full of shovels. "Hello, boys," he said. "*¡Libertad!*"

"*¡Libertad!*" they echoed raggedly. Some of them were still looking after the youngster who'd been sent away.

"These are your spades," Quinn said in his accented but fluent Spanish. "You will have the privilege of using them to make Sonora a better place." Most of them smiled at that, liking the idea.

"These are your spades," Felipe Rojas echoed. "You will have the privilege of taking care of them, of keeping them sharp, of keeping them shiny, of keeping their handles polished. You will take them everywhere you go in the Freedom Youth Corps. You will *sleep* with them, *por Dios*. And you will *enjoy* sleeping with them, more than you would with a woman. Do you hear me? *Do you hear me?* Answer when I talk to you!"

*"Sí, señor,"* they chorused in alarm.

Now Hipolito Rodriguez smiled, and he wasn't the only man his age who did. Rojas' rant sounded much like what sergeants had said at the training camp during the war, except they'd been talking about rifles, not spades. Rojas took a shovel from the wagon and tossed it, iron blade up, to the closest youth. The boy awkwardly caught it. Another shovel flew, and another, till every boy had one.

"Attention!" Rojas shouted. They came to what they imagined attention to be. There were as many versions as there were boys. Rodriguez smiled again. So did the rest of the fathers and other men in the square. They'd been through the mill. They knew what attention was, even if their sons didn't.

Felipe Rojas took a shovel from a youngster and showed the boys of the Freedom Youth Corps how to stand at attention, the tool lightly gripped in his right hand. More or less clumsily, the boys imitated him. He tossed the shovel back to the youth, who also came to attention.

Another sharp command (all of these were in English): "Shoulder—spades!" Again, the boys made a hash of it. One of them almost brained the youngster beside him. Hipolito Rodriguez didn't laugh at that. He remembered what a deadly weapon an entrenching tool could be.

Again, Rojas took the shovel from the boy. He stood at attention with it, then smoothly brought it up over his shoulder. After demonstrating once more, he returned it.

"Now you try," he told the youths. "Shoulder—spades!" They did their best. Rojas winced. "That was terrible," he said. "I've seen burros that could do a better job. But you'll improve. We'll practice it till your right shoulders grow calluses. You'll find out." His voice, like the voice of any proper drill sergeant making a promise like that, was full of gloating anticipation.

He showed them left face, right face, and about-face. He marched them, raggedly, across the square. No one hit anyone else with a shovel as they turned and countermarched. *Why* nobody hit anybody else

Rodriguez couldn't have said. He thought he ought to go light a candle in the church to show his gratitude to the Virgin for the miracle.

"I have one last piece of advice for you," Felipe Rojas said when the boys had got to their starting place without casualties. "Here it is. You've been fooling your fathers and talking back to your mothers ever since you found out you could get away with it. Don't try it with me, or with any other Freedom Youth Corps man. You'll be sorry if you do. You have no idea how sorry you'll be. But some of you will find out. Boys your age are damn fools. We'll get rid of some of that, though. You see if we don't."

Some of them—most of them—didn't believe him. No boys of that age believed they were fools. They thought they knew everything there was to know—certainly more than the idiot fathers they had the misfortune to be saddled with. They'd find out. And, in the Freedom Youth Corps, they wouldn't have to bang heads with their fathers while they were finding out. That might make the Corps worthwhile all by itself.

Robert Quinn drifted over to Rodriguez. "Two boys going in, eh, *señor*? Good for you, and good for them. They're likely-looking young men."

"They aren't young men yet," Rodriguez said. "They just think they are. That's why the Freedom Youth Corps will be good for them, I think."

"I think you are right, *Señor* Rodriguez," the Freedom Party organizer said. "This will teach them many of the things they will need to know if, for example, they are called into the Army."

Rodriguez looked at the English-speaker who'd come from the north. "How can they be called into the Army, *Señor* Quinn? There has been no conscription in *los Estados Confederados* since the end of the Great War."

"This is true," Quinn said. "Still, the Freedom Party aims to change many things. We want the country strong again. If we are not allowed to call up our own young men to serve the colors, are we strong or are we weak?"

"Weak, *señor,* without a doubt," Hipolito Rodriguez replied. "But *los Estados Unidos* are strong now. What will they do if we begin conscription once more?"

"This is not for you to worry about. It is not for me to worry about, either," Quinn said. "It is for Jake Featherston to take care of. And he will, *Señor* Rodriguez. You may rely on that." He spoke as certainly as the priests did of Resurrection.

And Rodriguez said, "Oh, I do." He meant it, too. Like so many others in the CSA, he wouldn't have joined the Freedom Party if he hadn't.

* * *

"**W**ell, well," Colonel Abner Dowling said, studying the *Salt Lake City Bee*. "Who would have thought it, Captain?"

"What's that, sir?" Angelo Toricelli asked.

Dowling tapped the story on page three with his fingernail. "The riots in Houston," he told his adjutant. "They just go on and on, now up, now down, world without end, amen." He was not a man immune to the pleasure of watching someone else struggle through a tough time. Serving under General George Custer, he'd had plenty of tough times of his own. He'd come to savor those that happened to other people, not least because they sometimes ended up getting him off the hook.

Captain Toricelli said, "Of course they go on and on. The Freedom Party in the CSA keeps stirring things up there. If we could seal off the border between Houston and Texas, we'd be able to put a lid on things there."

"I wish that were true, but I don't think it is," Dowling said. Toricelli looked miffed. Dowling remembered looking miffed plenty of times when General Custer said something particularly idiotic. Now the shoe was on the other foot. He'd been stuck then. His adjutant was now. And he didn't think he was being an idiot. He explained why: "The way things are these days, Captain, don't you believe the Confederates could pull strings just as well by wireless?"

"Pretty hard to smuggle rifles in by wireless," Toricelli remarked.

"If not from Texas, Houston could get them from Chihuahua," Dowling said. "To stop the traffic, we'd really need to seal our whole border with the Confederate States. I'd love to, but don't hold your breath. There's too much land, and not enough people to cover it. I wish things were different, but I don't think they are."

Toricelli pondered that. At last, reluctantly, he nodded. "I suppose you're right, sir," he said with a sigh. "If we can't seal off Utah, we probably won't be able to seal off Houston, either."

That stung. Dowling wished the USA would have been able to keep contraband out of the state where he was stationed. While he was at it, he wished for the moon. The Mormons had their caches of rifles. The reason they didn't use them was simple: enough soldiers held down Utah to make any uprising a slaughter. Even the locals understood that. However much they hated the U.S. Army, they knew what it could do.

"May I see the story, sir?" Captain Toricelli asked, and Dowling passed him the *Bee*. He zipped through; he read very fast. When he was done, he looked up and said, "They've got plenty of barrels down there, and it sounds like they're doing a good job. I wish we had some."

Dowling's experience with barrels during the Great War had not been altogether happy. Wanting to mass them against War Department orders, Custer had had him falsify reports that went in to Philadelphia. Custer had succeeded, and made himself into a hero and Dowling into a hero's adjutant. Custer had never thought about the price of failure. Dowling had. If things had gone wrong, they'd have been court-martialed side by side.

Maybe not thinking about the price of failure was what marked a hero. On the other hand, maybe it just marked a damn fool.

Still, despite Dowling's mixed feelings about barrels, Toricelli had a point. "We *could* use some here," Dowling admitted. "I'll take it up with Philadelphia. I wonder if they have any to spare, or if they're using them all in Houston."

"They'd better not be!" his adjutant exclaimed. That didn't mean they weren't, and both Dowling and Toricelli knew it.

That afternoon, Heber Young came to call on the commandant of Salt Lake City. The unofficial head of the proscribed Mormon church looked grave. "Colonel, have you provocateurs among the . . . believers of this state?" he asked, not naming the faith to which he couldn't legally belong.

"I have agents among them, certainly. I'd be derelict in my duty if I didn't," Dowling replied. "But provocateurs? No, sir. Why do you ask?"

"Because . . . certain individuals . . . have been urging a . . . more assertive course on us in our efforts to . . . regain our freedom of conscience." Young picked his words with enormous, and obvious, care. "It occurred to me that, if we become more assertive, the occupying authorities might use that as justification for more oppression."

*If we get out of line even a little, you'll squash us.* That was what he meant. Being a scrupulously polite man, he didn't quite come out and say it. Abner Dowling's jowls wobbled as he shook his head. "No, sir. I give you my word of honor: I have not done any such thing. My desire—and it is also my government's desire—is for peace and quiet in the state of Utah. I do not wish to do anything—anything at all—to disturb what peace and quiet we already have."

Heber Young eyed him. "I believe I believe you," he said at last, and Dowling couldn't help smiling at the scrupulous precision of his phrasing. Young continued, "One way to insure peace and quiet, of course, would be to grant us the liberties the citizens of the rest of the United States enjoy."

"There are certain difficulties involved with that, you know," Dowling said. "Your people's conduct during the Second Mexican War, the Mormon revolt of 1915, the assassination of General Pershing . . . How long do you suppose it would be, Mr. Young, before Utah made Houston seem a walk in the park by comparison?"

"I recognize the possibility, Colonel," Young replied, which was as much as he'd ever admitted. "But if you do not grant us our due liberties, would you not agree we will always be vulnerable to provocateurs? And I will take the liberty of asking you one other question before I go: if these men are not yours, who *does* give them their orders? For I am quite sure someone does. Good day." He got to his feet, set his somber homburg on his head, and departed.

Had Young been any other Mormon, Dowling would have called him back and demanded to know more. Dowling would have felt no compunctions about squeezing him if he'd denied knowing more, either. But Heber Young? No. His . . . *goodwill* was too strong a word. His tolerance toward the occupiers went a long way toward keeping the lid on Utah. Dowling didn't want to squander it.

And so Young left occupation headquarters in Salt Lake City undisturbed. But the question he'd asked before leaving lingered, and it disturbed Colonel Dowling more than a little. He hadn't been lying to Young when he said he had agents among the Mormons. The best of them, a man almost completely invisible, was a dusty little bookkeeper named Winthrop W. Webb. He seemed to know everything in the Mormon community, sometimes before it happened. If a rumor or an answer was floating in the air, he would find it and contrive to get it back to Dowling.

Getting hold of him, necessarily, was a roundabout business. Setting up a meeting was even more roundabout. Were Webb to be seen with Dowling, his usefulness—to say nothing of his life expectancy—would plummet. In due course, Dowling paid a discreet visit to a sporting house to which he was in the occasional habit of paying a discreet visit. Waiting for him in one of the upstairs bedrooms, instead of a perfumed blonde in frills and lace, was dusty little Winthrop W. Webb.

After they shook hands, Dowling sighed. "The sacrifices I make for my country."

"Don't worry, Colonel," Webb said with a small smile. "It'll be Betty again next time."

"Yes, I suppose—" Dowling broke off. How the devil did Webb know who his favorite was? Better not to ask, maybe. Maybe. Profoundly uneasy, Dowling told the spy what he'd heard from Heber Young.

Winthrop Webb nodded. "Yes, I know the people he's talking about—know of them, I should say. They're good at standing up at gatherings and popping off, and even better at disappearing afterwards. He's right. Somebody's backing them. I don't know who. No hard evidence. Like I say, they're good."

"Any guesses?" Dowling asked.

"I'm here to tell you the truth—I really don't know," Webb answered, deadpan.

For a moment, Dowling took him literally. Then he snorted and scowled and pointed south. "You think the Confederates are behind them?"

"Who gets helped if Utah goes up in smoke?" the agent said. "That's what I asked myself. If it's not Jake Featherston, I'll be damned if I know who it is."

"You think these Mormon hotheads Heber Young was talking about are getting their orders from Richmond, then?" Dowling leaned forward in excitement. "If they are—if we can show they are and make it stick—that'll *make* the president and the War Department move."

"Ha, says I," Winthrop Webb told him. "*Everybody* knows the Freedom Party's turned up the heat in Houston, and are we doing anything about it? Not that I can see."

"Houston's different, though." Dowling had played devil's advocate for Custer many times. Now he was doing it for himself. "It used to be part of Texas, part of Confederate territory. You can see why the CSA would think it still belongs to them and want it back. Same with Kentucky and Sequoyah, especially for the redskins in Sequoyah. You may not like it, but you can see it. It makes sense. But the Confederates have no business meddling in Utah. None. Zero. Zip. Utah's always belonged to the USA."

"Not the way the Mormons tell it," Webb said dryly. "But anyway, it's not that simple. These people who speak up and start trouble, they aren't from Richmond. They don't go back to some dingy sporting-house room"—he winked—"and report to somebody from Richmond. Whoever's behind this knows what he's doing. There are lots of links in the chain. The hotheads—hell, half of them never even *heard* of the goddamn Confederate States of America."

Dowling laughed, not that it was funny. "All right. I see what you're saying. What *can* we do, then, if we can't prove the Confederates are back of these fools?" He drummed his fingers on his thigh. "Not like there isn't a new hothead born every minute here. Maybe more often than that—Mormons have big families."

"They aren't supposed to drink, they aren't supposed to smoke, they aren't even supposed to have coffee. What the hell else have they got to do but screw?" Winthrop W. Webb said, which jerked more startled laughter from Dowling. The spy went on, "I don't know what we can do except hold the lid down tight and hope the bastards on the other side make a mistake. Sooner or later, everybody does."

"Mm." Dowling didn't much care for that, but no better ideas occurred to him, either. And then, as he was getting up to leave, one did: "I'll warn Heber Young some of the hotheads—provocateurs, he called them—are liable to be Confederate sympathizers."

"You think he'll believe you?" Webb asked, real curiosity in his voice. "Or will he just think you're looking for another excuse to sit on that church of his—you know, the one that officially doesn't exist?"

"I . . . don't know," Abner Dowling admitted after a pause. He and Young had a certain mutual respect. He thought he could rely on Young's honesty. But did the Mormon leader feel the same about him? Or was he, in Young's eyes, just the local head of the government that had spent the past fifty years and more oppressing Utah? "I've got to try, though, any which way."

When he went downstairs, the madam smiled as if he'd spent his time with Betty. Why not? He'd paid her as if he had. The girls in the parlor looked up from their hands of poker and bridge and fluttered their fingers at him as he left. But he'd never gone out the door of the sporting house less satisfied.


Everything in the white part of Augusta, Georgia, seemed normal. Autos and trucks chugged along the streets. A sign painter was putting a big SALE! sign in a shoe store's front window. A man came out of a saloon, took two steps, and then turned around and went back in. A workman with a bucket of cement carefully smoothed a square of sidewalk.

None of the white people on the sidewalk—or those who dodged into the street for a moment to avoid the wet cement—paid Scipio or the other Negroes among them any special attention. The riots that had leveled half the Terry were over, and the whites had put them out of their minds.

Scipio wished he could. His family was still sleeping in a church, and he knew how lucky he was. He still *had* a family. Nobody'd been killed. Nobody'd been worse than scratched. They'd even got their money out of the apartment before the building burned.

Luck.

Scipio walked past a wall plastered with election posters. SNOW FOR CONGRESS! they said. VOTE FREEDOM! Still four months to November, but Ed Snow's posters, featuring his plump, smiling face and a Freedom Party flag, were everywhere. A few Whig posters had gone up at about the same time. They'd come right down again, too. No new ones had gone up to take their place. Scipio had never seen any Radical Liberal posters this year.

Maybe nobody from the Rad Libs wanted to run against the Freedom Party. Maybe nobody dared run against it.

A cop coming down the street gave Scipio a hard stare. "You, nigger!" he snapped. "Let me see your passbook."

"Yes, suh." Scipio handed it over. For a while after the end of the Great War, nobody'd much worried about whether a black man had a passbook. Things had tightened up again before too long, though, and they'd got even worse after Jake Featherston won the presidency.

The cop made sure Scipio's photo matched his face. "Xerxes." He made a mess of the alias, but Scipio didn't presume to correct him. He looked Scipio up and down. "Why the hell you wearin' that damn penguin suit, boy, when the weather's like this?" His own gray uniform had darker gray sweat stains under the arms and at the collar.

"Suh, I waits tables at de Huntsman's Lodge," Scipio answered. Getting called *boy* by a man half his age rankled, too. He didn't let it show. Negroes who did let such resentment show often didn't live to grow old.

Grudgingly, a little frustrated that Scipio hadn't given him any excuse to raise hell, the policeman thrust the passbook back at him. "All right. Go on, then. Stay out of trouble," he said, adding, "Freedom!"

"Freedom!" Scipio echoed, sounding as hearty as he could. Satisfied, the cop walked on. So did Scipio, heart pounding and guts churning with everything he had to hold in. A colored man who didn't give back that *Freedom!* was also in trouble, sometimes deadly trouble. *A colored man born in the CSA is* born *in trouble,* Scipio thought. He'd always known that. He hadn't imagined how *much* trouble a colored man could be born into, though, not till the Freedom Party came to power.

The Huntsman's Lodge was probably the best restaurant in Augusta. It was certainly the fanciest and most expensive. "Hey there, Xerxes." The manager was a short, brisk fellow named Jerry Dover. "How are you?"

"Gettin' by." Scipio shrugged. "I thanks de Lord Jesus I's doin' dat much."

"Bunch of damn foolishness, not that anybody cares what I think," Dover said. "Bad for business."

He was a decent man, within the limits imposed on whites in the Confederate States. *Bad for business* and *damn foolishness* were as far as he would go in saying anything about the riots, but Scipio couldn't imagine him rampaging down into the Terry to rip up and destroy what little the Negroes of Augusta had.

Now he jerked a thumb in the direction of the kitchen. "You aren't on for half an hour. Get yourself some supper."

"Thank you kindly, suh," Scipio said. Waiters always ate where they worked. Even a white cook would feed them, and as for his colored assistants . . . In a place like this, though, the manager often tried to hold back the tide, not wanting to waste expensive food on the help. Not Dover. Scipio liked not having to sneak.

He liked the trout and brussels sprouts and delicate mashed potatoes he got, too. Bathsheba and the children were eating either soup-kitchen food or what they could find at the handful of cafés still open in the Terry. Part of Scipio felt guilty about getting meals like this. The rest reminded him it was food he didn't have to pay for. That counted, too.

He was at the tables the minute his shift started. Back and forth to the kitchen he went, bringing orders, taking food. To the customers, he was part of the furniture. He couldn't help wondering if any of them had gone down to the Terry to take from his people what small store of happiness they had. Maybe not. These men had too much money to need to feel the Negro as a threat. On the other hand . . . On the other hand, you never could tell.

He worked his shift. He made pretty good tip money. Everyone knew him as Xerxes. Nobody thought he was an educated fellow. The customer who'd seen him when he was Anne Colleton's butler had scared him half to death. And now he'd had to use that fancy accent again, had to use it with Bathsheba listening. The echoes from that hadn't even come close to dying down.

When midnight came, Scipio told Jerry Dover, "I see you tomorrow, suh."

"See you tomorrow," the white man echoed. "Be careful on the way home, you hear? Plenty of drunks out looking for trouble this time of night."

Spotting a black man would give them the excuse to start some, too. Scipio couldn't help saying, "Can't very well be careful goin' home, Mistuh Dover, on account of I ain't got no home. White folks done burn it down."

"I knew that," his boss said. "Telling you I'm sorry doesn't do you a hell of a lot of good, does it? Go on. Get out of here. Go back to your family."

That Scipio could do. He slipped out the kitchen door to the Huntsman's Lodge and down the alley behind the place. That made him harder to spot than if he'd gone right out onto the sidewalk. He took back streets and alleys south and east into the Terry. Telling when he got there wasn't hard. It wouldn't have been hard even before the riots: the edge of the Terry was where the street lights stopped.

He didn't dare relax once he got into the Negro district, either. Whites might have beaten him or shot him for the sport of it. Blacks would do the same to find out how much money he carried. The destruction of the riots had left plenty of people desperate—and some had been robbers before the riots, too.

No one troubled Scipio tonight. He made it back to the Godliness Baptist Church with nothing more dangerous than a stray cat (and not even a black one) crossing his path. Most of the people in the church were already asleep, on cots or on blankets spread over the pews.

Because a few men worked odd hours, the pastor had put up more blankets to give them a sheltered place to change. Scipio shed his formal clothes there and put on a nightshirt that fell down to his ankles. A cot by the one where his wife lay was empty. When he lay down, a sigh of relief escaped him. He'd been on his feet a long time. The cot was hard and lumpy, but weariness made it feel like a featherbed. He drifted toward sleep amidst the snores and occasional groans of several dozen people.

And then Bathsheba's voice, a thin thread of whisper, penetrated the rhythmic noise of heavy breathing: "How'd it go?"

He thought about pretending to have drifted off, but knew he couldn't get away with it. "Not bad," he whispered back.

The iron frame of Bathsheba's cot creaked as she shifted her weight. "Any trouble?" she asked.

He couldn't pretend he didn't know what she meant. Shaking his head, he answered, "Not today. *P*oliceman check my passbook, but dat's all. I pass. I's legal."

"Legal." His wife laughed softly. "Is you?"

"Xerxes, he legal," Scipio said, not liking the way this was going. "An' I ain't nobody but Xerxes. If I ain't Xerxes, who is?"

Bathsheba stopped laughing. "That ain't the right question. Right question is, if you ain't Xerxes, who *you* is?"

"I done tol' you everything." Scipio didn't like lying to Bathsheba. He lied here anyhow, and without hesitation. He liked talking about his years at Marshlands and his brief, hectic weeks in the Red Congaree Socialist Republic even less. He'd told her as little as he possibly could.

Trouble was, she knew it. Her bed creaked again, this time because she shook her head. "All them years we been together, and I never knew you could talk that way. I never *imagined* it. I lived with you. I had your babies. And you done hid that from me. You hid all the things that . . . that made it possible for you to talk that way." She didn't usually speak with such precision herself, but then, she didn't usually have to get across such a difficult idea, either. She was far from stupid—only ignorant. She went on, "It's like I never really knew you at all. Somebody you're in love with, that ain't right."

"I's sorry." He'd said that before, a great many times. It had done him exactly no good. He said something else he'd said before: "Don't much want to talk about none o' this on account of all dat ol' stuff still mighty dangerous. Anybody know too much . . ." He made a rattling noise deep in his throat, the sort of noise a man might make after the noose didn't break his neck and he hung, slowly strangling, on the gallows. "Dat why."

Bathsheba let out a small, exasperated hiss. "I ain't no sheriff. I ain't no *po*lice. I ain't no *goddamn* Freedom Party stalwart." She invested the swear word with infinite bitterness. "I love you. I love what I know of you, anyways. Turns out that ain't near as much as I reckoned it was, an' I don't quite know what to do about that. But do Jesus, Xerxes!" Scipio still hadn't told her his real name. That shamed him, but he didn't intend to do it, not even when Bathsheba added, "You know I never do nothin' to hurt you."

He did know that. He was as sure of it as he was of his own name— and he hoped no one else was sure of his name. Even so, he said, "Some things, dey too dangerous to say to anybody. Some things, you gits used to keepin' quiet. Dat's what I done." *That's what I'll keep on doing, as much as I can.*

Before Bathsheba could reply, an old man rose with a low groan from his cot and shuffled slowly and painfully toward the outhouses in back of the church. Their pungent reek filled the neighborhood. After a while, the old man came back. He groaned again when he lay down. A couple of minutes later, someone else got up. That reminded Bathsheba they weren't alone. They hadn't been alone together for more than a few minutes at a time since the riots. Scipio wasn't so young as he had been, but enough time had gone by since then to leave him acutely aware of that.

Bathsheba said, "All right. We don't finish now. But this ain't done, an' don't you think it is." She rolled over on her side, facing away from him. By her breathing, she soon slept. Scipio didn't, not for a long, long time.

Chester Martin and the skinny man who cadged handouts near his apartment looked at each other. The other man turned away. He hadn't shown up at the building site Martin suggested, and Martin hadn't given him a dime since it became clear he wouldn't show up. Martin saved his money for people who at least tried to help themselves.

The summer sun beat down on him as he walked on to the trolley stop. By late August, the worst heat was usually over in Toledo. Here in Los Angeles, he'd discovered, it was only beginning. It could stay ungodly hot—though not muggy—all the way into October.

He nodded to the other regulars at the trolley stop. This was a different crowd; he was getting up earlier than he had before, because his work these days was farther away. Go thirty miles in Toledo and you were almost to Sandusky. Go thirty miles from your apartment here and you hadn't even got out of the city limits.

*Clang!* Up came the trolley. Chester paid his fare and got two transfers. The first line took him west, past downtown. The second took him north, into Hollywood. And the last one carried him up over the Cahuenga Pass, into the San Fernando Valley.

The Valley, as people called it, was full of orange and walnut groves, wheat fields, and truck gardens. It wasn't full of houses. The farmland was so fine, Martin had trouble seeing why anybody would want to build houses on it. That, however, wasn't his worry, any more than grand strategy had been in the Army. Here, as there, he got his orders and did what he was told.

A couple of long streets sliced their way from east to west across the floor of the Valley: Ventura Boulevard near the southern mountains and Custer Way two or three miles farther north. Ventura Boulevard was the shopping district, such as it was. More and more houses with clapboard sides were going up near Custer Way. Martin had to lug his toolbox most of a mile from the last trolley stop to get to the tract where he worked.

"Morning, Chester," said Mordechai, the foreman. He looked at his watch. "Five minutes early."

"You didn't expect me to be late, did you?" Chester said. "Not me, not when you looked me up to let you know you had work for me."

After pausing to light a cigarette, the foreman blew a meditative smoke ring. It didn't last long, not with a little breeze stirring the air. "Well, that's *why* I got hold of you," Mordechai said. "I thought you were somebody I could count on. Some of these fellows . . ." He shook his head. "It's like they're doing you a favor if you tell 'em there's work."

Martin had some strong feelings about that. Not all of them, he suspected, were feelings Mordechai wanted him to have. He wished labor unions in the building trades were stronger. For that matter, he wished they existed at all. Bosses held absolute sway over who worked and who didn't, over how many hours and for how much money. As far as Chester was concerned, that was wrong as wrong could be. He'd accommodated himself to it because he *was* working. But that didn't mean it was right or fair.

And yet he had to admit that coin did have two sides. There *were* men who acted as Mordechai said. He could see why a boss wouldn't want them around. Where did you draw the line? Who decided? How? Those were all good questions—all political questions, to Chester's way of thinking. Again, he didn't suppose Mordechai would see them that way.

But he didn't figure he'd change the world this morning—and probably not tomorrow, either. Mordechai pointed him to the nearest house. "You know what needs doing. Take care of it."

"Right." Martin liked a foreman who said things like that. Some of them told him which nail to pound first, for heaven's sake. If he'd had his druthers, he would have pounded a nail—no, by God, a railroad spike—right up . . .

He chuckled. He would have liked to swing a sledgehammer that particular way. Dushan looked over at him. "What is funny?" he asked in his clotted accent.

"Nothing, really," Chester answered. He started driving nails in a way that didn't bother Mordechai. By the pained look on Dushan's face, it did bother him. Had he stayed out too late the night before and had a few drinks too many? It wouldn't have been the first time since Chester got to know him.

The Croat or whatever he was had revived somewhat by lunchtime: enough to lure a few suckers into a card game and likely pick up more money than he made in formal wages. To nobody in particular, Mordechai said, "When I was in the Navy, we'd have guys on the gun crew come in hung over on days where we were shooting. I don't ever recollect anybody dumb enough to do it more than once, though."

"I believe that, by God," Chester said. "Christ, it'd feel like blowing your head off, wouldn't it?"

"Now that you mention it, yes," the foreman said, in a way that suggested he knew exactly what he was talking about, and wished he didn't.

At the end of the day, Martin lined up in front of the paymaster, who handed him a five-dollar bill. As always, John Adams looked constipated. Chester didn't care. As long as the bill bought him five dollars' worth of whatever he needed, he wouldn't complain.

He sat through the long trolley ride without complaining, too, though the sun was low in the west when he finally got off near his apartment. Maybe that made it cooler here. He didn't think that was all, though—the Valley seemed hotter than the rest of Los Angeles.

As soon as he came in the door, he knew something was wrong: Rita never had been able to hide what she was thinking. Chester asked, "What is it, sweetheart? And don't tell me it's nothing, because I can see it's something."

"It's something." She took a letter from the cut-glass bowl on the hutch and handed it to him. "It's from your sister."

"What's Sue up to?" Martin asked, and then, before she could answer, "It's not my folks, is it?"

"No, thank God," his wife answered. "But your brother-in-law's lost his job."

"Oh, hell." Chester took the letter before adding, "Excuse me, sweetie." He tried hard not to talk like somebody who'd just escaped from the trenches. He read through the letter and shook his head. "That's rough. I thought the plate-glass plant would keep Otis forever. And they've got little Pete to worry about. Damn, damn, damn." He excused himself again.

"We've got to do whatever we can for them," Rita said.

Chester put down the letter and gave her a kiss. Sue and Pete and Otis Blake weren't kin of hers at all, except through him. He would have hesitated a little before saying what she'd just said, because money was still tight for them, too. "You're a brick, Rita," he told her.

She shrugged. "They helped out when your dad lost his job. What goes around ought to come around. And we can afford . . . some."

"Some, yeah. We've paid off what we owe Pa for the train tickets and all, anyhow. But there's still all the money he and my ma gave us to help us keep a roof over our heads when we were both out of work. Be a long time before we pay all that off—they carried us for a long time."

"They probably don't expect us to ever pay all that back," Rita said.

He nodded. "I know. But I don't always do what people expect, even when the people are my own folks. I don't really believe I'm back on my feet till I don't owe anybody anything."

His wife smiled at him. "I know how stubborn you are. If I don't, who would? You get all over town. Have you seen any plate-glass places that are looking for people? Have you seen any plate-glass places at all?"

"Not very many." He frowned, trying to remember. "No, not very many at all. It isn't a big thing here, the way it is back in Toledo. How come?" He read the letter again. "Oh. I missed that. They're thinking of coming out here." He clicked his tongue between his teeth. "No, I haven't seen much along those lines. I'm not saying there isn't anything, 'cause I haven't looked. But nothing's jumped out at me, either. I wonder what else Otis can do." *I wonder if I'll have to carry him till he finds out.* He didn't say that. Saying it might make it likelier to come true. *Don't give it a canary,* some guys in the Army had said. He didn't want to.

Rita said, "It would be funny, somebody owing us money instead of the other way around." That was an indirect way, a safe way, of getting at what Chester hadn't wanted to come right out and say. No canaries—*why canaries?* Martin wondered—flew.

After supper, they played double solitaire and slapped each other's hands grabbing the cards. A lot of the fellows at work didn't talk about anything but what they'd heard on the wireless the night before. Chester would have liked to have a wireless set himself. They were a lot cheaper than they had been only a few years before. If he kept working steadily, he could start saving for one—if that money didn't have to go to his brother-in-law instead.

*How do you get ahead?* he wondered. *Christ, how do you even stay where you are?* Socialists talked about capitalism pushing the bourgeoisie down into the proletariat. He'd never been bourgeois (a steelworker in Toledo? not likely!), but he knew what being declassed was all about just the same. It had frightened him into abandoning Socialism and voting Democratic—once. He didn't think he would do that again.

Rita started yawning before nine-thirty. That disappointed Chester, who'd hoped to persuade her to play something more exciting than double solitaire. She gave back a rather wan smile when he slipped an arm around her waist. Still, despite another yawn, she didn't say no. But she did yelp when he started playing with her breasts. "Careful," she said. "They've been awfully sore lately."

"Sorry, hon," he said. "I know they get that way sometimes when it's right before your. . . ." He paused and thought back. "When *was* your last time of the month?" He didn't always keep close track, but he did think she hadn't had to mess with pads for quite a while now.

Sure enough, she said, "Early last month—I'm late. I didn't want to say anything till I was sure, but I'm pretty sure now."

"A baby?" That squeak in Chester's voice was fear, all right. On top of everything else, how were they supposed to feed a baby? He wasn't even sure this apartment building allowed them. "How did that happen?"

"The usual way, I'm pretty sure," Rita answered. "We can call him Broken Rubber Martin." Chester laughed. He hadn't thought he could. And he almost forgot about other things till Rita said, "Aren't you going to go on? It feels nice, as long as you don't squeeze too hard."

"Does it?" Chester did go on. By the small sounds his wife made, it did feel nice. Before too long, he started to reach into the nightstand drawer for a safe. That made him laugh again. Why lock the barn door if the horse was long gone? He went ahead without one. And that felt mighty nice, too. No matter how good it felt, though, he started worrying again the second they finished. Rita fell asleep right away. He worried for a long time.

Clarence Potter looked into the mirror over the sink in his apartment. He thought he looked pretty sharp: polka-dot bow tie, white shirt with blue pinstripes, cream-colored linen jacket to fight the summer heat and humidity of Charleston, straw boater cocked at a jaunty angle. Then he let out a sour laugh. How he looked wouldn't matter a dime's worth when he got to the Whig meeting tonight. Nobody there would listen to him. Nobody there ever did.

He sometimes wondered why he kept going. Pigheadedness, he supposed. No, more than pigheadedness these days. He also had the feeling that somebody had to do something about the Freedom Party. If the Whigs didn't, if they couldn't, he didn't see anyone else who could.

That cool linen jacket also concealed a shoulder holster. Nobody had tried to give him a hard time yet. But he knew he was on a Freedom Party list. The Party was thorough, if not always swift. Some people had already disappeared. Potter didn't intend to go quietly. If the stalwarts wanted him, they would have to pay the price for him.

Out the door he went, whistling. No one lurked at the bottom of the stairs or, when he checked, out on the street. He nodded to himself. They were less likely to drop on him away from his flat, because they had more trouble knowing exactly where he was then. If they didn't want him now, they likely wouldn't for the rest of the day. Whistling still, he walked on toward Whig headquarters.

A couple of blocks from the headquarters, he ran into Braxton Donovan, who was heading in the same direction. The lawyer nodded. He had more patience with Potter than most local Whigs did.

"How goes it, shyster?" Potter asked. "They still haven't decided to call you a political and run you in?"

"Not yet," Donovan answered. He was a ruddy, fleshy man with an impressive pompadour. "Of course, now that the Supreme Court is gone, they're liable to get rid of all the others next, and then where will I be?"

"Up the creek," Potter answered, and Braxton Donovan ruefully nodded. Potter went on, "Why couldn't people see it's a damnfool thing to do, electing a party that said ahead of time it wouldn't play by the rules once it got in?"

"Because too many people don't care," Donovan said. He pulled out his pocket watch. Carrying one made him on the old-fashioned side—a typical attitude for a Whig. Potter, following postwar fashion, preferred a wristwatch. Donovan said, "We're early. You want to stop at the saloon across the street and hoist a couple?"

"Twist my arm," Potter said, holding it out. Donovan did, not too hard. "I give up," Potter announced at once. "Let's hoist a couple."

But when they turned the corner, they found a line of gray-uniformed policemen and Freedom Party stalwarts in white and butternut, the cops with drawn pistols—a couple of them had submachine guns instead—and the stalwarts with bludgeons, stretched in front of the entrance to the

Whig meeting hall. Angry Whigs milled about on the sidewalk and in the street, but nobody was going inside.

"What the hell's going on?" Potter said. Against a dozen policemen and twice that many stalwarts, the pistol under his left arm suddenly seemed a lot less important.

"I don't know, but I intend to find out." Braxton Donovan strode forward. In his fullest, roundest, plummiest courtroom voice, he demanded, "What is the meaning of this?"

One of the cops pointed a submachine gun at the lawyer's belly. Donovan stopped, most abruptly. A burst from a weapon like that could cut him in half. The policeman said, "No more political meetings. That there's our orders, and that there's what we're gonna make sure of."

"But you can't do that," Donovan protested. "It's against every law on the books."

"Braxton . . ." Potter said urgently. He took his friend's arm.

Donovan shook him off. "You want to listen to this other feller here," the cop said. This time, he didn't point the submachine gun—he aimed it. "By order of the governor in the interest of public safety, all political meetings except for the Freedom Party's are banned till after the election."

One of the stalwarts added, "And for as long as we feel like after that, too." Several of his buddies laughed.

Potter wondered whether Donovan would have a stroke right there on the spot. "Good God, are you people nuts?" the lawyer said. "I can go to Judge Shipley and get an injunction to stop this nonsense in thirty seconds flat. And *then* I file the lawsuits."

He was plainly convinced he had the big battalions on his side. The policeman, just as plainly, was convinced he didn't. So were the stalwarts. With a nasty grin, the one who'd spoken before said, "Judge Shipley resigned last night. Reasons of health." He leered.

What was going on had got through to Clarence Potter a little while before. The old rules didn't hold any more. In the new ones, the Freedom Party held—had grabbed—all the high cards. He watched Braxton Donovan figure that out. Donovan had been red, almost purple. Now he went deathly pale. "You wait till after the election," he whispered. "The people won't stand for this. They'll throw you out on your ear."

The policeman's finger twitched on the trigger of the submachine gun. Donovan flinched. The cop laughed. So did the Freedom Party stalwarts, in their crisp not-quite-uniforms. One of them said, "You don't get it, do you, pal? We *are* the people."

"I am going to declare this here an illegal assembly," the policeman said. "If you folks don't disperse, we *will* arrest you. Jails are crowded places these days. A lot of you big talkers end up in 'em for a lot longer than y'all expect. Run along now, or you'll be sorry."

Across the street and into the saloon counted as dispersing. Potter ordered a double gin and tonic, Braxton Donovan a double whiskey. "They can't do that," he said, tossing back the drink.

"They just did," Clarence Potter observed. "Question is, what can we do about it?"

Another Whig who'd taken refuge in the saloon said, "We've got to fight back."

"Not here," the bartender said. "You start talking politics in here, I get in trouble. I don't want no trouble. I don't want no trouble with nobody. Neither does the owner. You keep quiet about that stuff or I got to throw y'all out."

"This is how it goes," Potter said.

"How what goes?" Donovan asked.

"How the country goes—down the drain," Potter said. "The Freedom Party is doing its best to make sure we don't have elections any more—or, if we do, they don't mean anything. Its best is pretty goddamn good, too." He spoke in a low voice, in deference to the harassed-looking barkeep. Even that was an accommodation to what the Freedom Party had already accomplished.

Donovan snorted. "They won't get away with it. And when they do lose an election, there won't be enough jails to hold all of them, not even at the rate they're building."

"I hope you're right. I hope so, but I wouldn't count on it," Potter said. "Jake Featherston worries me. He's a son of a bitch, but he's a shrewd son of a bitch. The way he went after the Supreme Court . . . People will be studying that one for the next fifty years. Pass a law that's popular but unconstitutional, make the Court make the first move, and then land on it with both feet. Nobody much has complained since, not that I've heard."

"Who would dare, with the stalwarts ready to beat you if you try?"

But Potter shook his head. "It's more than that. If he'd really riled people when he did it, they would scream. They'd do more than scream. They'd stand up on their hind legs and tell him to go to hell. But they don't. Going ahead with that river project has given thousands of people jobs. It's given millions of people hope—hope for electricity, hope the rivers won't wash away their farms and their houses. They care more about that than they do about whether the bill's constitutional."

"Nonsense," Braxton Donovan said. "What could be more important than that?"

"You're a lawyer, Braxton," Potter answered patiently. "Think of ordinary people, farmers and factory hands. You ask them, they'd say staying dry and getting electric lights count for more. There are lots of them. And they vote Freedom."

"Even assuming you're right—which I don't, but assuming—what are we supposed to do about it?" Donovan asked. "You've got all the answers, so of course you've got that one, too, right?"

Potter stared down at his drink as if he'd never seen it before. He gulped the glass dry, then waved to the bartender for a refill. Only after he'd got it did he say, "Damn you, Braxton."

"Well, I love you, too," Donovan replied. "You didn't answer my question, you know."

"Yes, I do know that," Potter said gloomily. "I also know I don't have any answers for you. Nobody in the country has any answers for you."

"All right. As long as we understand each other." Donovan finished his second drink, then got to his feet. "I don't want another one after this. I just want to go home. That's about what we have left to us these days—our homes, I mean. They're still our castles . . . for the time being." He slipped out the door. It had grown dark outside, but not nearly so dark as Potter's mood.

*What do we do? What can we do?* The questions buzzed against his mind like trapped flies buzzing against a windowpane. Like the flies, he saw no way out. Even fighting the Freedom Party looked like a bad idea. Featherston's followers had been fighters from the start. They were better at it than the Whigs, much better at it than the Radical Liberals.

*If we can't fight them, and if they do whatever they please, no matter how illegal it is, to get what they want, what's left for us?* Buzz, buzz, buzz: another good question with no good answer visible.

"Maybe he'll go too far," Potter muttered. "Maybe he'll land us in a war with the United States. That'd fix him."

He despised the USA as much as any man in the CSA. That he could imagine the United States in the role of savior to the Confederate States said a lot about how he felt about the Freedom Party. None of what it said was good.

Two tall gins were plenty to make him feel wobbly on his pins when he rose from the barstool. A fellow in overalls came in just then and sat down at the bar. He ordered a beer. As the bartender drew it for him, he said, " 'Bout time they're shutting down those goddamn Whigs. Mess they got the country into, they ought to thank their lucky stars they aren't all hangin' from lamp posts."

That was a political opinion, too, but the barkeep didn't tell him to keep quiet. It was, of course, a political opinion favorable to the Freedom

Party. In the CSA these days, who could get in trouble for an opinion like that?

If Potter had had another gin in him, he would have called the bartender on it. If he'd had another couple of gins in him, he would have started a fight. But if he fought with every idiot he met in a saloon, he'd end up dead before too long. He went home instead. The cops didn't arrest him. The stalwarts didn't pound on him. In the CSA these days, that counted for freedom.

**S**ylvia Enos and Ernie lay side by side on her bed. He was as rigid as he would have been some hours after death. By the look on his face, he wished he were dead. "It is no good," he said, glaring straight up at the ceiling. "It is no goddamn good at all."

"Not tonight, sweetheart," Sylvia said. "But sometimes it is. Things don't always work perfect for a woman every time, either, you know."

"But I am a man. Sort of a man. A piece of a man." He raised up on one elbow to look down at himself. "A missing piece of a man. Times like this, I want to blow my brains out. One of these days . . ."

"You stop that." Sylvia put a hand over his mouth. Then, as if fearing that wasn't enough to drive such thoughts from his mind, she took the hand away and kissed him instead. "Don't be stupid, you hear me?"

"Is it stupid to want to be a man? Is it stupid to want to do what men can do?" He answered his own question by shaking his head. "I do not think so."

"It's stupid to talk that way. This . . . this is just one of those things, like . . . I don't know, like a bad leg, maybe. You have to make the best of it and do what you can to live your life. Sometimes things *are* all right, you know."

"Not often enough," he said. "It is not you, sweetheart. You do everything you know how to do. But it is no damn use. I might as well try to drive a nail with half the handle of a hammer. A wound like this is not like a leg. It goes to the heart of a man, to what *makes* him a man. And if it is not, *he* is not."

"I don't know what you're talking about. I don't want to know what you're talking about, either," Sylvia said. "All I know is, you're scaring me." George had never scared her. Infuriated her, yes, when he wanted other women after being away from her too long. But she could understand that, no matter how mad it made her. It was . . . Her mind groped till she found the word. It was normal, was what it was. It had none of the darkness that made Ernie's furious gloom so frightening.

Naked, he got to his feet and headed for the kitchen. "Christ, but I need a drink."

"Fix me one, too," Sylvia said.

"All right. I need my pipe, too. Cigarettes are not the same." Ernie never smoked the pipe in Sylvia's apartment. Cigarettes were all right, because she smoked, too. But pipe tobacco would have made the place smell funny to Mary Jane when she got home.

"Thanks," Sylvia said when he brought her whiskey over ice.

He gulped his, still in that black mood. "For a long time after I got wounded, I could not do anything with a woman," he said, his voice hard and flat. "Not anything. A dead man could do more. I wanted to. Oh, how I wanted to! But I could not."

"Ernie," she said nervously, "wouldn't it be better *not* to think about . . . about the bad times?"

She might as well have saved her breath. He went on as if she hadn't spoken: "I bought a rifle. I went hunting. I hunted and hunted. I shot more kinds of animals than you can think of. Sometimes, if you cannot love, killing will do."

"I told you once to cut that out," Sylvia said. "I'm going to tell you again. I don't like it when you talk that way. I don't like it a bit."

"Do you think I like what happened to me? Do you think I like what does not happen with me?" Ernie laughed a strange, harsh laugh. "If you do, you had better think again. Why this is hell, nor am I out of it."

That sounded like poetry, not quite like the way he usually talked. But Sylvia didn't know what it was from, and she was damned if she would ask him. She said, "You're the first man I've cared about since the Confederates killed my husband. If you think I'm going to let you get away, *you'd* better think again."

"If I decide to go, nobody will stop me." Somber pride rang in Ernie's voice. "Not you, not anybody. Do you know something?"

"What?" she asked warily.

"I am jealous of you. I am more jealous of you than I know how to say."

"Of me? How come?"

"You had your revenge. You went to the Confederate States. You knocked on Roger Kimball's door. When he opened it, you shot him. Your husband can rest easy."

*You were never a seaman,* Sylvia thought. Like most sailors, George

Enos had had a horror of dying at sea, of having his body end up food for fish and crabs. He'd had the horror, and then it had happened to him. Yes, she'd avenged herself, but poor George would never rest easy.

Ernie added, "I can never have my revenge. I do not know which English pilot shot me. He may not know he shot me. It was war, and I was a target. He went on his way afterwards. I hope he got shot down. I hope he burned all the way. But even then, it would be over for him. I go on, a quarter of a man."

"You're more of a man than you think you are." Sylvia pressed herself against him. "Do you think I'd want you to stay with me if you didn't make me happy?"

"Carpet munching," he muttered. "A bull dyke could do it better than I can."

"But that's not what I want," Sylvia said. "What I want is you, and you're plenty of man for me." If he really believed it, maybe he wouldn't be quite so ready to blow his brains out.

He was mule-stubborn, though. "I am not plenty of man for *me*, sweetheart." He finished the drink, got out of bed, got dressed, and left her apartment without another word and without a backwards glance. She wondered why that didn't infuriate her, as it would have if some different man had done it. She couldn't say. All she knew was, it didn't.

As things turned out, she was glad Ernie left, because she got a knock on the door about fifteen minutes later. She was in a housecoat by then, washing out the glasses that had held whiskey so she could put them away and so Mary Jane wouldn't notice they'd been out. She'd already dumped Ernie's cigarette butts down to the bottom of the wastepaper basket.

"Who is it?" she called, wondering if a neighbor wanted to chat or to borrow something. It was a little late for that, but not impossibly so.

"It's me—George." The voice was eerily like her dead husband's. She'd thought so ever since George Jr. went from a boy to a man.

She hurried to open the door. "What are you doing here?" she asked. "Why aren't you with Connie? Did you get drunk when your boat came back to T Wharf, and think you still live here instead of with your wife?"

"No, Ma. I just had a couple of drinks," he said, breathing whiskey fumes at her. *Good,* she thought. *He's less likely to notice the booze on my breath.* He went on, "I know where I live and all just fine. I'll go back there soon enough, too. But I wanted to stop by and say hello. You raised me, after all."

He was a big man, bigger than Ernie, wide-shouldered and solid and not at all inclined to talk frightening nonsense. How had he got so big? Hadn't he been a little boy raising hell in the Coal Board offices just a few months ago? So it seemed to her, anyhow. Slowly, she answered, "I must have done something right back then. I couldn't ask for a better son."

"Aw, Ma." Now she'd embarrassed him—easier when whiskey helped make him maudlin. He paused for a moment, then went on, "I want you to be happy. Mary Jane and I both want you to be happy."

"You both make me happy," Sylvia said. "You make me very happy."

"That's good, Ma." George Jr. hesitated again. "If . . . if you was to meet a fella who made you happy, neither one of us'd mind or anything. We talked it over one time. If he was a nice fella, I mean."

How much did they know about Ernie? Did they know anything? Sylvia thought Mary Jane might. Her daughter had never caught him here (though she'd come close a couple of times), but Sylvia wouldn't have been surprised if the neighbors gossiped. What were neighbors good for besides gossiping?

And how to answer George Jr.? Carefully, that was how. Sylvia said, "Well, that's sweet of both of you. If I find somebody like that, I'll remember what you said." She shook her head. She needed to tell him a little more: "You know, I'm a grownup myself. If I want to look for a fellow, I don't really need anybody's permission to go ahead and do it."

"Oh, no. I know that. I didn't mean you did. I just meant . . . you know. That we aren't upset or anything."

Not *that we wouldn't be upset*. They did know, then. Or they knew something, anyhow. Sylvia doubted they knew some of the things she'd been doing not too long before. Children always had trouble imagining their parents doing anything like that. And they wouldn't know how Ernie was mutilated and some of the makeshifts Sylvia and he had to use.

"As long as you're happy, that's what matters," George Jr. said.

"I am, dear," she answered. *Most of the time I am, anyhow. When Ernie starts talking about guns—that's a different story.*

"All right, Ma." Her son stooped and kissed her on the cheek. "I'm going to go on home. I hope they give me a little time before I have to head out again, but you never can tell." He touched the brim of his low, flat cap and ducked out of the apartment where he'd grown up, the apartment that would never be his home again.

The next morning, Sylvia left Mary Jane, who'd come in late, in bed asleep and went down to T Wharf to see what she could get in the way of seafood. With her husband and her son both fishermen, she had connections ordinary people could only envy. She bought some lovely scrod at a price that would have turned an ordinary housewife green, and, better yet, got the young cod without any jokes about the pluperfect subjunctive.

She didn't know how many times she'd heard those from fish dealers and fishermen. She did know it was too many.

She was on her way back to the flat when someone called her name. She turned. "Oh," she said. "Hello, Mr. Kennedy."

"Good morning to you, Mrs. Enos." As always, Joseph Kennedy's smile displayed too many teeth. It was not a friendly smile; it looked more like a threat. "So you prefer a hack writer to me, do you?"

"Ernie's no hack!" Sylvia said indignantly.

"Anyone who writes an 'as-told-to' book is a hack," Kennedy said, still smiling. He wanted to wound with those teeth; he wanted to bite. That Sylvia had said no to him was bearable as long as she said no to everyone else, too. That she'd said no to him and yes to somebody else . . . that irked him.

"He's a fine writer," Sylvia said. "Times are hard. Everybody's got to eat."

"Yes." Kennedy made the word into a hiss. "Everybody does. The campaign will start early next year, since President Hoover's going to run for reelection. You would have had a part in it, but. . . ." He shrugged. "You'd sooner have half a man."

Sylvia wanted to slap him in the face with a scrod. Instead, in a deadly voice, she answered, "Half of him makes a better man, and a bigger man, than all of you."

He went fishbelly pale under the brim of his boater. Sylvia hadn't bothered keeping quiet. Several people sniggered. A woman pointed at Kennedy. He fled. Sylvia knew she'd pay later, but oh, triumph was sweet for now.


The Alabama Correctional Camp (P) lay in the Black Belt, the cotton-growing part of the state, forty miles south of Montgomery and a hundred forty south of Birmingham. Except for his time in the Confederate Army and his stint down in the Empire of Mexico, Jefferson Pinkard had never been so far from home. The camp lay between cotton fields and pecan groves not far from a town of about a thousand people called Fort Deposit. Once upon a time, the fort had protected settlers from Indians. Now only the name was left to commemorate the stockade that had once stood there.

Fort Deposit did boast a train station, a little clapboard building with a roof that hung out over the track so people could board and leave a train when it was raining. And raining it was when Pinkard stood on the rickety platform by the track waiting for the northbound Louisville and Nashville Railroad train to take him up to Birmingham. He wore his warden's uniform, his Freedom Party pin on proud display on his left lapel. He kept hoping someone would want to argue politics, but nobody did.

Up chugged the train. It wheezed to a halt, iron wheels squealing against iron rails. Most of the people who got off and boarded were Negroes with work-weary faces and cardboard luggage. A couple of cars up at the front of the train were for whites, though. Jeff climbed in and sat down in one of those. A few minutes later, the train rattled north again.

Five hours later, the train came into the Louisville and Nashville station in Birmingham. The station was at Twentieth and Morris, only a few blocks west of the Sloss Works, where Pinkard had worked for so long. He took a cab back to his apartment closer to the center of town. The Freedom Party was picking up a good part of the tab for the place.

He didn't stay there long—only long enough to get out of uniform and into the white shirt and butternut trousers of a Freedom Party stalwart. He wasn't the only one wearing that almost-uniform who converged on Birmingham Party headquarters. Oh, no—far from it.

Inside Caleb Briggs had already started talking, warming up the men for what they would be doing. "Tomorrow is election day," rasped the dentist who headed the Party in Birmingham. His voice was only a ruin of its former self; he'd been gassed in the war, and he'd never recovered. "We got to make sure the fellows who get elected vote our way. *All* of 'em, y'all hear me?"

"Freedom!" the men roared, Pinkard loud among them.

Briggs nodded. "That's right. Freedom. We've already got the House in Richmond, and we'll keep it. But we got to get the Senate, too, and that's tougher, on account of the state legislatures pick the Senators. So we have to take care of those. Y'all reckon we can do it?"

"Yes!" the stalwarts shouted, and, "Hell, yes!" and a great many other things besides. The louder they yelled, the more excited they got.

"Good." Caleb Briggs grinned a wide, crooked grin. "Not so many Whig and Rad Lib gatherings as there used to be. But the Whigs are holding one tonight in Capitol Park, smack in the middle of town. We got to make sure they don't go through with it, and that they don't do any voting tomorrow. Make sure you grab your clubs and whatnot, and we aren't going there to take prisoners."

As the men assembled for the march on the park, they told stories of other elections, other brawls. A lot of them talked about 1933, when Jake Featherston won the presidency. Pinkard was one of the smaller number who could talk about 1921, when Featherston almost won. Nobody talked about the presidential election of 1927; the Party had wandered in the wilderness then. Even Jeff, a stalwart among stalwarts, had wondered if it would ever emerge.

Policemen tipped their hats to the advancing stalwarts. The dustup in the park that followed came almost as an anticlimax. The Whigs weren't what they had been two years earlier. They'd been fighting for their lives then, and known it. Now . . . Now it was as if they sensed it was all over but the shouting. A few stubborn men fought hard to hold back the Freedom Party avalanche, but only a few. The rest fled. So did the Whig candidate for governor, and just in time. The stalwarts would surely have beaten him had they caught him, and they might have strung him up.

"That'll teach those sons of bitches," somebody not far from Pinkard said.

"Yeah." Jeff nodded. "Not like it was in the old days, when the governor used to sic the National Guard on us to keep us from kicking up our heels."

"Folks know which side their bread is buttered on nowadays," the other stalwart said. "And what the hell? We're holding most of the bread now."

"That's right." Pinkard nodded again, emphatically. "And we're going to get the rest of it, too."

He wished he could go to a saloon and have a few drinks with his comrades, but Alabama remained stubbornly dry. Instead, he went home and slept in his own bed for the first time in months. He'd got used to the hard military cot down at the Alabama Correctional Camp (P). His mattress seemed squashy by comparison, and he woke up with a stiff back. Grumbling, he made a cup of coffee—just about all he had in the place—and got into the stalwarts' almost-uniform again.

When he went back to Freedom Party headquarters, Caleb Briggs sent him to a polling place a few blocks away. "I don't expect the police'll enforce the electioneering limits," Briggs rasped. "Case they do, don't pick a fight with 'em. Here." He handed Jeff and the other party men a sheet of newspaper-style photos of men's faces. "See if y'all can keep these bastards from getting to the booth. They're nothing but troublemaking trash."

Jeff grinned at the men with him. They were grinning, too. "You bet," he said, and took a cudgel from among those stuffed into a sheet-metal trash can. He thwacked the bludgeon into the palm of his left hand. This was the enjoyable part of the job. He pulled a quarter from his pocket, too. "Gonna buy some doughnuts before we get there," he said. "I'm empty inside."

The Confederate flag flew in front of an elementary-school auditorium. Sure enough, no one said a word, no policemen appeared, when the Freedom Party men stationed themselves right outside the door. Quite a few of the men going in to vote displayed Party pins, some without the black border that showed a new member, more with. They nodded and tipped their hats to the stalwarts as they went by. The call of "Freedom!" rang out again and again.

About half past eight, Pinkard nudged the stalwart nearest him. "There's one of the fuckers we're supposed to stop."

"Right," the other fellow said, and stepped into the would-be voter's path. "You better get the hell out of here, buddy, you know what's good for you."

"Are you saying I'm not allowed to exercise my Constitutional right to vote?" the man asked. He was bald, skinny, middle-aged, and wore a suit; he looked like a lawyer or somebody else too smart for his own good.

"He said you better get lost," Pinkard answered. "And you better, too, or you'll be real sorry."

"I will—as soon as I vote." The clever-looking guy started forward again.

Maybe he had guts. Maybe he was too stupid to know what was coming. All four stalwarts set on him, bludgeons rising and falling. "Freedom!" they shouted as the blows thudded home. Pinkard added, "You should've listened, you dumb asshole. You gonna vote now?" The bald man's wails rose above the thumps of the clubs and the stalwarts' battle cries.

At last, they let him go. He staggered away, face and scalp bloodied. He didn't try to go into the polling place, which proved they hadn't beaten *all* the brains out of him.

They beat up three or four other men from their sheet of photos; several more abruptly discovered urgent business elsewhere on seeing them waiting. The stalwarts saluted one another with their blood-spattered bludgeons each time that happened. Schoolchildren watched one beating. They laughed and cheered the stalwarts on. No policemen came to bother them. Pinkard hadn't expected that any would; the Party had been strong in police and fire departments across the CSA for years.

When the polls closed, a couple of Jeff's comrades headed home. He went back to Party headquarters. As he'd known they would, they had wireless sets blaring out election returns. They also had sandwiches and homebrew.

Results from the Confederate states on the East Coast had a good start on those in Alabama and farther west. "Looks like the Freedom Party landslide that started two years ago is still rolling downhill, folks," the announcer said. He sounded delighted with the news. People who didn't sound delighted the Freedom Party was doing well didn't last on the wireless. This fellow went on, "North Carolina's going to have a new governor, a Freedom Party man. Same with Georgia. And Party candidates are picking up seat after seat in the legislatures in the Carolinas and Florida. That makes races for the Senate likely to go Freedom, too."

Jefferson Pinkard turned to the closest stalwart and raised his glass of beer. "Here's to us, by Jesus! We've gone and done it. We sure as hell have."

"Looks like it," the other Party man agreed. He sported a mouse under one eye. He must have run into a Whig with more gumption than most. Pinkard hadn't.

After a while, Alabama returns and others from the western part of the Confederacy started coming in along with those from the Eastern seaboard. The only state where the Freedom Party didn't seem to be doing well was Louisiana, where the Radical Liberal governor had a solid organization of his own. Somebody not far from Jeff said, "He can laugh now, but that son of a bitch'll pay before long. You can count on it." Heads solemnly bobbed up and down, Pinkard's among them.

With restive Kentucky on its border, Tennessee went Freedom in a big way, and probably would have even without stalwarts outside polling places. With even more restless Sequoyah and stolen Houston on *its* borders, Texas voted Freedom more spectacularly still. Jeff went back to his apartment and to bed before many returns came in from Chihuahua and Sonora. For one thing, he was confident they'd turn out for the Party, too. For another, they were mostly greasers down there anyhow, and he'd had his fill of greasers fighting in the Empire of Mexico.

He got on the train again the next day, to go back to the Alabama Correctional Camp (P). Newsboys shouted election results. "Freedom Party claims vetoproof majority in both houses of Congress!" was one cry.

Conscious of a job well done, Jeff bought a paper. He read it as the train rumbled south from Birmingham. Then he let it fall to the floor and dozed: no, he didn't sleep well in his own bed any more.

He got rudely awakened just before the train pulled into Montgomery. He came within inches of getting killed. A bullet blew out the window by his seat, cracking past his head and spraying him with broken glass. More bullets stitched along the length of the car.

"Down! Get down, goddammit!" he shouted, and dove between his seat and the one in front. Quite a few of the men in the car—likely the ones who'd seen combat during the war—did the same thing. Like him, they knew machine-gun fire when they heard it. Screams and wails said some of the bullets hadn't missed—and that civilians were panicking. Before long, Pinkard's hands and knees were wet and sticky with someone's blood.

The last time anybody'd shot up a train in which he was riding, it had been Negro rebels when he was a private on his way to put down one of the Socialist republics the blacks had proclaimed in Georgia. Who was it this time? The country between Birmingham and Montgomery was full of farms and plantations . . . and the plantations were full of Negroes.

Coincidence? Or the start of a new uprising? Jeff didn't know—he had no way of knowing—but he muttered under his breath.

Flora Blackford didn't realize how much she'd missed the floor of Congress till she came back to Philadelphia. "Is it any wonder there is armed struggle against the Freedom Party in the Confederate States?" she demanded. "Is it any wonder at all, after the farce that went by the name of an election in that country two weeks ago?"

A Congressman—a Freedom Party Congressman—from Houston sprang to his feet. "How is that there election different from most of the ones y'all put on in what you call my state?"

He didn't want to be in the U.S. Congress at all. He would sooner have served in Richmond. "Excuse me, Mr. Mahon, but I have the floor," Flora said with icy courtesy. "May I go on?"

"That's right. Ride roughshod over me. You've been riding rough-shod over my state—what you call my state—ever since you tore us bleeding from Texas and made us join the USA."

"Tell the lady, George!" That was another Freedom Party man from Houston. Two more Congressmen, these from Kentucky, began singing "Dixie." Neither they nor their constituents wanted to belong to the United States, either.

*Bang! Bang! Bang!* Congressman La Follette of Wisconsin, the speaker of the House, plied his gavel with gusto. "The gentlemen are out of order," he declared. "The gentlemen will observe the rules of the House. Mrs. Blackford has the floor."

"This body is out of order!" George Mahon shouted. "This whole damn *country* is out of order!" The Kentucky Congressmen sang louder than ever.

*Bang! Bang! Bang!* "That will be quite enough!" Charles La Follette declared. "The sergeant-at-arms will eject from this chamber any individual flouting the rules of the House. Is that clear?"

"It's clear, all right," Mahon said. "It's clear that even though our own people elected us, you don't want to let us tell you what they want." But he sat down after that, and the rowdy singing stopped. The Freedom Party Congressmen knew La Follette meant what he said. He'd ejected them before. Flora wasn't sure how much good that did, though. Getting thrown out of Congress only made them bigger heroes back home.

"You may continue, Mrs. Blackford," La Follette said wearily. "Without further interruption, I very much hope."

"Thank you, Mr. Speaker," Flora said. "I rose to call upon the administration to take stronger action against the Confederate States than it has done up until this time. President Hoover stayed silent in the wake of the riots—I might even say, the pogrom—aimed against the black residents of the CSA and does not appear to recognize their legitimate right to rise against oppression and brutality. He—"

"The distinguished Congresswoman from New York worries more about the Negroes of the Confederate States not because they are black but because they are Red," another Congressman broke in. "Most people in the United States worry very little about them for any reason."

He wasn't a Freedom Party man. He was a rock-ribbed Democrat from Maine. Speaker La Follette gaveled him to silence, too, but not with the vehemence he'd used against the Freedom Party buffoons. And, to her dismay, Flora saw heads nodding in agreement with what the New Englander had said. The United States had only a handful of Negroes. Border patrols stayed busy keeping would-be colored refugees out. The USA wanted no more blacks; if anything, most people would have been happier with none at all.

Stubbornly, she said, "They are human beings, too, Congressman, endowed by their Creator with certain unalienable rights, among those being life, liberty, and the pursuit of happiness."

"Jefferson was a damned Virginian," the man from Maine sneered. "Give me Adams and Hamilton any day." More nods, these from all around the big room. Founding Fathers from states no longer in the USA had a low reputation north of the Mason-Dixon line these days, and had ever since the War of Secession.

"Do you deny, sir, that they are human beings?" Flora asked. "Do you deny that they possess those rights I named?"

"They are in a foreign country," the Congressman from Maine replied. "I deny that they are any business of the USA."

He got more nods, from fellow Democrats, from the handful of Republicans and Freedom Party men, and even from a few Socialists. To her dismay, Flora had seen that before. Socialists spoke on behalf of racial equality, but couldn't get too far ahead of the people who voted them into office. That was how they rationalized it, anyhow.

"Congressman Moran, would you say the same if these persecuted people were Irish?" Flora asked sweetly.

"Since they aren't Irish, the question does not apply." Moran was too smart to answer that one the way she asked it.

Because he was, she waited for Speaker La Follette to gavel down his interruption and then introduced her motion of censure against the Confederate States. She knew it would fail; the next motion passed censuring the Confederate States for the way they treated their Negroes would be the first. But she had to make the effort. It wasn't as if Jews didn't know pogroms, too. News out of Russia and the Kingdom of Poland (which bore about the same relationship to Germany as the Republic of Quebec did to the USA) wasn't good.

After the House adjourned, she went across the street to her office. A newsboy waving the *Philadelphia Inquirer* shouted, "Confederates ask to enlarge their army! Read all about it!"

"I certainly do want to read about that!" Flora exclaimed, and gave him a nickel. He handed her a paper, and smiled broadly when she didn't wait for change.

She spread the *Inquirer* out on her desk. That was the lead headline, all right. She zoomed through the story. President Featherston, apparently, had requested permission to boost the Confederate Army to a size significantly larger than that allowed by the treaty ending the Great War. Featherston was quoted as saying, "These soldiers will be used only for internal defense. We have uprisings against the lawful authority of our government in several states, and need the extra manpower to put them down."

Hoover hadn't said yes and hadn't said no. A Powel House spokesman had said the president of the United States would give the request serious consideration. Flora wondered what he would do. As a Democrat, he would normally favor a hard line against the CSA. But, as a Democrat, he would also normally favor putting down uprisings of the proletariat, no matter how justified they might be.

Flora wondered how she ought to feel about the request herself. Up till Jake Featherston became president of the Confederate States, the Socialists had favored a softer line with the CSA, easing the country's return to the family of nations. Some still did. How could the Confederacy become a normal country with a rebellion sputtering in its heartland? But how could one keep from sympathizing with the rebels, considering what they'd been through before picking up rifles (or, as Featherston claimed, cleaning the grease off the ones they'd hidden away in 1916)?

That last made up her mind. She dialed Powel House, wondering how long it would be before these newfangled telephones sent operators into extinction along with the passenger pigeon and the American bison. She worked her way through three secretaries before finally securing an appointment with President Hoover.

When she told her husband that evening what she'd done, Hosea Blackford made a sour face. "He won't listen to you. You're my wife. That's plenty of reason right there for him not to listen to you."

"This is foreign policy," Flora answered. "Foreign policy should be bipartisan. You said so yourself, often enough."

"This is Hoover." To put it mildly, Blackford did not care for his successor. "You'd do better to recommend the opposite of what you really want. You might have some chance of getting it then."

Powel House, on Third Street, was a three-story structure of red brick, with wide steps leading up to the broad porch and its wrought-iron railings. Philadelphia's last pre-Revolutionary mayor had lived there. Since the Second Mexican War, it had also replaced the White House in Washington as the chief presidential residence.

The reception hall onto which the street door opened was large and impressive, with highly polished mahogany wainscoting gleaming a mellow red-brown. The banister leading up to President Hoover's second-floor office was also of mahogany, the spindles fine examples of fancy lathework. When she'd lived here, Flora had often admired them. Now, worried as she was, she hardly gave them a glance.

Hoover's bulldog features twisted into a smile when she came in. "Good to see you, Mrs. Blackford." He waved her to a chair. "Please sit down. Make yourself comfortable." He didn't say, *Make yourself at home.* She'd been at home here. Had the election of 1932 turned out differently, she and Hosea would still be at home here. Hoover went on, "What can I do for you, Congresswoman?"

"Thank you for your time." Perhaps because she didn't like President Hoover, Flora took care to be especially polite. "I've come to ask you to tell President Featherston you do *not* approve of his proposed expansion of the Confederate Army. He will use it for nothing but the oppression of his own people."

"I agree. That is how he will use it," Hoover said, and astonished hope flamed in Flora. The president continued, "That is why I am disposed to permit the expansion."

Flora stared. "I don't understand . . . Mr. President."

"If I thought President Featherston intended to use his increased Army against the United States, I would oppose his enlargement of it with every fiber of my being. But I do believe he will use it only for the purpose he says he intends: putting down the Negro uprisings troubling several of his states. Any nation, whether friendly to the United States or not, is entitled to internal peace, stability, and security. If some ill-advised individuals disturb its tranquility, it has the right to use force to put them down."

"But, Mr. President, one of the reasons the Negroes are in arms against the CSA is that the white majority will not give them—how did you phrase it?—peace, stability, and tranquility," Flora answered. "The

Confederate States made their bed through oppression. Shouldn't they have to lie in it?"

"Radical elements have controlled blacks in the Confederate States for too long," Hoover said. "This is not their first rising, if you recall."

"Oh, yes. Their last one went a long way toward winning us the war," Flora replied. "Don't we owe them a debt of gratitude for that?"

The president thrust out his chin. "We owe no foreigners any debts," he said proudly. "We are at peace with the world. Even the Japanese." That was a dig at her husband, in whose presidency the war with Japan had broken out.

It was also an infallible sign she wouldn't get what she wanted. "I hope you will not regret this decision, Mr. President," she said, rising to her feet.

"My conscience is clear," Hoover said.

"Which is not the same as being right." Since she wouldn't get what she wanted, she did take the last word.


Grunting, Cincinnatus Driver eased the last sofa off his dolly and down to the floor of the furniture shop's storeroom. "Here you go, Mr. Averill. It's pretty furniture. I hope it sells good."

"Oh, Lord, so do I," the shopowner replied. He signed off on the paperwork Cincinnatus had given him, then handed back the clipboard.

"Obliged." Cincinnatus wheeled the dolly outside. Even though he'd been taking sofas and chairs and hassocks and chests of drawers off the truck for the past half hour and so was good and warm, the cold air flayed his face. Breathing it was like breathing knives. Snow crunched under his shoes. The winter looked to be as nasty as any he'd known since moving to Iowa.

He hoped the Ford would start, and breathed a sigh of relief when it did. He let the engine warm up before putting it in gear. That gave him a chance to pick up the folded copy of the *Des Moines Herald-Express* that lay on the seat. CONFEDERATE STALWARTS FLOCK TO ARMY, the headline read.

Cincinnatus muttered under his breath. That had nothing to do with Kentucky, but it had everything to do with blacks in the CSA. The new recruits would land on the Negro revolt with both feet. That would surely make more Negroes try to flee north. He wondered how many would make it into the USA.

*Not many,* he thought, throwing the paper down in disgust. *Not near enough.* A Jew or an Irishman could be welcome here. Even a Chinaman could, sometimes. But a Negro? Only the conquest of Kentucky had made Cincinnatus a U.S. citizen. And a Jew or an Irishman (though not a Chinaman) could easily pretend to be something he wasn't. A Negro? Cincinnatus shook his head. A black man *was* black, and nothing he could do would make him anything else.

Back in Kentucky, of course, Cincinnatus had known men called black who had blue eyes, and girls called black with freckles. They hadn't bought their features from the Sears, Roebuck catalogue or any of its smaller Confederate competitors. Nobody talked much about how they *had* come by them, but everybody knew.

Another story read, HOOVER PLANS REELECTION BID. Cincinnatus didn't bother reading that one. He'd voted Democratic ever since he'd been able to vote. He wanted the USA to keep the CSA down. As far as he was concerned, everything else ran second to that. And now Hoover had gone and betrayed his trust. Did that make it worth his while to vote Socialist later this year? He shrugged. He still had months and months to go before he needed to make up his mind.

He drove up to the railroad yards, got out of the truck and sat down on a bench with his pail to eat lunch. A couple of railroad dicks nodded to him as they went by; he was an accepted part of the landscape. One of the white men even tipped his cap. Cincinnatus made haste to return the gesture. No white in Kentucky would have done that with a black.

Half a dozen white truck drivers ate about fifty yards away. They didn't invite Cincinnatus over, and he didn't presume to join them without an invitation, though another white man did. Some things worked differently here from the way they did down in Kentucky, but others hadn't changed a bit.

Cincinnatus wasn't the only colored driver picking up cargo at the Des Moines yards, but the others seemed to be out hauling. It happened. He'd eaten a lot of lunches by himself. He took a big bite of his ham sandwich.

Shoeleather scrunched on gravel only a few feet away. Cincinnatus looked up. The black man coming toward him wasn't one of the usual drivers. That was the first thing Cincinnatus realized. The second thing was that he knew him anyway, though he hadn't seen him since moving away from Covington. "Lucullus!" he said in amazement. "What the hell you doin' here?"

"I been lookin' for you. Done found you now, too." Lucullus Wood stuck out his hand. Automatically, Cincinnatus shook it. When he'd come to Iowa, Lucullus had been on the cusp between boy and man: where Achilles was now. Today, Lucullus had a man's full and formidable presence. He'd also grown into a good deal of his father Apicius' heft.

"Lookin' for *me*? What for? I been gone from Covington a long time now. Don't want to go back, neither," Cincinnatus said.

The railroad dicks ambled past again, coming the other way. They gave Lucullus a hard stare. But, seeing that Cincinnatus knew him, they let him alone.

"Ain't just me. It's my old man," Lucullus said.

"What's Apicius want with me?" Cincinnatus asked in surprise and more than a little alarm. Lucullus' father wasn't just the best barbecue man between the Carolinas and Kansas City. He was also one of the leading Reds in Kentucky. During and after the war, he'd played a dangerous game with Confederate diehards and with Luther Bliss, the head of the Kentucky State Police. Having spent more time than he cared to in one of Luther Bliss' jails, Cincinnatus wanted nothing to do with him now. He pointed a finger at Lucullus. "Why'd old Apicius send you, anyways? Why don't he wire or write hisself a letter to me?"

"You know Pa ain't got his letters," Lucullus said, which was true but not fully responsive. Seeing Cincinnatus' impatience, the younger man went on, "He send me so I kin talk you into doin' what needs doin'."

"So you kin talk me into doin' what Apicius wants, you mean," Cincinnatus said, and Lucullus didn't deny it. "Well?" Cincinnatus asked. "Tell me what he wants an' why he wants *me*. Tell me quick, so I kin say no an' go on about my business."

"He wants you on account of you's a nigger with balls, and you's a nigger with a truck," Lucullus said. "Plenty o' black folks, they tryin' to get up to the USA from the CSA. You hear tell 'bout dat?"

"I hear tell," Cincinnatus admitted.

"You know 'bout the Underground Railroad back before the War o' Secession?" Lucullus asked. "Run slaves up into free country so they turn free themselves. That's what we do now. We run niggers up into the USA. An' we needs your help."

"You want me to go down there an' sneak black folks from the CSA up into the USA?" Cincinnatus asked.

Lucullus nodded. "That's right. What you say?"

Cincinnatus looked at him. He knew what Lucullus and Apicius were counting on: his urge to protect his own. But he had his own right here— Elizabeth, Achilles, and Amanda. He looked Lucullus straight in the eye and said, "No."

Lucullus' jaw dropped. "What?"

"No," Cincinnatus repeated. "That means I ain't gonna do it. Sorry you come all this way, but no anyhow. Tell your pa he should find hisself another nigger, one with rocks where his brains ought to be."

Now Lucullus started to get angry. "Why not?" he demanded.

"On account of whoever does this, he gonna get caught," Cincinnatus replied. "On account of I already been in Luther Bliss' jail once, and ain't nothin' or nobody make me mess with that man again. On account of I do anything you goddamn Reds don't like, I end up dead an' wishin' I was in Luther Bliss' goddamn jail. No. *Hell,* no."

He waited for Lucullus to remind him his mother and father still lived in Covington and bad things might happen to them if he didn't go along. He waited, but Lucullus said nothing of the kind. Maybe he knew it would do no good. He did say, "My pa, he ain't gonna be real happy with you."

"I ain't real happy with him, or with you, neither," Cincinnatus said. "You got a lot o' goddamn nerve, comin' up here an' tryin' to drag me back into that shit. I done gone away a long time ago, an' I ain't *never* goin' back." He was almost shouting. If he'd been any angrier, he would have hurled himself at Lucullus.

The younger man held out both hands, pale palms up, in a placating gesture. "All right. All right. I hears you. I tells my pa what you say." He left the railroad yard in a hurry.

"Who was that colored fella?" one of the railroad dicks asked Cincinnatus after Lucullus went away. Not *that other colored fella*, Cincinnatus noticed: they took him so much for granted, they almost forgot what color he was. *That* never would have happened in Kentucky, either. People there always paid attention to who was who. They were sometimes less overt about noticing than they were here in Iowa, but they always did.

"I used to know him when I was livin' down in Kentucky," Cincinnatus answered. "Ain't seen him for years till now."

"What did he want?"

"Tryin' to talk me into goin' back there. He had some kind o' business deal." Cincinnatus shrugged. "I ain't goin'. He's a fly-by-night."

"You must be rich, if he came all this way from Kentucky to try and take your money," the dick said. "He'll have a long, empty time going back. Thought he could play you for a sucker, did he?"

"Anybody reckon's I'm rich, he ain't never seen all the moths fly outa my wallet when I open it." Cincinnatus hesitated to admit even to himself that he was doing well.

Both railroad dicks laughed. "Yeah, well, I know that song," said the one who did most of the talking. "Don't I just, goddammit." He and his partner both strode off to prowl around trains.

Cincinnatus bolted the rest of his lunch. Then he went after work for the rest of the day. He got less than he wanted; wasting time with Lucullus had put him behind the other drivers. He muttered and fumed all afternoon. Not only had Lucullus bothered him, he'd cost him money. That hurt more.

When he got back to his apartment building at the end of that long, frustrating day, he found not only Elizabeth but also Mr. and Mrs. Chang from upstairs waiting in the lobby. Mrs. Chang spoke next to no English, but started yelling at him in Chinese the minute he walked in the door.

"Your foolish boy!" Mr. Chang shouted. "Foolish, foolish boy! What he think he do? He—" He broke down and started to cry.

Cincinnatus looked a question to Elizabeth. All this excitement was likely to mean only one thing. Sure enough, his wife nodded. "Achilles and Grace, they run off to get married," she said.

"Do Jesus!" Cincinnatus said softly. He didn't think that was a good idea—which put it mildly. But he didn't know what he—or the Changs—could do about it. His son and their daughter were of legal age. If they wanted to tie the knot, they could. Whether they would live happily ever after was liable to be a different story, but they weren't likely to worry about that now.

He held out his hand to Grace Chang's—no, to Grace Driver's—father. "Welcome to the family," he said. "I reckon either we make the best o' this or else we spend all our time fighting from here on out."

Mr. Chang looked at the hand for close to half a minute before finally taking it. "I got nothing against you. You good man," he said at last. "Your boy—against your boy I got plenty. But you, me—we no fight."

"That's about as much as I can ask for right now," Cincinnatus said. "Somehow or other, we'll get through it." The Changs didn't look as if they believed him. For that matter, neither did Elizabeth. And he hadn't said a word about Lucullus' visit yet.

Mort Pomeroy gave Mary a kiss on the cheek. He was bundled into an overcoat, with mittens and fur hat with earflaps. He was only going across the street to the diner, but in the middle of a blizzard all the clothes he could put on were none too many. "I'll see you tonight, sweetheart," he said.

"So long," Mary answered. "I've got plenty to keep me busy."

Her husband nodded, though that wouldn't have been true at the McGregor farm. Mort didn't realize how much harder life had been there. However much she loved him, Mary didn't intend to tell him, either. She didn't like keeping secrets from him, but thought she had no choice here.

He kissed her again and went out the door. She went to the window so she could watch him cross the street. She always did that. He knew it, too. He looked up, waving through the snow that blurred his outline. She waved back, and blew him another kiss. He jerked his head to show he'd got it.

As soon as Mort went into the diner, Mary washed the breakfast dishes. She put them in the drainer; she saw no point to drying them herself. Once she'd done that, she looked out the window again. An auto painted U.S. Army green-gray made its slow way up the street in Rosenfeld. Whoever was in it paid no attention to the Canadian woman looking down on him from the apartment building.

"One of these days, I'll *make* you pay attention," she muttered. "You see if I don't." She started to fix herself a fresh cup of tea, but stopped and shrugged instead. The cup she'd had with breakfast hadn't sat so well as she would have liked. Maybe the next one ought to wait till later.

Even without the tea, her heart beat faster when she got out the bomb-making gear she'd taken from the barn at the farm a year and a half before. After all this time, Mort had no idea the tools and explosives were here. He was busy in the diner's kitchen, but the kitchen pantries in the apartment were her place, and he left them alone.

She thought she knew as much as she needed to know about this business. Only the experiment, of course, would prove that one way or the other. She hadn't made the experiment yet.

A clock chimed the hour: eight o'clock. Not far away, the general store would be opening for business. It wasn't Henry Gibbon's store any more. Peter Karamanlides, the new owner, was a big-nosed Greek from Rochester, New York. His selection of merchandise was almost identical to what Gibbon's had been. His prices were, if anything, microscopically lower. Mary disliked him just the same, though she bought from him. A lot of things had to come from the general store, because nobody else in Rosenfeld carried them.

Karamanlides seemed decent enough. But here he was, one more Yank yankifying Canada. Mary wished there were Canadians buying general stores in Rochester instead, but there weren't, or she'd never heard of any.

She gave her attention back to the business at hand. Her father's bombs had always had wooden cases. Hers fit into a cardboard box. She could have made the same sort of case as Arthur McGregor had, but she'd decided not to. She didn't want investigators reminded of her father's work. That might make them look her way.

For the same reason, she didn't use the big tenpenny nails her father had. Thumbtacks would do the job well enough. She wound and carefully set an alarm clock, then even more carefully lowered it into the cardboard box. If she dropped it, if the impact made its bells clack against each other . . . *Pa never made a stupid mistake like that,* she told herself fiercely. *I won't, either.*

And she didn't, though a drop of sweat trickled down her forehead and between her eyes and fell from the tip of her nose onto the glass face of the clock. She wiped it away with a forefinger. Then she poured the thumbtacks into the box, put on the lid, and tied it shut with brown twine.

She yawned as she put on a heavy coat and a scarf to cover her red hair. Now she wished she'd had that second cup of tea after all. Well, no help for it. The coat was big and bulky. She had no trouble concealing the box under it. Out the door and down the stairs she went.

The general store was around the corner and two blocks away. Her heart pounded harder and harder as she walked towards it. Again, she spoke sternly to herself: *Father did this lots of times. You can, too. And you will.*

Hardly anyone was on the street yet. That was good. That was how she wanted things. The fewer people who saw her, the better. There was the post office. Wilf Rokeby would be getting ready to open up there, as he had for as long as she could remember. And here was the general store.

She jumped when the bell above the door jingled as she went in. "Good day to you, Mrs. Pomeroy," Karamanlides said from behind the counter. "What can I get for you today?" He chuckled. "So early, and I'm all yours."

She'd counted on being the only customer in the place. She hadn't counted on how hot it was inside. He had the potbellied stove going full blast. The sweat on her face now had nothing to do with nerves. She gave him her list, finishing, "And a pair of the strongest reading glasses you've got. I'll give them to my mother for her birthday." Her mother's birthday was indeed coming up in a few weeks.

Karamanlides piled goods on the counter, then said, "Excuse me. The glasses I keep in the back room." He disappeared.

Mary set the cardboard box on a bottom shelf. It didn't look much different from the boxes of epsom salts already sitting there. She left her coat open afterwards. That was all to the good. If she'd kept it closed much longer, the storekeeper would have started wondering why.

He came back with the spectacles. "I have a couple styles here. Which ones you like better? The lenses are the same in both." His accent wasn't just American; a faint trace of his native country lingered in it, too.

"Let me have the pair with the bronze frames," Mary answered. "What does it all come to?"

As Henry Gibbon would have, Karamanlides scribbled figures on a scrap of paper and added them up. "Three dollars and nineteen cents," he said after checking everything twice.

She gave him four dollar bills and checked to make sure the change was right. Then she took what she'd bought back to the apartment building. She put everything away. She didn't want Mort noticing she'd been to the general store this morning. She didn't think anyone but Karamanlides had seen her go in or come out.

She fell back into housework, but then broke off with a gasp. What would she do if the U.S. authorities decided to search the apartment just because she was her father's daughter? Stowing bomb-making tools in the kitchen was enough to keep Mort from knowing they were there. Hard-eyed men in green-gray uniforms? Probably—no, certainly—not. Having a really good hiding place didn't matter . . . so long as she didn't use the tools. But now she had.

Everything went into another cardboard box, this one considerably larger than the one waiting with the epsom salts. Then she took the box downstairs. Everybody in the building stashed things in the basement. It wasn't such a good hiding place as her father had found in the barn, but it would have to do for now. The Yanks would have trouble proving those tools were hers even if they did find them. She hoped they would, anyhow.

Halfway back up the stairs, Mary paused and yawned and yawned and yawned. She shook her head in amazement when she finally stopped. She couldn't remember the last time she'd felt this tired in the middle of the day. Finishing the climb felt like going up Mount Everest, which had recently killed a couple of German climbers who'd wanted to be the first to the summit.

When she returned to the apartment, she thought about fixing that cup of tea to perk herself up. But the last one had been so bitter, she just didn't feel like another. Her stomach lurched at the mere thought.

*What's wrong with me?* she thought, although she had at least the beginnings of a suspicion. She hadn't finished the morning dusting when she started yawning again. She sat down in the nearest chair, closed her eyes, and tilted her head back. *I'll just rest for a little. . . .* She didn't even finish the thought before sleep claimed her.

She woke with a start an hour and a half later, blinking and confused. Had it? Hadn't it? Had she slept through it if it had? She didn't think she could have, and yet. . . . A glance at a clock went some way toward reassuring her. It shouldn't have, not unless she'd done something wrong.

Feeling guilty about dozing off in the middle of the day, she got back to work. She should have been refreshed, but she kept wanting to start yawning again. Excitement that had nothing to do with waiting built in her. This wasn't her imagination; she couldn't remember the last time she'd taken a nap in the middle of the morning.

When the *bang!* came at last, it sounded less impressive than she'd expected. She'd heard a bomb go off once before, back during the war. She'd been a little girl then, and remembered the noise as seeming like the end of the world. This—was just a bang. The windows rattled briefly, and that was that. She was farther away now than she had been then. Maybe her bomb was smaller, too.

Before long, the town fire engine's siren screamed to life. Mary looked out the window. Some people, Mort among them, came out of the diner across the street to see what had happened. One of them pointed in the direction of the general store. Mary wondered if Mort would look up at her, but he didn't. In a way, she was sorry; in another way, relieved. He didn't automatically think of her as a bomber, then. If he didn't, maybe the U.S. occupiers wouldn't, either.

No one knocked on her door till her husband got home. She didn't need to ask him about the news. He was full of it: "Somebody blew Gibbon's general store—of course, it's not Gibbon's any more—to hell and gone. We haven't seen anything like this since—er, in a long time." *Since your father's day,* he'd started to say.

"I heard a boom. I didn't know what it was," Mary said.

"A bomb," her husband said solemnly. "The store went up in smoke. Big fire. If what's-his-name, the Greek, hadn't been in the back room, he would have gone up with it. As is, he got a nail or something right here." He patted his own left buttock. "He'll sit on a slant for weeks, I bet."

Mary laughed. She wasn't too sorry Karamanlides hadn't got badly hurt. She wondered whether she had the stomach to go on fighting the USA. *Pa wouldn't've cared who got hurt. They were just the enemy to him.*

"I have news, too," she said.

"What is it?" Mort sounded indulgent: what could be interesting or important after the bomb?

But Mary had an answer for him: "I'm going to have a baby."

His eyes went wide, wider, widest. "Are you sure?" he asked, a question men uncounted regret the moment it passes their lips.

But Mary, a good part of her mind on other things, let him down easy. All she said was, "Yes, very sure." Even if the U.S. occupiers didn't catch her, she doubted she would be doing much with the bomb-making tools for a while now.


**W**hen Jonathan Moss left his apartment these days, his hand was always on the stock of the pistol he carried. If anybody wanted to fight, he was ready. He took threats a lot more seriously than he had before. Major Sam Lopat had thought they were a pack of nonsense. Then occupation headquarters went up in smoke. The military prosecutor's opinions were no longer relevant.

Berlin, Ontario, had been quiet since the blast. Even new YANKS OUT! graffiti were harder to come by than they had been before the bomb went off. American soldiers had gone back to shooting first and asking questions later. The lawyer in Moss deplored that. The American in Canada in him thought it made him more likely to live to a ripe old age.

An armored car rattled down the street. The machine would have been hopelessly obsolete in time of war. But it was ideal for making terrorists and would-be revolutionaries think twice. A couple of the soldiers inside the machine jeered at Moss. Everybody around here knew who he was, Canucks and Americans alike.

Again, part of him savored that recognition and part of him could have done without it. He slid behind the wheel of his Model D Ford. He'd finally got rid of the Bucephalus, not only because it was old but also because it was distinctive. So far as he knew, it had been the only Bucephalus in Berlin, while there were four or five Model D's on this block alone.

*In obscurity there is strength,* he thought, and turned the key. Not only did the Ford start more readily than the Bucephalus had been in the habit of doing, he thought it less likely to have explosives waiting under the hood on any given day. He hadn't really worried about that, either, not till after occupation headquarters blew up.

He laughed as he put the motorcar in gear, not that it was really funny. Nothing like a bomb going off to concentrate the mind. When he got to the building that held his office, he didn't park the Ford in front of it, as he'd been in the habit of doing. Instead, he went on to a lot a couple of blocks away, a lot surrounded by barbed wire and patrolled by armed guards. SECURE PARKING, said the sign above the entrance. Moss gave the attendant twenty cents and drove in.

The sign might as well have read, PARKING FOR AMERICANS. The only Canadians who used it were a handful of collaborators. They were, of course, doubtless the ones who felt they needed it most.

Moss felt he needed it. That he felt he needed it infuriated him. Dammit, couldn't the Canucks see he was on their side? Evidently not. They only saw he was a Yank. If he came from south of the forty-ninth parallel, he had to be an enemy.

Most of the buildings in downtown Berlin had had their glass replaced since the bomb went off. Here and there, though, plywood sheets still covered those openings. Some people couldn't afford to reglaze. Some buildings simply stood empty; the business collapse had been no less savage here than anywhere else.

When he got to his office, he plugged in the hot plate and got some coffee going. The pot would be good in the morning, tolerable around noon, and battery acid towards evening. He knew he'd go right on drinking it anyway. How could anybody function without coffee? He yawned. Life was hard enough with it.

As soon as he'd poured the coffee, he started going through paperwork. Like a lot of busy men who worked for themselves, he was chronically behind. He had a better excuse than most, though. Since the bombing in Berlin, he'd had to try cases in Galt, in Guelph, in London, even in Toronto. That did nothing to make him more efficient. He was pleased with the record he'd managed to ring up despite the added difficulty of travel.

His first client came in at precisely nine o'clock. "Good morning, Mr. Jamieson." Moss rose to shake hands with him. "How are you today?"

"Tolerable, Mr. Moss." Lou Jamieson was a middle-aged man who walked with a limp. He had a very pale face that always bore a slight sheen of sweat or oil. His meat market was the biggest in Berlin. The occupying authorities kept accusing him of paying kickbacks to U.S. inspectors. Moss wouldn't have bet that he didn't, though of course lawyers didn't ask questions like that. Much of the evidence they'd had against him went up in smoke in the bombing. That hadn't kept them from going after him again; his trial, in London, was set to open the following week.

"What do you think they've got on me?" he asked now, lighting a cigarette.

"Well, that's a problem, you know," Moss answered. "This isn't an ordinary criminal proceeding. There's no pretrial discovery under occupation law. The military prosecutor can spring whatever surprises he wants in front of the judge."

Jamieson gestured with his right hand, leaving a trail of smoke from the cigarette. "Teach your granny to suck eggs, why don't you?" he said in a raspy baritone. "This ain't the first time they've had me up, you know. I've beaten this crap before. So what have they got on me?"

He expected Moss to know regardless of whether the Army told him. And Moss did. Even over in London—hell, even over in Toronto—he knew people who could tell him interesting things. Finding out cost him money, but that was one of the expenses of running a practice. "There's a lieutenant named Szymanski from the Inspectorate who's going to testify that you paid him off. He's going to name dates and amounts and what you wanted him not to see each time."

"Is he?" Jamieson's laugh had a wheezy sound to it. "You know Lucille Cheever?"

"Personally? No," Moss said, and Lou Jamieson laughed again. Dryly, Moss went on, "I know who she is, though." She ran the leading sporting house in Berlin, and had for years.

"That'll do." Jamieson stubbed out the cigarette and lit another one. "Ask her about Lieutenant Szymanski and Yolanda. She can name dates and amounts and what the damn Polack got each time. He has a wife and twins down in Pennsylvania. You hit him with that, what you want to bet he loses his memory?"

"Yolanda?" Moss echoed.

Jamieson nodded. "Yolanda. Big blond gal." His hands shaped an hourglass. "Big jugs, too. Gotta be better than what he was getting at home. 'Course, he's no bargain himself. He knows we know about Yolanda, he'll shut up."

"I'll take care of it." Moss didn't write down Lucille Cheever's name. He knew he would remember it—and the less in writing when he went on the shady side of the street, the better.

"What else they got?" Jamieson inquired.

"Unless somebody's pulling a fast one on me, he's their heavy artillery."

Jamieson snorted contemptuously. "Dumb assholes." Moss knew what that was likely to mean. He hadn't studied occupation law to help real crooks wiggle off the hook. But you couldn't turn down clients because you thought they were guilty. Jamieson went on, "If Szymanski's all they've got, we'll kick their asses. See you over in London." He fired up another cigarette and swaggered out of the office.

*And how do I explain talking to Lucille Cheever to Laura?* Moss wondered. He knew he would have to tell her. If he didn't and she found out later, that would be worse. He sighed. Northwestern Law School hadn't covered all the points of legal ethics it might have.

The telephone rang. "Jonathan Moss," he said crisply. It was occupation headquarters in Galt, announcing a delay in a case there: the prosecutor was in the hospital with a case of boils. "How . . . biblical," Moss murmured. The officer on the other end of the line hung up on him.

Chuckling, he went back to work. His next client came in fifteen minutes later. Clementine Schmidt was embroiled in what looked to be a permanent property dispute with the occupation authorities. Appeals over what was and what wasn't acceptable documentation that she owned the property she claimed to own dragged on and on. Since the war ended, military judges had changed their minds at least four times. All in all, it was not the USA's finest hour in handling Canadian affairs.

Miss Schmidt (Moss couldn't blame men for fighting shy of marrying such a disputatious woman) brandished a letter. In a voice ringing with triumph, she declared, "I have found my cousin, Maximilian."

"Have you?" Moss blinked. She'd been talking about Maximilian for years. He'd always assumed her cousin had died in the war.

But she nodded. "Yes, I have," she said triumphantly. "He fought in the Rockies and was badly wounded there. That is why he never came home." *It had nothing to do with you? Amazing,* Moss thought. His client went on, "He settled in a town called Kamloops, in British Columbia. And he remembers very well the situation of the property." She thrust the letter at him.

He rapidly read through it. When he'd finished, he nodded. "We'll definitely show this to the appellate judge when the time comes," he said. Miss Schmidt beamed. The letter was in fact a lot less ironclad than she seemed to think. Cousin Maximilian recalled that the family had owned the property in question once upon a time. He had no new documentation to prove that. If he'd lived out in Kamloops since being wounded, it wasn't likely that he would.

Clementine Schmidt was still elated that she'd found good old Cousin Max. Moss let her chortle, then eased her out of the office. He poured himself more coffee once she finally left. He was still drinking it when the postman knocked on the door. "Here you are, Mr. Moss," the fellow said, and dumped a pile of envelopes on what had been a nearly clean desk.

"Thanks." Moss surveyed the pile with something less than joy unalloyed. He sorted through the day's mail, separating it into piles: papers related to cases, advertisements, payments (only a couple of those—and why was he not surprised?), and things he couldn't readily classify.

He opened a plain envelope in that miscellaneous pile, then unfolded the sheet of paper inside it. Neatly printed on it in large letters were the words, WE HAVE NOT FORGOTTEN ABOUT YOU, YOU YANK SON OF A BITCH. WE HAVE NOT FORGOTTEN ABOUT YOUR WHORE OR HER BRAT, EITHER.

He stared in dismay. Since the bombing of occupation headquarters, he hadn't had a missive like this. He'd hoped he wouldn't. Considering what had happened to occupation headquarters, he couldn't very well ignore it. Whoever was behind this had proved he was playing for keeps.

His hand trembled as he reached for the telephone and rang up Galt. As bad luck would have it, he was connected to the officer with whom he'd cracked wise about the military prosecutor's boils. "You're not so goddamn funny when you need the Army, are you?" the other American said.

"Well, maybe not," Moss admitted. "I'm no fonder of being blown up than anybody else."

"Shows how much gratitude your clients have," the officer said.

"I doubt my clients are behind this," Moss said stiffly. The gibe stung all the same. He didn't know why Canadians wanted him dead, either. He'd spent his whole career fighting their legal battles—and winning quite a few of them. And this was the thanks he got?

"Bring in the paper," the man in Galt said. "We'll run it through the lab. I doubt they'll come up with anything, but you never know till you try."

"I'll do it," Moss said. Doing it right away meant canceling a meeting. He canceled it. Whoever was doing this, Moss wanted him caught. He didn't like living in fear. Somebody out there, though, didn't care what he liked.

# VI

Spring and snow went together in Quebec. Lucien Galtier drove with exaggerated care. He knew the Chevrolet would skid if he did anything heroic—which was to say, stupid or abrupt—on an icy road. The point of going to a dance, after all, was getting there in one piece. He wondered if he would have thought the same as a young buck courting Marie. Of course, back in those days before the turn of the century, only a few millionaires had had motorcars. It was hard to do anything too spectacularly idiotic in a carriage.

Marie . . . His hands tightened on the steering wheel. She was seven years dead, and half the time it felt as if she were just around the corner visiting neighbors and would be back any minute. The other half, Galtier knew she was gone, all right, and the knowledge was knives in his soul. Those were the black days. He'd heard time was supposed to heal such wounds. Maybe it did. The knives, now, didn't seem to have serrated edges.

A right turn, a left, and yes, there was the path leading to François Berlinguet's farmhouse and, even more to the point, to the barn nearby. Plenty of other autos and carriages and wagons sat by the house. Lucien found a vacant spot. He turned off his headlights and got out of the Chevrolet. Snow crunched under his shoes.

Lamplight spilled out of the barn door. So did the sweet strains of fiddle music. Then, suddenly, a whole band joined in. Galtier shook his head in bemusement. Back in his courting days, nobody had owned a phonograph, either. Music meant real, live musicians. It still could—those fiddlers were real, live human beings. But it didn't have to, not any more.

The band stopped. People in the barn laughed and clapped their hands.

Then the music started up again—someone must have turned the record over or put a new one on the phonograph. The live fiddlers joined in.

Lucien blinked against the bright lights inside the barn. He'd got used to the darkness driving over. Couples dipped and swirled in the cleared space in the middle. Men and women watched from the edges of the action. Some perched on chairs; others leaned against the wall. Quite a few of them were holding mugs of cider or beer or applejack. Galtier sidled toward a table not far from the fiddlers and the phonograph. Berlinguet's wife, Madeleine, a smiling woman of about forty-five, gave him a mug. He sipped. It was cider, cider with a stronger kick than beer.

"*Merci,*" he said. She nodded.

When the next tune ended, François Berlinguet, who was a few years older than Madeleine, pointed toward Lucien. "And here we have the most eligible bachelor in all of the county of Temiscouata, *Monsieur* Lucien Galtier!" His red face and raucous voice said he'd been drinking a lot of that potent cider.

The drunker the people were, the louder they cheered and clapped their hands. "God knows what a liar you are, François, and so do I," Lucien said. Berlinguet bowed, as if at a compliment. Galtier got a laugh. His host got a bigger one.

Trouble was, it hadn't been altogether a lie. Ever since he'd lost Marie, widows had been throwing themselves at Galtier. So had the daughters and granddaughters of friends, acquaintances, and optimistic strangers. He felt no urgent need for a second wife. He'd done his best to make that plain. No one seemed to want to listen to him.

Even though the phonograph was quiet, the fiddlers struck up a tune. People began to dance again. What Lucien noticed was how harsh and ragged the music seemed. When he was young, people had enjoyed whatever music their neighbors made. Some was better, some not quite so good, but what difference did it make?

It made a difference now. People measured neighbors' music not by the standards of other neighbors' music, but against the professionals who made records. What would have been fine a couple of generations before was anything but now. *We're spoiled,* Lucien thought. That hadn't occurred to him before, which made it no less true.

Berlinguet came over to him. "Will you be a wallflower?" he teased.

"If I want to," Galtier answered. "I can do just about anything I want to, it seems to me. I have the years for it."

"But you will break the hearts of all the pretty girls here," his host said. "How can they dance with you if you will not dance?"

"Now that, my friend, that is a truly interesting question," Lucien said. "And now I have another question for you as well: is it that they wish to dance with me, or is it that they wish to dance with my farm and my electricity and my Chevrolet?"

François Berlinguet did him the courtesy of taking him seriously. "It could be that some of them do wish to dance with the farm and the other things. But, you know, it could also be that some of them wish to dance with *you*. Will you take away their chance along with that of the others?"

"I do not know." Galtier shrugged a Gallic shrug. "Truly, I do not. The trouble is, how do I tell with a certainty the ones from the others?"

Before Berlinguet could answer, Dr. Leonard O'Doull and Galtier's daughter, Nicole, walked into the barn. With his long, angular body and fair, Irish-looking face, O'Doull always looked like a stranger in a crowd of Quebecois. But he wasn't a stranger here. He must have treated at least half the people in the barn. Men and women swarmed up to him. Some wanted to talk about their aches and pains. More, though, wanted to talk politics or gossip. Even if he did still sound a little—and only a little— like the American he was, he'd made a place for himself in and around Rivière-du-Loup.

Eventually, he and Nicole came over to Galtier. As François Berlinguet had, O'Doull said, "You're not dancing, *mon beau-père*. Do you think you will wear out all the sweet young things?"

"It could be," Lucien answered. "It could also be that I think they will wear me out. When I want to dance, I will dance. And if I do not care to . . . well, who will make me?"

Nicole grabbed his left hand. When she did, her husband plucked the mug of cider out of his right hand. "*I* will make you," she said, and dragged him out toward the middle of the floor. "You don't need to wonder why I want to dance with you, either." She understood him very well.

He wagged a finger at her. "Yes, I know why you want to dance with me. You want to make me look like a fool in front of the entire neighborhood. How is it that you have come down here from town?"

"I talked with Madeleine Berlinguet when she came up to sell some chickens, and she invited us," Nicole answered. "Before too long, you know, little Lucien will want to start coming to dances, too."

The idea that his grandson would soon be old enough to want to dance with girls rocked Galtier back on his heels. Had it really been so many years since little Lucien was born? It had, sure enough.

When the music started—fiddlers playing along with the phonograph—he had to remember where his feet went. Nicole didn't lead too obviously, for which he was grateful. And, once he'd been dancing a little while, he discovered he was having a good time. He didn't intend to admit that, but it was true.

After the song (an import from the USA, with lyrics translated into

French) ended, Leonard O'Doull came out and tapped Galtier on the shoulder. "Excuse me, *mon beau-père,* but I am going to dance this next dance with my wife."

"You think so, do you?" Galtier asked in mock anger. "Then what am I to do? Return to wallflowerdom?"

"Is that a word?" His son-in-law looked dubious. "You can go back if you like, or you can find some other lady and dance with her."

"Such choices you give me. I am not worthy," Galtier said, and Leonard O'Doull snorted. Now Lucien did feel like dancing. He touched a woman on the shoulder. He smiled. "Hello, Éloise. May I have this dance?"

"*Mais certainement,* Lucien." Éloise Granche was a widow of about Nicole's age. She'd lost her husband in a train wreck a little before Lucien lost Marie. If he hadn't known her before, he would have thought that was what gave her an air of calm perhaps too firmly held. In fact, she'd always been like that. Philippe Granche had drunk like a fish; maybe that had more to do with it.

The music started again. Galtier took her in his arms. She was two or three inches shorter than Marie had been, and plumper, too, but not so much that she didn't make a pleasant armful. She danced well. Lucien had to remind himself he needed to say such things.

"And you," she told him when he did. After a moment, she asked, "Is this your first time since . . . ?"

She let that hang, but Galtier understood perfectly well what she meant. "No, not quite," he answered, "but it still seems very strange. How long have you been dancing now?"

"A couple of years," Éloise said. "Yes, it is strange, isn't it? With Philippe, I always knew just what he would do. Other people are surprises, one after another."

"Yes!" He nodded. "They certainly seem to be. And not only on the dance floor, either. The world is a different place now."

"It certainly is for me," she said. "I wasn't so sure it would be for a man."

"Oh, yes. For this man, anyhow." Galtier didn't think he'd ever spoken of his love for Marie outside the bosom of his family. He didn't intend to start now. Even saying so much was more than he'd thought he would do.

Éloise Granche seemed to know what he meant even when he didn't say it. She said, "You have to go on. It's very hard at first, but you have to."

He nodded again. "So I've seen. It *was* hard at first." He hadn't spoken of that even with his family. There had been weeks—months—when he hadn't wanted to get out of bed, let alone get on with his life.

The music stopped. "Thank you for asking me," Éloise said. "That was very pleasant."

"I thought so, too." Lucien hesitated. He hadn't talked with anyone who knew what he was talking about before. She'd traveled down the same road as he. After the hesitation, he plunged: "Shall we also dance the next one?"

"I'd like to," she said briskly. "We've both made the same journey, haven't we?"

"I was just thinking that very thing!" he said in surprise. When he and Marie had the same thought at the same time, he'd taken it for granted. Why not? They'd spent forty years living in each other's pockets. When he did it with a near stranger . . . That was a surprise.

Éloise's shrug said it astonished her less than him. "It springs from what we were talking about, I think." The fiddlers began to play. She swayed forward. They started dancing again, this time without words.

Galtier wondered what Marie would say. Probably something like, *Try not to step on her toes, the way you always did on mine.* Éloise's eyes were closed as they spun around the barn. Her expression said she might have been listening to someone who wasn't there, too. But she was also very much with Lucien.

When the music stopped this time, they both walked over to the table to get some cider. They stood by the wall, talking of this and that, through the next dance—and the next. But Galtier didn't feel like a wallflower any more.


The USS *Remembrance* steamed south, accompanied by a couple of destroyers and a heavy cruiser. Lieutenant, Junior Grade, Sam Carsten smeared zinc-oxide ointment on his nose and the backs of his hands. He knew he would burn anyhow, but he wouldn't burn so badly this way.

Off to the east rose the bleak, almost lunar landscape of Baja California. The *Remembrance* and her companions sailed outside the three-mile limit the Empire of Mexico claimed, but not very far outside it. Their guns and the carrier's aeroplanes could have smashed up that coast or whatever little gunboats the Mexicans sent out to challenge them.

But the Mexicans sent out nothing. Cabo San Lucas wasn't much of a port. No, actually, that wasn't true. It had the makings of a fine harbor— or it would have, if only there were any fresh water close by. Since there wasn't, the protected bay went to waste except for an old gunboat or two and a few fishing trawlers.

Sam turned to Lieutenant Commander Harrison, the assistant officer of the deck. "Sir, may I make a suggestion?"

"Go ahead, Carsten," Roosevelt Harrison replied. The Annapolis ring on the younger officer's finger explained why he was where he was and Sam was where *he* was.

"Thank you, sir," replied Sam, who'd never expected to become an officer at all when he joined the Navy a few years before the Great War started. "The Confederates have a naval base at Guaymas, sir. Where we are and where we're headed, they might want to use us to give their submersible skippers some practice."

"They aren't supposed to have any submersibles," the assistant OOD said.

"Yes, sir. I know that, sir," Carsten said, and said no more.

Harrison considered. After a few seconds, he said, "You may have a point. I wouldn't trust those bastards as far as I could throw 'em." He cupped his hands in front of his mouth and raised his voice to a shout: "Attention on deck! All hands be alert for submarines in the neighborhood." Sailors hurried to the edge of the deck and peered in all directions, shielding their eyes from the glare of the sun with their palms. Lieutenant Commander Harrison gave his attention back to Sam. "A good thought. I don't believe they'd try anything even if they do have boats in the water, but you're right—stalking us would give them good practice."

"What happens if somebody does spot a periscope?" Carsten asked. "Do we drop ashcans on the submersible?"

"That's a damn good question, and I'm glad the skipper's the one who's got to answer it," Harrison said. "My guess would be no. The Confederates aren't allowed to have any submersibles, but how do we know whatever we spot isn't flying Maximilian's flag?" He and Sam exchanged wry grins; the Empire of Mexico could no more build submarines than it could aeroplane carriers. But where a boat was built had nothing to do with whose flag she flew.

"I don't suppose we can tell, sir," Sam allowed. "Still, if it looks like a boat's getting ready to fire something . . ."

"Then we're liable to have a war on our hands." The assistant OOD shivered, though the day was fine and warm. "Till I see a wake in the water, I won't order an attack on any submarine we spot. If the skipper has a different notion, that'll be up to him."

Sometimes not having rank was a comfort. Sam knew that from his days as a petty officer. If you weren't important enough to give any really important orders, you couldn't get into really big trouble. When he was a petty officer, he would have figured a lieutenant commander had the clout to screw up in a big way. From Harrison's point of view, though, that exalted status belonged only to the skipper.

Of course, Harrison wasn't thinking small. He was talking about starting a war. Back in Sam's petty-officer days, he couldn't have imagined a decision with that much riding on it. Even though he'd clawed his way up to officer's rank, carrying *that* much responsibility still didn't seem real to him.

It must have to Lieutenant Commander Harrison, though. A little later, Sam saw him talking on a telephone line that led straight to the bridge. And, not too long after that, elevators started lifting aeroplanes from the hangars belowdecks. Pilots raced to the aeroplanes, some of them putting on goggles as they ran. The *Remembrance* turned into the wind, what there was of it. One after another, the aeroplanes roared off the flight deck.

Were they hunting submersibles, too? Carsten couldn't think of anything else they might have in mind. Maybe Captain Stein thought that, if the Confederates were getting in some training, he might as well do the same thing. Or maybe the skipper just believed in wearing both suspenders and belt. In his place, Sam knew he would have.

He wished he could hang around the wireless shack and find out what the aeroplanes were seeing, but the skipper chose that moment to sound general quarters. Maybe it was a drill. Undoubtedly, most of the crew would figure it was. But maybe, too, one of the pilots had spotted something that made him jumpy. The *Remembrance* had been a nervous ship going through the Straits of Florida a few years before, and for many of the reasons also relevant today.

Sam's general-quarters station was deep in the bowels of the ship. He sighed as he hurried down to it. He still wished he had another post besides damage control. He'd been stuck with it for years now, but that didn't mean he liked it. He wished he could see, could be part of, what the ship was doing against its enemies. Cleaning up the mess after the guns and aeroplanes had failed to stop trouble was a lot less appealing.

It was to him, anyhow. Some people wouldn't have done anything else. Some people fancied sauerkraut, too—no accounting for taste. Lieutenant Commander Pottinger found damage control fascinating. He probably liked sauerkraut, too, though Carsten had never asked him about that.

By now, Hiram Pottinger had had more than a year to learn the ropes around the *Remembrance*. He really led the damage-control party, which he hadn't when he first boarded the carrier. Part of Sam chafed at losing the responsibility that had been his. The rest insisted he'd never wanted that particular responsibility in the first place.

"Do you know anything, Carsten?" Pottinger asked. "Have any idea why the captain called us to general quarters? You like to hang around on the flight deck." By the way he said it, that was a faintly—or maybe more than faintly—reprehensible habit for a damage-control man to have. Sam told what he'd seen and heard. Pottinger frowned. "Do you think it's the real McCoy?"

"Sir, I don't know for sure one way or the other," Carsten answered. "All I know is, it *could* be the McCoy."

"Yes." Pottinger nodded emphatically. "Of course, that's the way we have to treat every general-quarters call—something to remember."

He spoke now to the seamen and petty officers in the party, not to Sam. *Their* nods held varying degrees of impatience. They knew the truth of that better than he did. Most of them had served on the *Remembrance* when the war with Japan broke out. Pottinger hadn't. As far as Sam knew, he hadn't seen combat.

The damage-control party waited, down there in what they knew could easily become their tomb. A torpedo hit in the engine room, and the light bulbs that were the only illumination in this world of narrow steel corridors smelling of paint and oil and sweat would go out, trapping them in the darkness while, all too probably, the sea surged in around them.

*Maybe my trouble is too much imagination,* Sam thought unhappily. *Damage control's no place for somebody who sees all the things that can go wrong before they do.*

But that thought had hardly crossed his mind before the all-clear sounded. As always, sighs of relief accompanied it. If they seemed more heartfelt than usual this time . . . well, they did, that was all.

Reprehensible habit or not, Sam made a beeline for the flight deck as soon as he could leave his station. He soon found out the call to general quarters had been a drill, and hadn't sprung from sighting a submersible or anything else that could have been hostile. That was all to the good.

On steamed the *Remembrance*, into the Gulf of California. She was scrupulous about staying outside the territorial waters of both the Empire of Mexico and the Confederate States. Legally speaking, she was as much on the high seas as she would have been halfway out from San Francisco to the Sandwich Islands. Somehow, though, neither the Mexicans nor the Confederates seemed to feel that way.

A rusty gunboat flying the Mexican flag chugged out from La Paz to look her over. A Confederate coast-defense battleship, a much more serious threat, steamed into the Gulf from Guaymas. On the open sea, the *Remembrance* could easily have outrun her. Here in these narrow waters, the slow but heavily armored and armed ship had no trouble sticking close.

And, as they had in the Straits of Florida, aeroplanes flew over the *Remembrance*. Her own machines leaped into the air to warn off the intruders. The Confederacy was supposed to have no military aeroplanes, but. . . . Carsten waited for another general-quarters call. In his time as a seaman and petty officer, he'd served the carrier's five-inch guns. These days, they fired at aeroplanes as well as aiming at targets on land and sea.

When the alarm didn't come, Sam drifted over to the wireless shack. He let out a snort when he found out the strange aeroplanes overhead were labeled CONFEDERATE CITRUS COMPANY. "What's so funny, sir?" asked a wireless operator, a youngster who hadn't been aboard on that earlier cruise.

"That's the same outfit that eyeballed us when we sailed between Florida and Cuba," Carsten answered. "Do the Confederates even grow citrus over by Guaymas?"

"Damned if I know, uh, sir," the operator said. Sam didn't know, either. He did know the land there would have to be more fertile than the sorry, sun-baked soil of Baja California to give anybody even half a chance.

He didn't know the Confederate Citrus Company was a smoke screen to get around the military restrictions the armistice had imposed on the CSA. He didn't know, but he'd wondered even back in the Gulf of Mexico and the Caribbean. Here in the Gulf of California, he went from wondering to downright suspicion.

The wireless operator said, "Sir, shall we remind the skipper the name's the same now as it was then?"

"He's bound to remember," Sam said, but then, "Yes, go ahead and remind him. It can't hurt, and it might do some good."

He went back out to the flight deck. The aeroplanes from the Confederate Citrus Company seemed about as swift and maneuverable as the ones that had sprung into the air from the *Remembrance*'s flight deck. Why would an outfit that dealt with oranges and lemons and limes need machines like that? Carsten didn't know, but he got more suspicious.

About twenty minutes later, the aeroplanes that had flown out from the coast of Sonora suddenly went back the way they'd come. Rumor, which flew faster than any aeroplane, said Captain Stein had warned them he would have his pilots shoot them down if they lingered.

Sam didn't know if the rumor was true. If it was, he didn't know if it was connected to the reminder. But, when he got the news, he said only one word: "Good."

Through the coffeehouse's front window, Nellie Jacobs watched a tweedy man come out of the cobbler's shop across the street. The fellow's long, lean face bore an unhappy expression. She wasn't surprised; the shop had gone to the dogs in the more than three years since her husband, who'd had charge of it from not long after the turn of the century, passed away.

The tweedy man crossed the street, heading her way. He almost walked in front of an auto; the horn's angry bray pierced the plate glass. Nellie wasn't sure the man even realized the horn had been aimed at him. Once safe on the sidewalk again, he took a notebook out of a jacket pocket, consulted it, and then headed for her door.

She brightened. Business hadn't been brisk this morning. Business hadn't been brisk a lot of mornings lately, or afternoons, either. The man pulled at the door when he should have pushed. Realizing his mistake, he tried again. The bell over the door rang.

"What can I get you, sir?" Nellie asked from behind the counter.

"Oh." By the surprise in his voice, he hadn't thought of ordering anything. Then he nodded to himself, deciding he would. "A . . . a cup of coffee, please." He set a dime in front of Nellie. Tiny and shiny in silver, Theodore Roosevelt's toothy grin stared up at her.

"Here you are." She gave him the cup. "Cream and sugar right there." She didn't bother pointing them out to most people, but he might not have noticed without help.

"Thank you," he said, and used them. After a sudden, pleased smile at the coffee, he asked, "Excuse me, but were you acquainted with the gentleman who used to run the cobbler's shop across the street, Mr., uh"—he paused to check that little notebook again— "Harold Jacobs?"

"Was I *acquainted* with him?" Nellie echoed, scorn in her voice. "I should hope I was! Aren't I the mother of his daughter?"

"Oh!" The tweedy man brightened. "Is that why he wasn't there, then? Is he here? May I speak with him, please?"

She eyed him with even more scorn than she'd used while speaking. "Good luck, pal. I wish *I* could. He died in 1933. Who the devil are you, anyway?"

"My name is Maynard G. Ferguson, Mrs. Jacobs." Ferguson used the title with some hesitation, as if unsure she deserved it. She gave him a dirty look. He hurried on: "I am a professor of history at the University of Pittsburgh. I'm studying the way the United States gathered intelligence in Confederate-occupied Washington. Would you know anything about that?"

"I hope I would," Nellie answered. "Haven't I got my own Order of Remembrance, First Class, put on me by Teddy Roosevelt his own self, for the help I gave Hal during the war? What do you need to know?"

"Order of Remembrance, First Class?" Out came the notebook again.

After peering into it, Maynard Ferguson said, "Then you would be . . . Nellie Semphroch?"

"Not now," she said, as if to an idiot. "You said it yourself—I'm Nellie Jacobs."

"Yes. Of course." Ferguson scribbled in the little book. "Then you would know how information was smuggled out of the city and over to the U.S. lines?"

"I know pigeons were a part of it," Nellie said. "There was a fellow named . . . Oh, what was his name? Lou Pfeiffer, that was it! A fellow named Lou Pfeiffer who used to keep them. You could ask him about the details."

"Mr. Pfeiffer, unfortunately, is deceased. He died in. . . ." Professor Ferguson flipped through the pages of the notebook. "In 1927. In any case, I am not chiefly concerned with the pigeons. I am interested in the man to whom Mr. Jacobs—and every other man in the Washington spy ring—reported, a Mr. William Reach. Were you by any chance acquainted with *him*?"

Ice ran through Nellie. "With Bill Reach?" she said, through lips suddenly numb. "I knew him a little bit, but only a little bit." *And you can't prove anything else, God damn it, not now you can't.* "Why do you want to know about him in particular?"

"Primarily because he's such a man of mystery," Maynard Ferguson replied. "He conducted such an important intelligence campaign throughout the occupation, then disappeared without a trace just before U.S. soldiers retook Washington, D.C. I've been on the trail of that mystery for more than ten years now, ever since I started doing research on this topic, and I'm still hoping to get to the bottom of it."

*Well, you won't, not from me. You've just come to the end of the trail.* Nellie could have told what she knew, or at least some of it. It was safe enough now, with Hal dead. But she'd been keeping the secret so long, hugging it so tightly to herself, that letting go of it never once crossed her mind. She said, "My best guess is, he was killed in the shelling. An awful lot of people were."

Ferguson looked disappointed. "It could be, I suppose. Somehow, though, I want to believe he had a more dramatic end, and that someone still living knows what it was. He doesn't strike me as the type who would have gone quietly."

*A more dramatic end? He did.* Nellie still remembered the feel of the knife as she drove it into Bill Reach's chest. *And somebody does know, sure enough. But* you *never will.*

"If you don't know what happened to him, could you at least speak to what he was like?" the man from Pittsburgh asked.

"I didn't like him. He wasn't a gentleman, and he drank too much," Nellie said, and every word of that was true. "I have no idea how he got to be a spy. He was a reporter, wasn't he, back in the days before the war?"

"Yes, that's correct, with the *Star-News*," Ferguson said. "How did you know? You are the first person with whom I have spoken who did."

"I . . . used to know him back then," Nellie answered unwillingly. "I've lived in Washington all my life. I was here—I think I was five, or maybe seven—when the Confederates shelled us during the Second Mexican War."

"It was in 1881," Maynard Ferguson said. Maybe he was expecting her to tell him how old she'd been then, from which he could figure out exactly how old she was now. She wondered if he'd ever had anything to do with women before. After a moment, realizing she wasn't going to do anything of the sort, he asked, "Were you . . . romantically involved with Mr. Reach?"

"No," Nellie said at once, with great firmness. There hadn't been anything romantic about what passed between them in one hotel room or another. He'd laid his money on the dresser, and then she'd done what he paid for. Later, during the war, he'd decided that meant there was something between the two of them. Nellie knew better. She added, "He drank too much even way back then."

"Did he? How interesting!" By the way Professor Ferguson said it, the news really did interest him. "Impressive how he ran and organized a sophisticate spy ring while at the same time battling his drunkenness."

"I don't know what's so impressive about it," Nellie said with a sniff. "I saw him sitting right where you are when he was too drunk to know who I was even though he'd . . . known me before." She didn't want to put that pause there, but couldn't help herself. "You can't make me believe that was good for what he was doing."

"But information from Washington kept right on getting to Philadelphia even so," the professor said.

"Yes, and it kept right on getting to Philadelphia even when your precious Bill Reach spent time in jail on account of he stole something or other, or at least the Confederates thought he did," Nellie said.

Ferguson scribbled furiously. "That's fascinating," he said. "It's something else I hadn't heard of, too. I wonder if Confederate records survive to confirm your statement. Hard to guess; much was destroyed in the bombardment, and Reach also might have used an alias with them. But it's another avenue to explore. How do you suppose the ring continued to function with Reach in custody?"

"I'll tell you how—through my Hal, that's how," Nellie answered proudly. "You know TR gave him a Distinguished Service Cross, I expect. He didn't win that for playing tiddlywinks."

"I'm sure he didn't," Ferguson said. "I wish he were alive today so I could ask him about this entire important period."

"I wish he was alive today because I loved him and I miss him." When she first said she'd marry Hal, there at the end of the Great War, she hadn't dreamt how true that would be. What occasionally passed in their bedroom had next to nothing to do with it—with the large exception of causing Clara, who was the biggest surprise (and one of the most pleasant) Nellie had ever got. What made it true was that Hal had been a *good* man, and even Nellie, who had no use for the male half of the human race, couldn't possibly have had a different opinion.

"I'm sorry," the professor said. He was just being polite, though; Nellie could tell. He asked, "Is there anyone else who could possibly shed light on the way William Reach met his end in 1917, if that is what happened to him?"

"I can't think of anybody else," Nellie answered, which, again, was nothing but the truth. No one had been anywhere close by when Reach tried to rape her and she killed him.

But Professor Ferguson had ideas of his own. "What about your daughter, Edna"—flip, flip, flip went the notebook pages—"Semphroch?"

Even with his fancy research, he still got things wrong. "She's been Edna Grimes for a long time now," Nellie said, "and I guarantee she doesn't know anything about that." She did know about Nellie's scandalous background, though. Would she tell some professor what she knew? Nellie didn't think so, but wasn't a hundred percent sure. Edna had a mean streak in her that came out now and again.

"Didn't she receive a"—flip, flip, flip—"an Order of Remembrance, Second Class, at the same time as you were given your decoration?" Ferguson asked. "How can she be ignorant with that background?"

Nellie laughed in his face. "Easy as pie, that's how. She worked here with me, and sometimes I'd pass on things she told me, things she heard and I didn't. That's what she got her medal for. She would've married a Confederate officer, you know, if an artillery bombardment hadn't killed him on the way to the altar."

"Oh." Ferguson sounded faintly disappointed—and more than faintly revolted. He was old enough to have fought in the Great War. Like most men who were, he had no love for the Confederate States. He also seemed to have little understanding for what the people of Washington, who'd lived under Confederate occupation for more than two years, had gone through during that time. Nellie wasn't surprised. Few who hadn't lived here then *did* understand.

"You see?" Any which way, Nellie didn't want Ferguson talking to Edna. "Nobody knows nothing about Bill Reach."

Maynard Ferguson sighed. "I suppose not. I hope you realize how frustrating this is for me."

"I'm sorry," said Nellie, who was anything but. "Nothing I can do about it, though." *Nothing I will do about it, anyway.*

The professor left the coffeehouse, head down, shoulders slumped. Nellie put his cup in the sink. She'd never dreamt anybody would come poking after Bill Reach. But it didn't matter. In the end, it truly didn't. Only she knew the answer—only she knew, literally enough, where the body was buried—and she wasn't talking. Not now, not ever.

An aeroplane buzzed over the *Charles XI* as the French liner approached the Confederate coast. Anne Colleton glanced up at the machine, which roared past low enough for her to make out the words CONFEDERATE CITRUS COMPANY painted on the fuselage in big, bright orange letters. The lines of the aeroplane suggested falcon much more than grouse. She wondered why a citrus company needed such a swift, deadly-looking aircraft.

Beside her, Colonel Jean-Henri Jusserand watched the aeroplane speed back toward the Virginia coast. The Frenchman said, "I suspect it would not be too very difficult to fit this aeroplane with weapons. Would you not agree, *Mademoiselle* Colleton?"

"I would agree that am I an idiot," Anne replied, also in French. "I should have seen that for myself." She kicked at the decking, angry at missing something so obvious.

"But—" Colonel Jusserand stopped, just in time. Anne sent him a sour look. He'd been about to say something like, *But you are only a woman, Mademoiselle Colleton, so how could you be expected to notice such a thing?* Then, fortunately, he'd remembered Anne had spent the last two years in Paris, dickering with some of the more prominent people in *Action Française*—not always the people with fancy titles, but those who could promise results and mean it.

With wry amusement, Anne thought, *But you are only a boy, Colonel Jusserand, so how could you be expected to know anything?* Jusserand was in his mid-thirties, as young as he could be and still have fought in the Great War. He paid attention to Anne as a negotiator, but never once to her as a woman. She had fifteen years on him, give or take a couple. Most of the officers with whom she'd dealt were close contemporaries of the boyish colonel. *Action Française* had, so far, done a better job of pruning deadwood from the French Army than the Freedom Party had of purging the Confederate Army.

The *Charles XI* pressed on toward Norfolk. More aeroplanes buzzed by to examine the liner. All of them said CONFEDERATE CITRUS COMPANY. They shared the same sleek, dangerous look.

Colonel Jusserand asked, "Will there be an open display of these machines at the Olympic Games?"

"I don't know," Anne said. "I'm a stranger here myself." That held more truth than she felt comfortable admitting. She'd enjoyed her two years in France. She thought she'd helped her country while she was there. But, with Virginia in sight once more, she had to remember what she'd worked so hard to forget: that her time out of the CSA had also been an exile of sorts.

July in Norfolk brought memory flooding back. Though she was close to two hundred miles north of St. Matthews, the heat and humidity reminded her all too much of home. She'd never known weather like this in Paris. She wouldn't have been sorry not to renew acquaintance, either.

When the customs men saw her passport and Colonel Jusserand's, they very quickly became very respectful. "You're on our list, sir, ma'am," one of them said, touching the brim of his cap. He wore a snappier uniform than he would have when she left the Confederate States, one that made him look like a soldier rather than a functionary. "Our good list, I mean—we've got train tickets to Richmond waiting for both of you, and we'll get you to the station fast as we can."

He kept his promise, too. Anne wondered what sort of treatment she would have got had her name been on a different sort of list. She was just as glad not to have to find out.

Sweating in his brown wool uniform, Colonel Jusserand let out a sigh of relief when their railroad car proved air-conditioned. Anne found herself less delighted; too cold seemed as unpleasant as too hot. But she could add clothes for more warmth. She couldn't take them off outside, not if she wanted to stay decent.

With a cloud of coal smoke erupting from the stack, the locomotive began to roll. Jusserand stared at the countryside, which he was seeing for the first time. "How very many tractors and other farm machines there are," he remarked.

Anne nodded. "More than I remember seeing before I went to France," she said. "A lot more, as a matter of fact. Then there would have been nothing but sharecroppers working the land." *Sharecroppers* had come out in English. She thought for a moment before coming up with a French equivalent: "Tenant farmers."

"With so many machines, who needs men?" Colonel Jusserand said. "Where do you suppose the tenant farmers have gone?"

That was a good question. Anne answered it with no more than a shrug, for she didn't know, either. She did know most of the displaced sharecroppers were colored. Was it like this all over the CSA, or just in this stretch of Virginia? She couldn't guess. If this went on nationwide, what *would* the Confederacy do with all the displaced Negroes? One more question she couldn't answer. But, remembering what Negroes had done to the Marshlands plantation, remembering what they'd almost done to her, she hoped they got everything they deserved.

Night was falling when the train pulled into Richmond from the south. As soon as Anne descended to the platform, someone called her name. All she had to do was answer. As before, uniformed men whisked her and Colonel Jusserand away. She barely had time to note how many people in the station spoke with Yankee accents—men and women down from the USA to see the Olympic Games—before she and the Frenchman were in a motorcar bound for the Gray House.

No waiting in the waiting room this time, either. Jake Featherston saw them right away. "Congratulations," he told Anne. "I've read every report you sent. You did a first-rate job over there. First-rate, I tell you." He stuck out his hand and gave Colonel Jusserand a big, friendly smile. "And I'm damned pleased to meet you, Colonel. *Action Française*"—he didn't butcher the French too badly—"is doing the same thing for your country that the Freedom Party is for this one."

"Yes, I think so, too." Jusserand spoke good English, though Anne's French was even better. "*Revenge* is a sweet word, is it not?"

He couldn't have said anything better calculated to hit the Confederate president where he lived. "Oh, yes," Featherston said softly. "Oh, yes, indeed. None sweeter. So we *will* be able to count on France when the day comes?"

"That depends," Jusserand answered. "Can *we* count on the CSA if we first find that day?"

Here was something Anne hadn't seen before: someone hustling Jake Featherston. "Like you said, that depends." The president spoke carefully. "You start a fight with the Germans tomorrow afternoon, we'll have to sit out—we aren't ready yet. You give us the chance to get ready, we'll back you all the way."

In Paris, Anne and the Frenchmen with whom she'd dealt had gone round and round over that. The Kaiser's government watched the French as carefully as the United States watched the Confederate States, maybe more carefully. Colonel Jusserand thought so. He said, "You have the advantage over us. You are a large country, with more room to hide what you do not want your neighbors to see. With us, *les Boches* could be anywhere at any time."

"Since we've been good little boys, I don't know what you're talking about," Featherston answered. Even his grin didn't make those long, bony features handsome. But a smiling Jake Featherston made handsomer men seem insipid. Anne had thought so since the first time she met him, back in the days when she thought she could control him. She wasn't wrong very often. When she was, she wasn't wrong in a small way.

"How fortunate you are to have these Olympic Games," Jusserand murmured. "You show your own people and the world the Confederate States are once more a nation to be reckoned with."

"That's right. That's just exactly right," Featherston said. "You're a pretty sharp fellow, aren't you, Colonel?" The French officer did his best to look modest. His best, as Anne had seen, was unconvincing.

She asked, "How serious are the Negro uprisings, Mr. President? Some of the stories I heard in Paris played them down. The others made it sound as bad as 1915."

"That's crap. It's nothing like 1915—nothing, you hear?" Featherston's voice was hard and cold. "More than a nuisance, less than real trouble, you know what I mean? Bad enough so the USA couldn't say no when we asked to beef up the Army a bit—and we may beef it up a bit more than the damnyankees know about."

*He sounds . . . pleased the blacks are trying to hit back,* Anne realized. *He expected them to, and he was ready to take advantage of it.* She eyed the Confederate president with respect no less genuine for being reluctant. He always seemed to see a move or two further than anybody else.

Featherston went on, "But the hell with that for now." Colonel Jusserand looked shocked; he'd never have sworn in front of a woman. Featherston said, "You're here in Richmond when we've got the Olympics. You want to enjoy yourselves, right? Here." He scribbled on a couple of sheets of paper from a pad on his desk, then handed one to Anne, the other to the Frenchman. "Passes to whatever you want to see. Go on over to the ticket bureau and exchange 'em. Anybody gives you a hard time about it, let me know. I'll make the son of a bitch pay."

No one gave Anne anything close to a hard time. She found that instructive; people in the CSA took Featherston's orders seriously—or at least they'd learned they would be sorry if they didn't. Anne rode a bus to the enormous Olympic stadium on the northern outskirts of town. It hadn't existed when she'd left the country two years earlier. Now the great bowl of marble and concrete, Confederate and Party flags aflutter all around the rim, dominated the skyline in that part of Richmond. Other Olympic buildings and the village where the athletes lived surrounded the stadium.

In the stands near her, Anne heard American accents from both CSA and USA, clipped British tones, Irish brogues, and people speaking French, German, Spanish, Italian, and several languages she didn't recognize. For that matter, she had trouble following some of the French she heard. When the couple with the odd accent cheered the athletes from the Republic of Quebec, she understood why.

Black men from Haiti and Liberia competed along with everyone else. When a Haitian sprinter won a bronze medal, Jake Featherston looked as if he'd swallowed a big swig of lemon juice. In France, Anne had heard he'd had to accept the Negroes' participation on equal terms, like it or not: otherwise the Games would have gone elsewhere. She wondered how furious Featherston was, and whether he could extract any sort of revenge on the International Olympic Committee.

But that was a question only a handful of insiders would know about. To most citizens of the Confederate States, to most of the swarms of visitors from abroad, all that mattered was whether the Olympics came off well. By that standard, Featherston and the CSA were doing fine.

A Confederate runner narrowly beat a man from the USA in the 800-meter run. The crowd went wild. Anne clapped and yelled as loud as anyone else. She would never be behindhand in cheering for Confederate victories over the damnyankees. She wished there were more of them, and on fields different from the track. *One of these days,* she thought. *Maybe one of these days before too long.*

**W**ith a grunt, Clarence Potter rose from the seat he'd been occupying for what seemed like forever. He hadn't wanted to pay for a Pullman berth from Charleston up to the Confederate capital. Now he was paying in a different way: with a sore back, and with eyes gritty from lack of sleep. His seat had reclined, but not far enough. He'd managed to doze a bit on the way north, but he hadn't got nearly enough rest.

As he stood and grabbed his carpetbag from the rack above his head, the weight of the pistol in the shoulder holster reminded him of the weapon's presence. He wondered if Freedom Party goons would be waiting for him when he got off the train. If they were, they'd be sorry.

But no one troubled him on the platform or in the station. He hurried through the cavernous building, and got to the cab stand outside ahead of most of the other passengers, who'd had to go to the baggage car to retrieve their suitcases.

"Where to, pal?" asked the driver of the frontmost cab when Potter got in. The fellow added, "Freedom!"

"Freedom!" Potter echoed, hating the word. He felt the weight of the pistol again. "Ford's Hotel, across from Capitol Square."

"Right you are." The cabby put his auto—a middle-aged Ford imported from the USA—into gear, waiting for an opening in the traffic. "You here for the Olympics?"

"That's right." *Among other things,* Clarence Potter thought. "I know they started a couple of days ago, but I couldn't get away from work till now. These days, you hold on tight to a job if you've got one." He'd had more flexibility than he let on, but the driver didn't need to know that.

The fellow nodded. "Ain't it the truth?" he said. "Even this lousy job—I couldn't very well leave, could I? Not if I want my kids to eat, I couldn't. Business was crummy till the Games started, too—you'd best believe that."

"Oh, I do," Potter said solemnly. "Times aren't easy anywhere."

"Yeah." The driver pulled away from the curb. Behind him, the next cab moved up to wait for a passenger.

Richmond had changed since Potter last saw it. Of course, that had been during the dark days at the end of the Great War, when U.S. bombers were methodically knocking the Confederate capital flat. Now it seemed so fresh and clean, someone might have rubbed the buildings and even the sidewalks with soap and water. And maybe someone had, to give visitors the impression Jake Featherston wanted them to have. Potter wouldn't have been surprised.

Freedom Party stalwarts stood on every other corner. They weren't wearing their usual bludgeons, and were giving strangers directions. How long would they stay on their best behavior? Till the Olympics were over, no doubt, and not a minute longer.

In Capitol Square, a Mitcheltown—what the damnyankees called a Blackfordburgh: a shantytown full of people who'd lost their jobs and lost their homes—had flourished for years. It was gone now, with no sign it had ever existed. Where were those people? Were they all working? Potter laughed under his breath. Not likely. But they were out of sight, which was what mattered to the present masters of the CSA.

Ford's Hotel was a great white pile of a building, with Confederate flags flying everywhere on it. The cab wheezed to a stop in front of the entrance. Potter gave the driver half a dollar, which included a dime tip. He carried his bag up the low stairs leading into the hotel and past the doorman, an immensely tall, immensely fat Negro in a uniform gaudier than any the C.S. Army issued. Potter recalled the getup from his wartime visits to Richmond, though he didn't think this was the same man wearing it.

He checked in, got his room key, and put his clothes on hangers and into drawers, as if he were an ordinary traveler. Then he went downstairs again and spent five cents for a copy of the *Richmond Whig*, which gave him a schedule of Olympic events.

*President Featherston will watch the swimming competition tomorrow,* one story said, *to cheer on Richmond's own Peter Dawson, who will be aiming for the gold medal in the 400 and 800 meters.* Potter nodded slowly to himself. The swimming stadium would be a good place to try: much smaller than the great bowl where the athletes competed in track and field.

Every story in the paper seemed to glorify Featherston, the Freedom Party, the Olympics, Richmond, or all four at once. What made that particularly disgusting, as far as Potter was concerned, was that, up until the Freedom Party took power, the paper, as its name showed, had been strong for the Whigs. No more. Not many papers in the CSA persisted—or were still able to persist—in opposing the Freedom Party and the president.

"Which is why someone has to do something," Potter murmured. *And who better than me? I should have seen this coming before anybody else. Hell, I did see it coming, but I couldn't take Featherston seriously. My only consolation is, nobody else did, either.*

Without Jake Featherston, what would happen to the Freedom Party? Nothing good. Potter was sure of that. Featherston was the glue that held it together. Take him away, and the pieces would fly apart. They would have to . . . wouldn't they?

Potter ate a big steak and a mess of fries in the hotel restaurant. Then he went up to his room and turned on the wireless. It was full of stories about—what else?—Jake Featherston, the Freedom Party, the Olympics, Richmond, or all four at once. The wireless stories were very smooth, smoother than those in the paper. Whoever had put them together knew what he was doing.

The next morning, Potter ordered a plate of ham and eggs. *The condemned man ate a hearty meal. Well, why not?*

He got another taxi and took it to the swimming stadium. Tickets were three dollars apiece—not the worst daily wage for a working man. Potter set three brown banknotes on the counter, took his ticket, and went inside.

For a tense moment, the smell of chlorine rising from the huge swimming pool put him in mind of Great War gas attacks. He had to fight down panic—had to and did. Then he worked his way toward the presidential box. He couldn't get as close as he would have liked. Freedom Party guards in their almost-Army uniforms surrounded Jake Featherston. Potter sighed. He'd expected nothing different. He would have to wait for his chance, if it ever came.

He settled into his seat, right by an aisle that gave him at least the illusion of a chance to get away. He drummed his fingers on his thigh. How long would Featherston watch? Would he go do something else before Potter found a chance? *You'll find out,* Potter told himself. *Wait. See what happens.*

While he waited, he watched the swimmers. He cheered "Richmond's own Peter Dawson" as loudly as any of the men around him with their Freedom Party pins. He'd always thought of himself as a patriot. The difference was that, to him, Confederate patriotism didn't start and stop with the Party.

Dawson didn't win the gold in the 400 meters; a swimmer from Sweden did, by several lengths. But the hometown hero did win a silver medal. Better yet, he outkicked a man from the USA to do it. Cheers rang through the swimming stadium. After shaking the Swede's hand, Dawson pulled himself from the pool and waved to the crowd.

"Frankfurters! Git your frankfurters! Twenty-five cents! Frankfurters!" The colored vendor roamed up and down the aisles, hawking the sausages. Clarence Potter handed the man—whose graying hair said they were about of an age—a quarter. He got back a frankfurter on a bun wrapped in waxed paper. As Potter unwrapped it and began to eat, the Negro hurried up the aisle once more. "Frankfurters! Git your frankfurters!"

The medalists got up onto the victory stand. A pretty girl put the medals—gold, silver, bronze—around their necks. They all grinned and shook hands with one another. A band blared out what Potter presumed to be the Swedish national anthem, though he didn't recognize it. Up went the Swedish flag, yellow cross on blue. The Stars and Bars and the Stars and Stripes rose on flagpoles to its right and left.

When the anthem ended, the three young men descended from the platform. They were still chattering excitedly. Peter Dawson and the swimmer from the USA might have been friends. Maybe they were. Potter wondered how often they'd raced against each other, how well they knew each other.

"Frankfurters! Twenty-five cents! Git your frankfurters!" Here came the vendor again, distracting Potter—and everyone around him—from the joy of the moment. Back in the Roman days, vendors at the Colosseum selling dormice in honey had probably made people miss the best moments of lions devouring Christians.

The Negro paused by Potter, taking another frankfurter from the enameled metal box he wore at his waist. A sweat-stained canvas strap that went around his neck supported the box, leaving his hands free. He handed the sausage to a woman across the aisle, got back a dollar banknote, and gave her three quarters in change.

"Frankfurters! Git your frankfurters here!" The vendor stopped again, two or three steps farther down. For a moment, that meant nothing to Clarence Potter. Then he realized no one there had called or waved for a frankfurter. The Negro reached into the box just the same. What he pulled out this time wasn't a bun wrapped in waxed paper. It was a submachine gun with the stock sawed off short to make it easier to hide. With a wordless shout of fury and hate, he aimed it in Jake Featherston's direction and started shooting.

Guards toppled, wounded or dead. People screamed. The president of the CSA went down, too. Did he dive for cover, or was he hit? Potter didn't know. He *did* know the surviving guards were going to fill the Negro full of lead . . . and probably everyone around the fellow, including himself. With hardly any conscious thought, his own pistol sprang into his hand. He shot the Negro in the back of the head.

The colored man crumpled as if all his bones had turned to mush. He was surely dead before he hit the stairs. By sheer luck, the submachine gun didn't spray any more bullets when it clattered off the concrete. *You poor damned fool,* Potter thought. *If you'd only waited a little longer, I would have tried to do it for you. Now—sweet Jesus, maybe I've gone and saved Jake Featherston's worthless life.*

"Drop it!" Four Freedom Party guards screamed the words at the same time. They pointed Tredegars and submachine guns of their own at Potter. Very slowly and carefully, he laid down the pistol.

"Don't shoot him!" somebody close by called. "He just killed that goddamn nigger—and where the hell were *you?*"

"That's right!" someone else said, voice cracking with excitement. "He's a hero! He just saved President Featherston!"

Those rifle barrels didn't waver, but the guards held their fire. *Maybe I didn't save him,* Potter thought hopefully. *Maybe he got one right between the eyes. Maybe . . .*

But no. Jake Featherston stuck his head up. He had a pistol in his hand. He wouldn't have been easy meat for anyone. *With a little luck, he won't recognize me,* Potter thought. *He hasn't seen me for years, after all.*

Featherston's eyes widened. He recognized Potter, all right. Then one of his guards—who didn't—said, "This guy killed the nigger who was shootin' at you, sir." Other people called Potter a hero, too. Hero, here, was the last thing he wanted to be. But he was stuck with it—and so was Jake Featherston.

\* \* \*

Back in the Gray House, Jake Featherston gulped down a whiskey and set the glass on the presidential desk. Across the desk from him, Clarence Potter, annoyingly calm, sipped from a drink of his own. Jake said, "So you were sitting right there close to me, and you just happened to have a pistol in a shoulder holster."

"I didn't just happen to have it." Potter sounded annoyingly calm, too. "I'm an investigator. Some of the things I investigate are pretty unsavory. I always have a pistol where I can grab it in a hurry."

"And you never once thought of plugging me?" Featherston said.

"Of course not," Potter answered. His face said, *If I did, do you think I'm dumb enough to admit it?*

A silent aide set a piece of paper on Featherston's desk. His gaze flicked down it. When he was done, he eyed Potter again. "You've been a busy boy down in Charleston, haven't you? It's a wonder you're still running around loose."

"You come right out and admit that?" Potter said.

"Admit what?" Jake's smile was all teeth and no mirth. "You say I said it—you say I said it and you get anybody to print what you say—and I'll call you a liar to your face. How are you going to prove anything different?"

Potter took another sip from his drink. "A point." He wasn't just a cool customer. He was a cold fish.

"So what the hell am I going to do with you?" Jake wondered aloud. "You hate my guts, but you shot that nigger before any of my guards could."

He'd had bullets whistle past his ear before. The frankfurter seller who'd tried to do him in couldn't shoot worth a damn. The first couple of rounds had been near misses, but then the submachine gun had pulled up and to the right, as such weapons did all too often. Ten or twelve people were hurt, some of them badly, but not Jake. And, by failing, the Negro had handed the Freedom Party a whole new club with which to beat his race.

That could wait—for a little while, anyhow. "What *am* I going to do with you?" Featherston repeated.

With a shrug, Clarence Potter said, "Give me a medal and send me home."

Featherston shook his head. "Nope. You'd be back. And who knows? You might not miss. If I send you home, you'd have to have an accident pretty damn quick."

"You don't care what you say, do you?" Potter remarked. "You never did."

"I already told you, you're not going to make a liar out of me," Jake said. "Tell you what I'll do, though, since I owe you for this, and since you were damn near the only officer I knew during the war who had any sense at all." He leaned forward. "How'd you like to go back in the Army . . . Colonel Potter?"

In spite of Potter's calm façade, his eyes widened. "You mean that," he said slowly.

"Damn right I do. I can get some use out of you, and so can the country. About time we had some intelligence in Intelligence, goddammit. And I can keep an eye on you that way, too. What do you say?"

"If I tell you no, I wind up dead," Potter answered. "What do you think I'm going to say?"

*You can end up just as dead in a butternut uniform as you can in slacks and a jacket,* Jake thought. But he wasn't sorry Potter had said yes. The other man was a prim son of a bitch, but he had brains and he had nerve. He'd proved that during the war, in the swimming stadium, and—Jake's eyes again traveled down the list of some of the things Potter had done in Charleston—in between times, too, even if he'd been on the wrong side then. He could do the CSA a lot of good if he wanted to.

"All right, Colonel," Featherston said. "We'll go from there, then." He stuck out his hand. Potter didn't hesitate more than a heartbeat before shaking it.

Watching Potter walk out the door with a flunky reminded Jake of something else, a piece of business he wondered why he'd left unfinished. He picked up the telephone and spoke into the mouthpiece. He'd taken too many orders in his time. He liked giving them a lot better.

He had to wait a while before this order was carried out. Normally, he didn't like waiting. Here, though, he composed himself in patience and went through some of the endless paperwork on his desk. *If I'd known how much paperwork went with the job, I might've let Willy Knight be president of the Confederate States.* But he shook his head. That might be funny, but it wasn't true. The paperwork didn't just go with the job; in large measure, the paperwork *was* the job.

His secretary poked her head into the office. "General Stuart is here to see you, Mr. President."

"Thanks, Lulu." Jake's smile was large and predatory. "You send him right on in."

In marched Jeb Stuart Jr., his back as stiff as an old man could make it. He was a year or two past seventy, his chin beard and hair white, his uniform hanging slightly loose on a frame that had begun to shrink. He looked at Featherston with gray-blue eyes full of hate. His salute might have come from a rickety machine. "Mr. President," he said tonelessly.

"Hello, General," Featherston said, that fierce grin still on his face. "We meet again." He waved to a chair. "Sit down."

"I prefer to stand."

*"Sit down, I said,"* Jake snapped, and Stuart, startled, sank into the chair. Featherston nodded. "Remember the last time you paid a call on me, General? You were gloating, on account of I was down. You reckoned I was down for good. You weren't quite as smart as you reckoned, were you?"

"No, sir." Jeb Stuart Jr.'s voice remained stubbornly wooden.

"Do you recollect Clarence Potter, General Stuart?" Featherston asked. Doing his best to remain impassive, Stuart nodded. Featherston went on, "I just brought him back into the Army—rank of colonel."

"That is your privilege, Mr. President." Stuart did his best not to make things easy.

His best wasn't going to be good enough. Jake had the whip hand now. "Yeah," he said. "It is. You screwed his career over just as hard as you screwed mine. And for what? I'll tell you for what, God damn you. On account of we were right, that's what."

Jeb Stuart Jr. didn't answer. During the war, Jake had served in a battery commanded by Jeb Stuart III, his son. He'd suspected Pompey, the younger Stuart's colored servant, of being a Red. He'd said as much to Potter. Jeb Stuart III had used his family influence, and his father's, to get Pompey off the hook. The only trouble was, Pompey *had* been a Red. When that proved unmistakably clear, Jeb Stuart III had thrown his life away in combat rather than face the music. And Jeb Stuart Jr. had made sure neither Featherston nor Potter saw another promotion through the rest of the war.

"Did you reckon I'd forget, General Stuart?" Jake asked softly. "I never forget that kind of thing. Never, you hear me?"

"I hear you, Mr. President," Stuart said. "The high respect I hold for your office precludes my saying more."

"For my office, eh? Not for me?" Featherston waited. Again, Jeb Stuart Jr. didn't answer. Jake shrugged. He knew the older man blamed him for Jeb Stuart III's death. *Too damn bad,* he thought. In spite of his campaign promises, he'd walked softly around the Army up till now. He hadn't been quite ready to clean house. All of a sudden, he was—and surviving an assassination attempt would do wonders for his popularity, cushion whatever anger there might have been. "I accept your resignation, General."

That struck home. Stuart glared. He'd spent fifty-five years in the Confederate Army; he'd been a boy hero in the Second Mexican War, and had never known or wanted any other life. "You don't have it, you . . . you damned upstart!" he burst out.

Upstart? Jake knew he was one. The difference between him and Stuart—between him and all the swarms of Juniors and IIIs and IVs and Vs

in the CSA—was that he was proud of it. "No resignation?" he said. Jeb
Stuart Jr. shook his head. Featherston shrugged. "All right with me. In
that case, you're fired. Don't bother cleaning out your desk. Don't bother
about your pension, either. You're finished, as of now."

"I demand a court-martial," Stuart said furiously. "What are the
charges against me, damn you? I've been in the Army and risking my life
for my country since before you were a gleam in your white-trash father's
eye. And not even the president of the Confederate States of America has
the power to drum me out without my day in court."

"White trash, is it?" Featherston whispered. Jeb Stuart Jr. nodded
defiantly. "All right, Mr. Blueblood. All right," Jake said. "You want
charges, you stinking son of a bitch? I'll give you charges, by Christ!"
His voice rose and went harsh and rough as a rasp: "Yeah, I'll give you
charges. Charges are aiding and abetting your inbred idiot son, Captain
Jeb fucking Stuart III, in hiding that his prissy little nigger called Pompey
was really a goddamn Red. I'll take you down, cocksucker, and I'll take
your stinking brat down with you. There won't be a place in the CSA you
can hide in by the time I'm done with you two, you'll stink so bad. And
so will he."

The color drained from Jeb Stuart Jr.'s face. It wasn't just that no one
had talked to him like that in all his life. But no one had ever gone for the
jugular against him with such fiendish gusto. He was white as typing
paper when he found his voice, choking out, "You—You wouldn't. Not
even you would stoop so low."

Jake smiled savagely. "Try me. You want a court, that's what you'll
get."

"G-Give me a pen, God damn you," Stuart said. Featherston did, and
paper to go with it. The officer's hand shook as he wrote. He shoved the
paper back across the desk. *I resign from the Army of the Confederate
States, effective immediately,* he'd written, and a scrawled signature
below the words. "Does that satisfy you?"

"Damn right it does. I've been waiting for it for twenty years," Jake
answered. "Now get the hell out of here. You start feeling unhappy, just
remember you're getting off easy."

Jeb Stuart Jr. stormed from the office. He slammed the door as he
went. Jake laughed. He'd heard a lot of slams since becoming president.
This one didn't measure up to some of the others.

After a moment, Jake called, "Lulu?"

"Yes, Mr. President?" his secretary said.

"Give Saul Goldman a buzz for me, will you?" Featherston was
always polite to Lulu, if to nobody else. "Tell him I want to talk with him
right away."

When he said *right away* to Goldman, the skinny little Jew, who got the Freedom Party's message out to the country and the world, took him literally. He got to Jake's office within five minutes. "What can I do for you, Mr. President?"

"General Jeb Stuart Jr. just resigned." Featherston flourished the sheet of paper with the one-line message. "I'm going to tell you why he resigned, too." He gave Goldman the story of Jeb Stuart III and Pompey.

Goldman blinked. "You want me to announce that to the country? Are you sure?"

"Damn right I do. Damn right I am." Jake nodded emphatically. "Let people know why he left. Let 'em know we'll be cleaning out more useless time-servers soon, too. That's the angle I want you to take. Reckon you can handle it?"

"If that's what you want, Mr. President, that's what you'll get," Goldman said.

"That's what I want," Jake Featherston declared. And sure as hell, what he wanted, he got.

# VII

Jefferson Pinkard stood in line at the Odeum, waiting to buy a ticket. When he got up to the window, he shoved a quarter at the fellow behind it. He took the ticket and walked inside. After a pause at the concession stand, he went into the darkness of the theater, popcorn and a Dr. Hopper in hand.

He sat in the middle of a row, so people going by wouldn't make him spill the popcorn or the soda. As soon as he was settled, he started methodically munching away. No one else sat very close to him, maybe because of the noise. He didn't care. He wasn't there for company. He was there to kill a couple of hours.

The maroon velvet curtains slid back to either side of the stage, revealing the screen. In the back of the theater, the projector began to hum and whir. SMOKING IS PROHIBITED IN THIS AUDITORIUM appeared on the screen, then vanished.

Most of the people in the Odeum came from Fort Deposit. They leaned forward almost in unison, knowing the newsreel was coming up next. Pinkard leaned forward with them. Since coming to work at the Alabama Correctional Camp (P), he'd felt far more cut off from the world around him than he ever had up in Birmingham. If not for wireless and moving pictures, the outside world would hardly have touched this little Alabama town.

"In Richmond, the Olympic Games came to a magnificent conclusion!" the announcer blared. "The Confederate States have shown the world they are on the move again, thanks to President Featherston and the Freedom Party."

"Freedom!" somebody in the auditorium called, and the chant rang out. Jeff was glad to join it, but it didn't last; people couldn't chant and hear what the announcer was saying at the same time.

Confederate athletes with the C.S. battle flag on their shirtfronts ran and jumped and swam and flung javelins. Smiling, they posed with medals draped around their necks. President Featherston posed with them, shaking their hands in congratulations. He turned to face the camera and said, "We're a match for anybody—more than a match for anybody. And nothing's going to stop us from getting where we're going."

Suddenly, the camera cut away from the athletes. It lingered on the crumpled corpse of a black man, and on the submachine gun half visible under his body. "This stinking, worthless nigger tried to assassinate our beloved president, who sat watching the athletic competition," the announcer declared. "Thanks to the heroism of a Great War veteran, he paid the price for his murderous folly."

Another camera cut. The bespectacled white man standing beside Jake Featherston didn't look like a veteran; he put Pinkard more in mind of a professor. Featherston spoke again: "Those damn blacks—beg your pardon, folks—stabbed us in the back during the war. They're trying to do it again. This time, though, we're good and ready for 'em, and we won't let 'em get away with it."

Murmurs of agreement ran through the Odeum. Fort Deposit was in the Black Belt, but no black faces had been visible in the theater before the lights went down. Indeed, armed guards outside and on the roof made sure no marauding Negroes would cause trouble while the motion picture played.

At the Olympic closing ceremonies, smartly turned-out Confederate soldiers ringed the stadium, protecting it as the guards protected the theater here. Aeroplanes with the words CONFEDERATE CITRUS COMPANY painted in big letters on their sides streaked low above the stadium. They flew wingtip to wingtip, in formations only professional pilots who were also daredevils would have tried.

*They could fight if they had to,* Pinkard realized. He wondered if they were Great War veterans, or if they'd picked up their experience flying for Maximilian in the Mexican civil war. That didn't matter. Wherever they'd got it, they had the right stuff. So did the machines they flew: sleek low-winged metal monoplanes that made the slow, sputtering canvas-and-wire contraptions of the Great War seem like antiques by comparison.

After a moment's pause, the newsreel shifted subjects. VETERAN STEPS DOWN, a card said. "Jeb Stuart Jr., who first came to prominence in the Second Mexican War more than fifty years ago, has left the Confederate General Staff after revelations about his unfortunate role in failing to prevent the Red uprising of 1915," the announcer said. On the screen, Stuart looked ancient indeed, ancient and doddering. "President Featherston will soon name a younger, more vigorous replacement."

Other newsreel snippets showed dams rising in the Tennessee River valley, tractors plowing, and other machines harvesting. "Agriculture makes great strides," the announcer said proudly. "Each machine does the work of from six to six hundred lazy, shiftless sharecroppers." The camera panned across shabbily dressed colored men and women standing in front of shanties.

"And in lands stolen from the CSA after the war, in Sequoyah and the part of occupied Texas miscalled Houston . . ." The announcer fell silent. The pictures of dust in dunes, in drifts, in blowing, choking curtains, spoke for themselves. Leaning forward against a strong wind, a man lurched through drifted dust towards a farmhouse with a sagging roof. His slow, effortful journey seemed all but hopeless. So did the wail of a baby on the lap of a scrawny woman in a print dress. She sat on the front porch of a house whose fields lay dust-choked and baking under a merciless sky.

Gloating, the announcer said, "This is how the United States care for the lands they took from their rightful owners."

"Damnyankees," a woman behind Pinkard whispered.

After those grim scenes, the serial that followed came as something of a relief. It portrayed a pair of Confederate bunglers who'd ended up in the Army during the war and had escape after unlikely escape. Jeff knew it was ridiculous, but couldn't help laughing himself silly.

The main feature was more serious. It was a love story almost thwarted by a colored furniture dealer who kept casting lustful looks toward the perky blond heroine. Pinkard wanted to kick the Negro right in the teeth. That the people who'd made the motion picture might want him to react just like that never once crossed his mind.

He rose and stretched when the picture ended, well pleased that the black man had got what was coming to him. Then he left the theater and walked over to the bus that would take him back to the Alabama Correctional Camp (P). The bus was heavily armored, with thick wire grating over the windows. Pinkard wasn't the only white passenger who drew a pistol before boarding. Here at the edge of the Black Belt, rebellion still sizzled. He wanted to be able to fight back if the Negroes shot up the bus. His heart thudded in his chest when the machine got rolling.

It reached the Alabama Correctional Camp (P) without taking fire. Jeff breathed a sigh of relief when he got off. Two sandbagged machine-gun nests guarded the front entrance. They were new. Black raiders hadn't been shy about shooting into the camp, and didn't seem to care whether they hit guards or prisoners. New belts of barbed wire ringed the place, too. They were as much to keep marauders out as they were to keep inmates in.

Jeff's white skin was enough to get him past the machine-gun nests unchallenged. At what had been the entrance, another guard carefully scrutinized both him and his identity card. "Oh, for Christ's sake, Toby," he fumed, "you know goddamn well who I am."

"Yeah, I do," the lower-ranking guard said, "but I gotta be careful. There was that camp in Mississippi where one of the prisoners managed to sneak out with a phony card."

"You ever hear of anybody sneaking *in* with a phony card?" Jeff demanded. Toby only shrugged. Pinkard let it go. He couldn't complain too hard, not when the camp needed solid security.

A mosquito bit him on the back of the neck. He swatted and missed. Its buzz as it flew away sounded as if it were laughing at him. The camp lay quiet in the summer night. Snores floated out the windows of the prisoners' barracks. Men who'd proved too enthusiastic about being Whigs or Rad Libs weren't going anywhere—except for hasty trips to the latrines.

"What do you say, Jeff?" a guard called as Pinkard headed toward his much more comfortable barracks. "How was the picture?"

"Pretty good, Charlie," he answered. "Got to do something about those damn niggers, though. That one who took a shot at the president . . . " He caught himself yawning and didn't go on. Instead, he just said, "Freedom!"

"Freedom!" Charlie echoed. It was a handy word when you wanted to say something without bothering with a real conversation.

Pinkard's mattress creaked when he lay down. In the warm, muggy darkness, he was some little while falling asleep. He'd laid out the camp with room to grow. The expanded security perimeter had come from that extra room, which was fine. The land was there, for whatever reason. If it hadn't been, that would have caused a problem. As things were . . . As things were, he rolled over and slept.

Reveille woke him. He got out of bed, put on a fresh uniform, washed his face and shaved, and went out to look at morning roll call and inspection. The politicals were lined up in neat rows. They wore striped uniforms like any convicts, with a big white P stenciled on the chest and back of each shirt and the seat of each pair of trousers.

Guards counted them off and compared the tally to the number expected. When Pinkard saw the count start over again, he knew the numbers didn't match. The politicals groaned; they didn't get fed till everything checked out the way it was supposed to. One of them said, "Take off your shoes this time, goddammit!"

Without even pausing, a guard walking by backhanded the talky prisoner across the face. The political clapped his hands to his nose and mouth, whereupon the guard kicked him in the belly. He fell to the ground, writhing.

Jeff ate breakfast with assistant wardens not involved in the count. Ham and eggs and grits and good hot coffee filled him up nicely. When the count finally satisfied the guards making it, the prisoners got the very same breakfast—except for the ham and eggs and coffee.

One of the assistant wardens said, "I hear we've got some new fish coming in today."

"Yeah?" Jeff pricked his ears up. "What kind of new fish?"

"Blackfish," the other man answered.

"Niggers?" Pinkard said, and the other fellow nodded. Jeff swore. "How the hell are we going to keep 'em separate? Nobody said nothin' about niggers when we were laying out this place."

"What the devil difference does it make?" the other fellow said. "Half the bastards we've got in here—shit, more than half—they're already nigger-lovers. Let 'em stick together with their pals." He laughed.

To Jeff, it wasn't a laughing matter. "They'll make trouble," he said dolefully. He didn't want trouble—he didn't want trouble the prisoners started, anyhow. He wanted things to go smoothly. That made him look good.

With a shrug, the other assistant warden said, "They won't bust out, and that's all that matters. And how much trouble can they make? We've got the guns. Let 'em write the governor if they don't like it." He guffawed again. So did Pinkard—that was funny.

Sure enough, the colored prisoners came in a little before noon. Some of them were wounded, and went into the meager infirmary. The rest . . . The rest reminded Jeff of the Red rebels he'd fought just after he got conscripted into the C.S. Army. With them inside it, this camp would need more guards. He was morally certain of that. What, after all, did these skinny, somber Negroes have left to lose?


"Yankees go home! Yankees go home! Yankees go home!"

The endless chant worried Irving Morrell. He stood up in the cupola of his barrel, watching the crowd in the park in Lubbock. Trouble was in the air. He could feel it. It made the hair on his arms and at the back of his neck want to stand up, the way lightning did before it struck. Not enough men here, in the restless—hell, the rebellious—state of Houston; not enough barrels, either. They hadn't been able to clamp down on things here and make them stay quiet.

*What do you expect?* he asked himself. *We've got that long, long border with Confederate Texas, and agitators keep slipping over it. They keep sneaking guns across it, too, not that there weren't plenty here already.*

As if on cue—and it probably was—the crowd in the park changed their cry: "Plebiscite! Plebiscite! Plebiscite!" Morrell's worry eased, ever so slightly. Maybe they were less likely to do anything drastic if they were shouting for a chance to vote themselves back into the CSA.

From the gunner's seat, Sergeant Michael Pound said, "By God, sir, we ought to let Featherston have these bastards back. They'd be just as unruly for him as they are for us."

"I'm not going to tell you you're wrong, Sergeant, but that's not what our orders are," Morrell answered. "We're supposed to hold Houston, and so we will."

"Yes, sir." By his tone, Pound would sooner have dropped the place. Morrell had trouble blaming him. As far as he was concerned, the Confederates were welcome to what had been western Texas. But he didn't give orders like that. He only carried them out, or tried.

When trouble started, it started very quickly. The crowd was still chanting, "Plebiscite! Plebiscite!" Morrell barely heard the pop of a pistol over the chant and over the rumble of the barrel's engine. But he realized what was going on when a soldier in U.S. green-gray slumped to the ground, clutching at his belly.

The rest of the soldiers raised their rifles to their shoulders. The crowd, like most hostile crowds in Houston, had nerve. It surged forward, not back. Rocks and bottles started flying. The soldiers opened fire. So did people in the crowd who'd held back up till then.

Morrell ducked down into the turret. "It's going to hell," he told Pound. "Do what you have to do with the machine gun."

"Yes, sir," the gunner answered. "A couple of rounds of case shot from the main armament, too?"

Before Morrell could answer, three or four bullets spanged off the barrel's armor plate. "Whatever you think best," he said. "But we're going to dismiss this crowd if we have to kill everybody in it."

"Yes, sir," Michael Pound said crisply; that was an order he could appreciate. "Case shot!" he told the loader, and case shot he got. He had never been a man to do things by halves.

Despite the gunfire, Morrell stood up in the cupola again. He wanted to see what was going on. A bullet cracked past his ear. The turret traversed through a few degrees, bringing the main armament to bear on the heart of the crowd. The cannon bellowed at point-blank range. Barrels carried only a few rounds of case shot, for gunners seldom got the chance to use it. Sergeant Pound might have fired an enormous shotgun at the rioting Houstonians. The results weren't pretty, and another round hard on the heels of the first made them even more grisly.

People ran then. Not even trained troops could stand up to that kind of fire. Sergeant Pound and the bow gunner encouraged them with a series of short bursts from their machine guns. The other barrel in the park was firing its machine guns, too, and the soldiers were pouring volley after volley into the dissolving crowd. Such treatment might not make the Houstonians love the U.S. government, but would make them pay attention to it.

They had nerve, even if they had no brains to speak of. Some men lay down behind corpses and kept shooting at the U.S. soldiers. And a whiskey bottle with a smoking wick arced through the air and smashed on the front decking of Morrell's barrel.

It smashed, spilling flaming gasoline across the front of the machine. "God damn it!" Morrell shouted in furious but futile rage. What soldiers here in Houston called Featherston fizzes had proved surprisingly dangerous to barrels. Flames spread over paint and grease and dripped through every opening, no matter how tiny, in the fighting compartment. "Out!" Morrell yelled. "Everybody out!" He ducked back into the turret to scream the same message into the speaking tube, to make sure the driver and bow gunner heard him.

Then he scrambled out the cupola and down the side of the barrel. Escape hatches at the bow and on either side of the turret flew open. The rest of the crew got out through them, closely followed by growing clouds of black smoke. "Move away!" Sergeant Pound shouted. "When the ammo starts cooking off—"

Morrell needed no more encouragement. Neither did any of the other crewmen. They put as much ground between them and the doomed machine as they could. Morrell looked back over his shoulder. Smoke was pouring out of the cupola now, too. A moment later, the most spectacular fireworks display this side of the Fourth of July in Philadelphia finished the barrel.

"Do you know what we need, sir?" Pound said. "We need a good fire extinguisher in there. Could make a lot of difference."

"I'm not going to tell you you're wrong, because you're—" Morrell knew he was repeating himself. A bullet thudded into a tree trunk behind his head. He threw himself flat. So did the rest of the barrel crew. Lying on his belly, he finished with such aplomb as he could muster: "—not. But do you think you could remind me about it when I haven't got other things to worry about, like getting my ass shot off?"

"That was your ass, sir?" Michael Pound asked innocently, and Morrell snorted. Pound said, "I will, sir; I promise." Morrell believed him; he wouldn't forget something like that. The sergeant went on, "It did cross my mind just now for some reason or other."

"Really? Can't imagine why." Still prone, Morrell watched another Houstonian get ready to fling a Featherston fizz at the second barrel in the park. A U.S. soldier shot him in the arm before he could let fly. The incendiary dropped at his feet, broke, and engulfed him in flames. A shrieking torch, he ran every which way until at last, mercifully, he fell and did not rise.

"Serves him right," Sergeant Pound said savagely. Morrell would have been hard pressed to argue, and so didn't try.

What happened to the fizz-flinger sufficed to scare even the Houstonians. Still shouting, "Freedom!" they fled the park. Soldiers in green-gray moved among the wounded. They weren't helping them; they were methodically finishing them off, with single gunshots or with the bayonet.

"Grim work," Pound said, getting to his feet, "but necessary. Those people won't see reason, and so we might as well be rid of them."

"You kill everybody who doesn't want to see reason, people will get mighty thin on the ground mighty fast," Morrell remarked as he too got up and brushed off his coveralls.

"Oh, yes, sir," the sergeant agreed. "But if I kill everybody who won't see reason and who's trying to kill me, I'll sleep better of nights and I'm a lot likelier to live to get old and gray."

Sometimes perfect bloodthirstiness made perfect sense. This did seem to be one of those times. Morrell mournfully eyed the burning barrel, which still sent a thick column of black, stinking smoke up into the brassy sky.

Sergeant Pound looked toward the barrel, too. His thoughts, as usual, were completely practical: "I wonder how long they'll take to ship a replacement machine down here."

"Depends," Morrell said judiciously. "If Hoover wins the election come November, it'll be business as usual. But if it's Al Smith, and the Socialists get back in . . ." He shrugged.

Sergeant Pound made a sour face. So did the rest of the barrel crew. Pound said, "I'm going to vote for Hoover, too. What sane man wouldn't? And yet, you know, it's a funny thing. Charlie La Follette makes a ten times better vice president than what's-his-name running with Hoover— Borah, that's it."

"Bill Borah's got no brains to speak of. I won't argue that," Morrell said. "Still, you have to vote the party, and the man at the top of the ticket. Odds two presidents in a row would drop dead are pretty slim."

"Oh, yes, sir. Certainly. I said the same thing." Pound wasn't currying favor. Morrell didn't think such a ploy had ever occurred to the gunner. If it had, he would have become an officer years ago. He *had* said that, and was just reminding Morrell of it.

A lieutenant with a .45 still in his hand strode up to the barrel crew. Seeing Morrell's eagles, he started to come to attention. Morrell waved for him not to bother. "Aren't you glad we're in the USA, sir?" the young officer said. "If we're not careful, though, they'll send us to a country where the people don't like us."

Morrell clamped down hard on a laugh. If he started, he wasn't sure he could stop. "I've served in Canada, Lieutenant," he said carefully. "It's nothing like this. The Canucks don't like us, but even the ones who shoot at us aren't . . . wild men like these."

"Oh, good." Real relief showed in the lieutenant's voice. "I thought it was just me. I couldn't imagine how they held their ground so long with the punishment they took."

He might still have been making messes in his drawers when the Great War ended. Wearily, Morrell said, "People will do all kinds of mad things when their blood is up, son." He hadn't intended to add that last word, but the lieutenant had to be young enough to suit it, and hadn't seen a quarter of the things Morrell had. Only after a couple of seconds did Morrell realize that made the other man lucky, not unlucky.

The lieutenant had seen enough to keep a firm grip on fundamentals: "A lot of those bastards won't get their blood up again, on account of it's *out*."

"I know," Morrell said. "That's the way it's supposed to work."

"Yeah." Shaking his head, the lieutenant went away. His feet were unsteady, as if he'd had too much to drink. Morrell knew he hadn't. He'd simply seen too much. That could produce a hangover of its own, and one more painful than any that sprang from rotgut.

Sergeant Pound said, "We're alive and they're dead, and that's how I like it."

Ammunition was still cooking off inside the burning barrel. The flames had caught in the dry grass under it. Had the grass been less sparse, the fire would have spread farther and been more dangerous. Beyond the barrel lay the dead men—and a few women, too—who'd wanted to drag the state of Houston back into the CSA.

Morrell took a pack of cigarettes—Raleighs, from the Confederate States—out of the breast pocket of his coveralls and lit one. A moment later, he stubbed it out in the dirt. The smoke seemed to taste as greasy and nasty as the thick black stuff pouring from the barrel. He wondered if he'd ever want another cigarette again.

\* \* \*

"**I**t's all right, Ernie." Sylvia Enos heard the fright in her own voice, heard it and hated it. "It really is. That sort of thing can happen to any-body, not just to—" She broke off. She hadn't helped. Her hands folded into fists, nails biting the flesh of her palms.

"Not just to someone who got his dick shot off," Ernie finished for her, *his* voice flat and deadly. "Maybe it can. But there is a difference. For me, it happens all the goddamn time." He glared at her as if it were her fault. Half the time, these days, he seemed to think it was.

Sylvia twisted away from him on the narrow bed in his flat. She almost wished they hadn't succeeded so often when they were first start-ing out. Ernie had begun to think he could whenever he wanted to. He'd begun taking it—and her—for granted. Then, when he'd started failing again . . .

He reached down, plucked a bottle of whiskey off the floor, and took a big swig. "That won't help," Sylvia said. "It'll only make things worse." Drunk, he was always hopeless in bed. And when he proved hopeless, that made him meaner.

He laughed now. "Depends on what you mean by 'things.' " He took another long pull at the bottle. "I do not know why I go on. There does not seem to be much point." He reached into the drawer of the nightstand by the bed and pulled out a .45. He held it about a foot from his face, star-ing at it as if it were the most beautiful thing in the world.

"Ernie!" Sylvia wasn't frightened any more. She was terrified. She snatched the pistol out of his hand. "Leave this damned *thing* alone, do you hear me?"

He let her take it. She shuddered with relief. He didn't always, and he was much stronger than she was. When the black mood seized him . . . But now he smiled with a wounded tenderness that pierced and melted her heart even through her fear. "You never stop trying to make me into an angel, do you?" he said. "I am not an angel. I am from the other place."

"You're talking nonsense, is what you're doing." Sylvia got out of bed and started to dress. "What you need is sleep."

"What I need . . ." Ernie cupped what he had with one hand.

Sylvia thought about taking the .45 with her when she left. The only reason she didn't was that Ernie's apartment was a young arsenal. She couldn't carry off all the guns he owned.

She'd been standing on the corner waiting for a trolley at least five minutes before she realized her knees were shaking. When the streetcar came up, she staggered as she boarded it. She threw a nickel in the fare box, then all but fell into the closest seat. She looked down at her hands. They were shaking, too.

Her daughter Mary Jane was sitting in the kitchen drinking coffee when she walked into the apartment. "Hi, Ma," Mary Jane said cheerfully, and then, her smile fading and her jaw dropping, "My God, what happened to you? You're white as a sheet."

"Ernie." Sylvia poured herself coffee, put in cream and sugar, and then poured in a good slug of whiskey, too.

"Ma, that guy is nothing but trouble." Mary Jane spoke with the air of someone who knew what she was talking about. No doubt she did; at twenty-four she probably had more practical experience with men than did Sylvia, who'd found George, stuck with him, and then done very little till the writer came back into her life. Her daughter went on, "I know you've got a soft spot for him because he helped you with the book about Dad, but he's a little bit nuts, you know what I mean? Maybe he was good for you once, but he isn't any more."

Before answering, Sylvia took a big gulp of the improved coffee. It wasn't improved enough to suit her, so she put some more hooch in it. With a sigh, she said, "Chances are you're right. But—"

"Wait." Mary Jane held up a hand. "Stop. No buts. If he's trouble, if you *know* he's trouble, you don't walk to the nearest exit. You run."

"It's not that simple." Sylvia drank more of the coffee. She could feel the whiskey calming her. "You don't understand, honey. When he's right—and he is, most of the time—he's the sweetest man I ever knew, the sweetest man I ever imagined." That was true. Saying it, she almost forgot the cold weight of the .45 she'd wrenched from Ernie's hand.

"I don't know anything about that," Mary Jane admitted. "But I'll tell you what I do know. If he makes you come home looking like you just saw a ghost when he *isn't* right, you don't want anything to do with him."

"He's coping with more than most men ever have to. He's got this war wound. . . ." Sylvia had never gone into detail about Ernie's injury. She'd never even admitted they were lovers, though she was sure Mary Jane and George Jr. knew. Now shock and the potent coffee loosened her tongue. She explained what the wound was.

"Poor guy," Mary Jane said when she finished. "I'm sorry about that. It's terrible, and he can't do anything about it. Fine. Now I understand better why he's the way he is. But you're not the Red Cross, Ma. You can't go on giving like this when all you get back is grief. What if he decides to use you for a punching bag one of these days?"

"He wouldn't do that." But Sylvia was uncomfortably aware that she spoke without conviction.

Her daughter noticed, too. "How many times have you told me not to be dumb?"

"Lots." Sylvia managed a wry grin. "How many times have you listened?"

"A few, maybe." Mary Jane grinned, too. "But you're my mother. You're supposed to have good sense for both of us, right? Don't be dumb, Ma. You want to find somebody? Swell. Find somebody who doesn't scare you to death."

"I'll . . . think about it." Sylvia hadn't expected to say even that much. But she found herself continuing, "He's working on a book about how he got wounded, about driving an ambulance up in Quebec. He's let me see some of it. It's really good—and when he's writing, things go better." *Sometimes. Not tonight, but sometimes.*

Mary Jane threw her hands in the air. "Honest to God, Ma, I swear you didn't hear a word I said."

Sylvia shook her head and lit a cigarette. Mary Jane held out a hand. Sylvia passed her the pack. She leaned close to get a light from her mother. Sylvia said, "I heard you. But I'll do what I think I ought to, not what you think."

"All right, all right, all right." Mary Jane's smile had a wry twist to it. "I can't make you do anything. After all, *I'm* not *your* mother."

Sylvia laughed. She hadn't dreamt she'd be able to. But she did. Her daughter's company and some strongly fortified coffee made the terror she'd felt not long before seem distant and unreal.

A few days later, she had a visitor who surprised her. Joseph Kennedy simply showed up, assuming she'd be glad to see him. "Good day, Mrs. Enos," he said, and tipped his hat to her. "I hope we can rely on you to help get out the vote for Hoover and Borah."

"I didn't think I'd ever see you again after our . . . quarrel last year," Sylvia said. *And I hoped I wouldn't.*

He shrugged. "State Democratic headquarters reminded me how useful you've been. The Party comes first." By his face, he wished it didn't.

"I wondered whose side you'd be on this year," she remarked.

"Why?" Kennedy asked, in real surprise now. Then he laughed. "You mean because Al Smith is a Catholic, and so am I?" Sylvia nodded. Kennedy laughed again, louder this time. "My dear lady, the Pope is infallible. I believe that. Al Smith? If Al Smith were the Pope, I'd kiss his ring. Since he's not, I'm going to do my best to kick his . . . fanny."

Knowing it would be useless, Sylvia said, "Mr. Kennedy, I'm not your 'dear lady,' and I don't want to be."

"Well, Mrs. Enos, that's as may be," the Democratic organizer said.

"I'll tell you this, though: I have no idea what you see in that miserable hack of yours."

He'd made that crack before. "I told you, Ernie's no hack," Sylvia said. "He's a *writer!*"

Kennedy shrugged again. "If you say so." His dismissive tone said he wasn't about to change his mind. But he went on, "Never mind bedfellows, then. We'll keep this to politics. You've been helping the Democrats for a long time. Do you want another Socialist president now?"

"Well, no," Sylvia admitted. "You'll pay the same as you have the past couple of elections?"

"Of course," Kennedy answered, as if insulted she needed to ask. "I told you you'd been good. We pay for what we get."

*If state headquarters tells us to,* she thought. Still, the money was better than she could get any other way. Royalties from *I Sank Roger Kimball* were skimpy these days. There'd been talk of putting it out as one of the newfangled paperbound pocket books, but that hadn't happened yet, and she didn't know if it would. "It's a deal—as long as you keep your hands to yourself."

Joe Kennedy sighed. "You drive a hard bargain, Mrs. Enos, but yes, that's a deal." He held out his hand. Warily, Sylvia took it. She knew the only reason he stayed interested in her was that she stayed uninterested in him. But she couldn't stomach giving in to get him out of her hair.

The Democrats trotted her out at a rally near T Wharf a few days later. Party faithful listened as she told them this was no time to let a Socialist, someone who was bound to be soft on the Confederate States, take up residence in Powel House. The crowd clapped in all the right places. Because they did, Sylvia needed longer than she would have otherwise to realize her speech was falling flat.

Four years earlier, the Democrats, who'd lost three presidential elections in a row, had been hungry—more than hungry; desperate—to reclaim Powel House. And they'd done it, even if Calvin Coolidge had dropped dead before he could take the oath of office. But Hoover hadn't proved any better at fixing the collapse than Socialist Hosea Blackford had before him. And he was about as exciting as oatmeal without sugar. He was earnest. He worked hard. It wasn't enough.

Even before the last round of applause faded, Sylvia thought, *The Democrats are going to lose this time.* The feeling—no, the certainty—was irrational, but no less real for that.

Her eyes met those of Joe Kennedy, who stood on the platform with her. He was still clapping, but his smile seemed held on his face by force of will alone. *He knows,* she realized. *He's slimy, but he's not stupid. Yes, he knows.*

He gave back a shrug, as if to say, *This is my job, and I'm going to do it as well as I can no matter what happens.* Sylvia nodded in reply; that was something she understood. She could respect Kennedy the political operator, no matter what she thought about Kennedy the man.

As she stepped down from the platform, a new realization came to her. The election still lay a couple of months ahead. She was going to have to be a professional herself all through that time, going up on platforms and saying what needed to be said in spite of what she thought would happen in November. That wouldn't be easy. It might be harder than anything she'd ever tried before.

Her back stiffened. *I don't care whether it's easy or not. If Joe Kennedy can do it, so can I.*

Carl Martin was just starting to creep. Every minute or so, he'd forget how to move and flop down like a jellyfish. At six months, that didn't bother him. He thought it was funny. He'd try again after a while, when he remembered how to make his elbows work, and try to find something on the floor and stick it in his mouth. "Bwee!" he said proudly.

"You tell 'em, kid," Chester Martin agreed. He was pretty proud of his son, though he sometimes wondered how any baby ever lived to grow up. Some of the things Carl did, and of course did without thinking about them. . . . You had to watch him not just every minute, but every single second.

As if to prove the point, the junior member of the Martin family headed for a book of matches that shouldn't have been on the floor in the first place. Carl didn't want a cigarette. He wanted to find out what matches tasted like. Chester grabbed them before his son could. Carl clouded up and started to cry.

"You can't eat matches," Chester said. "They aren't good for you."

Telling something like that to a six-month-old, naturally, did no good at all. Carl kept on crying. And, because he was crying, he forgot to hold his head up. When it came down, he banged it on the floor. That really gave him something to cry about.

"What now?" Rita called from the kitchen.

Chester explained, as best he could over his son's din. He picked up the boy and cuddled him. The crying subsided. Chester pulled out his hankie and wiped snot off Carl's face. Carl didn't like that. He never did.

To distract him, Chester turned on the wireless. They'd bought the set not long after the baby was born. They couldn't quite afford it, but Rita had wanted it badly. Feeding the baby meant being up in the middle of the night a lot. She wanted it to stay dark then, to keep Carl from waking up.

Listening to music or news or a comedy show was better than sitting there all alone in the quiet.

Somebody knocked on the door. "There's Sue and Otis and Pete," Chester said.

"Oh, God, they're early!" Rita said. "Well, let 'em in. The fried chicken'll be done in about fifteen minutes."

When Chester's sister and brother-in-law and nephew came in, Sue exclaimed over the baby: "How big he's getting!"

"He's still tiny," said Pete, who at nine seemed to be shooting up like a weed himself, all shins and forearms and long skinny neck.

Otis Blake pointed to him. "I think this one's going to be a giraffe when he grows up."

Sue shook her head. "No, he won't. Giraffes eat vegetables." Pete made a horrible face at the very idea.

Having company over made Carl forget he'd been crying and stare about wide-eyed. Chester wondered, not for the first time, what babies made of the world. It had to be confusing as hell. He put his son down, went into the kitchen, and pulled four bottles of Burgermeister out of the icebox. He set one on the counter by Rita, who was turning chicken pieces, and brought the others out for himself and Sue and Otis.

His brother-in-law raised his beer in salute. "Here's to California," he said.

"I'll drink to that, by God," Chester said, and did. "This place has saved my life. Back in Toledo, I'd still be out of work."

"Oh, yes." Blake nodded vigorously. "Back in Toledo, I was out of work, too. I'm not making as much as I did back there when I had a job—"

"Unions here aren't what they were in Toledo," Chester broke in.

"I've seen that," Otis Blake agreed. "It'll come, I think. But I'm working, and I'm not broke or on the dole. The way things have been since the stock market went south, I can't complain."

"That's what years of hard times have done to us," Chester said. "They've made us satisfied with less than we used to have. It's not right."

"What can we do about it, though?" his sister asked.

Before Chester could answer, Rita called, "Supper's ready!" He felt like a prizefighter saved by the bell, because he didn't know. He remembered the years when he'd eaten chicken gizzards and hearts because he couldn't afford anything better. He'd even started to like them. Too often, though, he couldn't afford them or beef heart or tripe or any of the other cheap meats. He remembered plate after plate of noodles or potatoes and cabbage, too.

Now, though, he grabbed himself a drumstick. The crispy skin burned his fingers. "Ow!" he said. Along with green beans and fried potatoes, it made a tasty meal—and he could leave the gizzard and heart and neck to Pete, who, since he'd started eating them as a kid, remained convinced they were treats. Later, when Chester saw everybody else had plenty, he also snagged a thigh. After juicy dark meat, giblets weren't worth talking about, let alone eating.

Rita put Carl in his high chair and gave him small bits of food along with his bottle. He wound up wearing as much as he ate. He usually did. Pete watched in fascination. Sue said, "You used to eat that way, too." The boy shook his head, denying even the possibility.

After apple pie, Rita made coffee for the grownups. Carl got fussy. She changed him and put him to bed. Otis Blake lit a cigarette. "Who are you two going to vote for when the election gets here?" he asked.

"Hoover hasn't done anything much," Chester said.

"Hoover hasn't done anything, period," Rita said. "*I'm* voting for Al Smith. I don't know about him." She pointed at her husband. She still hadn't fully forgiven him for backing away from the Socialist camp in 1932.

He said, "I expect I'll vote for Smith, too. The only thing that bothers me about him is that he's never looked outside New York before now. I'm not sure he's tough enough to spit in Jake Featherston's eye if he has to."

His brother-in-law scratched his head. He had a wide, perfect, permanent part in the middle of his scalp; had the bullet that made it been even a fraction of an inch lower, Sue would never have got the chance to meet him after the war. He said, "Don't you think we need to worry about the USA more than we do about the CSA?"

"Not if another war's brewing," Chester said.

"Featherston fought in the last one," Blake said. "He couldn't be crazy enough to want to do that again. Besides, he's firing generals. Remember? That was in the paper this past summer."

"That's true. It was," Chester admitted. "I said I'd probably vote for Smith. I probably will."

"Me, too," Sue said. "Our folks are the only Democrats left in the family."

Otis Blake snorted. "Yeah, they're still Democrats even though your dad hasn't got a job and can't get one." He and Chester had both sent Stephen Douglas Martin money whenever they could afford to.

The Blakes didn't stay late. It was a Sunday night, with school ahead for Pete and work for Otis. After they left, Rita washed the dishes. Chester, who also had work in the morning, turned on the wireless before getting ready for bed. He found a news show.

"President Hoover vowed today to keep Houston in the United States regardless of Confederate pressure in the state," the announcer said. "He also accused Governor Smith of having too soft a policy on the Confederate States. 'Such well-meaning foolishness got the United States into trouble in the past two Socialist administrations,' Hoover said. 'I don't intend to go down that mistaken road. We must be strong first. Everything else springs from that.' "

Chester grunted. Foreign policy was the only area where he favored the Democrats' platform over the Socialists'. He shrugged. When you got right down to it, what happened in the USA counted for more than what happened outside. He'd voted against his class interest four years ago, and he'd spent most of the time since regretting it. He wouldn't make the same mistake twice.

The newscaster went on, "When asked for comment on the president's remarks, Governor Smith said, 'It's hard to keep people in a country where they don't want to stay. You would think the United States had learned that lesson after the War of Secession, but the present administration seems as thick-headed there as it does everywhere else.' "

*Take that,* Martin thought. He wasn't sure he agreed with Al Smith, but he liked the way the governor of New York came back swinging hard when Hoover attacked him. The announcer went on to talk about the dust storms that were picking up the soil of drought-ridden Kansas and Sequoyah and Houston and blowing it east, so the dust came down in New York City and even on the decks of ships out of sight of land in the Atlantic. The winds blew from west to east, so the dust storms didn't directly affect Los Angeles, but Martin had seen in newsreels how dreadful they were.

And farmers from the afflicted states were giving up any hope of bringing in a crop on their bone-dry farms. A lot of them were coming west by train or in rattletrap motorcars, looking for whatever work they could find. Two or three men who spoke with a twang had joined Chester's construction crew. They worked hard enough to satisfy even the exacting Mordechai, who thought anybody who didn't go home limp with exhaustion every night was a lazy son of a bitch.

Rita came out of the kitchen in the middle of the football scores. Since moving west himself, Chester had become passionately devoted to the fortunes of the Los Angeles Dons, the local franchise in the West Coast Football League. The Seattle Sharks, unfortunately, had smashed the hometown heroes, 31–10.

With an enormous yawn, Rita said, "I'm going to bed myself. He's been so fussy the past few nights. He must be cutting a tooth, but I can't find it yet. If he wakes up and he isn't hungry, I wish you'd take him tonight."

"All right." Chester did rock Carl back to sleep every once in a while.

When the alarm clock went off the next morning, he woke up happy. He hadn't heard a thing in the night, which meant the baby must have slept straight through. Or so he thought, till he got a look at Rita's wan, sleepy face. Reproachfully, she said, "You told me you'd take him, but you just lay there while he cried, till finally I got up and got him. He didn't want to go back to bed after that, either."

"I'm sorry," Martin said. "I never even heard him." That was nothing but the truth. Because he didn't usually get up when the baby cried, the noise Carl made didn't rouse him, though he'd shut off the alarm clock as soon as it rang.

His wife looked as if she had trouble believing him. "I don't see how you could have missed him. Half the neighbors must have heard," she said. But he kept protesting his innocence, and finally persuaded her. She rubbed bloodshot eyes. "I wish *I* could sleep through a racket like that."

Chester had slept through worse in the Great War. Bursting shells hadn't fazed him then, not unless they landed very close. A man could get used to anything. Absently, Chester scratched along the seam of his pajama bottoms. He'd got used to being lousy, too, and the vermin hid and laid their eggs in seams.

After strong coffee, scrambled eggs, and toast, he grabbed his tool kit and headed for the trolley stop. A man who had work clung to it. He didn't give anyone the chance to take it away. Martin knew what he had to do. He aimed to do it. One day, he wanted to have the money to buy a house. His father had never owned one, living in apartments all his days. *I can do better than that,* Martin thought—a great American war cry. *I can, and, by God, I will.*

**P**olite as usual, Heber Young nodded to Abner Dowling. "I am afraid, Colonel, that this is our final meeting," said the unofficial leader of the even more unofficial Mormon movement.

Dowling blinked "What's that you say, Mr. Young?" His mouth fell open. Several chins wobbled.

"I am very sorry, but I have concluded that the United States are not serious about negotiating with the people of Utah," Young said. "This being so, my continued presence no longer serves any useful purpose. I have better things to do with my time, to do with my life, than try to turn back the tide."

That was some sort of legend. Dowling knew as much, though he couldn't recall the details. He said, "I hope you'll reconsider, Mr. Young. I know you to be a man of good will and a man of good sense. Your people will be the losers if you walk away."

"So I have told myself many times—I am no less vain than any other man," Heber Young replied gravely. "Telling myself such fables has kept me coming here to your headquarters these past several years, even though I know President Hoover has tied your hands. I believe you would be more liberal if not constrained by orders from Philadelphia. After so many futile discussions, though, I find I no longer have the heart for any more."

"If you were any man but yourself, I would say the Confederate hotheads had got to you." Dowling didn't hide his anger and disappointment. "If you leave the scene, they *will* get to your people, and the results will not be happy." He didn't need Winthrop W. Webb's prediction to see that, but the spy's judgment here matched his own all too well.

"I shall have to take that chance," Young said. "I am still not altogether convinced these men serve the CSA and not the USA." He held up a hasty hand. "Please understand me, Colonel—I do not claim you are lying when you deny planting provocateurs among us. I believe you—you personally, that is. But whether someone else in the U.S. government is using such men . . . of that, I am less certain."

Abner Dowling grunted. He wasn't a hundred percent certain no U.S. officials were using provocateurs here in Utah, either. He wished he were, but he wasn't. Since he wasn't, he thought it wiser not to talk any more about that. Instead, he said, "You tell me you're unhappy with the orders I get from back East? I admit I haven't been happy about all of them myself."

"Because you are honest enough to admit such things, I've kept coming back to talk with you," Young said. "But no more. I am sorry, Colonel—I am very sorry, in fact—but enough is enough." He started to get to his feet and walk out of Dowling's office.

"Wait!" Dowling exclaimed.

"Why?" The Mormon was still polite, but implacable.

"Why? For the results of the election, that's why," the commandant of Salt Lake City answered. "If Smith beats Hoover, isn't it likely I'll have new orders after the first of next February?"

"Hmm." Heber Young had already taken his dark homburg by the brim. Now he hesitated: perhaps the first time Dowling had ever seen him indecisive. He set the hat back on the tree and returned to the chair across the desk from Dowling. "Now that is interesting, Colonel. That is very interesting. You *would* follow more liberal orders if you received them?"

"I am a soldier, sir. I am obliged to follow all legitimate orders I receive." Dowling didn't tell the Mormon leader he intended to vote for Hoover, or that he hoped the incumbent would trounce Al Smith. Young likely knew as much. But he had told the truth. As if to prove it, he said,

"Didn't I try to get public-works jobs for Utah just after Hoover took over?" The president had forbidden the scheme, but Young couldn't say he hadn't tried.

"You did," Young admitted. He rubbed his square chin. Then, abruptly, he nodded; once he had made up his mind, he didn't hesitate. "All right, Colonel Dowling. I will wait and see what happens in the election. If Hoover wins a second term, that will be the end of that. If Smith wins . . . If Smith wins, I will see what happens next. Good day." Now he did take his hat. Tipping it, he left.

Dowling allowed himself a sigh of relief. If Heber Young walked away from talks with the occupying authorities, that in itself might have been enough to ignite Utah. Dowling's career wasn't where it would have been if he hadn't spent so many years as George Custer's adjutant, but he still had hopes for it. With a Utah uprising on his record, he would have been dead in the water as far as hopes of getting stars on his shoulders one day went.

The telephone in the outer office rang. His own adjutant answered it. A moment later, the telephone on Dowling's desk rang. "Abner Dowling," he said crisply into the mouthpiece. He listened and nodded, though no one was there to see it. "That's very good news. Thanks for passing it on." He hung up.

Captain Toricelli came into the inner office, his face alight. "Barrels!" he said. "They're really going to give them to us!"

"I only started shouting for them a year or so ago," Dowling said. "The way things work back in Philadelphia, they're on the dead run."

"We could all have been dead by the time they got here," Captain Toricelli said.

"If we *had* died, that's the one thing I can think of that would have got them here faster," Dowling said. His adjutant laughed. He wondered why. He hadn't been kidding.

Being promised the machines didn't mean getting them right away. When they did arrive, he was grievously disappointed. He'd been hoping for new barrels, and what he got were Great War retreads. They must have come from Houston; most of them still showed fresh bullet scars and other combat-related damage to their armor.

"*I* can move faster than one of these things," Dowling said scornfully. Since he was built like a rolltop desk, that was unlikely to be true. But it wasn't *very* false, either. A man in good shape *could* outrun one of these snorting monsters. Dowling eyed the crewmen, duffel bags on their shoulders, who dismounted from passenger cars. "They take a couple of squads' worth of men apiece, too," he grumbled; he remembered that very well from Great War days.

"Yes, sir," Captain Toricelli answered. "But they're better than nothing."

"I suppose so," Dowling said unwillingly. Then he brightened, a little. "I suppose new barrels are coming off the line. They'd have to be, eh? They must be going straight to Houston—and to Kentucky now, too."

"That makes sense to me." Toricelli sounded faintly aggrieved. What was the world coming to when a superior started making sense?

Three days later, a pair of barrels rumbled up Temple Street and took up positions in Temple Square. Dowling thought that would be the least inflammatory way he could use them. Temple Square had been under guard ever since the U.S. Army leveled the Mormon Temple and killed the last stubborn defenders there. Bits of granite from the Temple were potent relics to Mormons who opposed the government. That struck Dowling as medieval, which made it no less true. Soldiers had always had orders to shoot to kill whenever anyone tried to abscond with a fragment.

Dowling wasn't particularly surprised when Heber Young paid him a call a few days later. He did his best to pretend he was, saying, "And to what do I owe the pleasure of your company this time, Mr. Young?"

"Those . . . horrible machines." Young was furious, and making only the barest effort to hide it. "How dare you pollute Temple Square with their presence?"

"For one thing, we've had soldiers in the square for years. The barrels just reinforce them," Dowling answered. "For another, I want people here to know we have them, and that we'll use them if we need to. It might—prevent rashness, I guess you'd say."

Heber Young shook his head. "More likely to provoke than to prevent."

"No." Dowling shook his head. "I am very sorry, sir, but I cannot agree. To my mind, the safety of my men and the protection of U.S. interests in Utah must come first."

"Those infernal machines promote neither," the Mormon leader insisted.

They looked at each other. Not for the first time, they found they were both using English but speaking two altogether different languages. "I would be derelict in my duties if I did not use barrels," Dowling said.

"Using them is what makes you derelict." Young eyed him, then sighed. "I see I do not persuade you. I don't suppose I should have expected to. Yet hope does spring eternal in the human breast. I tell you, Colonel, no good will come from your using these machines."

"Do you threaten me, Mr. Young?"

"Colonel, if I tell you the sun will come up tomorrow, is that a threat? I would not say so. I would call it a prediction based on what I know of past events. I would call this the same thing." He stood up, politely challenging Dowling to arrest him for sedition after he'd come and put his head in the lion's jaws. Dowling couldn't, and he knew it. The word that Heber Young languished in a U.S. prison would touch off insurrection, regardless of whether the barrels in Temple Square did. As Young turned to go, he added, "If the government were generous enough to grant me the franchise, you may rest assured I would vote for Al Smith, in the hope that such discussions as this one would become unnecessary. Good day, Colonel Dowling." Out he went, a man whose moral force somehow made him worth battalions.

Four days later, one of the barrels caught fire on the way from the U.S. base to its turn at Temple Square. All eighteen crewmen escaped, and nobody shot at them as they burst from the doomed machine's hatches. Word came to Dowling almost at once. Cursing, he left the base in an auto and zoomed down Temple toward the blazing barrel.

By the time he got there, the fire had already started touching off ammunition. The fireworks display was spectacular, with red tracer rounds zooming in all directions. A fire engine roared up not long after Dowling arrived. It started spraying water on the barrel from as far away as the stream from the hose would reach. That struck him as being about as futile as offering last rites to a man smashed by a speeding locomotive, but he didn't think it could do any harm, so he kept quiet about it.

"How did this happen?" he demanded of the barrel's commander, a captain named Witherspoon.

"Sir, I don't know." Witherspoon nursed a burned hand.

*He'll live,* Dowling thought savagely. "Was it sabotage?" he asked.

"Sir, I don't know," Captain Witherspoon repeated. "It could have been, but. . . ." He shrugged. "This machine has to be almost twenty years old. Plenty of things can go wrong with it any which way. A leak in a fuel line, a leak in an oil line . . ." Another shrug. He pointed toward the burning barrel, from which a thick cloud of black smoke rose. "We'll never know now, that's for damn sure."

"Yes. It is," Dowling said unhappily. Were people in Salt Lake City laughing because they'd got away with one? Worse, were people in Richmond laughing because *they'd* got away with one?

**K**aplan's, on the Lower East Side, was a delicatessen Flora Blackford hadn't visited for years. That got driven home the minute she walked in the door. She remembered the foxy-red hair of Lou Kaplan, the proprietor; it made you want to warm your hands over it. Kaplan was still behind the counter. These days, though, his hair was white.

These days, Flora's hair had more than a little gray in it, too. She saw her brother at a table in the corner. She waved. David Hamburger nodded. She hurried over to him. Her little brother had a double chin, tired eyes, and gray in his own hair. *The things time does to us!* Flora thought, sudden tears stinging her eyes. She blinked them away. "It's good to see you, David," she said. "It's been too long."

He shrugged. "I get by. I like being a tailor. I like it better than being a Congressman's brother, and a lot better than being a First Lady's brother. You can't say I ever bothered you for anything, the way important people's relatives do."

"Bothered me?" Flora shook her head. "I wish you would have. Most of the time, you wouldn't even talk to me. You don't visit. . . ."

"I don't get out much." David tapped the cane leaning against his chair. He'd lost a leg in the war, not far below the hip. He could walk with a prosthesis, but only painfully. As if to emphasize that, he pointed to the chair across from him and said, "Sit down, for heaven's sake. You know why I'm not going to get up till I have to."

Flora did sit. A waitress came over to her and David. They both ordered. The pause meant she didn't have to call him on what she knew to be an evasion. He was, after all, here at Kaplan's. He could have come to Socialist Party headquarters once in a while, too. He could have, but he hadn't.

Politics estranged them. Flora had never thought that could happen in her family, but it had. Her brother had come out of the war a staunch Democrat. It was as if, having been crippled, he didn't want his wound to have been in vain, and so joined the party that was hardest on the CSA.

Flora reached into the jar across the table, pulled out a pickled tomato, and bit into it. She smiled; the taste and the vinegar tang in the air and the crunch took her back to her childhood. "Can't get things like this in Dakota, or even down in Philadelphia," she said.

That won her a grudging smile from David. "No, I don't suppose you would," he said, and then fell silent again as the waitress brought his pastrami sandwich and Flora's corned beef on rye. He sipped from an egg cream, which had neither egg nor cream in it. Flora's drink was a seltzer with a shpritz of raspberry syrup on top, something else unmatchable outside of New York City.

"Is your family well?" Flora asked.

"Well enough," he answered. "Amazing how fast children grow."

She nodded; Joshua had taught her that. She said, "I'm glad—" and then broke off, hoping he would think she'd intended it for a complete sentence. David had feared no one would ever want to marry a one-legged man. She'd started to say she was glad he'd been wrong about that, but hadn't known how he would take it.

By his tight-lipped smile, he knew where she'd been going. But then he shrugged, visibly setting aside annoyance. He said, "These past couple of years, I see you've finally started to understand what nice people the Confederates really are. Better late than never, that's all I've got to say."

"It's not the Confederate people. It's the Freedom Party," Flora said. "Reactionaries have seized control of the apparatus of the state, the same as they have in France."

David Hamburger rolled his eyes. "I don't suppose that would have happened if the people hadn't voted them in, now would it?"

"Well . . ." Flora winced. Her brother's comment was painfully pungent, but that didn't mean it was wrong.

"Yes. Well," he said. "Listen, if it comes to a fight we'd better be ready. That's the big thing I wanted to tell you. We've got to, you hear me? Otherwise, this"—he made a fist and hit his artificial leg, which gave back a sound like knocking on a door—"was for nothing, and I don't think I could stand that."

"It won't come to war," Flora said in genuine alarm. "Not even Hoover thinks it'll come to war."

"Hoover's one of the best men we've ever had for getting things done," David said, "and one of the worst for figuring out what to do. That's how it looks to me, anyhow. Of course, I'm no political bigwig. *Nu,* am I right or am I *meshuggeh?*"

"You're a lot of things, but you're not *meshuggeh,*" Flora answered. He'd summed up Hoover better than most editorial columnists she'd seen. "I still think you worry too much about the CSA, though. They have more *tsuris* than we do."

"Just because you have *tsuris* doesn't mean you can't give it." David finished his sandwich. He used one hand to help lever himself upright. Taking hold of the cane, he said, "They'll send you back to Congress in a couple of days. I'm not telling you to listen to me—when did you ever? But keep your eyes open."

"I always do," Flora insisted. Her brother didn't argue. He just walked out of Kaplan's, with a slow, rolling gait like a drunken sailor's. That let the knee joint in the artificial leg lock each time he took a step, and kept it from buckling under him. Flora wanted to go after him, but what was the point? They hadn't had anything in common for years. A sad lunch talking politics proved as much, as if it needed proof.

That evening, she made a speech in a union hall, and got cheered till her ears rang. More loud cheers greeted her after her two speeches the day before the election. She shook hands till her own was swollen and sore—and she knew how to minimize the damage while she did it.

She expected she would win reelection, too. Her district was solidly Socialist; it had gone Democratic for a little while in the despair following the collapse, but then repented of its folly. What she didn't know— what nobody knew—was whether the country would have its revenge on Herbert Hoover, as it had had its revenge on her husband four years earlier.

Tuesday, November 3, was cold and rainy. Flora went out and voted early, so the reporters and photographers who waited at her polling place could get their stories and pictures into the papers before the polls closed. She knew her Democratic opponent was doing the same thing. This way, their appearances canceled each other out. If she hadn't come early, he would have grabbed an edge—a small one, but an edge nonetheless.

"I think Smith will whip him," Hosea Blackford said when Flora came back to their apartment after voting: he was still registered in Dakota, and had cast an absentee ballot. He'd stayed on the sidelines during the campaign. For one thing, his own reputation wouldn't help either Flora or the Socialist Party. For another, he was getting ever more fragile. He still managed pretty well as long as he stuck close to home. Out in crowds these days, though, he seemed not only frail but also slightly baffled. That worried Flora.

She took her son with her to Socialist Party headquarters for the Fourteenth Ward, then, but not her husband. Most of her family was there, too, although her nephew, Yossel, was serving out his time as a conscript on occupation duty in Canada, and David, as usual, gave the Socialists a wide berth.

Flora was glad Yossel had been sent north rather than down to Houston. That was a running sore that would not heal. Hoover had made a mess of things there, but Flora had no idea what a Socialist president might have done to make things better.

When she came in, Herman Bruck boomed, "Let's all welcome Congresswoman Hamburger!" He turned red as a bonfire. "Congresswoman Blackford!" he said, blushing still. "But I knew her when she *was* Congresswoman Hamburger."

He had, too. It was twenty years now—and where had the time gone?—since she'd beaten him for the nomination to this seat when Myron Zuckerman, the longtime incumbent, fell down a flight of stairs and broke his neck. If that hadn't happened . . .

With a shake of her head, Flora tried to drive that thought out of her mind. It wasn't easy. The past couple of years, there'd been a spate of what people called "worlds of if" novels. If the USA had won the War of Secession or the Second Mexican War, if the Negro uprising had succeeded in the CSA, if the Red uprising had succeeded in Russia . . . If, if, if. Dealing with the world as it was was hard enough for most people. Flora didn't think the "worlds of if" fad would last.

Bruck turned on a wireless set. He got loud music, and then, as he turned the dial, a quiz show. A couple of young women perked up at that, but he kept changing stations till he found one that was giving election returns. "With the polls just closing in New York . . ." the announcer said. A burst of static squelched him.

Another station farther down the dial came in better. It was announcing early returns from Massachusetts. Cheers rang out in the Socialist headquarters when the broadcaster said Smith was leading Hoover three to two. The station switched to an interview with a Boston Democratic leader. "Doesn't look good for us heah," the man said in a gravelly, New England–accented voice. "Have to hope Smith and Borah don't drag the local candidates down too fah."

"Thank you, Mr. Kennedy," the interviewer said.

"Yes, thank you, Mr. Kennedy!" Maria Tresca said. She and Flora grinned at each other. The two of them had been friends for more than twenty years, too. It was partly a matter of living in a largely Jewish district, partly sheer luck, that Flora and not Maria had succeeded in politics.

As soon as Flora heard Al Smith was ahead in Massachusetts, she knew the night would belong to the Socialists. And so it proved. She handily won her own race; her Democratic opponent called before eleven o'clock to throw in the towel. That brought more cheers in the headquarters, though by then everyone was starting to get hoarse. The air was blue with cigarette, cigar, and pipe smoke, which helped make throats raw.

President Hoover's spokesman kept issuing statements along the lines of, "The current trend cannot be overlooked, but the president will not concede the election before he is sure his victory is impossible."

Herman Bruck pulled out a bottle of champagne, an upper-class touch for the party of the proletariat. He brought Flora a glass—not a fancy flute, but an ordinary water glass. "Here's to Hoover! His victory is impossible!" he said.

*"Alevai, omayn!"* Flora drank. The bubbles tickled her nose.

Bruck had a glass, too. "Did you ever imagine, when we first started here, we would win Powel House, lose it, and win it back?" he asked. "Did you ever imagine you would be First Lady?"

"Don't be silly." She shook her head. "How could I? How could anyone?"

He leaned forward and kissed her on the cheek. People all around them cheered. Flora laughed. She wasn't so sure Herman had done it just to congratulate her. He'd been sweet on her before she won her first election and went to Philadelphia, even if she hadn't been sweet on him. Now they'd both been married to other people for years. But he just smiled when she wagged a finger at him, and everyone else laughed and cheered some more. On a night full of victory, she didn't push it.

# VIII

"**H**appy New Year, darlin'!" Scipio said to Bathsheba. "Do Jesus! I was borned in slavery days, I don't never reckon I lives to see 1937."

His wife sighed. "Better be a happy year," she said darkly. "Last couple-three sure ain't."

"We is on our feets," Scipio said. "We gots a place again." The flat wasn't much worse than the one they'd lived in before white rioters torched so much of the Terry, and they weren't paying much more for it. Compared to so many people who were still living in churches or in tents, they were amazingly lucky. That they'd managed to bring their money out with them had helped a lot. Money usually did.

Bathsheba refused to look on the bright side of things. "What happens the next time the buckra decide they gots to go after all the niggers in town? Where we stay then?"

"Ain't been bad"—Scipio corrected himself—"ain't been *too* bad since."

"Bully!" In Bathsheba's mouth, the old-fashioned white man's slang sounded poisonously sarcastic.

"We gots to go on. We gots to do what we kin." Scipio knew he was trying to convince himself as well as her.

"Wish we could go somewheres else," his wife said.

"Like where?" Scipio asked. She had no answer. He knew she wouldn't. The United States had made it very plain they didn't want any Negroes from the Confederate States, no matter what happened to blacks in the CSA. The Empire of Mexico was farther away and even less welcoming. "We is stuck where we's at."

"Gots to be some way." Like most people, Bathsheba saw what she wanted to see, regardless of whether it was really there.

He didn't try to argue with her. They'd argued too much lately. She still hadn't stopped nagging him about who he was and who and what he had been. He gave short answers, knowing that the more he said, the more dangerous it was for him. Short answers didn't satisfy her. She wanted to know—she was convinced she had the right to know—where and how and why and when he'd learned to talk like an educated white man. As far as he was concerned, the less said, the better. Secrecy had become deeply ingrained in him since he came to Augusta. Only by keeping his past secret did he, could he, survive.

Neither of them stayed up long after midnight. They had planned to get out with the children on New Year's Day, but a cold, nasty rainstorm rolling down from the north put paid to that. Instead, they spent the day cooped up in the flat. They were all on edge, Scipio's son and daughter from disappointment at an outing spoiled, himself and his wife over worry about what the new year might bring.

It was still raining the next day: the sort of steady, sullen rain that promised to hang around for days. January second was a Saturday. The Huntsman's Lodge, which had been closed for New Year's, reopened. Scipio put on his formal clothes, then put a raincoat of rubberized cloth on over them. With that and an umbrella, he left the block of flats full of a relief he dared not show.

He had no trouble getting to the Lodge. Because of the rain, only people who had to be out and about were, and no one seemed in the mood to harass a Negro. Also, the raincoat concealed the fancy jacket, wing-collared boiled shirt, and satin-striped trousers he wore beneath it. Not standing out in the crowd undoubtedly helped.

Jerry Dover greeted him when he came in the door: "How are you, Xerxes? Happy New Year!"

"I thanks you, suh. De same to you," Scipio answered. With Dover, the work came first. If you could do it well, nothing else mattered. If you couldn't, nothing else mattered, either, and he would send you packing. But if you could do it, he would stand by you. Scipio respected that, and responded to it.

Today, though, Dover didn't seem happy. "Got a few words to say when the whole crew comes in," he told Scipio. "Won't take long."

Anything that broke routine was worrisome. "What de trouble be?" Scipio asked.

His boss shook his head. "I'll tell you soon. I don't want to have to do this more than once. You'll hear, I promise."

That convinced Scipio the news, whatever it was, wouldn't be good. He couldn't do anything about it but wait. Naturally, one of the other waiters chose that day to show up late. When he finally did come in, he was so hung over, he could barely see. "New Year's Eve night befo' last," somebody told him. He managed a sheepish grin, then took two aspirins from his pocket and dry-swallowed them.

"Listen, people, anybody see a paper the past couple days or listen to news on the wireless?" Jerry Dover asked.

None of the waiters and assistant cooks and dishwashers and janitors said anything. Scipio might have bought a *Constitutionalist* if rain hadn't kept newsboys off the street. He wasn't sure how many of the other Negroes in the crew could read. Wireless? Sets were cheap these days, but nobody here got rich at his job.

"No?" Dover shrugged. "All right. I suppose you heard about the colored fellow who took a shot at President Featherston at the Olympics." Again, nobody said anything. *Too bad he missed,* was what Scipio was thinking. His boss went on, "There's an order from the president that colored folks—all colored folks—have got to pay a fine to the government on account of that. And there's an order that anybody who's got colored folks working for him has to take twenty dollars out of their pay and send it to Richmond to make sure that fine gets paid. So that's what'll happen. I'm sorry, but I can't do a thing about it."

"Twenty dollars?" The pained echo rose from the throats of all the men there. Twenty dollars was a lot of money—a week's wages for the ones who made the most, two weeks' for the rest. Scipio cursed softly under his breath. A twenty-dollar hole in his budget wouldn't be easy to fill. Somebody asked, "How is we supposed to git by without that money?"

Jerry Dover spread his hands. "I can't answer that. All I can tell you is, I don't dare try to duck this, not with what they'll do to me if I get caught."

From a lot of men, that would have been a polite lie. Scipio believed the manager of the Huntsman's Lodge; Dover treated the black men who worked for him like human beings. "Mistuh Dover, suh!" he called.

"What is it, Xerxes?"

"Kin you dock we a dollar, two dollars, a week, so it don't hurt so bad?"

"Yeah!" Several other men spoke up. Others nodded. One of the assistant cooks said, "I buys everything on the installment plan. I should oughta pay this here fine the same way."

But Dover shook his head. "I would if I could, but I can't. The order says it's got to come out of your next pay. It's *supposed* to hurt. That's why they're doing it. I'm sorry, Xerxes. It was a good idea."

Dully, Scipio nodded. *It's supposed to hurt.* He'd known that from the minute the Freedom Party won in 1933. No, he'd known it from the moment he first heard Jake Featherston speak in a park here in Augusta, back when the Party was young and small. He asked, "Mistuh Dover, suh, what keep de gummint from takin' away anudder twenty dollar from we whenever dey please?"

Jerry Dover looked startled. He was, within his limits, a decent man. Plainly, that hadn't occurred to him. It hadn't occurred to some of Scipio's fellow workers, either, not by their horrified exclamations. And Dover proved his honesty, for he answered, "I'll be damned if I know."

The Huntsman's Lodge was a glum place that night. Some of the men who came to dine there wore Freedom Party pins on their lapels. Somehow or other, waiters contrived to spill hot or greasy food on several of them, or on their wives or girlfriends. The whites were furious. The Negroes were apologetic. So was Jerry Dover. "I'm sure it was an accident, sir," he said repeatedly. "We have a very fine staff here, but they are human."

*Freedom Party men don't want to believe that,* Scipio thought. He'd taken his tiny revenge on a man with one of those enamel pins on his tuxedo jacket. Cleaning the jacket wouldn't come cheap, but it wouldn't come to twenty dollars, either.

By contrast, two or three waiters found themselves with unusually large tips. The men who gave them might have been silently saying they didn't approve of collective fines. You could always tell when a man got an unexpected tip. He would straighten and smile in delighted surprise before he could catch himself. Scipio kept hoping he would find a sympathetic customer like that. He kept hoping, and he kept being disappointed.

When he left the Lodge at half past twelve, the rain was still coming down. He didn't mind. Fewer troublemakers, white or black, were on the streets in weather like this. So he thought, anyhow. And, indeed, no one troubled him. But he was going up the front steps of his apartment building when he heard gunfire from the white part of town. It wasn't just a pistol shot; it was a regular fusillade from several Tredegars. Back during the brief and bloody history of the Congaree Socialist Republic, he'd come to know the sound of military rifles much better than he ever wanted to. Some things you didn't forget, no matter how much you wished you could.

"What was that?" Bathsheba asked worriedly when he went inside.

"Dunno," he answered. That was technically true, but he had his suspicions—his fears.

So did his wife. "You reckon some niggers doin' somethin' stupid?" She sounded frightened, too. And she didn't know about the fine the government was levying.

"Wouldn't be surprised. We all be sorry if they is. That one nigger, he shoot at the president. . . ." He told her of the fine.

"Twenty dollars!" Bathsheba's anguish was painful to hear. She knew how much that was, how badly it would hurt their finances.

"Ain't nothin' I kin do about it," Scipio said. More gunfire burst out in the white part of Augusta: Tredegars again, and then the smaller answering pops of pistols. Black attackers and roused whites fighting back with whatever weapons they had handy, Scipio judged.

A moment later, a hard hammering made him shiver, even though it wasn't close. Somebody had a machine gun. He'd seen what such reaping machines of death could do. By the way the rifle fire suddenly slacked off, the machine gun didn't belong to the raiders.

Bathsheba's face was a mask of pain. She had to be thinking the same thing. "Them poor boys," she whispered. "Them poor boys gettin' all shot up."

Scipio nodded heavily. But his pain wasn't just for the raiders who'd bitten off more than they could chew. *Bitter as wormwood,* Revelations said. He understood that now, where he never had before. "Them damn fools give de buckra de excuse to come down on we even harder'n ever."

"How they come down on us harder'n they already doin'?" his wife asked.

"Suppose Georgia fine de niggers in de state? Suppose Augusta fine de niggers in de city? Richmond do it. Dey reckons dey kin do it, too, mebbe," Scipio said. Bathsheba flinched as if he'd hit her, then reluctantly nodded. With the Freedom Party in the saddle, anything was possible, anything at all. That was a big part of what made it so frightening.

Another Inauguration Day. Nellie Jacobs wondered how many she'd seen. She hadn't gone to all of them. Work, indifference, and war had kept her away at one time or another. This year, though, February first fell on a fine, bright Monday. The temperature got up close to fifty. It might almost have been spring. She decided to close the coffeehouse and go hear what Al Smith had to say.

She took Clara with her: the high school closed for the day. That her younger daughter, her accidental daughter, should be in high school still struck her as amazing, to say nothing of unnatural. Hadn't Clara been born just a few weeks ago? That was how it seemed to Nellie. But Clara was taller than she was. She'd grown up while Nellie wasn't looking.

She'd grown snippy while Nellie wasn't looking, too. "Do we have to go with Edna and Merle and Armstrong?" she said.

The last name was the problem. Clara and Armstrong Grimes had never got along, not since she was a toddler and he was a baby. She didn't want to have anything to do with him, and she wasn't shy about letting the world know as much, either.

"He's my only grandson, and Edna's my daughter just as much as you are, Miss Smarty-Britches, and Merle Grimes is a good man—and I don't say that about many men," Nellie answered. "So you'll come along and act polite, or you'll find out you're not too big for me to warm your backside."

One of these days, that kind of argument wouldn't work. She'd have a fight on her hands if she tried it. She remembered that from dealing— trying to deal—with Edna. She got by with it today, though. Clara might be snippy, but she wasn't ready to fight back hard yet.

Merle Grimes wore his Purple Heart. Edna had on her Order of Remembrance, Second Class. Nellie wished she'd worn her medal. She'd earned it, where Edna hadn't come close to deserving hers.

They got pretty good bleacher seats on the Mall in front of the Washington Monument. Nellie remembered when it had been blasted down to a stump. Now it stood tall again. All it needed were hieroglyphics carved on the sides to make it seem perfectly Egyptian.

Nellie endured the parade of soldiers and workers and bands. They weren't what she'd come to see or hear, though they entranced both Clara and Edna, and Merle tapped the tip of his cane up and down between his feet in time to the music. Armstrong also seemed bored with parades and bands, but Armstrong made a habit of seeming bored with everything, so Nellie wasn't sure what that meant.

She leaned forward when the big black limousine carrying Hoover and Smith and La Follette pulled up to the platform on which the new president and vice president would take the oath of office. She hadn't voted for Smith, but she wanted to hear what he had to say for himself.

Chief Justice Cicero Pittman probably hadn't voted for Al Smith, either. He was a Hoover appointee, replacing at last the fierce and venerable Oliver Wendell Holmes, who was a veteran of the War of Secession: he'd outlasted even George Custer in public life. Pittman was round and benign-looking, unlike the hawk-faced, piratically mustached Holmes.

Charlie La Follette took the vice-presidential oath first. No outgoing vice president congratulated him, for Hoover, having been elected as vice president himself, had no replacement when propelled to the presidency on Calvin Coolidge's death. Hoover did rise to shake Al Smith's hand. The atmosphere on the platform was what diplomats called correct: people who despised one another did their best to behave as if they didn't.

After Chief Justice Pittman administered the oath of office to President Smith, the jurist sat down. Smith stayed behind the forest of microphones that would send his words to the crowd and take them across the country by wireless. His unruly shock of black hair tried to deny that he was in his early sixties, but his jowls affirmed it.

"Workers and people of the United States, I thank you from the bottom of my heart for bringing me here today." Al Smith's voice was raspy and full of New York City. "I have a lot of work to do, and I am going to do it. It is the people's work, and none is more important." Applause washed over him. He seemed to grow a couple of inches taller when it did. Nellie had seen that before with other politicians; Teddy Roosevelt and Upton Sinclair had both been the same way.

"Some folks said that because I am a Catholic, that was the kiss of death for my chances." As was his way, Smith met the issue head-on. Scorn in his voice, he continued, "They used to say the same thing about any Socialist's chances. What *I* say is, no matter how thin you slice it, it's still baloney."

Nellie joined the startled laughter. Up on the platform, Al Smith grinned. They didn't call him the Happy Warrior for nothing. "And what I say is, you've heard a lot of baloney about what I'll do and what I won't, especially about our newest states." President—no, former President— Hoover squirmed in his seat. Smith went on, "Let's look at the record. The record shows we won the war and we took Houston and Kentucky away from our Confederate neighbors at gunpoint. We didn't ask the people who were living there what they thought. We just went ahead and grabbed with both hands. Now we're paying the piper on account of that."

Merle Grimes started tapping his cane again—this time, Nellie judged, in anger. She needed a moment to realize Smith hadn't said a word about Sequoyah. But it was full of Indians, so what difference did that make?

"We have to find some way to straighten things out there," Smith said. "I don't know yet what that will be, but I intend to work with President Featherston to learn. If I need to, I will go to Richmond to seek it out."

For a moment, that didn't get applause. It got nothing but astonished silence. No president of the United States had ever said anything like it, not in all the years since the Confederate States rammed secession down the USA's throat. The cheers it did get after that long, amazed beat were all the more fervent because of the preceding surprise.

Nellie didn't join in them. She had her own ideas about Confederates, and cozying up to them wasn't one of those ideas. From then on, she stopped listening. Armstrong said to Edna, "Granny's falling asleep," but that wasn't true. She just wasn't interested any more. She almost told him so—she almost told the obnoxious brat where to go and how to get there—but it didn't seem worth the effort.

Next thing she remembered, loud clapping made her jump, so maybe her grandson hadn't been as wrong as she'd thought. Smith was done. *Armstrong's still obnoxious, though,* she thought, looking around furtively to make sure no one had paid too much attention to her lapse. Her voice was louder and cheerier than it had to be when she said, "Well, let's go back to my place."

"All right, Ma." Edna, by contrast, sounded oddly gentle.

"Are you all right, Ma?" Clara asked.

"I'm fine," Nellie declared. Then she stood up too quickly, and felt dizzy for a moment. *Oh, for God's sake,* she thought, mortified. *They're all going to think I'm nothing but a little old lady.*

Merle Grimes steadied her with a strong hand on her elbow. "Don't worry, Mother Jacobs," he said. "We'll get you home just fine."

"Thank you, Merle," Nellie said. "You're a good son-in-law." Merle smiled. Armstrong made a face. Merle was good and strict with him, and didn't put up with any guff, the way Edna sometimes did.

When they went back to the coffeehouse above which Nellie had lived for so many years, Edna and Clara both crowded into the kitchen with her as she took a big frying chicken out of the icebox. "Why don't you let us give you a hand, Ma?" Clara said. Edna nodded.

"You can stick me in a rest home the day I don't know how to cut up a chicken and put it in hot fat," Nellie said tartly. Her daughters looked at each other and both started to laugh. With identical shrugs, they retreated.

And then, with almost the first cut she made, Nellie got her own hand on the web between thumb and forefinger. She said something she hadn't said since her days as a working girl. Armstrong was sitting closest to her. His head came up in astonishment. She glared at him, defying him to make something of it or even to believe he'd heard what he thought he had. He looked away in a hurry.

Satisfied, Nellie went back to work. She didn't even bother washing her hands, not that it would have done much good when she was still messing with chicken pieces. Once the chicken was dredged in cornmeal and sizzling in the fat, she did rinse off. The wound hadn't bled much. She forgot about it.

Everyone said the chicken was the best she'd ever made. She thought so, too. It turned out crisp and juicy and not a bit greasy. Clara and Edna insisted that they wash the dishes. Triumphantly full, Nellie let them.

When she woke up a couple of days later with a sore hand, she had trouble even remembering what she'd done to it. Only when she looked down and saw how red and angry the cut looked did she nod to herself and think, *Oh, that's right—the chicken.* Then she went on about her business, favoring the hand as much as she could.

Clara noticed when she came home from school. "You ought to take that to a doctor, Ma," she said. "It doesn't look so good."

"Oh, don't be silly," Nellie said. "It'll get better. Besides, who can afford doctors?"

But the hand didn't get better, and the next day she started feeling weak and hot and run-down. Real alarm in her voice, Clara said, "I'm going to get the doctor over here right now." Nellie started to tell her not to bother, but then didn't. She didn't feel up to it—and besides, Clara was already out the door.

The doctor looked Nellie over, listened to her heart, took her pulse, and took her temperature. "What is it?" Nellie asked, though she was too miserable to care much about the answer.

"It's 104.4, Mrs. Jacobs," he said reluctantly. "You have blood poisoning, I'm afraid. It could be . . . serious. Do you understand me?"

When Nellie nodded, the room spun. Even so, she said, "Of course I do." After a moment, she added, "And the coffee, and the raspberries . . ." Even she had no idea what that meant. She tried to laugh, but didn't seem to have the strength.

"What do we do?" Clara asked from a million miles away.

"Keep her comfortable. Aspirin, to fight the fever. Soup, water, juice—whatever she can keep down," the doctor answered, his voice even more distant. "If she beats the infection, she'll be fine." He didn't say what would happen if she didn't. Clara didn't ask. Neither did Nellie. She knew. Her body knew, even if the fever clouded her mind.

She remembered very little of the next few days—and less and less as the time went on. In that same dim way, that way beneath consciousness, she knew she was fading, but she'd already faded so far that she had trouble caring. Above her, people seemed to appear and disappear as she drifted in and out of the real world: Clara, Edna, Merle, Armstrong. She would blink, and one would turn to another. It might have been magic.

Once, though, when she saw Edna, she knew there was something she had to say. After a struggle, she found it: "Bill Reach." Forcing out the name took all the strength she had.

"What is it, Ma?" Tears glinted off Edna's cheeks.

"Bill Reach," Nellie repeated, and Edna nodded, so she'd understood. Fighting for every word, Nellie went on, "Killed him. Stuck him. *Fuck* him."

"What's she saying?" asked someone off to the side: Armstrong.

"She's delirious," Edna said. "There was this crazy man during the war—he was a spy, or something. Hal would've known for sure. But she thinks she killed him."

"Did," Nellie said, or tried to say, but no one seemed to pay her any mind. *Isn't that the way it goes?* she thought as lucidity ebbed for the last time. *Isn't that* just *the way it goes? You tell the truth, and no one believes you.*

She felt burning hot, and then cold as the South Pole, and then . . . nothing at all.

"**W**here do you have to go today?" Laura asked as Jonathan Moss threw on his overcoat and jammed a wool hat down low on his head. As usual, April in Berlin, Ontario, was spring by the calendar but not by what it was doing outside. The sun shone brightly, but it shone on drifted snow from the storm that had just blown through—and another snowstorm or two might yet follow on the heels of this one.

"London," he answered, gulping the hot tea she'd set in front of him. Whatever warmth he could seize now would be welcome.

Dorothy's eyes got big and round. "You're driving all the way to England, Daddy?" his daughter asked. She was four, an age that seemed startling but not necessarily impossible.

Moss laughed. "No, sweetie—just over to London, here in Ontario. If the roads aren't clear, though, it'll seem like it's as far as England." He kissed Dorothy and Laura and headed for the door.

"London," his wife said behind him. "That's where I used to go when I needed something they didn't have in Arthur."

To someone who'd grown up in Chicago, the idea of London, Ontario, as the big city was pretty funny. Jonathan Moss didn't say so. He knew the things that were likely to spark quarrels with his wife, and tried to steer clear of them. Too many quarrels started out of a clear blue sky for him to want to look for more. Instead, with a wave, he ducked out the door and was gone.

Snow plows had gone over the road that ran west from Berlin. Moss didn't care to think about what the rock salt the road crews had put down was doing to his undercarriage and his fenders, and so, resolutely, he didn't. He drove past the military airstrip outside of London and let out a nostalgic sigh. He hadn't flown an aeroplane since coming home from the Great War. Unlike a lot of fliers, he'd never had the urge. Now, though, it tugged at him.

Tug or no, though, meeting the urge would have to wait. He had a trial scheduled at occupation headquarters in London.

His client, one Morris Metcalfe, was accused of bribing the occupying authorities to look the other way while he did some black-market liquor dealing. Metcalfe was a cadaverous man with none of the bounce and energy Lou Jamieson displayed. Moss suspected he was guilty, but the military prosecutor didn't have a strong case against him.

Moss made that plain at every turn. At last, the prosecutor, a captain named Gus Landels, complained to the judge: "How can I show he's guilty if all his lawyer has to do is say he's innocent?"

"How can I show he's innocent if all you have to do is say he's guilty?" Moss retorted, and thought the shot went home.

In the middle of the afternoon, the judge, a lieutenant colonel who looked as if he'd seen far too many cases, pronounced Metcalfe not guilty. Captain Landels looked disgusted. The judge pointed a finger at Morris Metcalfe. He said, "My personal opinion is that there's more here than meets the eye. I can't prove that, and you're probably lucky I can't. But I won't be surprised if I see you in this court again, and if you don't get off so easy."

Metcalfe looked back out of dead-fish eyes. "I resent that, your Honor," he said—he'd spent enough time in U.S. courts to know and use the proper form of address.

"I won't lose any sleep over it," the judge replied. "Case dismissed—for now."

After a limp handshake, Metcalfe disappeared with hardly a word of thanks for Moss. Captain Landels, noting that, let out a derisive snort. Moss shrugged. His only worry was extracting the balance of his fee from Metcalfe. But he thought he could do it. Like the judge, he believed the other man would need his services again before too long.

He went out to reclaim his Ford from the secure lot where he'd parked it—like Berlin, London had one. He was starting back to his home town when a flight of five fighting scouts—just plain fighters, they were calling them nowadays—zoomed down to land at the field outside of London.

He almost drove off the road. A block later, he *did* drive off the road—down a side street, toward the airstrip. Those lean, low-winged shapes drew him as a lodestone draws nails. They were as different from the machines he'd flown in the Great War as a thoroughbred was from a donkey. He tried to imagine what one of them would have done to a squadron of his kites. It would have knocked down the whole squadron without getting scratched; he was sure of that.

The rifle-toting guards at the airstrip weren't inclined to let him enter. His U.S. identification card finally persuaded them, though one rode along to escort him to the commandant's office. He caught a break there. The man in charge of the field, Major Rex Finley, had served in Ontario during the war. "I remember you," Finley said. "I was at the party after you made ace. You'd forgotten it was your fifth kill."

"That's me," Moss agreed cheerfully. "I'd forget my own head if my wife didn't nail it on me every morning."

Finley chuckled. "I know the feeling. Well, what can I do for you, Mr. Moss?" He bore down on Moss' civilian title.

"I saw the new fighters coming in for a landing," Moss said. "They're . . . quite something."

"The new Wright 27s? I should say so." Finley rubbed at his mustache, a thin strip of dark hair clinging tight to his upper lip. "And?"

"Could I sit in one?" The naked longing in Moss' voice startled even him. He hadn't felt anything like that since he'd fallen for Laura Secord long before she fell for him. "Please?"

Major Finley frowned. "I shouldn't. It's against about half a pound of regulations, and you know it as well as I do." Moss didn't say anything. He'd done all the pleading he could do if he wanted to keep his self-respect. The field commandant made a fist and smacked it into his other hand. "Come on. Officially, you know, you don't exist. You were never here. Got it?"

"Who, me?" Moss said. Finley laughed.

They walked out to the airstrip together. Major Finley said, "I've heard you spend your time getting Canucks off the hook."

To Moss' relief, he sounded curious, not hostile. "I do try," the lawyer answered. "It needs doing. Even if you lost the war, you need decent representation. Maybe you especially need it if you lost the war."

Sandbagged machine-gun nests protected the field. The soldiers in them looked very alert. Pointing to one of those nests, Finley said, "I'd be happier about having somebody representing the damn Canucks if all of 'em were convinced they *had* lost the damn war. But we both know it isn't so. That bomb over in Manitoba, and the big one in your town a couple of years ago . . ."

"Oh, yeah," Moss said. "That one almost caught me. Still, don't you think things would be worse if the Canadians decided the whole system was rigged against them?"

Shrugging, Finley answered, "Damned if I know. But then, they don't pay me to worry about politics—which is all to the good, far as I'm concerned."

Moss only half heard him. By then, they'd come up to the closest Wright 27. The air above the engine mount still shimmered with released heat. Two machine guns on this side of the mount fired through the prop; Moss assumed there were two more on the far side. He'd never flown an aeroplane that carried more than two machine guns. With four, he would have felt like the Grim Reaper in the sky. And yet he knew the armament was nothing out of the ordinary these days.

"You never piloted a machine that wasn't canvas and wire, did you?" Rex Finley asked, setting an affectionate hand on the blue-painted aluminum skin of the wing.

"Nope," Moss answered. "Started out in a Curtiss Super Hudson pusher, ended up in our copy of Kaiser Bill's Albatros. This is all new to me. Looks like a shark with wings. All you'd need to do would be to paint eyes and a mouth full of teeth on the front end."

"Not a half bad idea," Finley said. "Well, go on up."

The fighter, Moss discovered, had a mounting stirrup just in front of the left wing. He used the stirrup to climb up onto the wing. The aeroplane rocked under his weight. If he'd climbed onto the wing of one of the aeroplanes he'd flown in the Great War, though, odds were he would have stuck his foot straight through the doped fabric. The Wright 27 had a closed cockpit, for better streamlining and because the wind at the high speeds at which it flew would have played havoc with a pilot's vision, goggles or no. After some fumbling, Moss found the latch and slid back the canopy.

"Good thing I haven't got fat, or I'd never fit in here," he remarked as he settled himself in the seat.

Major Finley slammed the canopy shut above him. The cockpit smelled of leather and sweat and oil. Its being closed made it feel even more cramped than it really was. The instrument panel bristled with dials. Along with the altimeter, compass, airspeed indicator, inclinometer, and fuel gauge he was used to, instruments monitored engine performance in a dozen different ways, ammunition supply, propellor pitch, and the electrical system. The machine also boasted a wireless set, which had its own profusion of dials. *You'd need to go to college all over again to understand what half this stuff does,* Moss thought dizzily.

But the essentials hadn't changed. There was the stick, and there was the firing button on top of it. His right thumb found that button with unconscious ease. The gunsight in the fighter made what he'd used during the Great War seem a ten-cent toy by comparison.

He jerked when Finley rapped on the thick—armored?—glass with his knuckles. The base commandant gestured to show he should get out. With an odd reluctance, he nodded. Finley pushed back the canopy. Moss felt like a sardine getting out of its can as he extracted himself.

"What do you think?" Finley asked.

"That's . . . the cat's meow, all right." Moss hesitated, then plunged: "Any chance I could . . . fly it?"

"When was the last time you flew?" the officer inquired.

Moss wished he could lie, but judged that would make things worse, not better. With a sigh, he told the truth: "Not long after the Great War ended."

Rex Finley nodded. "About what I figured—and I would have kicked you off my field if you'd tried to tell me it was week before last. If you're going to take another stab at it, I want you to put in some time on trainers before you smash up a Wright machine. Even a trainer nowadays is a hotter crate than anything you've ever flown."

"I'll do that," Moss said at once. "Jesus, you bet I will. I figured you'd say you didn't want anything to do with me."

"Nope. You were an ace. You knew what you were doing up there," Finley said. "With any luck at all, you can find it again. And you know what? One of these days, we're liable to need more people like you again. Or do you think I'm wrong?" Moss wished he could have said yes, but that too would have been a lie.

After her time in Paris and Richmond—especially after her time in Paris—Anne Colleton found St. Matthews, South Carolina, much too small and confining. She did what she could to fight the feeling by making forays into Columbia and Charleston, but that helped only so much. She had to come back to the flat where she'd lived since Red Negroes almost killed her on the Marshlands plantation.

The Confederate government—or maybe it was the Freedom Party—had paid the rent on the flat while she was abroad. She hadn't had to put her worldly goods into storage and then exhume them when she took up her life in St. Matthews again. That was something, anyhow. Something . . . but not enough.

In Paris, she'd haggled over alliances and foreign affairs in her fluent French. In St. Matthews, people talked about the weather and crops and what they'd heard on the wireless the night before. But for the talk about the wireless, Anne had grown up on such conversation. It seemed all the more stifling now.

When her brother came over to visit one warm, muggy afternoon in late May, she burst out, "If I hear one more word about tractors and combines and harvesters, the loudmouth who says that word is going to be awfully sorry."

Tom Colleton shrugged. "Sorry, Sis," he said. "That stuff is important here. It's important all over the CSA."

"It's *boring*," Anne replied with great sincerity. "All the yahoos bragging about the fancy equipment they've got . . . They don't get that excited about the equipment in their drawers, for Christ's sake."

Her brother turned red. "You can't talk like that around here," he said, and then, before she could further scandalize him by asking why not, he went on, "Besides, tractors and such-like *are* important. You notice how many niggers have been coming through town lately?"

"I should say I have," Anne answered. "One more reason to keep guns where I can get at them in a hurry."

"Yeah, I know. Theft is up. That's a problem," Tom said. "But those niggers are sharecroppers who don't have work any more because the machinery's doing it instead of them. We don't need nearly so many people tied down to the land as we did when the Great War started."

Anne started to say, *And so?* Then she remembered that pushing hard for farm machinery was part of Featherston's program.

Before she could remark on that, Tom said, "I don't know what the towns'll do if all the niggers from the countryside stream into them at once. Do you know? Does the president?"

"If he does, he isn't telling me," Anne said.

"No? Too bad. He'd make a lot of friends if he came out and said what he has in mind. This is liable to hurt him when elections come around this fall."

That made Anne smile. She couldn't help herself. "Do you think anything will get in the way of the Freedom Party at election time? Anything at all?"

Her brother's face was a study in astonishment. "But there've always been elections," he said.

"The Freedom Party is in." Anne might have been an adult reproving a child's naïveté. "It's going to stay in till it gets where it's going and the Confederate States get where they're going."

"Christ!" Tom said. "I don't think I much care for that."

"Tom . . ." Now Anne spoke urgently, warning him against disaster. "Do you realize how big a chance you're taking saying that even to me? If you say it to somebody else—and it could be somebody you trust—you're liable to end up in more trouble than you've ever imagined."

Tom Colleton started to say something else. Very visibly, he changed his mind. But he couldn't let it go. He asked, "And you work with these people? You work for these people?" By the way he looked at her, he might have been seeing her for the first time.

But Anne didn't hesitate before she nodded. "I sure do," she said. "Because they're going to take the CSA where I want us to go—right back up to the top."

"I'd sooner—" Her brother caught himself again. His face twisted. "All right, Sis. I'll shut up. If I talk too goddamn much, I'm liable to end up in a camp with a big P stenciled on the back of my shirt. Isn't that right?"

She winced. "Not if you're talking to me."

"That isn't what you said a minute ago."

"I just wanted to remind you that you need to be careful. And you do."

"Because if I'm not careful, I *will* end up in a camp." That was statement, not question. Tom paused to light a cigarette. After a couple of long, angry puffs, he added, "If that's where the Freedom Party is taking the country, to hell with me if I want to go along. Am I a nigger? Or am I a white man who can stand up on his hind legs and speak his mind if he wants to?"

"We've all got to give up something if we're going to get revenge on the USA," Anne said soothingly. "The Yankees put up with keeping quiet and doing what they were told and standing in line for rationed goods for thirty years so they could get even with us."

The coal on that cigarette glowed a fierce, fiery red when Tom took another drag. Smoke fumed from him as he replied, "They didn't give up elections, did they? They didn't stop talking when they felt like talking. Even during the war, the Socialists were telling the Democrats to go to the devil. You should've heard some of the mouthy prisoners we caught up in Virginia."

"Yes, they had elections," Anne said. "They had them, but how much did they matter? From the Second Mexican War up till they licked us in the Great War, the Democrats won every single time. So they had them. They kept people happy with them. But the elections didn't really *count*. Maybe the Freedom Party will keep on doing that, so people will stay happy. I don't know. The Whigs here did."

"And when the Whigs lost, they got out of office and handed things over to Featherston, the way they were supposed to." Tom stubbed out the cigarette, then lit another one. "If the Freedom Party loses, will it do the same?"

*No,* Anne thought. She decided she didn't want to be that blunt, so she answered, "I don't see the Freedom Party losing any time soon. People have work where they didn't before. I was in Richmond for the Olympics. I saw what a hit they were. People are proud again. They *want* to vote Freedom."

Before the war, Tom had been content, even eager, for her to do his thinking for him. He wasn't any more. He was his own man now. Through the haze of tobacco smoke around him—he might have been putting up a smoke screen—he said, "You didn't answer my question."

*I know I didn't. You weren't supposed to notice.* Anne said, "I don't think the Freedom Party will lose an election for quite a while—not one that's really important to it, anyway—except maybe in Louisiana, and that hardly counts."

It still wasn't a direct answer. It seemed to come close enough. Tom said, "All Featherston needs is a crown, like the one the Emperor of Mexico wears."

"Think whatever you want," Anne said wearily. "You care about your family, though. Be careful where you shoot off your mouth. Please."

"Why? Don't you have dear old Jake wrapped around your finger?"

Anne's lips skinned back from her teeth in what was anything but a smile. At that, the question could have been worse; at least he'd asked about her finger and not some other part of her anatomy. She had to hide a small shiver as she answered, "Don't be stupid, Tom. Anybody who's ever tried to get Jake Featherston to do what he wants—or what she wants—has ended up either sorry or dead. And before you ask, I think it's more luck than anything else that I'm still here."

More than her words, she thought, her tone got through to Tom. His eyes, blue as her own, went wide. He blurted, "Sweet Jesus Christ, Anne, you're scared to death of him!"

"Anybody who's met him and who isn't is a fool," she said. "Standing up against him is like standing up to a hurricane. You can yell and scream and fight and carry on, but he'll blow you over just the same."

He laughed. She'd known he would, and she'd known why. Sure enough, he said, "That's how people talk about you, you know."

"Oh, yes." She waved the words aside for now; she'd assess the hurt later. For the time being, she wanted to make sure she was understood: "But he's . . . he's *serious* about things. He's serious *all* the time. And what he wants, happens. I don't always know how it does, but it does. Think about it. The Whigs had run things here for as long as the Confederate States were a country. If *they* couldn't stop Jake Featherston—and they damned well couldn't—what can? Nothing. Nobody."

Tom Colleton shook his head in disbelief. "You talk about him like he really is a hurricane. He's just a man, Sis."

Anne shook her head, too. "Oh, he's a man, all right. He sleeps. He eats. He goes to the toilet." That jerked a startled laugh out of her brother. She went on, "He'll die one of these days. If that nigger had shot him at the Olympics, he'd've died right then. But as long as he's alive, he's not *just* a man. For a long time, I thought he was, too. So did a lot of people. Look what's happened since. We were wrong, every single one of us."

Another cigarette out of the pack. The scrape and flare of another match. The harsh stink of sulfur before the mellower smell of tobacco smoke. Tom blew a smoke ring up toward the ceiling, maybe to give himself time to think. He said, "I never reckoned anybody could make you talk like that."

"Did you think I did?" she flared. "But Jake *does* make me talk that way. And you'd better be careful how you talk, too. If you do anything stupid, I can't protect you. Have you got that? *I can't.* Featherston and the stalwarts will do whatever they want. Oh, he might listen to me if I beg hard enough. He might. I've done some useful things for him, and he might throw me a bone. But I walked away from the Freedom Party once, remember? I thought he was finished, and I went back to the Whigs. He never forgets something like that. He might use you to pay me back, too. Don't give him the chance. Please."

Had she ever said *please* to him before? Oh, she'd said it. She must have. Everybody did, for politeness' sake. But had she ever meant it the way she had twice in the past five minutes? She didn't think so. Children meant *please*, especially when they got into trouble. Usually, grownups didn't have to.

Her desperate urgency must have got through to her brother. He put out the latest cigarette—by now, the ashtray was full of butts—and got to his feet. "All right," he said. "I'll keep quiet. But it's not for your sake. It's for Bertha and the kids."

"I don't care why. Just do it," Anne said. He left the flat without another word. She thought he'd slam the door, but he didn't. The restraint was worse. It felt like a slap in the face. She wondered if they would ever have anything to say to each other again.

Lucien Galtier looked up at the sky. The sun was sliding down toward the northwest, but it wouldn't set for a long time yet. When summer days came to the country by Rivière-du-Loup, they lasted. Long days meant short nights. He'd always thought that was good. It let him get more work done and spend more time with his family. Now . . . Now, suddenly, he wondered.

Oh, the work went on. He couldn't imagine the work stopping altogether. If the work stopped, wasn't that a sure sign he was dead? He could still do the work, too. He took a certain somber pride in that. True, he wasn't young any more. But he was still strong. Thinking about that made him laugh.

He was walking back from weeding the potato plot, hoe on his shoulder like a soldier's rifle, when an auto came up the track from the road toward his farmhouse. He picked up the pace, like a soldier going from ordinary march to double time. That machine belonged to the O'Doulls.

Sure enough, his son-in-law got out of the motorcar and stood there waiting for him. "A good day to you!" Galtier called to Dr. Leonard O'Doull. "And what brings you here?"

"What brings me here?" O'Doull patted the iron flank of the motorcar. "My automobile, what else?"

"Thank you so much." Lucien unshouldered the hoe and made as if to swing it, like a soldier starting bayonet drill. "Let me ask the question another way, then: why have you come here?"

"Oh! Why?" What he meant might not have occurred to Dr. O'Doull before. Galtier didn't believe that for a moment, but his son-in-law played the role of a suddenly enlightened one well. "I had some business at the hospital"—he pointed to the big building the U.S. Army had run up on Galtier's land during the war—"and I thought I would stop by as long as I was so close."

"Good. I'm glad you did. Come inside, if you like. We can have a little something to drink, smoke a cigar—with an afternoon's weeding behind me, I could use a cigar, and I could truly use a drink."

His son-in-law laughed. "Motion carried by acclamation, without a dissenting voice."

Lucien stowed the hoe in the barn. He and Leonard O'Doull went into the house through the door that led to the kitchen. Galtier knew the place wasn't so clean and neat as it had been when Marie was alive. All he could do was hope she wouldn't have been too displeased with the way he kept it up. He busied himself pouring a couple of glasses of applejack, and handed one to the American who'd married Nicole.

*"Merci beaucoup."* Dr. O'Doull reached into a jacket pocket and took out two cigars. He gave one to Galtier. "Here you are. I delivered a baby boy yesterday. These are part of the reward from the father."

"I thank you. I thank him. Come—let's go into the front room." When they'd sat down, when they had the cigars going, Lucien raised his glass of homemade Calvados. *"Salut!"* he said, and drank.

So did O'Doull. After a good swig, he whistled softly. "Son of a bitch," he said in English, a tongue he used these days only when taken by surprise. He sipped again, more cautiously, and returned to French: "Potent stuff."

"Yes, a strong batch," Lucien agreed. Quality varied wildly from one jug to the next, as was only to be expected when people made the stuff in small stills with no tedious government regulations or even more tedious taxes. "Strong, but good. So . . . How wags your world?"

"Well enough, if I didn't set fire to my liver there," Leonard O'Doull replied. "For myself, for Nicole and little Lucien, all is well, as I hope it is for you."

"As you say, well enough." Galtier puffed on the cigar. He'd had better. Whoever the new father was, he was a cheapskate. He paused. "All is well for your family, you say, which is good. All is not so well some-where else?" He wasn't sure he'd heard that in the doctor's voice, but thought he had.

And O'Doull nodded. "I am not nearly so sure I like the direction in which I see the world headed."

Galtier tried to make sense of that. "What man ever does?"

"*Non, mon beau-père,* not like that," O'Doull said. "Not the little thoughts that make a man wonder if he is all he should be. When I say the world, I mean . . . the world." His expansive gesture not only took in the whole world, it nearly knocked over a lamp on the table next to the sofa where he sat. Maybe the applejack was hitting hard and fast. Maybe, too, he did have something big on his mind.

"And what of the world?" Lucien Galtier asked. "Most of it goes its way far from here. When I remember how things were when that was not so, I think this is not so bad. I can do without soldiers and bombs and such things on my doorstep. That ambulance driver I saw, poor fellow, wounded in his very manhood . . ." He shuddered and sipped again from his own drink.

"If you will recall, though, helping the wounded is why I first came to Quebec." O'Doull picked up his glass. Instead of drinking, he stared at the pale yellow apple brandy. "I have been comfortable here for many years, forgetting the world and by the world forgot. But I fear one day I may have to go back to my proper craft, healing the wounded once more."

"Here? In Quebec?" Lucien shook his head. "I do not believe it."

"Nor I," O'Doull replied with a sweet, sad smile. "But the world, poor thing, is wider than Quebec, and wilder, too, worse luck. And I am a doctor, and I am an American, and if my country should ever need me in another war—"

"God forbid!" Galtier broke in, and crossed himself.

"Yes. God forbid." Leonard O'Doull nodded. "So the world said in 1914. But God did not forbid. And so, if He should happen to be watch-ing a football match again . . ." Lucien laughed at the delicious blas-phemy. His son-in-law was not in a laughing mood. O'Doull went on, "If that happens, how could I stay quiet here, attending to cases of measles and rheumatism? That would be a waste of everything for which I trained."

The worst part of it was, what he said made sense to Galtier. Soberly—in spite of the applejack—the farmer said, "All I can tell you is, may this not come to pass."

"Yes. May it not, indeed." O'Doull knocked back the rest of his drink. After he got over the coughing fit that followed—the stuff was too strong for such cavalier treatment—he said, "Thank you for letting me share my darkness with you."

"*C'est rien,*" Lucien replied. "And it is nothing because who but you saw *my* darkness not so long ago?" *Who but you caused it?* he thought. But that wasn't fair, and he knew as much. O'Doull had only diagnosed the trouble Marie already had.

"Between the *Action Française* and the Freedom Party and the Silver Shirts in England, the world is a nastier place than it was ten years ago," O'Doull said. "And in Russia, the Tsar seems to think the Jews cause all his problems, and no one seems to want to stay in Austria-Hungary except the Austrians and the Hungarians, and even the Hungarians are not so sure. And the Turks treat the Armenians as the Russians treat the Jews, and—"

"And you Americans hold down English-speaking Canada." Galtier hadn't expected to say that. It just popped out. He wondered if his son-in-law would be offended.

But Leonard O'Doull only nodded. "Yes. And that. Small next to some of the others, I believe, but no less real even so." He got to his feet. "And now I had better leave. If you ask me to have another drink, I'll say yes, and then I'll be too drunk to go back to Rivière-du-Loup, and Nicole will be unhappy with me—and with you." He gave a curiously old-fashioned bow, then made his way to the door, and to his motorcar.

Galtier wasn't going anywhere that night. He made himself another drink, and poured it all down. Maybe it helped him go to sleep. After O'Doull's dark fantasies, he needed all the help he could get.

When Sunday came, he drove into Rivière-du-Loup to hear Mass. As he'd got into the habit of doing the past few months, he stopped at Éloise Granche's house to give her a ride into town. "*Bonjour,* Lucien," she said as he opened the passenger-side door of the Chevrolet for her. "You look very handsome today."

"I thank you . . . for not buying new spectacles any time lately," he replied. She laughed. He went on, "Now, I do not need spectacles of any sort to know what a pretty woman I am lucky enough to have with me."

"How you do go on," she said, but indulgently.

When they got to the church, Éloise saw some lady friends and went to chat with them. Lucien sat in the bosom of his family. Nothing could have been more decorous. Nicole said, "How nice that you were able to bring Mme. Granche again." Lucien nodded. The service started a moment later.

After taking communion, Galtier led Éloise Granche back to his auto. As they'd driven north, so they went south. When he stopped by the house, she said, "Would you care to come in for a cup of tea?"

"Thank you. I'd like that. I can't stay long, though," he replied.

They went inside. Everything was quiet and peaceful—and dark, for Éloise had no electricity. She turned. Lucien took her in his arms. A moment later, they were holding each other and kissing and murmuring endearments, for all the world as if they were a couple of youngsters discovering love for the very first time.

Laughing, exulting in his strength, Lucien lifted her into his arms and carried her upstairs to the bedroom. "Be careful!" Éloise exclaimed. "You'll hurt yourself." He laughed some more. She said that every time. He hadn't hurt himself yet, and didn't seem likely to. And the soft feel of her made the way his heart pounded till he gently set her on the bed seem altogether worthwhile.

Before too long, his heart was pounding again, from an even more pleasurable exertion. "Oh, Lucien!" Éloise gasped, urging him on. Her nails dug into his back. "So sweet," she murmured, eyes half closed. "*So* sweet."

Afterwards, he gave her a kiss as he lay beside her. His heart was still drumming, harder than it would have when he was a younger man. He had more trouble catching his breath, too, than he would have when he and Marie were newlyweds.

"One of these days," he said, "we should have Father Guillaume say the words over us."

Women were supposed to be the ones who wanted such things, but Éloise shook her head, as she had several times before. "Not necessary," she said. "Better if he doesn't, in fact. It would only complicate matters with both our families. If we marry, it turns into a question of patrimonies. If we don't, then this is . . . what it is, that's all. I like it better this way."

Lucien set a hand on his chest and mimed complete exhaustion. "I don't think I could like it better than this," he said. Éloise laughed again. They laughed a lot when they were alone together. Neither one of them had done much laughing for a long time before. And that, to Lucien, mattered almost as much as the other.

Cincinnatus Driver wasn't an old man. No one—except his son, of course—could have accused him of being an old man. He was strong. His hair was—mostly—dark. He remained three years on the good side of fifty. None of that, though, had kept him from turning into a grandfather.

Karen Driver wiggled in his arms. He was getting used to holding a baby all over again. Karen weighed no more than a big cat, which is to say, nothing to speak of. He was getting used to the way she looked, too.

Her skin was lighter than his, but not quite the coffee-with-cream color of Negroes with a fair amount of white blood. She had her mother's narrow eyes with the folds of skin at the inner corners, too.

"She's going to be beautiful," Cincinnatus said. "She's *already* beautiful."

"Thank you," Grace Driver said softly. Cincinnatus and Elizabeth had accepted her more readily than her folks accepted Achilles. The child helped and hurt at the same time. The Changs did love the baby, but Grace's mother blamed her for not having a boy . . . among other things.

Karen stopped wiggling, screwed up her little face, and grunted. Cincinnatus laughed. He had no trouble remembering what that meant. He handed her to her mother. "She done made a mess in her drawers," he said. He was just Karen's granddad. He didn't have to clean her up himself.

"I'll take care of her," Grace said, and changed the baby's diaper.

Cincinnatus turned to his son. "How you doin'?" he asked.

"I'm all right," Achilles answered, more of Iowa than of Kentucky in his accent. Cincinnatus knew his son would have said the same thing if he were living on the street and eating what he could fish out of garbage cans. Achilles had his own full measure of the family's stubbornness. But he wasn't on the street; he continued, "That clerking job of mine isn't what you'd call exciting, but I can pay my bills. I won't get rich, but I'm doing fine."

"Good. That's good." Cincinnatus had been on his own when he was younger than Achilles was now, but he hadn't had to worry about a family then. And a young black in Confederate Kentucky hadn't had the hopes and dreams of one in U.S. Iowa. Cincinnatus had been brutally sure he wouldn't, couldn't, get very far ahead of the game. Achilles could aspire to more. He might not get it, but if he didn't he'd have to blame himself as well as the system under which he lived. Down in the CSA, the system gave any Negro an easy excuse for failure.

"Let me have my grandbaby," Elizabeth said, and reached for Karen. Elizabeth took to being a grandmother with none of the doubts about age and the like that troubled Cincinnatus. And Karen fascinated Amanda, who at fourteen was plenty old enough to help take care of her niece.

"How you doin' with your folks these days?" Cincinnatus asked Grace.

Before she could answer, Achilles said, "Well, her daddy hasn't called me a nigger, but he sure has come close."

"I didn't ask how *you* was doin' with Mr. Chang," Cincinnatus said sharply. "I asked how Grace was."

"It is still hard," she answered. "It is still very hard, like Achilles said.

My father and especially my mother are not modern people. They think of China all the time. They don't think we are all Americans. They don't think we are all the same."

Achilles stirred at that. "Pa doesn't think we're all the same, either. He thinks colored people are down at the bottom of the pile."

"That ain't so," Cincinnatus said.

"The . . . heck it isn't," Achilles retorted.

"No." Cincinnatus shook his head. "I never said that, and I don't believe it. What I say is, white folks reckon black folks is on the bottom o' the pile. An' that's the Lord's truth. If you was old enough to recollect what it was like livin' in Kentucky when it belonged to the Confederate States, you'd know it, too."

"But we aren't in the Confederate States any more," Achilles pointed out.

"But white folks is still white folks." That wasn't Cincinnatus; it was Elizabeth. The two older people thought as one on this question. If anything, Elizabeth was more cautious about rocking the boat than her husband.

Grace's smile was sad. She held up a hand to stop Achilles when he would have come back with a hot answer. That hand *did* stop him, too, as Cincinnatus noted with surprise and more than a little respect. She said, "My parents sound the same about this. But times have changed. If times hadn't changed, would Achilles and I be together?"

"Times has changed—some," Cincinnatus said. "They ain't changed enough. You look at the black folks runnin' away from the Confederate States. You look at how the USA don't let 'em cross the border. President Hoover, President Smith, that don't matter—it don't change. The USA don't want nothin' to do with us, an' that's how come I say things ain't changed enough."

He waited to see how Grace would respond to that. She shrugged and said, "Maybe." He wondered what that was supposed to mean. Probably that he hadn't convinced her, but she was too polite to say so. She didn't always come out and say what she thought. Cincinnatus had already noticed that.

He asked, "You going to visit your folks while you're here? Only one flight up."

Grace shook her head. "Not much point. They don't want to see us."

"Don't they want to see their grandbaby?" Cincinnatus pointed to Karen.

His son answered: "I'm not Chinese. I'm just a spook." His voice was harsh and cold.

"That's not quite fair," Grace said. "They wouldn't like it if you were white, either."

"Well, maybe not," Achilles admitted. "They don't quite hate me, the way I've seen some white men do. They can make themselves be polite. I even used to think they were pretty nice, till the two of us started getting serious. But they sure don't want you to be married to me, and the baby hasn't made 'em change their minds about that."

His wife sighed. "I know. It's sad. They came to America to find a better life than they could have had in China. They got one, too. But they're still Chinese first and American afterwards."

"We came here to Iowa to get a better life, too," Cincinnatus said. "I'm glad I'm livin' in the United States and not in the Confederate States no more—'specially nowadays. God help the poor niggers in the CSA nowadays."

Achilles and Grace left a little later. Cincinnatus walked to the stairway with them, hoping they would change their mind and go upstairs to visit the Changs after all. But they didn't. They went down to the street, carrying the baby with them. He sighed and went back to the apartment. Elizabeth's raised eyebrows asked a question. Cincinnatus shook his head.

His wife sighed. "That's so sad, they cut off from half their family. Don't seem right. Don't seem right at all. You ain't got family, you ain't got nothin'."

"And the baby's so *cute*," Amanda said. "How can you not love a little baby?"

Cincinnatus smiled. "You love everybody, honey." That was true. Amanda was a sweet-natured child. Because she liked almost everyone, she thought everybody should like everybody else. And if all the people in the world had been like her, everybody would have. Sooner or later, though, she would have to realize not everyone worked the way she did. Cincinnatus hoped she wouldn't get hurt too badly finding that out.

Elizabeth said, "I reckon Grace's folks love the baby, all right. The one they got trouble with is your brother."

Not even Amanda believed everybody ought to love Achilles. *She* loved him, yes, but sometimes even she had to work at it. Especially when she was smaller, he'd sometimes made her life miserable, as an older brother was only too likely to do with a younger sister.

The next morning, Cincinnatus gulped an extra cup of coffee before he hit the road. He stopped on the way to the railroad yards to buy a copy of the *Herald-Express*. As usual, he read the paper in snatches at stop signs and traffic lights, and not for the front-page stories but for the ones on the inside pages, the stories the editors—and most people in Des Moines—didn't think were so important.

Who in Des Moines, for instance, got excited about a page-three story whose headline said KENTUCKY STATE POLICE DISBANDED? Kentucky had rejoined the USA before Houston had, and had been much less troublesome. But the Freedom Party had done very well in the last elections there, and this was the result.

How many comfortable Iowans knew the Kentucky State Police might better have been called the Kentucky Secret Police? The Kentucky State Police had been the instrument the USA used to make sure the state stayed loyal to Philadelphia. Cincinnatus knew Luther Bliss, the head of the outfit, all too well. Just thinking of Bliss' light brown eyes, the color of a hunting dog's, was enough to make him break out in a cold sweat. He'd spent a couple of years in prison on account of the Kentucky State Police.

And now they were disbanding? Cincinnatus whistled softly. "Do Jesus!" he muttered. "Who hold that state down?" And what would happen to their longtime head, who'd spent a generation stomping on everything the Freedom Party stood for? Would the new winners in Kentucky hang him from a lamp post?

Cincinnatus got his answer to that in the very next paragraph. *State Police Chief Luther Bliss,* the story said, *is on a fact-finding trip to Pennsylvania, and was unavailable for comment.* When Cincinnatus saw that, he chuckled grimly. Bliss was either lucky or—giving him credit no less real for being reluctant—sly to have escaped Kentucky when his foes grabbed hold of the reins.

*President Smith is conferring with the Secretary of War and the Secretary of the Interior about the present situation in Kentucky,* the story continued. *A statement from Philadelphia is expected within the next few days.*

Would the U.S. government send more troops to Kentucky to force the state to rescind what it had done? Or would it send enough soldiers to hold things down without the Kentucky State Police? The only thing Cincinnatus couldn't imagine the administration doing was nothing. After all, Kentucky's southern border was also the USA's southern border these days.

Behind Cincinnatus, a horn blared. He jumped and put the truck in gear. He'd been reading and woolgathering while traffic piled up. He would have honked, too, if someone else did something like that.

He didn't get to finish the story, then, till he stopped at another red light. When he did, ice ran through him, for the last sentence read, *Governor Ruby Laffoon pledges to make good on a campaign promise to explore a plebiscite on whether Kentucky should belong to the United States or to the Confederate States.*

"They can't do that!" Cincinnatus exclaimed. He hoped they couldn't, anyhow. His father and mother still lived in Covington. If the Stars and Bars replaced the Stars and Stripes . . . He shivered, though the day was warm and muggy, even so early in the morning. "Got to git them out o' there." For Negroes, what nightmare could be worse than returning to the CSA with the Freedom Party in the saddle?

# IX

The Manitoba prairie seemed to roll on forever. Above, puffy white clouds drifted across the blue sky. Mary Pomeroy watched a hawk circle in lazy spirals high overhead. The hawk would be watching, too, for rabbits or gophers. To it, a picnic on a farm wouldn't mean a thing.

Mary couldn't watch the hawk for long. She had to watch her own son like a hawk. Alexander Arthur Pomeroy's first birthday was the occasion for the picnic. He'd just figured out how to put one foot in front of him without falling down, which made him all the more dangerous to himself. Alexander didn't know that, of course. To him, walking was the most wonderful thing in the world.

Something went into his mouth. Mary tossed the drumstick she'd been gnawing onto a plate and grabbed her son. "What have you got there?" she said sharply.

"Mama!" Alexander said. Then, as her forefinger snaked into his mouth, he let out an indignant wail. *Something* there . . . She fished it out—a blade of grass. *Not so bad,* she thought, wiping her hand on her checked skirt. She'd taken a used match and a dead fly out of his mouth at one time or another. She didn't want to think about the things he might have swallowed. None of them seemed to have done him any harm, anyhow.

Maude McGregor watched her daughter with a faint smile on her face. "I don't know how many times I had to do that with you," she said. "Then there was the pearl button I found in your diaper."

"Was there?" Mary said, and her mother nodded. Mary glanced toward her husband. Mort Pomeroy was doing his polite best to pretend he hadn't heard, but he turned red all the same. Of course, he'd grown up in town, not on a farm. Mary had dealt with droppings of one kind or another ever since she learned how to walk: talking about them didn't faze her.

Her older sister, who still lived on a farm, was the same way. "I've had a surprise or two changing my kids, too," Julia Marble said. She lay on a blanket on her side, propped up on one elbow. Her belly bulged; another chip off the Marble block was due in about six weeks. Her husband, Kenneth, and mother-in-law rode herd on her children. She couldn't move fast enough now to do it herself.

Mary remembered that beached-whale feeling from her own pregnancy. "Don't you wish it was over?" she asked Julia.

"Oh, Lord, yes," her sister answered. Their mother nodded at that, too, and so did Beth Marble, Kenneth's mother.

"Hand me another beer, would you, dear?" Mary said to her husband. Mort pulled a Moosehead from the picnic hamper. He opened it with a church key and gave it to her. "Thanks," she told him. Nothing went better with fried chicken than the intense hoppiness of beer. She smiled. "That's nice."

He nodded. "It is, isn't it? We get some Hamm's at the diner, too, because Yanks will order it when they eat, but I wouldn't bring it here."

"I hope not," Kenneth Marble said. "I've had Yank beer. They strain it through the kidneys of a sick horse and then bottle it, eh?"

Mort started to nod again, then blinked and made a peculiar noise, half snort, half giggle. Beth Marble laughed out loud. So did Mary, who was always ready to say or hear unkind things about the USA. So did her mother, which surprised and pleased her; Maude McGregor didn't find a whole lot to laugh about these days.

Fried chicken. Homemade potato salad. Deviled eggs. Fresh-baked bread. Apple pie. Mary made a pig of herself, and enjoyed doing it, too. She changed Alexander's soggy diaper and cuddled him, then set him down on the blanket when he fell asleep.

After a while, the picnickers headed back to Maude McGregor's house. Mort carried Alexander. Mary carried the hamper, which was much lighter than it had been when they put it in the motorcar back in Rosenfeld. Julia said, "Mary and I will take care of the dishes."

"That's all right," Mary said. "I can do them. You should stay off your feet."

"I don't mind, even if I have to run to the outhouse all the time now," her sister said. "We can talk while we do them. We don't get the chance much any more, not the way we used to when we both lived here."

"That's sweet," Beth Marble said. "I was going to tell you I'd help, but now I won't. I'll be lazy instead." She laughed at that. So did Julia. Her mother-in-law was one of the least lazy people around.

Before Mary got married, she'd taken working the pump handle every so often while she did dishes for granted. Now she had to remind herself to do it, and it made her shoulder ache. "Running water's spoiled me," she said sheepishly.

"Well, you're living in town now," Julia said. "We always knew it was different."

"It sure is. We didn't know how much," Mary said. "Electricity . . . It beats kerosene all hollow."

"I bet it does," Julia said. "Like I said, a lot of things are different in town. I know that." She lowered her voice and added, "But I'm afraid some things haven't changed at all."

"What's that supposed to mean?" Mary asked, scrubbing at a frying pan. The breading and chicken skin at the bottom didn't want to come off. She used more elbow grease.

In that same quiet voice, Julia answered, "I think you know. I almost died when I heard somebody put a bomb in the general store. I think Ma probably did, too. If anything happened to you, I don't think we could stand it, not after Alexander and Pa."

"I don't know what you're talking about," said Mary, who knew perfectly well. "Besides, that was a year and a half ago now—more than a year and a half ago. Nobody ever thought I had anything to do with it till now."

Her sister set a glass in the dish drainer. In the front room, Mort was telling a joke. Mary recognized his tone, though she couldn't make out the words. That ought to mean nobody in the front room could make out what she and Julia were saying. "You're lucky," Julia told her. "And like I said before, the two of us don't get the chance to talk like we used to."

"If you're going to talk about things like this . . ." Mary said.

Julia's smile was anything but amused. "I know you. So does Ma. You've hated the Yanks since you were this high." She set a hand where her waist had been. "And you know what Pa did. The Americans never found his tools. Did you?"

"Even if I had, I wouldn't say anything," Mary answered. "People who know things can tell them. That's how the last uprising got betrayed. Some folks blabbed, and they're rich and happy. And other folks hanged on account of it."

"Do you think I would do anything like that?" Julia asked indignantly.

"No, dear. Hand me that platter, would you?" Mary scrubbed at it. "But it doesn't matter, because I haven't told you anything. There isn't anything *to* tell. Nobody knows where Pa hid his tools. If the Yanks couldn't find them, you don't think I could, do you?"

After that, they worked together in tense silence for some little while. Julia said, "I never thought the day would come when my own sister lied to me."

That hurt. Mary scrubbed away, her head down. "I didn't lie," she said in a low, furious voice. "I told you there was nothing to talk about, and there isn't. And if you call me a liar, there *won't* be anything to talk about, not ever."

"Tell me you didn't put that bomb in the general store, then," Julia said.

"I didn't put it there," Mary said. Julia's jaw dropped. Mary added, "And if you don't believe me, you can go to the devil."

She lied without hesitation. Her family was and always had been sternly Presbyterian. Here, though, she had no compunctions. She'd seen her father, a man of somber rectitude if ever there was one, lie the same way. Some things were too important to trust to anyone but yourself. Other people, even a sister you loved, could let you down. Better not to give them the chance.

And the lie worked. Julia put her arms around Mary. Because of her bulging belly, the embrace was awkward, but Julia plainly meant it. "I'm so sorry, dear," she said. "I *did* think you had something to do with it, and it left me petrified. Ma, too. We've talked about it, though I don't think she'd ever get up the nerve to say so."

Mary didn't think so, either. When her father was making bombs, her mother had never asked him about it. She'd known. She'd known full well. But she'd kept quiet. That had always been her way. As the older sister, though, Julia had always thought she could poke her nose into Mary's business whenever she felt like it. That was how it seemed to Mary, anyhow. She never stopped to wonder if it looked any different to Julia.

They finished the dishes. When they went into the living room, Mort asked, "What were you two gossiping about in there?"

"Men," Mary answered.

In the same breath, Julia said, "Horses."

"How to tell the difference between them," Mary said. That got a laugh from Julia and their mother and Beth Marble. Mort and Kenneth Marble didn't seem to think it was quite so funny.

On the drive back to Rosenfeld, Mary held Alexander on her lap. He put up with that for a while, but then started to fuss. He wanted to crawl around in the auto. No matter what he wanted, Mary didn't let him. Who could guess what kinds of fascinating things he'd find to stick in his mouth down there?

"It's a different world, your mother's farm," Mort remarked as he pulled to a stop in front of their apartment building.

"I've thought the same thing," Mary said. "No running water, no electricity . . . I didn't know what they were like till I married you."

"No indoor plumbing, either. And that privy . . ." Her husband held his nose. Alexander thought that was funny. He tried to hold his little button of a nose, and almost stuck a finger in his eye.

"I didn't even think about it when I lived there," Mary said. She'd had to use the privy while she was there, though. The stink was enough to make her eyes cross. It wasn't so bad in the wintertime—but during the winter, you didn't want to expose any part of your anatomy to the cold.

"What we've got here is better," Mort said. "A lot better."

"Of course it is," Mary said. "We've got each other." That made Mort smile, which was what she'd had in mind. She didn't talk about what Canada didn't have: freedom, independence, its own laws, its own people running its shops, its own police in the streets, its own soldiers guarding the frontiers.

Mort knew his country lacked all those things, too. But Mary didn't want to remind him about them, lest he wonder if she'd put the bomb in the general store. It wasn't that she didn't trust him. If she hadn't trusted him, she never would have married him. But some burdens, she remained convinced, had to be borne alone. This was one of them.

She carried Alexander Arthur Pomeroy up the stairs. Her brother's name went on. So did her father's. And so did the quiet war they'd waged against the USA.

Election Day brought Hipolito Rodriguez into Baroyeca to vote. It also brought him in to make sure things went the way they were supposed to. He thought people had learned their lessons during the election of 1933, when Jake Featherston became president of the CSA, and from the revenge on the Freedom Party's foes that followed. But 1933 was four years gone by now. Sometimes people forgot lessons . . . or needed to be reminded.

Rodriguez's trip into town this year was different from the ones that had gone before. With him strode Miguel and Jorge. Both of his older sons had finished their time in the Freedom Youth Corps. Now they were strong young men, broad-shouldered, deep-chested, hard-muscled, both of them several inches taller than their father. They weren't old enough to vote yet, but they were old enough and tough enough to knock heads if heads needed knocking.

A new set of poles marched down from the mountains, parallel to the ones that had brought the telegraph into Baroyeca for generations. Those were spindly and sun-faded; they leaned now this way, now that. The new poles, by contrast, were perfectly spaced. They were thicker than the poles that held the telegraph wire, and every one stood perfectly straight. Even the wire on them, wrapped in its heavy coat of black insulation, seemed altogether stronger and tougher than the wire for the telegraph.

Pointing to the line of new poles, Miguel said, "We did that." Pride rang in his voice.

"I know you did," Hipolito Rodriguez answered. "And I'm proud of you. Who would have thought Baroyeca would have its own electricity?"

A falcon spiraled down and perched on a power pole a couple of hundred yards away. It didn't stay long. As the Rodriguezes drew near, it flew off again, screeching shrilly. It landed on a telegraph pole, but flew up at once when the pole shifted under its weight.

Jorge said, "Somebody's going to have to take care of those telegraph poles one of these days before too long."

His father had a pretty good idea who those somebodies might be. The Freedom Youth Corps was made for projects like that. It always had plenty of eager, active bodies, and it didn't pay any of them very well. When he got into Baroyeca, he saw boys from the Youth Corps, working under the direction of a master mason from another town, laying bricks for a new town hall and jail. They labored like men possessed, with a rhythm alien to Sonora, where things generally found their own pace. Not here; this was a breath of businesslike Virginia or North Carolina set down at the far end of the Confederate States.

Miguel and Jorge watched the youths with a mixture of scorn for those younger than themselves and respect for what they were doing. Miguel said, "They may be clumsy, but they aren't lazy." He spoke in English. It was the language of the Youth Corps, and seemed to be the language he and Jorge always used these days to think and talk about work.

The two of them weren't lazy now that they'd come back to the farm. They pitched into chores with an enthusiasm Hipolito Rodriguez found almost frightening. They ate them up and went looking for more. His own natural pace was slower. He used *mañana* to mean one of these days, when he got around to it. They used the word scornfully, to mean something that would never get done. He stopped using the word so much. The Youth Corps attitude began rubbing off on him.

This year, the polling place was in the *alcalde*'s front room. Several Freedom Party stalwarts stood just outside. They waved to Hipolito as he came up. Carlos Ruiz had a list in his hand. Pointing to it, Rodriguez asked, "Did any of those fellows try to vote this time?"

"Only one," Ruiz answered. "We gave him a set of lumps and sent him home."

Rodriguez walked inside to cast his ballot. He voted the straight Freedom Party ticket. The way the ballot was printed, that was easy. Voting for the Whigs or the Radical Liberals was much harder. He put the completed ballot in the box. "Hipolito Rodriguez has voted," intoned the clerk in charge of the box. Hearing his name spoken so seriously always made him feel important. Another clerk wrote a line through his name on the registration roster so he couldn't vote twice.

He wondered how much difference that made. The people who would count the ballots were Freedom Party men. Back in the days when Sonora had been in the Radical Liberals' pockets, Rodriguez had often wondered how much announced counts had to do with real ones. He still did. The Freedom Party seized advantages whenever and however it could.

After voting, he took his sons to Freedom Party headquarters. Robert Quinn had seen them before, but not lately. "*Por Dios, Señor* Rodriguez, you did not tell me you were raising football players," he said in his deliberate Spanish. "Where did you get these enormous young men?"

Miguel and Jorge both stood even taller and threw back their shoulders to make them look wider. They liked the idea of being football players. The new U.S.-style game, with forward passing, had really caught on in Sonora since the Great War. Some open ground, goal posts, and a ball were all you needed.

Miguel said, "All the good food we got in the Freedom Youth Corps helped us finish growing." He'd said the same thing to Rodriguez not long after coming home, and in the same—English—words. Rodriguez guessed he'd heard it a lot in the Corps. Hastily, though, Miguel added, "We eat well at home, too," and Jorge nodded. Their mother had been hurt when they praised the food they'd eaten in the Freedom Youth Corps.

Quinn nodded now. "I'm sure you do," he said, still in Spanish. He bent over backwards not to seem to be ramming English down anyone's throat. In that, he and other Freedom Party men in Sonora were the opposite of a lot of English-speakers Rodriguez had known. The Freedom Youth Corps operated mostly in English, but the younger generation was already more at home in the language of most of the Confederate States. Quinn went on, "And what will you do now that you've been discharged from the Corps?"

"Help Father on the farm for now, sir," Jorge said.

"I wish we could do something more for the country, though," Miguel said.

"It could be the day will come when you can," Quinn answered smoothly.

*Miguel wants to be conscripted. That's what he's saying, though he doesn't even know it.* The realization struck Rodriguez like a thunderbolt. And Jorge was nodding. *I'll talk with them,* their father thought. *He* hadn't wanted to be conscripted. But when his time came, during the war, the government was shooting young men in Sonora who refused to report. He'd gone in and taken his chances with Yankee lead. He was still here, so he supposed he'd done the right thing.

Robert Quinn went on, "Meanwhile, of course, doing things for the *Partido de Libertad* is almost the same as doing things for *los Estados Confederados.* Your father is a good man, a patriotic man. You'll follow in his footsteps, eh?"

Miguel and Jorge both nodded then. Rodriguez said, "I will tell you what I am. I am a man who is lucky in his sons."

"There is no luck better than that," Quinn said. "Do you want to grab a club and take the afternoon shift on watching the polling place? Bring your boys along; let them see how it's done. Then come back here. Now that we have electricity, I've got a wireless set to let us hear returns." He pointed to the box on his desk.

"Good," Rodriguez said, nodding to the wireless almost as if it were a person. "We will see you here, then, after the polls close. Come on, boys."

Out they went, and back to the *alcalde*'s house. When Miguel and Jorge saw that one of the men outside the polling place with their father was Felipe Rojas, who'd shown them the ropes when they joined the Freedom Youth Corps, they were very impressed. When they saw that Rojas didn't roar at their father like the wrath of God, but treated him as an equal and a friend, they were even more impressed. Rodriguez carefully concealed his amusement.

And then his amusement dried up and blew away, for here came Don Gustavo, his old *patrón*, straight for the polling place. Don Gustavo's name was on the list Felipe Rojas held. He came up to the Freedom Party men as if he were still a great power in the land, the power he'd been before 1933. His white shirt and string tie, his sharply creased black trousers and wide-brimmed black felt hat, his silver belt buckle and patent-leather shoes, all declared that he was no peasant, but a person of consequence. So did his thin little mustache and his prominent belly.

*"Buenos días,"* he said, affably enough. "Excuse me, please, for I am going to vote." He had nerve. He'd come without bodyguards. More than once, the men loyal to him had come up against those who followed the Freedom Party. They'd come off second best every time, and paid a heavy price in blood. Now Don Gustavo was doing his bold best to pretend none of that had ever happened.

No matter how bold that best was, it wasn't going to get him into the polling place. "Freedom!" Felipe Rojas said in English. "You would do better, *señor,* to go home and stay there in peace."

Don Gustavo's nostrils flared angrily. "You speak of freedom, and yet you say I am not free to vote?" *He* stuck to Spanish, and Spanish of almost Castilian purity. His face was fiery red. Scorn came off him in waves. His hand slid toward his pocket. By the way the pocket sagged, a small pistol hid there.

Hipolito Rodriguez tightened his grip on his club. "Don't do that, *señor,*" he said. "You may shoot us. You may even march in there and vote. But if you do, you are a dead man. Your family will die with you. The *Partido de Libertad* knows how to take revenge. Do you doubt it?"

He waited. Slowly, the high color faded from Don Gustavo's cheeks and forehead, leaving him almost corpse-pale. He'd seen how the Freedom Party struck back. "Damn you," he said. The Party men answered not a word. Don Gustavo's shoulders sagged. He turned and walked away.

"*¡Bueno, papa!*" Jorge said softly. Hipolito Rodriguez was only a peasant doing his best to make a living from a farm that could have been bigger and could have been on better land, but for the moment he felt ten feet tall.

Felipe Rojas took a pencil from a trouser pocket and checked Don Gustavo's name off on the list of those who weren't going to vote. The tiny sound the pencil point made on the paper was the sound of a system centuries old, a system that had endured under the flag of Spain, the flag of Mexico, and the flag of the Confederate States, falling to ruin.

"He backed down, did he?" Quinn said when the Freedom Party men returned to Party headquarters. "He's not a hundred percent stupid, then, is he? He knows things have changed in Sonora, and changed for the better, too."

The sound of the wireless set was another sound of change. The announcer, who spoke mostly English, but an English larded with Spanish words and turns of phrase, told of one Freedom Party victory after another in Congressional races and in state and local elections. The whole Confederacy lined up behind President Featherston and the party he'd built.

Well, almost the whole Confederacy. Rodriguez said, "He does not talk about the elections in Louisiana."

Robert Quinn frowned, as if he wished Rodriguez hadn't noticed. "Louisiana is . . . a problem," he admitted. "But the Freedom Party solves problems. You can count on that."

\* \* \*

The *Remembrance* was a great ship. Her displacement matched that of any battleship in the U.S. Navy. All the same, the storm in the Atlantic flung the aeroplane carrier around like a toy boat in a bathtub also inhabited by a rambunctious four-year-old. Sam Carsten was glad he had a strong stomach. Plenty of sailors didn't; the air in the ship's corridors carried a faint but constant reek of vomit.

Somewhere off to the east lay the coast of North Carolina. The *Remembrance* and her aeroplanes were supposed to be keeping an eye on what the Confederates were up to. In weather and seas like this, she could neither launch aeroplanes nor land them once launched. About all she could do was pick up this, that, and the other thing in the wireless shack.

When Carsten wasn't on duty, he spent a fair amount of time hanging around in the shack finding out whatever he could. A lot of the wireless traffic coming out of the CSA was in Morse, which he understood only haltingly. A lot of it was in code, which not even the sailors taking it down understood. But every now and then they tuned in to stations from Wilmington or Elizabeth City or Norfolk up in Virginia. Those fascinated him. Up until about the time his father was born, the USA and the CSA had been one country. Half an hour of listening to Confederate wireless was plenty to show him they'd gone their separate ways since the War of Secession.

Oh, the music the Confederates played wasn't that much different from what he would have heard on a U.S. station. Even there, though, the Confederates' tunes often had wilder rhythms to them than any band in the USA would have used. Carsten had heard people say that was because a lot of musicians in the CSA were Negroes. He didn't know if it was true, but he'd heard it.

In between songs, the advertisements were all but identical to their U.S. equivalents. That made perfect sense to him. People trying to separate other people from their money probably sounded the same regardless of whether they were speaking English or Italian or Japanese or Hindustani. A hustler was a hustler, no matter where he lived.

But when the news came on, Sam knew he was hearing voices from another country. For one thing, all the stations carried the same stories, word for word. Sam had thought so, and the men in the wireless shack confirmed his impression. The broadcasters were all getting their scripts from the same place. And, by the way things sounded, that place was a Freedom Party office somewhere in Richmond.

As far as the wireless was concerned, the Freedom Party could do no wrong. Jesus might have walked on water, but, if you listened to the smooth-voiced men in the wireless web, Freedom Party officials from President Featherston down to Homer Duffy, the dogcatcher in Pig

Scratch, South Carolina, walked on air, and choirs of angels burst into song behind them whenever they deigned to open their mouths and let the masses benefit from their godlike wisdom.

That especially held true when the announcers introduced a speech by Jake Featherston. To listen to them, Moses was coming down from Mount Sinai to enlighten an undeserving and sinful people. It wasn't just an act, either, or Carsten didn't think it was. They meant it, and they expected everybody listening to feel the same way.

"I'm Jake Featherston, and I'm here to tell you the truth," the Confederate president would say in his harsh accent, and then he'd spew out lies and hate. If he spoke in front of an audience, people would go nuts, whooping and hollering and cheering to beat the band. If he was by himself for a talk, the broadcaster would sugarcoat it afterwards.

"Do the Confederates really believe the crap that guy puts out?" Sam asked after a particularly virulent tirade from Featherston about colored terrorists.

One of the yeomen in the wireless shack shrugged. "If they say they don't, sir, they end up slightly dead," he answered. "Or more than slightly."

"Besides," the other yeoman added, "they can't say anything against the government, not in public they can't."

"Is it a country or a jail?" Carsten asked.

"Near as I can tell, sir," the second yeoman said, "it's a jail."

The more time Sam spent in the wireless shack, the more he was inclined to agree with the man who monitored signals coming out of the CSA. The other thing he noticed was that everybody on the wireless sounded happy about being in jail. If people in the Confederate States were unhappy about anything that was going on in their country, they didn't say so where any large number of other people had the chance to hear them.

When Carsten remarked on that, one of the yeomen said, "You're close, sir, but you're not quite right. When you hear 'em talk about Louisiana, you'll think the devil lives there."

Little by little, Sam discovered the man was right. It took a while. The men who read the news didn't like talking about Louisiana, any more than Sam's mother had liked talking about the facts of life. Sometimes, though, they couldn't help it. They sounded as if they were gloating when they noted how the state militia there was having trouble putting down Negro uprisings within its borders. Whenever Governor Long made a speech the broadcasters couldn't ignore, they went out of their way to heap scorn on it. They even seemed to celebrate when the New Orleans

Tigers, the number-one football team in the state, lost to elevens from Atlanta or Richmond.

"Why do the rest of the Confederate States hate Louisiana?" Carsten asked in the officers' mess one day at suppertime.

"You've noticed that, have you, Lieutenant?" Commander Dan Cressy said.

"Uh, yes, sir," Sam replied, more than a little nervously: Cressy was the *Remembrance*'s executive officer, answerable to no one aboard the carrier except Captain Stein. Attracting his attention could be good or could be anything but, depending on why you attracted it.

"Anyone else here notice it?" Cressy inquired, sipping his coffee. He had a long, thin, pale, highly intelligent face, and a pair of the coldest gray eyes Sam had ever seen. Like any good exec, he acted like a son of a bitch so the skipper didn't have to. A lot of people said he wasn't acting. Rumor had it that he translated Latin poetry in his quarters. Carsten had no idea if that particular rumor was true. Commander Cressy waited, but none of the other officers in the mess said anything. He set down the thick white china mug and nodded to Sam. "Very good, Lieutenant. You're dead right, of course; Louisiana is the pariah of the CSA. How did you come to realize that?"

*Why didn't the rest of you notice that?* bubbled just below the surface of his voice. Three or four officers sent Sam resentful looks. He was the least senior man in the mess except an ensign just out of Annapolis—and that smooth-cheeked ensign had a much brighter future in the Navy than a middle-aged mustang. Picking his words with care, Sam answered, "That sure is the way it sounds on the wireless, sir."

He wondered whether Commander Cressy would land on him like a ton of bricks for listening to the wireless. But Cressy didn't. His eyes stayed cold—Carsten didn't think they *could* warm up—but the light in them was undoubtedly approval. "Good," he said. "The more ways you can find out about the enemy, the better." Formally, of course, the Confederate States weren't the enemy. But among the fruit salad on Cressy's chest was the ribbon for a Purple Heart. He'd got a broken ankle aboard a U.S. destroyer torpedoed by a C.S. submersible in 1916. After another sip of coffee, he went on, "But you asked why, didn't you?"

"Uh, yes, sir," Carsten said.

The exec nodded again. "That's always the right question, because everything else comes out of it. Not what. Not how. Why. Know why, and what and how and often when and where and who take care of themselves. This time, why is pretty easy. Louisiana is the only Confederate state the Freedom Party doesn't own lock, stock, and barrel. Long, the governor there, is a Radical Liberal, and he's pulled off the same kind of coup inside the state as the Freedom Party has in the rest of the CSA. Outside of Louisiana, what Jake Featherston says, goes. Inside Louisiana, it's what Governor Long says."

Carsten nodded. That told him what he needed to know, all right. It also raised another question: "Can he get away with it?"

Before Commander Cressy could answer that, the general-quarters klaxon started hooting. Cressy and Carsten and all the other officers sprang to their feet. The exec said, "We'll take this up another time, if you like. Meanwhile . . ." Meanwhile, he was the first one out the door, trotting toward his station on the bridge.

Sam was only a step behind Cressy. As he hurried to his own post down in the bowels of the *Remembrance*, he wondered how many times he'd gone to general quarters, either as a drill or during real combat. He wouldn't have cared to give a precise number, but it had to be up in the hundreds.

He also wondered whether this was a drill or the real thing. You always did, if you had any sense. He heard sailors asking one another the same question as they clattered up and down iron staircases and rushed along corridors. Nobody seemed to have an answer, which was par for the course.

He was panting a little when he got to his own post. *Too goddamn many cigarettes,* he thought. *They're hell on the wind.* Thinking of them made him want one. But the smoking lamp went out during general quarters. The pack stayed in his pocket.

"What's up, sir?" asked one of the sailors in the damage-control party.

"Beats me," Sam answered. "Here's Lieutenant Commander Pottinger, though. Maybe he knows." He turned to the officer who headed the damage-control party. "You know what's going on, sir?"

"I think so," Hiram Pottinger said. "Don't know for a fact, but the scuttlebutt is, somebody spotted a periscope off to port."

That produced excited chatter from the sailors in the party. One of them, an enormous redhead named Charlie Fitzpatrick, asked the cogent question: "Whose?"

"Subs don't usually fly flags on top of their periscopes," Pottinger said dryly. "In these waters, though, that boat isn't awfully goddamn likely to be Japanese."

The sailors laughed. But then somebody said, "The Confederates aren't supposed to have any submersibles," and the laughter stopped. Everybody in the U.S. Navy was convinced the CSA had quite a few things the armistice at the end of the war forbade. Carsten remembered those sleek aeroplanes with CONFEDERATE CITRUS COMPANY painted on their sides. They hadn't been armed—he didn't think they had, anyhow—but they'd looked mighty ready to take guns.

"No way to know the submarine *is* Confederate," Pottinger said. "It could be British or French, too."

That didn't make Sam any happier. The British, who'd been beaten but not crushed, had been allowed a few submarines after the war. The French hadn't. But Kaiser Bill's Germany wasn't pushing them about that. For one thing, the Kaiser was an old, old man these days. For another, the *Action Française* regime, like the Freedom Party in the CSA, wanted to do some pushing of its own. And, for a third, Germany kept looking anxiously toward the Balkans, where restive South Slavs were making Austria-Hungary totter the same way they had a quarter of a century before.

Fifteen minutes later, the all-clear sounded. Carsten warily accepted it. But, as he headed up to the flight deck, he couldn't help wondering how long things would stay all clear.

The southbound train hurried through the night. Anne Colleton had done a lot of traveling, and a lot of sleeping in Pullman cars. She had trouble sleeping now. Here in Mississippi, she couldn't help wondering if machine-gun fire would stitch its way along the side of the train, or if a charge of dynamite buried in the roadbed would blow the engine off the tracks. The Confederate Army was doing its best to put down the simmering Negro uprising, but guerrillas weren't easy to quell. As soon as they hid their guns, they looked like any other sharecroppers. And plenty of blacks who wouldn't go out bushwhacking themselves would lie for and conceal the ones who did.

This wasn't a revolt like the one in 1915. That one had hoped to topple the Confederacy, and had come too close to success. This was more like a sore that didn't want to heal. Anne feared Jake Featherston and the Freedom Party had pushed blacks too hard after taking power—pushed them too hard without being able to crush them if they did rise up. Now the country had to pay for that lack of foresight.

Eventually, she did doze off. When she woke, the sky was getting light. Nobody had shot up the train. She yawned enormously, trying to drive away sleep. A few minutes later, a colored steward came by with a pot of coffee. She all but mugged him to get her hands on a cup. Even as she drank it, though, she wondered if the man had any connection to the guerrillas. You never could tell. She'd found that out the hard way.

She knew to the minute when the train passed from Mississippi down into Louisiana. Billboards with Jake Featherston's picture and Freedom Party slogans disappeared, to be replaced by those with Governor Long's picture and his slogans. Long called himself a Radical Liberal, but in fact he was just as much a strongman in Louisiana as Featherston was in the CSA as a whole. He'd learned a lot from the way the Freedom Party had risen, learned and applied the knowledge in his own state.

Fortified by that cup of coffee, Anne got dressed and went to the dining car for breakfast. She was just finishing when the conductor came through, calling, "Baton Rouge! Next stop is Baton Rouge!"

She went back to her compartment, threw her nightclothes into a suitcase, and waited for the train to stop. A porter came to collect the luggage: another Negro, and so another man to wonder about, no matter how fulsomely he thanked her for the tip she gave him.

Flashbulbs burst in a startling fusillade when she got down onto the platform from the Pullman car. "Welcome to Louisiana, Miss Colleton!" boomed a pudgy, dark-haired man in his mid-forties: Governor Huey Long. He swarmed forward, first to shake her hand, then to plant a kiss on her cheek. More flashbulbs popped. The papers in Louisiana were as much in his pocket as those in the rest of the Confederacy were in Jake Featherston's.

"Thank you very much," Anne answered, slightly dazed. "I hadn't expected such a fancy reception." She'd expected to be met by a driver and possibly bodyguards, and to be whisked from the station to the state Capitol.

But Huey Long didn't operate that way. "Anything worth doing is worth overdoing," he declared, and turned to play to the crowd on the platform. "Ain't that right, folks?"

People burst into noisy applause. "You tell 'em, Kingfish!" a woman called, as if to a preacher. Long lacked some of President Featherston's fiery intensity, but he seemed a more likable, more *human* figure. They both got what they wanted—people did as they told them to—but by different roads. That *ain't* was a nice touch. Huey Long had a law degree; such language wasn't part of the way he usually talked. But he brought it out naturally, using it to connect with the crowd.

"Come on," he told Anne. "Let's get on over to the statehouse and talk." She nodded. That was what Jake Featherston had sent her to Louisiana to do.

The governor's limousine was a Bentley with a hood as long as a battleship. Featherston would never have set foot in such a flashy motorcar. He had, so to speak, risen from the ranks, and didn't want to lose the common touch. Governor Long, by contrast, reveled in luxury.

Motorcycles ridden by state troopers preceded and followed the limousine. So did police cars with red lights flashing and sirens blaring. Long turned the short trip from the station to the Capitol into a procession. More photographers were waiting for him and Anne as they went up the steps into the impressively domed building.

Hard-faced guards surrounded them going up those steps. More guards waited at the entranceway. Still more patrolled the corridors. However much Huey Long posed as a friend of the people, he didn't trust them very far. A horde of sweepers also patrolled the hallways, and kept them spotlessly clean.

"If I'm rushing you, just sing out," Long told Anne. "You want to go to a hotel and freshen up, maybe even take a day to rest, it's all right by me."

"Thank you, but I'm fine," she said. "I'm here now. We may as well talk now, don't you think?"

"However you want it, that's how it'll be," he said grandly. "Suppose you go on and tell me *why* you're here."

"That's simple, Governor: I'm here to deliver a message for President Featherston," Anne answered. "You must understand that, or you wouldn't have given me such a . . . splendid reception."

"Well, now, I want you to know it was my pleasure," Long said, and then, as if relishing the phrase, repeated it: "My pleasure. I'll be glad to listen to this here message, whatever it is, even though I have trouble seeing what sort of a message the president of the CSA would want to send to me. I'm just minding my business here in Louisiana, and I reckon he ought to do the same outside my state."

"That's . . . part of what the message is about," Anne replied, much more nervous here than she'd ever been while dealing with *Action Française*. If Governor Long didn't like what she had to say, she might not get home to South Carolina.

He nodded now, though, all graciousness. "Go on, then," he told her.

"You understand that this is unofficial," Anne said. "If you quote me, the president will either call you a liar or say I wasn't speaking for him." Long nodded impatiently. He'd trumpet what came next anyhow, and Featherston would disown it. But now the formalities of things unofficial had been observed, so Anne went on, "You could call this a warning, Governor. If you don't bring Louisiana into line with the rest of the CSA, you'll be sorry."

Huey Long scowled. "Bring it into line, you say? What's that supposed to mean? Knuckle under to the Freedom Party? Pardon my French, Miss Colleton, but I'll be damned if I'll do that."

*You'll be damned if you don't,* Anne thought. Aloud, she said, "The president is concerned about the direction you're taking Louisiana in."

"I'm not doing anything he hasn't done," Long said.

He was right, of course. But he'd started later, and had only a state to work in. That wasn't enough, not when he was up against the rest of the country. If he didn't see that . . . If he didn't see that, maybe he was too full of himself to see it. Anne said, "You'd do better not to get all stiff-necked about this, Governor. The president is very determined."

"What's he going to do? Invade my state?" Long snorted, ridiculing the mere idea. "If he does, we'll fight, by God. I'm just as good a Confederate patriot as he is any day of the week."

Despite his threat, he didn't take the idea seriously. Anne did. One thing she was sure of: Jake Featherston would tolerate no threats to his own authority. She said, "I don't know what he'll do. Whatever it is, do you really think you could stop it? This is only one state, after all."

"I'll take my chances," said the governor of Louisiana. "We haven't seen much freedom since the Freedom Party took over. But Featherston can't run again in 1939; it's against the Confederate Constitution. I think maybe I can whip anybody else in the Party. Willy Knight?" He gave a contemptuous shrug. "If he hadn't climbed onto Featherston's coattails, he'd still be a loudmouthed Texas nobody."

He wasn't wrong about that, either, or about the single six-year term to which the Confederate president was limited. More than once, Anne had wondered what Jake Featherston intended to do about that. What *could* he do? She didn't know. To Huey Long, she said, "That's all, then. I've told you what I came here to tell you. I have a reservation at the Excelsior. May I go there?" It wasn't an idle question; Long might want to hold her hostage. "Just so you know, the president won't pay ransom or anything like that to get me back."

"Oh, yes. I know. Run along," Long said. "You're not a big enough centipede in my shoe to get excited about."

That stung. Of all the things Anne least wanted to be called, *small-time* ranked high on the list. Smiling as if he knew as much, Long escorted her to the limousine. The driver put the car into gear without asking where she was going. Five minutes later, he pulled up in front of the Excelsior. "Here you are, ma'am."

"Thank you." She tipped him. A colored bellboy put her suitcases on a cart and wheeled them into the hotel. Anne went to the front desk. After fuming while she waited in line, she gave her name to the clerk.

"Oh, yes, Miss Colleton. Of course. And how are you this lovely afternoon?"

Anne hesitated a split second before answering. She'd expected to hear that precise question, but not so soon. "Tired," she told him. If she'd said, *Just fine,* the world would have been a different place. She didn't know how, not for certain, but one response meant one thing, the other something else.

The clerk's face showed none of that. With a sympathetic smile, he said, "You take it easy here. We've got fine rooms, and the best restaurant in town, too."

"All right. I'll try it." She collected her room key and went upstairs, the bellboy trailing along behind her. She tipped him and the elevator operator, then unpacked and indulged in the luxury of a bath before going down to the best restaurant in town. It lived up to the desk clerk's description. She soon saw why: a lot of the plump, prosperous men who ate there were Louisiana legislators. Talk of power and of business filled the air.

The restaurant gave a view of Roselawn, the street that led north to the Capitol. Anne was about halfway through an excellent plate of lamb chops when chaos suddenly erupted outside. Sirens screaming and red lights blazing, police cars and ambulances raced toward the statehouse.

Several of the important men in the restaurant wondered what was going on, some of them loudly and profanely. A telephone in the corridor that led to the place jangled. A waiter hurried from the corridor to one of the tables full of prominent people. A handsome, gray-haired man went back with him.

A moment later, curses as explosive as any Anne had ever heard filled the air. The gray-haired man rushed back into the room, crying, "Governor Long's been shot! Shot, I tell you! Nigger janitor was carrying a gun! Goddamn nigger's dead, but Governor Long, he's hurt bad!"

Pandemonium filled the restaurant. Men sprang to their feet shouting frightful oaths. Women screamed. A few men screamed, too. Anne went right on eating her lamb chops. She was supposed to get out of town tomorrow, and hoped the state authorities would let her leave. If they started wondering what connection she had to a desk clerk and a desperate janitor . . . All she knew about was one code phrase. No. She knew one other thing. When Jake Featherston gave her this assignment, she'd known better than to ask too many questions.

"**Y**ou can't do this to me," the silver-haired lawyer insisted. "It violates every tenet of the Constitution of the Confederate States of America."

Jefferson Pinkard shrugged broad shoulders. "If I had the time, I could tell you there's martial law in Louisiana, and so whatever the Constitution's got to say doesn't matter worth a hill of beans. If I had time, I could do that. But I don't have time. And so—" He slapped the lawyer in the face, then backhanded him with a return stroke. Then he punched the silver-haired fellow in the pit of the stomach. The man tried to double up, but the guards who had hold of him wouldn't let him. In friendly tones, Pinkard asked, "See what I mean?"

He wondered if the lawyer would say something stupid and need another dose. Some of these people did. They'd run things in Louisiana for a long time, and had trouble figuring out they weren't in charge any more. They ran their mouths off, and they paid for it. Oh, yes, they paid plenty.

This one, though, seemed smarter than most. He also needed half a minute or so to catch his breath before he could say anything at all. "I get it," he choked out, his face gray with pain.

A little disappointed, Jeff jerked a thumb toward the interior of the camp. "Take him away," he said, and the guards did. Jeff laughed. He wondered if the men who'd voted to build camps in Louisiana ever imagined they'd wind up in them. He doubted it; people didn't work that way.

But, whether people believed it or not, things changed mighty easily. Huey Long had imitated in miniature Jake Featherston's system of running up prison camps to hold people who might cause trouble for him. With Long dead, with the president declaring martial law in Louisiana "to deal with the vile terrorism of black insurrection," the Freedom Party and all its apparatus had swooped down on the state like a hawk swooping down on a plump chicken. Men who'd defied the Freedom Party since long before 1933 were finally getting what was coming to them.

The swoop came so hard and fast, state officials hadn't had any chance to resist. President Featherston declared martial law the minute he heard Governor Long was dead. Soldiers and Freedom Party guards and stalwarts swarmed into Louisiana from north, east, and west. So many of them had been in Texas and Mississippi and Arkansas, so very close to the border, that Pinkard wondered if they hadn't waited there for Long's assassination. He wondered, but he kept quiet. Men who shot off their mouths about things like that didn't run prison camps; they got locked up in them. And besides, Jeff was more inclined to see this whole operation as good planning than as an invasion.

Long's wardens had used a little more imagination on the names of their prisons than the Freedom Party bothered with. This one, just outside Alexandria, was called Camp Dependable. That amused Jeff, not least because the fellow who had been in charge of this place was now an inmate here.

So was one of Huey Long's brothers. The other had suffered an unfortunate accident shortly after the forces necessary for martial law began entering Louisiana. Jeff had heard—unofficially, of course—that the "accident" involved a burst of machine-gun fire. That wasn't in the papers or on the wireless. He couldn't prove it was true. But he wouldn't have been surprised, either.

He went out to the perimeter of Camp Dependable. Freedom Party stalwarts were strengthening it with more barbed wire. It already had more machine-gun emplacements than Long's people had been able to afford. Martial law had been declared to put down the Negro insurrection in Louisiana. That insurrection still simmered, and still needed defending against. Somehow, though, just about all the inmates in the prison camp were white men who'd backed Huey Long to the hilt.

"Everything tight?" Pinkard asked a helmeted Freedom Party guard who manned a machine gun.

"You bet, Warden," the man answered. "Tight as a fifty-dollar whore's snatch."

Pinkard laughed. "That's the way it's supposed to be," he said, and continued on his rounds. "Freedom!" he added over his shoulder.

"Freedom!" the machine gunner echoed. That greeting hadn't been heard much here since Huey Long seized the reins. With martial law in place, though, with Louisiana being brought into line with the rest of the Confederate States, *Freedom!* here now had the importance it deserved.

A few hundred yards away, motorcars rolled along the highway that ran down to New Orleans. Governor Long had done a lot for the roads in the state. Building roads meant lots of jobs. Out in the rest of the CSA, President Featherston's dam-building program did the same thing.

Only after he'd tramped the entire perimeter did Pinkard relax a little. He'd got into the habit down in the Empire of Mexico. There, he hadn't been able to rely on the guards as much as he would have liked. If he didn't see things with his own eyes, he couldn't know for sure how they were going. He still remained convinced he had a better chance of heading off trouble if he kept an eye on everything himself.

With a couple of guards, he also strode through the interior of Camp Dependable. Having an escort was part of regulations. Where he didn't make the rules, he followed them. Making people follow the rules was the point of a prison camp, after all. But, rules or no rules, he didn't much worry about being taken hostage. New prisoners had tried that once with another warden, a couple of days after Governor Long died. The ensuing massacre showed what they could expect if they tried it again.

"Hey, Warden!" somebody called. "Can we get better food?"

"You'll get what the regulations say you get," Pinkard answered. "And you'll be sorry if you whine about it. You understand?"

The prisoner didn't answer. He wore his striped uniform—regulation in Louisiana—with an odd sort of pride. He'd sounded like an educated man when he asked the question. Jeff wondered what he'd been before Huey Long's rule collapsed. A lawyer? A professor? A writer? Whatever he'd been, he was only a prisoner now. And he hadn't really figured out how to be a prisoner, or he wouldn't have kept quiet when the warden asked him a question. Pinkard nodded to the guards. He needed to do no more than that. They fell on the man and beat him up. He howled, which helped him not at all. The other prisoners nearby watched, wide-eyed. None of them said a word or tried to interfere. They were learning.

When the beating ended, the guards stepped back. They weren't even mussed. Slowly, painfully, blood running down his face, the prisoner struggled to his feet. "You understand?" Jeff asked him again.

"Yes, Warden," he choked out.

"Stand at attention when you speak to the warden, you worthless sack of shit," a guard growled.

The prisoner did his best. It wasn't very good, since he could hardly stand upright at all. Here, though, making the effort counted. "Yes, Warden," he repeated, and then, warily, he added, "Sorry, Warden."

"Sorry doesn't cut the mustard," Pinkard snapped. "What are you?"

"What—?" The prisoner frowned. One of the guards snarled in hungry eagerness. He snarled a little too soon, though, and gave the man a hint. "I'm a worthless sack of shit, Warden!" he blurted.

Pinkard answered with a brusque nod and a handful of words: "Grits and water—ten days."

He waited. If the prisoner protested, if he even blinked, he would be a lot sorrier than he was already. But he only stayed at attention and tried to look as if he'd got good news. Pinkard nodded again and walked on. He would have less trouble from here on out with everybody who'd watched and listened.

No one gave him any more lip till he got to the infirmary. Then it came not from a prisoner but from a white-coated doctor. "Warden, if these men keep getting rations of hominy grits and a little fatback and nothing else, you'll see more cases of pellagra than you can shake a stick at."

"What else am I supposed to feed them?" Jeff asked.

"Vegetables. Fruits. Wheat flour," the doctor said. "They haven't been here very long, but some of them are already starting to show symptoms."

"Feeding 'em that other stuff'd cost more money, wouldn't it?" Pinkard asked.

"Well, yes," the man in the white coat admitted. "But pellagra's no joke. It will kill. It's only the past few years we've found out that something missing from the diet causes it. Do you want to burden yourself with a lot of disease you can easily prevent?"

Jeff shrugged. "I don't know about that. What I do know is, these people are enemies of the Confederate States. They don't deserve anything fancy. We'll go on the way we have been, thank you very much."

He waited. He couldn't punish the doctor the way he'd punished the prisoner. The doctor was only trying to do his job. He was supposed to be politically sound. He took a look at the guards standing behind Pinkard and visibly wilted. "All right," he said. "But I did want to keep you informed."

"Fine," Pinkard said. "I'm informed. Freedom!" This time, the handy word meant, *Shut up and stop bothering me.*

"Freedom!" the doctor echoed. He couldn't say anything else.

Barbed wire separated the warden's office and quarters and the guards' quarters from the prisoners' barracks. Pinkard nodded to himself when he passed out of the area where the prisoners lived. They were nothing but trouble. That was even more true here than it had been in Alabama. There, Whigs and Rad Libs had guessed for a long time what would happen to them once the Freedom Party came out on top. Not here in Louisiana, not after Long got in. The Rad Libs here had thought they'd stay on top forever.

As Pinkard went up the stairs of the mess hall to grab himself a snack (*he* had a lot more choices than grits and fatback), a flight of aeroplanes buzzed by overhead. They were painted in bright colors. Instead of the C.S. battle flag, they had CONFEDERATE CITRUS COMPANY painted on wings and fuselage. But they meant business. When Confederate forces entered Louisiana after Governor Long was gunned down, a few state policemen and militiamen had tried to resist. They didn't try for long, not after those CONFEDERATE CITRUS COMPANY machines bombed and machine-gunned them from the sky. And the aeroplanes had been useful since, too, pounding Negro guerrillas who hid in swamps and bays inaccessible except from above.

The Confederate States weren't supposed to have aeroplanes that carried bombs and machine guns. That was what the United States had been saying since 1917, anyhow. President Smith had sent President Featherston a note about it. Jeff remembered hearing about that on the wireless set in his quarters. And President Featherston had written back, too, saying they were armed only for internal-security reasons, and that the CSA would take the weapons off as soon as things calmed down again.

So far, the USA hadn't said anything more. It had been two or three weeks now since the first protest. As far as Jeff could see, that meant his country had got away with it. He grinned as he went into the mess hall. The damnyankees had been kicking the Confederate States around for more than twenty years, but their day was ending. The CSA could walk proud again. Could . . . and would.

A colored cook fixed him a big, meaty roast-beef sandwich with all the trimmings. He got himself a cup of coffee, rich and pale with cream and full of sugar. Mayonnaise ran down his chin when he took a big bite of the sandwich. Life wasn't bad. No, sir, not bad at all.

Every time Clarence Potter put on his uniform, he looked in the mirror to see if he was dreaming. No dream: butternut tunic, a colonel's three stars on each collar patch. The cut of the tunic was slightly different from what he'd worn in the Great War. It was looser, less binding under the arms, and the collar didn't try to choke him every time he turned his head. Whoever'd redesigned it had realized a man might have to move and fight while he had it on.

Going to the War Department offices in Richmond seemed a dream, too, although he'd been doing it for a year and a half now. The sentries outside the building stiffened to attention and saluted when he went by. He returned the salutes as if he'd done it every day since the war ended. The first few times he'd saluted, though, he'd been painfully, embarrassingly, rusty.

More visitors to the War Department walked up the stairs near the entrance or paused to ask the sergeant sitting at a desk with an INFORMATION sign where they needed to go. The sergeant was plump and friendly and helpful. Few people went down the corridor past his desk. Another sign marked it: AUTHORIZED PERSONNEL ONLY.

The friendly sergeant nodded to Potter as he strode by. He went halfway down the corridor with the intimidating sign, then opened a door labeled SUPPLIES & REQUISITIONS. With careful, even fussy, precision, he closed the door behind him.

Three more guards stood on the other side of that door. Instead of bayoneted Tredegars, two of them carried submachine guns: short, ugly weapons good for nothing but turning men into hamburger at close range. The third guard had a .45 instead. He said, "Your identification, Colonel?"

As always, Potter produced the card with his photograph on it. As always, the guard gave it a once-over to make sure photo matched face. Satisfied, the man with the .45—who'd been careful not to get in his comrades' line of fire—stepped back. He pointed to the log sheet on a table past the guards. Potter put the card back in his wallet, then logged himself in. He looked at his watch before adding the time: 0642. He'd had to get used to military hours again, too.

Stairs led down from the door marked SUPPLIES & REQUISITIONS. The room where Potter worked was in a subbasement, several stories below street level. Down here, fans whirred to keep air circulating. It felt musty anyhow. In the summer, it was air-conditioned like a fancy cinema house; it would have been unbearable otherwise.

Potter sat down at his desk and started going through U.S. newspapers, most of them a day, or two, or three, out of date. *Know your enemy* had to be the oldest rule in intelligence work. Papers in the USA talked too much. They talked about all sorts of things the government would have been happier to see unsaid: movements of soldiers, of barrels, of aeroplanes, of ships; stories of what was made where, and how much, and *for* how much; railroad schedules; pieces about how the bureaucracy worked and, often, how it failed to work. Papers in the CSA had been the same way before the Freedom Party took over. They offered much less to would-be spies now.

Every so often, Clarence Potter remembered he'd come up to Richmond to assassinate President Featherston. He knew why he'd come up here to do it, too. He still believed just about everything he had during the 1936 Olympics. But he wasn't interested in shooting Featherston any more. He had too many other things going on.

He'd known Featherston was shrewd. But he hadn't realized just *how* clever the president of the CSA was, not till he saw from the inside the way Featherston operated. After shooting the Negro who'd opened fire on Featherston before he could himself, Potter could have been patted on the back and then suffered a dreadful accident. Instead, Featherston had done something even nastier: he'd given Potter a job he really wanted to do, a job he could do well, and a job where who his boss was didn't matter a bit.

"Oh, yes," Potter murmured when that thought crossed his mind. "I'd want revenge on the USA no matter who the president was."

Featherston hadn't used him in the subjugation of Louisiana. Potter hadn't even known that was in the works till it happened—which was, all by itself, a sign of good security. There were all sorts of things he didn't need to know and would be better off not knowing. The people who'd planned and brought off the Louisiana operation didn't know what he was up to, either. He hoped like hell they didn't, anyhow.

He was banging away at a typewriter, putting together a report on U.S. Navy movements out of New York harbor, when his nine o'clock appointment showed up ten minutes early. Randolph Davidson's collar tabs bore the two bars of a first lieutenant. He was in his late twenties, blond, blue-eyed, with very red cheeks and a little wisp of a mustache. Saluting, he said, "Reporting as ordered, Colonel Potter."

Potter cocked his head to one side, listening intently, weighing, judging. "Not bad," he said in judicious tones. "How did you come to sound so much like a damnyankee?" He sounded a lot like one himself; the intonations he'd picked up at Yale before the war had stuck.

"After the war, sir, my father did a lot of business in Ohio and Indiana," Davidson answered. "The whole family lived up there, and I went to school there."

"You'd certainly convince anyone on this side of the border," Potter said.

The younger man looked unhappy. "I know *that*, sir. People don't trust me on account of the way I talk. I swear I'd be a captain now if I sounded like I came from Mississippi."

"I understand. I've had some trouble along those lines myself," Potter said in sympathy. "Now the next question is, could you pass for a damnyankee on the *other* side of the border?"

Davidson didn't answer right away. Those blue eyes of his widened, and became even bluer in the process. "So *that's* what this is all about," he breathed.

"That's right." Potter spoke like one of his Yale professors: "This is what happens when two countries that don't like each other use the same language. You can usually tell somebody from Mississippi apart from somebody from Michigan without much trouble. Usually. But, with the right set of documents, somebody who sounds like a damnyankee can go up north and *be* a damnyankee—and do all sorts of other interesting things besides. What do you think of that, Lieutenant?"

"When do I start?" Davidson said.

"It's not quite so simple," Clarence Potter said with a smile. "You've got some training to do." *And we've got some more checks to do.* "But you look good. You *sound* good."

"Thank you very much, sir," Davidson said, where most Confederate citizens would have answered, *Thank you kindly.* Potter nodded approval. The younger man's grin said he knew what Potter was approving.

"I will be in touch with you, Lieutenant," Potter said. "You can count on that."

"Yes, sir!" Davidson also knew dismissal when he heard it. He got to his feet and saluted. "Freedom!"

That word still rankled. It reminded Clarence Potter of what he had been. He didn't care to think about how the man who'd redonned Confederate uniform had come to Richmond with a pistol in his pocket. He wanted to pretend he hadn't heard the word. He wanted to, but he couldn't. Lieutenant Davidson was definitely a man who spoke with a Yankee accent. That didn't mean he wasn't also a Freedom Party spy checking on the loyalty of a suspect officer.

*I'm old news now,* Potter thought. *If anything happens to me, it won't even show up in the papers. I can't afford to make people worry about me.* The calculation—one he'd gone through before—took less than a heartbeat. "Freedom!" he echoed, not with the enthusiasm of a stalwart but in a crisp, businesslike, military way.

Davidson left the underground office. Potter scribbled a couple of notes to himself. They both had to do with the background checks he'd have to make on the officer who'd gone to school in Ohio and Indiana. Some of those checks might show whether Davidson was reporting back to the Freedom Party. Others might show whether he was reporting back to U.S. Army Intelligence headquarters in Philadelphia.

Potter muttered under his breath. That was the chance he took when running this kind of operation. Somebody who sounded like a damnyankee was liable to *be* a damnyankee. The CSA spied on the USA, but the USA also spied on the CSA. If the United States could slide a spy into Confederate Intelligence, that could be worth a corps of ordinary soldiers when a second round of fighting broke out. Facing a foe who spoke your language was a two-edged sword, and could cut both ways. Anyone who didn't realize that was a fool.

"I hope I'm not a fool," Potter muttered as he went back to plugging away at his paperwork. "I hope I'm not that kind of fool, anyhow."

How could you know, though? How could you be sure? During the Great War, Potter had worried more about the tactical level than the strategic. This new job was more complex, less well defined. Here, he couldn't write something along the lines of, *Interrogation of U.S. prisoners indicates an attack in map sector A-17 will commence at 0530 day after tomorrow.* What he was looking for was subtler, more evanescent— and when he thought he saw it, he had to make sure he wasn't just seeing something his U.S. opposite number (for he surely had one) wanted him to see.

"Damn you," he said under his breath. That was aimed at Jake Featherston, but Potter knew better than to name names. Someone might be— someone almost certainly was—listening to him.

The trouble was, Featherston had known exactly what made Potter tick. *I solve puzzles. I'm good at it. Point me at something and I will get to the bottom of it. Tell me it helps my country—no, let me see with my own eyes that it helps my country—and I'll dig four times as hard to get to the bottom of it.*

Above Potter's head, the fans in the ventilation system went on whirring. The sound got to be part of him after a while. If it ever stopped, he'd probably exclaim, "What was that?" The vibration had made his fillings ache when he first came here. No more. Now it seemed as basic, as essential, as the endless swirl of blood through his veins.

A major walked past him. "After twelve," the man said. "You going to work through lunch, Colonel?"

Potter looked at his watch in amazement. Where had the morning gone? He'd done more plugging than he thought. "Not me," he said, and got to his feet. Intelligence had its own mess hall—*the secret lunchroom,* he thought with wry amusement—so men who dealt in hidden things could talk shop with no one else the wiser.

He got himself a pastrami sandwich—a taste he'd acquired in Connecticut, and not one widely shared in the CSA—and a glass of Dr. Hopper, then sat down at a table. He had it to himself. Even after a year and a half, he was still new here, still not really one of the gang. A lot of the officers in Intelligence, the elite in the C.S. Army, had served through the lean and hungry times after the Great War. They had their own cliques, and didn't readily invite johnny-come-latelies to join. They were still deciding what to make of him, too. Some of them despised Jake Featherston. Others thought him the Second Coming. With one foot in both those camps, Potter didn't fit either.

And so, instead of gabbing, he listened. *You learn more that way,* he told himself. A Yankee spy would have learned a lot, especially hearing the way names like Kentucky and Houston got thrown around. Potter had suspected that much even before he came back to Intelligence. As anyone would, he liked finding out he was right.

**S**now swirled through the air. Colonel Abner Dowling stood at stiff attention, ignoring the raw weather. Even when a flake hit him in the eye, he didn't—he wouldn't—blink. *I'll be damned if I let Salt Lake City get the best of me now,* he thought stubbornly. A military band struck up "The Star-Spangled Banner." Beside Dowling, his adjutant drew himself up even straighter than he had been.

When the last notes of the National Anthem died away, Dowling moved: he marched forward half a dozen paces to face the newly elected governor of Utah, who stood waiting in a black suit an undertaker might have worn. A mechanism might have given Dowling's salute. "Governor Young," he said.

Heber Young returned a nod at least as precisely machined. "Colonel Dowling," he replied, his tone as cool and formal as the officer's.

Flashbulbs popped, recording the moment for posterity. Purple and green spots filled Dowling's vision. He did his best not to blink on account of the flashbulbs, either. "Governor Young," he said, "at the order of President Smith, Utah is now taking its place as a state like any other in the United States, its long military occupation coming to an end. I wish you and your fellow citizens good fortune in years to come, and hope with all my heart that the peace and tranquility established here may long continue."

"Thank you very much, Colonel Dowling," Governor Young replied, and more flashbulbs popped. "We of Utah have waited a long time for this moment. Now that our government is in our own hands once more, you may rest assured that we will be diligent and careful in serving the public good."

*He's as big a liar as I am,* Dowling thought. Utah wasn't a land of peace and tranquility, and the new civilian government—the new Mormon government, since Latter-Day Saints held all the elected offices in the executive and solid majorities in both houses of the Legislature—would do whatever it damn well pleased.

Young went on, "For more than half a century now, the United States have persisted in believing that the people of Utah are different from others who call the USA home. At last, we will have the opportunity to show the country—to show the entire world—that that is not so. We are our own masters once more, and we will make the most of it."

Dowling listened politely, which took effort. Young hadn't mentioned a few things. Polygamy was one. Disloyalty was another. After an attempted secession during the Second Mexican War, an armed rebellion during the Great War, and an assassination in front of Dowling's own eyes, were the people of Utah really no different from others who called the USA home? Dowling had his doubts.

But President Smith evidently didn't, and Smith's opinion carried a lot more weight than Dowling's (even if Dowling himself carried a lot more weight than Smith). Removing the U.S. garrison from Utah would save millions of dollars that might be better spent elsewhere—provided the state didn't go up in flames and cost more money, not less. *We'll find out,* Dowling thought.

"I will work closely with the government of the United States to make sure peace prevails," Heber Young said. "Utah has been born again. With God's help, our liberty will long endure."

He nodded once more to Dowling. What did that mean? *Get out, you son of a bitch, and don't come back?* Probably, though Young, a thorough gentleman, would never have said such a thing.

Dowling gave him another salute, to show that civilian authority in the United States was superior to military. Then the commandant—now the former commandant—of Salt Lake City did a smart about-face and marched back to his men. The ceremony was over. Civilian rule had returned to Utah for the first time in more than fifty years.

Trucks waited to take the soldiers to the train station. Dowling and Captain Toricelli went in a green-gray automobile instead. Toricelli said, "Five minutes after we leave the state, the Mormon Temple will start going up again."

"What makes you think they'll wait that long?" Dowling asked, and his adjutant laughed, though he hadn't been joking. He went on, "How much do you want to bet that gilded statue of the angel Moroni will go on top of the new Temple, too?"

"Sorry, sir, but I won't touch that one," Captain Toricelli answered. The gilded copper statue that had surmounted the old Mormon Temple had disappeared before U.S. artillery and aerial bombs brought the building down in 1916. The occupying authorities had put up a huge reward for information leading to its discovery. In more than twenty years, no one had ever claimed that reward, and the statue remained undiscovered.

"I wonder what the Mormons will do now that they're legal again," Dowling said in musing tones.

"Young had to promise they wouldn't bring back polygamy," Toricelli said. "The president did squeeze that much out of him."

"Bully," Dowling replied, at which his adjutant, a much younger man, looked at him as if amazed anyone could say such a thing. Dowling's ears heated. His taste in slang had crystallized before the Great War. If he sounded old-fashioned . . . then he did, that was all.

No one shot at the auto or the trucks on the way to the station. Dowling had wondered if his men would have to fight their way out of Salt Lake City, but the withdrawal hadn't had any trouble. Maybe the Mormons didn't want to do anything to give Al Smith an excuse for changing his mind. Dowling wouldn't have, either, not in their shoes, but you never could tell with fanatics.

The Mormons did find ways to make their feelings known. Pictures and banners with beehives—their symbol of industry and the emblem of the Republic of Deseret they'd tried to set up—were everywhere. And Dowling saw the word FREEDOM! painted on more than a few walls and fences. Maybe that just meant the locals were glad to be getting out from under U.S. military occupation. But maybe it meant some of them really were as cozy with Jake Featherston's party and the Confederate States as Winthrop W. Webb had feared.

Dowling hoped the skinny little spy was safe. As far as he knew, no one had ever figured out that Webb worked for the occupying authorities. But, again, you never could tell.

At the station, most of the soldiers filed into ordinary second-class passenger cars. They would sleep—if they slept—in seats that didn't recline. Dowling and Toricelli shared a Pullman car. Dowling remembered train rides with General Custer. He didn't think he was as big a nuisance as Custer had been.

No matter what he thought, he'd never broached the subject to Captain Toricelli. Custer was a great hero to the USA, but not to Abner Dowling. As Dowling knew too well, no man was a hero to his adjutant, any more than he was to his valet. Toricelli stayed polite. That sufficed.

With a squeal of the whistle and a series of jerks, the train began to move. Toricelli said, "I won't be sorry to get out of Utah, sir, and that's the Lord's truth."

"Neither will I," Dowling allowed. "I wonder what the big brains in Philadelphia will do with me now."

He had to wait and see. He'd spent ten years as Custer's adjutant (and if that wasn't cruel and unusual punishment, he didn't know what would be) and all the time since in Utah. What next? He'd proved he could put up with cranky old men and religious fanatics. What else did that suit him for? He himself couldn't have said. Maybe the General Staff back in the *de facto* capital would have some idea.

Military engineers kept the train tracks in Utah free of mines. Dowling hoped they were on the job as the Army garrison left the state. He also hoped trains wouldn't start blowing up once the engineers stopped patrolling the tracks.

When the train passed from Utah to Colorado, Dowling let out a silent sigh of relief. Or maybe it wasn't so silent, for Captain Toricelli said, "By God, it really is good to get out, isn't it?"

"I spent fourteen years in the middle of Mormon country," Dowling answered. "After that, Captain, wouldn't *you* be glad to get away?"

His adjutant thought it over, but only for a moment. "Hell, yes!" he said. "I've been there too damn long myself."

The farther east the train got, the more Dowling wondered what sort of orders would wait for him in Philadelphia. All he knew was that he was ordered to the War Department. That could mean anything or nothing. He wondered if he still had any sort of career ahead of him, or if they would assign him to the shore defense of Nebraska or something of the sort. The farther east the train got, the more he worried, too. He was an outspoken Democrat, who'd been adjutant to one of the most outspoken Democrats of all time, and he was coming home in the middle of a Socialist administration. He'd met omens he liked better.

Captain Toricelli seemed immune to such worries. But Toricelli was only a captain. Dowling was a colonel. He'd been a colonel a long time. If he didn't get stars on his shoulders pretty soon, he never would. And a superannuated colonel was as pathetic as any other unloved old maid.

On the way to Philadelphia, the train went through Illinois and Indiana and Ohio, not through Kentucky. Going through Kentucky was less dangerous than going through Houston, but only a little. Freedom Party men, whether homegrown or imported from the CSA, made life there a pretty fair approximation of hell. Long military occupation and memories of a lost uprising had helped cow the Mormons. Nothing seemed to cow the militants in the states taken from the Confederacy.

"Think of it this way, sir," Captain Toricelli said when Dowling remarked on that. "When we put them down, our men are getting real combat training."

Dowling was tempted to go, *Bully!* again, but feared his adjutant wouldn't understand. Instead, he said, "Well, so we are, but the Confederates get it, too."

"Yes, sir. That's true." Toricelli might have bitten into a lemon at the prospect. Then he brightened. "They don't if we kill all of them."

"Right," Dowling said. There was bloodthirstiness the irascible George Armstrong Custer himself would have approved of.

Even a luxurious Pullman car palled after a few days. Dowling began to wish he'd taken an airliner from Salt Lake City. More and more people were flying these days. Still, he doubted the government would have held still for the added expense.

The train was going through Pittsburgh when he saw flags flying at half staff. Alarm shot through him. "What's gone wrong?" he asked Captain Toricelli, but his adjutant, of course, had no better way of knowing than he did. No one else on the train seemed to have any idea, either. All he could do was sit there and fret till it pulled into the station in downtown Philadelphia.

He hurried off, intending to ask the first man he saw what had happened. But a General Staff lieutenant colonel was waiting on the platform, and greeted him with, "Welcome to Philadelphia, Brigadier General Dowling. I'm John Abell." He saluted, then stuck out his hand.

In a crimson daze of delight, Dowling shook it. He heard Captain Toricelli's congratulations with half an ear. Lieutenant Colonel Abell led him to a waiting motorcar. *They think I've done something worthwhile with my time after all,* he thought. He'd wondered, as any man might.

Not for hours afterwards did he think about the flags again. It hadn't been a disaster after all, he learned: only a sign of mourning for the passing of former President Hosea Blackford.


Flora Blackford felt empty inside, empty and stunned. The rational part of her mind insisted that she shouldn't have. Hosea had been getting frail for years, failing for months, dying for weeks. He'd lived a long, full life, fuller than he could ever have imagined it before he chanced to meet Abraham Lincoln on a train ride through Dakota Territory. He'd risen from nothing to president of the United States, and he'd died peacefully, without much pain.

And Flora had loved him, and being without him felt like being without part of herself. That made the emptiness. No matter what the rational part of her mind told her, she felt as if she'd just walked in front of a train.

Joshua took it harder yet. Her son wasn't quite fourteen. He didn't have even the defenses and rationalizations Flora could throw up against what had happened. She knew Joshua was a child born late in the autumn of Hosea's life, that her husband had been lucky to see their son grow up as far as he had. All Joshua knew was that he'd just lost his father. To a boy heading toward manhood, losing a parent was more a betrayal than anything else. Your mother and father were supposed to be there for you, and be there for you forever.

In their New York apartment, Flora said, "Think of Cousin Yossel. He never got to see his father at all, because his father got killed before Yossel was born. You knew your father your whole life up till now, and you'll remember him and be proud of him as long as you live."

"That's why I miss him so much!" Joshua said, his voice cracking between the treble it had been and the baritone it would be. Tears ran down his face. He fought each spasm of sobs, fought and lost. A few years younger, and crying would still have seemed natural to him; he would have done it without self-consciousness. Now, though, he was near enough a man to take tears hard.

Flora held him. "I know, dear. I know," she said. "So do I." Joshua let himself be soothed for a little while, then broke free of her with a man's sudden heedless strength and bolted for his bedroom. He slammed the door behind him, but it couldn't muffle the pain-filled sound of fresh sobs. Flora started to go after him, but checked herself. What good would it do? He was entitled to his grief.

The telephone rang. Flora stared at it with something close to hatred. Hosea was only one day dead, and she'd already lost track of how many reporters and wireless interviewers she'd hung up on. She'd put out a statement summing up her husband's accomplishments and her own sorrow, but did that satisfy them? Not even close. The more she had to deal with them, the more convinced she grew that they were all a pack of ghouls.

Staring at the telephone didn't make it shut up. Muttering under her breath, she went over to it and picked it up. "Hello?"

"Flora, dear, this is Al Smith." That rough New York voice couldn't have belonged to anybody else. "I just wanted to call and let you know how sorry I am."

"Thank you very much, Mr. President." Flora mentally apologized to the telephone. "Thank you *very* much. I appreciate that, believe me."

"He was a good man. He did everything he could. The collapse wasn't his fault, and fixing it isn't easy." The president sighed. "Hoover found that out, and I'm doing the same damn thing. Not fair he should be stuck with the memory of it."

"I know," Flora answered. "I've been saying the same thing since 1929. The next person who pays attention will be the first."

"*I'm* paying attention," Smith said. "The services will be out West?"

"That's right. He wanted to be buried in Dakota. That was home for him. I'll do what he would have wanted."

"Good. That's good." Across the miles, Flora could all but see the president nod. "You have any trouble dealing with a *goyishe* preacher?"

In spite of everything, she laughed. The USA was a special country, all right, and New York a special state—where else would a Catholic leader come out with a perfectly fitting bit of Yiddish? "Everything seems all right so far," she answered.

"Fine," Smith said. "He gives you any *tsuris*, though, you tell him to talk to me. *I'll* fix him—you see if I don't."

"Thank you," Flora said. That made quite a picture, too: a Catholic president offering to browbeat a Methodist minister. She went on, "Joshua and I are going to fly back to Dakota this afternoon. We'll finish making arrangements on the spot, and we'll be ready when . . . when Hosea gets there." Her husband's body was coming by special train.

"Charlie will come out to the funeral," Smith said.

Now Flora found herself nodding. When Hosea was vice president, one of his duties had been going to important people's funerals, too. La Follette would only follow a long tradition there. And Al Smith himself didn't want to seem too closely associated with Hosea Blackford even in death: people still blamed Blackford for the business collapse, and Smith didn't want that to rub off on him no matter how unfair it was. Flora said, "President Sinclair has already left for Dakota."

"He can afford to," Smith answered. "He's not going to run again year after next." Yes, they were both thinking along the same lines.

"And Hoover asked if he was welcome," she added.

"What did you tell *him*?" the president asked. "He's not going to run again, either, not after the way I kicked his *tukhus*." More Yiddish, jut as fitting.

"I said yes," Flora replied. "I don't agree with a lot of the things he did—Hosea couldn't stand a lot of the things he did—but he's an honest man. You have to respect that."

"If you ask me, he's a stiff-necked, sour prig," Smith said, "but have it your own way." Flora didn't think that verdict was wrong. Maybe she had a bit of stiff-necked prig in herself, too, though, even if she did hope she wasn't sour. The president went on, "If there's anything I can do, you let me know, you hear? Don't be shy about it."

"I won't," she promised. They said their good-byes. As soon as she hung up the telephone, she started running around again. Too many things to do before she had to leave for the airport, not enough time to do them.

The airport itself was in Newark. New York City had a major airport under construction—largesse from a hometown president, and many, many jobs for local workers, all paid with federal money—but it wouldn't be done for another couple of years. The aeroplane was a twin-engined Curtiss Skymaster. It carried thirty-two people in reasonable comfort west to Omaha. Flora and Joshua spent the night in a hotel there, then boarded a smaller Ford trimotor for the trip north to Bismarck.

That flight was like falling back through time. The Ford was smaller, with corrugated-metal skin rather than smooth aluminum. The seats inside were smaller, too, and more cramped. When the aeroplane took off, it was noisier, too. It didn't fly so high, either, which meant the ride was bumpier. They flew around a storm on the prairie. Even the rough air on the outskirts was plenty to make Flora glad the airline provided airsickness bags. She turned out not to need hers, and neither did Joshua, but some of the other passengers weren't so lucky. The rest of the flight was unpleasant even with the bags. Without them . . . Well, without them it would have been worse.

A black limousine waited at the field on the outskirts of Bismarck. It took her down to the little town of Frankfort, on the James River. Hosea Blackford's nephew, William, owned a farm just outside of Frankfort; the former president would lie in the churchyard there. William Blackford and Flora weren't far from the same age. The farmer and the Congresswoman from New York City were about as different as two Americans could be, but they had an odd sort of liking. And the farm fascinated Joshua. So did William's daughter, Katie, who was blond and blue-eyed and very pretty. Flora watched that with more than a little amusement.

William Blackford did, too. "Maybe you'll have to bring the boy out some other time," he said, his voice dry.

"Maybe I will." Flora couldn't keep herself from smiling. "Or maybe you could visit New York or Philadelphia."

Her husband's nephew shook his head. "No, thanks. For one thing, you don't mean me. And I've seen Philadelphia. I don't care to go back. More people on the sidewalks, I think, than there are in all of Dakota." He wasn't far wrong, and Flora knew it. He went on, "I grew up with elbow room. I don't know what to do without it."

Flora had grown up with none whatsoever. Her family had crowded a cold-water flat, and they'd taken in boarders besides to help make ends meet. She took people and noise as much for granted as William Blackford took wide open spaces and peace and quiet. "The first time Hosea brought me to Dakota, I felt like a bug on a plate," she said. "There was too much country, too much sky, and not enough me."

"I've heard folks from back East say that before," her host replied, nodding. "I reckon it's heads to my tails, but—" He broke off, alarm on his face. "Here, let me get you a handkerchief."

"I have one." Flora reached into her handbag, pulled out a square of linen, and dabbed at her eyes. "Sometimes it catches me by surprise, that's all. I remember the good times I had with Hosea, the things he showed me, and then I remember we won't have any more, and . . . this happens." She blew her nose.

William Blackford nodded. "I know how that goes, sure enough. I lost a brother in the war. Now and again, I'll still think about going trout fishing with Ted, just like it was day before yesterday when we did it last. And I'll be . . . darned if I don't still puddle up every once in a while, too."

Three days later, dignitaries and reporters crowded Frankfort's tiny white clapboard church. The building might have come straight from New England. The enormous sweep of the horizon beyond it, though, could only have belonged to the West. Waiting had torn at Flora. Now she sympathized more than ever with the Jewish custom of holding the funeral as quickly as possible after death. These days in between were nothing but a torment.

The Reverend Albert Talbot had a face like a fish, with pale skin, big blue eyes, and a perpetually pursed mouth. His eulogy, to Flora's ears, was purely conventional, and caught little of what Hosea Blackford had stood for, little of what he had *been*. She started to get angry, wondering if she should have sicced President Smith on him after all.

But she didn't need long to decide the answer was no. Everyone else in the church, including Joshua, seemed satisfied with, even moved by, those ordinary phrases. That was what really mattered. As long as the minister's audience went away pleased with what they heard, nothing else counted for much.

And the vice president and two former presidents of the United States served as pallbearers, helping Joshua and William Blackford and a more distant relative carry the coffin out to the graveyard under that vast sky.

"He was a good man—a fine man," Upton Sinclair said.

"He was indeed," Herbert Hoover agreed. They nodded to each other, and to Flora. Socialist and Democrat, they agreed on very little, but they would not quarrel about that. Flora nodded, too, though more tears stung her eyes. Here, they were both right.

Brigadier General Daniel MacArthur was not a happy man. Colonel Irving Morrell had trouble blaming his superior. MacArthur's cigarette holder jerked in his mouth. By all appearances, the U.S. commandant in Houston was having trouble not biting right on through the holder.

"Ridiculous!" he burst out. "Absolutely ridiculous! How are we supposed to keep this state in the USA if we go easy on all the rebels and traitors inside it?"

Morrell gave him the only answer he could: "Sir, I'll be damned if I know."

"May Houston and everybody in it be damned!" MacArthur growled. "That would be just what it—and they—deserve. It's a running sore. We ought to cauterize it with hot metal."

He meant hot lead, from rifles and machine guns. Morrell didn't disagree—on the contrary. He said, "It's hard to operate where everybody in the country where you're stationed wants you to go to the devil and does his best to send you there. I thought Canada was bad. Next to this, Canada was a walk in the park."

"Next to this, hell is a walk in the park, Colonel." MacArthur gestured to the officers' club bartender. "Another one, Aristotle."

"Yes, suh, General, suh." Aristotle did the honors, then slid the whiskey across the bar to MacArthur. *Well,* he's *loyal, anyway,* Morrell thought. Any Negro who preferred Jake Featherston to Al Smith wasn't just a traitor—he was certifiably insane. Morrell wished Houston held more Negroes; they would have made a useful counterweight to all the pro-Confederate fanatics. But they were thin on the ground here.

After a sip—no, a gulp—from the new drink, Daniel MacArthur went on, "By God, Colonel, there were stretches of the front during the Great War where a man was safer than he is in Houston today. During the war, only cowards got shot in the back. Here, it can happen to anybody at any hour of the day or night."

"Yes, sir," Morrell agreed mournfully. "Taking hostages after someone does get shot hasn't worked so well as I wish it would have."

MacArthur looked disgusted—not with him, but with Houston, and perhaps with the world. "Some of these sons of bitches seem *glad* to die. It's not that I'm not glad to see them dead, either, but. . . ."

"Yes, sir. But." Morrell turned the word into a complete, and gloomy, sentence. He went on, "I think we're doing a better job of making martyrs for the Freedom Party than we are of making people decide not to take shots at us."

"Unfortunately, you are correct. Even more unfortunately, I don't know what to do about it." MacArthur stubbed out the cigarette. He stuck another one in the holder, lit it, and puffed moodily. Then he looked at the pack. " 'Finest quality tobacco from the Confederate States of America,' " he read, and made as if to throw it away. Reluctantly, he checked himself. "God damn it to hell and gone, they *do* have the best tobacco."

"Yes, sir," Morrell agreed. "When they asked for a cease-fire in 1917, the officer who came into our lines with a white flag gave me one of his smokes. After three years of the chopped hay and horse turds we called cigarettes, it was like going to heaven."

"I'd like to send half this state to heaven, assuming anybody here would go in that direction," MacArthur growled. "But even that wouldn't do much good." He finished the whiskey with another gulp. Instead of asking for another refill, he sprang to his feet and stalked out of the officers' club, trailing smoke from his cigarette. He was hot enough, he might have trailed smoke without it.

"Your glass is empty, suh," Aristotle said to Morrell. "You want I should get you another one?"

"No, thanks," he answered. "You've lived here a good long time, haven't you?" He waited for the bartender to nod, then said, "All right. Fine. What would *you* do to keep Houston in the USA?"

The black man's eyes widened. "Me, suh?" He needed a moment to realize Morrell meant the question seriously—after the time Morrell had had in Houston, he would have meant it seriously if he'd asked it of an alley cat. Aristotle said, "I reckon the first thing you do is, you blow off that Jake Featherston's head."

"I reckon you're absolutely, one hundred percent right," Morrell said. The real Greek philosopher couldn't have solved the problem better. If anything would do the job, that was it. Unfortunately . . . "Suppose we can't?"

"In that case, suh, I dunno," Aristotle said. "But I know one thing. You Yankees ever decide you leavin' this here state, you take me with you, you hear?"

"I hear you." What Morrell heard was naked terror in the man's voice. He soothed him as he would have soothed a frightened horse: "Don't you worry. We've been here twenty years. We aren't going anywhere."

"Not even if they have one o' them plebi—whatever the hell you call them things?" Aristotle asked.

"I don't think you need to fret about that," Colonel Morrell told him. "We paid for Houston in blood. I don't expect we'll give it back at the ballot box."

That seemed to get through to the bartender. He pulled out a rag from under the bar and ran it over the already gleaming polished wood. Though Aristotle seemed happier, Morrell was anything but. The colored man probably didn't pay much attention to what Al Smith said. Because of the nature of Morrell's duties, he had to. He didn't like what he'd heard. Talk of democracy and self-determination sounded very noble. He'd had some things to say on the subject himself, when the Ottoman Turks were persecuting Armenians. But when democracy and self-determination ran up against a country's need to defend itself . . .

Morrell supposed the United States could lose Houston without hurting themselves too badly, though losing the oil found in the 1920s would be a nuisance—and seeing it fall into Confederate hands would be a bigger one. The same applied to Sequoyah, where the Indians most cordially despised the U.S. occupiers, who hadn't even deigned to let the state enter the USA. Losing Kentucky, though, wouldn't be a nuisance. Losing Kentucky would be a disaster. During the War of Secession, Lincoln had said he hoped to have God on his side but he had to have Kentucky. Losing the war and the state, he'd proved to have neither.

"I take it back. Let me have another drink," Morrell said suddenly.

Aristotle fixed it for him. "On the house, suh," he said. "You done set my mind at ease, and I'm right grateful."

"Thanks." Morrell felt guilty about taking the free drink, but couldn't insist on paying without making the barkeep worry again. Morrell was worried himself. If the northern border of the Confederate States returned to the Ohio River, why had so many soldiers from the United States died to push that frontier south? What had they died for? Anything at all? Morrell couldn't see it.

But if President Smith let a plebiscite go forward, Houston, Sequoyah, and Kentucky would all vote to return to the CSA. Morrell was sure of that. And if Smith didn't let the plebiscite go forward, Jake Featherston could cuss him up one side and down the other for trampling on those wonderful things, democracy and self-determination.

Featherston had done some trampling on them himself, but not that much. He might well have won a completely honest election, and Morrell was painfully aware of it. (That Featherston had triumphed in elections with a third of his country's population disenfranchised never once crossed Morrell's mind. Negroes were politically invisible to him, as they were to most whites in the USA.)

Morrell swallowed his guilt and his worries along with the free drink. Then he left the officers' club. Fences and sandbags guarded against snipers as he made his way to Bachelor Officers' Quarters. He was sick of BOQ, but he didn't intend to bring Agnes and Mildred down from Fort Leavenworth. He got paid to risk his life for his country. The people he loved didn't.

More sandbags and barbed wire and machine-gun emplacements

protected the barrels outside of Lubbock. Morrell went out to them early the next morning. A few enthusiastic Houstonians had tried to sneak in and sabotage them in spite of the defenses. The locals' next of kin were surely most unhappy. The would-be saboteurs themselves no longer cared one way or the other. But no one had ever caught the enterprising fellows who'd lobbed mortar rounds into the U.S. encampment from somewhere inside Lubbock. Large rewards for their capture had been highly publicized, but nobody in Houston seemed interested in collecting that kind of reward.

Crewmen started showing up only a couple of minutes after Morrell got to the barrel park. "Good morning, sir," Sergeant Michael Pound said. "I thought I'd beat you here."

Sometimes he did, which annoyed Morrell. "Not today," he answered. "I spent too much of last night thinking about the way things look."

Pound shook his head. "You're braver than I am, sir. That's a dangerous thing to do these days."

"What would you do if you were king?" Morrell asked, interested to see what the sergeant would come up with.

"Abdicate," Pound said at once, which jerked a laugh out of him. The underofficer went on, "It's a lousy time to be a king, sir. All these damned democrats around—small-*d*, of course. But if I had my druthers, I'd smash the Confederate States now, before Jake Featherston uses our own better instincts to steal territory from us that we really ought to keep . . . and before he starts building barrels the way he's building tractors these days."

That marched much too well with what Morrell was thinking—right down to the remark about tractors. A factory that turned out engines or caterpillar treads for one type of vehicle wouldn't have much trouble converting to make parts for another type.

Before long, a squad of three barrels was rumbling through the streets of Lubbock. YANKEES GO HOME! was amongst the mildest of the graffiti on the walls these days. So was FREEDOM! A lot of messages told what the scribblers wanted to do with everyone in the state government of Houston who didn't belong to the Freedom Party. Morrell had seen a good deal in his time. Some of those suggestions sickened him.

Freedom Party banners flew everywhere. The reversed-color C.S. battle flag was legal, being the symbol of a political party like the Socialists' red flag and the Democrats' donkey. Morrell thought Socialist Al Smith was a donkey to let that inflammatory flag fly here, but Smith did. *Featherston uses our own better instincts to steal from us.* Michael Pound's words came back uncomfortably.

And then a middle-aged man on the street pulled out a pistol and fired at Morrell, who as usual rode with his head and shoulders and upper torso out of the cupola so he could get a better look at what was going on. The bullet clanged off the barrel's armor plate. Morrell ducked. The turret machine gun of the barrel behind him chattered. When Morrell stood straight again a moment later, he had his own .45 out and ready.

No need. The shooter was down in a pool of blood, the pistol still in his outstretched hand. A man and a woman who'd been near him were down, too, the man writhing and howling, the woman very still, her skirt flipped up carelessly over one gartered thigh. Plainly, she wouldn't rise again.

Screams filled the air after the gunfire stopped. People who'd thrown themselves flat when it started now cautiously got to their feet. A woman looked from the corpse of the man who'd tried to plug Morrell to him, then back again. She pointed a red-nailed finger at the U.S. officer in the barrel and shrieked one word: "Murderer!"

Jonathan Moss pushed the stick forward. The nose of the Wright 27 went down. He opened the throttle. The fighter dove like a stooping hawk— dove faster than any hawk dreamt of flying. Acceleration shoved him back in the seat. He eyed the airspeed indicator with something like awe—320, now 330! That was easily three times as fast as a Great War fighting scout could have flown, and he wasn't giving the aeroplane everything it had.

He watched the altimeter unwind at an awesome rate, too. *If I don't pull up pretty soon, I'm going to make a big hole in the ground. Major Finley won't be very happy with me if I do that. Neither will Laura.*

Reluctantly, he pulled back on the stick. He did it a little at a time, not all at once. He had a good notion of the fighter's limits. Even so, the wings groaned at the force they had to withstand. Pulling out of a dive like this would have torn the wings right off a machine built of wood and canvas. His vision grayed for a couple of seconds as blood poured down out of his brain, but then color returned.

"Jesus!" he said hoarsely when he was flying level once more. He caressed the curved side of the cockpit as if it were the curve of a lover. He'd never known, never imagined, an aeroplane that could do things like this.

He looked around, wondering where the hell he was. Puffy cloud shadows dappled the green and gold geometry of Ontario fields and woodlots. Then he spotted the Thames. The river naturally led his eye back to London. The Labatt's brewery was much the biggest building in town. Once he spied it, he also knew where the airfield outside would be.

As he flew back toward the field, the wireless set in the cockpit crackled to life: "A-47, this is A-49. Do you read me? Over."

A-49 was another fighter. Moss peered here and there till he spotted him at ten o'clock high. "I read you loud and clear, A-49. Go ahead. Over." He had to make himself remember to thumb the transmit button. He'd never had to worry about wireless chatter in the Great War.

"Up for a dogfight, old-timer?" the pilot of A-49 asked. *Punk kid,* Moss thought scornfully. The younger man went on, "Loser buys the beer at the officers' club. Over."

"You're on, sonny boy. Over and out," Moss snapped. With altitude, the other pilot had the edge. Moss pulled back on the stick to climb. He gave the fighter all the gas he had so he wouldn't lose too much airspeed. His opponent zoomed toward him. He spun away, heading for one of those pretty little clouds. He beat the other fighter to it, then snapped sharply to his left, still climbing for all the Wright was worth.

A moment later, he whooped like a wild man. The guy in A-49 had done just what Moss thought he would: flown straight through the cloud and looked around for him. That wasn't good enough, not anywhere close. Moss dove on his foe from behind. Of itself, his thumb went to the firing button atop the stick. He pulled his nose up and fired past the other aeroplane.

A startled squawk came from the wireless set at the sight of tracer rounds streaking by. Laughing exultantly, Moss said, "Sonny boy, you are dead as shoe leather. That beer's going to taste mighty good. Over."

"How did you do that?" The pilot of A-49 had to remember to say, "Over."

"I was playing these games when you were a gleam in your old man's eye," Moss answered. "The aeroplanes change. The tricks don't, or not much. Shall we go on in now?"

"Yeah." The young fighter pilot, like any good flier, had thought he was the hottest thing in the sky. Chagrin filled his voice when he discovered he wasn't, or at least not today.

Moss had to find the Thames and London and the airstrip all over again. He was slower doing that than the kid in A-49, and wasn't ashamed to follow the other fighter in. He had to remind himself to lower his landing gear, too; that was one more thing he hadn't had to worry about during the Great War.

He jounced the landing, hard enough to make his teeth click. But A-47 came to a stop before the end of the runway. The prop spun down to immobility. Moss pulled back the canopy and got out of the fighter. Only then, with the breeze on him, did he realize he was drenched in sweat. The dogfight had squeezed it out of him. *He'd* known it wasn't real, but his body hadn't.

Major Rex Finley came trotting up. "Those were your tracers?" he demanded. Moss nodded. Finley put hands on hips. "I wouldn't have been very happy if you'd shot Jimmy down. Neither would he, as a matter of fact."

"Sorry," said Moss, who was anything but. "He challenged me. He called me an old man. I whipped him, and I wanted to make damn sure he knew it." He waved to the other pilot, who walked toward him shaking his head. "Who's buying that beer?"

"Looks like I am," Jimmy said ruefully. Sweat plastered his dark-blond hair to his head and glistened on his face. His body had thought it was the real thing, too. He caught Major Finley's eye. "He got me good, sir. He knows what he's doing up there."

"Well, we've had to scrape some rust off," Finley remarked. Moss nodded. He couldn't argue with that. He hadn't flown for twenty years, and the state of the art had changed. But Finley nodded. "I've seen worse."

"Thanks," Moss said. "I don't know why I gave this up. It's more fun than . . . damn near anything I can think of. I guess when the war ended I just wanted to get back to what I was doing beforehand."

Major Finley nodded. "A lot of people did." He'd stayed in uniform himself, of course, doing his job so most people in the USA could get back to what they'd been doing beforehand. Moss knew as much. Finley had to know he knew, but none of that showed in the officer's voice as he went on, "Of course, having fun isn't the only reason you're doing this. Not a whole lot of folks get to have fun with the taxpayer footing the bill."

"Congressmen—that's about it," Moss agreed. Finley and Jimmy both laughed.

Laughing or not, though, Finley said, "That's about the size of it, yeah. So all right—you've proved you can still play on the first team. I'm not talking about conscripting you. But if we run into trouble, can we count on you?"

Jonathan Moss let out a long breath before he answered. "Yes," he said at last. "But if you try to put me in the air to shoot up Canucks in another rising . . . well, I'm not the best man for that job, and you or whoever else I serve under had better know it ahead of time."

"The Army knows who your wife is and what you've been doing since you moved up to Canada," Finley said dryly. "We do sometimes have to break parts in our machine. We try not to put parts into places where they're bound to break."

Thinking back to his own flying days, Moss decided Finley was probably right. Not certainly—nothing that had to do with the Army was certain—but probably. He said, "How about that beer now? It'll taste twice as good with somebody else buying." The grin Jimmy gave him was half sheepish, half *I'll get you next time.* Jonathan's grin said only one thing. *Oh, no, you won't.*

But Moss wasn't grinning when he drove back to Berlin. He understood why Major Finley worried about where his pilots would come from. The USA had been holding Canada down for more than twenty years now. The Canucks showed no sign of wanting to become Americans, none at all, despite a generation's worth of schooling and propaganda. But the United States couldn't just turn them loose and wave good-bye. If they did, the British would be back twenty minutes later. And then . . . "Encirclement," Moss muttered. That had been the U.S. strategic nightmare from the end of the War of Secession to the end of the Great War. With the Confederate States feeling their oats again, encirclement would be a disaster.

The way the world looked wasn't the only reason Moss' grin slipped on the way home. "Daddy!" Dorothy squealed when he walked in the door, and did her best to tackle him. That best was pretty good; it would have drawn a penalty on any football field from Edmonton down to Hermosillo.

"Hi, sweetie." Moss squeezed his daughter, too, though not with intent to maim. "Where's your mom?"

"I'm here," Laura called from the kitchen. "Where else would I be?"

After disentangling himself from Dorothy, Moss went into the kitchen and gave his wife a kiss. She kissed him back, but not with any great enthusiasm. "What smells good?" he asked, pretending he didn't notice.

"Roast pork," she said, and then, "Did you have a good time shooting up the countryside?"

Her voice had an edge to it. "I didn't shoot up the countryside," Moss answered steadily. "I would have shot down one American half my age if this were the real thing."

He'd hoped the prospect of a Yank going down in flames would cheer Laura, but it didn't. She said, "If anything really happened, the two of you would fly on the same side—and you'd fly against Canada. Are you going to tell me I'm wrong?"

"They wouldn't do that to me," Moss said. "I was talking about it with Major Finley."

"Ha!" she said. "If fighting started, they'd do whatever they pleased."

She could have been right. But Jonathan shook his head. "No, I don't think so. They know what I've been doing since I came to Canada. They want people they can trust to carry out their orders, and I don't think I qualify."

"Are you sure? Isn't it likely they just want Yanks who know how to fly?"

That paralleled Moss' own worries too closely for comfort. Angry because it did, he snapped, "You sound like those Canadians who want to murder me because I was born in the United States, no matter what I've tried to do up here."

Laura turned red. "There are Canadians who want to murder me, too, because you were born in the United States. Me!" She sounded furious. She was descended from, and named for, the first Laura Secord, who in the War of 1812 had done for the Canadians what Paul Revere had for the Americans in the Revolution: warned of oncoming enemy soldiers and saved the day. Laura was proud of her ancestry, and was as much a Canadian patriot as her ancestor had been.

"Yes, I know that," Moss said. "If you think it doesn't worry me, you're crazy."

*Hostages to fortune,* he thought unhappily. "If anything happened to you and Dorothy, I'd—"

"You'd what?" Laura broke in. "Hop in an aeroplane and machine-gun my people from the sky for revenge? That's not the right answer, you know."

Maybe it wasn't. It was exactly what Moss had been thinking. He knew he couldn't say that to his wife. He kissed her again instead. She looked as if she would rather have gone on arguing. To his relief, she didn't.

Hipolito Rodriguez hadn't been on a train for a long time: not since he laid down his rifle at the end of the Great War and came home to Baroyeca from west Texas. Then he'd had the taste of defeat in his mouth, sour as vomit after too much beer. Now, as the car rattled and jounced toward Hermosillo along the twisting track, he was having the time of his life.

Why not? Many of his friends from Baroyeca rode with him: among others, Carlos Ruiz and Felipe Rojas and Robert Quinn, who'd brought the Freedom Party to his home town. And better yet, Jorge and Miguel rode with him, too. What could be better than going into action with your own sons at your side? Nothing he could think of.

Everybody in the car seemed to feel the same way. Men chattered and sang snatches of Freedom Party songs and passed bottles of tequila and whiskey back and forth. Nobody got drunk, but a lot of people got happy. Rodriguez knew he was happy.

He kept an eye on his boys. He didn't want them making fools of themselves and embarrassing him in front of his comrades. But they did fine. They mostly stared out the window, watching the landscape change. Even in the Freedom Youth Corps, they hadn't gone so far from home.

As the crow flew, Hermosillo was about 150 miles northwest of Baroyeca. The railroad line from the little mining town to the capital of Sonora was no crow. It went west from Baroyeca to Buenavista, south to Terim, west to Guaymas on the coast, and then, at last, north to Hermosillo. That made the journey take twice as long as it would have by a more direct route, but Rodriguez didn't mind. No, he didn't mind at all.

He nodded to Robert Quinn. "*Gracias, muchas gracias, señor,* for arranging to have the Freedom Party pay for our fares. We never would have been able to come otherwise."

"*El gusto es mio,*" Quinn answered with a smile. "The pleasure is also that of the *Partido de Libertad*. This is important business we are going to tend to in Hermosillo. We need all the help we can get. We need it, and we are going to have it. No one can stop us. No one at all."

Hipolito Rodriguez nodded again. "No. Of course not." Hadn't he seen Don Gustavo, his one-time *patrón,* turned away from the polling place in Baroyeca? Hadn't he helped turn him away? Yes, indeed, nothing could stop the Freedom Party.

They got into Hermosillo late that afternoon. It was as big a city as Rodriguez had ever seen—big enough to make his sons' eyes bug out of their heads. The train station stood a couple of miles north of downtown. Rodriguez wondered whether they would have to march down to the Plaza Zaragoza, the square where they would go into action, but buses draped with PARTIDO DE LIBERTAD banners waited for them. The men from Baroyeca weren't the only Freedom Party members who'd come to Hermosillo on the train. By the time everybody filed aboard the buses, there weren't many empty seats.

The ridge line of the Cerro de la Campaña rose higher in the southern sky as the buses rolled down toward the Plaza Zaragoza. Rodriguez noted the hill only peripherally. He was used to mountains. The profusion of houses and shops and restaurants and motorcars was something else again. More than half the signs, he noted, were in English, which had a stronger hold in the city than in the Sonoran countryside.

Hermosillo's two grandest monuments stood on either side of the Plaza Zaragoza. To the west was the Catedral de la Asunción, to the east the Palacio de Gobierno. A cathedral had stood next to the plaza since the eighteenth century. When Sonora passed from the Empire of Mexico to the Confederate States in the early 1880s, the original adobe building had been crumbling into ruin. The replacement, not completed till the early years of the twentieth century, dwarfed its predecessor in size and splendor. With its two great bell towers and elaborate ornamentation, it put Rodriguez in mind of a gigantic white wedding cake.

It dwarfed the Palacio de Gobierno on the other side of the square, though that brick-and-adobe structure was impressive in its own right. And, since the Palacio de Gobierno housed the governor and legislature of the state of Sonora, it was of more immediate concern to the Freedom Party than the cathedral. God could take care of Himself. Secular affairs needed a nudge in the right direction.

Freedom Party men already jammed the Plaza Zaragoza. They greeted the latest set of newcomers with calls of, "Freedom!" and "¡Libertad!" and handed out signs, some in Spanish, others in English. Rodriguez looked up at the one he got. In English, it said, REPEAL THE SEVEN WORDS!

Robert Quinn translated for him, knowing he didn't have much written English: "Abrogan las siete palabras." The Freedom Party man went on, "You understand what that means?"

"Oh, sí, sí," Rodriguez said. "The Constitution."

"That's right." Quinn nodded. "The way it is now, it says"—he switched from Spanish to English—" 'The Executive power shall be vested in a President of the Confederate States of America. He and the Vice-President shall hold their offices for the term of six years; but the President shall not be reeligible.' "

"But if we take out the last seven words, President Featherston can run again next year," Rodriguez said.

"Exactamente," Quinn agreed. "That's what the Constitutional amendment the legislature is debating will do. South Carolina and Mississippi demanded that the Congress in Richmond call a Constitutional convention, so it did, and the convention reported out this amendment. As soon as two-thirds of the states in the CSA ratify it, it becomes the new law."

"It will become law, won't it?" Rodriguez asked anxiously.

"Oh, yes. Absolutamente." Quinn grinned. "The Partido de Libertad has a big majority in both houses of the legislature here in Sonora, and in all the other states it needs to pass the amendment. This demonstration is mostly for show. But show is an important part of politics, too, eh?"

"Yes." Rodriguez's time in the Freedom Party had left him sure of that. "If people see many other people want the change made, they will all be happy with it."

"Just so. You are a clever fellow, *Señor* Rodriguez." Quinn hesitated, then asked, "Have you ever thought of doing anything but farming?"

"Not for myself. It's what I know, and I am not ready to move to the big city to try something else," Rodriguez answered. "For my sons, though—well, who knows?"

The sun sank toward the western horizon. Rodriguez's belly growled and rumbled. He wondered what he would eat, and if he would eat anything. Quinn hadn't told him to bring food along. He wished the Freedom Party man would have; even a few tortillas would have helped hold emptiness at bay.

But he started worrying too soon. Here and there, fires began to burn in the Plaza Zaragoza. The savory smell of cooking meat rose from them. "Form lines!" somebody shouted. "Form lines to the nearest fires! Form lines, and you'll all be fed!"

A lot of the Freedom Party followers were veterans. They knew how to queue up. Some of the younger fellows in the plaza milled about at first, but not for long. Shouts and elbows got them into place.

A woman whose features said she had more Spanish blood than Indian handed Rodriguez two rolled tortillas filled with *carne asada* when he got to the head of the line. *"Gracias, señora,"* he said.

*"De nada,"* she answered. *"¡Libertad!"*

*"¡Libertad!"* he echoed, and then got out of the way so she could feed the man behind him. He took a big bite from one of the tortillas. *Carne asada* was a Sonoran specialty; the grilled, spicy beef came with chilies that made him long for a cold beer to put out the fire in his mouth.

He looked around hopefully, but didn't see anybody passing out bottles of beer. After a while, though, he did hear someone calling, *"¡Agua! Agua fresca aquí."* He got into another line, eating as he snaked forward. A dipperful of fresh water gave him most of what he wanted, though he still would rather have had beer.

He wondered if anyone would pass out blankets. Nobody did. He hadn't slept on bare ground since the Great War ended. He also wondered if his sons would complain, but they didn't. He supposed they'd spent their fair share of time sleeping outdoors in the Freedom Youth Corps. They knew enough to close up with him and several other men. The night got chilly, but all that body warmth kept anyone from having too bad a time.

Rodriguez woke before sunup. He didn't remember getting so stiff and sore in the trenches in Texas. Of course, that had been half a lifetime earlier. When Miguel and Jorge climbed to their feet, they seemed fresh enough. More lines formed, these for tortillas for breakfast and for strong coffee partly tamed with lots of cream.

More Freedom Party men came into the square in the early morning hours. They dressed like townsfolk, not peasants. Rodriguez guessed they were native Hermosillans. They didn't need feeding, but they got their signs on the edge of the plaza. Things had to look right.

And things had to sound right. When the real demonstration got under way a little past nine, the chants had been carefully organized. *"¡Abrogan las siete palabras!"* the Freedom Party men roared in rhythmic unison, and then, in English, "Repeal the seven words!" After that came choruses of, "Featherston!" and *"¡Libertad!"* and "Freedom!" Then the cycle began again.

Newsreel cameras filmed the crowd in the Plaza Zaragoza. Rodriguez wondered how many state capitals had chanting crowds putting pressure on legislators and governors. Enough. He was sure of that. The Freedom Party would make sure the Constitutional amendment took effect well before next year's elections.

Not everything that happened in the Plaza Zaragoza was official and planned in advance. Somebody behind Rodriguez tapped him on the shoulder. When he looked around, a man with a big black mustache passed him a flask. He swigged, expecting tequila. Good brandy ran down his throat instead. *"¡Madre de Dios!"* he said reverently, and handed the flask to Jorge, who stood next to him. His son gulped, coughed, and then grinned.

The bells in the cathedral had just struck twelve when a man in a somber black suit came out of the Palacio de Gobierno. He held up his hands. Little by little, the demonstrators stopped their choruses. "I am pleased to inform you," he called in English, "that the amendment to our dear Confederate Constitution has passed both houses of the legislature of Sonora. We have voted to repeal the seven words! Freedom!" Then he said the same thing in Spanish.

The Plaza Zaragoza went wild. Men threw hats in the air. Others threw their signs in the air. Still others cursed when those came down— they were heavy enough to hurt. "Freedom!" some shouted. Others yelled, *"¡Libertad!"*

Rodriguez shouted in Spanish, then in English, and then in Spanish again. Which language he used didn't seem to matter. The Freedom Party had won. Jake Featherston had won. That made him feel as if he'd won, too.

Someone started a new chant: "Nothing can stop us!" He gladly joined in. How could he not believe that, when it was so obviously true?

\* \* \*

**A**rmstrong Grimes didn't want to get out of bed. He mumbled and tried to stick his head under the pillow when his mother shook him awake. "Get up!" Edna Grimes said sharply. "Annie's already eating breakfast. You don't want your father coming in here, do you? You'd better not, that's all I've got to tell you."

He didn't. With a last resentful mutter, he got to his feet and went into the bathroom to take a leak and brush his teeth and splash cold water on his face. He looked at himself in the mirror, trying to decide whether he needed to shave. He had his mother's long, oval face, but his coloring was darker, more like his father's. "Hell with it," he said to his reflection. He'd shaved the day before, and at sixteen he didn't have much more than peach fuzz to begin with. He also had pimples, which made shaving even less fun than it would have been otherwise.

Back to his room. He put on a checked shirt and a pair of slacks. He would rather have worn blue jeans, but his father wouldn't let him get away with it, not when he was going to high school. Some of his friends wore dungarees all the time. He'd pointed that out to his old man— pointed it out in loud, shrill, piercing tones. It hadn't done him any good at all. Merle Grimes wasn't a man to bellow and carry on. But once he said no, he wasn't a man to change his mind, either.

With a martyred sigh, Armstrong carried his three-ring binder and the books he'd brought home the night before out to the kitchen. Annie, who was four, was making a mess of a bowl of oatmeal. Armstrong's mother had a plate of scrambled eggs and toast and a glass of milk waiting for him. His father was digging into a similar breakfast, except he had coffee instead of milk. "Morning," he said.

"Morning, Pa," Armstrong answered. Breakfast resigned him to being up.

Then his father had to go and ask, "Did you get all your homework done?"

"Yes, Pa," Armstrong said. *As much of it as I understood, anyhow,* he added, but only to himself. His junior year, which had started two weeks earlier, hadn't been much fun so far. If algebra wasn't something Satan had invented to torment indifferent students, he couldn't imagine what it was.

"You'd better keep your grades up, then," Merle Grimes said. *He* could do algebra. Armstrong gave him a resentful look. His father could do algebra with effortless ease. What he couldn't do was show Armstrong how he did it. *Because this is how it works,* he'd say, and wave his hands and cast a spell (that was how it looked to Armstrong, anyway) and come up with the right answer. And when Armstrong tried waving *his* hands . . . he'd add when he should have subtracted, or he'd forget what to do with a negative number, or he'd just stare at a problem in helpless horror, with no idea how to start it, let alone finish.

His father got his pipe going and worked his way through the newspaper. He didn't have to get to the office till half past eight, so he could take his time. Armstrong had to be at Roosevelt High at eight o'clock sharp, or else the truant officer would start sniffing around. That meant he had to gobble his breakfast—no great hardship for a sixteen-year-old boy, but he didn't like getting up from the table while his old man lingered.

Annie waved good-bye. His mother called, "So long, son," as he went out the front door. His only answer was a grunt. As soon as he got around the corner, he lit a cigarette. The first drag made him cough. He felt woozy and lightheaded and a little sick; he was just learning to smoke. Then his heart beat harder and he felt more alert. He enjoyed that feeling, even if it wasn't the main reason he'd started smoking. People he liked smoked. So did people he wanted to be like. That counted for more.

He smoked two cigarettes on the way to Roosevelt, but made sure the pack was out of sight before he got to the campus. Smoking there was against the rules. The principal had a big paddle in his office, and he wasn't shy about using it.

"Morning, Armstrong," a boy called.

"Hey, Joe," Armstrong answered. "Can I get some answers to the algebra from you?"

Joe shook his head. "I don't know how they do that stuff. I'm gonna flunk, and my old man's gonna beat hell out of me."

"Me, too," Armstrong said dolefully. He still had a couple of periods to go before he had to turn in the math homework, such as it was. He didn't look forward to English literature, which he had first, with any great enthusiasm, either. Memorizing chunks of *The Canterbury Tales* in the original incomprehensible Middle English wasn't his idea of fun. But getting walloped because he didn't do it also wasn't his idea of fun, so he tried.

English Lit did have one compensation. He sat next to Lucy Houlihan, a redhead who had to be one of the three or four prettiest girls at Roosevelt High. That would have been even better had Lucy had the slightest idea he existed. But she didn't. She had a boyfriend: Frankie Sprague, the star tailback on the Regiment. Still, she couldn't shoot Armstrong for looking at her, as long as he didn't drool too much while he was doing it.

The textbook, naturally, didn't include "The Miller's Tale." Herb

Rosen, one of the class brains, had found out about it, and started whispering. By the time the whispers got to Armstrong, they were pretty distorted, but the piece still sounded juicier than anything the class *was* studying. He wondered why they couldn't read the good stuff instead of boring crap about sweet showers.

A trail of sniggers ran through the class. "The Miller's Tale" would do that. "And what is so funny?" Miss Loomis inquired. She was a tall, muscular spinster with a baritone voice. She didn't use a paddle. She wielded a ruler instead, with deadly effect. Nobody said anything. The sniggers didn't stop, but they did ease. Miss Loomis looked at the students over the tops of her half-glasses. "That will be quite enough of that," she declared, and got on with the lesson.

As soon as Miss Loomis turned back to the blackboard, Lucy asked Armstrong, "Why *is* everybody laughing?" She hadn't heard, then. Well, some guys would be shy about saying such things to a girl.

Armstrong wasn't shy about anything—and having Lucy notice him for any reason at all was a reasonable facsimile of heaven. He gleefully told her everything he'd heard about "The Miller's Tale." Odds were, Chaucer wouldn't have recognized it. It was still plenty to make Lucy turn pink. Armstrong watched the blush in fascination—so much fascination that he didn't notice Miss Loomis bearing down on him.

*Whack!* The ruler scorched his knuckles. He jumped and yelped in pain. Miss Loomis fixed him with a glare that would have paralyzed Jake Featherston. "That will be enough of that," she said, and marched back up to the front of the classroom.

Lucy, damn her, didn't even say she was sorry.

He was glad to flee English Lit for government, even though Miss Thornton, who taught it, was almost as big a battle-axe as Miss Loomis. She didn't look so formidable, being round rather than tall, with a bosom about the size of the USS *Remembrance*. But she was a stickler for detail. And, naturally, she picked on him. "Why is the new Confederate Constitutional amendment so important?" she demanded.

"Uh," he said, and said no more. He remembered his father saying something about the amendment, but couldn't remember what to save his life—or his grade.

"Zero," Miss Thornton said crisply, and wrote it in the roll book. She asked Herb Rosen. Herb didn't just read Chaucer for fun; he even read textbooks for fun.

"Because now their president can be elected for lots of terms, not just one," he answered. "It looks like the Freedom Party is setting things up for him to be president for life."

A girl stuck up her hand. Miss Thornton nodded to her. She said, "I don't think that's true. Our presidents can be elected more than once, and nobody's ever been president for life."

"That's because we've got a custom of stopping after two terms. Even Teddy Roosevelt lost when he tried for a third one," Herb said. That touched off a discussion about the role of unwritten custom in government.

Armstrong Grimes listened with no more than half an ear. Somebody was going to be on top, and somebody else was going to get it in the neck. That was how things worked, as far as he could see, and nobody could do anything much about it. The most you could do was try to be the fellow who came out on top.

Miss Thornton left him alone for the rest of the period. But when the class ended, he had to go on to algebra, and he got it in the neck. Mr. Marr, the algebra teacher, had lost his right arm during the war. He'd had to teach himself to write and eat lefthanded. He'd done it, too, and come away convinced that anybody could teach himself to do anything. But Armstrong hadn't been able to teach himself to do algebra.

He had to go up to the board to try a problem. He butchered it. Mr. Marr glared at him. "If you multiplied one side of the equation by six, why didn't you multiply the other side by six, too?" he snapped.

"Uh, I don't know," Armstrong answered helplessly.

"Well, *that's* obvious," Mr. Marr said. "Sit down." He did the problem himself. When he did it, it looked easy. Multiply, subtract, and what do you know? X equals seven. Armstrong knew he wouldn't be able to do it himself, not if he lived to be a hundred.

"Not your day today," somebody said when the bell rang and they escaped to lunch: a period's worth of freedom.

"No kidding," Armstrong said. "They can't teach for beans, and I'm the one who gets in trouble on account of it." That a lot of the other students in his classes were having no trouble at all didn't occur to him. Far easier to blame his teachers than himself.

After lunch came chemistry. He'd had hopes for chemistry. If they'd shown him how to make things that blew up, he would have worked hard. But learning that lithium was always +1, oxygen was always -2, and carbon was ±4 left him cold. He staggered through a quiz, and hoped he got a C.

Wood shop went better. His hands had some skill in them, even if he'd never make a big brain. He was making a spice rack for the kitchen, and everything was going about as well as it could. Mr. Walsh stopped and watched him work with a file and sandpaper. The shop teacher nodded. "Not bad, Grimes," he said. "You keep it up, and you'll have no trouble finding a job when you get out of high school."

The only reason Armstrong intended to graduate was that he knew his old man would murder him if he didn't. He didn't tell that to Mr. Walsh. If the teacher hadn't heard it a million times before, he would have been amazed.

At last PE, and Armstrong came into his own. He was stronger and faster than most of the other boys in his class, and he reveled in it. And from PE he went straight to football practice. He was only a second-string defensive end, but he threw himself into every play as if his life depended on it. The harder he practiced, the more playing time he'd get when the game came Friday night.

And there across from him, taking snaps in the single wing, was Frankie goddamn Sprague. *Think you're going to get your hand under Lucy Houlihan's blouse, do you?* Armstrong spun past the tackle trying to block him, steamrollered the fullback, and knocked Frankie Sprague right on his ass.

# XI

"**I**'m off." Chester Martin blew Rita a kiss and Carl another one. His wife and their son sent kisses through the air back toward him, too. He was glad to get them as he went out the door and headed for the bus stop.

It had rained the day before, the first rain of the season in Los Angeles. The sky was a brilliant blue now, as if the rain had washed it clean. Even late in October, the weather would get up into the seventies. Chester remembered Toledo with a fondness that diminished every year he stayed in California. You couldn't beat this weather no matter how hard you tried.

A bum slept in a doorway, a blanket wrapped around him. Living here without money was easier than it was in the eastern USA, because people didn't have to worry so much about shelter. Idly, Martin wondered if Florida and Cuba had more than their share of out-of-work people in the CSA for the same reason.

He needed a southbound trolley today. He was heading down to Hawthorne, a suburb south of the airport and not far from the beach. Mordechai's crew was running up a pair of apartment buildings. People with jobs kept moving to Southern California, too, and they all needed places to live.

When the trolley rolled up, Martin threw his nickel in the fare box, paid two cents more for a transfer, and then sat down with his toolbox in his lap. Even though that toolbox was a sign he had work to go to, he didn't stop worrying. The way things were these days, who could? He wondered if he would be able to go on working after Mordechai retired. The foreman with the missing fingers on his right hand had to be past sixty. Whoever replaced him might have new favorites who needed jobs. In a trade without a union, that sort of thing was always a worry.

Posters praising candidates for the upcoming Congressional elections sprouted like toadstools on walls and fences and telephone poles: Democratic red, white, and blue against Socialist red and, here and there, Republican green. Trying to guess who'd win by seeing who had the most posters up was a mug's game, which didn't mean people didn't play it all the time. By the way things looked here, the two big parties were running neck and neck. Outside of a few states in the Midwest, Republicans had a hard time getting elected. Their ideas were stuck between those of the Democrats and the Socialists, and old-timers still associated them with the nineteenth-century disasters the USA had suffered under Lincoln and Blaine.

Martin changed lines on El Segundo. He got off the trolley at Hawthorne Boulevard and walked two blocks south and three blocks east. Mordechai waved to him when he came up, calling, "Morning, Chester."

"Morning," Martin answered. About half the crew—who lived all over the Los Angeles area—were already there. It was still only a quarter to eight. Chester didn't expect many people to show up after eight o'clock. You did that more than once—twice if you were lucky—and some hungry son of a bitch would grab your job with both hands.

This morning, only Dushan came in late. He was plainly hung over. Mordechai said something to him. He nodded in a gingerly way, then got to work. He depended on construction work less than most of the other men, for he could make cards and dice behave the way he wanted them to. That let him—or he thought that let him—get away with showing up late every once in a while.

He buckled down willingly enough, even if the banging of hammers made him turn pale. The fellow working alongside Chester, a big Pole named Stan, said, "Goddamn if Dushan don't look like a vampire left out in the sun."

The past few years, there'd been a lot of films about vampires and werewolves and other things that should have been dead but weren't. That probably put the comparison in Stan's mind. It was good enough to make Martin nod. All the same, he said, "Don't let Dushan hear that. He's from the old country, and he's liable to take it the wrong way."

"Let him. I ain't afraid," Stan said. He was bigger and younger than Dushan, so he had reason to be confident. Still . . .

"Don't push it." Now Chester sounded a plain warning. "Why start trouble?"

"You're not my grandma," Stan said. But, to Martin's relief, he went back to driving nails and let Dushan alone.

It didn't last. Chester might have known it wouldn't. Something in him *had* known it wouldn't. But he couldn't do anything but watch when the trouble started. He was two stories up, nailing rafters to the roof pole, when Stan got in front of Dushan down on the ground and made as if to drive a stake through his heart.

Dushan looked at him for half a second. Then, his cold face revealing nothing of what he intended, he kicked Stan in the crotch. Had his booted foot gone home as he intended, there wouldn't have been a fight, because Stan wouldn't have been able to give him one. But, maybe because of his hangover, the kick got Stan in the hipbone rather than somewhere more intimate.

Stan roared with pain. But he didn't fall over clutching at himself, which was what Dushan had had in mind. Instead, he surged forward and grappled with the other man. They fell to the ground, slugging and gouging and spitting out a couple of different flavors of guttural, consonant-filled Slavic curses.

"Oh, for Christ's sake!" Chester descended as fast as he could. He was cursing, too, almost as angry at himself as he was at Stan and Dushan. He'd seen trouble coming, but he hadn't been able to stop it.

"Fight! Fight!" The shout brought construction workers running, just as it would have brought kids running on a high-school campus. Most of the workers only stood around and watched without trying to break it up. It was entertainment, something to liven up the day, something to talk about over the supper table tonight.

"Come on, let's get 'em apart," Chester said. Still enjoying the show, the men at his side looked at him as if he were crazy—till Mordechai got there a few seconds later.

Not much made Mordechai mad. Anything that slowed down work and threatened the job would do the trick, though. Swearing like the veteran Navy man he was, he shoved through the crowd of workers, most of whom were twice his size and half his age. Seeing that, Chester did some pushing and shoving of his own. The two of them grabbed Dushan and Stan and pulled them apart. Once they actually started doing that, they got some belated help from the other men.

Dushan twisted in Chester's grasp, trying to wade back into the scrap. That might have been more for form's sake than anything else. He hadn't been getting the better of it. He had a bloody nose and a black eye and a scraped cheek. He'd hung a pretty good mouse on Stan, too, but the Pole hadn't taken anywhere near so much damage as he had.

"What the hell happened here?" Mordechai couldn't have sounded more disgusted if he'd tried for a week.

Dushan and Stan both gave highly colored versions of recent events. Some of the builders who'd been watching supported one of them, some the other, and some gave versions of their own that had very little to do with anything that had really gone on—that was how it seemed to Chester, anyhow.

Mordechai listened for a little while, then threw up his hands. "Enough!" he said. "Too goddamn much." He used his mutilated right hand to point first to Stan, then to Dushan. Somehow, his two missing fingers made the gesture seem even more contemptuous than it would have otherwise. "You're fired, and you're fired, too. Get the fuck out of here, both of you. I don't want to see either one of your goddamn ugly mugs again, either. And you both blow all of today's pay."

A sigh went through the workers. Nobody'd expected anything different. Dushan never changed expression. Stan said, "Fuck you, asshole," but his bravado rang hollow. Word would get around, and get around quick. He'd have a tough time landing construction work from here on out. He was just an ordinary worker, easily replaceable by another ordinary worker.

If Mordechai had stopped there, nothing more would have come of it. But he was furious, and he held the whip hand. "And the rest of you pussies," he said, glaring at the men around him, "the rest of you pussies lose half a day's pay for standing around while all this shit was going on."

"That's not fair!" Chester Martin exclaimed. Several other men muttered and grumbled, but he was the one who spoke out loud.

Mordechai glowered. "You don't like it, you know what you can do about it."

He meant, *nothing*. But Martin wasn't a veteran of union strife in Toledo for nothing, or to take nothing lying down. "Yeah," he said stonily. "I know what I can do about it."

As soon as people went back to work, he started doing it. He hadn't done any union agitating for years, but he still knew how. Some of the men didn't want to listen to him. "You're gonna get your ass fired, and everybody else's, too," was something he heard more than once.

But others were ready to go along. Mordechai had hit too hard when he punished workers for something they hadn't done. And a lot of the men who'd come to California to find jobs had belonged to unions back East. They remembered the gains they'd made, gains they'd had to throw away to find any work at all out here.

"We've got to spread the word," Chester warned. "If we just strike at this site, they'll crush us. But if we strike at *all* the building sites around Los Angeles, the bosses will have to deal with us." He hoped they would, anyhow. And if they didn't . . . well, he'd gone on strike before.

When he got his pay at the end of the day—half a day's pay for a whole day's hard work—he said, "I'm taking this under protest."

The paymaster shrugged. "Take it and like it or take it and stick it up your ass." He had a couple of bully boys with pistols behind him to make sure the payroll stayed safe. He could afford to talk tough—or thought he could, anyhow.

Martin thought he was playing into the workers' hands. Several other men said, "I'm taking this under protest," too. The paymaster went right on shrugging. He didn't see the resentment he was raising—either that or, secure in his power, he just didn't care.

That evening, when Chester told Rita what had happened, she looked at him for a long time before asking, "Are you sure you want to go through with this?" He knew what she meant; now that he had a child, he'd given fortune a hostage.

He sighed. "Do you want me to knuckle under?"

His wife bit her lip. After half a minute's silence, she said, "No. They'll own you if you do." He kissed her. He'd thought—he'd hoped— she would say that. She was a stronger Socialist than he was.

He spent the next few weeks working his shift during the day and agitating during his free time. He talked with workers. He talked with Socialist Party officials. The Socialists gained seats in the House and Senate—and in the California legislature—in the off-year elections. That strengthened his hand. He hoped it did, anyhow.

One morning early in December, he got to the construction site at the same time as a pickup truck. Instead of going in to work, he grabbed a sign from the back of the truck. He wasn't the only one who did. Inside of two minutes, three dozen UNFAIR! signs went up in a picket line. Picketers were hitting other sites all over town, too. "On strike!" Chester and the other men shouted. "Join us!" They cursed a worker who crossed the picket line. Another worker thought better of it.

"You sons of bitches!" Mordechai shouted. "You'll pay for this!"

"We've paid too much for too long already," Chester answered, wondering how much he would have to pay from here on out.

As soon as the engineer waved and the red light in the studio came on, Jake Featherston leaned toward the microphone like a lover toward his beloved. "I'm Jake Featherston, and I'm here to tell you the truth." He wondered how many times he'd said that over the years. He always believed it, at least while he was talking.

"Truth is, for the past twenty years and more, the United States of America have been holding on to what doesn't belong to them. At the end of the war, the USA stole Kentucky and Sequoyah and what they call Houston. The people in those states don't want to belong to the USA. They've made it plain every way they know how that they don't want to belong to the USA, but the United States government doesn't want to listen to them."

He paused to let that sink in, then went on, "If they held fair and honest elections in those places, the people there would show what they wanted. They would show they want to come home to the Confederate States of America. President Smith knows that as well as I do. He's a clever man, and I reckon he's an honest man."

He didn't think Smith was anything close to clever, and couldn't have cared less whether he was honest. He did want to butter up the president of the United States. He had his reasons: "I challenge President Smith to allow plebiscites in Kentucky and Sequoyah and what they call Houston. I challenge him to abide by the results of those plebiscites. I challenge him, after the Confederate States win those plebiscites, to let those states come home."

Featherston banged his fist down on the table. The microphone jumped a little. He loved sound effects like that. They made people pay attention to what he was saying. "President Smith has talked big about what he'd do to restore peace in the stolen states. He's talked big, but he hasn't done anything much. He's even said he'd come to Richmond to hash things out. He's said that, but he hasn't done it. I tell him he's welcome here, and I'd like to talk to him.

"And I tell him one more thing, something he'd better listen to. Back during the war, the USA helped our niggers when they rose up against us. Well, that was wartime, and maybe we can let bygones be bygones on account of it was. But the blacks still don't know their proper place, and the United States are still sneaking weapons down across the border to 'em. That has got to stop. It's cost us a lot of lives and it's cost us a lot of money to keep the niggers in check. We've had to bump up the size of the Army. We've even had to put guns and bombs on our aeroplanes. It's been expensive. We could have done better things with that money. We could have, but we didn't get the chance. And that's the USA's fault."

Inside, he was laughing. Here he was, blaming the United States for what he'd most wanted to do anyhow. The black guerrillas had given him the perfect excuse for rearming. Even the USA hadn't squawked much about it. Had the guerrillas been white, he thought the USA would have. But the United States loved Negroes hardly more than the Confederate States did. They'd made it very plain they didn't want the ones who tried to flee to the north.

He didn't know whether the United States were arming the guerrillas. He knew he would have if he were in charge in Philadelphia. But coming up with U.S.-made weapons and putting them in the hands of dead Negroes so photographers could snap pictures of them was the easiest thing in the world.

"President Smith says the United States want peace. They act like they want trouble. We would rather have peace, too. But if they think we can't handle trouble, they had better think again."

That was a bluff, nothing else but. If the United States pushed hard against the Confederate States, he hadn't a prayer of resisting. But the USA had seemed ever more reluctant to hang on to their conquests. If they couldn't even manage that, they weren't very likely to do anything more.

In the control room, the engineer held up a hand, fingers spread: five minutes. Jake nodded to show he'd seen the signal. He'd had a good notion of what the time was, but he wanted to make sure everything ran smoothly. "North America is a big place," he said. "We're not all crowded together, the way they are in Europe. There's room on this continent for two great countries—maybe even for three, if the United States ever bother to recollect what they've done up in the north." A smile that was half snarl flitted across his face. He enjoyed nothing more than sticking a needle in the USA. "If the United States think the Confederate States can't be great again, if they think we *shouldn't* be great again, then they had better think again about that, too.

"All we really want is for them to take their noses out of our affairs, to take them out and to keep them out. That's what good neighbors do. Bad neighbors get doors slammed in their faces, and they deserve it, too. But I don't really expect we'll have any trouble. If they're just reasonable, we'll get on fine."

To Featherston, *if they're just reasonable* meant *if they do what I want*. That the phrase could mean anything else never occurred to him. He'd just said the last word when the engineer drew a finger across his throat and the red light went out. Jake got to his feet and stretched. As usual, Saul Goldman waited for him right outside the studio door. Goldman's title—director of communications—didn't sound like much, any more than the little Jew looked like much. But it meant that Goldman was in charge of the way the Freedom Party and the Confederate States presented themselves to the world.

"Good job, Mr. President," he said now.

"Thank you kindly, Saul," Jake answered. He spent more politeness on Goldman than on most people, a recognition of how valuable he thought the other man was. The Party and the CSA could get by without a lot of fellows who brought only fanaticism. Losing somebody with brains would have hurt much more. Brains were harder to come by.

Goldman said, "You do remember you've got the rally tonight? That's going to be the speech about agriculture and about the dams and electricity."

"I remember," Jake said indulgently. "Got to talk about what's going on inside the country. That's what most folks worry about first. Wouldn't want anything to go wrong with my reelection." He laughed. Nothing would go wrong. But saying the word felt good. Up till now, no elected Confederate president had, or could have, been reelected. Now that the amendment had repealed those seven nasty words, though, Jake could go on about his business without worrying about leaving office after only six years. He clapped Goldman on the back. "You did real good with the campaign for the amendment, too."

"Thank you, Mr. President," Goldman said. "You're the one who will have to make it worthwhile."

"And I intend to," Featherston said.

He was feeling pretty cocky as he strode out of the studio and got into his armored limousine. "Back to the Gray House?" the driver asked.

"That's right, Virgil," Jake answered. Virgil Joyner had been driving him for years—ever since the Party struggled for survival after Grady Calkins assassinated President Hampton. Featherston trusted him as far as he trusted anybody.

Outriders on motorcycles pulled away from the curb before the limousine got going. Featherston didn't believe in taking chances he didn't have to. He wanted to make sure he got to enjoy his second term.

The limousine glided past Capitol Square. Everything there was clean and tidy and orderly. No more shantytown right at the heart of the CSA. All the hungry squatters had been cleared away well before the Olympics, and they hadn't come back. Freedom Party stalwarts made damn sure they didn't come back.

But instead of turning left to go up Shockoe Hill to the presidential residence, the driver hit the brakes. "What the hell?" Jake said.

"There's a wreck up ahead," Joyner answered. "We'll have to go around."

Sure enough, not just two but three autos had tangled at the corner of Twelfth and Capitol. Steam jetted from smashed radiators. Drivers and passengers stood by the wreckage arguing about who'd done what to whom.

Joyner blew his horn, which did no good at all. Featherston's outriders descended from the motorcycles to push the wreckage out of the way, which was a lot more practical.

Another big motorcar raced down Twelfth Street. It screeched to a stop on the far side of the accident. Three men in the white shirts and butternut trousers of Freedom Party stalwarts got out. Jake didn't think anything about that till they raised submachine guns and started shooting.

"Get the hell out of here!" he shouted as his guards started falling.

The men who were dressed like stalwarts—or, worse, really *were* stalwarts—ran forward, shooting as they ran. One of them fell, which meant they hadn't picked off all the outriders, but the others came on.

Virgil Joyner put the limousine in reverse, but it could only limp— the assassins had shot out the two front tires. Their bullets starred the windscreen. Pretty soon, they'd punch through; even bulletproof glass could take only so much. Rifle rounds would have smashed through the glass right away.

Featherston and his driver both had .45s—not the best weapons to use against submachine guns, but a hell of a lot better than nothing. A heartbeat before the windscreen finally blew in and sprayed fragments of glass all over the passenger compartment, Jake threw himself flat in the back seat. Bullets thudded into the upholstery just above his head.

And then the stream of bullets punishing the limousine stopped. That meant at least one of the bastards out there had gone through a whole magazine's worth of ammunition and needed to reload. Featherston popped up and fired out through the hole the assassins had shot in the windscreen. With a pistol, you had to aim. You couldn't just spray bullets around and hope some of them would hit something. One of the gunmen started to grab for his face. He never finished the motion. Instead, he crumpled to the ground, the back of his head blown to red ruin as the round that killed him tore out.

The limousine's horn blared. That was Joyner's body slumping forward onto the button—the assassins' fire had struck home after all. *One son of a bitch left,* Jake thought: *one son of a bitch and me. And I'm the meanest s.o.b. this country ever saw.*

If he'd been out there, he would have jumped up on the hood, stuck the submachine gun through the now-shattered windscreen, and finished the job. The last surviving assassin didn't. Maybe losing two of his buddies had unnerved him. *Must be a kid,* went through Featherston's mind. *He's never seen action before, and he doesn't quite know what to do.*

What the assassin did was go around to the side of the motorcar where Jake had been sitting. He grabbed for the door handle, intending to yank the door open and shoot through the gap.

What he intended wasn't what he got. Featherston kicked the door from the inside with both feet, using all his strength. It caught the assassin in the midsection. With a startled squawk, he went down on his wallet. He hung on to the submachine gun, but he was still trying to swing it back toward the limousine when Jake shot him in the belly. He was trying to shoot him in the balls, but didn't quite get what he wanted. The assassin's shriek was satisfying enough as things were. Featherston's next shot, more carefully aimed, blew off the bottom half of his face.

Ears ringing, Jake looked around for more trouble. He didn't see any, only cops and ordinary people running toward the limousine to find out what the hell had happened. All of a sudden, he regretted that last vengeful shot. With just a bullet in the gut, the last assassin might have lived long enough to tell him a lot about what the hell had happened. As things were, he was dying fast and couldn't talk even if he wanted to.

"But I'll find out anyhow," Jake said, and nodded slowly to show how much he meant it. "Oh, yes. You just bet I will."

Even now, the Negroes of Augusta managed to snatch fun where they could. The joint called the Ten of Clubs was a case in point. Its sign showed the card for which it was named: lots of black spots on a white background. Scipio got the joke. He was sure everybody who lived in the Terry got it. So far, no white man seemed to have figured it out, which only made it more delicious.

He and Bathsheba paid fifty cents each at the door. Drinks weren't cheap, either. But the best bands came to the Ten of Clubs. If you wanted to cut a rug in the Terry, this was *the* place to do it.

Scipio slipped the headwaiter another half dollar for a tiny table by the dance floor. He pulled out one of the chairs so Bathsheba could sit down. "You spoil me," she said, smiling.

"Hope so," Scipio answered. His butler's training back at Marshlands made such politesse automatic in him. His wife still didn't know about that, and she'd pretty much given up nagging him to explain how he could pull a different way of speaking out of the woodwork just when they needed it most.

He ordered a bottle of beer, Bathsheba a whiskey. The air was thick with cigarette smoke, cheap perfume, and sweat. People wore what finery they had. Jewelry flashed on the women. Most of it was cheap costume jewelry, but in the dim light of the Ten of Clubs rhinestones did duty for diamonds, colored glass for rubies and sapphires.

A comic in white tie and tails several sizes too big for him came out and stood behind the microphone. Surveying the audience, he sadly shook his head. "You ain't here for me. You is here for the band. You don't make my life no easier, you know."

He was right, of course. People in the shabby little night spot *were* waiting for the band, which was on a tour that took it to colored districts of major towns all over the Confederate States. A heckler called, "Why don't you shut up and go away?"

How many hecklers had the funny man faced, and faced down, during his own years on the road? Hundreds, surely. "You ain't gonna git rid o' me that easy," he answered now. " 'Sides, ain't it sweet how the white folks loves the president just as much as we does?"

That brought not only giggles but a few horrified gasps from the crowd. The papers had been full of Jake Featherston's latest escape from assassination. These assailants had been white. From everything Scipio could gather, they'd been Freedom Party men unhappy with Featherston for seeking a second term. Nobody in public said much about who might have been behind them. Nobody said anything at all about imposing a fine on the white community like the one that had been taken from the CSA's Negroes after that frankfurter-seller tried to ventilate the president at the Olympics. That surprised Scipio not a bit.

Bathsheba leaned forward and said, "He got nerve."

"He gots more nerve'n he gots sense," Scipio replied. Even in a place like this—maybe especially in a place like this—informers were bound to be listening. Plenty of Negroes would betray their own people for a little money or simply for the privilege of being left alone by Freedom Party goons. Scipio thought they were fools. Whatever tiny advantages they got wouldn't last long. But a lot of men—and women—couldn't see past the end of their noses.

"When I heard they was shootin' at the president, I prayed," the comic said. "I tell you, I got down on my knees an' prayed. I prayed, God keep Mistuh Featherston . . . a long ways away from me."

More giggles. More gasps, too. Scipio wondered again whether the comic had more nerve than sense. He skated awfully close to the line. In fact, he likely skated right over the line. In how many towns, in how many rooms full of strangers, had he told jokes like that and got away with them?

Then Scipio had another thought, one that chilled him worse than the December weather outside. Maybe the funny man wasn't worried about informers. Maybe he was an informer himself. Maybe he was trying to smoke out rebellious Negroes in the audience. They would come to him because he said what they were thinking, and then . . . then they'd be sorry.

Scipio shivered again. He didn't know that was true. That it could even occur to him was a measure of the time he lived in.

"Reckon you heard Satchmo and the Rhythm Aces is from New Orleans," the comic went on with a sly leer. "But I reckon you don't know why they is *from* New Orleans an' not *in* New Orleans." He paused, setting up his punch line: "The Freedom Party gits in there, they gits *outa* there."

It might even have been true. A lot of bands from New Orleans *had* started touring when Huey Long met an assassin who, unlike those who'd tried for Jake Featherston, had known how to shoot straight. Had Long been easier on Negroes than the Freedom Party? He couldn't have been much tougher. And any which way, a joke about the Party was bound to draw a laugh from this crowd.

That only made Scipio wonder again whether the funny man was a stalking horse for the people he pretended to mock. No way to know, not for sure, but even the question spoiled his enjoyment of the comic's lines. He ordered another overpriced beer.

After what seemed a very long time, the comic retreated and Satchmo and the Rhythm Aces came out. The trumpeter who led the band was an engagingly ugly fellow with a froglike bass voice. When he raised the horn to his lips and began to play, Scipio's eyes went wide, not only at the sounds he produced but also at the way his cheeks swelled up. He looked like a frog, too: like a spring peeper calling from a tree.

But the way he played made Scipio and everybody else forget about the way he looked. In his hands, that trumpet didn't just speak. It laughed and it moaned and it wept. And when it did, everyone who heard it wanted to do the same.

The Rhythm Aces—fiddler, sax man, bass man, drummer—couldn't have backed him better. And the music that poured from the band sent people hurrying from their seats and onto the dance floor. Now and again, in the Huntsman's Lodge, Scipio had heard rich white men sneering about nigger music. But the wilder, freer rhythms blacks enjoyed had also infected whites' music in the Confederate States. You could hardly find a song or a record on the wireless that didn't sound as if the musicians, no matter how white, had been listening to what came out of New Orleans and Mobile and Atlanta and other towns with a lively colored music scene. Sometimes they didn't seem to know it themselves. But the alert ear could always tell, especially when a song from the USA got played for comparison. Music from north of the border wasn't necessarily bad, but it was *different*: more staid, less surprising.

Even in the Confederate States, though, white musicians borrowed only some of the trimmings from what blacks played for themselves and among themselves. Any white band that played like Satchmo and the Rhythm Aces—assuming a white band could do any such thing, which struck Scipio as unlikely—would have been booed off the stage . . . or, just possibly, idolized.

Before Scipio could decide which, Bathsheba reached out and tapped him on the arm. "Why you sittin' there?" she demanded. "Let's us dance!"

"All right. We do dat." He got to his feet. He wasn't the most enthusiastic dancer God ever made, but you didn't come to the Ten of Clubs if you didn't want to get out on the floor.

He wasn't the most athletic dancer God ever made, either. He never had been; he'd always owned too much of a sense of his own dignity to let loose as fully as a lot of people, and he wasn't so young as he had been, either. He did his best, knowing Bathsheba's was better—and, as he watched some of the youngsters cavort, knowing there were things he hadn't even imagined. Some of the moves they made were as far beyond him as Satchmo's music was beyond a bored Army bugler.

He shrugged—and found himself trying to do it so it fit the beat. He must have managed; Bathsheba didn't seem too exasperated. All the same, he felt like a sparrow among hummingbirds that could hover and fly backwards and zoom straight up and do a million other things no ordinary bird could ever hope to manage.

Satchmo seemed ready to play all night. Eyes bugging out of his head, trumpet aimed at the sky as if to let God and the angels hear, he wailed on and on. Scipio wasn't ready to dance all night, though his wife might have been. But when he mimed exhaustion, she went back to the table with him so he could catch his breath. He realized that while out on the floor he hadn't once thought about Jake Featherston or the sorry plight of Negroes in the CSA. The music had driven all his worries clean out of his head. He might almost have been making love. He laughed. Some of the young couples out there might almost have been making love while they danced. For all he knew, maybe some of them had.

At two in the morning, the manager said, "We gots to close. We git in trouble with the *po*lice if we don't. I's right sorry, but I don't want no trouble with the *po*lice, not the way things is."

A few people grumbled, but nobody really raised a fuss. The way things were these days, a black man had to be crazy to court trouble with the police in Augusta or anywhere else. Scipio and Bathsheba got their coats and hats from the girl who'd checked them and walked out into the night.

The Terry was quiet—almost deserted but for the people leaving the Ten of Clubs. A chilly drizzle had begun to fall. The crowd scattered quickly. The Negro district remained technically under curfew, though the cops hadn't bothered enforcing it lately. Still, nobody wanted to get caught and beaten up or shaken down.

Bathsheba hoisted an umbrella. Scipio, who didn't have one, pulled his hat low on his forehead and looked down toward the ground to keep the rain out of his eyes. "Lord, I'm so glad tomorrow's Sunday," his wife said.

He shook his head. "*Today* Sunday. It be Sunday coupla hours now. Do Jesus, I thanks de Lawd we ain't got to work." Most Sundays, he would have gone to church to thank the Lord. Bathsheba believed, even if he had trouble. This morning, though, it looked as if they would both sleep in, and so would the children.

He turned a corner, then stopped short. Men were moving up ahead. He couldn't see much—street lights in the Terry hadn't worked for years. But if those weren't rifles being passed back and forth . . . If they weren't, he'd never seen any. He turned around and, without a word, signed for Bathsheba to back away, raising a finger to his lips to show she needed to be quiet while she did it.

For a wonder, she didn't argue. For a bigger wonder, none of those men with rifles came after them. Maybe they'd been so intent on their own business, they hadn't noticed the people who'd spotted them. Maybe the drizzle had helped, too.

Whatever the reason, Scipio knew he was lucky to get away in one piece. He and Bathsheba took a different street home. As they made their escape, a snatch of whistled music pursued them. It wasn't any tune Satchmo and the Rhythm Aces played, but he'd heard it before just the same. It was the "Internationale."

Reds had come—come back—to the Terry. They'd come back, and they had guns.


"Holy Jesus!" One of the yeomen in the USS *Remembrance*'s wireless shack yanked off his earphones and stared at his pal. "You hear that, Zach?"

"Sure as hell did," Zach answered, scribbling furiously on the pad in front of him.

"What's up?" Sam Carsten asked. As usual when not on duty, he was killing time in the wireless shack. It was warm—the aeroplane carrier cruised between Florida and the U.S.-occupied Bahamas—but at least he was out of the sun. He wished the yeomen weren't wearing earphones. That way, he could have heard whatever it was, too. But they liked to get rid of distractions from the outside world—nosy officers, for instance— when they listened to Morse.

Zach finished writing, then dropped the pencil. "Signal going out in clear to the Confederate Army and Navy, sir," he answered. "Their vice president—Willy Knight, his name is—has resigned, and he's under arrest."

"Christ!" Sam said. The other yeoman—his name was Freddy—was on the phone to the bridge with the news. Carsten heard a startled squawk on the other end of the line when it went through. He felt like squawking himself. Instead, he asked, "How come, for the love of Mike?"

"Story they're giving out is, he was the fellow behind the stalwarts who tried to take out Featherston a couple weeks ago," Zach said.

"Christ!" Carsten repeated, louder and with more emphasis this time. "That's the kind of crap that happens in Argentina or Nicaragua or one of those places, not up here."

"Yes, sir." The yeoman nodded. He knew better than to come right out and contradict an officer, no matter how stupid that officer had just been. He got his barb in, all right, but politely: "Except it just did."

"Well, what do they do now?" Sam asked. "They arrested Knight, you say? They going to give him a blindfold and a cigarette and stand him up against a wall?"

"No report on that, sir," Zach answered. "Only an alert. He has resigned. He has been arrested. No orders issued in his name are to be obeyed."

Sam wondered exactly what that meant, too. Had Willy Knight tried to get the Army, or some of it, to move against Jake Featherston? If he had, it didn't sound as if he'd had much luck. Luck or not, though, nobody in either the USA or the CSA had ever tried to play that particular game before.

"He wanted to put on a Napoleon suit, but it turned out to be three sizes too big," Sam judged. Both yeomen in the wireless shack nodded this time.

He hung around the wireless shack, hoping for more details, but no more seemed forthcoming. About ten minutes later, the klaxons began to hoot, ordering the crew to general quarters. He thought it was a drill. He hoped it was a drill. He got down to his station in the bowels of the *Remembrance* in jig time even so.

"What the hell's going on, sir?" a sailor in the damage-control party asked. "They ain't sprung one of these on us in a while."

"I'm not sure," said Sam, who had a pretty good idea. "Maybe Lieutenant Commander Pottinger knows more about it than I do."

But when Pottinger got there half a minute later, he said, "Now what?" in tones mightily aggrieved. He proceeded to explain himself: "I was in the head, God damn it, when the hooters started screeching."

A couple of sailors smiled. Nobody laughed. That had happened to every man who'd been in the Navy more than a few months. Carsten said, "Well, sir, I don't know for certain, but. . . ." He told what he'd heard about Willy Knight.

"Shit." Pottinger didn't usually talk that way; maybe his recent misadventure preyed on his mind. He gathered himself and went on, "What the hell are the Confederates going to do now?"

"Beats me, sir," Sam answered. "But I expect it explains the general-quarters call: they want to make damn sure they don't go and do it to us."

"Makes sense," Pottinger agreed. He shifted uncomfortably. "If they keep us here too long, though, I'm going to need a honey bucket." Again, nobody laughed. Carsten approved of an officer who wouldn't abandon his post even in the face of what would ordinarily have been an urgent need.

The all-clear sounded before Lieutenant Commander Pottinger was reduced to such indignities. The officer in charge of the damage-control party left with dignified haste.

Carsten headed back to the wireless shack. He found the door closed against snoopy interlopers like himself. Somebody on the *Remembrance* was taking the news out of the CSA very seriously indeed. Sam's suspicions fell on Commander Cressy. Taking things seriously was how the exec earned his pay.

Balked from getting more news, Sam went out on the flight deck. By the rumors flying among the sailors there, the powers that be had shut the door to the wireless shack too late. Somebody claimed Willy Knight had already been shot. Somebody else said he was still in jail, awaiting trial as a U.S. spy. A grizzled bosun insisted Knight had been trying to flee up into Maryland when he was caught. Other claims seemed to spring from thin air.

Some of them were probably true. Sam had no idea which, though. He listened to them all, admiring the ones he found most impressive. He might have done the same thing watching girls on a street corner in a liberty port.

The *Remembrance* pitched a little as she steamed south, but the sea was a lot calmer here than it would have been in the open waters of the North Atlantic at this time of year. The sun shone down out of a sky mostly blue. In these latitudes, even the winter sun could burn Sam's tender hide. Sea birds scudded along the breeze or dove into the ocean after fish.

But that buzz Carsten heard didn't come from gulls or petrels. Those were aeroplane motors—and they weren't the motors of the machines aboard the *Remembrance*. This was a different note. Peering west, Sam saw several brightly painted aeroplanes nearing the carrier. They zoomed past low enough for him to read the words CONFEDERATE CITRUS COMPANY on their sides.

A sailor saluted the machines from the CSA with his middle finger. Another man said, "I hear those bastards all have guns in 'em these days."

Sam had heard the same thing. As with the news about Willy Knight, he didn't know how much to believe, but there was probably a fire somewhere under all that smoke. A petty officer said, "We ought to splash a couple of 'em, fish 'em out of the drink, and damn well see for ourselves."

That took things right to the edge, because a lot of sailors were nodding. Sam felt he had to draw back a step or two, and he did: "We don't shoot at them unless they shoot first, or unless we get orders from the skipper, which means orders from the Navy Department back in Philadelphia."

That petty officer muttered something Carsten decided he didn't have to notice in any official way. Just as well, too, for it wasn't a compliment. The fellow knew he was a mustang, and wondered why he took the attitudes of ordinary officers. That was what it amounted to, anyhow; the way the petty officer put it, it would have knocked down one of those CONFEDERATE CITRUS COMPANY machines without bothering about the carrier's antiaircraft guns.

Both the flyby and the news out of the CSA got kicked around in the officers' mess that evening. The foulmouthed petty officer might have been surprised, for a lot of the officers he'd sneered at agreed with him. "Those Confederate bastards are just poking at us, seeing how much they can get away with," was a common sentiment. "We ought to break their fingers for 'em, remind 'em who won the last war."

"Maybe this business with Knight means they'll start fighting among themselves and leave us alone for a while," a lieutenant said.

"Don't bet on it." Commander Cressy entered the fray with his usual authority. "If they'd got rid of Featherston, then, maybe. The way things are, he just gets the excuse to clamp down harder."

"Wonder if Knight really was spying for us," a lieutenant commander said.

*In your dreams,* Carsten thought. He didn't say that, not to an officer two grades senior to him, but he held the opinion very strongly.

And he wasn't the only one, for the executive officer snorted and said, "Not likely. He's done us too much harm over the years to make it easy to believe he was on our side all along. But we can deny it till we're blue in the face, and that won't do us any good."

"Wonder what excuse Knight had for getting rid of him," someone said. "Whatever it was, too bad it didn't work."

"Featherston is going to run again, and Knight didn't think he should," Sam said. "Knight figured *he* was going to get elected this coming November, but their Constitutional amendment screwed his chances."

"Could be," Commander Cressy said. "Could be, but we don't know for sure. The Confederates are saying Knight was the guy behind those fellows who tried to shoot Featherston, but how do we know that's true? Far as I can see, we don't. Featherston might be using the assassination attempt as an excuse to get rid of Knight, regardless of whether he really had anything to do with it."

That cynical assessment stopped talk in its tracks. At last, Lieutenant Commander Pottinger whistled in reluctant admiration. "You don't believe in anything, do you, sir?" he said.

"Not without evidence," Cressy answered at once. "We haven't got any, except for what the Confederate wireless says. And the Confederate wireless lies. It lies like a drunk telling his wife what happened to the grocery money. Are you going to trust it just because it says something you might want to hear?"

Again, no one spoke for a little while. Sam eyed the exec with real respect. He *had* believed the wireless reports from the CSA. They were the only news he had, so why not believe them? He hadn't found any reason not to, but Commander Cressy had—and a damn good reason, too.

"Makes it harder to figure out what the Confederates are up to if we can't believe anything they say," he remarked.

"That's not our worry," Cressy said. "The way I look at things is, we don't believe any of it till we either have evidence of our own that we should or until our superiors tell us what's true and what isn't. You can bet they've got spies inside the CSA finding out what the straight dope is."

*I hope they do. They'd be damn fools if they didn't,* Carsten thought. That cheered him, but not for long. A lifetime in the Navy had convinced him that a lot of his superiors *were* damn fools, and the only thing he could do about it was try to keep them from causing as much harm as possible.

He did say, "I wonder how many spies the Confederates have in the USA."

Nobody answered the question, which produced a chilly silence in the wardroom. He might have started talking about whorehouses he'd known at a women's club meeting. The *Remembrance*'s officers were willing enough to think about their own spies, but not about the other fellow's.

Commander Cressy looked thoughtful, though he didn't say anything. But then, Commander Cressy always looked thoughtful, so Sam wasn't sure how much that proved, or whether it proved anything at all.

Every once in a while, Boston cast up a mild, springlike day, even if the calendar said it was early February. If it was a Saturday, too, well, all the better. People who'd stayed indoors as much as they could since winter slammed down emerged from their nests, blinking at the watery sunshine and the pale blue sky. They might almost have been animals coming out of hibernation.

Sylvia Enos certainly felt that way. With the mercury in the high forties—one reckless weatherman on the wireless even talked about the fifties—she wanted to be out and doing things. She didn't need to worry about long johns or overcoat or mittens or thick wool muffler. All she had to do was throw a sweater on over her blouse and go outside. And, gratefully, she did.

Mary Jane didn't even bother with a sweater, perhaps because her blouse was wool, perhaps because she wanted to show off while she had the chance. Sylvia minded that impulse less than she'd thought she would in a daughter. Mary Jane was heading from her mid- toward her late twenties, and hadn't snagged a husband yet. She didn't seem unduly worried about it, either. As far as Sylvia was concerned, a little display might be in order.

They went to Quincy Market, next to Faneuil Hall. The grasshopper on the weather vane atop Faneuil Hall showed the wind coming out of the south. Pointing to it, Sylvia said, "That's the only good thing from the Confederate States: the weather, I mean." She paused to light a cigarette, then shook her head. "No, I take it back. Their tobacco's nice, too. The rest? Forget it."

"Let me have one of those, will you?" Mary Jane said. Sylvia handed her the pack, then leaned close to give her a light. Mary Jane sucked in smoke. She blew it out and nodded. "That's pretty good, all right."

A sailor on leave whistled at her. She ignored him. Sylvia would have ignored him, too. He was a little bowlegged fellow with a face like a ferret's. Ten seconds later, he whistled at another woman. She didn't pay any attention to him, either.

Mary Jane said, "How's Ernie? Or don't I want to know?"

"He's not that bad," Sylvia said defensively. "He's been . . . sweet lately. His writing is going better. That always helps." Ernie said it helped him starve slow instead of fast. As long as Sylvia had known him, though, he'd always managed to make at least some kind of living from his typewriter.

"Hurrah," Mary Jane said. "Hasn't pulled a gun on you lately?"

"Not lately," Sylvia agreed.

"I don't care how sweet he is. He's trouble," her daughter said.

She was probably right. No—she *was* right, and Sylvia knew it. That didn't mean she wanted to dump Ernie. If she'd wanted to, she would have long since. The whiff of danger he brought to things excited her. (Actually, it was a good deal more than a whiff, but Sylvia refused to dwell on that.) And, if anything, his . . . shortcoming posed a challenge. When she pleased him, she knew she'd accomplished something.

How to put that into words? "He may be trouble, but he's never dull."

"He may not be dull, but he's trouble," her daughter said.

Again, Sylvia didn't argue. She just kept walking past the stalls and shops of Quincy Market. People sold everything from home-canned chowder and oyster stew to books to frying pans to furniture to jewelry to hats. Mary Jane admired sterling-silver cups that aped ones made by Paul Revere. Sylvia admired the cups, too, but not their prices. Those horrified her. "They're for rich tourists," she said.

"I know," Mary Jane answered. "But they are pretty."

Someone—not a tourist, by his accent, which was purest Boston—took a silver gravy boat up to the shopkeeper and peeled green bills out of his wallet. Sylvia sighed. "It must be fun to be able to afford nice things," she said.

Mary Jane pointed to a new stall across the way. "Those look nice," she said, "and they might not be too expensive."

Sylvia read the sign: " 'Clogston's Quilts.' " She shivered, knowing winter wasn't over in spite of this mild day. "Some of the blankets are getting pretty ratty, all right. Let's go have a look."

The quilts on display made a rainbow under a roof of waterproof canvas. They were carefully laid out with an eye to which colors went with others, and that only made the display more enticing. Some duplicated colonial patterns, while others were brightly modern.

"Hello, ladies," said the proprietor, a pleasant woman in her early forties with a wide smile and very white teeth. "Help you with something?"

"Do you make all these?" Mary Jane blurted.

"I sure do. Chris Clogston, at your service." She dipped her head in the same brisk way a man running a shop might have used. "When you don't see me here, you'll find me at the sewing machine."

"When do you sleep, Mrs.—uh, Miss—Clogston?" Sylvia asked, awkwardly changing the question when she noticed the other woman wore no ring.

"Sleep? What's that? I just hang myself in a corner now and then to get the wrinkles out." Chris Clogston laughed. It was a good laugh, a laugh that invited anyone who heard it to share the joke. She went on, "I *do* stay busy, but I like making quilts, picking out the colors and making sure everything is strong and will last. It doesn't seem like work. And it beats the stuffing"—she laughed again—"out of going to a factory every day."

"Oh, yes." Sylvia had done her share of that and more. "What sort of living do you make, if you don't mind my asking?"

"I'm still here," the shopkeeper answered. "Actually, I'm new *here*, new in Quincy Market. The rent for this space is twice what I paid where I was before, but I get a lot more customers, so it's worth it." Her gray eyes widened a little. "And what can I interest you in?"

"That one's pretty." Sylvia pointed.

Chris Clogston nodded, seeming pleased. "I'm glad you like it. That pattern's been in the family for I don't know how long—since before the Revolution, anyhow. I'm a ninth-generation Clogston in America. John, the first one we know about, came to Boston before 1740, out of Belfast."

"Wow," Mary Jane said.

"Wow is right," Sylvia said. "I can't trace my pedigree back past my great-grandfather, and I don't know much about him."

"My granny was mad for family history, and she gave me some of the bug," Chris Clogston said. She picked up the quilt. "Now, this particular one is stuffed with cotton. I also make it stuffed with goose down if you want it extra warm. That will cost you more, though."

"How much is this one, and how much would it be with the down?" Sylvia asked.

"This one's $4.45," the quiltmaker answered. "It's nice and toasty, too—don't get me wrong. If you want it with goose down, though, it goes up to $7.75."

Sylvia didn't need to think about whether she could afford the down-stuffed quilt; she knew she couldn't. The cotton . . . Even the cotton was a reach, but she said, "I'll take it."

"You won't be sorry," Chris Clogston said. "It'll last you a lifetime."

Mary Jane pointed to a small quilt in pink and blue. "Let's get that one, too, for George and Connie's baby." Sylvia hesitated, not because she didn't like the quilt but because she couldn't afford to spend the money. Mary Jane said, "Don't worry, Ma. I'll spring for it. It'll use up some overtime I got last week." She grinned. "Easy come, easy go."

The small quilt cost $2.25. Mary Jane did pay, and didn't blink. Sylvia hadn't known about the overtime. She wondered if it was mythical. She didn't quarrel with her daughter, though. George and Connie would be happy to have the quilt for their little boy.

"Thank you very much, ladies," Chris Clogston called as Sylvia and Mary Jane left the stall.

"Thank *you*," Sylvia answered, well pleased with the quilt she'd bought. She looked up at the blue sky and the bravely shining sun. "I wonder how long this weather will hold."

"As long as it does," Mary Jane said. "We just have to enjoy it till it's gone."

"I intend to," Sylvia said, and then, after a few steps through the crowded Quincy Market, "It's like that with Ernie and me, too, you know."

Mary Jane only shrugged. "I can't talk sense into your head about that. I've tried, and it doesn't work. But I still don't think he's good for you."

"Good for me?" Sylvia hadn't worried about that. "He's . . . interesting. Things happen when he's around, and you never know beforehand what they'll be."

"Maybe," Mary Jane said, "but some of the time I bet you wish you did."

She was right. Sylvia knew it. Ernie had frightened her in ways no one else had matched, or even approached. She sometimes—often—thought he was most in earnest when his mood turned blackest. Even so . . . "Never a dull moment," she said. "That counts for something, too."

"Pa would have said the same thing, wouldn't he, after his destroyer dodged a torpedo?" Mary Jane replied. "But one day the destroyer didn't dodge, and that's how come I hardly remember my own father."

"Yes, that's right," Sylvia said. "I paid him back, though." Roger Kimball was dead, sure enough. But that didn't, wouldn't, couldn't, bring George Enos, Senior, back to life. Mary Jane would never have the memories she was missing. All Sylvia had left were her memories.

Mary Jane changed the subject as abruptly as anyone could: "Let's go over to the Union Oyster House for an early supper. I can't remember the last time I was there."

"Why not?" Sylvia said, thinking *in for a penny, in for a pound.* They'd already spent a lot of money today; after that, what was a little more? The Union Oyster House was only a couple of blocks from the market square. The building in which it operated had stood on the same spot since the early eighteenth century. The restaurant itself had been there for more than a hundred years. People said Daniel Webster had drunk at the cramped little bar.

Almost everything about the Union Oyster House was cramped and little, from the stairs people descended to get down to the main level to the panes of glass in the windows to the tiny wooden booths into which diners squeezed. Sylvia and Mary Jane snagged a booth with no trouble—they got in ahead of the evening rush.

The one place where the restaurant didn't stint was on the portions. The plates of fried oysters and fried potatoes a harried-looking waiter set in front of the two women would have fed a couple of lumberjacks, or possibly a couple of football teams. "How am I going to eat all that?" Sylvia asked. Then she did. Mary Jane cleaned her plate, too.

Going home happily full, carrying things they'd wanted to buy, made a good end to a good day. And two men on the trolley car stood up to give Sylvia and her daughter their seats. That didn't happen all the time, either.

Spread on the bed, the quilt looked even finer than it had in Chris Clogston's stall. It promised to be warm, too. Sylvia wanted to burrow under it right then and there.

"How about that, Ma?" Mary Jane said.

Sylvia nodded. "Yes. How about that?" She wondered what Ernie would say when he saw the quilt. *Probably something sarcastic,* she thought. *Well, if he does, too bad for him.*


Lucien Galtier cleaned the farmhouse as if his life depended on it. He was not the sort of slob a lot of men living by themselves would have been. Marie wouldn't have liked that, and he took his wife's opinions more seriously now that she was gone than he had while she was there to enforce them. But he knew he couldn't hope to match the standard she set, and he hadn't tried. He'd set his own, less strict, standard and lived up to that.

Now, though, he tried to match what Marie would have done. That meant a lot of extra scrubbing and dusting. It meant cleaning out corners where dirt lingered—though he still didn't attack the corners with needles, as Marie might have done. It meant putting things in closets and deciding what was too far gone even to linger in a closet any more. It meant a lot of extra work.

He did the extra work not merely from a sense of duty but from a sense of pride. He was going to bring Éloise Granche here, and he wanted everything perfect. If she thought he lived like a pig in a sty . . . *Well, so what?* some part of him jeered. *She doesn't want to marry you anyhow.*

He ignored the internal scoffing. He didn't so much think it wrong as think it irrelevant. Seeing a clean house wouldn't make Éloise change her mind and want to live here. When she spoke of patrimony and the problems marriage would cause both families, she was firm, she was decisive—and, as far as Lucien could see, she was dead right.

That wasn't why he worked till his lungs burned and his heart pounded and his chest ached: worked harder than he did on the farm at any time of the year but harvest. He worked himself into a panting tizzy for one of the oldest reasons in the world: he wanted to impress the woman he cared about. They were already lovers; impressing her wouldn't get him anything but a smile and perhaps a quick, offhand compliment. He knew that. His mother hadn't raised a fool. Hoping to see that smile kept him slaving away with a smile on his own face.

After he couldn't find anything else left to clean, he cleaned himself. He made lavish, even extravagant, use of water he heated on the stove. On a warmer day, he could have luxuriated in the steaming tub for a long time, letting the hot water soak the kinks out of his back. But water didn't stay hot forever, not in winter in Quebec it didn't. When it started to cool off, which it did all too soon, he got out and dried off in a hurry.

He thought about putting on his black wool suit when he went to get Éloise: thought about it and discarded the notion in the next breath. She would think someone had died, and he was on his way to the funeral. And besides, the suit smelled so strongly of mothballs, it would have made her eyes water. It stayed in the closet. He put on the clothes he would have worn to a dance—work clothes, but the best he had, and also impeccably clean. If he wouldn't go to Éloise's reeking of mothballs, he wouldn't go reeking of stale sweat, either.

He'd just set a warm wool cap on his head and was putting on his overcoat when someone knocked on the door. *"Tabernac!"* he snarled. Who the devil would come bothering him now, when he had more important things to worry about than a neighbor who'd run out of chicken feed?

Before he went to the door, he shrugged on his overcoat. *I was just going out* would cut any visit short. With dramatic suddenness, he threw the door open. Whoever was out there, Lucien intended to make him feel guilty.

Dr. Leonard O'Doull stared at him, surprised but not visibly afflicted with guilt.

"What have we here?" Galtier's son-in-law asked. "Is it that you are so eager to escape my company?"

*Yes,* Galtier thought, but he couldn't say that. "I was about to go out for a drive," he replied.

"In this?" O'Doull waved at the swirling snow. Now he sounded more than surprised; he sounded astonished. "Me, I had to come down to the hospital today, and from the hospital it is but a short hop here. But why would you go out for a drive if you don't have to?"

"To visit a friend," Lucien replied, which was part of the truth, though he was careful to say *un ami* and not *une amie*: he didn't want O'Doull knowing his friend was of the feminine persuasion. Realizing his son-in-law wouldn't disappear in the wind, he stepped aside. "Come in. No point letting the heat out of the house."

"No, certainly not." O'Doull did come in, and stamped snow all over the tidy entry hall. Lucien did his best not to wince. Slowly, he shed his own coat and cap. Leonard O'Doull slithered out of his overcoat with a sigh of relief. He went on, "I won't keep you long, since it's plain you have such important business elsewhere."

Galtier pretended not to notice the sarcasm. "Unfortunately, I do," he said, which made O'Doull raise a gingery eyebrow. Lucien waved him to the couch. "But sit down. What sort of gossip have you heard at the hospital?"

"At the hospital? Nothing much." O'Doull stretched his long legs out in front of him. To Galtier's relief, he didn't put his feet up on the table, as he'd sometimes been known to do. "Still, though, gossip does come to a doctor's office."

"Does it?" Lucien said tonelessly.

"Well, yes, as a matter of fact, it does," his son-in-law replied. "And it could even be that the gossip that comes is true, though I did not think so before I knocked on your door."

"Since you have not told me what this gossip is, I have no idea whether it is true or not," Lucien said. "Should I care?" Were people starting to talk about Éloise and him?

Leonard O'Doull didn't directly answer that. Instead, he asked, "*Mon beau-père,* are you a happy man?"

That question took Galtier by surprise. He thought for a moment, then answered, "Most of the time, I am too busy working even to wonder."

"All right. Never mind." Dr. O'Doull smiled. "I hope, when you do have time away from your work, I hope you are happy, however you get to be that way. I hope so, and so does Nicole. And I have talked with Charles and Georges and Denise. They all feel the same way. I have not talked with your other two daughters, but I am sure they would agree."

"Are you? Would they?" Lucien said. "And why is everyone so intimately concerned with my happiness?" That didn't quite take the bull by the horns, but it came close.

O'Doull smiled at him. "Because of the gossip, as I said."

"Well? And what is this gossip? And why are you acting like an old woman and listening to it?" There. Now Lucien would find out whatever there was to find out.

So he thought, anyhow. But O'Doull only smiled and said, "That it could be you have some reason for happiness."

"Well, if I do, that reason is not a *beau-fils* who comes around snooping after what I am doing," Lucien said pointedly.

This time, Leonard O'Doull laughed out loud. "As if you never did any snooping of your own," he said. The only comeback Galtier found for that was dignified silence, so he used it. But even silence made his son-in-law laugh at him. O'Doull got to his feet.

"Well, *mon beau-père,* I won't keep you any more. I hope you find happiness wherever you can."

He didn't even wait for an answer. He just put on his hat and overcoat and left. Through the howl of the wind, Lucien heard his son-in-law's old

Ford roar to flatulent life. The motorcar sputtered up the path from the farmhouse to the road. Then its noise faded away.

As soon as quiet returned, Lucien put on his own warm clothes again. He hoped the Chevrolet would start. It did. The battery might be going, but it wasn't quite gone. He let the engine get good and warm, then put the auto in gear and drove off to Éloise Granche's.

"What kept you?" she said when he knocked on the door. "I expected you half an hour ago."

"My son-in-law paid me a call," he answered with a shrug. "From what Leonard says, there may be some gossip about us. Do you mind? Does it bother you?"

"No, not at all," Éloise said with a shrug of her own. "I've always expected it. We should be grateful it's taken this long to show up."

"Who knows whether it has?" Lucien said. "It's taken this long for one of us to hear about it, yes. But that's different. Who knows how long people have been mumbling this, that, or the other thing?"

Éloise looked thoughtful. Slowly, she nodded. "Yes, it could be that you are right. Still, it is a small thing. Shall we go?"

"Certainly," Lucien replied. He held the passenger door of the Chevrolet open for her, then went around to the driver's side. Again, the motorcar started. Lucien surreptitiously patted the steering wheel. The machine might be less reliable than a horse, but it was doing what it was supposed to do.

Hardly any traffic was on the road as he drove back to his own farmhouse. The autos and trucks that did appear seemed to come out of nowhere, loom enormously for a moment through the swirling snow, and then disappear as abruptly as they'd come into view. "Everything goes by so fast," Éloise murmured.

*"Tu as raison,"* Galtier said. "That was what gave me the hardest time when I learned to drive after the war." Up till then, he hadn't had a prayer of affording a motorcar. Only a bargain with the Americans for the land they'd taken from his farm for their hospital had let him do it. He went on, "In a buggy or a wagon, you have time to look away from the road and back again. In a motorcar? No. *Mon Dieu,* no. If you do not pay attention every moment, you will have a wreck."

He got back to his house without having a wreck. He was anxious even so as he handed Éloise out of the Chevrolet. The anxiety grew on the short walk to the front door. *He* thought the place was reasonably tidy. But what did he know? What did he really know? He was only a man, after all.

When he opened the door, he distracted Éloise for a moment by flipping the switch and turning on a lamp across the room. "Electricity," she said, and nodded to herself. "Yes, I knew you had it. It's so much brighter and finer than kerosene."

A moment later, Lucien wondered whether that fine, bright light was what he wanted. It would let her see every flaw in his housekeeping. Mercifully, though, she didn't seem inclined to be critical. She let him guide her through the house, every so often nodding again.

"Very nice," she said when the tour was done. "Very nice indeed. I am glad you're comfortable. I have worried about you living here by yourself." She raised an eyebrow. "Somehow, though, I doubt everything is *quite* so neat when you are not having company over."

Lucien looked back at her, nothing but innocence on his face. "Why, my sweet, what can you possibly mean by that?"

Éloise started to explain exactly what she meant. Then she caught the glint in his eye and started to laugh instead. "You!" she said fondly. "You are a devil, aren't you?"

"If I am, it is because you make me one," Galtier answered. He took her in his arms to show just what kind of devil she made him. Her lips were sweet against his. She didn't kiss quite like Marie—but she was probably thinking he didn't kiss like her dead husband. And so what, either way? They were kissing each other, and nothing else mattered, not right then.

# XII

Cincinnatus Driver wasn't happy about walking upstairs from his apartment. He knew he should have been happy. Knowing that only made him more unhappy yet. He sighed and muttered something under his breath. The more you looked at it, the more you lived it, the more complicated life got.

He knocked on the door of the apartment just above his. The wireless was on inside, pretty loud. He had to knock twice before anybody in there heard him. Suddenly, the wireless got softer. A few seconds later, the door opened.

"Evenin', Mr. Chang," Cincinnatus said. "How are you today?"

"Oh. Hello, Mr. Driver," said the father of Cincinnatus' daughter-in-law. Joey Chang was polite. He'd always stayed polite with Cincinnatus, even if he didn't much care to have Achilles in his family. He hesitated, then brightened. "I just make new batch of beer. You want some?" If Cincinnatus had come up about homebrew, then maybe they wouldn't have to talk about . . . other things.

And Cincinnatus smiled and nodded and said, "I'd love to have some, for true." He meant every word of it. Iowa was a dry state, with liquor of any kind hard to come by. And Chang made damn good beer. But that wasn't why Cincinnatus had come upstairs. "I got some news you need to know."

"News?" Mr. Chang asked, and Cincinnatus nodded again. The Chinaman sighed, much as Cincinnatus had while climbing the stairs. He stepped aside. "You come in, you tell me news."

"Thank you kindly," Cincinnatus said. "Evenin', Mrs. Chang," he called to the woman sitting close by the wireless set. It was playing a comedy about a trolley driver and his friend who worked in a sewer.

Cincinnatus wondered how much Mrs. Chang followed; her English wasn't as good as her husband's.

As if to underscore that, Joey Chang spoke to her in Chinese. She answered in the same language. Cincinnatus understood not a word, but she didn't sound happy. Mr. Chang sighed again, on exactly the same note. He lit a cigarette, then offered Cincinnatus one. Once they were both smoking, he said, "What is this news?"

"Achilles and Grace, they gonna have themselves another baby toward the end of the year," Cincinnatus answered.

"Baby?" Mrs. Chang said sharply. She might not have a whole lot of English, but she sure understood that.

"Yes, ma'am. That's right," Cincinnatus said.

"This is good news. Here, you wait." Joey Chang went into the kitchen. He came back half a minute later with three small glasses. He gave one to his wife, one to Cincinnatus, and kept the third for himself. "A baby. *Kampai!*" he said, and knocked back his glass.

"Mud in your eye." Cincinnatus followed suit. This wasn't beer. It scorched his gullet all the way down, and exploded like a bomb when it hit his stomach. "Whew!" He eyed the empty glass with respect. "You make that yourself?"

"Not me." Chang shook his head. "This place too small for proper still. Beer easy. Can make beer anywhere. But need more room for still, need place where neighbors no smell . . . smoke." He scowled; that wasn't the word he wanted. After a moment, he found the right one: "Fumes. Neighbors no smell fumes. For this, I trade plenty beer with fellow I know. You want more?"

"If you've got it to spare, I wouldn't mind another one. Don't want to put you to no trouble, though."

"No trouble." Mr. Chang took Cincinnatus' glass and disappeared into the kitchen again. When he returned, he had a refill, too. This time, Cincinnatus sipped cautiously instead of sending the hooch down the hatch. It was some kind of brandy, not whiskey, and strong enough to grow hair on his chest—or on Joey Chang's chest, which was a bigger challenge. "Another baby," Chang murmured, his eyes for a few seconds soft and far away. "Grandfather again."

"Yeah," Cincinnatus said dreamily. Then he pointed at Mr. Chang. "You'd like it a lot better if you saw the new baby when it comes—and if you saw the grandbaby you already got once in a while."

"I know. I know." Chang stared down into the glass he held. "But Grace, she run off, she get married when we say no. She not do what her mother, her father say. She marry fellow who is not Chinese. Things hard on account of that."

He was a little man, more than a head shorter than Cincinnatus. But he spoke with enormous pride. *Reckon he'd say the same thing if I was white, too,* Cincinnatus thought, bemused. He hadn't imagined a Chinaman could also look down his nose at whites. The mere idea broadened his mental horizon.

Mrs. Chang spoke, a sharp, singsong rattle of Chinese. Her husband answered in the same language, then returned to English for Cincinnatus' benefit: "She say, we not angry because your boy colored fellow. We angry because Grace disobey us. For Chinese, this is very bad. Hard to forgive."

"Don't know nothin' about that," said Cincinnatus, who suspected Chang was lying some for politeness' sake, but wasn't quite sure. He went on, "I do know you ain't just missin' out on Grace, though. You missin' out on your grandbaby. You gonna be missin' out on *two* grandbabies. Your pride worth all that?"

Now Mr. Chang spoke in Chinese—translating the question, Cincinnatus figured. Mrs. Chang answered right away. Again, her tone said everything Cincinnatus needed to know. *You bet your life pride is worth it.* That was what she'd told him, all right. Cincinnatus wondered whether Mr. Chang would show any backbone. From everything the Negro had seen, Mrs. Chang was the one who said, *Jump, frog!* Her husband asked, *How high?* on the way up.

But he said something more, and then something more, and then something more again. After his last sally, Mrs. Chang burst into tears. Embarrassed, Cincinnatus turned away. "I better go," he mumbled.

"All right, you go," Mr. Chang said. "But you see Achilles and Grace, you say they can come by here. We be glad to see them. This go on too long." Mrs. Chang protested again. Her husband, for a wonder, overrode her. They were still arguing when Cincinnatus slipped out the door and went downstairs.

"Well?" Elizabeth asked when he walked into their apartment.

"Mr. Chang say they can come visit," Cincinnatus answered, and his wife's face lit up. He raised a warning hand. "Mrs. Chang ain't very happy about it. Pretty fair chance she make him change his mind."

Elizabeth sighed. "They's powerful proud folks," she said. Cincinnatus walked over and gave her a kiss. She eyed him with as much suspicion as pleasure. "What's that for?"

"On account of that's the very same word the Changs used when they was talkin' about themselves," he said, "and only a clever lady like you would figure it out all on her lonesome."

"That a fact?" Elizabeth said. Cincinnatus solemnly nodded. She wagged a finger at him. "I tell you a fact: you only talk so sweet to me when you want something—an' I generally know what it is you want."

If she hadn't been smiling, the words would have flayed. As things were, Cincinnatus laughed. "Sure enough, you got what I want," he said. Elizabeth snorted. Cincinnatus laughed again. But, though he might have been trying to butter her up, he hadn't been lying. He hoped she felt the same way. She'd never given him any signs she didn't.

When he came home two or three days later, Elizabeth pointed to an envelope on the kitchen table. "You got a letter from Covington," she said. She hadn't opened it. She'd acquired her letters only after they came to Iowa, and still didn't read fluently. They also had a family rule that mail belonged to the person whose name was on the envelope, and to nobody else.

Cincinnatus eyed the envelope with a mixture of pleasure and apprehension. His father and mother still lived in Kentucky, and they did write to him every so often—or rather, they had a literate neighbor do it, for they couldn't read or write. He was always glad to hear from them, and always suspicious when he did. Back in the 1920s, the Kentucky State Police had used a false message from them to lure him to Covington, and flung him into jail for sedition as soon as he got off the train.

He opened the envelope and took out the sheet of paper inside. He was frowning when he put it down. "What's it say?" Elizabeth asked.

"He says Ma's startin' to forget things, act like she was a little child again." Cincinnatus scowled at the letter. Up till now, Livia had always been the rock at which the family anchored. Seneca's health had been shaky now and again, but hardly ever hers. Tears stung Cincinnatus' eyes. This wasn't anything a doctor could fix, either; he knew that too well.

"That's hard to bear, sweetheart. That's right hard to bear," Elizabeth said. Both her parents, though, were long dead, so her sympathy went only so far. Sudden anxiety sharpened her voice as she asked, "He don't want you to go down there? He better not, after all you went through."

"No, no." Cincinnatus shook his head. "He say my pa's managin' for now." But then he shook his head in a different, more thoughtful way. "Reckon maybe I could, though. Ain't no more Kentucky State Police to fling me in jail."

"Sure ain't." But that wasn't agreement from his wife. It was sarcasm. "And there ain't on account o' the Freedom Party's runnin' things in Kentucky nowadays. Freedom Party fellers, they love to have another nigger come down to their state an' commence to raisin' trouble."

"I wouldn't raise no trouble," Cincinnatus said. "All I'd be doin' was seein' my own mother while she's still on this earth."

Elizabeth shook her finger at him as if he were a naughty little boy. "You stay right here where you belong."

"Ain't goin' nowhere. Already told you that. But things ain't as bad as you think in Kentucky, and that's the truth. Yeah, they got them Freedom Party fellers runnin' things now, but they can't do like they done down in the Confederate States—can't beat up all the folks who don't like 'em and keep them folks from votin'. They lose the next election, they's gone."

"You goes down there, you's gone," Elizabeth said. " 'Sides, you goes down there, what's Amanda an' me supposed to do for money? It don't grow on trees—or if it do, I ain't found the nursery what sells it."

"Even if I was to go, I wouldn't be gone long," Cincinnatus said. "It'd be to see my ma, say good-bye to her while she still know who I am. That kind of forgettin', it just gits worse an' worse. Somebody live long enough, he don't even know who he is, let alone anybody else."

Elizabeth softened slightly. "That's so," she admitted, and hugged Cincinnatus. "All right. We take it like it comes, see how she do. If you got to go, then you got to go, and that's all there is to it."

She started to let go of Cincinnatus, but now he squeezed her. "I love you," he said. "You're the best thing ever happen to me."

"I better be," Elizabeth said, "on account of you don't know how to stay out of trouble on your own." Cincinnatus wanted to resent that or get angry about it. He wanted to, but found he couldn't.

"No," Alexander Arthur Pomeroy declared, like a tycoon declining a merger offer. Mary had just asked him if he wanted a nap. At two and a half, he was liable to mean that no, too, and to be fussy and cranky at night because he hadn't had it. One of these days before too long, he'd stop taking naps for good, and then Mary wouldn't get any rest from dawn till dusk, either. She looked forward to that day with something less than delight. Most of Alec's milestones had delighted her: first tooth, first step, first word. Last nap, though, last nap was different.

Of course, Alec might also have been saying no just for the sake of saying no. He did that a lot. From what other mothers said, every two-year-old went through the same maddening phase. Maddening though it was, it could also be funny. Slyly pitching her voice the same way as she had when asking him if he wanted a nap, Mary said, "Alec, do you want a cookie?"

"No," he said again, a pint-sized captain of industry. Then he realized he'd made a dreadful mistake. The horror on his face matched anything in the moving pictures. "Yes!" he exclaimed. "Cookie! Want cookie!" He started to cry.

Mary gave him a vanilla wafer. He calmed down. The way he'd wailed, though, said he needed a nap whether he wanted one or not. She didn't ask again, but scooped him up, sat down in the rocking chair, and started reading a story. She kept her tone deliberately bland. After about ten minutes, Alec's eyes sagged shut. She rocked a little longer, then carried him to his crib.

She put him down with care; sometimes his head would bob up if she wasn't gentle. But not today. Mary let out a sigh of relief. Now she had anywhere from half an hour to an hour and a half to herself. Time had been a luxury more precious than ermine, more precious than rubies, ever since Alec was born.

"Coffee!" Mary said, and headed for the kitchen. She'd always liked tea better. Come to that, she still did like tea better. But coffee had one unquestionable advantage: it was stronger. With a baby—now a toddler—in the house, strength counted. She'd long since given up trying to figure out how far behind on sleep she was.

A gently steaming cup beside her, she sat down in the rocking chair again, this time by herself. She unfolded the *Rosenfeld Register* and prepared to make the most of her free time. The *Register* was just a weekly, and so didn't bother with much news from abroad, but it did have one foreign story on the front page: CONFEDERATE STATES RESUME CONSCRIPTION! President Featherston of the CSA said he was doing it because of the continuing national emergency in the country, and blamed rebellious blacks. President Smith of the USA hadn't said anything by the time the *Register* went to press.

Mary glanced over to the wireless set. She couldn't remember anything Smith had said since the *Register* went to press, either. She thought about turning on the set and listening to some news, but she didn't have the energy to get up. Whatever the president of the USA said, she'd find out sooner or later.

Regardless of what President Smith said, Mary knew what she thought. If the Confederates weren't getting ready to spit in their northern neighbor's eye, she would have been surprised. She hoped they spat good and hard.

During the war, Canada and the Confederates had been on the same side. She'd wondered about that then; the Confederate States hadn't hung out a lamp of liberty for all the world to see. They still didn't, by all appearances. But, whether they did or not, one ancient rule had still applied: the enemy of my enemy is my friend.

These days, Mary would gladly have allied with the Devil against the United States. Only trouble was, Old Scratch appeared uninterested in the deal—or maybe he'd taken up residence in Philadelphia. As for her country, it remained subjugated. She saw no grand uprising on the horizon. The Canadians had tried that once: tried, failed, and seemed to decide not to repeat the experiment.

That left Mary furious. She wanted to be part of something bigger than herself, something more than a rebellion of one. Other people made bombs, too, and made more of them; she read and heard about the bangs every so often, and had the feeling the papers and wireless didn't talk about all of them. The others attacked real soldiers and administrators, too, the way her father had. They didn't limit themselves to a Greek who'd come up to Canada to run a general store.

Mary looked up toward the heavens and asked God, or perhaps her father, *Well, what else could I do?* Other parts of life had got in the way of her thirst for revenge. One of those other parts was working in the diner across the street. Another was sleeping in the crib. She knew next to nothing about the people who planted other bombs, but she would have bet they didn't have babies to worry about.

Local stories filled most of the *Register*'s pages: local stories and local advertising. The wedding announcements and obituaries were as stylized as the serials that ran ahead of main features on the cinema screen. If you'd seen one, you'd seen them all; only names and dates changed.

As for the ads, many of those were even more formulaic than the announcements. Peter Karamanlides bought space to plug his store every week. So did Dr. Shipley, the painless dentist. Mary often wondered why, when they had the only general store and dentist's office for miles around. The same applied to the laundry and the haberdasher and to the newspaper itself. If you didn't use their services, whose would you use?

Advertisements from farmers often followed formulas, too. Those for stud services did: *offspring to stand and walk* was the stock phrase. If the offspring did, fine; if not, the stud fee had to be refunded. But some of those ads were different. There was no standard format, for instance, for selling a piano.

There was no formula for the little stories speckled through the inner pages of the *Rosenfeld Register*, either. The editor, no doubt, would have called them "human interest" pieces. Mary sometimes wondered about the sanity of any human being who was interested in stories about a two-headed calf nursed by two different cows or a man who pulled a boxcar with his teeth—and false teeth, at that.

But she looked at the filler pieces herself. A story about a mother cat nursing an orphaned puppy could make her smile. So could one about two former sweethearts who'd both moved away from the small town where they grew up, then didn't see each other for twenty-five years till they were standing in line at the same Toronto cinema. One had never married; the other was a widower. They'd fallen in love all over again.

Some of those "human interest" stories made Mary grit her teeth, because propaganda poisoned them. The one about the Yank flier who'd requalified as a fighter pilot after twenty years away from aeroplanes was particularly sappy; she had to resist the impulse to crumple up the *Register* and throw it across the living room. The last paragraph said, *Our bold hero, now also a successful barrister specializing in occupation affairs, is married to the former Laura Secord, a descendant of the "Paul Revere of Canada," who had the same name. They have one daughter. Thus we see that the two lands are becoming ever more closely intertwined.*

Mary saw nothing of the sort. What she saw was a traitor living high on the hog because she'd married a Yank. And hadn't Laura Secord been one of the people who'd betrayed the uprising in the 1920s? Mary nodded to herself. She was sure she remembered that. She wouldn't forget the name, not when she'd learned it in school before the Yanks started changing what was taught. Had the woman been intertwined with this Yank flier even then? The lewd image was enough to make Mary's cheeks heat.

She'd promised herself vengeance on the people who'd made the uprising fail. She'd promised, and then she hadn't delivered. Her father would have been ashamed of her. Up there in heaven, Arthur McGregor probably *was* ashamed of her.

"I'll take care of it," she whispered. "I'll take care of it if it's the last thing I ever do."

Then she had to take care of something else, because Alec woke up with a yell: "Pooping potty!" That was his signal that he needed to use the toilet—or, sometimes, that he'd just gone. Mary rushed in to lift him out of the crib and see which it was this time.

"You're dry!" she exclaimed in glad surprise after a hasty check—he did have accidents in his sleep.

"Dry as a fly," he answered, echoing one of the things she said to him.

"What a good boy!" Mary took him out of the crib, gave him a kiss, and stood him on a stool in front of the toilet. He did his business, and almost all of it went where it was supposed to go. Mary cleaned up the rest with toilet paper. "What a good boy!" she said again. Another woman in the block of flats insisted babies didn't turn into people till they were toilet-trained. Mary thought that went too far . . . most of the time.

His clothes set to rights, Alec went off to play. Mary went off to keep at least one eye on him while he was playing, to make sure he didn't knock over a table or pull a lamp down on his head or try to swallow a big mouthful of dust or stick his finger in an electric socket or do any of the other interesting and creative things small children did in their unending effort not to live to grow up.

This afternoon, he made a beeline for the ashtray. "Oh, no, you don't!" Mary said, and got there first. He'd tried that before. Once, he'd managed to swallow one of Mort's cigarette butts, as he'd proved by puking it up. Keeping an eye on her son, Mary understood how her mother had come to have gray hair.

Every so often, she cast a longing glance across the street at the diner. When Mort got back, she'd have another pair of eyes in the flat to keep watch on Alec. One toddler left two parents only slightly outnumbered. Dealing with Alec by herself, Mary often felt not just outnumbered but overwhelmed.

But when Mort did come home, he sank down into the rocking chair with a bottle of Moosehead and complained about how busy he'd been all day at the diner. "Lord, it's good to get off my feet," he said.

"I have the same feeling when Alec takes a nap," Mary said pointedly.

Her husband didn't take the point. "It was a madhouse over there today," he said. "We made good money, but they kept us hopping."

"Alec always keeps me hopping," Mary said.

"This little fellow? This little fellow here?" Mort grabbed Alec and stuck him on his lap. Alec squealed with glee and cuddled up. *If I tried that, he'd pitch a fit. Either that or he'd just jump off ten seconds later,* Mary thought. Mort ruffled the toddler's fine sandy hair. "You're not so tough, are you?"

"Tough!" Alec yelled gleefully. "Tough!"

"You're not so tough," Mort said again, and turned him upside down. Alec squealed in delight. Mary hid a sigh by turning away. Mort could do things with their son that she couldn't. She'd seen that very early on. He could get Alec to pay attention and do what he was told when she couldn't. Maybe it was just that he had a deep, rumbling man's voice. Maybe it was that he was gone more and Alec wanted to please him while he was around. Whatever it was, it was unquestionably real.

So was Laura Secord's treason. *Alec has his father,* Mary thought. *I made a promise to mine a long time ago. I haven't kept it yet, but that doesn't mean I won't. Oh, no. It doesn't mean that at all.* She nodded to herself. Then she smiled. She wasn't annoyed at Mort any more, not even a little bit.

Conscripts were filling out the ranks of the Confederate Army. It got stronger week by week. Confederate aeroplanes carried guns and bombs. The fastest Confederate fighters could go up against anything the USA built. And the United States, while they'd grumbled, hadn't done anything *but* grumble. As far as Clarence Potter was concerned, that would do for a miracle till a bigger one came along.

Jake Featherston had thought it would work like this. If it hadn't, whether Featherston got—extorted—the right to run for a second term wouldn't have mattered a hill of beans' worth. The country would have thrown him out on his ear if the USA didn't take care of the job.

The Confederate States were ever so much stronger than they had been. Potter knew just how strong they were—and how strong the United States were. A fight would have been no contest. But no fight came. Featherston had been sure none would. And he'd been right.

"By God, he's earned a second term for that," Potter muttered at his desk down below the War Department building.

He shook his head in something halfway between bemusement and horror. *Did I say that? Did I say that?* he wondered. *By God, I did. I meant it, too.* He'd spent more than fifteen years as one of Jake Featherston's sincerest enemies—sincerest, because he'd known Featherston longer and better than any of the other people who couldn't stand him. And now he had to admit Jake had known what he was doing after all.

Potter wouldn't have dreamt the USA would sit quiet and let the CSA rearm. He would have thought—hell, he *had* thought—you'd have to be crazy to take a chance like that. Featherston had taken the chance, and he'd got away with it.

So what did that make him? A crazy man saw things nobody else could see. But what about someone who saw things nobody else could see—but that turned out to be there after all? There was a word for people like that, too. The word was *genius*. Potter didn't like using that word about Jake Featherston. He still remembered the weight of the revolver he'd carried up to the Olympic swimming stadium, intending to get rid of Jake once for all.

But he hadn't. He'd got rid of the colored would-be assassin instead, and the whole world was different on account of it. He looked down at his butternut uniform. He wouldn't have put that on again, not in a million years.

Here he sat, analyzing reports from Confederates in the USA who talked as if they'd grown up there. The reports, of course, weren't addressed WAR DEPARTMENT, RICHMOND, VIRGINIA, CSA. Somehow, that might have made even the sleepy United States open eyes wide and perhaps raise an eyebrow. Instead, the letters and telegrams had come to a variety of businesses scattered all over the Confederate States. They were all coded, too, so they didn't talk directly about barrels or aeroplanes. Not all the codes were particularly subtle, but they'd defeat casual snoopers.

Potter wished the reports could come straight to him. As things were, he got them anywhere from several hours to several days after they reached the CSA. As long as the United States and Confederate States stayed at peace, the delay didn't matter too much. If they ever went to war . . .

He laughed at himself. If the USA and the CSA went to war again, the only way letters and telegrams crossed the border would be through the International Red Cross. He suspected—no, he knew—they would be a lot slower than they were now.

He drummed his fingers on the desk, took off his spectacles and carefully polished them, replaced them on his nose, and then did some more drumming. However much he despised the USA, he hoped another war wouldn't come. The Confederacy would be fighting out of its weight, and all the more so because the United States had no second front against Canada this time.

Did Jake Featherston see that? It seemed pretty plain to Potter. As far as he could tell from cautious conversations, it seemed pretty plain to most of the officers in the War Department. The trouble was, of course, that Featherston wasn't an officer, and never had been one. He was a jumped-up sergeant, remarkably shrewd, but not trained to look at the big picture. How much would that matter? If it really came to another fight, the president would surely be shrewd enough to let trained commanders take charge of things.

Potter's musings were interrupted when a uniformed officer—not a soldier, he realized after a moment, but a Freedom Party guard—strode up to his desk, saluted, and barked out, "Freedom!"

"Freedom!" Potter echoed in more crisply military tones. "And what can I do for you, ah, Chief Assault Leader?" The other officer wore a captain's three bars on either side of his collar, but Party guards had their own titles of rank. Potter didn't know if they thought the Army's weren't good enough for them, or if they thought those were too good. It wasn't the sort of question he could ask, not if he wanted to keep wearing his uniform and not one with a big P stenciled on the back.

"Sir, I am ordered to bring you to the president at once," the chief assault leader answered.

"Ordered, are you? Well, then, you'd better do it, eh?" Potter said, pushing back his chair and stowing papers in a drawer that locked. The Freedom Party guard nodded seriously. Clarence Potter didn't smile. He'd been pretty sure a man who became a Party guard wouldn't recognize irony if it piddled on his shiny black boots. He asked, "Do you know what this is about?"

"No, sir," the officer said. "I have my orders. A motorcar is waiting outside." He turned and marched, machinelike, toward the stairs. Potter followed at a more human amble.

The motorcar was a Birmingham painted butternut. It flew a Freedom Party flag, though, not the Confederate battle flag an Army vehicle would have sported. Potter and the stone-faced chief assault leader got in. The driver, also a Freedom Party guard, whisked them away from the War Department and up Shockoe Hill to the presidential residence.

A bodyguard there relieved Potter of his pistol. That was routine these days. If the guard knew Potter had once carried a pistol intending to use it on the president, he gave no sign.

"Reporting as ordered, sir," Potter said when the captain—no, the chief assault leader—took him into Featherston's office. Formality helped. If he spoke to the president of the CSA, he wouldn't have to think—so much—about the fiery, foul-mouthed artillery sergeant he'd known during the war, wouldn't have to think that the sergeant and the president were one and the same.

"Good to see you, Colonel. Sit down," Jake Featherston replied, returning the salute. Maybe he was using formality to suppress memory, too. As soon as Potter was in the chair, Featherston waved to the Party officer. "That'll be all, Randy. You just run along. Close the door on your way out." Randy looked unhappy, but he did what everybody seemed to do around Featherston: he obeyed. The president turned back to Clarence Potter and got straight to business: "I need more from your people in Kentucky."

"Sir?" Potter needed a moment to shift gears.

Featherston's scowl made him look like an angry, hungry wolf. "Kentucky," he repeated impatiently. "Things are heating up there, and I'm going to want to know more about what's going on. I'm going to want to be able to make things happen there, too."

"*I* haven't got but a handful of men in Kentucky, Mr. President," Potter said. "My specialty is people who talk like Yankees, and that's not what we mostly use there, because the accent is closer to our own. Men from Tennessee don't stand out in Kentucky the way they would in Pennsylvania or Kansas."

"I know what you've got in Kentucky." Featherston reeled off the names and positions of almost all of Potter's men in the state. He wasn't looking at a list. He knew them, knew them by heart. Those names and supporting details had surely gone to him in one report or another, but that he'd remembered them. . . . Clarence Potter was more nearly flabbergasted than impressed at that grasp of detail. *I didn't know he had it in him,* he thought. The president went on, "The point is, three or four of your people are in slots with the state government or a city government where they can be useful to us *because* everybody reckons they're Yankees."

"They can do *some* of that," Potter said cautiously, "but not too much. If they don't act like what they're supposed to be, they'll make the real Yankees wonder why they don't. That wouldn't be good. The last thing we want is to make the United States suspicious."

This time, Featherston's scowl was of a different sort. Potter had no trouble identifying it, though: it was the scowl of a man who wasn't used to people telling him anything he didn't want to hear. *Well, too damn bad,* the intelligence officer thought. *You're the one who brought me back into the Army. Now you have to take the consequences. I'm not one of your Party hacks, and you'd better remember it.*

"You telling me you can't do what I need?" The president's voice was harsh and dangerous.

Potter shook his head. "No, sir. That's not what I said at all. But I am asking you to make sure in your own mind that what you get now is worth the risk of losing a lot later on. If the damnyankees start looking hard for Confederate spies, they're bound to find some. And if they find some, they'll look for more, and. . . ."

"All right." Featherston held up a hand. "I see what you're saying. But what's the point of having all these goddamn spies in place if we can't get any use out of 'em?"

"We *do* get use out of them," Potter said; for all his grasp of detail, Jake Featherston *was* missing the big picture here. "We get information. Without it, we're blind. That's really what they're there for, as far as we're concerned. If they step out of their roles, they may give themselves away."

Featherston grunted. His eyes showed his own hard suspicion. Regardless of whether his guards did, he remembered the pistol in Clarence Potter's pocket, and he had to know why Potter had had it there. "If we can't use our people to nudge things along there, how the hell do we do it?" he snapped.

"We can use our people. The ones I run just aren't the right set of tools for the job," Potter answered. "Demonstrations, riots, stories in the papers, wireless shows . . . We can do all that. About the most my men can do is pretend they haven't seen telegrams, things like that. If they try to do much more, the fellows they work for will start giving them fishy stares. Do you see what I'm saying?"

He waited for Jake Featherston to blow. As long as he'd known him, Featherston had had a short fuse. Now the president of the CSA didn't have anybody set above him to make him pull back. If he wanted to lose his temper, he could, and who would say boo?

But Potter had been as cool and dispassionate as he could, and the president seemed to respond well to that, or at least not to take it as a threat. "All right, then," he said. "We'll try that, and see how it works. I do want to leave your people in place, on account of we're not done with Kentucky. Oh, no. We're not done, not by a long shot. That state is *ours*, and I aim to get it back."

Clarence Potter could have found any number of things about which to disagree with the president of the Confederate States. Not about getting Kentucky back, though. He stood, came to attention, and saluted. "Yes, sir!" he said.

Flora Blackford remembered when going out on the floor of Congress had been a thrill. It wasn't any more. Not these days. The Freedom Party Congressmen from Houston and Kentucky made sure of that. They weren't there to do the nation's business. They were there to disrupt it, and they were good at that. The pair of Representatives Utah had elected after the end of the military occupation weren't much better. They seemed more interested in complaining about what had happened over the past twenty—sometimes, over the past sixty—years than in trying to make the next two better.

Congressman Nephi Pratt was complaining even as Flora took her seat. "I accept your correction with all due humility, Mr. Speaker," he was saying. "I would have been more fully abreast of these matters had the government not labored so long and hard to suppress my creed and oppress my state, thereby depriving me of the opportunity to participate in the decisions made by this august body since the end of the war."

Up jumped a young pepperpot Democrat from New Mexico. "Perhaps the distinguished gentleman will state on the record in which direction he pointed a gun during the war: at the foes of the United States or at her soldiers."

Pratt was a portly man with a mane of white hair. He tossed it angrily now. "I need not answer that—"

"You just did, seems to me," the Democrat shot back.

"Mr. Speaker, I resent the imputation," Pratt said.

"Mr. Speaker, *I* resent having to share the chamber with a damned traitor," the Congressman from New Mexico said.

*Bang! Bang! Bang!* The Speaker's gavel descended like the crack of doom. "Mr. Pratt, Mr. Goldwater, you are both out of order," he said. "Any further outbursts from either of you, and I will have the sergeant-at-arms remove you from the floor."

"The United States hanged my grandfather," Nephi Pratt said. "I see things have not changed much since."

"He had it coming, by God," Congressman Goldwater snapped.

*Bang! Bang! Bang!* "Sergeant-at-arms!" Congressman Cannon of Missouri said. The Speaker looked thoroughly disgusted as he continued, "You and your assistants are to escort the two contentious gentlemen to separate waiting rooms, in which places they shall remain until they see fit to comport themselves in civilized fashion."

Congressman Pratt left the room with majestic dignity. Congressman Goldwater shouted, "Defense of the truth is no vice! I should not be removed." He scuffled with the men who tried to take him away, and landed one solid blow before they did.

All the Freedom Party men stood up and cheered at the chaos they, for once, had not created. That made Flora signal to the Speaker, a fellow Socialist. He pointed back, intoning, "The chair recognizes the distinguished Congresswoman from New York, Mrs. Blackford."

"Thank you, Mr. Speaker." She waited till the din died down a little, then said, "In my opinion, the Freedom Party has been the source of most of the problems and most of the bad manners in both houses of Congress, even if members of other parties have caught the disease from it. The Freedom Party—"

She couldn't go on, not right away, for the House chamber echoed with angry shouts from the Freedom Party Congressmen and cries of "Hear! Hear!" from Socialists, Republicans, and even a good many Democrats. Speaker Cannon again plied the gavel with might and main. At last, something like quiet returned.

Flora resumed: "The Freedom Party, as I was saying before its Congressmen so neatly proved my point, differs from other parties in the United States in one particular: that its members do not truly wish to take part in the serious business of making this country a better place."

To her surprise—indeed, to her amazement—Congressman Mahon of Houston sprang to his feet, crying, "Mr. Speaker! Mr. Speaker! If the distinguished Congresswoman from New York will yield . . ."

The sight of a Freedom Party man following proper parliamentary procedure must have astonished Congressman Cannon as much as it did Flora. "Mrs. Blackford?" the Speaker asked.

"I will yield for a brief statement or question," Flora said. "Not for a harangue."

Even that didn't upset Mahon. "I will be brief," he promised. Flora nodded. The Speaker pointed to the Houstonian. Mahon said, "I would like to note that the Freedom Party Representatives do not wish to serve our states here in Philadelphia or in Washington. We—"

This time, shouts of, "Shame!" drowned him out. The Speaker of the House rapped furiously for order. With some reluctance, he said, "The gentleman from Houston has the floor. He may continue."

"Thank you, Mr. Speaker," Mahon said, willing to be courteous since the presiding officer of the House had ruled in his favor. "We don't care to be here, I say, because we would rather represent our states in Richmond, since they rightfully belong to the Confederate States of America!"

"Freedom! Freedom! Freedom!" his fellow Freedom Party members chanted, and, "Plebiscite! Plebiscite! Plebiscite!"

Roars of, "Treason!" and, "Never!" came from Democrats, Republicans, and some Socialists. Again, Speaker Cannon had to ply his gavel with might and main to restore quiet—or at least lower the noise. He might have done better by firing a pistol round into the ceiling. But if he'd had a pistol, other Congressmen would have, too, and they might have aimed them at one another. The Speaker said, "Mrs. Blackford has the floor. You may go on, Mrs. Blackford."

"Thank you, Mr. Speaker," Flora said. "However much pleasure most of us would take from no longer having the company of the members from the Freedom Party, I am also certain more than a few of us would not care to give them the satisfaction of gaining anything they want, simply because they have made themselves so obnoxious to us."

That brought jeers from the Congressmen from Houston and Kentucky, jeers largely drowned out by a storm of applause from Representatives of other parties. Flora wasn't particularly proud of herself despite the applause. She knew she'd sunk to the Freedom Party's level in condemning it.

*Hosea wouldn't have done that,* she thought. When he'd been a Congressman, Hosea Blackford had got on well with everyone—he'd got on better with reactionary Democrats than Flora ever had. But the men from the Freedom Party weren't just reactionaries. They were reactionaries on the march, in the same way as the Reds in the failed uprisings in the CSA and Russia had been radicals on the march. Up till the past few years, the world hadn't had to worry about revolutionary reaction. It did now.

Wearily, Speaker Cannon fought yet again for order. When he finally got it, he spoke in wistful tones: "Do you suppose we could possibly return to discussion of the trade bill before us at the moment?"

They did go on. In due course, the Speaker let Congressman Pratt and Congressman Goldwater return to the floor. They started sniping at each other again, but within—sometimes narrowly within—the rules of House decorum. The Freedom Party Congressmen from Houston and Kentucky went back to ignoring the rules, as they usually did. They cared nothing for them, and admitted as much. They didn't want to be here in the first place, and seemed to operate on the theory that, if they made all the colleagues hate and despise them, their states became more likely to leave the USA for the CSA. What worried Flora was that they might well prove right.

Thanks to their unending shenanigans—and thanks to the basically uninspiring nature of trade bills—the day crawled past on hands and knees. Speaker Cannon didn't look for a motion to adjourn till well past six that evening. When he did, a throng of Representatives tried to make it and another throng tried to second it. Wearily, the members left the floor.

Competition for cabs outside was as fierce as anything that had gone on within the hallowed hall. Flora, normally polite and gentle, brawled with the best of them. She wanted to get home to Joshua as fast as she could. Thanks to a judicious elbow, she quickly won a ride.

Her son looked up from his homework in surprise when she came through the door. "Hello," he said, his voice at fifteen as deep as a man's. "I didn't expect you back so soon. Weren't you going to do some office work before you came here?"

"The session ran long, so I came . . ." Flora's voice trailed away, also in surprise—not at what he'd said but at what she smelled. "That's cigarette smoke. When did you start smoking cigarettes?"

"Last year, not long after Father died," Joshua answered, resolutely nonchalant. "Everybody at school does it, and it doesn't hurt anything."

"It hurts me that you've been sneaking cigarettes behind my back," Flora said. "If you thought I wouldn't mind, why didn't you come out and tell me?"

"Well . . ." Her son looked uncomfortable, but he finally said, "Mostly because you're so old-fashioned about some things."

"Old-fashioned?" Flora yelped. If that wasn't the most unkind cut of all for someone who'd always prided herself on her radicalism, she couldn't imagine what would be. "I am not!"

"Oh, yeah?" Joshua said, a colloquialism that made his mother incline more toward reaction than radicalism. He went on, "If you weren't old-fashioned, you wouldn't flabble about cigarettes." As fifteen-year-old boys are wont to do, he acted monstrously proud of his own logic.

Flora blinked at the slang, then figured out what it had to mean. "I don't flabble about cigarettes—for grownups," she said. Instead of seeming pleased that she'd understood him, Joshua merely looked scornful that she was trying to speak his language. She might have guessed he would. Suppressing a sigh, she forged ahead: "No matter what you think, you're not a grownup yet."

"Father was smoking cigarettes when he was fifteen," Joshua said.

He was right about that, however much Flora wished he weren't. "Your father grew up on a farm in the middle of nowhere," she answered. "When he was fifteen, he was going to the bathroom in a privy, bathing once a month, and eating food his folks had cooked over buffalo chips. Do you want to imitate him there, too?"

For a moment, she thought he would say bathing once a month didn't sound so bad. But he visibly changed his mind and changed the subject: "If cigarettes are so terrible, how come everybody smokes them?"

"Not everybody does."

"Just about!" Joshua said, by which he doubtless meant three or four people he liked did.

This time, Flora didn't suppress her sigh. She knew a losing fight when she saw one, and she saw one here. Whether she liked it or not, Joshua was going to smoke. She said, "From now on, you don't need to sneak any more." That made him happy. She wished it would have made her happy, too.

Sylvia Enos came out of the moving-picture theater with Ernie. She looked happy—she'd liked the film. He didn't, and hadn't. "What was wrong with it?" she asked. "It was exciting, and it had a good love story."

"What was wrong with it?" he echoed. "I will tell you what was wrong. The men who made it never saw war. They were boys in 1914. They had to be. Either that or they were cowards. Half the things in the film could not have happened. Soldiers would have gone to the guardhouse for the other half."

"It's only a story," Sylvia said. "It's not supposed to be true."

"But it pretends to be true," Ernie said. "That offends me."

She didn't want him angry. When he got angry, he got angry at the whole world, not just at what had bothered him in the first place. She said, "Let's go somewhere, and we'll have a couple of drinks, and we'll forget about it."

"All right," he said. "That film deserves forgetting."

They ended up having more than a couple of drinks—considerably more, in Ernie's case. Then they went back to Sylvia's apartment. Mary Jane was out with friends, and wouldn't be back till late. They had the place to themselves. Sober or drunk, Ernie made a conscientious lover. He did what he needed to do to make Sylvia happy. Then she tried to do the same for him. She'd had pretty good luck with that lately. Not tonight, though. Try as she would, nothing happened.

She did her best to make light of it, saying, "See what those last couple of cocktails will do to you?"

"My cock has more wrong with it than cocktails," Ernie answered, which was unfortunately true. "Half-cocked," he muttered. That was what

Sylvia thought she heard, anyhow. He shook his head. "It is no good. It is no goddamn good at all."

"That's not true," Sylvia exclaimed. "It was fine just last week."

He didn't want to listen. "No good at all," he said again. "Sometimes I wonder why the hell I bother. What is the use? There is no use. I know that. I know that much too well."

"Don't be silly," Sylvia told him. "It can happen to anybody at all, not just to you."

"It does not happen to a real man," Ernie said. "That is what it means to be a real man. And what am I?" His laugh told what he thought he was. "A leftover. Something from the scrap heap. I ought to go to Spain. I could fight there." A Nationalist uprising backed by France and Britain had half the country up in arms against King Alfonso XIII. Kaiser Wilhelm had belatedly sent the Monarchists weapons to resist their would-be overthrowers, but things didn't look good for them even so.

Sylvia shook her head. "What does shooting people have to do with—this?" She set her hand on the part, or part of a part, that hadn't quite worked.

Ernie twisted away, kicking the quilt she'd got from Chris Clogston down onto the floor. "You do not understand. I knew you would not understand. Damn you anyway." He all but jumped out of the bed they'd shared and started putting on his clothes.

"Maybe I would understand, if you'd talk sense once in a while," Sylvia said.

"You are only a woman. What do you know?" Ernie stormed out of the apartment, slamming the door behind him. Sylvia sighed as she picked up the quilt and put on a nightgown. This sort of thing had happened before. It would probably happen again. She sighed once more, went into the bathroom to brush her teeth, and then came back and fell asleep. Whatever time Mary Jane came in, Sylvia never heard it.

George Jr., his wife, Connie, and their children came over for supper the next evening. Sylvia enjoyed spoiling her grandchildren. Bill, the baby boy for whom Mary Jane had bought another quilt, was toddling now. Sylvia also enjoyed listening to her son's stories about life on a fishing boat. They took her back to the days when her husband had told the same kind of stories. Hard to believe George was more than twenty years dead. Hard to believe, but true.

"And how are you, Ma?" George Jr. asked. "How's Ernie? Sis said you went to the cinema with him last night."

He sounded earnest himself. The pun made Sylvia laugh a little. *He wants me to be happy*, she thought. *He really does. That's sweet.* But she had to answer. "He's been better," she said slowly. "But he's been worse, too."

Her son's sigh had an indulgent quality, one that made her wonder who'd raised whom. "You really ought to—" he began.

Sylvia held up a hand and cut him off. "I really ought to do whatever *I* think is the best thing for me to do. And *you* really ought to"—she enjoyed turning George Jr.'s phrase back on him—"mind your own beeswax."

"Give up, George," Connie said. "You don't let her tell you what to do. How can you blame her if she doesn't want to let you tell her?"

"That's right." Sylvia beamed at her daughter-in-law.

"Fine. I give up. Here—I'm throwing in the towel." George Jr. took his napkin off his lap and tossed it into the middle of the table. "But I'm going to tell you one more thing before I shut up."

"I know what you're going to say." Sylvia held up her hand again, like a cop stopping traffic. "I don't want to hear it."

"I don't care. I'm going to say it anyway." George Jr. stuck out his chin and looked stubborn. "That guy is bad news, Ma. There. I'm done."

"About time, too." Sylvia knew her son was right. Ernie was, or could be, bad news. She would have known even if Mary Jane hadn't told her the same thing. The feel of danger—within limits—was part of what made him attractive. Whether he would ever break those limits . . . But he hadn't—quite—in all the time Sylvia had known him. And he had reasons for being the way he was. Sylvia didn't think George Jr. knew about those. She couldn't very well talk about such things with a man, and especially not with her son.

She wondered whether George Jr. could keep from bringing up Ernie again for the rest of the evening. She would have bet against it, but he managed. That made time pass a lot more pleasantly. Only when he and his family were leaving did he say, "Take care of yourself, Ma."

"And haven't I been doing that since before you were born?" Sylvia said. "A fisherman's wife who can't take care of herself is in a pretty sorry state, that's all I've got to tell you." She looked to Connie. "Am I right or am I wrong?"

"Oh, you're right, all right," her daughter-in-law said.

"You bet I am." Sylvia spoke with great certainty. Fishermen were away at sea so much, their wives had to do things on their own behalf. If the wives didn't, nobody would or could. And Sylvia had gone from fisherman's wife to fisherman's widow. Nobody gave a widow a helping hand. She'd discovered that the hard way.

For that matter, no elves emerged from the walls to help her with the dishes. She did them herself, the way she always had. She couldn't go to bed without being angry at herself till they were done. Her hard-earned, hard-learned self-reliance ran deep.

And when Ernie showed up at her door with flowers two days later to ask her out the next Saturday, she didn't say no. She didn't even ask him if he would behave himself. A question like that would just have made him angry and all the more determined to act up. She couldn't blame him for that, not when she felt the same way herself.

When Saturday came, he took her to the Union Oyster House. She smiled, remembering her last visit there with Mary Jane. Unlike Mary Jane, though, Ernie washed down his fried oysters with several stiff drinks. "Are you sure you want to do that?" Sylvia picked her words with care. He did have more trouble in the bedroom when he was drunk—and he had plenty when he was sober. And when he was drunk, he had a harder time coping with the trouble he had.

But he didn't want to listen to her tonight, any more than she'd wanted to listen to George Jr. earlier in the week. "I am fine. Just fine," he said loudly. The way he said it proved he was nothing of the sort, but also proved he would pay no attention if she tried to tell him so.

*If you can't lick 'em, join 'em,* she thought, and waved to the waiter for another drink of her own. After another one, and then another one yet, she stopped worrying—at any rate, she stopped caring—about how many Ernie had had, though he kept pouring them down, too. She took him by the arm. "Where shall we go?" she asked, laughing at how bold and brassy she sounded.

"We will go back to my place," he answered. "And when we get there, we will see what comes up." That made Sylvia laugh, too, though Ernie wasn't joking the way another man might have. In fact, he seemed to be trying to persuade himself something *would* come up. Under his leer, or perhaps stirred into it, was enough desperation to give Sylvia pause, though she was a long way from sober herself.

"Maybe we ought to have some coffee or something first," she said.

Ernie took her arm. "Come on," he said, and effortlessly hauled her up out of the booth. He was very strong, even if he didn't show it all the time. She went along with him, thinking, *The walk will sober him up. It may even sober me up, too.*

Her head still buzzed when they got to Ernie's apartment. She didn't want to think about what it would feel like in the morning. But the morning seemed a million miles away. Ernie closed the door behind them, then took her in his arms and kissed her, hard. He tasted of whiskey and pipe tobacco. He picked her up and carried her into the cramped little bedroom and half set, half dropped her on the bed.

"Come on," he said again, and started taking off his clothes.

Sylvia did the same, quickly. His strength and the whiskey in her and the taste and smell of him all combined to excite her. If he'd been any other man, he would have thrown himself on her and done what he wanted to do. But he couldn't. He hadn't been able to do anything like that for more than twenty years. If he was going anywhere, she would have to get him there. She sat up and leaned forward and took what there was of him in her mouth as he stood by the side of the bed.

And nothing happened. He groaned again and again, but always in frustration, not release. Try as she would, it was no use. She did everything she knew how to do. Nothing helped. Sweat ran down his face, down his chest. "Damn you," he muttered, and then, "Damn me."

She looked up at him. "What do you want?" she asked. "I'll do anything you think will do you good. You know I will."

She'd turned on the lamp by the bed a little while before. Sometimes watching helped him. Not tonight. He looked at her, looked through her. His eyes might have belonged to a dead man. His voice sounded as if it came from the other side of the grave, too: "It makes no difference, not any more."

"What do you mean?" she said. "Of course it does. Next time, we'll—" She broke off. "What are you doing?"

The blued metal of the pistol he took out of the nightstand gleamed dully in the lamplight. "Nothing matters any more," he said, and pointed it at the side of his own head.

"*No!*" He'd played such games before. This time, Sylvia didn't think he was playing. She grabbed for the pistol. Ernie cursed and hit her. She tried to knee him in the crotch. He twisted away. They wrestled, both of them shouting, both of them swearing, there on the bedroom floor.

Loud as the end of the world, the pistol went off. She never knew whether he'd intended to shoot her. It made no difference. It didn't matter. The bullet tore into her chest, and the world was nothing but pain and darkness.

As if from very far away, Ernie shouted, "Sylvia! Don't die! Damn you, I love you!" She tried to say something, but blood filled her mouth. From even further away, she heard another shot, and the thump of a falling body, and then nothing, nothing at all.


Jefferson Pinkard was not a happy man. He'd come to Louisiana to help run a camp for political prisoners, and what had they gone and done? They'd taken out most of the politicals and filled the camp full of colored guerrillas. The politicals had been sober, civilized, middle-aged men who did as they were told. The Negroes, on the other hand . . .

Though Pinkard didn't want to admit it, even to himself, the captured Negroes scared him to death. They had taken up arms against the Confederate States not in hope of victory—as the colored Reds had a generation earlier—but because they simply couldn't stand the way things were. Now that they'd been taken prisoner, they expected nothing from the men into whose hands they'd fallen. They expected nothing—and they were seldom disappointed.

Camp Dependable was a rougher place now than it had been when inoffensive politicals filled it. These days, guards always carried submachine guns. They carried the weapons with safeties off, and they always traveled in pairs in areas where prisoners went. So far, the blacks hadn't managed to steal a submachine gun from a guard. Jeff hoped that record would last. He wondered if it could.

He had other worries, too, though not of the life-and-death sort. Just keeping track of the prisoners was a record-keeper's worst nightmare. They didn't come into the camp with passbooks in the pockets of their dungarees. He assumed most of the names they gave were false. Even had those names been genuine, they wouldn't have helped much. Negroes in the CSA had never been allowed to take surnames, as they were in the USA. With passbooks, the powers that be didn't have too much trouble sorting out who was who. Without them . . .

The camp had an underofficer who specialized in taking fingerprints and forwarding them to Baton Rouge and to Richmond for identification. If the people in Baton Rouge and Richmond had cared as much as Pinkard did about matching those fingerprints to the ones in their files, he would have been happier. As things were, he wasn't sure who most of his prisoners were. The only thing he was sure of was that they had good reason for concealing their identity.

"We've got to be careful, dammit," he would tell the guards every morning. "These nigger bastards don't want to argue with us like the politicals did. They want to kill us. That's why they're here. Thing we can't do is give 'em the chance."

Work parties that left the barbed-wire perimeter of the camp made him especially nervous. The blacks who went out on road-building details and other hard labor were chained to one another. They wore balls and chains on their left ankles. They couldn't possibly run. So Jeff told himself. He worried even so.

And it was all his baby. When the politicals had gone off to another camp, the warden at Camp Dependable had gone with them. "You made this place a going concern," he told Pinkard before he went away. "You know it best, and that makes you best suited to keeping these black devils in line here."

Maybe he'd even been right. Regardless of whether he had, Jeff didn't love him and never would. The then-warden had had a choice between an easy job and a hard one. He'd taken the easy one himself and left the hard one to somebody else. If he'd fought in the war, he would have sent patrols forward while he stayed in a nice, safe dugout in his own trench line. Jeff had known officers like that. He'd despised them, too.

Higher rank. Fancier emblems on his collar tabs. A bigger paycheck every month. Pinkard approved of all those things. But he didn't approve of the way he'd got them.

He checked the clock in his office. Half past five. About time for the working party to come back. Pinkard heaved himself out of the swivel chair, which creaked under his weight. He headed for the front gate. He always liked to watch the gangs come in. If he could get a report on the spot, he didn't give the guards a chance to come up with any lies. He knew such things happened. He'd done the like himself, and didn't want it done to him.

His timing was good. He got to the gate two or three minutes before the work party returned. The Negroes clanked along, slowed by their chains and the weights attached to their ankles—and slowed also by doing work they didn't want to do and coming back to a place where they didn't want to be.

"How did it go?" Jeff called to the chief guard, a stocky, hard-faced man named Mercer Scott.

"Another day," Scott answered with a shrug. He shifted a plug of tobacco and spat a stream of brown juice on the ground. "Three niggers keeled over. Two of 'em croaked, and we flung 'em in the swamp. The other one got back up on his feet when we thumped him a couple times. Lazy bastard just wanted a break. I'll break his black ass, he tries that kind of shit with me." He spat again.

"Who died?" Pinkard asked. "I've got to try and keep the records straight, you know."

"Yeah, yeah." Mercer Scott screwed his face into a parody of deep thought. "One was that mincing little faggot named Dionysus. He's been poorly since that big buck beat him up last month. And the other one . . . Hell, who was the other one?" He turned to another guard. "Who was the other nigger we pitched in the swamp, Bob?"

"The skinny bastard," Bob answered. "Cicero, that's his name."

"Oh, yeah. That's right. I couldn't recollect if he was today or yesterday." Scott turned to Jeff. "That's who it was, all right. Dionysus and Cicero. No loss, either one of 'em."

Pinkard nodded and scribbled a note to himself. The camp held several Ciceros, but only one of them was in this work gang, so he wouldn't have any trouble with that. He said, "Good enough. Make sure the count matches, then bring 'em on inside." A mosquito lit on the back of his wrist. He smashed it. Hell might have more mosquitoes than Louisiana, but he wasn't sure anyplace else did.

One by one, the Negroes counted off. The reek of their unwashed bodies was harsh in Pinkard's nostrils. The guards smelled nearly as ripe. In this heat and humidity, everybody stank.

One of Pinkard's aides pounded on the door to his quarters at half past twelve that night. He woke up grabbing for his pistol. Nobody would bother him at that time of night for anything but trouble. As far as he was concerned, trouble came in two flavors: escape and uprising. "What the hell?" he demanded, throwing the door open in just his pajamas.

"Warden, they need you at the front gate right away," the aide said.

Jeff shoved his feet into slippers and jammed his hat down onto his head so people would have some idea of who he was. "I'm coming," he said. "What am I walking into?"

"I don't exactly know," the aide answered, and Jeff wanted to clobber him with the pistol. He went on, "There's folks from Richmond there. Reckon they'll tell you what you need to know."

"From Richmond?" Pinkard's mind raced. Was he in trouble? What kind of trouble could he be in? He couldn't think of anything he'd screwed up. He'd done his job here. He'd done it back in Alabama, too. He'd been a good Freedom Party man since the days just after the war, and he'd stayed in the Party through the hard times after Grady Calkins shot President Hampton. Hell, he'd broken up with his wife because Emily was fooling around on him on nights when he went to meetings. "Get out of my way, goddammit." He pushed past the aide and hustled to the gate.

None of the guards said a word about what he had on. He could deal with them later, when he was in proper uniform. The men at the gate wore the regalia of Freedom Party guards, high-ranking ones. Their cold, hard faces would have scared the bejesus out of even a thoroughgoing son of a bitch like Mercer Scott. "You are Jefferson Pinkard?" one of them asked. He didn't say anything about how Pinkard was dressed, either.

"That's right," Jeff answered. "Who the—devil are you?"

"Chief Assault Band Leader Ben Chapman." The accent wasn't Virginia; it was Alabama, much like Pinkard's own. "I have a prisoner to deliver to this camp. You are to acknowledge receipt."

"You do? I am?" Pinkard said. The Party officer nodded. "Well, who the hell is he?" Jeff asked testily. "And what are you doing bringing him here in the middle of the goddamn night?"

"Orders," Chapman said, as if orders were the most important thing in the world. Well, maybe he had a point there. "And the prisoner is"—he lowered his voice so Pinkard could hear but the guards at the front gate couldn't—"a fellow by the name of Willy Knight."

"Holy Jesus!" Jeff exploded. Having the vice president of the CSA—well, the former vice president, after his resignation and imprisonment (to say nothing of his impeachment and conviction)—in his prison camp was the last thing he wanted. The responsibility if something went wrong . . . and things were only too likely to go wrong. "Didn't anybody tell you this here camp is full of niggers?"

Chief Assault Band Leader Chapman shrugged. He had an athlete's grace, and an athlete's watchful eyes, too. "Goddamn spooks deserve whatever happens to 'em," he said. "And the goddamn son of a bitch we brought down here deserves whatever happens to him, too. Nobody will say a word if he comes out of this place feet first."

That took a load off Pinkard's mind. But, still cautious, he asked, "Will you put that in writing?"

"Nothing about this business goes down in writing," Chief Assault Band Leader Chapman said scornfully. "Nothing except your name on the form that says we got Knight here in one piece."

"I might have known," Jeff muttered, and Chapman nodded, as if to say, *Yes, you might have.* With a sigh, the warden nodded, too. "I'll sign—as soon as I see him, so I can make sure he *is* in one piece."

"Right." Ben Chapman turned to his henchmen. "Bring him on up." The door to a motorcar at the edge of Camp Dependable's lights opened and then slammed shut. More Freedom Party guards hustled someone forward. Chapman pointed. "See for yourself," he told Pinkard.

It was Willy Knight. Jeff had seen him in Birmingham on the campaign trail. He was still tall and blond and still, in a way, handsome. But, where he had been full of piss and vinegar, he was thin to the point of gauntness, and suffering haunted his face—especially the eyes. "Go ahead and laugh," he said to Pinkard. "One of these days, the son of a bitch will turn on you, too."

"Shut up, you bastard," Chief Assault Band Leader Chapman told him. Chapman thrust a clipboard and a pen at Jeff. "You've seen him. Sign." Jeff did. His men took charge of the fallen Confederate hero and led him into the camp.

# XIII

**H**ipolito Rodriguez had never been a rich man. He was reasonably confident he would never be a rich man. But he was and always had been a proud man. The Confederate States were and always had been a proud nation. And Sonora and Chihuahua were and always had been states where pride counted for even more than it did elsewhere in the CSA. A poor man who could hold his head up often gathered more respect than a rich man who could not meet his neighbors' eyes.

When Rodriguez brought his youngest son into Baroyeca, he strode along with pride unusual even for him. Pedro seemed a good deal more diffident than his father—or maybe his feet hurt. He had on the sturdy shoes he'd got from the Freedom Youth Corps. He hadn't worn them much since getting out of the Corps a few months earlier; sandals were plenty good for farm work. But he didn't want to seem like a peasant when he came into town.

"They will make a man of you," Rodriguez said as he and Pedro started up the main street toward the *alcalde*'s residence.

"I thought the Freedom Youth Corps already did that," his son replied. He was taller than Hipolito Rodriguez, and wider through the shoulders, too. Like his brothers, he spoke more English than Spanish these days—except, sometimes, with his mother.

"I have nothing bad to say about the Freedom Youth Corps," Rodriguez told him. "But it is what its name says it is: it is a thing for youths. The Army of the Confederate States of America is a thing for men."

He hadn't thought about it that way when he was conscripted. He remembered as much, remembered very clearly. But times had changed.

He'd gone into the Confederate Army in the middle of the Great War and been thrown straight into action, first against Red Negroes in Georgia and then against the USA in west Texas. His son would serve in peacetime. With luck, he would get his hitch out of the way and come back to the farm without ever firing a shot in anger. Rodriguez hoped so, anyhow. When you were shooting in anger, the people on the other side had a nasty habit of shooting back. He didn't know how he'd come through the war unwounded. Luck, no doubt, luck and the Virgin watching over him.

Out of Jaime Diaz's general store came Felipe Rojas. When Pedro saw the Freedom Youth Corps drillmaster, he automatically stiffened to attention right there in the middle of the street. Rojas' smile showed several gold teeth. "You don't need to do that today, Pedro," he said. "I don't give you orders any more."

"Just as well that he stay in practice," Hipolito Rodriguez said. "I've brought him into town to report, because he's been conscripted."

"Has he?" Rojas' eyes widened. "How the years do get on. He would be old enough, of course, but still, it hardly seems possible. Not so long since we had rifles in our own hands, is it?"

"No, indeed. I was just thinking that," Rodriguez said. Of course, they'd both had Tredegars in their hands a lot more recently than they'd been mustered out of the Army. They'd shown the big landowners who'd run things in Sonora for so long that the Freedom Party was the new power in the land, and that anyone who thought otherwise had better think again.

"A soldier." Rojas slapped Rodriguez's son on the back with a big, hard hand. "He'll do well. What we showed him in the Youth Corps will help him, and he's a fine young man. Yes, I'm sure he'll do very well indeed."

"We'd better go on to the *alcalde*'s residence," Rodriguez said. "I wouldn't want him to get in trouble for reporting late."

"No, that wouldn't be the right way to start," Felipe Rojas agreed. He clapped Pedro on the back again. "Go with God, and God go with you. You'll be fine. I know you will. Show them what we taught you. They'll build on that."

"*Sí, señor. Gracias, señor,*" Pedro said proudly.

Another youth and his father were also at the *alcalde*'s residence. He and Pedro started chattering. They'd gone to school together and served in the Freedom Youth Corps together, and now they were going into the Army together. Rodriguez shook his head. *It hardly seems possible,* Rojas had said, and wasn't that the truth? No matter how it seemed, though, it was the truth. The years had a way of piling on whether you looked at them or not.

His son had to fill out most of the inevitable paperwork, but there was plenty for Hipolito, too, because Pedro was of course under twenty-one. He signed his name a dozen times, mostly without bothering to look at what he was signing. More than half the forms were in English, anyhow, and he read it less well than he spoke it.

At last, it was done. Essentially, he'd deeded his son to the Confederate States. He hugged Pedro and kissed him on both cheeks. "Be strong," he said. "Do what they tell you and be strong." Then he left the *alcalde*'s residence in a hurry, so neither the clerk there nor his son would see him cry.

He headed for *La Culebra Verde*. If he wasn't entitled to drown some sorrows after giving his son to the Army, when could he? Not even Magdalena would complain about that . . . he hoped.

Before he got to the Green Snake, though, a couple of young men he'd never seen before came up to him. They were both dirty and ragged and weary-looking. One was barefoot; the other wore a pair of sandals that had more patches than original shoe leather. *"Buenos días, señor,"* the barefoot man said in Spanish. "Do you by any chance need someone to help you with your work?"

"No, for I have three strong sons, thank God," Rodriguez answered in the same tongue. Out of curiosity, he switched to English: "Do you know this language?"

*"No, señor. Lo siento mucho,"* the stranger said. *"Solamente español."*

Rodriguez had expected nothing different. Dropping back into Spanish himself, he asked, "From which province in the Empire of Mexico do you come?"

Both newcomers in Baroyeca looked alarmed. The man with the patched sandals, who was older and stockier than his friend, replied, "You have made a mistake, *señor*. Like you, we are citizens of *los Estados Confederados*."

"Bullshit," Rodriguez said in English. They couldn't even understand that, and he couldn't imagine a Sonoran or Chihuahuan who didn't. He returned to Spanish: "Don't tell me lies. Do you think I'm too stupid to know the difference? Times are hard here, but I know they're worse south of the border."

The ragged men sighed in equally ragged unison. That older fellow said, "Very well, *señor. Usted tiene razón.* We have come from near Mocorito in Sinaloa province." Rodriguez nodded, unsurprised; Sinaloa lay just south of Sonora. The other man went on, "We have to have work, or we will starve. So will our families, if we cannot send them money."

"It is as I told you—I have no work for you to do," Rodriguez said. "If you keep looking, though, maybe you will find someone who does."

He waited to see what would happen next. If the Sinaloans were hungry enough, desperate enough, or maybe just stupid enough, they might try to get his money without working. If they did, he aimed to fight back. But their shoulders slumped and they went on down the street. As they went, they exclaimed about how fine and fancy everything was. If that didn't prove they weren't from the CSA, Rodriguez couldn't think of what would.

He wondered if they would find someone who'd pay them. They weren't the first men from the Empire of Mexico he'd seen passing through Baroyeca. He was sure they wouldn't be the last. Even though the town now boasted electricity, it was a backwater in Sonora, and Sonora was a backwater in the CSA. By the standards prevailing farther south, though, even a Confederate backwater seemed rich and bustling.

*I have a dollar in my pocket,* he thought. *To those fellows, that makes me a rich man. God help them, poor devils.*

He walked into *La Culebra Verde.* Robert Quinn sat at the bar, drinking a bottle of beer. "*Hola, Señor* Rodriguez," he said. "What brings you to Baroyeca this morning?"

"Pedro reports to the Confederate Army today," Rodriguez answered. "I came in with him to fill out papers and to say good-bye."

"Congratulations to you and congratulations to him," Quinn said in his deliberate Spanish. "This is a good time to be a young man in the Confederate States. We aren't going to be pushed around any more."

Rodriguez wasn't so sure whether that made this a good time or a bad one. He almost said as much. Then he remembered the two men from Sinaloa who thought times in the CSA were better than those in the Empire of Mexico. He spoke of them instead, meanwhile sitting down beside the Freedom Party man and ordering a beer for himself.

Quinn nodded. "More and more men keep coming north," he said. "Enough of them do find work to encourage others. We are trying to tighten things at the border, but"—he shrugged—"it is not an easy job."

"If they do work no one else will or no one else can, I do not suppose it is so very bad," Rodriguez said, sipping his beer. "But if they take jobs away from Confederates . . . That would not be good at all."

"We have to take care of ourselves first," Quinn agreed. After another pull at his beer, Hipolito Rodriguez began to laugh. Quinn cocked his head to one side, a quizzical look on his face. "What is the joke?"

"In other parts of the Confederate States, people worry the same way about Sonorans and Chihuahuans taking their jobs."

"Yes, they do, some. Not so much as they used to, I do not think," Quinn answered seriously. "They have seen that people who come from these parts are good and loyal and work hard. And they have seen that *los mallates* are the worst enemies the Confederate States have."

"Yes." Rodriguez said the same thing in English—"Niggers"—just to show he knew it. "In this country, *los mallates* are nothing but trouble. They have never been anything but trouble. *Los Estados Confederados* would be better off without them."

Quinn waved to the bartender. "Another beer for me, Rafael, and another for my friend here as well." He turned back to Rodriguez. "It is because you understand this that you are a member of the *Partido de Libertad*."

"Is it?" After thinking that over, Rodriguez shook his head. "No. I am sorry, but no. That is not the reason."

The bartender set the beers in front of his customers. Robert Quinn gave him a quarter and waved away his five cents' change. After a sip that left foam on his upper lip, he asked, "Why, then?"

"I'll tell you why." Rodriguez drank from his beer, too. "I joined the Freedom Party because it was the only one in Sonora that didn't take me for granted. You really wanted to have me for a member. And you want vengeance against *los Estados Unidos*. Men from *los Estados Unidos* tried to kill me. I have not forgotten. I want vengeance against them, too." *But if Pedro fights them, they will shoot back.* He took a big sip from his new beer. Life wasn't simple, dammit.

"Ah, yes, the United States," Quinn said, as if reminded of the existence of a nation he'd forgotten—and been glad to forget. "Well, my friend, you are right about that. Every dog has its day, but theirs has gone on for too long."

"If we fight, can we beat them?" Rodriguez asked.

"I am no general," the Freedom Party man replied. "But I will tell you this: if Jake Featherston says we can beat them, then we can."

Somewhere up ahead—somewhere not very far up ahead—the state of Houston and the USA ended, and the state of Texas and the CSA began. Colonel Irving Morrell bounced along in a command car. *Bounced* was the operative word, too, for the command car's springs had seen better years, while the roads in these parts went from bad to worse.

However bad its springs might have been, though, its pintle-mounted machine gun was in excellent working order. Morrell had carefully checked it before setting out. If it hadn't been in excellent working order, he wouldn't have got into the command car in the first place.

Above the growl of the engine, the driver, a weather-beaten private named Charlie Satcher, said, "Looks quiet enough."

"It always looks quiet enough," Morrell answered. "Then they start shooting at us."

Satcher nodded. "Big country," he remarked.

"Really? I hadn't noticed," Morrell said, deadpan. The driver started to say something, caught himself, and grunted out a little laughter instead.

It was a very big country indeed. The horizon seemed to stretch for ever and ever. The sun beat down out of a great blue bowl of a sky. The only motion in the landscape was the tan trail of dust the command car had kicked up, slowly dispersing in the breeze, that and— Morrell suddenly swung the machine gun to the right, and as suddenly took his hands off the triggers. That was only a roadrunner, loping through the dry brush with a lizard's tail hanging out of the side of its mouth.

"Nothing but miles and miles of miles and miles," Charlie Satcher said, as if he were the first one ever to bring out the line.

"Not quite nothing," Morrell answered. "Somewhere out there, those Freedom Party fanatics are bringing guns and ammo into Houston."

Calling them fanatics made him feel better. If he could paint them as villains, even if only in his own mind, he could do a better job of trying to deal with them. When he wasn't thinking of them as fanatics, he had to think of them as tough, clever foes. Not all of them belonged to the Freedom Party. Nobody in the Confederate States had much liked losing Houston, and not many people in Houston liked being part of the USA, either. The people who did like it kept quiet. If they didn't keep quiet, their neighbors made them pay.

"Miles and miles of miles and miles." Satcher liked to hear himself talk.

Again, he wasn't wrong. The Confederates put up a few border checkpoints between Texas and Houston, but only a few, and they mostly cared about things passing into Texas, not things leaving it. As far as they were concerned, things passing from Texas into Houston didn't really cross a border. If the United States felt otherwise, then it was up to the United States to do something about it.

And the United States hadn't. Even with all the unrest—hell, the out-and-out rebellion—in Houston, the United States hadn't. Morrell understood why. It would have cost too much, in money and in men. The USA would have had to put up barbed-wire emplacements the whole length of the border, and would have had to man them with an army. It would have been almost like a trench line from the Great War. No government, Democrat or Socialist, had been willing to do the work or deploy the manpower. And so the border remained porous, and so rebellion went right on simmering.

All that unhappy musing flew out of Morrell's head the moment he spotted a plume of dust not much different from the one his command car was kicking up. This one, though, was coming from the east and heading west: heading straight into Houston. He had every reason to be where he was and doing what he was doing. Did that other auto? *Fat chance,* he thought.

He tapped Charlie Satcher on the shoulder. "You see that?" he said, pointing.

The driver nodded. "Sure as hell do, Colonel. What do you want to do about it?"

"Stop the son of a bitch," Morrell answered.

"He may not want to stop," Satcher observed.

"I know." Morrell reached for the machine-gun triggers. "We have to persuade him he does want to after all—he just doesn't know it quite yet."

"Persuade him." The driver's grin showed a broken front tooth. "Right you are, sir." He turned toward the motorcar that was raising the other dust trail.

Excitement flowered in Morrell. He was going into action, all on his own. He'd seen plenty of action in Houston, much of it brutal and unpleasant. Armored warfare against people who flung Featherston fizzes couldn't very well be anything but brutal and unpleasant. This, though, this seemed different. This was fox and hound, cat and mouse. It was out in the open, too. Nobody could fling a bottle of flaming gasoline from a window and then disappear.

Before long, whoever was in the other motorcar spotted the one that held Morrell and his driver. Whoever he was, he kept on coming. Maybe that meant he was an innocent, though what an innocent would be doing sneaking over the border was beyond Morrell. More likely, it meant he hadn't recognized the command car for what it was.

As the two machines got closer, Morrell's driver said, "They've got a lot of people in there—and what's that one bastard sticking out the window?"

A muzzle flash said it was a rifle. Nothing hit the command car—not for lack of effort, Morrell was sure. "Which side of the border is he on, do you think?" he asked.

"If he's shooting at me, he's on the side where I can shoot back," Satcher answered without hesitation.

"I like the way you think," Morrell said. The fellow with the rifle in the other motorcar fired again. This time, a bullet slammed into the command car. It must not have hit anything vital, because the machine kept running, and no steam or smoke or flame burst from its innards.

Morrell squeezed the machine gun's triggers. Brass cartridge cases flew from the breech and clattered down around his feet. Tracers guided the stream of bullets towards and then into the other motorcar. Smoke immediately poured from its engine compartment. It skidded to a stop. The doors on the far side flew open. Several men got out and ran. A bullet knocked one of them down. Another man shot at Morrell from behind the automobile. Morrell hosed bullets back at him. The motorcar caught fire. The rifleman had to pull away from it. That made him an easier target. Down he went, too.

And once the auto started burning, it didn't want to stop. As soon as the flames reached the passenger compartment, ammunition started cooking off. Some of the rounds were tracers. They gave the fire a Fourth of July feel.

"Ha!" Charlie Satcher said. "They *were* running guns."

"Did you expect anything different?" Morrell asked. The driver shook his head.

A bullet cracked past Morrell's head. That wasn't one from the fireworks display in the motorcar—it had been deliberately aimed. He ducked, not that that would have done him any good had the round been on target. He'd known only a handful of men who could go through a fire fight without that involuntary reaction. It wasn't cowardice, just human nature.

He tapped the driver on the back and pointed. "Go around there and give me a better shot at that fellow."

"Right." Satcher steered the car in the direction Morrell indicated. The rifleman from the auto coming out of Texas scrambled away, trying to keep the burning vehicle between the command car and himself.

That scramble proved his undoing. He was behind the trunk when either the fire or one of the rounds going off in the passenger compartment reached what the men from Texas had been carrying there. The explosion sent flaming chunks of motorcar flying in all directions. One slammed down about a hundred feet in front of the command car; Satcher almost rolled it steering clear.

No more aimed shots came, though Morrell needed a little while to be sure of that, because rounds did keep cooking off every now and then with a *pop-pop-pop* that would have been merry if he hadn't known what caused it. He got a look at the Texan who'd been shooting at him, and wished he hadn't. The rear bumper had torn off the man's head and his left arm.

The grim sight didn't unduly upset his driver. "For all I care, they can bury the bastard in a jam tin," Satcher said, "either that or leave him out for the buzzards. If I was a buzzard, I'd sooner eat skunk any day of the week."

His words seemed to come from a long way off. Firing the machine gun left Morrell's ears temporarily stunned. He hoped the stunning was temporary, anyhow. Some of it probably wasn't. He knew he didn't hear as well as he had when he was younger. Would he go altogether deaf in another ten or twenty years? He shrugged. Not much he could do about that. It wasn't the rarest ailment among soldiers.

"Sir?" Charlie Satcher said.

"What is it?" Morrell's own voice seemed distant, too.

"I heard you had balls," the driver answered. "The guy who told me, though, he didn't know the half of it."

Morrell shrugged. The motion told him how tense his shoulders had got in the fire fight. He didn't think of himself as particularly brave. When the shooting started, he didn't think much at all. Reaction took over. "They started it, Charlie," he answered.

"Yeah," Satcher said admiringly. "And you sure as hell finished it."

"I wonder which side of the border we're on." Morrell shrugged again. "Doesn't matter much, not when their auto went up like that. Nobody can say they weren't running guns into Houston."

"Damn well better not try," the driver said. "Me, I thought I was gonna shit myself when that goddamn back seat landed in front of us."

"Back seat? Is that what it was?" Morrell said. Charlie Satcher nodded. Morrell managed a laugh. "I've got to tell you, I didn't notice. I was busy just then. You did a hell of a job getting around it. I noticed that."

"Neither one of us would've been real happy if I hit it," Satcher said. Morrell couldn't very well argue with that. The driver asked, "Shall we head on back to Lubbock, sir?"

"I think we'd better," Morrell replied. "I want to report to General MacArthur, and he'll want to report to the War Department. I suppose *they'll* report to the president, or maybe to the State Department. Somebody will have to figure out how loud we squawk."

"Squawk, hell," Satcher said. "We don't scream our heads off, they deserve to roll like that last Confederate fucker's."

Morrell only shrugged. "I won't tell you you're wrong, but the people in Philly are liable to. Because I can tell you what Richmond's going to say. Richmond's going to say they didn't know anything about these fellows, they didn't have anything to do with them, and they aren't responsible for them."

"My ass," Charlie Satcher said succinctly.

"Now that you mention it, yes," Morrell agreed, and the driver laughed. But Morrell went on, "You know it's crap, I know it's crap, and Jake goddamn Featherston knows it's crap, too, but how do you go about proving it's crap?"

"Screw proving it," Satcher said. "Blow the bastards to hell and gone anyway."

"I *do* like the way you think," Morrell said.


Brigadier General Abner Dowling remembered George Armstrong Custer. There had been times—a great many times—when Dowling's dearest wish would have been to forget entirely the officer whose adjutant he'd been for so long. Things didn't seem to work that way, though. All those years with Custer had marked him for life. Scarred him for life, he would have been inclined to say in his less charitable moments. This was one of those days.

When Dowling thought of Custer nowadays, he thought of the general after the Great War, when Custer had come back to Philadelphia to fill an office and count corks and write elaborate reports on the best deployment of paper clips in the U.S. Army. With nothing real, nothing important, to do, Custer had wanted to jump out of a window. Dowling often thought the only thing that stopped him was his office's being on the ground floor.

And now Dowling knew exactly how his superior had felt. Since coming back from Salt Lake City after the occupation of Utah ended, he'd filled an office and written elaborate reports on the best way to transport rubber bands to combat units. That was how it seemed, anyhow. He was on the shelf, and he was damned if he knew how to get off again.

If he was going to be stuck in Philadelphia, he'd hoped the War Department might at least channel reports of what was going on in Utah through him. He'd spent a lot of years—a lot of thankless years—in the state. He wondered if Winthrop W. Webb was still in business, or if the Mormons had figured out who Webb's real bosses were and arranged an accident for him.

Try as Dowling would, he couldn't find out. Somebody in the War Department was surely tending to affairs in Utah. Whoever it was, it wasn't Dowling. He couldn't even find out who it was. The only thing his efforts to find out got him was a visit from Lieutenant Colonel John Abell.

The more Dowling saw the General Staff officer, the less he liked him, even though Abell had been the one who'd told him he'd made general-officer grade. The man was slim and pale—downright bloodless, in fact. Had the U.S. Army been made up of ghosts rather than men, he would have been one of the handsomest ones in it. As things were, he made Dowling want to turn up the heat in the office even though the day was warm.

"Sir, you have been poking your nose into matters that do not concern you," Abell said. "We discourage that."

*We? You have a tapeworm?* Dowling wondered. He remembered Irving Morrell talking about Abell during the war. At the time, he'd been sure Morrell was exaggerating. Now he found the other man had been speaking the gospel truth. He eyed the General Staff lieutenant colonel's lean, pallid countenance and picked his words with care: "I don't believe Utah's affairs can fail to concern me, not when I was there so long."

"If the War Department feels otherwise, why should you disagree?" Lieutenant Colonel Abell inquired.

"Because if I had anything to do with Utah, I could be useful to the Department," Dowling answered. "With what people have me doing now—I mean, not doing now—I'm useless. Useful is better."

"Don't you trust the judgment of your superiors as to what is useful and what is not?" Abell asked silkily.

By the way spoke, he might have been one of those superiors, even if Dowling outranked him. *General Staff officers,* Dowling thought scornfully, and tried not to let his annoyance show. Even if Abell had a lower grade, he enjoyed much better connections. And so, still speaking carefully, Dowling said, "A quartermaster sergeant could do most of what I've been doing since I came back here, whereas I've got some specialized knowledge no sergeant can match. Using me without using that knowledge is inefficient."

"Possibly," Abell said, which meant he wasn't about to admit it. "A pleasure talking to you." He got to his feet and started for the door. With a hand on the knob, he turned back. "You know Colonel Morrell, don't you?"

"Oh, yes." Dowling nodded. "We worked together on the breakthrough that took Nashville." That might have been impolitic, since the breakthrough had violated War Department doctrine on how to use barrels. Dowling didn't much care, since it had also gone a long way toward making the Confederates throw in the towel.

"How interesting," Lieutenant Colonel Abell said with a smile that displayed a lot of expensive dentistry. And then, silent as a specter, he was gone. Dowling wondered if he ought to have his office exorcised.

He'd hoped Abell's questions would lead to something better in the way of work. For the next couple of weeks, his hopes were disappointed. He read about Irving Morrell's encounter with gun runners on the border between Texas and Houston in the newspapers. Nobody in the War

Department asked him about it in any official way. He wondered why Abell had bothered confirming that they were acquainted. *The better to blackball me,* he thought.

But, somewhat to his surprise, he did see the General Staff officer again. When John Abell next appeared—materialized?—in his office, the lieutenant colonel's face bore a smile that seemed less than perfectly friendly. "So you are friends with Colonel Morrell, are you?" Abell said, a note of challenge in his voice. "And you've done the same sort of work, have you?"

Dowling hadn't said he was friends with Morrell. He admired Morrell's talent; what Morrell thought of him he wasn't nearly so sure. But, sensing that a yes would annoy Lieutenant Colonel Abell more than a no, he nodded defiantly and said, "That's right."

"Very well, Brigadier General Dowling. In that case, I have some orders for you." Abell spoke as if washing his hands of him.

To Dowling, anything would have been better than what he was doing now. "And those orders are . . . ?" he asked eagerly.

Abell heard that eagerness. It made him blink. By the fruit salad on his chest, he'd stayed in Philadelphia through the Great War. He no doubt thought his role more important than those of soldiers who actually went out and fought the enemy, too. He might even have been right, but Dowling didn't care to dwell on that. "Sir, you will be sent to Kentucky," he said now. "Your duty there will be similar to Colonel Morrell's in Houston: you will help control agitation against the government of the United States. This *does* also relate to your experience in Utah, would you not agree?"

"Yes, I'd say that's true," Dowling answered cautiously. "You're coming as close as you can without a real war to sending me into combat, aren't you?"

"Isn't that what you wanted?" Abell asked with sardonic satisfaction.

But that satisfaction slipped when Dowling gave him another yes instead of a no, saying, "You bet it is. I've wanted to get into the field for years. They wouldn't take me away from Utah when we fought the Japs, dammit."

"Well, you're going to get your wish." Lieutenant Colonel Abell plainly thought he was out of his mind.

"When do I leave?" Dowling asked. "Where exactly do I go? All over Kentucky, or somewhere in particular?"

"I don't have the precise details yet," Abell said. "I assure you, they will be passed on in good time. In the meanwhile, you are to continue with the duties you have already been assigned."

"Thank you so much," Dowling said sourly. The General Staff officer took no notice of his tone, which might have been just as well. Abell departed with a salute that mocked military courtesy instead of reinforcing it. Now Dowling was the one who ignored the slight. He would have ignored not only a slight but a large if that meant escaping from Philadelphia.

Knowing the speed at which the War Department moved, he expected *in good time* to mean a month or six weeks. In reality, he got his orders eleven days after Lieutenant Colonel Abell's visit. On reflection, he was less surprised than at first glance. The military bureaucrats in War Department headquarters were probably as glad to see him gone as he was to go. He'd been General Custer's right-hand man, after all, and Custer and the War Department had got along like rattlesnake and roadrunner—and who'd ended up eating whom was anybody's guess.

He was on a train the next day, bound for Kentucky. He could have left Philadelphia even sooner if he'd wanted to take an airliner. He was content to stay on the ground. When he was a boy, there'd been no such things as airliners. When he was a boy, there'd been no such things as aeroplanes (or airplanes, as he saw the word spelled more and more often in newspapers and magazines). If one of them could carry two dozen people in reasonable comfort three or four times as fast as a train or a motorcar ran . . . *That's nice,* Dowling thought. In an emergency, he would have flown. Without an emergency, no.

For one thing, trains boasted dining cars. Nothing he'd heard about food on airliners tempted him to sample it. The meals aboard the Pennsylvania Railroad's *Cincinnati Limited*, on the other hand, fully measured up to Dowling's exacting standards. He was sorry to have to leave the train and cross the Ohio into Kentucky.

It was late afternoon when a driver took him from Cincinnati over the bridges across the river and into Covington. A long line of northbound autos waited to cross the bridge. "What's their trouble?" Dowling asked.

"They have to be searched, sir," the driver answered. "You're new here, aren't you? We don't want those Freedom Party bastards running guns and explosives up into the real United States."

*The real United States.* Those four words spoke volumes. Dowling had ordered such precautions himself in Utah. He hadn't thought they would be necessary here, but maybe he'd been naive. *You're new here, aren't you?* That spoke volumes, too. This game was being played for keeps.

No one fired at his motorcar on the way to the local Army encampment. No one fired, but he got plenty of hints he was in hostile country just the same. The graffiti shouted FREEDOM! or CSA! They showed either a blue or a red St. Andrew's cross: quick takes on the Confederate battle flag and the Freedom Party banner based on it.

In Utah, the occupation authorities would have cracked down on people who scribbled such things. In Utah, though, the occupation authorities had been the only formal power in the land. Here . . . Here there was also the state government—and that was in the hands of the Freedom Party. The Army faced an uphill fight it hadn't had to worry about farther west.

"You want to hear something funny, sir?" the driver said as the green-gray Ford pulled up in front of BOQ.

"I," Dowling answered most sincerely, "would love to hear something funny."

"You know who our biggest backers here are?" the soldier asked.

"From everything I saw, I wondered if we *had* any backers here," Dowling said.

"Oh, we do, sir. There's one bunch of folks in this town—one bunch of folks in this whole goddamn state—who'd do anything in the world for us, anything at all. That's the niggers. They don't want one goddamn thing to do with the Confederate States, and can you blame 'em?"

"Not me," Dowling admitted, but he couldn't see how they'd help much, either.


A chilly, nasty rain fell on Augusta, Georgia. Scipio didn't like the rain. He had to put on a long coat and rubber overshoes and to carry an umbrella to protect the tuxedo he had to wear at the Huntsman's Lodge. Newsboys hawking their papers doubtless liked the rain even less. They got their copies of the *Constitutionalist* wrapped in yellow wax paper, but it didn't always keep them dry. Customers who bought a newspaper with the consistency of bread soaked in milk were apt to say unkind things—and to demand a fresh copy without forking over another five cents.

"Election today!" the newsboys shouted from under their umbrellas. "President Featherston seeking second term!"

Scipio didn't buy a paper. Why would he want a *Constitutionalist* when Jake Featherston was violating everything the Confederate Constitution had stood for since before the first shot was fired in the War of Secession? Oh, Featherston had rammed through the amendment that let him run again, but so what? Even a blind man could see that was a put-up job.

And even a blind man could see the election was a put-up job, too. Yes, the Whigs and the Radical Liberals had nominated candidates, but they had only a slightly better chance of winning than Scipio would have if he'd run against the incumbent president. The Freedom Party dominated the wireless web and the newspapers; the other candidates got only brief and unflattering mention. Despite the rain, Freedom Party stalwarts prowled outside polling places. Freedom Party officials would count most of the votes. Jake Featherston wouldn't lose.

With a snort, Scipio walked past another newsboy. As if elections applied to him or the likes of him anyway! He'd never had any choice in who ruled the Confederate States, and he never would. He wondered how many of the black men who'd earned the franchise fighting for the CSA in the Great War still had the nerve to try to use it. He also wondered how many of those who tried succeeded.

Not many and even fewer, unless he missed his guess.

As usual, he got to the Huntsman's Lodge in good time. He shed the coat and galoshes with sighs of relief, and hung the umbrella on a peg so it dripped down onto the rug in a hallway. Then he went into the kitchen to remind himself of the day's specials. At least this was Tuesday, not Monday. They wouldn't be making specials out of whatever hadn't moved over the weekend.

"Evening, Xerxes," Jerry Dover said. "How are you?"

"Tolerable, suh," Scipio told the manager. "I's tolerable. How you is?"

"Not bad," Dover answered. "Can we talk a little?"

"Yes, suh. What you want?" Scipio did his best not to sound too alarmed. Whenever a boss said something like that, it usually meant trouble.

Dover said, "You're a hell of a good worker, Xerxes, don't get me wrong. You read and write and cipher better than most white men I know. What I want to ask you is, do you have to talk the way you do?"

"This heah onliest way I knows how to talk," Scipio answered. That, of course, wasn't true, as Bathsheba could have testified. If he hadn't been able to sound like an educated white man, they and their children would have died in the riots after the Freedom Party took power.

But if he talked that way without direst need, some white man or other who heard him would connect his voice with the Marshlands plantation and Anne Colleton—whereupon, very shortly, he would be dead.

"Would you be willing to take lessons?" Jerry Dover asked, not knowing he could have given them instead.

"Once upon a time, I try dat," Scipio lied. "It don't do no good. I still sounds like dis."

"I could make it worth your while," Dover said. "Menander the headwaiter's going to retire before too long—he's been sickly for a while now, you know. You'd be the perfect fellow to take his place—if you didn't talk like such a nigger. Everything else? I know you can do it. But you got to sound better."

Scipio wondered if he could fake the lessons and end up sounding a little better than he did now, but not a lot. He had his doubts. Dover wasn't wrong: unless he sounded like a college-trained white (which the restaurant manager didn't know he could do at all), he sounded like someone who'd come straight from the swamps by the Congaree. That wouldn't do for a headwaiter. Compromise between the two dialects? He saw none. He also saw danger in sounding even a little like the way he had at Marshlands. He couldn't afford to be recognized, not after he'd been a spokesman for the Congaree Socialist Republic. He'd been coerced into playing that role, but who would care? No one at all.

And so, not without regret, he said, "Reckon I better stay where I is."

Dover exhaled angrily. "Dammit, where's your get-up-and-go? And if you tell me it got up and went, I'll kick your ass, so help me Hannah."

He might have meant it literally. Scipio shrugged. "Sorry, Mistuh Dover, suh. You is a good boss." He meant that. "But you gots to see, I never want to be nobody's boss a-tall."

"All right. All right, dammit. Why didn't you say that sooner?" Jerry Dover remained disgusted, but he wasn't furious any more—now he faced something he understood, or at any rate something he thought he did. "I've seen it before. You don't want to play the white man over your own people, is that it?"

"Yes, suh," Scipio said gratefully. "Dat just it." There was even some truth in what he said. He hadn't wanted to open up his own café in the Terry for exactly that reason. He'd told other Negroes what to do for years in his role as butler at Marshlands, and hadn't cared for it a bit. It was less important to him than his other reason for turning the manager down, but it was there.

Dover said, "If you want to know what I think, I think you're a damn fool. Somebody's got to do it. Why not you instead of somebody else? Especially why not you if you feel that way? Wouldn't you make a better boss than some other buck who did it just to show what a slave driver he could be?"

He was shrewd. He was very shrewd, in fact, to use that last argument and to contrast Scipio, who remembered slave drivers, with one. If not wanting to boss other blacks had been the only thing troubling Scipio, the restaurant manager might have persuaded him. As it was, he shrugged again and said, "Mebbe"—disagreeing too openly with a white man wasn't smart, either.

His boss knew what that *mebbe* meant. Dover waved him away. "Go on. Go to work, then. I'd fire some people for telling me no, but you're too good to lose. If you don't want the extra money, I won't pay you."

With a sigh of relief, Scipio went into the dining room. Tonight, he felt much better about dealing with customers than with his own boss. The Huntsman's Lodge was not the sort of place that kept a wireless set blaring away while people ate, but he got his share of the news anyway. Sure enough, Jake Featherston was easily winning a second term. All the whites in the restaurant seemed happy about it. Every so often, somebody at one table or another would call out, "Freedom!" and glasses would go high in salute. No one asked Scipio's opinion. He didn't offer it, and wouldn't have if asked. He did pocket some larger tips than usual, as often happened when people were happy.

The rain had stopped by the time he headed for home: a little past twelve. He'd gone about half a block from the restaurant when a rattling, wheezing Birmingham pulled up to the curb alongside of him. A young black man got out. He and Scipio eyed each other for a moment. Scipio's heart thudded in his chest. All too often, Negroes stole from other Negroes, not least because whites cared little about that kind of crime.

But then the youngster grinned disarmingly. "You ain't never seen me, grandpa. You know what I'm sayin'? You ain't never seen this here motorcar, neither."

Was he fooling around with someone else's woman? That was the first thing that occurred to Scipio: no, the second, for that *grandpa* rankled. Still, if the required price was no higher, he could meet it. "Ain't never seen who?" he said, peering around as if someone invisible had spoken.

He got another grin for that. "In the groove, grandpa."

"Somebody talkin' to me?" Again, Scipio pretended not to see the man right in front of him. Then he started back down the street toward the Terry. Behind him, the young Negro laughed. He walked warily even so, ready to run in case the other fellow came after him. But nothing happened. The man who'd parked the Birmingham might have forgotten all about him.

By the time he woke up the next morning, he'd just about forgotten the young man. Bathsheba, who had to go to her cleaning job much earlier than he needed to leave for the Huntsman's Lodge, was heading out the door when an explosion tore through the morning air.

"Do Jesus!" Scipio exclaimed. The windows rattled and shook. He thought they might break, but they didn't.

"What was that?" Antoinette asked.

"That was somethin' blowin' up," Scipio said heavily. "Mebbe it was an accident. But mebbe it was a bomb, too."

"Oh, sweet Jesus, who'd want to blow things up?" Bathsheba burst out. "Ain't we seen enough sufferin'?" Out she went, shaking her head.

When Scipio headed for work later that day, he had to take a detour to get to the Huntsman's Lodge. He got a glimpse of the street where the bomb had gone off. The building closest to where it went off had fallen down. Windows or pieces of façade were missing from several others. It wasn't till he looked down the street from above the Huntsman's Lodge that he realized just where the explosion had taken place. *You ain't never seen me,* that grinning young Negro had said. *You ain't never seen this here motorcar, neither.* Nobody would ever see it again. Scipio was sure of that. *How* much dynamite had it held?

Enough. More than enough. Even here, a good long block from where the bomb had gone off, there were bloodstains under Scipio's shoes. How many dead? How many hurt? Plenty. He could see that. "Do Jesus!" he said again.

Only shards of glass jagged as knives remained in the windows of the Huntsman's Lodge. The door had a jagged hole in it. As Scipio started to go in, a policeman barked, "Let me see your passbook, boy." He handed it over. The policeman matched the photograph and his face, then gave it back. "You work here?"

"Yes, suh," Scipio said. "I's a waiter. You kin go ask Mistuh Dover, suh."

"Never mind," the gray-uniformed cop said impatiently. "You see anything funny when you went home last night? Anything at all that wasn't regular?"

Scipio looked at him. He wore a Freedom Party pin next to his badge. "No, suh," the black man answered. "I didn't seen nothin'. I didn't see nobody. Jus' go home an' mind my business."

The policeman snarled in frustration. "*Somebody* must have, dammit. We catch the son of a bitch who did this, he'll be begging to die before we're through."

"Yes, suh," Scipio repeated in studiously neutral tones. "Kin I go to work, suh?" The cop didn't say no. Scipio walked into the Huntsman's Lodge without another word.

**W**ith their third Socialist president in office, with a Socialist working majority in both houses of Congress, the United States should have been a country where labor had the advantage on capital. They should have been. As Chester Martin had bitterly discovered, they weren't—and nowhere was that truer than in Los Angeles.

When construction workers picketed a site, goons often came out in force to break up their picket lines. The cops backed the goons. So did the newspapers. As far as the *Los Angeles Times* was concerned, strikers were

Red revolutionaries who deserved hanging—shooting was too good for them.

Chester remembered the days of the steel-mill strikes in Toledo. Next to this, those had been good times. That, to him, was a genuinely frightening thought. But it was also true. Back in Toledo, he'd had a feeling of solidarity with his fellow strikers, a feeling that their hour was come round at last. They'd been doing something epoch-making: winning strikes that had always been lost before, paving the way for Socialist victories at the polls that had never been seen before.

What was another strike nowadays? Just another strike. Some were won; more were lost. Nobody except the immediate parties—and the *Times*—got very excited about most of them, and even the immediate parties didn't always bother. The strikes put Chester in mind of some of the later battles on the Roanoke River front during the Great War. They would tear up the landscape and cause a lot of damage and pain to both sides, but things wouldn't change much no matter who won. Either way, the next fight on the same ground would loom around the corner.

When he said as much to Rita one morning before heading out to the latest picket line, she frowned. "That wasn't what you told me when you first led the construction workers out on strike," she said. "Then you thought you were doing something worth doing, something important."

"I know." He tried to recapture the feeling of outrage, the feeling of urgency, he'd had then. It wasn't easy. It was, after more than a year, next to impossible. "Too much has happened since, and not much of it good. Have we got enough money for groceries this week?"

His wife nodded. "And for the rent when the first rolls around. You're making as much as an agitator as you ever did building houses."

"Swell," he said. "When I build a house, though, I've got something to show for it, something I can see, something people can live in. Same when I was making steel. Once I was done, it was there. It was real. I don't even know that I'm doing any good by agitating. Plenty of people *aren't* making as much money now as they were before we started striking."

"They will, though. They'll make a lot more if you get your just demands." A solid Socialist—more solid than Chester—Rita assumed the demands were just. He'd been sure of that at the beginning of the strikes. He wasn't sure of anything any more.

He shook his head. He was sure of one thing: he had to get out the door to get to the picket line by the time the construction crew got to the site. Some of the workers were leery of crossing picket lines, and the ones who were were usually the real builders, the men who knew what they were doing. Half the time, the scabs the contractors hired to take strikers' places couldn't tell a chisel from a brace-and-bit. Chester wouldn't have wanted to live in a house put up by such half-trained workers.

The sun hadn't risen. December days in Los Angeles were longer than they were in Toledo, but sunrise still came late. And, by Los Angeles standards, it was cold: it had dropped down into the forties. Chester Martin found the idea that that could be chilly laughable. He wore a denim jacket over a cotton shirt and a pair of dungarees. He might have put on the same outfit in April in Toledo. In December, he would have frozen to death with it. But his real cold-weather gear had sat at the back of the closet for years. He'd finally given most of his winter-weight coats and heavy wool mufflers to the Salvation Army. He didn't think he would ever need to wear that kind of outfit again.

He had to watch where he was going as he made his way down to the trolley stop. One thing where Toledo beat Los Angeles hollow was street lights. They were few and far between here. Whole neighborhoods—his, for instance—did without them altogether. Long winter nights made that especially noticeable.

Street lights or not, the southbound trolley came on time. Chester tossed his nickel in the fare box and bought a couple of transfers, too. He rode down toward the suburbs, where most of the building was going on right now. Dawn came as he rattled along. It was a leaden dawn, the sky full of gray clouds. He wondered if it would rain. That would shut things down better than any picket line. Probably not, though. Even by Los Angeles standards, 1939 had been a dry year.

Torrance, where he got off, reminded him of Gardena, the little town to the north of it where he'd started building houses after coming to California. Groves of figs and walnuts and oranges and lemons and alligator pears still flourished. Truck gardens, many of them run by farmers from Japan, shipped strawberries and lettuce and carrots and other produce to half the country, thanks to refrigerated freight cars. And, here and there, clusters of houses with clapboard sides mostly painted white sprouted among the greenery.

At the site where the picket line went up, the houses were still sawdust-smelling wooden skeletons. Strike headquarters was a big tent on a vacant lot two blocks away. Four or five burly men guarded the tent day and night. Contractors had tried to get the police to remove it, but the man who owned the lot was a good Socialist, and wouldn't swear out a trespassing complaint.

One of the guards tipped his battered fedora to Chester. "Mornin'," he said. "Pot of coffee's going inside, you want a cup."

"Good deal," Chester said. "Any trouble?"

All the guards shook their heads. "Not a bit," answered the one who'd spoken before. "Bastards don't bother anybody they figure he'll fight back." This time, all of his friends nodded.

That wasn't true. The class enemies and their lackeys weren't cowards. They defended their interests no less earnestly than proletarians. Things would have been easier if they hadn't. Chester said nothing about that. Why hurt the guards' morale?

He just ducked into the tent. Sure enough, a coffeepot perked above the blue flame on some canned heat. Several not very clean cups sat on a card table nearby. He'd drunk from far worse during the war. There was a sugar bowl, but no cream. Sugar would do. He poured himself a cup, quickly drained it, and took a picket sign. It said, SHAME! and UNFAIR TO WORKERS!, so it could be used in almost any strike. The handle was a good, solid piece of wood. Tear off the sign, and it turned into a formidable bludgeon.

Shouldering the sign, Martin went back outside. Another picket was walking across the lot toward the tent. "Morning, John," Chester called.

"Morning," John answered. "Chilly today."

"You say so." Chester smiled. No, he didn't think he'd ever get used to Los Angeles notions about weather.

He had a good picket line in place around the houses under construction before many workers started showing up. Some turned away, as if glad for an excuse not to go to work. Others squared their shoulders and crossed the line. The pickets showered them with abuse. They had to watch what they said; some of the scabs could have been plainclothes cops. General curses and insults were all right. Threats like, *We know where you live,* or, *Wait till you get off work,* could land a man in jail on an assault charge. Lawyers were expensive. Using them drained a strike fund in a hurry.

Around and around and around. In a field across the street, crows and Brewer's blackbirds with golden eyes pecked for worms and bugs and seeds. Hammers started banging at the construction site. The pickets cursed. "Scabs!" they shouted. Around and around and around.

Halfway through the morning, a white-haired, sun-browned man in a windbreaker fell into step with Chester. The man was missing most of two fingers from his right hand. "What the hell you want, Mordechai?" Martin asked.

"To talk with you, if you care to talk," the foreman answered. "Some of this mess is my fault. Maybe I can help fix it. Decent chop-suey joint around the corner and a block and a half down. I'll buy you lunch, if you'll let me."

Chester considered. The ex-Navy man was a pretty good guy, even if he had sold out to the exploiters. "I'll eat with you," Chester said. "I won't let you buy for me."

"Deal," Mordechai said at once.

"And no sneaking in more scabs at lunchtime, the way you guys have done before," Martin said. Mordechai nodded. Chester studied him. If he was a liar, he was a fine one. Chester nodded, too. "All right. We'll do that."

At noon, they walked to the chop-suey place together. It wasn't bad. Martin had certainly had worse. He ate without saying much. If Mordechai wanted to talk, *he* could talk. After a while, he did: "How can we settle this? I flew off the handle, and people have paid for it all over town. You can have your job back. No trouble there. Same with most of the people on your side."

"If you would've said that then, I'd've slobbered all over you, I'd've been so happy. Now?" Chester shook his head. "If I give in now, I sell out my pals. I can't do that. The people you work for have got to recognize that the union's come to Los Angeles. We don't want the moon, but they've got to bargain with us, and they've got to do it in good faith."

Mordechai frowned. He ate another forkful of strange vegetables and bits of fried meat. "If you think they'll recognize the union, that's wanting the moon, and the stars to boot."

With a shrug, Chester answered, "I figured you'd say that. So what the hell have we got to talk about? We'll go on with the class struggle and see how this round comes out."

"Oh, don't give me that Socialist crap," Mordechai said impatiently.

"It isn't crap." Chester set his jaw. "It works. If it worked in the steel mills in Toledo, it'll work here, too. How do you like being a scab?"

Mordechai's weathered features darkened with anger. "Don't you call me that."

"Well, what else are you?"

"I'm a foreman. And I'm a damn good one, too, by God." Pride rang in Mordechai's voice.

"I never said you weren't," Chester answered. "You're a damn fine foreman—most of the time. But that doesn't mean you—or some prick who's a foreman, too—can act like Jesus Christ on roller skates whenever you want. *That's* why we need a union."

Despite his mutilated hand, Mordechai ate faster than Chester did. He finished lunch and pushed his chair back from the table. "Afraid you were right," he said. "This was just a waste of time. You're not going to win this strike, though, you know. You can't."

"They said that in Toledo, too. They were wrong there. And you're wrong now. Sooner or later, a construction outfit will decide they'd rather not have all this trouble, and they'll give us a contract we can live with."

"Don't hold your breath," Mordechai advised. He tossed down a quarter. The silver coin rang sweetly. He walked out. Chester set his own quarter beside it and also headed back to the half-built tract. The strike would go on.

January in the North Atlantic tested a ship's construction. The endless storms and enormous seas tested a man's construction, too. The USS *Remembrance* handsomely passed the test. Sam Carsten wasn't so sure about his own innards. He had a good stomach, but the endless rolling and pitching started to make him feel as if he were riding a horse that hadn't been broken. And he had to strap himself to his bed every night to keep from winding up on the deck. He always hated that.

It needed doing, though. One sailor who slept in a top bunk forgot the strap and broke his arm when he fell out. To add insult to injury—in the most literal sense of the words—the captain busted him to ordinary seaman, too. Sam didn't suppose he'd lose officer's rank if he pulled a rock like that, but he didn't care to find out, either.

He was up and about when general quarters came. Getting to his station in the bowels of the *Remembrance* without breaking his neck was an adventure in this kind of weather, but he did it. He cussed most of the way there, though. The skipper had to be in an especially nasty mood to order general quarters in seas like this. It was bound to be just a drill, too. The United States weren't at war with anybody.

Besides, at the moment the carrier wasn't anything more than an oversized light cruiser, anyhow. No way in hell she could launch her airplanes in seas like this. That left her with guns to defend herself, and she didn't pack a whole lot of firepower—not that kind of firepower.

Lieutenant Commander Pottinger arrived at their station at the same time as Sam did. Panting, he asked, "Do you think it's true, Lieutenant?"

"Do I think what's true, sir?" Sam asked in turn. He was panting, too. He'd been in the Navy thirty years now. These mad dashes weren't so easy as they had been once upon a time.

"Why the captain called the general quarters," Pottinger answered.

"I can't begin to tell you, sir," Sam said. "I just heard the hooter and ran like hell. What do you know?"

"I ran like hell, too," the head of the damage-control party said. "Some men heading the other way said we'd spotted a Royal Navy ship, or maybe a Royal Navy squadron."

"I heard the same thing, sir," a sailor named Szczerbiakowicz said. "Damned if I know whether it's true, but I heard it."

"Did you, Eyechart?" Carsten used Szczerbiakowicz's universal nickname; nobody but another Pole could have hoped to pronounce his real one. Sam turned to Lieutenant Commander Pottinger. "If that's so, sir, you think the limeys mean trouble?"

"I couldn't begin to tell you," Pottinger replied. "But I think maybe the skipper thinks they might."

"Yes, sir. Does seem that way, doesn't it?" Sam looked at all the faces in the damage-control party. He realized he was the only one there old enough to have been at sea during the Great War. Even more than the way his heart pounded after the run to general quarters, that told him how many years he was carrying. He said, "The Royal Navy's a damn good outfit. They were still on their feet in 1917. We never did knock 'em flat; we starved England into quitting when we finally shut down the grain and beef imports from Argentina."

The *Remembrance* rolled steeply. Everybody grabbed for a handhold to steady himself. The ship straightened, then rolled back the other way. Eyechart Szczerbiakowicz said, "I don't care how good they are, sir. What can they do to us in seas like this?"

"Damned if I know," Sam said, talking like the petty officer he had been rather than the officer he was. "I'll tell you this, though: I sure as hell don't want to find out the hard way."

Nobody disagreed with him. Nobody wanted to see anything happen to the *Remembrance*. The men might not remember the Great War, but most of them had been through the inconclusive scrap against the Japanese. They knew too well how vulnerable to disaster even the mightiest warship could be. Huddling down here far below the main deck, away from fresh air and natural light, only served as a reminder. No one would do this if he didn't have to.

When the all-clear sounded, Sam let out a sigh of relief. Maybe the seas were too high to let the limeys launch torpedoes or to allow for accurate gunnery, but he didn't want to have to see by experiment.

As he left his station, he laughed at himself. For one thing, as he'd thought before, the United States were at peace with Britain, even if the two countries were a long way from friendly with each other. For another, he didn't know for a fact that there were any Royal Navy ships within a hundred miles of the *Remembrance*. Along with everybody else in the damage-control party, he'd been building castles in the air.

Sailors coming from other stations were also buzzing about the limeys. If they were wrong, they were all wrong the same way. Carsten shrugged. If he'd had a dollar for every time he'd seen unanimous rumor prove mistaken, he could have quit the Navy and lived ashore in style.

He headed for the officers' mess, both to grab a sandwich and some coffee and to find out what was going on from some people who might actually know. When he got there, he discovered that most of the other officers were as much in the dark as he was.

Before too long, though, Commander Cressy came into the mess. Every head swung toward the executive officer. Sam was far too junior to ask the question about which he was so curious, but that didn't matter, because a lieutenant commander from engineering did it for him: "Did we really bump into the limeys, sir?"

The exec paused to time the ship's roll and put cream in his coffee with the least likelihood of spilling it all over the deck. That done, he nodded. "We sure as hell did. Oh, not literally, but in dirty weather like this we have to worry about that, too: can't spot anything till it's right on top of you."

"They're patrolling farther west than they have for a while," another officer said.

"I know." Commander Cressy nodded again, not very happily. "We have no agreement with them that says they can't, but they haven't up till now. They still have a long reach, damn them."

"Think they could link up with the Confederates, sir?" Sam asked.

"Now isn't that an interesting question?" Cressy said. "You have a way of asking interesting questions, Carsten." Almost shyly, Sam dipped his head at the praise—if that was what it was. The exec went on, "The short answer is, I don't know. For that matter, the long answer is I don't know, too. We haven't spotted the Confederates doing a whole lot to build up their surface fleet—some destroyers and cruisers, but no new battleships, no carriers. They would have a devil of a time building those without our noticing. Submersibles . . . Submersibles are a different story, I'm afraid."

The officer who'd first asked about the Royal Navy was a flame-haired Irishman named George Toohey. He said, "They started building those fuckers—pardon my French, sir—years before that Featherston bastard grabbed the reins. You can bet they haven't stopped since."

"We should have made 'em say uncle the second we caught 'em at it," another lieutenant commander said. "It would have saved us a lot of grief. Their boats gave us fits in the last war. They're liable to do worse than that if we ever have to tangle with them again."

Nobody said he was wrong. Nobody in the Navy—nobody Sam Carsten had ever heard, anyhow—would have said he was wrong. But

Commander Cressy only shrugged. "No use crying over spilt milk," he said crisply. "We're stuck with the world we've got, not the one that might have been. For better or worse, the political will to clamp down tight wasn't there. If we ever do have another war, God forbid, I think we'll see Royal Navy subs—and French ones, too—refitting in Confederate harbors, and C.S. boats doing the same thing on the other side of the Atlantic." His smile bared sharp white teeth. "Makes our job a little more interesting, doesn't it, gentlemen?"

"They won't be using Bermuda or the Bahamas or Canada as bases against us, anyway," Lieutenant Commander Toohey said. "Not this time around, they won't."

"Or Newfoundland, either." Commander Cressy was relentlessly precise.

"If the Confederate States have a lot of submarines, holding on to the Bahamas could get expensive," Sam remarked. "Long haul down from Philadelphia and New York City, and every mile of it right past their coast."

A very young ensign said, "Baltimore's closer."

Cressy withered him with a glance. "A look at the map would remind you that Baltimore also lies within Chesapeake Bay. One assumes the mouth of the bay will be thoroughly mined. One also assumes the Confederates in Norfolk will not sleep through the commencement of hostilities." The ensign turned pink. He left the mess in a hurry. The exec was imperturbable. "Shall we go on discussing reasonable possibilities?"

"Even if the Confederates don't have carriers, how many land-based bombers have they got?" a lieutenant asked.

That struck Sam as a possibility altogether too reasonable. He said, "I was aboard the *Dakota* in 1917, when British bombers attacked her from the Argentine mainland. That wasn't much fun—and the airplanes now are a lot better than they used to be."

Commander Cressy nodded. "One reason we have carriers is to keep land-based aircraft off our fleets. Even so, though, the days of operating battleships in coastal waters may be gone for good."

The lieutenant who'd asked about land-based bombers said, "In that case, sir, why do we keep building them?"

"I am not the right person to whom to direct that particular question, Mr. Hutton," the exec replied. "I suggest you ask your Congressman, your Senators, and the Secretary of the Navy. You may be sure, I have done so." His smile was cynical. "You may also be sure, my letters have done just as much good as you would expect."

Carsten had been in the Navy his entire adult life. He understood how the top brass thought. "We got some use out of battleships in the last war," he said, "so of course we'll need them in the next one."

"Yes. Of course." But that wasn't agreement from the executive officer. It was raw sarcasm. "By that way of thinking, it's a miracle we have any carriers at all these days." Another of those frightening smiles. "But of course we know everything is exactly the way it should be in this best of all possible worlds. Don't we, gentlemen?"

No one in the officers' mess quite knew how to answer that. Sam hoped somebody in the Navy Department did.

# XIV

If it had been up to Armstrong Grimes, he would have dropped out of high school as soon as he could and gone to work. He wanted everything work could give him: money, money, and, well, money. He didn't think his mother would have minded. She and Aunt Clara were keeping Granny's coffeehouse going to bring in extra cash.

Armstrong snickered and cursed at the same time. He'd never liked his aunt, and it was mutual. They were only a couple of years apart, but these days the gap seemed wide as the Grand Canyon. Clara had escaped from school, while Armstrong was still stuck in it.

Not matter what he thought, his old man was bound and determined that he get his high-school diploma. Armstrong quarreled with his father, but he'd never had the nerve to take things too far. Merle Grimes walked with a permanent limp, yes, but that was no sign of weakness. It as much as said, *Don't mess with me, punk. The Confederates shot me and I kept going, so why the devil should I be afraid of you?*

And so Armstrong had to endure another six months of Theodore Roosevelt High School before he could escape into the real world. He said as much one night, resentfully, over supper.

His father laughed. "Once you do graduate, you'll probably be conscripted. Two years in the Army will show you what's real, all right."

"They don't conscript everybody in a whole year-class, the way they did in your day," Armstrong said. "I've got a pretty good chance of just being able to get on with my life."

"Your country is part of your life," Merle Grimes said. "If you don't help it, why should it help you?"

"I would if we go to war or something," Armstrong said. "But now . . . ?" He spread his hands, as if that would tell his father what he wanted instead of a green-gray uniform. Heading the list were his own apartment, his own auto, and a good-looking girlfriend the first two items would impress.

"The peacetime Army is a steady place," his father said. "The way things are these days, that counts for a lot. Who knows what'll be out there? If your grades were better . . ." He gave his son a dirty look.

"So I'm no greasy grind," Armstrong said, returning it with interest. "I do good enough to get by."

"Good enough to get by isn't good enough," his father insisted. As far as Armstrong was concerned, he might have been speaking Chinese.

On the way to school the next morning, Armstrong lit his first cigarette of the day. He didn't smoke all that much, because his father didn't like him doing it around the house. The first drag he took made him a little sick and gave him a little buzz, both at the same time.

He didn't pay much attention in class. He *would* get by, and he knew it. The teachers couldn't do anything to make him study harder, not when he would escape their clutches for good in a few months. A lot of the seniors, especially the boys, acted the same way.

More because he was a senior than for anything in particular he'd done—his football career had been decent, but no more than decent—he found himself a big man on campus. The younger kids all looked up to him. He'd had that happen before, when he'd worked his way up from first grade all the way to eighth in elementary school. As an eighth-grader, he'd been a big shot. Then, all of a sudden, he'd been nothing but a freshman at Roosevelt, and freshmen were nobodies. He'd spent the rest of his time here getting back on top.

He was on his way from math to U.S. government when he stopped so suddenly, the kid behind him bumped into him. He hardly even noticed. He'd just had a very nasty thought. Once he got out of high school, he'd fall right down to the bottom of the totem pole again. He wouldn't be a big man on campus. He'd be a kid, fighting for a break against men twice his age. How long before he got back on top again? Twenty years? Ever?

Armstrong tried to imagine twenty years. He couldn't—it was longer than he'd been alive. In twenty years, he'd be close to forty, and if forty wasn't old, what was? He'd intended to sneak another smoke in the boys' room on the way to government, but he didn't. Worrying about falling to the bottom of the totem pole had slowed him down, and he didn't want to be tardy. They still handed out swats to kids who came in late, even to seniors.

Mr. Wiedemann, the government teacher, walked with a limp almost identical to that of Armstrong's father. He wore the ribbon for a Purple

Heart on his lapel, so he'd been hurt during the war, too. "We don't look at secession the way we did before 1863," he said. "Can anyone tell me why we don't?" Several hands shot into the air. Armstrong's wasn't one of them, but Wiedemann pointed at him anyway. "Grimes!"

He didn't need to be one of the big brains to figure that out. "On account of the Confederate States," he said.

"Very good." Mr. Wiedemann had a wide sarcastic streak. As long as he wasn't aiming it at you, it made him pretty funny to listen to. "And from 1863 to the Great War, what happened to the border between the USA and the CSA?" He cupped a hand behind his ear. "Don't everybody talk at once."

"Nothing," a girl said without raising her hand.

She would have got in trouble if she were wrong, but Wiedemann nodded. "Very good. For a long time, people thought that border would never change. Were they right?"

Herb Rosen, the greasiest grind in the whole class, stuck up his hand. Everyone said he would end up at Harvard if he could make it into the quota for Jews there. The government teacher pointed to him. Herb said, "Maybe they were."

That made Armstrong sit up a little straighter. He knew the United States had taken land away from the Confederate States. The way his father went on, he would have needed to be dead not to know it. It wasn't the answer Mr. Wiedemann had expected, either. The teacher said, "Suppose you explain yourself." He didn't come right out and call Herb a blockhead. When it came to splitting hairs, Herb could hold his own with anybody, and he'd won a couple of arguments with Wiedemann in class. No one else could claim that.

Now Herb said, "The way things are going, Kentucky and Houston will end up back in the CSA, and maybe Sequoyah, too."

"God help us if you're right," Mr. Wiedemann said. "Why did we spend so much money and so much blood and so much pain to win them if we're going to give them back to the Confederate States?" He tapped the end of his walking stick against the floor as he spoke. Armstrong didn't think he knew he was doing it.

Like Armstrong, Herb Rosen hadn't been born while the Great War was going on. For him, it was as much ancient history as the reign of Caesar Augustus. Unlike the teacher, who'd done his own bleeding and hurting, Herb could think and talk about that time dispassionately. "That's the point I'm trying to make, Mr. Wiedemann. We took them, but did we really win them? Wouldn't most of the people in those states sooner live in the CSA than the USA? Isn't that why we've never let them have a plebiscite to decide?"

Mr. Wiedemann turned a blotchy purplish color. "What are you saying?" he asked, his voice shaking. "Are you saying we were wrong to take the spoils of victory? Are you saying we should have left the Confederates on the banks of the Ohio—and in easy artillery range of this very classroom?"

That last got home to Armstrong. His mother and grandmother had had plenty of stories of what Washington was like under bombardment. Most of them had to do with the long U.S. barrage that had preceded the reconquest of the city, but they'd talked about the Confederate shelling before the occupation, too. His mother didn't go on about those things the way she had when he was younger, but she still talked about them every now and again.

Herb, plainly, had struck a nerve. Armstrong wondered if he would back down. Kids who got too far under the skin of grownups usually regretted it. They might be clever, but grownups were the ones with the clout.

"I'm saying things have changed since the War of Secession." Herb sounded brash as ever. "Back then, states were more important than countries. Didn't you say Kentucky even declared itself neutral after the war started, and for a long time the USA and the CSA both had to honor that?"

"Yes, I did say that," Mr. Wiedemann admitted, "but I don't see what—"

Herb charged ahead: "Can you imagine a state trying to be neutral during the Great War? Things were different. Countries counted most. You thought, *I live in the United States,* or, *I'm a Confederate.* You didn't think, *I'm a New Yorker* first, or *I'm from Georgia.* And so when we took Kentucky and Houston away from the CSA, the people there didn't stop thinking they were Confederates, the way their grandfathers might have. I'm saying that's why we've had so much trouble. The Germans have, too, haven't they, in Alsace and Lorraine?"

Before the government teacher could answer, the bell rang. Wiedemann looked like a prizefighter who'd been saved by it. "Dismissed," he croaked, and sat down behind his desk.

Armstrong didn't usually have much to do with Herb Rosen. In the tightly tribal world of high school, they traveled in different packs. As they left the classroom, though, he made a point of going up to Herb. "Boy, you tied him in knots," he said admiringly.

Herb shrugged skinny shoulders. "I like to try to get to the bottom of things. It's interesting, you know what I mean?"

"Till just now, I didn't think government class *could* be interesting," Armstrong said. And, had he been coming out of math or science or literature, he would have said the same thing.

Herb blinked behind thick glasses. He looked just like what he was: a smart little sheeny. Armstrong realized he'd taken him by surprise, first by speaking to him at all and then by what he'd said. After another blink, Herb said, "It's like putting a puzzle together for me. I want to see where all the pieces go."

Only once in a while, as today, did Armstrong get the feeling there was a bigger puzzle that held pieces in a pattern. Keeping track of one piece at a time seemed plenty hard enough to him. He said, "You see more of them than old man Wiedemann does."

"I hope so," Herb Rosen answered. "He doesn't know all that much."

He surprised Armstrong again. Teachers knew more about what they taught than Armstrong did himself, so he'd always been willing to believe they knew a lot. Believing anything else hadn't even occurred to him. Now it did. He suddenly saw teachers as people like store clerks or truck drivers or trombone players: all doing their jobs, some good at them, some not so good. They weren't little tin gods, even if they wanted kids to think they were.

"You're all right, you know?" Armstrong said.

Herb blinked again, then beamed. He'd probably been wondering if he was going to get the snot knocked out of him. "You, too," he said, and hurried off to his next class. Armstrong went off to his, too, in what was, for him, an unusually thoughtful state of mind.

Cincinnatus Driver sighed as he pulled his truck over to the curb in front of his apartment building. He was angry at himself when he got out of the truck. It was a big, growling Studebaker, only two years old. The hauling business had been good lately. It would have been better yet if he could have got Achilles to throw in with him. He could have afforded a second truck—and if they'd had two, they would have had more before very long. Cincinnatus could see himself as somebody in charge of a real trucking outfit.

Trouble was, Achilles didn't want to drive a truck. He would have made more money than he did clerking, but he didn't want to come home to Grace and his children dog-tired every night, with beat-up hands and an aching back. Part of Cincinnatus scorned his son for being soft. Another part, though, admired Achilles for getting by on brains instead of brawn.

Cincinnatus went into the lobby of the apartment building and checked his mail. He sighed again once he had, this time in relief: no letter from his parents' neighbor in Covington. That meant no more news about his slowly failing mother. But even the relief held sorrow. It didn't mean his mother was getting better. She wasn't. She wouldn't. Once you went into your second childhood, you didn't come out again.

He trudged up the stairs to his flat. How tired he really was washed over him then. His back felt as if he'd been carrying an elephant up a mountain ever since he got up in the morning. He looked forward to a long soak in a hot tub. That would get some of the kinks out. When he went upstairs, he also understood exactly why his son wanted no part of the business he'd spent so long building up. If Achilles didn't have to, why would he want to feel like this?

*And what happens if you throw your back out?* Cincinnatus didn't want to think about that, but sometimes—especially when things in there ached more than usual—he couldn't help it. He knew what would happen. He'd be in trouble, and so would his whole family.

The key went into the lock. He opened the door. Amanda sat at the dining-room table doing homework. Her face was set in concentration. Her tongue stuck out of the corner of her mouth. Cincinnatus smiled. His daughter never noticed when she did that. *Both my children gonna graduate high school,* he thought, and the smile got wider. That wasn't bad at all, not for a black man who hadn't been allowed to go to school at all growing up in Confederate Kentucky. He'd learned to read catch as catch can, and he'd had to be careful about letting white people know he could do it. Iowa wasn't paradise—far from it—but it was better than what he'd known when he was small.

"Hello, sweetheart," he said.

Amanda jumped. "I didn't hear you open the door."

"I know. You was—*were*—thinkin' about your schoolwork."

"Test tomorrow," she said, and sank down into that sea of study.

Cincinnatus went into the kitchen. Elizabeth was wrapping spiced ground beef in cabbage leaves. Cincinnatus' mouth watered; he loved pigs in blankets. His wife looked over her shoulder. He gave her a quick kiss. "How's things?" she asked.

"Not bad," he answered. "Busy day. I'm tired."

"Sore, too, I bet," Elizabeth said. "I can see it, way you move." He nodded. She wasn't wrong. She went on, "Why don't you take your bath now an' soak for a while? These ain't gonna be ready for at least half an hour."

"All right, I do that," Cincinnatus said. "I was thinkin' comin' up the stairs, hot water feel good. Maybe I put the wireless set in the hall so I can listen to it in there, too. That way, I don't have to turn it on so loud, it'll bother Amanda."

"Well, go on, then," Elizabeth told him. "Longer you stand here talkin', less time you got to git clean and git warm."

When they moved in, it had been a cold-water flat. They'd been happy enough because it had electricity, which they'd done without in Covington. Heating water on the stove hadn't seemed like much. These past few years, though, the building had changed hands, and the new owner had put a water heater in the basement along with the furnace. The rent had gone up a few dollars a month to pay for it, but Cincinnatus didn't know a single tenant who was inclined to complain. All the hot water you wanted, without having to heat it and carry it . . . If that wasn't a bargain, he didn't know what was.

He put the wireless on the floor in the hall, and ran it back to a plug in the bedroom with an extension cord. If he left the door open a couple of inches, he could hear just fine. He picked the station that would carry the football game in a little while. The Tri-State Association wasn't a top league, but the Des Moines Hawks were one of the two or three best teams—and they were playing Keokuk, a doormat, tonight.

"Dutch will be along at half past the hour with the game," the announcer said earnestly. "First, though, here is the news."

Soaking in a steaming tub, Cincinnatus was inclined to be tolerant. "Go on, then. Tell me," he said.

The announcer did, starting with the latest scandal at the State House. It sounded as if some Socialist legislators were going to spend some time in quarters less fancy than their present offices, but you never could tell. More than a few politicians here had managed to wiggle off the hook.

Farm news came next. Most of Iowa was farm country. They took prices for grain and hogs and cattle seriously here. They had to; an awful lot of people either made a decent living or didn't, depending on whether those prices went up or down.

Only after the local and state news did the announcer bother to admit a wider world was out there. President Smith remained optimistic, or said he did, that an old-age pension bill would finally fight its way through Congress. The Socialists had been saying that for years. The Democrats had been filibustering for years. Smith was quoted as saying, "If they vote against it, they'll pay at the polls next November, and they'll deserve to." Cincinnatus had long since decided he would believe in the pension when he saw his first check.

Someone in Houston had taken a shot at the U.S. commandant there. He'd missed, and been killed by the officer's guards for his trouble. Someone in Sequoyah had blown up an oil well. "A spectacular fireball," the announcer said, "and damage in the hundreds of thousands of dollars." He sounded almost gleeful about having such exciting news to read.

"And in Kentucky," he went on, "a plot to wreck the bridges crossing from Covington to Cincinnati was foiled by the vigilance of soldiers commanded by Brigadier General Abner Dowling. Dowling is quoted as saying Kentucky will stay in the USA as long as he is in charge there, and radicals and agitators had better get used to the idea." Cincinnatus was sure the man on the wireless would have been more cheerful if he'd got to talk about the bridges falling into the Ohio River.

In the CSA, an auto bomb had gone off in Montgomery, killing four—three whites and a Negro—and wounding seventeen. The newsman said, "Like most of the recent rash of auto bombs, this is surely the work of Negro guerrillas, although no one has claimed responsibility for it. In Richmond, President Featherston has vowed vengeance for the attack, and has stated that, if necessary, he will hold the entire colored community responsible for the actions of the bombers, who, in his words, 'are cowards destroying innocent lives but afraid to come out and fight like men.' "

Cincinnatus snorted. If you fought somebody stronger than you were, you had to be a fool to meet him face to face. Cincinnatus despised the idea of blowing up innocent bystanders. But he also despised what the Freedom Party was doing to blacks in the Confederacy. How could he blame them for hitting back with whatever weapons they found?

"In South America, talks between Venezuela and the Empire of Brazil on their latest border dispute are said to have made some progress," the announcer said. "However, Argentina and Chile have recalled their ambassadors from each other's capitals. They are said to be closer to war with each other than at any time since 1917." Cincinnatus remembered that one of the South American countries had been on the USA's side in the Great War, the other on the CSA's. Sprawling there in the nice, warm tub, he couldn't have said which was which. They were both too far away.

"King Charles of France has demanded a plebiscite in Alsace and Lorraine, much as President Featherston has demanded a similar vote in Kentucky and Houston," the announcer declared. "No immediate reply is expected from Kaiser Wilhelm's government, not least because of the Kaiser's failing health. In Britain, Prime Minister Churchill announced his support for the French demand, saying, 'The Germans have decided only to be undecided, resolved to be irresolute, adamant for drift, solid for fluidity, all-powerful to be impotent.' "

From what Cincinnatus had seen in the papers, this Churchill was a reactionary. The only reason he was prime minister was that the Conservatives had named him to the post to keep the Silver Shirts from eating their party the way the Socialists had eaten the Republicans in the USA. He was an old man, and cartoonists liked to show him with jowls like a bulldog's. But he could turn a phrase.

"Churchill has also introduced a bill instituting conscription in Britain," the newsman went on. "In his speech in the House of Commons, he said, 'Come on now, all you young men, all over the kingdom. You are needed more than ever now to fill the gap of a generation shorn by the war. You must take your place in life's fighting line. Raise the glorious flags again; advance them upon the new enemies.' He pointed to the achievements of the British Unicorn Legion in Spain, and its role in helping the Nationalists seize Madrid from the German-backed Monarchists. 'Surely Wellington would have praised their pluck,' he said, amidst loud applause."

Who was Wellington? Cincinnatus supposed the British knew. Achilles and Amanda might have known, too. He had no idea himself.

He didn't much care, either. After giving the day's stock-market figures (dismal, as usual) and the weather forecast (not much better), the newsman went away. The excited background mutter from a packed football stadium came out of the wireless speaker. "Hello, Hawks fans. A very pleasant good evening to you, wherever you may be," the sportscaster said. "This is your pal Dutch, bringing you tonight's game between Des Moines and the Keokuk Colonels. Des Moines has to be the favorite, but you've got to watch out for Keokuk because they're coming off a win against Waterloo, and . . ."

"Ahhh." Cincinnatus knew he would enjoy hearing the game regardless of whether the Hawks won or lost. Even if it was 49-7 at the half, Dutch would find a way to keep the broadcast exciting till the final gun sounded. Dutch could read the telephone book and make it interesting. If there ever was a great communicator, he was the man.

And then, with the Hawks driving ("There they go again!" Dutch said after yet another gain), Elizabeth spoiled things by yelling, "Supper's ready!" Cincinnatus didn't want to get out of the tub, but he did.

Jonathan Moss was chewing a piece of roast beef when Dorothy looked across the table at him and asked, "Daddy, why are you a damned Yank?"

He didn't choke. It took an effort, but he didn't. After carefully swallowing, he looked not at his little girl but at his wife. Laura shook her head. "I've never called you that, Jonathan—well, never where Dorothy could hear."

He believed her. She was straightforward in what she thought and said; he couldn't imagine her lying about it to his face. Turning back to Dorothy, he asked, "Who called me that, dear?"

"Some of the kids at school," she answered. "They said Mommy was a collabo-something. I don't know what that means."

Laura turned red. She bit her lip. She knew what it meant, too well. Quickly, Jonathan said, "It means those kids don't know what they're talking about, that's what."

"Oh," Dorothy said. "All right." She went back to her supper.

But it wasn't all right, and Jonathan knew it. He read stories to Dorothy while Laura did the dishes. They all listened to the wireless for a while. Dorothy changed into a long flannel nightgown, brushed her teeth, and came out clutching her favorite doll for good-night kisses.

After she'd gone to bed, Laura looked at Jonathan and said, "Hello, you damned Yank."

He didn't say, *Hello, you collaborator,* or even, *Hello, you collabo-something.* That would only have made things worse. He just shook his head and said, "Kids."

"She'll know what a collaborator is soon enough," Laura said bitterly. He wouldn't be able to escape the word by not mentioning it, then. He hadn't really thought he would, though he had hoped. His wife went on, "The schoolchildren will make sure of that."

"She'll know you're not a collaborator, too," Moss said. "You still can't stand Yanks, even though you married one. And there are plenty of Yanks who'd say I'm the collaborator—collaborator with Canucks, I mean."

"Not as many as there used to be," Laura said. "Not since you started flying again."

"Ha! Shows what you know," Moss told her. "You should hear the way the fellows at the airdrome outside of London needle me."

"I don't want to hear them. I don't want anything to do with them," she answered. "If I did, I really would be a collaborator." She glared at him, daring him to tell her she was wrong.

He didn't want to argue about it. They argued enough—they argued too much—without looking for reasons to lock horns. He said, "I want to review those papers I brought home. I'm going to have to put in a lot of work on that appeal when I get to the office tomorrow."

A military judge had sentenced one of his clients to five years for lying about his past in the Canadian military when applying for a liquor-store license. Moss was convinced the judge had ignored the evidence. He thought he had a decent chance of getting the verdict overturned; the military courts in occupied Canada weren't nearly so bad nowadays as they had been shortly after the war.

But he also wanted to remind Laura of what he did for a living—what he'd been doing for years. To his relief, she nodded. "All right," she said. "Will it bother you if the wireless stays on? I like the music program that's coming up next."

"I don't mind a bit," he said. "I won't even notice it."

As he headed out the door the next morning, he wondered if he should have asked Dorothy which children at the local elementary school were calling Laura and him names. That probably said something about how their parents felt about the U.S. occupiers. He shook his head. He didn't want to know.

The sun shone on soot-streaked snow. As usual in early March, Berlin was a gloomy, frozen place. Moss warily looked around before getting into his auto. He saw nothing out of the ordinary. Relieved but not reassured, he got in and started the motor. The day seemed just like any other. All the same, he didn't go to his law office by the route he'd used the day before. He'd had too many threats to care to make things easy for anyone who might want him dead. And, while the bomb that had blown up occupation headquarters hadn't been aimed at him in particular, it would have killed him just the same if he'd been there when it went off. He came by his caution honestly.

Getting out of the Ford and walking half a block to the office building was another small, thoughtful stretch of time. No matter how he went from his block of flats to the office, he got there in the end. Somebody could be waiting.

Nobody was, not today, not outside, not in the lobby, not on the stairs, not in the office. Moss nodded to himself. Now he could get on with business. He lit a cigarette, plugged in the hot plate, and got a pot of coffee going. The first cup would be good. He prepared to enjoy it. By the end of the day, the pot would be mud and battery acid. He knew he'd go right on pouring more from it.

He was his own secretary. He could have afforded to hire a typist, but the idea had never once crossed his mind. He started pounding away on a typewriter not much younger and not much lighter than he was. The letters that appeared on the sheet of paper were grayer than he would have liked. When he looked in the desk drawer to see if he had a new ribbon, he found he didn't. He muttered under his breath; he thought he'd bought two the last time he needed them. Either he hadn't, or this was the second and not the first. Before long, he would have to go shopping again. Ribbons for this ancient model were getting hard to come by.

He'd dealt with some ordinary correspondence and was working on the appeal when his first client of the day came in. "Mr. Godfrey, isn't it?" Moss said, turning the swivel chair away from the typewriter stand and toward the front of the office. "How are you today, sir?"

"I'll do, Mr. Moss, thank you." Toby Godfrey did not look like the plump, red-faced English squire his name might have suggested. He was skinny and sallow and wore a perpetually worried expression. Since the occupation authorities were taking a long and pointed look at his affairs, he had reason to wear that kind of look, but Moss suspected he'd had it long before the Great War started.

"Let me check your file, Mr. Godfrey." Jonathan got up and pulled it out of a steel four-drawer cabinet. Looking at what was there reminded him of what wasn't. "You were going to get me your certificate of discharge and your certificate of acceptance." A Canadian man who'd fought in the Great War and couldn't prove he had accepted U.S. authority after the surrender in 1917 had a very hard time of it indeed if he ever came to the notice of a military court.

Godfrey coughed: a wet sound, half embarrassed; half, perhaps, tubercular. "I have the certificate of discharge," he said. "As for the other . . ." He coughed again. "I would, of course, be happy to sign a certificate of acceptance now. That would be better than nothing, wouldn't it?"

"A little," Moss said glumly. A military prosecutor would claim Godfrey had signed the certificate only because of his dispute with the occupying authorities. He would also claim everything Godfrey had done over the past twenty-odd years was illegal because he'd done it without having a certificate on file. A military judge would be inclined to listen to that kind of argument, too, because occupation law presumed the worst about men who'd tried to kill U.S. soldiers.

"I'm sure you'll do your best," Godfrey said.

"If you can't find that certificate, I'm making bricks without straw," Moss warned. "You'd do better trying to settle—if they will."

"But I've lived a quiet, peaceable life since 1917. No one can say otherwise," Toby Godfrey protested. "That must count for something!"

"A little," Moss said again, even more glumly than before.

Godfrey seemed not to hear that glumness—seemed to refuse to hear it, in fact. Clients were often like that: full of their own hopes and fears, they became deaf and blind to anything that ran against whatever they already had in their minds. The Canadian said, "I'm sure you'll do your very best, Mr. Moss."

Moss nodded. "I will. But I tell you frankly, I've taken a lot of cases where I liked the odds better. If you can arrange a compromise with the occupying authorities . . ."

Godfrey wouldn't hear of it. He must have thought it was a way of asking for more money, for he set ten crisp, new ten-dollar bills on the desk. "Your very, very best, Mr. Moss." He didn't even wait for a reply. He got up and stuck out his hand. Moss took it. His client left the office.

Moss scooped up the money. *I'll have to mail him a receipt,* he thought, sighing. He would do his best. If you were fighting a foe too much bigger and stronger than you were, sometimes your best wasn't good enough. The Canadians had found out all about that during the Great War, and Jonathan Moss had been one of the men who taught them the lesson.

He turned the swivel chair back to the typewriter stand and started banging away again. He'd just got up a good head of steam when somebody knocked on the door. "Come in," he called. *Who the devil?* went through his mind. Clients didn't usually knock, and he had no one scheduled till the afternoon. The mailman didn't knock, either. Besides, the mail wouldn't get here for at least another hour. Just in case, Moss' hand found the pistol he'd taken to keeping in a desk drawer.

In walked Major Rex Finley. Moss pulled his hand out of the drawer. "Hello, Major," he said. "This is a surprise. What brings you here?"

"A government-issue Chevy, and I hope it'll bring me back to London, too," answered the officer who commanded the airdrome there.

Laughing, Jonathan pointed to the chair across from his desk and said, "Well, sit down and tell me what I can do for you."

"I've come to say good-bye," Finley said. "I've been transferred to Wright Field, outside of Dayton, Ohio. Captain Trotter will be in charge of things here from now on. You'll be able to keep flying. Don't worry about that. Before too long, we may want every trained man we can find." His voice had an edge to it.

"Dayton," Moss said musingly. "That's down toward the border, isn't it?"

Major Finley nodded. "It sure is, and it'll be even closer if there's a plebiscite in Kentucky and we lose." Neither of them said anything after that for a little while. If there was a plebiscite, the USA would lose. Everything Moss knew about Kentucky told him as much. By Finley's expression, he had the same opinion.

At last, Moss asked, "Do you really think it will come to . . . that?"

"I don't know," Finley replied. "I don't know, but I wouldn't be surprised."

"Well, well." Moss whistled tunelessly. "Do you want to go out and get drunk?"

"Too early in the day for me," Finley said with genuine regret. "And, like I said, I have to be able to drive back to London. But don't let me stop you."

"I've got work to do myself." Jonathan looked for a silver lining: "Maybe we're wrong. Here's hoping we're wrong."

Major Finley nodded. "Yes. Here's hoping." But he didn't sound as if he believed it.

\* \* \*

Mary Pomeroy cut up pieces of fried pork chop and put them on Alec's plate along with some string beans. Her son ate string beans only under protest. He would eat them, though, and only rarely required threats of imminent bodily harm. Not even threats of imminent bodily harm would make him eat spinach. Bodily harm itself wouldn't; Mary and Mort had both made the experiment, which had left everyone in the family unhappy.

Mort dug in. "That's good," he said.

"Thanks," Mary answered. "What's the news at the diner?"

"Not a whole lot," her husband said. "Two different tables of Yank soldiers talking about whether there'll be a whatchamacallit down south."

"A plebiscite?" Mary asked.

Mort nodded. "That's it. I hear it a dozen times a day, and I never remember it."

"If there is one, the people down there will vote to leave the United States. They'll vote to be Confederates again," Mary said.

"I suppose so." Mort lit a cigarette. He didn't care one way or the other.

That he didn't care disappointed Mary. She did her best not to let it infuriate her. "What do you suppose would happen if we had one of those plebiscites here in Canada?" she asked.

Mort didn't answer right away. He was blowing smoke rings for Alec. He was good at it; he could send them out one after another. His son watched in goggle-eyed fascination. Only when Mort ran out of smoke did he shrug and say, "I don't know."

"Don't you think we'd vote to be Canadians again, to be free again?" Mary blazed. "Don't you think we'd vote to send the Yanks packing?"

"I suppose so." But Mort still didn't sound very excited. "But we're not going to get to vote, you know."

"Why not?" Mary said. "If the people in those states ever get to, we should, too. I don't want to be a Yank any more than somebody in Houston does."

After another virtuoso set of smoke rings, Mort said, "I'll tell you why not. Because those other places have the Confederate States shouting for 'em all the time. Who's going to shout for us? We can't even shout for ourselves."

Canadians didn't shout, or not very much. One surefire way to tell Yanks in Canada was by how much noise they made. Mary didn't just want to shout. She wanted to scream. "We ought to be shouting for ourselves. We're just as much a country as the United States are."

"I suppose we could be, if—" Mort began.

Alec interrupted: "More smoke rings, Daddy!"

But Mort stubbed out the cigarette in an ashtray. "Next time I light up, sport," he told the little boy, and turned back to Mary. "I suppose we could be, if they let us," he said, picking up where he'd left off. "But they aren't going to let us, and there's nobody who can make them let us. We're stuck. We might as well get used to it. If we do, maybe they'll ease up on us a little more."

Mary had never imagined hating her husband. She came unpleasantly close to it now. Mort wasn't a collaborator. Mary never would have had anything to do with him if he were, no matter how he stirred her. But he was—what would you call somebody like him?—an accommodator, that was it. He knew he was a Canadian. He even liked being a Canadian, and was proud of it. He didn't think staying a Canadian was worth a big fight, though. All he wanted to do was get along from one day to the next.

More and more Canadians seemed to be accommodators these days. That made Mary want to scream, too. Accommodate enough, accommodate long enough, and you weren't a Canadian any more, were you? Not as far as she could see. Didn't you turn into a pale imitation of a Yank instead?

"You want to go to the cinema Saturday night?" Mort asked. "The new film about Roosevelt's Unauthorized Regiment is supposed to be good. And they say Marion Morrison makes a first-rate TR."

"I don't think so," Mary said tightly, fighting hard against despair. Mort already sounded like a pale imitation of a Yank. He would have denied it if she'd called him on it. She didn't. She didn't want a fight. Life was too short, wasn't it?

*If you don't fight, aren't you giving up, too?* she asked herself. She supposed that was partly true, but only partly. She still cared about the wrongs the Americans had committed in occupying her country. She didn't, she wouldn't, forget.

"Oh," Mort said. "Almost slipped my mind."

"What?" Mary asked.

"You know Freddy Halliday?" Mort said. That was a silly question; Rosenfeld wasn't such a big town that everybody didn't know everybody else. Mary nodded impatiently. Her husband went on, "He says the public library really will open in two weeks. He says, 'Cross my heart and hope to die.' "

"Do you think it will happen?" Mary asked. Freddy Halliday had been trying to bring a public library to Rosenfeld for years. He hadn't had much luck till lately. Now he actually had a building a few doors down from the general store. He had it because the pharmacist who was supposed to come up from Minneapolis had got cold feet, but he did have it.

Whether he had anything besides the building was a subject of much speculation in town.

"He *says* he has a permit from the occupying authorities in Winnipeg and a budget and books," Mort answered. "I don't know if he really does. If he doesn't, we ought to ride him out of town on a rail, to teach him not to get our hopes up."

"*My* hopes are up," Mary said. "You can have as much fun in a library as you can at the cinema, and it doesn't cost you anything." She turned to Alec. "I wonder if it'll have any children's books for you."

"Read me a story?" Alec asked, cued by the word *books*.

"After supper," Mary said. That made Alec shovel food into his mouth like a stoker fueling a fast freight. Mary hoped most stokers had better aim than her little boy did.

It began to look as if Freddy Halliday had all the things he claimed he had. A brass plaque that said ROSENFELD PUBLIC LIBRARY went up above the door to the forsaken pharmacy. A formidably stout maiden lady, a Miss Montague, moved into a ground-floor flat in the Pomeroys' block of flats and began spending all her waking hours in the building. A large truck brought crates of something to the place. If those crates didn't hold books, what *was* in them?

The promised opening day came . . . and went. Everybody in town joked about it—everybody except Freddy Halliday, who remained resolutely upbeat. A week later, the Rosenfeld Public Library did in fact open its doors.

Mary wasn't there for the opening. Alec came down with a cold, which meant he had to stay home, which meant she had to stay home, too. She didn't get to the library for another week. It was a bright spring day, the sky a deep, almost painful, blue overhead. The few white clouds dappling it only made the glorious color deeper. Out on the farms beyond the edge of town, people would be taking advantage of this glorious weather to plant. Mary could just enjoy it. Walking along with Alec's little hand in hers, she felt guilty about not doing more.

In the library, Miss Montague sat behind a large wooden desk and under an almost equally large QUIET, PLEASE! sign. She did smile at Alec, and pointed to, sure enough, the children's section. She didn't even breathe fire when Alec whooped with delight at finding books he hadn't seen before.

Mary arranged to get a library card for herself and one for Mort. She stole brief glimpses of novels and nonfiction books, encyclopedias and magazines and newspapers. "Look at all the telephone books," she said, trying to keep Alec interested so she could go on looking around. "You can find out the telephone number of anybody in Canada or the United States." She refused even to name the Republic of Quebec, stolen from her country as Kentucky and Houston had been stolen from the CSA.

"Why?" Alec asked her.

"So you can call them if you want to."

"But we don't got a telephone."

"Don't *have* a telephone. But if we did, we could."

"Why?" Alec asked again.

That string of questions could go on all day. Knowing as much, Mary said, "And here's a book of maps of the whole world." The big, colorful atlas distracted Alec.

It also distracted Mary, but only for a little while. *If I could call anybody, who would it be? What would I say?* The thought was enough to make her dizzy. She'd used a telephone only a handful of times in her life. The diner had one, but the flat didn't, and of course there hadn't been one on the farm. If she had a telephone, and if the farm had one, too, she supposed she would talk to her mother whenever she got the chance. She couldn't think of anyone else except her sister Julia she wanted to call. The people she knew in Rosenfeld she could visit whenever she pleased, while no telephone would ever let her talk with her brother or her father.

But even if she didn't have a telephone, lots of people in Canada and even more in the USA did. The telephone book for Toronto, for instance, had to be an inch and a half thick. Mary pulled it off the shelf—she didn't care even to open a telephone book from the United States. The first name she looked for was McGregor, the one she'd been born with. She found almost a page of McGregors, each name with not only a telephone number but also an address beside it. *That must be handy,* she thought, *especially in a big city where you don't know where everybody else lives.* After the McGregors, she checked the Pomeroys. There weren't so many of them—only a little more than a column's worth. She smiled at the obvious superiority of her own birth name. But then, when she saw the seven pages of Smiths, she decided quantity didn't make quality.

Alec got impatient watching his mother flip pages back and forth. "Want to go home," he said.

"Hush," Mary told him. "Don't talk loud in the library."

"Want to go *home*." Alec didn't care where he was, and knew where he wanted to be.

"All right," Mary said. She was ready to go, too. But then, as they were on their way out, she suddenly stopped. Alec tugged at the pleats of her skirt. "Wait a second," she told him, and went over to the librarian's desk. "Excuse me, Miss Montague, but could I borrow a pencil and a little piece of paper?"

"Why, of course." The librarian gave them to her.

Alec's face clouded up when she went back. "It'll only be a minute," she said. "I want to see something." He didn't burst into tears on the spot, which was something. If he had, she would have had to take him home—and she would have warmed his fanny, too.

As things were, she found what she was looking for inside of two minutes. She wrote down what she needed to know, gave the pencil back to Miss Montague with a nod of thanks, and walked out of the library. Alec behaved on the way back. Why not? He was getting what he wanted. As Mary walked past the building that housed the *Rosenfeld Register*, she gave the newspaper a nod of thanks, too.

Lucien Galtier started up his motorcar. The Chevrolet roared to life right away. He'd finally had to replace the battery. The new one was much stronger than the old one had been, but he still grumbled at the expense. When he was driving a horse, he hadn't had to buy new pieces for it every so often.

Once the motor warmed up, he put the auto in gear and drove up toward Rivière-du-Loup. Today was his sixty-somethingeth birthday (he didn't care to contemplate the exact number), and Nicole and Dr. Leonard O'Doull had invited him to their house for supper to celebrate.

Part of him wondered why people celebrated getting older. Another part, the part that still ached for Marie, told him the answer: because the alternative was *not* getting older, and that was dreadfully final.

It had been a quarter of a century now since war's clawed hand raked across the countryside. Young men said you couldn't see the scars any more. Lucien knew better. Time had softened those wounds, but they were still there if you knew where to look. And shells still lay buried in the ground. Every so often, they worked their way to the surface. Most of the time, *démineurs* took them away and disposed of them. Once in a while, one of them went off when a plowshare struck it or it suffered some other mischance of that sort. The Great War was still killing people, and would go on killing for years to come.

He drove past the post office. The Republic of Quebec's fleur-de-lys flag fluttered in the breeze in front of it. He was used to that flag now, but it still didn't feel like the flag of his country. He didn't suppose it ever would, not when he'd spent his first forty years in the province of Quebec rather than the Republic. Were things better now? Worse? Or just different? For the life of him, he had trouble saying.

There was the house where Nicole lived with Leonard O'Doull. He parked in front of the walk that led to the front porch. The grass on the lawn was green again. When he got out of the auto, he took the key with him. On the farm, he left it in the ignition half the time. That probably wouldn't do here in town, where a stranger might hop in and decide to go for a spin.

The door opened before he could knock. There stood his oldest grandson. By what magic had Lucien O'Doull grown taller than the man for whom he was named? "Happy birthday, *mon grandpère*," he said. "Come in." That same magic, whatever it was, had given him a man-deep voice, too.

"*Merci*," Lucien Galtier said, and then, after an appreciative sniff, "What smells so good?" An instant later, he held up a hand. "No, don't tell me. I'll find out."

He followed his grandson down the short entry hall to the living room. As soon as he got there, a flashbulb went off in his face. What sounded like a million people shouted, "*Surprise!*"

"'*Osti*," Lucien muttered, flinching with what was indeed surprise—shock probably came closer. With a large purplish-green spot swimming in front of his eyes, he needed a moment to see how jammed with people the living room was. He'd expected Nicole and Leonard and little Lucien, and they were there, but so were Denise and Charles and Georges and Susanne and Jeanne and their spouses and their children. And, he realized after another startled heartbeat, so was Éloise Granche.

"*Surprise!*" they all shouted again, even louder than before. Nicole wriggled through the crowd and kissed Galtier on the cheek. "Happy birthday, *cher papa*!" Her husband raised the camera again. Another flashbulb froze the moment.

Lucien was at least partly braced for the second blast of light. He wagged a finger at his offspring. "You are a pack of devils, every one of you," he said. "You did your best to make this the last surprise I would ever have, this side of the Pearly Gates." He mimed clutching his breast and falling over dead.

His children and grandchildren laughed and cheered. Éloise Granche said, "If they are a pack of devils, where do you suppose they get it?" That brought more laughter yet. Éloise rose from the sofa and threaded her way past children and out to Lucien. As Nicole had, she said, "Happy birthday," and kissed Galtier. Leonard O'Doull took yet another photograph.

"Well, well," Lucien said. "I suspect you have all been plotting this for a very long time."

"Oh, no, Papa." Georges shook his head. "Your American son-in-law drove round to our houses a couple of hours ago, and since we weren't doing anything special tonight. . . ."

"Nonsense," Galtier said. If there hadn't been so many women and children there, he would have said something more colorful than that. But *nonsense* would do. His younger son's head had always been full of it. Most of the grownups had glasses close by them, some full, some empty. Plaintively, Galtier asked, "Could it be that I might get something to drink?"

"Well, seeing that it *is* your birthday," Leonard O'Doull said with the air of a man granting a great concession. "And it could also be that I should prescribe something for that green-around-the-gills look you have. Would you like whiskey or apple brandy?"

"Yes," Galtier said: a reply worthy of Georges.

His son-in-law made a face at him. "Which, you cantankerous creature?"

"Apple brandy, by choice," Lucien answered. He would drink whiskey readily enough, but he wasn't wild about it. He turned to Éloise. "And what are you doing here?"

"Why, wishing you a happy birthday, of course," she answered demurely. "I hope it *is* a happy birthday?"

"It seems to be, so far," he answered; coming right out and admitting he was happy struck him as a show of weakness. He turned to Leonard O'Doull. "You see? You have been listening to gossip again."

"And what if I have?" O'Doull replied. "Are you complaining?"

"Me? Not at all. I am glad I am here. I am glad everyone is here," Galtier said. "And I do mean everyone." He smiled at Éloise. He wanted to kiss her again, but he wouldn't do that, not in front of his children and grandchildren. They might—most of the ones old enough to understand surely did—know he and Éloise were more than friends, but there was a difference between knowing and showing. One little kiss had been all right. Two would have been excessive. The difference mattered to him. That it might matter much less to his offspring never once crossed his mind.

Nicole disappeared into the kitchen. When she came out, it was with some of the most arresting words in any language: "Supper's ready!"

Fried chicken, lamb fragrant with garlic, rabbits stewed with plums, fresh spinach and peas, stewed turnips, endless snowy mounds of mashed potatoes, plenty of whiskey and applejack and beer to wash them down . . . Any man who couldn't be happy after a feast like that wasn't trying hard enough. Lucien ate till he wanted to curl up on his chair and go to sleep. Nor was he the only one who went above and beyond the call of duty; Georges could easily have built a whole new chicken from the mound of bones on his plate.

Everyone groaned with horrified pleasure when Nicole brought out an enormous birthday cake. A single large candle topped it. Leonard O'Doull grinned evilly at Lucien. "We did not want to put a candle for each year," he said, "for fear you would burn the house down when you tried to blow them out."

"An old man hasn't got enough wind to blow out that many candles anyhow," Georges put in.

"I gave you the strap when you were little," Lucien told his younger son, "but not enough of it, I see. Well, *le bon Dieu* is still listening. I did not know 'Dishonor thy father and mother' was one of the commandments."

"Don't be silly. I wouldn't think of saying a word against *maman*." Georges' face was the picture of innocence. Galtier snorted.

Charles struck a match and lit the candle. "Blow it out, Papa, so we can eat the cake," he said sensibly. Unlike Georges, he had no wildness in him, but he made a good, solid man.

Blow it out Lucien did. Everybody cheered. Nicole cut the cake. She gave her father the first piece. He had no idea how he found room for it, but he did. His children and their spouses groaned as they ate. His grandchildren might have been a swarm of locusts. Lucien marveled that they left any of the cake undevoured.

"Now," Nicole said briskly, "presents."

Galtier tried to wave them away. "That I am here with my family is enough—more than enough," he said. Nobody listened to him. He hadn't thought anyone would. Now that he'd made the protest, he could enjoy his gifts and not be thought greedy.

From Charles, he got a soft tweed jacket better suited to a gentleman of leisure than to a working farmer. That was how it seemed to him, anyhow. But Éloise said, "It's perfect to wear to a dance." He hadn't thought of that. Once she said it, though, he saw she was right.

Georges gave him a fancy pipe and some even fancier tobacco. When he opened the tin, the rich fragrance filled the room. *"Calisse,"* he said reverently. "That smells so good, I won't even have to smoke it . . . And what's this?"

*This* came from Nicole and Leonard O'Doull. It was a big bottle of real Calvados, not the imitations turned out by local craftsmen who didn't care for the Republic of Quebec's tedious excise-tax regulations. " 'This fine brandy is patronized by his Majesty, King Charles XI, King of France,' " Galtier read from the label.

*"Mais certainement,"* his son-in-law said. "I personally wrestled this very bottle from King Charles' own hands."

"You certainly are a muttonhead," Lucien said.

Éloise Granche gave him a maroon wool sweater. Everyone said it was very handsome. Again, Lucien thought it finer than what he usually wore, but it was thick and warm. It would do nicely in spring and fall and, under a coat, in wintertime, too. "I hope you like it," Éloise said.

"I do, very much," he said. "It is always pleasant when a friend thinks of me." He spoke with a straight face. Éloise nodded. So did Galtier's children and their spouses. Most of his grandchildren were too young to care one way or the other. Decorum was preserved.

Later, when he was carrying booty out to the Chevrolet, Éloise said, "Could you give me a ride back to my house, *cher* Lucien? I would not care to impose on Dr. O'Doull to drive me both ways."

"It would be no trouble at all," Leonard O'Doull said politely.

"No, no, don't put yourself to the trouble," Galtier said. "Everyone has done so much for me today. It would be my pleasure to do this." His son-in-law let himself be persuaded.

"I hope you had a happy birthday," Éloise said as they rolled out of Rivière-du-Loup and into the countryside.

"Very happy." Now Lucien could admit it. He chuckled. "I have not had a surprise party since I was eight years old."

When they pulled up in front of her house, she smiled and asked, "And is there anything else you might like for your birthday?"

"It could be," he said. "Yes, it could be." They went inside together.

Except from the roof of the U.S. embassy, the Stars and Stripes had not flown in Richmond for almost eighty years. Only a handful of ancient men and women remembered the days when Virginia was one of the United States. Now, though, as Jake Featherston waited in the June heat inside the railroad station to receive the special train southbound from Washington, U.S. and C.S. flags flew side by side throughout the Confederate capital. No president of the United States had ever made an official visit to Richmond . . . till now.

Featherston wore the uniform of a Freedom Party guard, almost identical in cut and color to that of the Confederate Army. The summerweight cotton cloth was cooler and more comfortable than a suit would have been. With Jake's rangy height, the uniform was also much more impressive on him.

Photographers snapped away. Newsreel cameras ground out footage. Reporters waited for quotes. Jake reminded himself that he had to be extra careful about what he did and said in public. The Confederate press crews would make him look and sound the way he and Saul Goldman thought he should. The crews from the USA were a different story, though. Half—more than half—of them were here hoping to see him look and sound like a fool. And he couldn't keep them out of the CSA, not when President Smith was coming. *Just have to be smarter than they are,* he thought, and smiled a little nastily. *Shouldn't be hard.*

A stalwart in white shirt and butternut trousers put down a telephone and hurried over to him. "The train's about two minutes away, boss," he said.

"Thanks, Ozzie," Jake answered. The stalwart drew back. *Are you loyal?* Featherston wondered. *Are you really loyal?* Ever since Willy Knight tried to do him in, he'd wondered about almost everyone around him—everyone except Ferd Koenig and Saul Goldman and a handful of other old campaigners. He'd chosen his new vice president, a senator from Tennessee named Donald Partridge, not least because Don was an amiable nonentity who couldn't hope to threaten him.

Here came Al Smith's train. Schoolchildren on the platform started waving the Stars and Stripes and the Stars and Bars. A military band struck up "The Battle Cry of Freedom," a tune both sides had used—with different lyrics—during the War of Secession.

The train came to a stop. A colored attendant brought up the little stepped platform people used to descend to the station. Freedom Party guards—not stalwarts, who were less likely to be trustworthy—with submachine guns fanned out to make sure there were no unfortunate international incidents. The door to Smith's Pullman car opened. The first men out were the U.S. president's bodyguards. They wore civilian suits, not butternut uniforms, but otherwise were stamped from the same hard-faced mold as the Freedom Party men.

When President Smith himself emerged, the band began to play "The Star-Spangled Banner," a tune heard as seldom in Richmond as the Stars and Stripes were seen. Under a jaunty fedora, Smith's hair was snow white. He looked older and wearier than Jake Featherston had expected. But he managed a smile for the swarm of cameramen and reporters, and walked up to Jake with a friendly nod. "Pleased t'meetcha, Mr. President," he said.

"Right pleased to meet you, too, Mr. President," Jake answered. Flash photographs and the newsreel cameras recorded their handshake for posterity. Jake had heard Al Smith on the wireless and in newsreels. He'd found the other president's New York City accent hard to follow then. It proved no easier in person. Smith highlighted sounds anyone from the Confederate States would have swallowed, and chopped up what a Confederate would have stretched out.

"Looking forward to hashing things out wit' you," Smith said.

"Welcome to Richmond," Featherston said. "About time we did sit down and talk face to face. Best way to settle things." *Best way for you to give me what I want.*

"You betcha," Smith said. Jake took that to be agreement. The military band switched from the U.S. national anthem to "Dixie." President Smith took off his hat and stood at attention.

Also at attention beside him, Jake Featherston admitted to himself it was a nice touch. When the Confederate anthem ended, Jake said, "Shall we go on to the Gray House and do a little horse-trading?"

"That's a deal," Al Smith said.

Surrounded by bodyguards from both countries—who eyed one another almost as warily as they examined bystanders—the two presidents went out to Featherston's new limousine. The previous motorcar had been armored. This one could have been a barrel, except it didn't have a turret. Anyone who tried to murder the president of the CSA while he was in it was wasting his time.

Unfortunately, with the thick windows rolled up, traveling in the limousine was about as hot as traveling in a barrel. Al Smith promptly rolled his down a few inches. "They want to take a shot at me, they can take a shot at me," he said. "At least I won't roast."

"Suits me." Jake did his best to stay nonchalant. His guards and Smith's were probably all having conniptions. *Well, too damn bad,* he thought.

The parade route from the station to the Gray House jogged once. That way, Smith—and the reporters with him—didn't see the damage from an auto bomb Red Negroes had set off two days before. Featherston hated the black man who'd come up with that tactic. It did a lot of damage, it spread even more fear, and it was damned hard to defend against. Too many Negroes, too many motorcars—how could you check them all? You couldn't, worse luck.

If President Smith noticed the jog, he was too polite to say so. He smiled out at the flag-waving children and adults lining the route. "Nice crowd," he said, with no trace of irony Featherston could hear. Did that mean he didn't realize they'd been specially brought out for the occasion? Jake hoped so.

When they got to the Gray House, Smith stared at it with interest. *Comparing it to the White House,* Jake thought, *or to that place in Philadelphia.*

They posed for more pictures in the downstairs reception hall, and then in Jake's office. Then they shooed the photographers out of the room. "Care for a drink before we get down to business?" Featherston asked. He'd heard Al Smith could put it away pretty good, and he wasn't so bad himself.

"Sure. Why not?" the president of the USA said.

A colored servant brought a bottle of hundred-proof bourbon, some ice cubes, and two glasses. Jake did the honors himself. He raised his glass to Al Smith. "Mud in your eye," he said. They both drank.

"Ah!" Smith said. "That's the straight goods." He took another sip. Anyone that whiskey didn't faze had seen the bottom of more than one glass in his day, sure as hell.

After Featherston poured refills, he said, "You know what I want, Mr. President. You know what's right, too, by God." As far as he was concerned, the two were one and the same. "Let the people choose. We'll take our chances with that."

"And in the meantime, you'll keep murdering anybody in Kentucky and Houston who doesn't go along," Smith said.

"We haven't got anything to do with that." Jake lied without compunction.

The president of the USA let out a laugh that was half a cough. "My ass."

Featherston blinked. Nobody'd come right out and called him a liar for a long time. He said, "You're just afraid of a plebiscite on account of you know what'll happen."

"If I was afraid of a plebiscite, I wouldn't be here," Al Smith answered. "But if we go that way, I've got some conditions of my own."

"Let's hear 'em," Jake said. Maybe he wouldn't be able to grab everything on the table. If he got it served to him course by course, though, that would do.

"First thing is, no bloodshed in the time before the plebiscite," Smith said. "If people are going to vote, let 'em vote without being afraid."

"If you call a plebiscite, I expect the folks in the occupied states will be happy enough to go along with that," Featherston said at once. He could rein in most of his people, and say the ones he didn't rein in weren't his fault. Besides, everybody knew by now what the Freedom Party could do. It wouldn't have to add much more in the runup to a plebiscite to keep the message fresh.

"All right. Number two, then," Al Smith said. "You want the people to vote, the people should vote. All the people—everybody over twenty-one in Houston and Kentucky and Sequoyah."

"I've been saying that all along," Jake answered. Despite his thunderings, he didn't know if he would win in Sequoyah. Settlers from the USA had flooded into it since the war. Before, the Confederates had kept white settlement slow out of deference to the Five Civilized Tribes of Indians, who'd helped so much in the War of Secession. The United States had

always been hard on Indians, which was why the Creeks and the Chero-
kees and the rest were so loyal to the CSA.

But President Smith shook his head. "I don't think you get it. When I
say everybody, I mean *everybody*. Whites and Negroes."

"Whites *and* Negroes?" Jake was genuinely shocked. That hadn't
even occurred to him. "Niggers've never been able to vote in the CSA.
They sure as hell won't vote once they come back, either. Hell, they can't
vote in those states now."

"They'll vote in the plebiscite," Smith said. "They've got surnames
these days. We can keep track of 'em, make sure it's fair and honest. They
aren't slaves any more. In the USA, they're citizens, even if they don't
vote. If they're going to change countries, they have to be able to help
make the choice."

Jake considered. Smith had neatly turned the tables on him. He'd
been yelling, *Let the people vote!* Now Smith said, *Let* all *the people
vote!* How could he say no to that without looking like a fool? He
couldn't, and he knew it. "All right, goddammit," he ground out. That
made Sequoyah even iffier, but he didn't think it would hurt—except as
far as precedent went—in Kentucky or Houston.

Smith seemed a little surprised he'd accepted, even if grudgingly. He
gave his next condition: "Any state that changes hands stays demilitarized
for twenty-five years."

"That's a bargain." Jake didn't hesitate for even a moment there. He
knew he would break the deal inside of twenty-five days. He could
always manufacture incidents to give him an excuse—or maybe, if the
blacks got uppity, he wouldn't have to manufacture any. "What else?"

"These have to be your *last* demands as far as territorial changes go,"
Smith said. That would leave the United States with part of Virginia, part
of Arkansas, part of Sonora—maybe enough to claim they'd still made a
profit on the war.

"Well, of course," Featherston said, again without hesitation. *If I get
that much, I'll get the rest, too—you bet I will.* "Anything else?"

"Yes—one more thing," the U.S. president said. "We can announce
an agreement now, but I don't think the vote itself oughta come before
1941. We should have a proper campaign—let both sides be heard."

"What?" Featherston frowned, wondering what sort of fast one Smith
was trying to pull there. Then, suddenly, he laughed. Al Smith would run
for reelection in November. He wanted to be able to say he'd made peace
with the Confederate States, but he didn't want to have to hand over any
territory to them before Election Day. Afterwards, he'd have plenty of
time to repair the damage. *He thinks so, anyway.* "All right, Mr. President," Jake said. "You've got yourself a deal."

# XV

Anne Colleton had heard that people danced in the streets in Richmond when Woodrow Wilson declared war on the United States. Now the newsboys here shouted, "Plebiscite!"—and people danced in the street. Maybe that was because they thought there wouldn't be a war now. But maybe—and, odds were, more likely—it was because they thought the Confederate States would finally get back what they'd lost in the war.

She thought as much herself. She felt proud of herself for backing the right horse. Before the Freedom Party came to power, who would have believed the United States would ever even think of turning loose the lands they'd stolen from the CSA? But the stolen states had grown too hot to hold on to; the United States kept burning their fingers. And if that wasn't Jake Featherston's doing, whose was it? *The right horse, sure enough,* Anne thought smugly.

Celebrations in Capitol Square, across the street from Ford's Hotel, were noisy enough to keep her awake at night. She hadn't thought of that when she checked in. There were, of course, plenty of worse problems to have, even if she needed her sleep more regularly than she had when she was younger.

She was in Richmond to pay a call on the French embassy. Some of the men with whom she'd conferred in Paris years before had risen in prominence since. She could talk with one of them informally but still leave him certain he understood where the Confederate government stood. She hadn't had much chance to speak French lately, but she expected her accent wouldn't be too barbarous.

Across from the French embassy east of Capitol Square stood the much bigger building housing the U.S. embassy. A man-high fence of pointed iron palings protected the neoclassical white marble pile above which flew the Stars and Stripes. Anne understood why the U.S. embassy needed that kind of protection. How many times had her countrymen wanted to give it what they thought it deserved?

But not today. Today people cheered the U.S. military guards in their green-gray uniforms. The guards stood impassive at the entrance to the embassy. Their faces showed nothing of what they were thinking. All the same, Anne wondered what that would be. How happy did the prospect of a plebiscite in the annexed states make them?

*Not very, I hope.*

Colonel Jean-Henri Jusserand had been French military attaché in the Confederate States since sailing across the Atlantic with Anne aboard the *Charles XI.* "So good to see you again, *Mademoiselle* Colleton," he said, bowing over her hand. "It has been too long a time."

"Yes, I think so, too," she said. "I hope you are well?"

"I must confess, the weather here in summer is a trial," Jusserand replied. "Other than that, though, yes, thank you. And I must also say that I am full of admiration for the extraordinary achievement of your government. *C'est formidable!*"

"*Merci beaucoup,*" Anne said. "I hope that France will soon have similar good fortune with respect to Alsace and Lorraine."

Colonel Jusserand's narrow, intelligent face twisted. "Who can say? The Germans delay and delay. They delay endlessly. And we cannot even tax them for it overmuch, for the Kaiser delays dying. He delays and delays, delays—almost—endlessly. And while he is dying, what can be decided? Why, nothing, of course."

"There are ways to make them decide," Anne murmured.

"To go to war, do you mean?" the military attaché asked. Anne nodded. Jusserand sighed. "It is not so simple. I wish it were, but it is not. We have to know what the English will do, and the Russians, and the Italians. Until we are sure, how can we move? The *Boches* have beaten us twice in a lifetime. If we lose for a third time, we are ruined forever."

"When we came across the Atlantic from France to the Confederate States a few years ago, your country was ahead of mine," Anne said. "You poked and prodded at the Germans, while we could not do much with the United States. Things are different now. *C'est dommage.*"

The Frenchman's eyes flashed. "Yes, it is a pity," he agreed. "You will understand, I hope, that there are those who wish to move faster. And we wish to be certain that if we do move, we shall not move alone. If the United States are not distracted, if they land on our back while we face the German Empire . . ."

Anne had gone to the French embassy to pass along a message. Now she saw she was getting one in return. "I do not believe, my dear Colonel, that you need concern yourself on that score."

"Ah? *Vraiment?*" Colonel Jusserand looked alert. "May I pass this interesting news on to my superiors—unofficially, of course?"

"Yes—as long as it is unofficially," Anne answered.

He nodded. They understood each other. After some small talk, she stood to go. He bowed over her hand. He even kissed it. But it was politeness, and politeness only. No spark leaped. Anne could tell. That politeness felt like a little death. *Twenty years ago, he would have drunk champagne from my slipper,* she thought bitterly as she left the embassy. She hated the calendar, hated the mirror and what it showed her every morning. *A handsome woman, that's what you are.* She would almost rather have been ugly. Then she wouldn't have to remember the beauty she had been not so long ago.

She had walked to the French embassy. It was only three blocks from her hotel. She thought hard about taking a taxi back. All the heat and humidity had manifested themselves while she talked with Colonel Jusserand. The sun beat down from a sky like enameled brass. The air was thick as porridge. Sweat rivered off her and had nowhere to go. Every step felt enervating.

Stubbornly, she kept on. The hotel bar was air-conditioned. Just then, she would have crawled through broken glass to get out of the heat. Not many whites were on the sidewalks, though plenty drove past. But most of the pedestrians were Negroes.

By their clothes, a lot of them hadn't been in Richmond long. She had no trouble recognizing sharecroppers thrown off the land as farming grew increasingly mechanized. She'd seen plenty of them in St. Matthews. Some of them turned to odd jobs in town, others to petty theft. The big farms, the farms that raised cotton and tobacco and grain, seemed to get on fine without them. Tractors and harvesters could do the work of scores, even hundreds, of men.

" 'Scuse me, ma'am, but could you spare me a quarter?" a gaunt colored man asked, touching the brim of his straw hat. "I's powerful hungry."

Anne walked past him as if he didn't exist. She heard him sigh behind her. How many times had whites pretended not to see him? She didn't care if he thought she was heartless. He'd been old enough to carry a rifle in the uprisings during the war. As far as she was concerned, that meant she couldn't trust him. She was glad a good number of policemen and Freedom Party stalwarts tramped along the streets.

She walked past three or four more black beggars before getting back to Ford's Hotel. One of them cursed softly when she went by without taking notice of him. He couldn't have been in Richmond long, or he would have got used to being ignored. At the hotel, the colored doorman in his magnificent uniform smiled and bowed as he held the door open for her. Before the war, she would have taken that subservience as no less than her due. Now she wondered what lay behind it—wondered and had no trouble coming up with a nasty answer.

When she strode into the bar, she let out a sigh of relief. The cold air gushing from the vents seemed a blessing from on high. She ordered a gin and tonic and took the drink back to a small table. Five minutes later, she was fighting not to shiver. She'd never imagined that air conditioning could be too effective, but it was here. She felt as if she'd gone from sub-tropical Richmond to somewhere just north of the Arctic Circle.

A bespectacled officer—a colonel, she saw by the three stars on his collar tabs—sitting at the bar picked up his drink and carried it over to her table. "May I join you?" he asked, his accent sounding more like a Yankee's than that of a man from the CSA.

"Clarence!" she said, and sprang to her feet to give him a hug. "Wonderful to see you again—it's been years. I remember when you got your name in the papers at the Olympics, but I'd forgotten they put you back in uniform."

"Had to find something to do with me," Clarence Potter answered lightly, but with a hint of bitterness underneath. "How have you been, Anne? You still look damn good."

She couldn't remember the last time a man told her something like that and sounded as if he meant it. When she and Clarence had briefly been lovers down in South Carolina, nothing personal drove them apart, but she'd backed the Freedom Party while he despised Jake Featherston. Despite the saying, politics had unmade them as bedfellows.

"I'm—well enough," she said. She and Potter both sat down. She couldn't help asking, "What do you think of the plebiscites?"

"I'm amazed," he said simply. "If you'd told me five years ago that we could annoy the United States into calling elections they're bound to lose, if you'd told me we could get Kentucky back without going to war, I would have said you were out of your ever-loving mind. That's what I would have said, but I would have been wrong."

Not many men, as Anne knew too well, ever admitted they were wrong for any reason. All the same, she couldn't help asking, "And what do you think of the president now? He's sharper than you figured."

"I never figured he wasn't sharp. I figured he was crazy." Potter didn't hold his voice down. He'd never been shy about saying what he thought, and he'd never worried much about what might come after that. After a sip at his own drink—another gin and tonic, Anne saw—he went on, "If he is crazy, though, he's crazy like a fox, so maybe I'm the one who was crazy all along. You can't argue with what he's accomplished."

She noticed he still separated the accomplishments from the man. In the CSA these days, people were encouraged—to put it mildly—to think of Jake Featherston and his accomplishments as going together. No, Clarence had never been one to join the common herd. Anne didn't mind that; neither had she. "What are you doing in the Army these days?" she asked.

"Intelligence, same as before," he answered, and then not another word. Given the four he had used, that wasn't surprising. After a moment, he asked a question of his own: "Why did you come up to Richmond?"

*"Parce que je peut parler français bien,"* she said.

It didn't faze him. He nodded as if she'd given him a puzzle piece he needed. He hesitated again, then asked, "How long are you going to be here?"

"Another few days." She looked him in the eye. "Shall we make the most of it?" She'd never been coy, and the older she got, the less point to it she saw.

That didn't faze him, either. He nodded again. "Why not?" he said.


Colonel Irving Morrell didn't think he'd ever seen people dance in the streets before, not outside of a bad musical comedy on the cinema screen. Here in Lubbock, people were dancing in the streets, dancing and singing, "Plebiscite!" and, "Yanks out!" and whatever other lovely lyrics they could make up.

The people of the state of Houston had been his fellow citizens ever since it joined the USA after the Great War. If he'd been carrying a machine gun instead of the .45 on his belt, he would have gunned down every single one of them he saw, and he would have smiled while he did it, too.

Sergeant Michael Pound, who strode down the sidewalk with him, was every bit as appalled as he was. "What are they going to do with us, sir, once we have to get out of this state?" the gunner asked.

"I don't know," Morrell said tightly. He'd tried not to think about that. He couldn't help thinking about it, but he'd done his best not to.

Sergeant Pound, on the other hand, seemed to take a perverse pleasure in analyzing what had just happened. *He probably enjoys picking scabs off to watch things bleed, too,* Morrell thought. "This is a defeat, sir—nothing but a defeat," Pound said. "How many divisions would those Confederate sons of bitches have needed to run us out of here? More than they've got, by God—I'll tell you that."

"Democracy," Morrell answered. "Will of the people. President Smith says so."

Before Sergeant Pound could reply—could say something that might perhaps have been prejudicial to good discipline—one of the local revelers whirled up to the U.S. soldiers and jeered, "Now you damnyankee bastards can get your asses out of Texas and go to hell where you belong."

Colonel Morrell did not pause to discuss the niceties of the situation with him. He punched him in the nose instead. Sergeant Pound kicked the reveler on the way down. He didn't get up again.

"Anybody else?" Morrell asked. The .45 had left its holster and appeared in his right hand with almost magical speed.

Before President Smith and President Featherston agreed on the plebiscite, the U.S. officer would have touched off a riot by slugging a Houstonian. Now the rest of the dancers left him and Sergeant Pound alone. They'd already got most of what they wanted, and Morrell knew they would get the rest as soon as the votes from the plebiscite were counted. And most of them didn't want to give the U.S. Army big, overt provocations any more. Those could jeopardize what they'd been screaming for.

Sergeant Pound must have been thinking along with Morrell, for he said, "Freedom Party goons will probably thump that big-mouthed son of a bitch harder than we ever did."

"Good," Morrell said, and said no more.

A woman—a genteel-looking, middle-aged woman—said something inflammatory about U.S. soldiers and their affections for their mothers. Morrell still held the .45 in his hand. Ever so slightly, his index finger tightened on the trigger. He willed it to relax. After a few seconds, the rebellious digit obeyed his will.

An Army truck took Morrell and Pound out of Lubbock and back to the Army base outside of town. As far as Morrell could tell, Army bases and colored districts were the only parts of Houston where anybody still gave a damn about the USA.

A young lieutenant waylaid Morrell as soon as he jumped down from the truck. "Sir, Brigadier General MacArthur wants to see you in his office right away."

"Thank you," Morrell said, in lieu of something more pungent. Sergeant Pound went on his way, a free man. Morrell sighed. The guards outside MacArthur's office glowered at him despite his uniform as he approached, but relaxed and passed him through when they recognized him and decided he wasn't an assassin in disguise. He saluted Daniel MacArthur. "Reporting as ordered, sir."

The lantern-jawed U.S. commander in Houston returned the salute, then waved Morrell to a chair. "Easier to fiddle sitting down while Rome burns, eh, Colonel?"

"Sir, I just had the pleasure of coldcocking one of those goddamn Houstonian bastards." Morrell explained exactly what he'd done on the streets of Lubbock, and why. The only thing he didn't do was name Michael Pound. The responsibility was his, not the sergeant's.

MacArthur heard him out. "I have two things to say about that," the general said when he was done. "The first is, by this time tomorrow Jake Featherston's pet wireless stations will be baying about another damnyankee atrocity in the occupied lands."

Morrell's opinion about where the president of the CSA could stick his wireless stations was anatomically improbable, but no less heartfelt on account of that. "Sideways," he added.

"Indeed." Daniel MacArthur stuck a cigarette into the long, long holder he affected. He lit it and blew out a cloud of smoke. "The second thing I have to say, Colonel, is that I'm jealous. You have no idea how jealous I am. You keep managing to hit back, while I've had to turn the other cheek again and again and again. It's enough to make me wonder about Christianity; it truly is."

"Er, yes, sir," Morrell said, not knowing how else to respond to that. "On the whole, though, things have been a lot quieter since President Smith agreed to the plebiscite."

"Of *course* they have!" Brigadier General MacArthur exploded. "The miserable fool has given the Confederate States exactly what they've always wanted. Is it any wonder that they're willing to take it?"

"No wonder at all," Morrell agreed. "Sir, if Smith had told Featherston to go jump in a lake, do you think the Confederates would have gone to war with us over Houston and Kentucky and Sequoyah?"

"I would have liked to see them try," MacArthur answered with a contemptuous snort. "I don't care how fast they're rearming. There is such a thing as fighting out of your weight. That's what infuriates me so: they'll likely win with the ballot box what they couldn't on the battlefield."

Morrell wondered about that. Hadn't Houston and Kentucky and Sequoyah *been* battlefields for the past several years? That was the way it seemed to him. The Confederates' sympathizers had taken a lot more casualties than they'd inflicted on the U.S. Army and U.S. sympathizers in the disputed states, but they hadn't cared. They'd thought it was all worthwhile. The United States hadn't held the same opinion about the losses they'd suffered. In the end, that made all the difference.

Daniel MacArthur saw things the same way. "We have sustained a total, unmitigated defeat," he said. Michael Pound had said the same thing, without the fancy adjectives. Being a general entitled MacArthur to use them. In fine rhetorical fettle, he went on, "Do not let us blind our-selves. The road to the Ohio, the road that points to Pittsburgh and the Great Lakes, has been broken. Throughout these days, the president has believed in addressing Mr. Featherston with the language of sweet rea-sonableness. I have always believed he was more open to the language of the mailed fist."

"Yes, sir," Morrell said. "I wish I could have punched him instead of that fanatic a little while ago."

"Punched whom?" MacArthur asked. "Smith or Featherston?"

That was an interesting question—to say nothing of inflammatory. It was so interesting, Morrell pretended he hadn't heard it. He asked a ques-tion of his own: "If things really have quieted down around here, sir, what do we do till they finally hold the plebiscite?"

"We get ready to leave," MacArthur said bluntly. "Or do you think the USA will win the vote?"

"If we were going to win this vote, sir, they wouldn't need the Army to hold the lid on here," Morrell said.

MacArthur nodded. "That's how I see it, too. The other thing we'll do is make sure all the eligible niggers in Houston come out and vote in the plebiscite."

"It won't help," Morrell said. "We'll still lose."

"I am aware of that, thank you." Daniel MacArthur might have been talking to the village idiot. Colonel Morrell's ears heated. His superior went on, "Nevertheless, the more independence those people show, the more trouble they'll cause the Confederate State after we lose the elec-tion."

"Well, yes, sir," Morrell allowed. "But they won't cause all *that* much trouble, on account of there aren't enough of them in Houston. And the Confederates have never been shy about shooting Negroes whenever they thought they needed to. With Featherston in the saddle, they don't even think twice."

"Have you any other observations to make?" MacArthur asked icily.

"No, sir." Morrell knew he couldn't very well observe that Brigadier General MacArthur had a thin skin and couldn't stand having anybody disagree with him. It was true enough—MacArthur's chagrin just now showed how true it was—but the other officer would only get angrier if he said so.

Sure enough, MacArthur imperiously—and imperially—pointed toward the door with the cigarette holder. "In that case, Colonel, you are dismissed."

Morrell gave him a salute extravagant in its adoration. His about-face would have won praise from a drill sergeant on a West Point parade ground. As he marched out of the brigadier general's office, though, he reflected that he was probably wasting irony. MacArthur would accept the gestures as no less than his due. Back during the war, General Custer had shown the same sort of blindness.

Come to think of it, MacArthur had served under Custer during the war. Had he learned that sort of arrogance from the past master? Possible, Morrell decided, but not likely. Odds were MacArthur would have been a cocksure son of a bitch even if he'd never met George Armstrong Custer.

The guards outside the office saluted Morrell. He returned their salutes in proper casual style. They hadn't done anything to raise his blood pressure. No, that distinction belonged to the U.S. commandant in Houston—and to all the Houstonians who didn't want to belong to the United States. He blamed them less than he blamed Daniel MacArthur. He and MacArthur were supposed to be on the same side.

Instead of going back to BOQ and getting drunk at the bar or brooding in his hot, airless little cubicle, Morrell headed over to the barrel park. The big, lumbering machines were always breaking down. Even when they weren't broken down, they needed constant maintenance to keep running the way they were supposed to. Getting his hands and his uniform dirty was at least as good a way of blowing off steam as getting a snootful of whiskey—and he wouldn't have a thick head in the morning, either.

He wasn't surprised to find Michael Pound in the barrel park fiddling with a carburetor. "Hello, sir," the sergeant said. "And how is the Grand High Panjandrum today?"

"I'm going to pretend I didn't hear that," Morrell said, sternly suppressing the urge to snicker. "And you're goddamn lucky I'm going to pretend I didn't hear it, too."

"Yes, sir," Sergeant Pound said innocently. "Well, in that case, how is Brigadier General MacArthur?" He sounded no more respectful than he had a moment earlier.

Since Irving Morrell wasn't feeling particularly respectful toward the commandant, he overlooked the sergeant's tone this time. "Brigadier General MacArthur doubts that the USA can win the upcoming plebiscite," Morrell said. "He is unhappy about returning Houston to the CSA." That was like canned rations—it kept the substance and lost the flavor. And was there any U.S. soldier in Houston happy about returning Houston to the Confederacy? If there was, Morrell hadn't met him.

Sergeant Pound asked, "Does he suggest anything we can actually do about it?"

"Such as?" Morrell said. "President Smith has the right to do what he wants here. If he thinks a plebiscite is a good idea, he can order one."

"If he thinks a plebiscite is a good idea, he's an idiot," Pound said. "We'll pay for it down the road. Probably not very far down the road, either."

Once more, Morrell wished he thought the sergeant was wrong.

Colonel Clarence Potter was about as happy as a naturally dour man could be. Part of his somber joy came from the upcoming plebiscite. For more than twenty years, he'd wanted to see the stolen states brought back into the Confederacy, and now it seemed they would be. He gave Jake Featherston all the credit in the world for that. He gave it reluctantly, but not insincerely. He'd thought Jake was out of his mind. Maybe Jake was, but he'd read Al Smith like a book.

And part of Potter's present happiness had very little to do with Jake Featherston—at least directly. He'd never been a man who had extraordinary luck with women. He'd never married, and he'd never come particularly close to marrying. Like a fisherman, he had sometimes talked about the one that got away. For him, that had been Anne Colleton.

They'd always got on well down in South Carolina. But he hadn't been able to stand the Freedom Party, and she'd ended up backing it. That had been plenty to keep the two of them from staying together. Potter had thought he would never see her again, except possibly over gunsights—and he hadn't been sure which of them would be aiming the gun.

Now . . . Now, lazy in the afterglow, he sprawled on the bed in Ford's Hotel. "You see?" he said. "You just wanted me to tell you I was wrong."

"Well, of course," Anne answered, and poked him in the ribs. "What else does a woman want to hear from a man?"

"How about, 'I love you'? How about, 'You're beautiful'?" Potter suggested.

"Those are nice, too," she agreed with a smile. "As far as I'm concerned, though, nothing's better than, 'You were right.' "

He believed her. He didn't tell her so. She was too likely to take it the wrong way, to think he meant she was tough and bossy. And, as a matter of fact, he *did* think she was tough and bossy. To his way of thinking, though, that was a compliment. He had as little use for a woman who couldn't take care of herself as for a man who couldn't take care of himself.

"You *are* beautiful, you know," he said.

The smile didn't just fade. It blew out like a candle flame. "I used to be," she said bleakly. "You don't need to butter me up, Clarence. I know what's there when I look in the mirror."

"You're not young any more. So what?" Potter shrugged. The motion made the mattress shake beneath him. "I'm no spring chicken these days, either. And have you looked at *all* of you in a mirror lately?" He ran a hand along the length of her. "You've got nothing to worry about."

"Like hell I don't," Anne said. "My tits sag, I'm thick in the middle, and I'm spread in the butt."

"You're not young any more. So what?" he said again. "You still look damn good. I might lie, but do you think *he* would? He's either sincere or he doesn't work at all, especially at my age."

Anne laughed. A moment later, though, she rolled over onto her stomach and started sobbing into her pillow. Startled, Potter put a hand on her shoulder. She shook it off.

"What's the matter?" he asked, honestly bewildered.

"You son of a bitch," she said, her voice muffled. "I don't remember the last time a man made me cry. I didn't think anybody could any more. And then you went and did it."

"I didn't mean to," he said.

"I know." She sat up, a wry smile on her tear-streaked face. "If you'd been trying, you couldn't have done it in a million years. You caught me off-guard—and look what happened."

"No, no, no." Potter shook his head. "That's what the United States are supposed to say to us one of these days."

Anne laughed, but she nodded, too. "Oh, yes." She leaned forward. He'd caught her interest in a different way—which was probably just as well, since he wasn't good for more than one round a day himself any more. She asked, "How likely is it? How soon?"

He shrugged again. "All I know is what I read in the newspapers, like that comic from Sequoyah says."

Anne Colleton laughed again, this time at him. "Tell me another one, *Colonel* Potter. If you can't tell me, who can?"

"The president, most likely," Potter answered. "But believe me, he doesn't confide in colonels." That wasn't altogether true. From things Potter had heard, and from others that had crossed his desk, he could make what he thought were some pretty good guesses about how things might go. He didn't tell her what they were. With another woman, he would have been joking about the president. But Anne knew Jake Featherston. Could Jake put her up to finding out whether one Clarence Potter, colonel in Intelligence, ran off at the mouth? Potter didn't think so, but he wasn't a hundred percent sure.

She pointed an accusing, red-tipped fingernail at him. "So you won't talk, eh?"

"Not me. Not a word. Nothing but name, rank, and pay number." He rattled them off. "Wild horses couldn't pull more out of me."

"Who said anything about wild horses?" Anne's voice went soft and breathy. A mischievous glint sparked in her eyes. "Wild horses went out with the covered wagons. What we do these days is . . ." She started doing it.

After a while, Potter discovered there were still days when he was good for more than one round—with sufficient encouragement, that is. Panting, his heart pounding, he said, "My goodness. Torture's certainly come up in the world since the last time I ran into it."

"I should hope so. This is a high-class outfit here." As if to prove as much, Anne pulled up the sheet and daintily dabbed at her chin. Then she assumed what she fondly imagined to be a U.S. accent and said, "So tell me the score, Colonel."

"If it's all the same to you, I think I'd rather hold out for more torture," he said.

She poked him in the ribs again, hard enough to come closer to torture than he'd looked for. "Monster!" she said. He made as if to salute. She made as if to poke him one more time. Instead, she aimed that forefinger at him once more, this time as if it were the barrel of a Tredegar. "All right, you . . . you impossible person. Be that way. Don't tell me what you know. Tell me what you think. You can't get in trouble for thinking."

As seriously as he could, Potter answered, "I think that, if I tell you what I think, I'll get in trouble for telling you what I think." She started to get angry. So did he. He went on, "Dammit, Anne, what do you think my job is? Finding out secrets and keeping them, that's what. How long do you think I could do it if I ran my mouth like a heavy freight tearing downhill with the brakes gone?"

Every once in a while, when she heard the plain truth, it would disarm her completely. Clarence remembered that from the days of their unhappy affair in South Carolina. It was one of the things he'd liked most about her then. Now he saw it again. "I hadn't looked at it like that," she admitted in a small voice. "Never mind."

He sat up in bed, put on his glasses, and swung his feet down to the carpet, still wondering whether he'd passed his own test, hers, or Jake Featherston's. Through the gauzy curtains on the window, he could see people bustling along the paths in Capitol Square and others lying on the grass in the shade of the trees, doing their best to fight the oppressive weather.

On the sidewalk down below the window, a Negro said, "Spare some change for a hungry man? . . . Spare some change for a hungry man? . . . Spare some change for—? Oh, God bless you, ma'am!"

"I wouldn't give a nigger a dime," Anne said coldly. "I wouldn't give a nigger a penny, by God. If they can't find work, to hell with them. Let 'em starve."

Clarence judiciously pursed his lips. "A lot more of them looking for work these days, you know, with tractors and farm machinery driving sharecroppers off the land."

"Yes, I've seen that. So what?" she said. "If they can't figure out some way or another to make themselves useful, who needs them? The whole country would be better off without them."

"Would it? I wonder. Who'd do the nigger work without niggers?"

"Machines could do a lot of it, the way they do on a farm," Anne answered.

"Some of it, anyway," Clarence admitted. "But where are you going to get a machine that waits on tables or cuts somebody's hair? If we didn't have niggers, whites would need to do things like that." He started getting dressed.

"It could happen," Anne said stubbornly. "I do all sorts of things for myself I used to have servants do back before the war."

"I suppose so," Potter said. "Nigger work must get done in the USA, too, and they don't have that many niggers to do it. But things are different here. An awful lot of whites here say, 'I may be poor and stupid, but by God I'm white, and I'm better off than those niggers, and I don't have to do the things they do.' " Slyly, he added, "An awful lot of them vote Freedom, too."

Anne Colleton didn't rise to the bait. She just nodded. "I know they do. But if they didn't have any choice, they'd do what needs doing. If we had another war, we could even make them feel patriotic about doing what needs doing."

At first, Potter thought that was one of the most monstrously cynical things he'd ever heard, and he'd heard some doozies. Then he realized that, no matter how cynical it was, it probably wasn't wrong. He leaned over and kissed her. "Do you want to write that down and pass it on to the president, or do you want me to do it?" he asked.

"Whichever you please," she answered. "But what do you want to bet he's already thought of it himself?"

Clarence thought it over. He didn't need to think very long. "I won't touch that one," he said. "You're bound to be right." Featherston was plenty cynical enough to use patriotism to get people to do what he wanted—and plenty good enough at leading to get them to follow.

"One of us ought to do it," Anne said, "just on the off chance it hasn't occurred to him."

"I'll take care of it, then," Potter said, knotting his butternut tie. "Unless you really want to, I mean."

"No, it's all right. Go ahead." Anne laughed. "The funny thing is, here we are, both trying to give him good advice, and he doesn't trust either one of us as far as he can throw us."

"We've known him too long, and we've known him too well, and at one point or another we've both stood up and told him no," Potter said. "That doesn't happen to him very often, and he doesn't much like it."

"True." Anne laughed again, on a lower, less amused, note. "And now we're both following his orders even so. Everybody follows his orders these days."

"He's the president." Potter set his shiny-peaked officer's cap on his head. "He's the president, and he's been right. How do you lick a combination like that? As far as I can see, you're better off joining him."

Would he have said that before Jake Featherston brought him back into the Army? He knew he wouldn't. But that was almost four years ago now. And in serving Featherston, he also served his country. His country counted most. So he told himself, and told himself, and. . . .

G eorge Enos carefully coiled the last line that had held *Sweet Sue* to T Wharf. The fishing boat's diesel rumbled under his feet. Pungent exhaust poured from the stack. The *Sweet Sue* began to move, although for the first few seconds it seemed more as if the boat were standing still and the wharf sliding away from it. But then there could be no doubt. The fishing boat was leaving Boston and Boston harbor behind. George let out a slightly hung-over sigh of relief.

He'd been putting to sea for his entire adult life, almost half of his thirty years, but he'd never been so glad to watch his home town slide below the horizon as he had this past year and a little more. If he didn't have to look at Boston, he didn't have to be reminded—so much—of the place where that writer son of a bitch had shot his mother and then shot himself. He'd told her Ernie was no goddamn good for her, told her and told her. His sister had told her the same thing. Fat lot of good it did.

*I shouldn't have just talked,* he thought for the thousandth time. *I should have kicked the crap out of that bastard.* His fists clenched. His jaw knotted. His teeth ground. He hadn't done it, and it was too late now. It would always be too late.

He was so lost in his own gloom, he jumped when somebody clapped him on the back. "How you doin' Junior?" Johnny O'Shea asked.

"I'm all right, Johnny," George answered. It wasn't really true, but the older man couldn't do anything about what ailed him. Nobody could, not even himself.

"You looked a little green there," O'Shea said, fiddling with one upturned end of his old-fashioned gray Kaiser Bill mustache. He was a wiry little fellow whose strength and endurance belied his sixty years. He and a few other old-timers who'd known George's father were the only ones who called him Junior. George didn't mind. Anything that helped him connect to his old man was welcome. George had only vague memories of him. He'd been just seven when that Confederate submersible sank the USS *Ericsson*. Before that, his father had been in the Navy or on a fishing boat most of the time.

*If the* Sweet Sue *sinks tomorrow, my kids won't remember me at all. They're too little.* That was a hell of a cheerful thought with which to put to sea.

He realized he hadn't answered Johnny. "A little too much beer last night, that's all," he said. "I'll be all right." Talking about the other would have shown weakness. He refused.

O'Shea's laugh showed missing teeth, a few stubs stained almost the color of tobacco juice, and a plug of chewing tobacco big enough to choke a Clydesdale. "A little too much beer?" he said. "A little? Sweet Jesus Christ, what a milk-and-cookies lot we've raised up to take our places when we're gone. When I was your age and I'd be going out to sea the next morning, I'd drink till I couldn't see and fuck till I couldn't get it up for a month afterwards and let the skipper worry about having me on board when we got going. If you're gonna do these things, for God's sake do 'em right."

George had made sure Connie had something to remember him by, too. That was one of the reasons he hadn't drunk too much to excess. If you didn't know who you were, your John Henry wouldn't know who he was, either.

He was damned if he felt like talking about what he'd done in the bedroom, though. Instead, his voice sly, he asked, "How about last night for you, then?"

"Oh, I got drunk," O'Shea said. "Take enough aspirins, drink enough coffee, and that ain't so bad the next day. And I found me a girl, too. But I'll tell you something, Junior, and it's a goddamn fact. Enough fucking so you can't get it up for the next month is a hell of a lot less when you're my age than it is when you're yours." He spat a stream of tobacco juice into the sea.

A lot of men would have sounded bitter saying something like that.

Johnny O'Shea thought it was funny. He slapped George on the back and went off to chin with one of the other fishermen.

He got even less in the way of response from Carlo Lombardi than he had from George. Aspirins and coffee might have been enough to beat Johnny's hangover, but Carlo looked as if he'd been ridden hard and put away wet. Under his perennial five-o'-clock shadow, his face was fish-belly pale. He had a hat jammed down low over his eyes to shield them from the sun, and they were nothing but bloodshot slits. He answered O'Shea in monosyllables, and then stopped answering him at all. Johnny thought that was funny, too. George didn't. He'd been where Carlo was a few times—well, maybe more than a few times—and he hadn't enjoyed it a bit.

A couple of the other fishermen looked as much the worse for wear as Lombardi. By the time they got out to the Grand Bank, they'd be sober enough. The only liquor aboard the *Sweet Sue* was a bottle of medicinal brandy under lock and key in the galley. Every so often, Captain Albert would dole out a nip as a reward for a job well done. Davey Hatton, whose territory the galley was, had also been known to pour out a little brandy every now and then, but that was unofficial, even if the skipper winked at it.

Back in George's father's day, most fishing boats leaving T Wharf had made for Georges Bank, about five hundred miles offshore. Some still did, but Georges Bank had been fished so hard for so long, it didn't yield what it had. The Grand Bank, though, out by Newfoundland, seemed inexhaustible. Some people said Basque fishermen had been taking cod and tuna there since before Columbus discovered America. George Enos didn't know anything about that one way or the other. He did know there were a hell of a lot of fish left.

Boston sank below the edge of the sea. He wasn't sorry to see it go, or all the little islands that marked the way into the harbor. A couple of miles off to port, a U.S. Navy minesweeper—not a very big warship, but a giant when measured against fishing boats—opened up with its guns. A few seconds later, a big column of water rose from the Atlantic. The flat, harsh crack of the explosion took ten or twelve seconds to reach the *Sweet Sue*. When it did, Carlo Lombardi looked as if he wished his head would fall off, or maybe as if it just had.

George felt the blast in his teeth and sinuses, too. Even so, he nodded in satisfaction. "There's one mine we won't have to worry about any more," he muttered. During the war, the USA had mined the approaches to Boston harbor to a faretheewell, to make sure Confederate and British raiders and submarines couldn't sneak in and raise hell. And the Confederates had sown mines to give U.S. shipping a hard time.

Some of those mines still floated in place. Some of the ones that had been moored came loose with the passage of years and drifted free, a menace to navigation. Fishing boats and the occasional freighter blew up and sank with all hands. Finding mines and disposing of them had kept the Navy hopping since the end of the war.

And how long would it be before the Navy stopped sweeping for mines and started laying them again? George didn't like the headlines coming out of the states that had changed hands between the CSA and the USA. President Smith was loudly declaring he'd removed the last reasons for war on the North American continent. George hoped he was right. As far as he could see, everybody hoped the president was right.

Gulls glided along overhead. They always followed fishing boats, hoping for handouts from the garbage and offal that went over the side. They did better when the boats were farther out to sea and actually fishing, but that didn't keep them from being optimistic whenever they saw fishermen.

George stopped in the cramped little galley for a mug of coffee. He took it up to the *Sweet Sue*'s bow and drank it there. The hot, sweet, creamy brew and the fresh breeze from the fishing boat's passage helped submerge the last of his headache. His cure wasn't so drastic as Johnny O'Shea's, but he hadn't hurt himself so badly the night before, either.

Going out to the Grand Bank was a long haul. Once the ocean surrounded the *Sweet Sue* on all sides, she might not have been moving at all. No landscape changed to prove she was. Every so often, she would pass an inbound fishing boat. Captain Albert would get on the wireless then, doing his best to find out exactly where the fish were biting best.

*When my old man went to sea, his boat didn't even have wireless,* George thought. He remembered his mother saying his father hadn't know that crazy Serb had blown up the Austrian archduke till he got back to T Wharf after a fishing trip. And when a Confederate commerce raider captured him and sank his boat, his skipper back then hadn't been able to yell for help. He'd been interned in North Carolina for months before the Confederates finally let him go.

On George's first night in the tiny, cramped bunk up at the bow, he tossed and turned and slept very badly. He always did his first night at sea. He'd got used to a bed that didn't shift under him, to one where he could roll over without falling out, to one where he could sit up suddenly without banging his head—hell, to one with Connie in it, sweet and warm and mostly willing. He knew he'd be all right tomorrow, but tonight was tough.

More coffee persuaded his eyes they really did want to stay open the next morning. He poured in the cream as if there were no tomorrow. So did everybody else. Even on ice, it wouldn't stay fresh through the cruise, so they enjoyed it while they could. By the same token, Davey Hatton did up enormous plates of scrambled eggs for the fishermen.

"By God, Cookie, yesterday I'd've puked these up," Johnny O'Shea said. "This morning, they're goddamn good." He shoveled another forkful into his face.

Hatton was a round, red-faced man with a barbed wit. "If somebody'd lit a match under your nose yesterday, he could've used your breath for a blowtorch," he replied. "Today you're on your way to remembering your name."

"Fuck you," Johnny said sweetly.

The cook nodded. "There—you see? I knew that was it." The men in the crowded galley laughed. Even Johnny laughed—he knew he'd lost that round.

When the *Sweet Sue* finally got out to the Grand Bank, there was little more time for laughter. Boats from the USA, the CSA, the Republic of Quebec, occupied Canada and Newfoundland, Britain, Ireland, France, and Portugal bobbed here and there on the ocean. Captain Albert found a place at the edge of one pack of boats and started fishing.

George lost track of how many big hooks he baited with frozen squid. The process was as automatic as breathing for him. If he'd thought about it, he probably would have stuck himself. Every so often, somebody did. Then it was the nasty business of pushing the barb through and snipping it off, the even nastier business of iodine, and, if a man hadn't had one in a while, a tetanus shot from the first-aid kit. And, with his hand bandaged, he'd go back to fixing hooks.

But when the lines came in . . . when the lines came in, work really started. Gaffing a wriggling tuna that weighed as much as a man, gutting it, kicking the offal over the side, and getting the fish into the ice in the hold went on hour after hour. Sometimes it wouldn't be a tuna—it would be a tuna head, proof that a shark had found the fish first. Off the hook, over the side. Sometimes a shark would be on the hook. Gaff him, gut him so he stayed dead, and pitch him overboard.

The endless fishing went on for the next three weeks. By then, the *Sweet Sue* had more than twenty tons of tuna in her hold and rode noticeably lower in the water than she had when she set out from T Wharf. George still didn't know how good a trip it was. He wouldn't till the skipper sold the tuna. But he knew he was finally ready to head back to Boston. After all, he had to remind his kids who he was.

Brigadier General Abner Dowling was not a happy man. He felt betrayed not only by the War Department—which would have been nothing tremendously unusual—but also by the entire government of the United States. Having the whole government gang up on him didn't happen every day.

But Dowling certainly felt it had happened here. He'd come to Covington to help keep Kentucky in the United States. He'd got a good start on doing just that, too. And then Al Smith had jerked the rug out from under him by going to Richmond and agreeing to a plebiscite. The only way the USA could win that plebiscite would be for Jesus Christ to appear in Louisville and curse Jake Featherston with words that glowed like burning coals—and even then it would be close.

Now, ironically, what Dowling was watching over was the presidential election campaign. Up till Al Smith said there would be a plebiscite after all, he couldn't have got elected dog catcher in Kentucky. Now Red Socialist posters were everywhere in Covington. They showed Smith's face and the slogan, THE HAPPY WARRIOR—HE'S KEPT US OUT OF WAR. More went up all the time, too.

The Democrats were running Senator Bob Taft—son of longtime Congressman William Howard Taft—from across the river in Ohio. In a normal year, he would have scored well in conservative Kentucky. This wasn't a normal year, nor was Kentucky a normal state. The Freedom Party had ambushed the local Democrats from the right, and the Freedom Party, taking its cue from Richmond, was loudly for Smith.

Besides, Taft had denounced the plebiscite. Like most Democrats, he remained in favor of holding on to the gains the USA had made in the Great War. That would have doomed him here anyway.

"Isn't it grand?" Dowling said at supper one evening. "Kentucky will vote Socialist in February, and then it'll vote Freedom in January. Tell me how that makes sense."

All the officers with whom he was eating were junior to him, of course. None of them ventured to claim that it didn't make sense, or that he was worrying too much. A major did say, "At least the Freedom Party is on its best behavior from now until January."

"Bully!" Dowling exploded, which made the younger officers look at one another. He caught the looks, and knew why they made them. They didn't say *bully*, and they thought only dinosaurs—anyone who remembered the nineteenth century certainly qualified—did. Dowling was too exercised to care. He went on, "Of course those bastards will be on their best behavior. They don't have to blow things up any more to get what they want. All they have to do is wait. Wouldn't you be on your best behavior, too?"

"Uh, yes, sir," the major replied. "The only trouble is, their being quiet goes a long way toward making our presence here irrelevant, wouldn't you say?"

"Like hell I would," Dowling growled. "If we weren't here, if we weren't doing the job we're supposed to do, how much worse would things be?"

The major, being only a major, did not presume to contradict. That helped ease Dowling's mind—a little. He kept up a bold front not least for the sake of the men he commanded. He wasn't about to admit he thought his presence in Kentucky was irrelevant. He wouldn't admit it to anyone but himself, anyhow.

When he looked at the name of the man with whom he had his first appointment the next morning, it rang a bell. He went through some files and nodded to himself. The homework he'd done before taking command in Covington had paid off. "Good morning, Mr. Wood," he said when the man strode into his office. "And what can I do for you today?"

Lucullus Wood held out his hand. Dowling reached out and shook it with, he hoped, no noticeable hesitation, even if he wasn't used to treating a Negro as his social equal. Wood was in his early or mid-thirties: a wide-shouldered man, blocky rather than fat, with high cheekbones and an arched nose that argued he might have a little Indian blood in him. Without preamble, he said, "Kentucky got troubles, General."

"Yes, indeed." Dowling's voice was dry. "Do you aim to stop them or cause more?"

Before answering, Wood sat down across from Dowling. Dowling hadn't invited him to, but he didn't say anything. When the black man smiled, he looked like a predatory beast. "Depends on for who you mean," he answered, adding, "Reckon you know who I am, then."

"When I got here, they told me you made the best barbecue in town," Dowling said. "I've tried it. They were right."

"Hell they was." Lucullus Wood sounded affronted. "I make the best barbecue in the whole goddamn state. So did my old man."

Dowling looked down at the notes he'd taken. "Your father was . . . Apicius Wood. I hope I'm saying that right." He waited for the Negro to nod, then went on, "And one after the other, you and he have been the two biggest Reds in town. Or are you the two biggest Reds in the whole goddamn state?"

Woods blinked at that. After a moment, he decided to laugh. "Maybe he was. Maybe I is. Maybe we ain't never been," he said. "Folks who talk about that stuff, they don't always do it. Folks who do it, they don't always talk about it."

"Well, if you don't do it, if you've never done it, why am I wasting my time talking to you?" Dowling asked. "Tell me what you've got on your mind, and we'll see if we can do some business."

Lucullus Wood blinked again. "You ain't what I reckoned you would be," he said slowly.

Abner Dowling's shrug made his chins quiver. "Life is full of surprises. Now come on, Mr. Wood. Piss or get off the pot."

"Come January, a lot of colored folks is gonna want to git the hell out of Kentucky," Wood said. "Reckon you got some notion why."

"We won't stop them," Dowling answered. "They're U.S. citizens. We will respect that. Some whites will want to leave the state, too."

"Some. A few." Wood spoke with dismissive scorn. "Some colored folks, though, some colored folks is gonna stay. Dunno how many, but some will. Some damn fools in every crowd, I suppose."

"If I were a Negro, I wouldn't stay in Kentucky," Dowling said.

Wood's eyes went to the shiny silver star on the right shoulderboard of Dowling's green-gray uniform. "Don't suppose they lets no damn fools turn into generals," he remarked.

As far as Dowling was concerned, that only proved the colored man didn't know as much about the U.S. Army as he thought he did. Custer, for instance, had worn four stars, not just one. But Custer, while doubtless often a fool, had been a very peculiar kind of fool, and so. . . . With an effort, Dowling tore his thoughts away from the man he'd served for so long. "Fair enough," he said to Lucullus Wood. "I'm sure you're right about what will happen. Some Negroes will stay here. Some people don't know to get out of a burning building till too late, either. But if the U.S. Army has to leave Kentucky after the plebiscite, what concern to us are they?"

"If we was white folks, you wouldn't talk like that about us." Wood didn't try to hide his scorn. Dowling wondered if a Negro had ever reproached him like that before. He didn't think so. He hadn't dealt with a whole lot of Negroes—not many people in the USA had—and the ones he had dealt with were all in subordinate positions. After a deep, angry exhalation, Wood went on, "You reckon the niggers in Kentucky gonna like all them damn white bastards runnin' around yellin', 'Freedom!' all the goddamn time?"

"I wouldn't," Dowling answered. If *he'd* called Negroes niggers, Lucullus Wood might have tried to murder him. Being one himself, Wood could use the label. But then that thought slipped away and another took its place: "What do you suppose they'll want to do about it?"

Anger dropped away from Wood like a discarded cloak. "No, General, you ain't no damn fool. You got to understand, I ain't in love with the USA. Revolution comin' to y'all, too. But we gots to make a popular front with whoever's on our side even a little when it comes to them Freedom Party cocksuckers."

"How much of a nuisance do you think your people can be, and how much help do you want from the United States?" Dowling asked. "The more we can set up before the plebiscite, the better off we'll be."

"More we kin set up before the plebiscite, better off the USA'll be," Wood said cynically. "Ain't gonna be no more good times for the niggers here after that. But I figure we kin raise some kind of trouble for the Confederates when they comes marchin' back in here."

"It would be nice if you could arrange as much for them as the Freedom Party fanatics did for us here and in Houston," Dowling said.

"Be nice for y'all, yeah, but don't hold your breath, on account of it ain't gonna happen," Wood said. "Lots mo' white folks here and down there than there is niggers. Revolutionary, he got to swim like a fish in the school of the people. Us blackfish, we is a smaller school."

He didn't sound like an educated man. But when it came to the business of revolution, he spoke with an expert's authority. Abner Dowling found himself nodding. "I suppose you're right," he said regretfully. "But if you people just happened to find some wireless sets and rifles and explosives lying around, you might figure out what to do with them, eh?"

"We might." Lucullus Wood nodded, too. "Yes, suh, General, we just might cipher out what they's for."

*I ought to get War Department authorization for this,* Dowling thought. He rejected the notion the minute it occurred to him. The War Department might not want to get officially involved in resisting Confederate occupation. Then again, some of the people in the War Department might just get cold feet. *I'm here. They put me in charge. I'll take care of things, God damn it.*

"All right, then," he said. "We'll see to that. And I know you're not doing us any special favors. But what works against the CSA works for the USA. That's how things are."

Wood nodded again. "That's how things is," he agreed. "We is fellow travelers on this here road for a while, even if we's goin' different places."

"Fellow travelers." Brigadier General Dowling tasted the phrase. "Yes, I can live with that."

"You been fair to me, General, so I be fair to you," Wood said. "Come the revolution, we go different ways. Come the revolution, I reckon I try an' kill you. Nothin' personal, you understand, but you is one o' the 'pressors, and you got to go to the wall."

"Fair is fair," Dowling said, "so I'll tell you something, too. You want to be careful about threatening a man with a weapon in his hand. He has a nasty habit of shooting back." With a sour smile, he too added, "Nothing personal."

"Sure enough," the Negro said imperturbably. "Them Freedom Party fellas, they done found that out down further south. Reckon mebbe we teach 'em some new lessons here in Kentucky. Is that a bargain?"

"That's a bargain." Dowling heaved himself to his feet and held out his right hand once more. Lucullus Wood took it. The Negro dipped his head and sauntered out of Dowling's office. Dowling looked down at his own right palm. Had he ever shaken a colored man's hand before today? He didn't think so. Kentucky was proving educational in all sorts of ways.

"Sorry, kid." The man who shook his head at Armstrong Grimes didn't sound sorry at all. He sounded as if he'd said the same thing a million times before. He doubtless sounded that way because he had. "I can't use you. I want somebody with experience."

Armstrong had heard that a million times since finally escaping high school. His temper, which had never been long, snapped. "How the hell am I supposed to get experience if nobody'll hire me on account of I don't have any?"

"Life's tough," the man in the hiring office answered, which meant, *To hell with you, Jack. I've got mine.* He lit a cigarette, but didn't quite blow smoke in Armstrong's face. Maybe his first long drag made him feel a little more like a human being, because he unbent enough to say, "One way to do it is to odd-job for a while. Sometimes you can get hired by the day even if somebody doesn't want you for keeps."

"Yeah, I've tried some of that," Armstrong said. "But it's a day on and a week off. It'll take me forever to do enough of anything to get the experience to make anybody want to take me on for good, and I'll starve to death in the meantime."

The man looked him over. "Other thing you could do is join the Army. You're a big, strong fellow. They'll take you unless you just got out of jail—maybe even if you just got out of jail, the way things are nowadays. You can sure as hell learn a trade in there."

"Maybe," Armstrong said. His father had made the same suggestion—made it loudly and pointedly, in fact. That would have prejudiced him against the idea even if he'd liked it to begin with. "They don't pay you anything much in the Army, and you're stuck there for three years if you volunteer."

"Have it your way, pal. You think I give a rat's ass about what you do, you've got another think coming." The clerk behind the desk looked up at the line of poor, hungry men desperate for work. "Next!"

Seething, Armstrong stormed out of the hiring office. If he hadn't thought the clerk would sic the cops on him, he would have whaled the stuffing out of the bastard. Sitting there like a little tin Jesus, who the hell did he think he was? But the answer to that was mournfully obvious. *He thinks he's a man who's got a job, and the son of a bitch is right.*

Armstrong inquired at a furniture factory, a trucking company, and a joint that made Polish sausages before heading for home. No luck anywhere. His old man wanted him out there trying—insisted on it, as a matter of fact. If he didn't pound the pavement, he wouldn't get fed. Merle Grimes had been most painfully clear about that. Armstrong wished he thought his father were bluffing. Since he didn't . . .

When he got home, he found his mother in tears. He hadn't seen that since Granny died. "What happened?" he exclaimed.

Without a word, she held out an envelope to him. His name was typed on it. The return address was printed in an old-fashioned, hard-to-read typeface:

### Government of the United States, War Department.

Another, smaller line below that said:

#### Office of Selection for Service.

"Oh," he said. It felt like a punch in the breadbasket. He'd known it was possible, of course, but he hadn't thought it was likely. "Oh, shit."

Edna Grimes nodded. "That's what I said, too, Armstrong, when I saw the damn thing. But there's nothing you can do about it. If they conscript you and you pass the physical, you've got to go."

"Yeah." Armstrong nodded glumly. From some of the things he'd heard, the only way to flunk the physical was not to have a pulse, too. He did his best to look on the bright side of things: "If they conscript me, it's only for two years. That's a year less than I'd spend if I joined up on my own."

"I know. But still . . ." His mother gave him a hug of the sort he hadn't had from her in years. "You're my baby, Armstrong. I don't want you going off to be a soldier. What if we have another war?"

Being his mother's baby didn't appeal to Armstrong. Fighting a war did—if you were going to be a soldier, what point was there to being one when nothing was happening? None he could see. That he might get hurt or killed never crossed his mind. He was, after all, only eighteen. But he was smart enough to know that, if he told his mother what he really thought, she'd pitch a fit. So, as soothingly as he could, he said, "There won't be any war, Ma. We're giving the Confederates those pleb-whatchamacallits, so they've got nothing left to fight about."

"Jesus, I hope you're right," his mother said. "Some people, though, if you give 'em an inch, they'll want to take a mile. The way the Freedom Party carries on, I'm afraid they're like that."

Armstrong's little sister met the news that he was going to go off and be a soldier with complete equanimity. "So long," Annie said. "When do you leave?"

"Not tonight, you little brat," he said. She stuck out her tongue at him. He wanted to belt her a good one, but he knew he couldn't. She'd just go yelling to their mother, and then he'd end up in trouble. Annie was almost as big a pest as Aunt Clara, who would no doubt hope he never came back when he went off to wherever they'd ship him for training.

When his father got home and found out, though, he slapped Armstrong on the back and poured him a good-sized slug of whiskey, something he'd never done before. "Congratulations, son!" Merle Grimes said. "They'll make a man out of you."

Since Armstrong was already convinced he was a man, that impressed him less than it might have. To show what tough stuff he was, he took a big gulp of the whiskey. He hadn't done a lot of drinking. The hooch felt like battery acid going down the pipe, and exploded like a bomb in his stomach. "That's good," he wheezed in a voice that sounded like a ghost of its former self.

"Glad you like it," his father answered gravely. If he knew that Armstrong had just injured himself, he was polite enough not to let on. That was more discretion than he was in the habit of showing. He took a smaller sip from his own glass and asked, "When do you go in for your preinduction physical?"

"Next Wednesday," Armstrong said. "I can hardly wait."

He meant that ironically, but Merle Grimes took it seriously. "Good," he said. "That's real good. You ought to be eager to do something for your country. It's been taking care of you all along."

"Right," Armstrong said tightly. He could have done without his father sounding like a goddamn recruiting poster.

Next Wednesday, naturally, rain poured down in buckets. Armstrong had to walk three blocks from the trolley stop to the building where the government doctors waited to get their hands on him. He was half soaked by the time he made it inside. Seeing several other guys his own age who were just as bedraggled as he was made him feel a little better. More fellows with wet hair and pimples came in the door after him, too.

A pair of clerks marched into the room. At the same time as one was saying, "Line up in alphabetical order by last name," the other declared, "Line up according to height."

After some confusion, alphabetical order won. Armstrong would have ended up about the same place either way. As a G, he was fairly close to the head of the line but not right at it. He was also taller than most of the young men there for their physicals, but not a real beanpole, either. He had a chance to look things over before the system got to work on him.

First came the paperwork. He would have bet money on that. His old man made a living pushing papers around for the government, and had plenty to do. Armstrong filled out about a million forms and carried them with him to the eye chart, which came next. The fellow in front of him had some trouble. "I can see the little bastards just fine," he told the guy in the white coat in charge of the test. "Only thing is, I can't no way read 'em."

"Let me see your paperwork," the man in the white coat said. Armstrong got a glimpse of a couple of pages, too. Just about everything was blank. The man in charge of the test frowned. "You're illiterate?" Seeing the puzzled look on the young man's face, he tried again: "You can't read and write?"

" 'Fraid not," the youth said. "I can sign my name. That's about the size of it."

"Didn't you go to school?"

"A couple years. I never was much good, though. I been workin' ever since."

"Well, uh, Slaughter, no matter how good a name you've got for a soldier, you need to be able to read and write to enter the Army. You're not even in the right place in line. You'll be excused from conscription. I don't know if your exclusion will be permanent or if they'll class you as fit for service in an emergency. But we won't take you now." He glanced towards Armstrong Grimes. "Next!"

Armstrong thought about pretending he couldn't read, too. Too late, though—he'd already filled out his paperwork and done it right. He stepped up to the line and went down the chart as far as he could, switching eyes when the man in the white coat told him to.

"Give me your papers," the man said, then nodded. "You've passed here. Proceed to the next station."

He saw even more guys in white coats than he had at the Polish sausage works where he'd tried to get a job. They measured and weighed him. One of them listened to his heart. Another one took his blood pressure. Another one—this one with a brand new pair of rubber gloves—told him to drop his pants, turn his head to one side, and cough. As he did, the man grabbed him in some highly intimate places. "No rupture," he said, and wrote on Armstrong's papers. "Now bend over and grab your ankles."

"What?" Armstrong said in alarm. "You're not going to—"

But the man in the white coat was already doing it. That was a lot less pleasant than being told to turn his head and cough. "Prostate gland normal," the man said. He took off the gloves and tossed them into a corrugated-iron trash can. Then he wrote on the papers again. As soon as he gave them back, he started putting on a fresh pair of gloves.

"You must go through a lot of those," Armstrong said. He pulled up his pants in a hurry, still stinging a little.

"You bet I do, sonny," the man in the white coat agreed. "All things considered, would you rather I didn't?" Armstrong hastily shook his head. "Well, neither would I," the man said. "Go on to the next station."

They drew blood there. A big, strapping fellow passed out just as Armstrong arrived. The fellow with the hypodermic syringe put it down in a hurry and managed to keep the big young man from banging his head on the floor. He dragged him off to one side and glared at Armstrong. "*You're* not going to faint on me, are you? This guy was the third one today. Roll up your sleeve."

"I don't think I am," Armstrong said. "What do you need to do this for, anyway?"

"See if you're anemic. See if you've got a social disease. See what your blood group is for transfusions. Hold still, now." The man swabbed the inside of his elbow with alcohol. The needle bit. Armstrong looked away as the syringe filled with blood. He felt a little queasy, but only a little. The man yanked out the needle, stuck a piece of cotton fluff on the puncture, and slapped adhesive tape over it. He wrote on Armstrong's papers. "That's it. You're done."

"Did I pass?" Armstrong asked.

"Unless you're anemic as hell or you've got syphilis, you did," the man replied. "You're healthy as a horse. You'll make a hell of a soldier."

"Oh, boy," Armstrong said.

# XVI

"**H**e's kept us out of war." Flora Blackford repeated the Socialist Party slogan to a street-corner crowd in her district. "He's kept us out of war, and he's done everything he could to keep food on the working man's table. If you want to see what the Democrats will do about that, look at what Herbert Hoover did. Nothing, that's what."

People in the mostly proletarian crowd clapped their hands. A sprinkling of hecklers at the back started a chant: "Taft! Taft! Robert Taft!"

Flora pointed at them. "I served in Congress with Senator Taft's father. William Howard Taft was an honorable man. So is Robert Taft. I don't say any differently. But I do say this: Senator Taft would be horrified at the way his supporters are bringing Freedom Party tactics into this campaign."

That got more applause. Next to nobody in this strongly Socialist district had a good word to say about Jake Featherston's gang. But one of the hecklers yelled, "Al Smith's the one who's in bed with the Freedom Party!"

"Al Smith is against war. I am against war. I had a brother-in-law killed and a brother badly wounded in the Great War," Flora said. "If you are going to tell me you are for war—if you are going to tell me Senator Taft is for war—you will have a hard time selling that to the people of this district."

"Taft is for keeping Kentucky and Houston," the heckler called.

"How can you keep a state in the country when its own people don't want to be here?" Flora asked. "That was the lesson of the War of Secession—you can't. Some things you can buy at too high a price."

The crowd applauded again, but less enthusiastically than before. Flora understood why: they wanted to have their cake and eat it, too; to have peace and to hold on to Kentucky and Houston. She wanted the same thing. She understood the people who said the USA had sacrificed too much even to think about giving back the two states. At least half the time, she felt that way herself. She would have liked the idea much better if it didn't involve giving them back to Jake Featherston.

"I don't love the Freedom Party," she said. "But it is in power in the Confederate States, and we can't very well pretend it isn't and hope it will go away. What can we do if we don't try to deal with it?" She was trying to convince herself as well as her audience, and she knew it.

"I'd sock it in the nose!" that iron-lunged heckler yelled. "Taft will sock it in the nose!"

"No, he won't." Flora shook her head. "If he does, he'll have a war on his hands, and I can't believe he wants one. He may talk tough, but his foreign policy won't look much different from President Smith's. And his domestic policy . . ." She rolled her eyes. "He grows like an onion—with his head in the ground." She said it in English. Some of the people her age and older in the crowd echoed it in Yiddish.

She managed to get through the rest of her speech without too much harassment. She had a pretty good idea why, too: the Democrats didn't think they could beat her. She'd never lost an election in this district. The Democrats had elected a candidate here while she was First Lady, but she'd trounced him as soon as she returned to the hustings.

At the end, she said, "If you're in favor of what President Smith has done, you'll vote for him again, and you'll vote for me. If you're not, you'll vote for Taft. It's about that simple, my friends. Forward with Smith or back with Taft?"

She stepped down from the platform with applause ringing in her ears. When she'd started agitating for the Socialists, she hadn't had a platform—not a real one. She'd made her first few speeches standing on crates or beer barrels. She was right around the corner from the Croton Brewery, where she'd spoken at the outbreak of the Great War. She'd opposed war then; she still did. In 1914, her party hadn't gone along with her. This year, it did.

*Why aren't I happier, then?* she wondered.

In 1914, the Confederate States hadn't been that different from the United States. Most of the oppressed proletariat in the CSA had been black, but capitalists had oppressed workers almost as savagely in the USA. Now . . . Things were different now.

A middle-aged man in a homburg limped up to her, leaning on a stick. "Good speech," he said. A Soldiers' Circle pin showing a sword through his conscription year in a silver circle sparkled on his lapel.

"Thank you, David," Flora said with a sigh. That her own brother could belong to a reactionary organization like the Soldiers' Circle—and not only belong but wear the pin that showed he was proud to belong—had always dismayed her. The Soldiers' Circle wasn't the Freedom Party, but some of its higher-ups wished it were.

"Good speech," David Hamburger repeated, "but I'm still going to vote for Taft."

"I hadn't expected anything different," she said. David had gone into the Great War a Socialist like the rest of the family. He'd come out a conservative Democrat. He'd also come out with one leg gone above the knee. Flora had no doubt the two were related.

She asked, "And will you vote for Chaim Cohen, too?" Cohen was the latest Democrat to try to unseat her.

Her brother turned red. "No," he said. "I don't like all of your ideas—I don't like most of your ideas—but I know you're honest. And you're family. I don't let family down."

"Being family isn't reason enough to vote for me," she said.

"I think it is." David laughed. "And you may not like my politics, but at least I care about things. Did you see your sisters or your other brother or Mother and Father at your speech?"

Now Flora was the one who had to say, "No." Sophie and Esther and Isaac had their own lives, and lived them. They were proud when she won reelection, but they didn't even come to Socialist Party headquarters any more. As for her parents . . . "Mother and Father don't get out as much as they did."

"I know. They're getting old." David shook his head. "They've *got* old. *Bis hindert und tzvantzik yuhr.*"

*"Omayn,"* Flora said automatically, though she know her mother and father wouldn't live to 120 years. People didn't, however much you wished they would. A stab of loss and longing for Hosea pierced her. She was grateful her parents had lived to grow old. So many people didn't, even in the modern world.

"Have you got plans for tonight, or can you go to dinner with your reactionary tailor of a little brother?" David asked.

"I can go," Flora said. "And it's on me. I know I make more money than you do." She knew she made a lot more money than he did, but she didn't want to say so out loud.

With his usual touchy pride, David said, "I'm doing all right." He'd never asked her or anybody else for a dime, so she supposed he was. With a wry grin, though, he went on, "I'll let you buy. Don't think I won't. How does that go? 'From each according to her abilities, to each according to his needs'? Something like that, anyhow."

"I never heard anybody quote—I mean misquote—Marx to figure out who's getting dinner before," Flora said, and she couldn't help laughing. "Since I'm buying, how does Kornblatt's sound?"

"Let's go," her brother said, so the delicatessen must have sounded good.

When they got there, he ordered brisket and a schooner of beer. Flora chose stuffed cabbage, which just wasn't the same in Philadelphia. What she got at Kornblatt's wasn't the same as what she'd helped her mother make when she lived on the Lower East Side all the time, but it came closer.

David attacked the brisket as if he hadn't eaten in weeks. He'd devoured almost all of it before he looked up and said, "You really think we ought to give back what we won in the war? Give it back to those 'Freedom'-yelling *mamzrim*?"

"If the people who live there don't want to be part of the country, how can we keep them?" Flora asked.

"They were pretty quiet till Featherston started stirring them up," David said, which was true, or at least close to true. He speared his last bite of meat, chewed it, swallowed, and went on, "If we're not doing the same thing with the *shvartzers* in the CSA, we're missing a hell of a chance."

"I don't know anything about that," Flora said.

"Somebody ought to," her brother said, and somebody probably did. If the United States weren't trying to use Negroes in the Confederate States to make life difficult for the government there, then the War Department was indeed falling down on the job. Flora disliked a lot of the people and policies in the War Department, but she did not think the men at the top there were fools. Over almost a quarter of a century of public life, she'd learned the difference between someone who couldn't do his job and someone who simply disagreed with her about what the job should be.

"Say what you want," she told David, "but we'd just have endless trouble if we tried to keep those states."

David didn't reply with words, not right away. Instead, he rapped his artificial leg with his knuckles. By the sound that came from it, he might almost have been knocking on a door; it was made of wood and canvas and leather and metal. "You know how many men like me there are in the USA—men without legs, men without arms, men without eyes, men without faces? If we don't keep what we won, why did we get shot and blown up and gassed? Answer me that one, and then I'll say good-bye to Kentucky and Houston and Sequoyah."

"There is no answer," Flora said. "Sometimes something looks like a good idea when you do it but turns out not to be later on. Or haven't you ever had that happen?"

"Oh, yes. I've seen that. Who hasn't? But this one is kind of large to treat that way. And what do we do if giving back those states turns out to be that same kind of mistake? Taking them again would get expensive."

"I don't know," Flora said.

"Well, that's honest, anyhow. I said you were," her brother replied. "Does Al Smith know? Does anybody in the whole wide world know?"

"How can anybody know?" Flora asked, as reasonably as she could. "We'll just have to see how things turn out, that's all."

David paused to light a cigarette. He blew smoke up toward the ceiling, then said, "Seems to me that's a better reason for not doing something than for doing it. But I'm no politician, so what do I know?"

"It's going to happen." Flora knew she sounded uncomfortable. She couldn't help it. She went on, "If it makes you that unhappy, the thing to do *is* to vote for Taft. I think it will work out all right. I hope it does."

"I hope it does, too. But I don't think so. The Confederates on the banks of the Ohio again?" David Hamburger shook his head. "We had to worry about that for years, and then we didn't, and now we will again."

"When they were on the Ohio, they didn't cross it in the last war," Flora said.

"They didn't have barrels then. They didn't have bombers then, either," her brother said.

"Even if they do get it back, they've promised to leave it demilitarized afterwards," Flora said.

"Oh, yes. They've promised." David nodded. "So tell me—how far do you trust Jake Featherston's promises?"

Flora wished he hadn't asked that. She'd deplored Featherston in the U.S. Congress long before he was elected. She liked him no better, trusted him no further, now that he was president of the CSA. As she had on the stump, she said, "He's there. We have to deal with him." Her brother let the words fall flat, which left them sounding much worse than if he'd tried to answer them.


Chester Martin faced Election Day with all the enthusiasm of a man going to a doctor to have a painful boil lanced. His efforts to build a construction workers' union in antilabor Los Angeles had got strong backing from the Socialist Party. How could he forget that? He couldn't. But he couldn't make himself like the upcoming plebiscite, either.

His wife had no doubts. "I don't want another war," Rita said. "I lost my first husband in the last one." She hardly ever spoke of him, but now she went on, "Why should anybody else have to go through what I did? If we don't have to fight, that's good news to me."

But Chester answered, "Who says we won't?"

"Al Smith does, that's who." Rita sent him an exasperated stare. "Or are you going to vote for a Democrat for president again? Look how well that turned out the last time."

"I don't know. I'm thinking about it," Chester said. Rita looked even more exasperated. She'd always been a Socialist. He'd been a Democrat through the Great War, but the only time he'd voted for a Democratic presidential candidate was in 1932, when he'd chosen Calvin Coolidge over Hosea Blackford. Blackford had had three and a half years to end the business collapse, and hadn't done it. Coolidge, of course, dropped dead three weeks before taking office, and Herbert Hoover, his running mate, hadn't done it, either. For that matter, neither had Smith. Chester went on, "Giving back so much of what we fought for sticks in my craw."

"Giving the country back to the Democrats sticks in my craw," Rita said. "Do you think Taft cares about what you're trying to do here? If you do, you're nuts. His father didn't stand with the producers, and neither does he."

That had an unpleasant ring of truth. Plenty of people would think local issues were the most important ones in the election. Half the time, Chester did. But, the other half of the time, he didn't. He said, "If the Confederates want Houston and Kentucky back and then they're done, that's one thing."

"They say that's all," Rita reminded him.

He nodded. "I know what they say. But Jake Featherston says all sorts of things. If he gets them back and starts putting soldiers into them, that's a different story. If he does that, we've got trouble on our hands."

"Even if he does, we can beat the Confederates again if we have to," Rita said. "If we tell them to pull back, they'd have to back down, wouldn't they?"

"Who knows? The point is, we shouldn't have to find out." Chester muttered unhappily to himself. He wanted a party with a strong foreign policy, and he also wanted a party with a strong domestic policy. Trouble was, the Democrats offered the one and the Socialists the other. He couldn't have both. "Maybe I ought to vote for the Republicans. Then I'd have the worst of both worlds."

"Funny. Funny like a crutch," his wife said. "Well, I can't tell you what to do, but I know what I'm going to."

Chester didn't. He went through October and into November unsure and unhappy. Autumn in Los Angeles was nothing like what it had been

in Toledo. It was the one season of the year where he might have preferred his old home town. Trees didn't blaze with color here. Most of
them didn't even lose their leaves. The air didn't turn crisp and clean,
either. It rained once, toward the end of October. That was the only real
way to tell summer was gone for good. The Sunday before the election, it
was back up to eighty-one. That wouldn't have happened in Toledo, but
there was nothing wrong with sixty-one, either. Forty-one and twenty-one
were different, to say nothing of one. Los Angeles might see forty-one as
a low. Twenty-one? One? Never.

Picketing was a lot easier when you weren't freezing while you carried a sign. Chester and his fellow construction workers kept on getting
help from the local Socialist Party. He did grumble about the plebiscite
with Party men, but never very loudly. Like most people, he was shy
about biting the hand that fed him. The Socialists probably wouldn't have
dropped support for his young, struggling union if they knew he might
vote for Taft, but why take chances?

Houses and apartment buildings and factories and shops went up all
over Los Angeles and the surrounding suburbs, but not many went up
without pickets around the construction sites. The *Los Angeles Times* kept
screaming that the pickets were nothing but a bunch of dirty Reds who
ought to be burned alive because hanging was too good for them. But the
*Times* screamed that about everything it didn't like, and it didn't like
much. Strikers and cops began to learn to get along, if not to love one
another. Even the insults and cries of, "Scab!" as men crossed the picket
line came to have a certain ritualistic quality to them.

November 5 dawned bright and clear, though the day plainly wouldn't
reach the eighties. "What are you going to do?" Rita asked at breakfast.

"Vote." Martin reached for the pepper shaker and spread pungent
black flakes over his fried eggs.

Rita made an irritated noise. "How?"

"Oh, about like this." He mimed picking up a stamp and making an X
on a ballot with it.

"Thank you so much." Somehow, no sarcasm flayed like a spouse's.
His wife asked a question he couldn't evade: "Who are you going to vote
for?"

"To tell you the truth, honey, I won't know till I get inside the voting
booth," Chester answered.

"If you don't vote for Al Smith, you'll end up sorry," Rita said. "You
were when you didn't vote for Blackford eight years ago."

"I know I was. I think Coolidge might have been better than Hoover,
but we'll never know about that, will we?" He spread butter and grape
jam on a piece of toast, then started to throw out the empty jam jar.

"Don't do that," Rita said. "I'll wash it out and use it for a glass. Jelly glasses are better for Carl—they don't hold as much as real ones, and they're thick, so they don't break as easy if he drops them."

"All right," Martin said with his mouth full. He put the jam jar back on the table. When he finished the toast, he gave Rita a quick, greasy kiss, stuck a cloth cap on his head, and hurried out the door. Rita took a deep breath, as if to call something after him, but she didn't. She must have realized it wouldn't change his mind.

The polling place was in the auditorium of an elementary school three or four blocks from the apartment. Chester got there as it opened. As always, the child-sized chairs made him smile. Once upon a time, he'd fit into seats like those. No more, no more. He gave his name and address to the white-mustached man in charge of the list. The man matched it against the entry, then handed him a ballot. "Take any empty voting booth," he droned. How many times had he said that, and in how many elections? How many more would he say it today?

There it was, the big question, right at the top of the ballot. Smith or Taft? Taft or Smith? Chester ignored the Republicans' candidate. Not many people outside of his native Indiana cared about the businessman they'd nominated, which meant they weren't about to win with Willkie. Besides, how could a Wendell hope to prevail against the brute simplicity of Al and Bob? Smith or Taft? Taft or Smith?

Chester stamped the X by Taft's name, hoping he was doing the right thing. Had he voted for Smith, he would have had the same hope, and would have been just as unsure of himself. *It's done, anyhow,* he thought, and went down the rest of the ballot in a hurry. Most of the candidates he voted for were Socialists. That salved his conscience, at least a little.

He carried the finished ballot back to the table where he'd got it. Another old man took it, folded it, and thrust it through the slot in the ballot box. "Mr. Martin has voted," he intoned, the words as formal and unchanging as any this side of the Mass.

Having voted, Chester Martin hurried to the trolley stop. He rode across town to Westwood, not far from the Pacific and even closer to the southern campus of the University of California. Orange groves were going down, houses were going up, and union labor, as usual in Los Angeles, was being ignored.

"Hey, Chester!" another organizer called as he came up. "You vote yet?"

"Sure did, before I came here," Martin answered. Westwood wasn't bright and sunny. Fog lingered here, and probably wouldn't burn off till midmorning. "How about you, Ralph?"

"I'll take care of it on the way home," Ralph answered. "Who'd you vote for?" He winked and laughed uproariously. He was sure he already knew, which meant Chester didn't have to tell him. Under the circumstances, that came as something of a relief.

The strikers carried their picket signs around and around the construction site. They stayed on the sidewalk. Once, at a different site, a man had stumbled and gone onto what would be a lawn. The cops nabbed him for trespassing. Not here, not today.

"Scabs!" the picketers shouted—along with other things, even less complimentary—when workers crossed the picket line and went into the construction site. They had to watch what they said, too. The police had been known to run strikers in for public obscenity. Still, endearments like "You stinking sack of manure!" got the message across.

Most of the strikebreakers went in with their heads down. Watching them cross the picket line was one thing that made Chester glad he'd chosen this side. He had yet to see a scab who didn't act as if his conscience bothered him. A man might go and decide he had to eat any way he could, but he seldom seemed happy about it.

One of the scabs here, a big man on whom the picketers had showered a lot of abuse, finally got fed up and shouted back: "Wait till the Pinkertons get into town, you bastards! They'll kick your asses but good!"

Not one but two foremen ran up to the strikebreaker. They both started cussing him up one side and down the other. The cops didn't jug them for the language they used, any more than they'd arrested the scab.

Chester didn't stop marching or yelling. But he sure as hell did prick up his ears. If the bosses were bringing in Pinkerton men, they were going to try breaking the union. The more notice he had about that, the better he could fight back, because the Pinkertons, notorious union-busters, fought dirty, really dirty. If he'd been one of those foremen, he would have cussed out that scab, too, for tipping the other side's hand.

At lunch, Ralph came up to him and said, "Pinkertons, is it? Well, there'll be a hot time in the old town tonight."

"You bet there will," Chester said. "We can lick 'em, though. They're bastards, sure as hell, but we can lick 'em. And if we do, what have the bosses got left to throw at us? Soldiers? Whose side would they be on?"

"Pinkertons." Ralph made a disgusted face. "I fought those fuckers years ago, in Pittsburgh. Never thought I'd see their ugly mugs again."

Martin nodded. "Same with me in Toledo. They're goons, all right. You think we're going to back down, though? I sure as hell don't. I've got brass knucks, and I can always get a .45 if it looks like I need one."

The other union man looked worried. "You gotta be careful with that, though. You pull it, the cops have the perfect excuse to blow you to kingdom come."

"I know. I know. Like I said, I did this before," Chester said. "But I know something else, too—if they get us on the run, we're in trouble. I don't aim to let that happen."

Cincinnatus Driver refused to buy a paper as he steered his truck toward the railroad yard. He was too disgusted to want to hear anything more about Al Smith's reelection than he had the night before on the wireless. He'd stayed up till the West Coast returns came in, and poured down three cups of coffee to try to make up for not enough sleep. Taft, behind in the race, had needed to sweep the Coast to win enough electoral votes to overtake the president. He'd won in California, but lost Oregon and Washington—and the election.

*They're gonna hold the plebiscite,* Cincinnatus thought dolefully. *They're gonna hold it, and the Confederate States are gonna win.* That meant he had to get his mother and father out of Kentucky before it left the USA and returned to the CSA. He knew what being a Negro in the Confederate States was like—and it was bound to be even worse now, under Jake Featherston and the Freedom Party, than it had been before the Great War.

He wished his mother were in better shape than she was. He could have sent his father and her train fare, and they would have ended up in Des Moines not long afterwards. As things were, with her sinking ever deeper into her second childhood, he knew he would have to go down to Covington to help his father bring her out. Elizabeth wouldn't like it—he didn't like it himself—but he saw no way around it.

He pulled into the railroad yard at a quarter to seven, yawning despite all the coffee. When he jumped out of his trunk and hurried over to see what cargoes he could pick up, first one railroad dick and then another waved to him. He was accepted here. He belonged. He never remembered belonging in Covington—certainly not in any part of it where he bumped up against white men. The first conductor whose train he approached greeted him with, "Hey, Cincinnatus. How you doing?"

"Not bad, Jack," he answered. He never would have called a white man in Covington by his first name. "What you got?"

But Jack felt like gabbing. "Four more years of Smith," he said. "I'm happy. My son got conscripted not long ago, and I don't want him getting shot at. I saw too goddamn much of that myself twenty-five years ago."

That gave Cincinnatus a new slant on things. He'd been shot at during the Great War, too, if only as a truck driver behind the lines. But he didn't have to worry about Achilles getting conscripted. The USA didn't conscript Negroes, any more than the CSA did. If war came, Achilles would be as safe as anybody. Even so, Cincinnatus said, "You won't find anybody colored who wants to go back to livin' in the Confederate States."

By the way Jack blinked, he'd no more thought about that than Cincinnatus had worried about conscription. The white man said, "I don't suppose there's enough colored folks to change the vote, though."

Cincinnatus grimaced. That was painfully true. Not wanting to dwell on the likely fate of Kentucky (and Houston, and perhaps Sequoyah, but Kentucky mattered most to him), he asked again, "What you got here?"

"Furniture," Jack said, and Cincinnatus' eyes lit up. He and Jack haggled for a while, but not too long. He loaded the truck as full as he could, then roared off for the shops taking delivery. If he got rid of everything in a hurry, he thought he could be back for another equally profitable load by lunchtime.

He was, too. Plenty of things held back a colored man: fewer in the USA than in the CSA, but still plenty. Adding laziness on top of everything else would only have made matters worse. Cincinnatus was a lot of different things. Whatever he was, though, he'd never been afraid of hard work.

His back ached when he pulled up to the apartment building that night, but the money in the pocket of his overalls made the ache seem worthwhile. He opened the mailbox in the lobby, crumpled up the advertising circulars, and winced when he saw a letter with a Covington postmark and the sprawling handwriting of his father's neighbor. News from Covington was unlikely to be good. Because he wished he didn't have to find out what the letter said, he carried it upstairs without opening it.

When he walked in, Amanda was doing homework. He smiled at her. *Gonna have me two high-school graduates soon,* he thought proudly. *That ain't bad for a Kentucky nigger who never went to school at all.*

From the kitchen came the crackle and the mouth-watering smell of frying chicken. Cincinnatus went in to say hello to Elizabeth, who was turning pieces with long-handled tongs. After a quick kiss, she asked, "What you got there?"

"Letter from Covington."

"Oh." She understood his hesitation, but asked the next question anyhow: "What's it say?"

"Don't know yet. Ain't opened it," he said. The look his wife sent him was sympathetic and impatient at the same time. He tore off the end of the envelope, took out the letter, unfolded it, and read. By the time he got to the end, his face was as long as the train from which he'd taken off furniture.

"What is it?" Elizabeth asked.

"I got to git down there. Got to do it quick," Cincinnatus said heavily. "Neighbor says my mama, she start wanderin' off every chance she get. Pa turn his back on her half a minute, she out the door an' lookin' for the house where she growed up. Can't have that. She liable to git lost for good, or git run over on account of she go out in the street and don't look where she goin'." Stress and the thought of Covington made his accent thicken.

Elizabeth sighed. Then hot fat spattered, and she yipped and jerked back her hand. She said, "I reckon maybe you do, but, Lord, I wish you didn't."

"So do I, on account of Ma and on account of I don't want to go back to Kentucky, neither," Cincinnatus said. "But it ain't always what you want to do. Sometimes it's what you got to do." He waited. Elizabeth sighed again, then reluctantly nodded.

He bought a round-trip train ticket, knowing he would have to get one-way fares for his parents in Covington. He sent the neighbor down there a wire to let him know when he'd be getting into town. Then he stuffed a few days' clothes and sundries into a beat-up suitcase and went to the railroad station to catch the eastbound train.

It pulled into Covington at eleven that night. The neighbor, Menander Pershing, stood on the platform with his father. Cincinnatus' father looked older and smaller and wearier than Cincinnatus had dreamt he would. After embracing him, Cincinnatus looked nervously across the brightly lit platform.

"Ain't none o' them Kentucky State *Po*lice this time," Seneca Driver said. He'd been born a slave, and still talked like it. After so long hearing the accents of the white Midwest, Cincinnatus found his father's way of speaking strange and ignorant-sounding, even though he'd sounded like that himself when he was a boy. His father hadn't even had a surname (and neither had he) till they'd all taken the same one after Kentucky returned to the USA in the Great War.

Cincinnatus couldn't help looking around some more. As far as he could tell, nobody was paying any attention to him. Little by little, he began to relax. "Freedom Party don't give you no trouble?" he asked.

"Don't want trouble from nobody," his father said. "I minds my business, an' I don't git none."

"Ain't too bad," Menander Pershing added. He was about Cincinnatus' age, lean, with a few threads of gray in his close-cropped hair. He fixed autos for a living, and wore a mechanic's greasy overalls. "They reckon they win come January, so they bein' quiet till then." He jerked a thumb toward the exit. "Come on. I got my motorcar out in the lot."

U.S. soldiers were searching some passengers' bags as they left the station. The men in green-gray waved Seneca and his companions through without bothering. It might have been the first time in his life when being colored made things easier for him. The soldiers didn't think Negroes would back the Freedom Party no matter what. They were likely to be right, too.

Menander Pershing's auto was an elderly Oldsmobile, but its motor purred when he started it. Getting in, Cincinnatus asked, "How's Ma?"

"Well, she sleepin' now. That's how I come away," his father answered. "You see in the mornin', that's all." He wouldn't say anything more.

Even by moonlight, the house where Cincinnatus' parents lived was smaller and shabbier than he remembered. He lay down on the rickety sofa in the front room and got what sleep he could.

In the morning, heartbreak began. His father had to introduce him to his mother; she didn't recognize him on her own. After she came out of the kitchen with a cup of coffee in her hand, she looked at him and said, "Who are you?"

"I'm Cincinnatus, Ma," he said quietly, and felt the sting of tears.

As long as they stayed in the room together, she seemed to know who he was. When she left to go to the outhouse, though, she came back and looked at him as if she'd never seen him before in her life. As far as she knew, she hadn't. Fighting the stab at his heart, he introduced himself again.

"She like that," Cincinnatus' father said sadly. "She still know me all the time. She better, after all these years. But she don't know nobody else, not so it stick."

Cincinnatus pounded a fist into his thigh. "Damn!"

"Don't you talk like that, young man! I switch you if you cuss in the house!" For two sentences, his mother sounded just the way she had when he was thirteen. Hearing that *damn* might have flipped a switch in her head. Old things seemed more familiar to her than new ones. But then her eyes went vague again. She forgot her own annoyance. Seeing her forget might have been harder to bear than anything.

Or so Cincinnatus thought, till he too went out back to use the outhouse—a fixture he hadn't had to worry about for many years—and returned to find his father rushing out to get him. "She run off!" Seneca cried. "I go back in the kitchen for a minute, and she run off!"

"Do Jesus!" Cincinnatus exclaimed. "We got to find her." He and his father hurried out to the front yard. Cincinnatus looked left and right. No sign of her. "You go this way," he told his father. "I'll go that way. She ain't gone real far."

Off he went, quick as he could. When he got to a corner, he hesitated.

Up or down? Either way might prove a dreadful mistake—and he had the chance for another one at every corner he came to. Swearing under his breath, he dog-trotted along the street. Each time he came to a corner, his curses got louder.

But luck was with him. He rounded one last corner and there she was, on the far side of the street, strolling along as if she knew just where she was going. "Ma!" Cincinnatus yelled. "Ma!" She paid no attention to him. Maybe she didn't hear. Maybe she'd forgotten a grown man could call her his mother.

Cincinnatus ran out into the street after her—and his luck abruptly changed. He remembered a squeal of brakes, a shout, and an impact . . . and then, nothing.

When he woke, he wanted that nothing back. One leg was on fire. Someone was taking a sledgehammer to his head. He opened his eyes a crack. Everything was white. For a moment, he thought it was heaven. Then, blearily, he realized it had to be a hospital.

He made a noise. A nurse appeared, as if by magic. He tried to talk. At last, after some effort, he succeeded: "Wha' happen?"

"Fractured tibia and fibula," she said briskly. "Fractured skull, too. When they brought you in a week ago, they didn't think you'd make it. You must have a hard head. You had to be nuts, running out there like that. The guy in the auto never had a chance to stop. And how are you going to pay your bills?"

That was the least of his worries. His wits didn't want to work. The injury? Drugs? Whatever it was, he tried to fight it. "Ma?" he asked. The nurse only shrugged. "Got to get out of here," he said.

She shook her head. "Not till you're better. And you aren't going anywhere for quite a while, believe you me you're not."

"Plebiscite," he said in dismay. The nurse shrugged again. Cincinnatus drifted back into unconsciousness. If he whimpered, it might have been pain and not fear. Pain was what the nurse took it for, anyhow. She gave him another shot of morphine.


**W**inter in Covington, Kentucky, was of positively Yankee fury. Anne Colleton didn't care for it a bit. But she didn't complain, either. She'd pulled every wire she could reach to get to be a Confederate election inspector. Now that she was here, she intended to make the most of it.

Disapproval stuck out like spines from the fat brigadier general who commanded the local U.S. garrison. He knew what was going to happen when the votes were cast on Tuesday. He knew, but he couldn't do one damned thing about it.

Anne disliked the idea of Negroes voting in the plebiscite as much as Brigadier General Rowling (she thought that was his name, but wasn't quite sure—he wasn't worth remembering, anyhow) disliked the idea of the plebiscite itself. She had grumbled about that.

Brigadier General—Rowling?—wouldn't listen. He said, "Your president agreed to it, so you're stuck with it."

She had no answer for that. What Jake Featherston said, went. "Let them enjoy it while they can, then," she said, "because they sure won't be doing any voting after Kentucky comes back where it belongs."

The U.S. officer scowled. She'd hoped he would. He said, "Maybe you'd like to go into the colored district yourself on Tuesday so you can see everything is on the up and up?"

"I'm not afraid, if that's what you mean," she said.

"Bully for you," said the fat man from the United States. Anne couldn't remember the last time she'd heard anyone say *bully*, even sardonically.

January 7, 1941, dawned clear and cold. Anne Colleton got up to see the sun rise to make sure she missed none of the plebiscite. Polls opened at seven. Polling places were officially marked by the Stars and Stripes and the Stars and Bars flying in front of them—and unofficially by the armed U.S. soldiers who stood outside each one to make sure there was no trouble. Jake Featherston had offered to send Confederate soldiers into Kentucky and Houston and Sequoyah to help with that, but President Smith had told him no, and he hadn't pushed it. For the moment, they remained U.S. territory.

*For the moment,* Anne thought with a ferocious smile.

Both the USA and the CSA had poll watchers at every polling place. They checked the men and women who came in to vote against the lists of those who were eligible. Every now and then, they would argue. Both sides kept lists of contested voters. If the plebiscite turned out to be close, those lists would turn into weapons. In Kentucky and Houston, at least, Anne didn't think the vote would be close.

She did go into the colored part of Covington. Her motorcar flew the Stars and Bars from the wireless aerial. In most of Covington, people had cheered when they saw it. In the colored district . . . Anne wished she'd thought to take down the flag.

Some of the U.S. poll watchers in the colored part of town were Negroes: young men who'd grown up and got an education while Kentucky belonged to the USA. Because the voting rolls for Negroes were new and imperfect, they bickered constantly with their C.S. counterparts, and argued with them as if they believed they were just as good as whites. In the Confederate States, that would have been a death sentence.

One of the Confederate poll watchers said as much: "When this here state goes back where it belongs, you better recollect what happens to uppity niggers, Lucullus."

The Negro—Lucullus—looked steadily back at him. "You better recollect what happens when you push folks too far," he answered. "You push 'em so far they don't care if they lives or dies, why should they care if *you* lives or dies?"

"Talk is cheap," the white man fleered. Lucullus said not a word. Anne feared he'd won the exchange.

When she came out of the polling place—a little storefront church—she discovered her auto had a smashed windscreen (though they said *windshield* in the USA). Her driver was out of the motorcar, hopping mad and yelling at a U.S. soldier: "Why the hell didn't you stop that goddamn nigger? He flung a brick right in front of your nose, and you just stood there."

"I'm sorry, sir." The green-gray-clad soldier sounded anything but sorry. By his accent, he was from nowhere near Kentucky. "I didn't see a thing."

"What is your name?" Anne demanded. "I'm going to report you to your commanding officer."

"Jenkins, ma'am. Rudy Jenkins," the soldier answered. "And you can report as much as you please, but I won't lose any sleep over it."

She thought about telling him where to go and how to get there in the sort of language he would use himself—thought about it and decided it would do no good. Oh, she intended to give his name to that stuffed pork chop in a brigadier general's uniform, but she was sure that would do her no good, either. Jenkins might get a public slap on the wrist, but he was bound to get some private congratulations along with it.

She turned to the driver. "Just take us on to the next stop. This fellow can laugh as much as he pleases, but he'll be leaving soon, and we're going to stay."

The driver fumed. But Rudy Jenkins fumed even more. Anne nodded to herself. She'd done that right.

Before she left the colored district, the auto picked up a couple of more dents. The driver plainly wanted to curse some more; her presence in the motorcar inhibited him. "To hell with these goddamn bastards," she said, her voice crisp. "From now on, no one will give a shit what they think. Right?"

"Uh, yes, ma'am." He sounded scandalized. She smiled; she'd heard a lot of men sound that way. On they went, to a new polling place in the white part of town. There, Freedom Party stalwarts waving Party flags paraded just outside the hundred-foot electioneering limit. The U.S. soldiers by the polling place looked as if they wanted to shoot the men in white shirts and butternut trousers. The stalwarts were careful not to give them an excuse.

Anne went from one polling place to another till the polls closed at eight o'clock. Then the driver took her to the Covington city hall, where the votes would be counted. As at the polling places, both the USA and the CSA had observers present to make sure the count went straight.

Watching it progress, Anne found more people in Covington voting to stay in the United States than she would have liked: certainly more than the Negro vote—and what a mad notion that was!—accounted for. Some of the whites who'd grown up in the USA must have been too lazy to want a change. Even so, returning to the Confederacy took an early lead in Covington, and never lost it.

Wireless sets blared in the white-painted, windowless, smoke-filled room where the ballots were tallied. They let the counters and the observers keep track of what was going on in the rest of Kentucky and in the other states where there were plebiscites. Return to the CSA held the same sort of lead in Kentucky as a whole as it did in Covington—less than Anne would have liked, but plenty to win. Houston was going for the CSA in a rout: better than three to one. Sequoyah . . . Sequoyah gave the damnyankees something to smile about, because the people there seemed to be choosing to stay in the United States.

The tally in Covington finished about half past one. By then, Anne's driver had fallen asleep in a folding chair. She eyed him in some admiration; she didn't think she could have done that in a quiet room, let alone in the noisy chaos at city hall. He jerked and almost fell out of the chair when she shook him awake again. She was sorry about that, but not sorry enough to keep from doing it.

Noisy chaos roiled through the rest of Covington, too, as she saw on the short trip back to her hotel. Freedom Party stalwarts and others who backed the CSA danced in the streets, waving Party flags, the Stars and Bars, and the Confederate battle flag. A lot of them were drunk. They cheered the Confederate flag on the aerial of Anne's battered auto. Somehow, the cheers turned into a rousing chorus of "Dixie."

Anne wondered if the celebrants would go into the colored district and take their revenge on Covington's Negroes for voting to stay in the USA— or for having the nerve to vote at all. Maybe the U.S. soldiers who still patrolled the town would keep them from doing that. But any Negroes who stayed in Covington after Kentucky changed hands wouldn't have a happy time of it. Anne supposed a lot of them would go while the going was good. *The United States are welcome to them,* she thought.

She snatched a few hours' sleep. When she came downstairs for breakfast, she got a copy of the *Covington Chronicle*. The banner headline summed things up:

### UNTIED STATES!

A smaller subhead below gave the details:

#### KENTUCKY, HOUSTON RETURN TO CSA!
#### SEQUOYAH STAYS UNDER STARS AND STRIPES!

After bacon and eggs and lots of coffee, Anne paid a call on the U.S. commandant in Covington. "The people have spoken, Brigadier General," she said—and if she was gloating, she thought she had good reason to.

A cup of coffee steamed on the fat officer's desk. He looked to have had even less sleep than she had. "The people are a bunch of damned fools," he said. "They elected Featherston, didn't they?"

"I don't talk about your president that way," she said.

"Why not? I do." The commandant swigged from the coffee cup. He got down to business: "Under the agreement, we have thirty days to withdraw our men. Yours are not to follow. Kentucky will stay demilitarized. U.S. citizens wishing to leave the state may do so until it passes under Confederate sovereignty. A lot of them, I expect, will already have made plans to do so."

"Collaborators and niggers," Anne said scornfully. "You can have 'em."

"They'll do all right for themselves in the United States," the U.S. general predicted. "And I'll give you—and your president—some free advice, too."

"Free advice?" Anne didn't laugh in his face, but she came close. "I'm sure it's worth every penny you charge for it."

She hoped that would make him angry. If it did, he didn't show it. He just nodded, setting his chins in motion, and said, "Oh, no doubt. Well, I'll give it to you anyway, mostly 'cause I know you won't listen to it."

Anne could simply have turned her back and walked out the door. Instead, with ill-concealed impatience, she said, "Go ahead, then. Get it over with."

"Thanks a lot." The U.S. officer wasn't bad at sarcasm, either, even if he was built like a zeppelin. "If you people are smart, you won't land on this state too hard. You won the plebiscite, yes. But you didn't win it by as much as you thought you would, and you can't tell me any different. If you come down on Kentucky with both feet, you'll have about as much fun holding it down as we have since the last war."

That made more sense than Anne wished it did—enough that she decided to mention it in her report to President Featherston. She wouldn't suggest that he follow the fat man's advice; she knew better. But noting it as an item of intelligence wouldn't hurt.

She also decided she would note the way—Rowling? she had to check that—had spoken of the last war. Unless she altogether misread his tone, he was already thinking about the next one.

As had been his habit since the days of the Mexican civil war, Jefferson Pinkard prowled the barracks in the prison camp he ran in Louisiana. Camp Dependable wouldn't boil over while his back was turned.

It might boil over anyway. He knew that. The black prisoners in the camp had little to lose. They'd been captured in arms against the Confederate States. Nothing good was going to happen to them. They only thing that kept them in line was the certain knowledge that they would die if they rose up against the guards. Jeff's endless prowling was designed not least to make sure they stayed certain of that.

Whenever he stepped into a barracks, he had a pistol in his hand and half a squad of guards with submachine guns at his back. The Negro captives jumped down from their bunks and sprang to attention as soon as he came in. They were certain of what would happen if they didn't show him that courtesy, too.

"You, boy!" Pinkard pointed to one of them, a big, muscular buck. "Give me your name and number and where you were captured."

"I's Plutarch, suh," the Negro replied. He rattled off the camp number, finishing, "I was cotched up in Franklin Parish, suh. Some damn nigger sell me out. I ever find out who, dat one dead coon."

A lot of prisoners here had similar complaints. Some Negroes didn't want guerrilla war in their back yards. The ones who didn't had to be careful with what they did and said, though. A lot of them had ended up gruesomely dead when the men they were trying to betray took vengeance.

"Any complaints?" Pinkard asked.

Plutarch nodded. "I ain't got enough to eat, I ain't got enough to wear, an' I's *here.* 'Side from that, everything fine."

"Funny nigger," growled one of the guards behind Pinkard. "You'll laugh outa the other side of your face pretty damn quick, funny nigger."

Several of the other blacks in the barracks had smiled and nodded at what Plutarch had to say. None had been rash enough to laugh out loud. Now even the men who'd smiled tried to pretend they hadn't. Pinkard said, "You get the same rations and same clothes as everybody else. And if you didn't want to be here, you never should have picked up a gun."

"Huh!" Plutarch said. "White folks rise up against what they don't like, they's heroes. Black folks do the same, we's goddamn niggers."

"Bet your ass you are, boy," that guard said.

"There's a difference," Pinkard said.

Plutarch nodded. "Sure enough is. Y'all won. We lost. Ain't no bigger difference'n dat." That wasn't the difference Jeff had had in mind, which didn't mean the prisoner was wrong. Pinkard poked through the barracks. He knew how things were supposed to be, and carefully checked out everything that didn't match the pattern. Nothing looked like the start of an escape attempt, but you couldn't be sure without a thorough inspection.

On to the next barracks. As before, prisoners tumbled out of their bunks and stood at stiff attention. There was one difference here, though: Willy Knight dwelt in Barracks Six. The tall, blond, former vice president stood out from the black men all around him like a snowball in a coal field.

He was not the man he had been when Freedom Party guards brought him to Camp Dependable. He was scrawnier; camp rations weren't enough to let anybody keep the weight he'd come in with. He was dirtier, too—water for washing was in short supply. And, in an odd way, he was tougher than he had been. That he'd been tough enough to stay alive surprised Jeff Pinkard, who wouldn't have given him the chance of a snowball: a snowball in hell.

Hell this might well have been. But none of the Negro inhabitants here had taken advantage of the chance to get rid of a Freedom Party big shot. That surprised Pinkard, too—it did, but then again, it didn't. The blacks might have suspected Knight was in here as much as bait as for any other reason. Anybody who harmed him was liable to pay the price.

They might not have been wrong, either. For the moment, Jeff's orders were to look the other way if anything happened to Willy Knight. But one telegram could change that, and could change it days or weeks or months after something nasty happened to the ex–vice president.

Almost as if Knight were any other prisoner, Pinkard pointed at him and snapped, "You! Give me your name and number!" He couldn't make himself call another white *boy*.

Knight repeated his name and camp number, then added, "I was captured in Richmond, Virginia, trying to save the country."

"I want something from you, I'll ask for it," Jeff said.

The guard who'd growled at Plutarch growled at Willy Knight, too: "You really want to catch hell, just go on runnin' your mouth."

Knight shut up. The first time someone had said something like that to him, he'd asked what could be worse than coming to the camp to begin with. The guards had spent the next couple of weeks showing him what could be worse. Another way he was different now was that he didn't have any front teeth. He'd learned something, but not everything, about keeping quiet.

Pinkard didn't ask him if he had any complaints. Even if Knight did, nobody was going to do anything about them. That being so, why waste time and breath?

The warden did inspect Barracks Six with care unusual even for him. If some of the colored prisoners escaped, that would be a misfortune. He'd get called on the carpet. If Willy Knight escaped, that would be a catastrophe. Somebody's head would have to roll, and he knew whose. He might end up in one of these hard, narrow bunks himself—or they might simply shoot him and get it over with. Nobody, but nobody, was going to escape from Barracks Six.

Everything seemed shipshape. Pinkard didn't trust the way things seemed. He had no reason not to. He just didn't. He took out a little book and scribbled a note to himself. Half the men in here would get cleared out before the day was done, to be replaced by prisoners from other barracks. If plots were stirring, that would slow them down. People would have to figure out who could be trusted and who couldn't. *I better stick a new informer or two in here, too,* Jeff thought. The less that went on without his knowing it, the better the camp ran.

He was heading for the next barracks when a guard came up to him with a yellow envelope. "This here wire just came in, boss," the man said, and thrust it at him.

"What the hell?" Pinkard took the envelope, opened it, and extracted the telegram inside. "What the *hell*?" he said again, this time in tones of deep dismay.

"What's the matter?" the guard asked.

"What's the matter?" Jeff would echo anybody, not just himself. "I'll tell you what's the matter. We're going to get a new shipment of prisoners, that's what—a big new shipment of prisoners. Nice of 'em to let us know, wasn't it? They're supposed to start comin' in this afternoon."

"A new shipment of prisoners?" The guard proved he could repeat what he'd just heard, too. Then he exploded, much as Jeff wanted to do. "Jesus H. Christ! Where the hell we gonna put 'em? We already got niggers swingin' from the rafters. Shit, we got niggers comin' out our assholes, is what we got."

"You know that, Wes, and I know that, and anybody who knows one goddamn thing about this here camp knows it, too," Pinkard said. "But you know what else? The folks in Richmond don't know it. Either that or they just don't give a fuck." He looked around more than a little frantically. "Where am I gonna put all them nigger bastards? How am I gonna stop 'em from runnin' away? Christ! How are we gonna feed 'em? This here don't say word one about extra rations."

Wes frowned. Then he shrugged. "Split up what you get with as many mouths as we got inside. What the hell else can you do?"

"Damfino." Jefferson Pinkard shook his head in deep discontent. "Prisoners we got are already hungry as can be on what we're feeding 'em. Nothin' left to scrounge off the countryside. If they got to make do with three-quarters as much—or maybe only half as much: how can I guess?—they're gonna start starving to death in jigtime."

"You don't need to get your bowels in an uproar about it, boss," Wes said. "They're only niggers, for Chrissake. Ain't like you was starvin' Uncle Henry and Aunt Daisy."

"Oh, hell, I know that," Pinkard said. "But this is all just a bunch of crap." His sense of order, of propriety, was offended. "If they send us extra men, they oughta send us the extra rations to go with 'em. Ain't fair if they don't. It's like in the Bible where old what's-his-name—Pharaoh—made the Jews make bricks without straw." He wanted things to work the way they were supposed to.

"Reckon the sheenies had it coming to 'em, same as the coons do now," Wes said.

But Pinkard shook his head. "No. You give somebody something to do, you got to give him the chance to do it, too. And Richmond *ain't*."

"Send 'em a wire back," the guard suggested.

"Maybe I will." But Jeff doubted he would. If the big boys got the idea he couldn't handle whatever they threw at him, they'd toss him out on his ear and put in somebody who wouldn't say shit if he had a mouthful.

As promised—threatened?—the new shipment of colored prisoners did come in that afternoon. Pinkard had his clerks as ready as they could be. They got swamped anyway. It would have been worse if they hadn't been braced. That was the most Jeff could say for it. The shipment was even larger than he'd expected. For a little while, he feared he wouldn't be able to shoehorn everybody inside the barbed-wire perimeter.

He did manage that, though he had prisoners curled up on bare ground between barracks without a blanket to call their own. The cooks served out the supper ration, share and share alike. The new prisoners ate like starving wolves. Pinkard wondered how long they'd gone with even less, or with nothing. By their gaunt faces and hollow cheeks, some of them had gone quite a while. The men already inside Camp Dependable grumbled at what they got. They didn't grumble too loud, though; if they had, they would have offended people who'd been through worse.

About midnight, a thunderstorm loosed an artillery barrage of rain on the prison camp. The new prisoners struggled to get into the barracks: it was either that or sink into what rapidly became a bottomless gumbo of mud. Not all of them could. The buildings simply would not hold so many men.

*We'll see pneumonia in a few days,* Jeff thought, lying in bed while lightning raved. *They'll die like flies, especially if nobody ups the ration.*

He shrugged. His initial panic had receded. What could he do about this? Nothing he could see, except ride herd on things the best way he knew how. It wasn't as if the prisoners hadn't done plenty of things that made them deserve to be here. Anybody who came here deserved to be here, by the very nature of things. Jake Featherston had got Kentucky and Houston back for the Confederate States. If that didn't prove he knew what was what, nothing could. Nodding to himself—*figured that one out*—Pinkard rolled over and went back to sleep.

Hipolito Rodriguez had always been better at saving money than most of his neighbors. That Magdalena had the same sort of thrifty temperament certainly helped. Some of the people around Baroyeca thought of him as a damned *judio*. He didn't lose any sleep about those people's opinions. In general, he didn't think much of them, either.

He did believe that working hard and hanging on to as much cash as he could paid off sooner or later. *Sooner or later* often simply meant *later*. He wasn't rich. He wasn't about to get rich any time soon. But he didn't mind living more comfortably when the chance came along.

And it was coming. He could see it coming, in the most literal sense of the words: a row of poles stretching out along the road from Baroyeca that ran alongside his farm. Every day, the Freedom Youth Corps planted more of them, as if they were some crop that would grow.

Electricity had come to the town a few years earlier. That it should come to the farms outside of town . . . Rodriguez hadn't been sure he would live to see the day, but here it was, and he was going to take advantage of it. He'd had the money to pay an electrician to wire the house before the poles reached it. He'd had enough to buy electric lamps and the bulbs that went with them, too. And he'd had enough for a surprise for Magdalena. The surprise waited in the barn. (He also dreamt of buying an automobile, and a tractor to take the place of the mule. He knew that was and would stay a dream, but savored it anyhow.)

The day came when the poles reached and marched past his house. That turned out to be something of an anticlimax, for the wires that made the poles anything more than dead trees hadn't yet come so far. Still, looking out at the long shadows the poles cast in the low January sun, he nodded to himself. Those poles were the visible harbingers of a new way of life.

Three days later, the electrical wires arrived. Freedom Youth Corps boys strung them from pole to pole under the supervision of a foul-mouthed electrician from Hermosillo. Even Rodriguez, who'd done his time in the Army, heard some things he'd never run into before. For the boys from the Freedom Youth Corps, this had to be part of their training that they hadn't expected.

Baroyeca's electrician was a moon-faced man named César Calderon. He never swore. The day after the wires passed the farmhouse, he came out on a mule that made the one Rodriguez owned seem like a thoroughbred by comparison. He ran a wire from the closest power pole to the fuse box he'd installed on the side of the house. He tested the circuits with a device that glowed when the current was flowing. Seeing it light up made Rodriguez swell with pride.

"*¿Todo está bien?*" he asked.

Calderon nodded. "Oh, yes. Everything is fine, exactly how it should be. If you like, you can plug in a lamp and turn it on."

Fingers trembling, Rodriguez did. He pushed the little knob below the light bulb. The motion felt strange, unnatural, unpracticed. The knob clicked into the new position. The light came on. It was even brighter than Rodriguez had expected.

Magdalena crossed herself. "*Madre de Dios*," she whispered. "It's like having the sun in the house."

Rodriguez solemnly shook hands with the electrician. "*Muchas gracias.*"

"*De nada*," Calderon replied. But it wasn't nothing, and they both knew it. Calderon packed up his tools, climbed onto the mule, and rode away. Rodriguez turned off the lamp and turned it on again. Yes, the electricity stayed even after the electrician went away. Rodriguez had thought it would, but he hadn't been quite sure. When he lit a kerosene lamp, he understood what was going on: the flame from the match made the wick and the kerosene that soaked up through it burn. But what really happened when he pushed that little knob? The light came on. How? Why? He couldn't have said.

But even if he didn't know how it worked, he knew that it worked. And knowing that it worked was plenty. He turned out the lamp again—they didn't really need it right this minute—and headed out to the barn, telling Magdalena, "I'll be back," over his shoulder.

The crate was large, heavy, and unwieldy. He'd brought it to the farm from Baroyeca in the wagon. Now it rested on a sledge. He'd been warned to keep it upright; bad things would happen, he was told, if it went over on its side. He didn't want bad things to happen, not after the money he'd spent. He dragged the crate out of the barn and toward the farmhouse.

Magdalena came outside. "What have you got there?" she asked.

Hipolito Rodriguez smiled. He'd made a point of coming back from town after sundown, so she wouldn't see what was in the wagon. "It's—a box," he said.

*"Muchas gracias,"* Magdalena replied with icy sarcasm. "And what is in the box?"

"Why, another box, of course," he replied, which won him a glare from his wife. By then, he'd hauled the crate to the base of the steps. He went back to the barn for a hammer, which he used to pull up the nails holding the crate closed. "You don't believe me? Here, I'll show you."

"Show me what?" Magdalena demanded. But then she gave a little gasp, for, just as Rodriguez had planned, the front panel of the crate fell away. She stared at him. "Is that—?"

He nodded. *"Sí,* sweetheart. It's a refrigerator."

She crossed herself again. She did that several times a day. It was nothing out of the ordinary. Then she started to cry. That made him hurry up the stairs and take her in his arms, because she hardly ever did it. She sobbed on his shoulder for a few seconds. At last, pulling away, she said, "I never thought we would have electricity. Even when we got electricity, I never thought we would have one of these. And I wanted one. I wanted one so much." She suddenly looked anxious. "But can we afford it?"

"It wasn't as much as I thought it would be," he answered. "And it isn't supposed to use that much electricity. Look." He wrestled off the rest of the crate. That done, he opened the refrigerator door. "In the freezer compartment, it even makes its own ice in little trays."

"What will they think of next?" Magdalena whispered. "A few years ago, I don't think there was any ice in all of Baroyeca. Who in the whole town had ever seen ice?"

"Anyone who'd gone north to fight *los Estados Unidos.*" Rodriguez shivered at the memory. And he'd only been in Texas. The men who'd fought in Kentucky and Tennessee had had it worse. "I have seen ice, *por Dios,* and I wish I hadn't."

"You'd seen God make ice," Magdalena said with a snort. "Had you ever seen people making ice?"

"Even the people had it up there," he said. "They're richer than we are. But we're gaining. I know we are. I didn't used to think so, not before the Freedom Party won. Now I'm sure of it."

"Electricity," his wife said, as if the one word proved everything that needed proving. As far as Rodriguez was concerned, it did.

He went back and closed the refrigerator's door. Then, grunting with effort, he picked up the machine and carried it up the stairs. It wasn't any taller than his navel, but it was plenty heavy. He'd found that out getting the crate into the wagon in the first place. When he set it down on the porch, the boards groaned under the weight. "Open the door for me, please," he said, and Magdalena did.

The kitchen wasn't far. *A good thing, too,* Rodriguez thought. He set the refrigerator against the wall near an outlet and plugged it in. It started to hum: not loudly, but noticeably. He hadn't known it would do that. He cocked his head to one side, listening and wondering how annoying it would be. Would he get used to it, or would it start to drive him crazy? He didn't know, but he expected he'd find out.

Magdalena came in to stare at the new arrival in the kitchen. "Is it cold yet?"

"I don't know." Rodriguez opened the door and stuck his hand inside. "It feels cooler, anyhow, I think." He took out the ice-cube trays. "Fill these with water. We'll see how long they take to freeze."

"All right." Magdalena did. Carefully, she put the trays back into the freezer compartment, closed its door, and closed the refrigerator door. The hum, which had got louder with the door open, quieted down again. "Not too bad," Magdalena murmured, and Hipolito nodded; he'd been thinking the same thing. She went on, "We have lamps. We have this wonderful refrigerator." She pronounced the unfamiliar word with care. "Do you know what I would like next, when we can afford it?"

"No. What?" Rodriguez hadn't begun to think about what might come after the refrigerator.

But Magdalena had. "A wireless set," she said at once. "That has to be the most wonderful invention in the whole world. Music and people talking here inside our own house whenever we want them—what could be more marvelous?"

"I don't know." Rodriguez hadn't heard the wireless all that often himself. It had brought returns from the last election to Freedom Party headquarters. The cantina had a set, too, one that usually played love songs. He shrugged. "If you want one, I suppose we can do that one of these days. They aren't too expensive."

"I *do* want one," Magdalena said emphatically. "If we have a wireless set, we can hear everything that happens as soon as it happens. We wouldn't be on a farm outside a little town in a state most of *los Estados Confederados* don't care about. We would be in New Orleans or Richmond itself."

Rodriguez laughed. "Now I understand," he said. "You want the wireless set so you can catch up on gossip all over the world."

His wife poked him in the ribs. He squirmed. He wasn't usually ticklish, but she'd found a sensitive spot. She said, "And you never gossip at all when you visit *La Culebra Verde*."

"That's different," he declared. Magdalena didn't say anything, which made him wonder how it was different. He tried his best: "Men talk about important things."

Magdalena laughed in his face. Evidently his best wasn't good enough. But she let him down easy, asking, "Is it ice yet?"

"Let's find out." He opened the refrigerator door. The air that came out was definitely chilly now. The water in the ice-cube trays was still water, though. He touched it with a fingertip. "It's getting colder."

Magdalena touched it, too. She nodded and closed the door. They stood there in front of the refrigerator, listening to the soft hum of the future.

# XVII

In the officers' mess on the USS *Remembrance*, Commander Dan Cressy nodded to Sam Carsten. "Well, Lieutenant, you called that one," the exec said.

"Called which one, sir?" Sam asked. The carrier was rolling, but not too badly. He had no trouble staying in his chair.

"There are reports of Confederate soldiers assembling near the borders of Kentucky and Houston," Cressy answered. "What do you want to bet they'll be marching in as soon as we finish pulling out, just the way you said they would?"

"Sir, if you think I'm happy to be right, you're wrong," Sam said. "What happens if they do go in?"

Commander Cressy shrugged. "I don't know. I hope President Smith does. He'd better. Somebody had better, anyhow."

"If they go in, won't it take a war to get them out?" That was Lieutenant Commander Hiram Pottinger, Carsten's superior on the damage-control party.

Nobody in the officers' mess said anything for some little while after that. They knew what war meant. Not many of them besides Sam had served in the Great War, but they'd all been through the inconclusive Pacific War against Japan.

"A lot will depend on what happens in Europe," Commander Cressy said.

"France is starting to whoop and holler about Alsace and Lorraine," Sam said meditatively. "I saw an *Action Française* riot before those boys came to power. I don't think they'll take no for an answer. They're just as sure they've got God on their side as Jake Featherston is."

"And the Russians are squawking about Poland, and they're starting to squawk about the Ukraine, too," Cressy said. "And the limeys are growling at the micks, and ain't we got fun?"

Sam sighed. He wished for a cigarette, but the smoking lamp was out. "We're going to hell in a handbasket all over again," he said. "Didn't anybody learn anything the last time around?"

"I'll tell you one thing we didn't learn," the *Remembrance*'s exec said. "We didn't learn to make sure the sons of bitches who lost took so many lumps, they couldn't get back up on their feet and have another try. And I'm afraid we're going to have to pay for it."

Lieutenant Commander Pottinger said, "They've learned something in South America, anyhow. Argentina and the Empire of Brazil are cuddling up, even if Argentina and Chile are yelling again."

"Sir, that's good news for Britain, not for us," Carsten said. "If there is a war, it means Brazil will let Argentina ship food through its territorial waters and then make the short hop across the Atlantic to French West Africa, same as happened the last time."

"How do you know so much about that?" Commander Cressy asked, as if to say, *You're a mustang, so you're not supposed to know much of anything.*

"Sir, I was there, in the *Dakota*," Sam answered. Cressy was a young hotshot. He had more book learning and learned faster than anyone Sam had ever seen. If war did come, he would likely have flag rank by the time it was done, assuming he lived. But he did sometimes forget that people could also learn by good, old-fashioned experience.

The other side of the coin was, Sam had only been a petty officer then. Officers also had the unfortunate habit of believing that men who weren't didn't know anything. (Petty officers, of course, were just as sure that officers' heads either had nothing in them or were full of rocks.)

"We can lick the Confederates," Pottinger said. "We did it before, and this time we won't have to take on Canada, too."

Everyone in the mess nodded. Somebody—Sam didn't see who—said, "Goddamn Japs'll try and sucker punch us in the Pacific when we're busy close to home."

More nods. Sam said, "They did that in the last war—the last big war, I mean. I was there for that, too."

Something in his tone made Commander Cressy's gaze sharpen. "The *Dakota* was the ship that went on that wild circle through the Battle of the Three Navies, wasn't she?"

"Yes, sir," Carsten said. "One of the hits we took jammed our steering, so all we could do *was* circle—either that or stand still, and the Japs or the limeys would have blown us out of the water if we had."

"You've had an . . . interesting career, haven't you?" the exec said.

"Sir, I've been lucky," Sam answered. "Closest I came to buying a plot was from the Spanish influenza after the war. That almost did me in. Otherwise, hardly a scratch."

"They tried taking the Sandwich Islands away from us in the Pacific War." Hiram Pottinger went on with the main argument: "Odds are the bastards will try it again. And if they do, the Pacific coast had better look out."

Nobody argued with him. After the wake-up call the Japanese had given Los Angeles in 1932, nobody could. They'd built their Navy to fight far out into the Pacific, and so had the United States. If the two countries ever went at each other with everything they had . . .

"If we go at the Japs full bore, instead of doing a half-assed job of it the way we did the last time, we'll lick 'em," Sam said.

Commander Cressy nodded. "If we could do that, we would," he said. "But if we're at war with Japan any time soon, we're also likely to be at war with the Confederate States. And if we're at war with the CSA, we aren't going to be able to hit the Japs with everything we've got. And they've built up a tidy little empire for themselves since the last war."

That was true enough. Japan had owned Chosen, Formosa, and the Philippines going into the Great War. Since then, she'd gained a lot of influence in China and quietly acquired Indochina from France and the oil-rich East Indies from Holland. In the aftermath of defeat, Britain hadn't been able to do anything but grumble and hope she could hold on to Malaya and Singapore if she ever got on Japan's bad side. But, since the limeys and the Japs both worried about the USA, they put up with each other.

"If they hit us again, those sons of bitches are going to put a rock in their fist," somebody predicted gloomily.

"Well, gentlemen, that's why we wear the uniform." Commander Cressy got to his feet. He was always sharply turned out. Sam envied him the knife-edged creases in his trousers. His own clothes were clean, but they weren't what you'd call pressed. Neither were those of anybody else in the officers' mess—except the exec's. Cressy nodded to the other men and left, ignoring the ship's motion with the air of a man who'd known worse.

Sam stayed long enough to drink another cup of coffee. Then he left the mess, too. As often happened, the officers' bull session went aimless and foolish without Cressy's sharp wit to steer it along. The exec also had the rank to make that wit felt. Sam thought he might have done some steering, too, but he was junior in grade, too damn old, and a mustang to boot. Nobody would take him seriously.

More than a little wistfully, he went up to the flight deck. He wished he had more to do with sending airplanes off into battle. That was why he'd wanted to serve on the *Remembrance* in the first place. He'd done good work, useful work, in damage control since returning to the ship as an officer. He knew that. He was even proud of it. But it still wasn't what he wanted to be doing.

Mechanics in coveralls had the cowl off a fighter's engine. They were puttering with a fuel line, puttering and muttering and now and then swearing like sailors. *Funny how that works,* Carsten thought, smiling at the bad language that flavored the conversation the way pepper flavored scrambled eggs.

The fighter itself was a far cry from the wire-and-canvas two-deckers that had flown off the *Remembrance* when Sam first came aboard her. It was a sleek, aluminum-skinned one-decker with folding wings, so the belowdecks hangar could hold more of its kind. Because of the strengthening it needed to cope with being sent forth with a kick from a catapult and landing with an arrester hook, it was a little heavier and a little slower than a top land-based fighter—a little, but not much.

Carsten looked out to sea. As always, destroyers shepherded the *Remembrance* on all sides. The way things were these days, you just couldn't tell. If the Confederates or the limeys wanted to use a submersible to get in a quick knee in the nuts, those destroyers were the ones that would have to make sure they couldn't. He'd served aboard a ship not much different from them. Compared to the *Remembrance*, they were insanely crowded. They were also much more vulnerable to weather and the sea. But they did a job no other kind of vessel could do.

For that matter, so did the *Remembrance* herself. With her aircraft, she could project U.S. power farther than any battleship's big guns. All by herself, she could make the Royal Navy thoughtful about poking its nose into the western Atlantic. Because of that, Sam was surprised when, half an hour later, the carrier suddenly picked up speed—the flight deck throbbed under his feet as the engines began working harder—and swung toward the west. Like any good sheepdogs, the destroyers stayed with her.

"What's going on, sir?" Sam called to the officer of the deck.

"Beats me," that worthy replied.

She kept on steaming west all the rest of that day and into the night. By the time the sun came up astern of her the next morning, rumor had already declared that she was bound for Boston or Providence or New York or Philadelphia or Baltimore to be scrapped or refitted or to have the captain court-martialed or because she was running low on beans. Sam didn't believe the skipper had done anything to deserve a court-martial. Past that, he kept an open mind.

She turned out to be heading for the Boston Naval Yard. The powers that be admitted as much before she'd been steaming west for a day. They remained close-mouthed about why she'd been called in to port early in her cruise. Maybe she really was running low on beans. Sam couldn't have proved she wasn't. Sailors hoped for shore leave while she stayed in port.

When she came in, a tugboat guided her into Boston harbor. By the way the tug dodged and zigged, Carsten suspected the minelayers had been busy. That saddened him, but didn't surprise him very much.

More tugs nudged the *Remembrance* up against a quay. It was snowing hard, the temperature down close to zero. That didn't keep a swarm of electrician's mates and machinist's mates led by several officers from coming aboard and going straight to work. By all appearances, the refit rumor had been true.

But what were the technicians fitting? Sam couldn't figure it out on his own, and nobody seemed willing to talk. Whatever it was, it involved some funny-looking revolving installations atop the island, and a bunch of new gear inside the armored command center. After a little while, Sam stopped asking questions. Whenever he did, people looked at him as if he were a traitor. He went on about his own business and watched from the corner of his eye. Sooner or later, he figured, he'd find out.

Lucien Galtier stretched uncomfortably as he shooed another hen off the nest to see if she'd laid. She hadn't; his fingers found no new egg. The hen clucked at the indignity. Galtier went on to the next nest. He grunted when he reached into it. The grunt was part satisfaction, for he found an egg there, and part unhappiness, for he still couldn't get rid of the tightness in his chest.

No help for it. Even if he had pulled something in there, the work didn't go away. He finished gathering eggs, fed the animals and mucked out their stalls, and did everything else in the barn that needed doing. Then he picked up the basket of eggs, pulled his hat down on his forehead, lowered the earflaps and tied them under his chin, pulled the thick wool muffler Nicole had knitted up to cover his mouth and nose, and left the barn.

That first breath of outside air was as bad as he'd known it would be. He might have inhaled a lungful of daggers. It was cold inside the barn with the animals' body heat and an oil heater warming things up and with the wooden walls keeping out wind and snow. Outside, in the space between the barn and the farmhouse, it was a good deal worse than merely cold.

Snow blew horizontally out of the northwest. It had a good running start by the time it got to his farm. It stung his eyes and tried to freeze them shut. Despite hat and muffler and heavy coat and sweater and stout dungarees and woolen, itchy long johns, the wind started sucking heat from his body the instant it touched him.

In the swirling white, he could hardly see the house ahead. He'd known worse blizzards, but not many. If he missed the house, he'd freeze out here. That happened to a luckless farmer or two every winter in Quebec.

Lucien didn't miss. He staggered up the stairs, opened the kitchen door, lurched inside, and slammed it shut behind him. *"Calisse!"* he muttered. He shook himself like a dog. Snow flew everywhere. The stove was already hot, but he built up the fire in it and stood in front of it, gratefully soaking up the warmth.

Only after he'd done that did he worry about the clumps of melting snow on the floor. He cleaned up as best he could. Then he went back to the stove and made himself a pot of coffee. He gulped it down as hot as he could stand it. He wanted to be warm inside and out.

Outside, the wind kept howling. He watched the blowing, swirling whiteness and sent it some thoughts that weren't compliments. There was supposed to be a dance tomorrow night. If the blizzard went on roaring, how would anybody get to it?

He turned on the wireless set in the front room. The wireless was a splendid companion for a man who lived by himself. It made interesting noise, and he didn't have to respond unless he wanted to. Music poured out of the speaker. Right now, though, he didn't care for music. He changed the station. He wanted to find out whether they were going to get another foot and a half of snow before tomorrow night.

But the wireless stations blathered on about what they were interested in, not about what he was interested in. That was the drawback of the marvelous machine. He didn't have to respond to it unless he wanted to, but it didn't have to respond to him at all.

He went from station to station for the next twenty minutes, until the top of the hour, and not one of them seemed the least bit interested in the weather outside. For all they cared, it could have been summer out there, with blue sky and warm sun. It could have been, but he knew it wasn't.

At the top of the hour, every station gave forth with five minutes of news. It was as if they suddenly remembered they were part of the wider world after all. Lucien listened impatiently to accounts of riots in the Ukraine and Austria-Hungary and celebrations on the border between the United States and the Confederate States. All he wanted was a simple weather report, and nobody seemed willing to give him one.

Finally, at the very tail end of one of the newscasts, an announcer grudgingly said, "Our storm is expected to blow itself out by this afternoon. Snow will end before nightfall, and tomorrow will be clear and a little warmer." Two sentences, and then the music resumed.

In January in Quebec, *a little warmer* didn't mean *warm*. Lucien knew that all too well. He also knew the weather forecasters lied in their teeth about one time in three. Even so, he had reason to hope. Without hope, what was a man? Nothing worth mentioning.

Sure enough, that afternoon the wind dropped and the snow stopped falling. The sun came out and peeped around, as if surprised at everything that had happened since the last time it showed its face. It might have been embarrassed at what it saw, for it set half an hour later.

The night was long and cold, as January nights were. Lucien woke when it was still dark. He threw on his clothes and went out to the outhouse. The sky was brilliantly clear. Ribbons and curtains of aurora blazed in the north. He yawned and nodded, acknowledging that they were there. Then he trudged back to the farmhouse.

He was eating fried eggs when a snowplow grumbled by. The main road would be clear, then. Who could guess whether the little side roads to Éloise Granche's house would be, though, and the ones from there to the dance?

"Well," he said, "I will just have to find out."

Before he could find out, he had to do some shoveling to let his auto get to the main road. That was hard work, and would have been for a man half his age. His heart was pounding before he finished, but finish he did. Under all those layers of warm clothes, sweat ran down his sides. He went back in and heated water for a bath. That helped soak out some of the kinks in his back, though others refused to disappear.

When evening came, he used a little more hot water, this time for a shave. He scraped his chin and cheeks with a straight razor he'd been using since before the turn of the century. None of these newfangled safety razors and blades for him. He stropped the razor on a thick, smooth piece of leather before it touched his face. If his shave wasn't smooth, he had only himself to blame, not some factory down in the United States.

He dressed in clothes he might have worn to town: dark trousers, clean white shirt, and his least disreputable hat. The overcoat he put on had seen better days, but overcoats always got a lot of use in Quebec. Whistling a tune he'd heard on the wireless, he went out to the Chevrolet.

"I want no trouble from you," he told the auto, as if it were the horse with which he'd had so many philosophical discussions over the years. The Chevrolet was old, but it knew better than to argue with him. It started right up.

Despite the snowplow and the rock salt it had laid down, the roads would still be icy. Galtier drove with care, and made sure he kept plenty of room between himself and other motorists—not that many others were out and about. He didn't miss the traffic. He knew he wouldn't be able to stop in a hurry.

He left the paved road and bumped along rutted dirt lanes till he came to the farm where Éloise Granche lived. The dim, buttery light of kerosene lamps poured out through her windows; she still had no electricity. He stopped the engine, wagged a finger at the Chevrolet to remind it to start up again, and went up the steps and knocked on the door.

"Hello," she said with a smile. Then she was in his arms and they kissed hungrily for a long time.

Still holding her, he said, "When we do that, I want to forget all about the dance."

"We can, if you want to," she answered. "Would you rather just stay here?"

Regretfully, Galtier shook his head. "That would be a lot of staying for not much staying power, I'm afraid. If I were half my age, I would say yes."

"If you were half your age, I wouldn't want anything to do with you—not for that, anyhow," Éloise said. "We'll go to the dance, then, and we'll come back, and who knows what will happen after that?"

"Who indeed?" Lucien kissed her again, then led her out to the motorcar.

That wagged finger did its job. The auto started up again without any fuss. The dance was at Pierre Turcot's, not far from the little town of St.-Modèste. A rowdy sprawl of motorcars and wagons and buggies surrounded Turcot's barn when the Chevrolet pulled up. Lucien handed Éloise out of the motorcar. They went in side by side.

People waved and called their names and hurried up to greet them. By now, they'd been together long enough that all their neighbors took them for granted. They might almost have been a married couple. Lucien's son Georges was already out on the floor dancing. He waved to Lucien and blew Éloise a kiss.

"Georges can be very foolish," Éloise remarked. She eyed Galtier. "I wonder where he gets it."

"I haven't the faintest idea," he answered with such dignity as he could muster.

The fiddlers and drummer and accordion player took a break. Pierre Turcot wound up a phonograph and put a record on it. The dancing went on. The musicians on the record played and sang better than the home-grown talent. Lucien had noticed that before. He wondered if the problem would kill off homegrown talent after a while. But once he started whirling Éloise around the floor, he stopped worrying about it.

They danced. They snacked and drank some of the potent punch Pierre had set out and danced some more. People talked about politics in the city of Quebec and the price of potatoes and who was fooling around with whom. Lucien didn't think he and Éloise were high on the gossip list these days. Why get excited about old news?

Somewhere between ten and eleven, Éloise turned to him and said, "Shall we go?"

He smiled. "Yes, let's."

They went back to her house in companionable silence. When they got there, he got out first so he could open the door on her side. "Such a gentleman," she said. "Would you like to come in for a little while?"

"Why not?"

They drank some applejack. One of Éloise's neighbors had cooked it up. It was a good batch, almost as good as if it weren't bootleg. And then, as they had a good many times before, they went upstairs to her bedroom.

Everything was dark in there, but Lucien knew where the bed was. He sat down on one side of it and got out of his clothes. When he was naked, he reached out. His hand found Éloise's bare, warm flesh.

They kissed and caressed each other. Lucien's heart pounded with excitement. Heart still pounding, he rolled onto his back. Éloise straddled him. She liked riding him, and he found it easier than the other way round.

"Oh, Lucien," she whispered.

He didn't answer. As his delight mounted, so did the thudding in his chest. He could hardly breathe. He'd never felt anything like this, not in all his years, not with Marie, not with Éloise, not with anyone. Pleasure shot through him. So did pain, pain in his chest, pain stabbing up his arm. Pain . . . He groaned and clutched at Éloise. In an instant, the darkness in the bedroom became darkness absolute.

"Lucien?" Éloise exclaimed. He never heard her scream, or anything else, ever again.

Scipio might have known it would happen one of these days. Hell, he *had* known it might happen one of these days. The Huntsman's Lodge was the best restaurant in Augusta. No other place even compared. If Anne Colleton ever came to town, this was where she'd have dinner.

And there she sat, at a table against the far wall, talking animatedly with several local big shots. Scipio hadn't seen her for twenty years or so, but he had not the slightest doubt. She'd aged very well, even if he wouldn't have called her beautiful any more. And she still sounded as terrifyingly self-assured as she ever had, maybe even more so.

As befit its status as a fancy place to eat, the Huntsman's Lodge was dimly lit. Scipio didn't think she recognized him. He was just another colored waiter, not one serving her table. He thanked heaven he hadn't let Jerry Dover talk him into taking the headwaiter's post. Then he would have had to escort her party to the table, and she would have been bound to notice him.

Even now, he wasn't sure she hadn't. She always held her cards close to her chest. He didn't want to go anywhere near that table. He didn't want to speak, for fear she would know his voice. He spent as much time as he could in the kitchens. The cooks gave him quizzical looks; he didn't get paid for roasting prime rib or doing exotic things with lobster tails.

His boss knew it, too. "What the hell you doing hiding in there, Xerxes?" Jerry Dover demanded indignantly. "Get your ass out and wait tables."

"I's sorry, suh," Scipio answered. "But I gots to tell you, I's feelin' right poorly tonight."

Dover didn't say anything for a little while. His eyes raked Scipio. "You know," he remarked at last, "there's niggers I'd fire on the spot, they tried to use that kind of line on me."

"Yes, suh," Scipio said stolidly. Firing was the least of his worries right now.

"You ain't one of 'em, though. You never tried shirking on me before," the restaurant manager said. He astonished Scipio by reaching out to put a palm on his forehead. "You don't have a fever. At least it isn't the grippe. You need to go home? Go on, then, if you've a mind to."

"I thanks you kindly, suh." As he had years before with John Oglethorpe, Scipio needed to remind himself that white men could be decent. He found it especially remarkable now, with the Freedom Party in the saddle for the past seven years. Things were set up to give whites every excuse to be bastards, and a lot of them didn't need much excuse. "Somehow or other, I finds a way to pay you back." He felt like the mouse talking to the lion in the fable. But the mouse actually had found a way to do it. How could he?

Dover only shrugged. He wasn't worrying about it. "Get the hell out of here," he said. "You got your reasons, whatever they are. I've known you for a while now. You don't fuck around with me. So get."

Scipio got. He wasn't used to being out on the street so early. He made a beeline for the Terry. The sooner he got into his own part of town, the safer he'd feel.

Then he heard a gunshot down an unlit alleyway, a scream, and the sound of running feet. Maybe he wasn't so safe in the Terry after all. Whites preyed on blacks, but blacks also preyed on one another. He wondered why. His own people had so little. Why not try to rob whites, who enjoyed so much more? Unfortunately, an answer occurred to him almost at once. If a Negro robbed a white, the police moved heaven and earth to catch him. If he robbed another Negro, they yawned and went about their business.

"Hey, nigger!" A woman's voice, all rum and honey, called from the darkness. "You in your fancy clothes, I show you a good time like you ain't never seen." Scipio didn't even turn to look. He just kept walking. "Cocksuckin' faggot!" the woman yelled after him, all the sweetness gone.

Bathsheba stared when Scipio came into the apartment so early. "What you doin' here?" she demanded. "I jus' put the chillun to bed."

He'd been trying to figure out what to tell her ever since he left the Huntsman's Lodge. "Once upon a time, you asked me how I came to be able to speak like this," he answered in soft, precise, educated white man's English. Bathsheba's eyes went wide. The only time he'd ever spoken like that in her hearing was to save their lives in the rioting not long after the Freedom Party took over. Now he had to tell the truth, or some of it. In that same dialect, he went on, "A long time ago, I was in the upper ranks of one of the Socialist Republics we tried to set up. Someone came into the restaurant tonight who knew me in those days. I'm not certain whether she recognized me, but she might have. She's . . . very sharp." Seeing Anne Colleton forcibly reminded him how sharp she was.

"You learn to talk like dat on account of you was a Red?" Bathsheba asked.

Scipio shook his head. "No. I was useful to the Reds because I could already talk like this. I . . . I was a butler, a rich person's butler in South Carolina." There. Now she knew—knew enough, anyhow.

He waited for her to shout at him for not telling his secret years before. But she didn't. "If you was a big Red, no wonder you don't say nothin'," she told him. "What we do now?"

"Dunno." He fell back into the slurred speech of the Congaree Negro. Talking in that other voice took him off to a world that had died in fire and blood and hate—but also a world where he'd grown to manhood. The contrasts terrified him. "Mebbe nuttin'. Mebbe run fas' as we kin."

"How?" Bathsheba asked, and he didn't have a good answer for her. Passbooks were checked these days as they'd never been before the war. Any black without a good reason for being where he was—and without the papers to back up that reason—was in trouble. People talked about camps. No one knew much about them, though; they were easy to get into, much harder to leave.

Even so, he said, "Better we takes de chance. They catches me . . ."

He didn't go on. If they caught him and realized who he was, he wouldn't last ten minutes. No trial. No procedure. They'd just shoot him.

Bathsheba was still staring at him. His wife clucked sadly, a sound of reproach: self-reproach, he realized when she said, "I shoulda pussected what you was." He needed a heartbeat or two to figure out that she meant *suspected*. She went on, "If you was a Red, you had to hide out. And you was smart, gettin' out o' the state where you was at."

"I weren't no Red, not down deep, not for real an' for true," Scipio said. "But dey suck me in. I don't go 'long wid dey, dey shoots me jus' like de buckra shoots me." That was the truth. Cassius and Cherry and the rest of the Reds on the Marshlands plantation had been in deadly earnest. Confidence in their doctrine had sustained them—till rifles and what little else they got from the USA ran up against the whole panoply of modern war, and till they discovered their oppressors wouldn't vanish simply because they were called reactionaries.

Bathsheba's mind went in a different direction. Suddenly, she said, "I bet Xerxes ain't even your right name."

"Is now. Has been fo' years."

"What your mama call you?"

"Scipio," he said, and wondered how long it had been since he'd spoken his own name. More than twenty years; he was sure of that.

"Scipio." Bathsheba tasted it, then slowly shook her head. "Reckon I like Xerxes better. I's used to it." She sent him an anxious look. "You ain't mad?"

"Do Jesus, no!" he exclaimed. "You go an' forget you ever hear de other one. Dat name get around, de buckra after we fo' sure. Dey still remembers me in South Carolina." Was that pride in his voice? After all these years, after all that terror, after being sure at the time that he was walking into a disaster (and after proving righter than even he'd imagined), was that pride? God help him, it was.

His wife gave him a kiss. "Good." She was proud of him, too, proud of him for what had to be the stupidest thing he'd ever done in his life. Madness. It had to be madness. There was no sensible explanation for it. But no sooner had that thought crossed his mind than Bathsheba said, "Every once in a while—Lord, more'n every once in a while—them white folks *deserves* a whack in the chops, they truly does."

And that did make sense. When things were bad, you tried your best to make them better. How didn't matter much. "Let's go to bed," he said.

"How you mean dat?" Bathsheba asked.

Now he kissed her. "However you wants, sweetheart."

He went up to the Huntsman's Lodge the next day with a certain amount of apprehension. He checked the autos parked near the restaurant with special care. None of them looked as if it belonged to either the police or Freedom Party goons. He had to go to work. If he didn't, he wouldn't eat, and neither would his family. In he went.

Jerry Dover met him just inside the door. "Go home," the manager said bluntly. "Get the hell out of here. You're still sick. You'll be sick another couple of days, too."

Scipio blinked. "What you say?"

"Go home," Dover repeated. "Damn Freedom Party woman asking all kinds of questions about you."

Ice congealed in Scipio's belly. He might have known Anne Colleton would spot him. Did she ever miss a trick? "What you say to she?" he asked, already hearing hounds baying on his trail.

"I told her you ain't who she thinks you are. I told her you been working here since 1911," Jerry Dover answered. His eyes twinkled.

"God bless you, Mistuh Dover, but when she catch you in de lie—"

"She ain't gonna catch me." Dover grinned at him. "I showed her papers from back then to prove it."

"How you do dat?" Now Scipio was all at sea.

Still grinning, the manager said, " 'Cause a nigger named Xerxes did work here then. He was only here a couple months, but those were the papers I showed her. Bastard stole like a son of a bitch. That's why they canned his ass. I heard one of the owners bitching about it not too long after we hired you. The name stuck in my head, and so I watched you close after that, but old Oglethorpe was right—you're first-rate. Anyway, this here gal like to shit, I'll tell you. You don't ever want to tell that one she's wrong. She ain't got no wedding ring, and I can see why."

That made a perfect thumbnail sketch of the Anne Colleton Scipio had known. She would have thought she had him at last—and then she would have seen her hope snatched away. No, she wouldn't be happy, not even a little bit. "God bless you, Mistuh Dover," Scipio said again.

"Go home," Jerry Dover repeated once more. "She may come back and try to raise some more trouble for you. I don't want that. I need you here too bad. And don't get your bowels in an uproar. I'll pay your wages."

Home Scipio went, in a happy daze. Safe—really safe—from Anne Colleton at last! He was back in the Terry before he realized this wonderful silver lining had a cloud. Maybe he was free of Anne Colleton. But now Jerry Dover had a hold on him. Miss Anne had been far away. Dover was right here in town. If he ever decided to go to the police . . . Scipio shivered, but he kept on walking.

*   *   *

"**I**'m Jake Featherston, and I'm here to tell you the truth," the president of the Confederate States said into the microphone as soon as the engineer behind the glass wall gave him the high sign. "And the truth is, folks, that Kentucky is ours again and Texas is whole again and our country is a long way back towards being what it's supposed to be again.

"The people spoke, and the Yankees had to listen. The people said they were sick and tired of being stuck in the USA. They came back where they belonged. The Stars and Bars are flying in Lubbock and San Antonio and Frankfort and Louisville. We took back what was ours, because that was how the people wanted it."

He didn't say anything about losing the plebiscite in Sequoyah. The papers and the wireless in the CSA hadn't said much about it, either. People got the news he wanted them to have, slanted the way he wanted it to go. Oh, his coverage wasn't perfect. By the nature of things, it couldn't be. Too many people could also pick up wireless stations from across the U.S. border. But not a lot of them did. Confederates and Yankees had disliked and distrusted one another for a long time now.

"Here and there along the border, the Yankees are still holding on to what's ours: in Sonora, in Arizona, in Arkansas, and right here in Virginia," Jake continued. "Al Smith tried to make me promise I wouldn't talk about those things if we had the elections last month, but I don't call that an honest kind of promise. No, sir, folks, I don't call it honest at all, not even a little bit. He was saying, 'I'll give you back some of what's yours if you forget about the rest of what's yours.' Now you tell me, friends—is that fair? Is that right?"

*Bang!* He slammed his fist down on the table, a favorite trick of his. "I tell you it's not fair! I tell you it's not right! And I tell you that the Confederate States of America deserve to be whole again! The CSA *will* be whole again! This here that we've done now is only the beginning. We don't want trouble with the United States. We don't want trouble with anybody. But we want what's ours, and we're going to get it!"

He ended just as the light went red. This wasn't one of his long speeches, only a little one to remind people that he'd got back two of the states the Whigs had lost. He stood up, stretched, and left the studio.

As always, Saul Goldman waited for him outside in the hallway. "Good speech, Mr. President," the director of communications said. "I don't think you can make a bad one."

"Thanks, Saul," Featherston answered. "We have a lot of things to take care of over the next few weeks. You've got the incident simmering?"

"Oh, yes." The little Jew nodded. "We'll have something worked up if they don't take care of things for us. They're liable to, you know."

Jake nodded. "Hell, of course I know. But we'll be able to get the story out the way we want it if it's our incident to begin with."

Bodyguards came up alongside of Saul Goldman. Goldman nodded to them in an absent-minded way. He didn't take security as seriously as he should have. Of course, nobody was gunning for him, either. Featherston didn't have the luxury of making that assumption. He nodded to the men in the butternut uniforms. They carried submachine guns at an identical angle. Their expressions were also identical: tough and watchful. Jake was watchful, too, though he tried not to let it show. Party stalwarts had tried to bump him off once. Could he really trust Party guards? If he couldn't, could he trust anybody in the whole wide world?

The guards led him out into the street. They spread out before he got into his new armored limousine. With Virgil Joyner shot dead, his driver was new, too. He missed Virgil. He missed anybody who'd known him in the old days and stuck with him through thick and thin. Harold Stowe, the new man, was probably a better driver than Joyner had been. Jake didn't care. The man was—and acted like—a servant, not a drinking buddy.

"Back to the Gray House, Harold," Featherston said. Harold. He sighed to himself. Stowe didn't even go by Hal or Hank or anything interesting.

"Right, Mr. President," the driver said, and put the limousine in gear. Jake sighed again, a little louder this time. Virgil Joyner had called him *Sarge*. He'd had the right, too. Not many people did, not any more.

Climbing Shockoe Hill was hard work for the heavy limousine. There'd been an ice storm the night before. Despite rock salt on the road, the going was still slippery. They crawled to the top in first gear.

When he strode back into the presidential residence, his secretary met him just inside the door. "You know you're scheduled to meet with Lieutenant General Forrest in ten minutes, don't you, sir?" she said, as if sure he'd forgotten.

"Yes, Lulu, I do know that," he said. "Let me go to the office and look at a couple of things, and I'll be ready for him."

An officer named Nathan Bedford Forrest III should have raised Featherston's hackles. He'd campaigned against all the Juniors and IIIs and even VIs who clung to power in the CSA by virtue of what their ancestors had done, and who hadn't done anything much on their own. But, for one thing, the first Nathan Bedford Forrest had been as much of a self-made son of a bitch as Jake was, and he'd been proud of it, too. And, for another, his great-grandson wasn't a Great War General Staff relic. He'd been too young even to fight in the trenches from 1914 to 1917. He was a hell of a soldier now, though, with notions of how to use barrels as radical as his illustrious ancestor's ideas about horses. Featherston liked the way he thought.

At the moment, though, Forrest looked worried. "Sir, if the Yankees decide to jump us for moving troops into Kentucky and west Texas"—he wouldn't call it Houston, refusing to recognize the validity of the name—"they'll whip us. They can do it. If you don't see that, you'll land the country in a hell of a mess."

"I never said they couldn't," Featherston answered. "But they won't."

Nathan Bedford Forrest III looked exasperated. The first officer to bear the name had been a rawboned man who looked a bit like Jake Featherston. His descendant had a rounder face, though he kept his great-grandfather's dangerous eyes. They looked all the more dangerous when he glowered. "Why won't they? You've promised to keep those states demilitarized, and you're going back on your solemn word. What better excuse do they need?"

"If they attack me for moving my men into my states, they've got a war on their hands," Jake said calmly. "I'm telling you, General, they don't have the stomach for it."

"And I'm telling you, Mr. President, you'll take the country down in ruins if you're wrong." The first Nathan Bedford Forrest had had a reputation for speaking his mind. His great-grandson took after him.

"To hell with the country," Featherston said. Nathan Bedford Forrest III gasped. Jake went on, "I've got twenty dollars of my own money against twenty dollars of yours, General. The damnyankees won't move."

Forrest frowned. "You sound mighty damn sure of yourself, Mr. President."

"I am mighty damn sure of myself," Jake Featherston answered. "That's my job. Suppose you let me tend to it while you tend to yours."

"I *am* tending to my job," Nathan Bedford Forrest III said. "If I didn't point out to you that we're liable to have a problem here, I wouldn't be tending to it. The damnyankees outweigh us. They're always going to outweigh us. Remember how much trouble the Germans had against the Tsar's armies in the Great War? That wasn't because one Russian was as good a soldier as one German. It was because there were a hell of a lot of Russians. There are a hell of a lot of soldiers in the USA, too."

Jake Featherston nodded. "They'll be able to outnumber us, like you said. That means we'll just have to outquick 'em. You going to tell me we can't do that?" His voice developed a hard and ugly rasp. If General Forrest was going to tell him something along those lines, he'd be sorry.

"No, sir." Forrest didn't try. "We've got the airplanes, and we've got the barrels, and we've got the trucks, too. We'll run 'em ragged." Like

Jake, like most of the Confederates who were really involved with them, he called barrels by the name they had in the USA. Some of the men who'd done their service well away from the trenches still used the British name instead: tanks. Featherston found that a useless affectation. But the general wasn't through, for he added, "If there is a war, sir, we'd better win it pretty damn fast. If we don't, we've got troubles. They're bigger than we are, like I say, and they can take more punishment. We don't want to get into a slugging match with them. Do you hear what I'm saying?"

"I hear you," Jake said coldly. "You make yourself very plain."

"Good. That's good. I want you to understand me," Nathan Bedford Forrest III said. "If I have a choice, I'd just as soon see us not have a war at all. Three years of the last one should have been enough to satisfy us for the rest of our days."

Three years of war hadn't been enough to satisfy Jake Featherston. He'd fought with undiminished hatred from beginning to end. Some of that hatred had been aimed at the Yankees, the rest at his own side. He'd had plenty to go around. He still did. "General, I don't need to explain my policies to you. I just need you to carry them out," he said. "Is that plain enough for you, or shall I draw you a picture?"

Nathan Bedford Forrest III looked back at him. "Oh, that's plain enough," he answered. "But if you're being a damn fool, sir, don't you think somebody has the duty to come out and tell you so?"

"People told me that before I got Kentucky and Houston back," Jake said in a low, furious voice. "Was I right, or were they? People told me that when I brought dams and electricity into the Tennessee Valley. Was I right, or were they? People told me that when I made damn sure the farms in this country had the mechanical gear they needed, so we wouldn't get stuck relying on niggers we can't trust. Was I right, or were they?"

"Damned if I know about that last one," Forrest said. "Now we've got those niggers robbing houses in town instead." Featherston waited. The general nodded. "All right, sir. I get your point. But you'd better be able to take my twenty dollars. That's all I've got to say."

"Look here, General—I hope there won't be a war, too," Featherston said. "But one way or the other, the Confederate States are going to get what we want. We deserve it, it's our right to have it, and we're going to get it. Is *that* plain enough for you? Thanks to the Whigs, we've been waiting for almost twenty-five years. That's too damn long. We can't wait forever."

"Yes, sir. Whatever you decide needs doing, we'll try our best to give it to you," Forrest said. "Doing that is our job. Figuring out what we need—that's yours." He got to his feet, saluted, and left.

Jake looked after him. As the door closed, he said, "I know what needs doing," though Nathan Bedford Forrest III could not hear him. "And by God, I aim to do it."

Mary Pomeroy paused with a forkful of scrambled eggs halfway to her mouth. "It's not fair!" she said. "The Yanks let Kentucky and Houston vote on where they wanted to go, and now they're back in the CSA. If they let *us* vote, the Americans would be gone from here so fast, it would make your head swim."

Mort Pomeroy chewed up a mouthful of bacon—Canadian bacon, not the skinny strips that went by the name in the USA—before saying, "They let that Sequoyah place vote, too, and it voted to stay in the United States."

Red curls flew as Mary tossed her head. "At least it had a choice. The Yanks don't give us any."

"I can't do anything about that." Mort ate another chunk of bacon. He might have been chewing on his words, too. After swallowing the bacon, he spat out the words: "And neither can you."

She bridled. The Yanks had shot her brother for trying to do something about the occupation. Her father had fought a one-man war against the USA till his own bomb blew him up instead of General Custer, for whom it was intended. Mort braced himself, regretting what he'd said and getting ready for an argument. Before she could answer him, Alec spoke from his high chair: "More bacon?" He was wild for bacon and ham and sausage—anything salty, in fact.

"Sure, sweetheart," Mary told him, and gave him some. While she cut it up for him, she wondered what to say to her husband. In the end, all that came out was, "Maybe you're right. Maybe I can't."

Mort blinked, plainly thinking he'd got off easy. He waited for her to come out with something else. When she didn't, he decided to count his blessings. He finished his bacon and eggs, his toast and jam, and his tea. Then he got into his overcoat, hat, and earmuffs for the trip across the street to the diner. It was warmer today than it had been lately; the high might get up into double digits. On the other hand, it might not, too.

Mary also finished her breakfast. Then she let Alec chase little pieces of bacon around his plate with his fork as long as he ate one every so often. When it stopped being breakfast and turned into playtime, she extracted him from the high chair and carried him over to the sink so she could wash his greasy face. He liked that no better than he ever did, and he was getting big enough to put up a pretty good fight. But she was still bigger, and so, whether he liked it or not, the grease came off.

She read to him for a while. He liked *Queen Zixi of Ix*, even if a Yank had written it. She didn't suppose L. Frank Baum had particularly disliked Canada. The book gave no sign that he'd ever heard of it—or of the United States, either. Hard to go wrong with a world so thoroughly imaginary.

When Alec started to fidget in her lap, she let him down to play. She didn't have to watch him quite every second these days; he was old enough not to stick everything into his mouth the instant he saw it. That let Mary go into the kitchen and play with something of her own.

Alec wandered in to watch. "Whatcha doing?" he asked.

"Fixing something," Mary answered.

"Is it busted?" he asked. "It don't look busted."

"Doesn't," Mary said. "It doesn't look busted."

"If it doesn't look busted, how come you're fixing it?"

Conversations with children could be surreal. By now, Mary had got used to that, or as used to the unpredictable as you could get. She said, "I'm not fixing it like that. I'm fixing it up."

"Are you making it fancy-like?"

She shook her head. "No, I'm just taking care of what needs taking care of." That didn't mean much to Alec. It didn't mean much to her, either. She didn't care. It kept him from asking too many more questions, which was what she'd had in mind. She worked on it for a while, then put it away. Before too long, it would be done.

"Can we go out and play?" Alec asked.

"No. It's too cold."

"Can we throw snowballs? I'll bop you in the nose with one."

"No. It's even too cold to throw snowballs."

"How can it be too cold to throw snowballs?" Alec was disbelieving. "It's not too cold to snow."

"It's too cold for people to go out there unless they have to."

"Daddy went out there."

"He just went across the street to the diner. And he didn't stop to throw snowballs at anybody." Mary still wondered how Mort had come to be *daddy* to Alec. Her own father had always been *pa* to her. She hadn't looked for anything like that to change. But change it had.

"Sometimes Daddy throws snowballs," Alec said.

Mary couldn't very well deny that. They'd had a memorable snowball fight only a few weeks before. But she said, "He doesn't do it on days like this. On days like this, he stays inside where it's warm as much as he can."

Alec went to a window and looked out. "There's people out there."

"I know there are people out there. Sometimes you have to go to the general store or to the dentist. Sometimes you have to deliver letters and things, the way the postman does." The Yanks called him the mailman. Mary refused to. She'd been calling him the postman since she learned to talk, and she wasn't about to change now. She still called the last letter of the alphabet *zed*, too. She wondered if Alec would after he started going to school. Yanks said *zee*, which struck her as insufferably . . . American.

"Do you have to go to the general store, Mommy?" Alec asked hopefully.

"No. I've got everything I need right here," Mary answered. She wasn't *ma*, either. She wondered why not. How had the language changed while she wasn't looking? She couldn't have said, but it had.

Cleaning and dusting here took only a fraction of the time they would have back on the farm. She didn't have any livestock to worry about, either. How many times had she gone out to the barn no matter what the weather was like, to feed the animals and collect eggs and muck out? She didn't have a number, but she knew it would have been a large one. Animals needed tending, rain or shine or blizzard. Back on the farm, if she had a moment to relax, it probably meant she'd forgotten something that needed doing. Here, she could sit down and smoke a cigarette and read a book or listen to the wireless without feeling guilty about leaving work undone.

Except for electric lights, the wireless was the best thing about electricity she'd found. And there were replacements of sorts for electric lights: gas lamps, or even the kerosene lanterns her mother still used out on the farm. What could replace the wireless, for immediacy or for entertainment? Nothing she could imagine.

No sooner had that thought crossed her mind, though, than she remembered a story the *Rosenfeld Register* had run not so long before. People were starting to figure out how to send moving pictures the same way they sent wireless signals. Apparently they'd broadcast pictures of a football game in New York City. But the sets cost more than a thousand dollars. Mary didn't suppose they'd ever come down to where an ordinary person could afford them.

During the middle of the afternoon, she started boiling a beef tongue in a big iron pot. Tongue was one of her favorite foods. Alec liked it, too. So did Mort, but he preferred it with cloves stuck in it. Back on the farm, they'd always done it simply with carrots and onions and potatoes and whatever other vegetables they happened to have. Today she made it the way her husband liked.

He sniffed when he got back from the diner. "I know what that is!" he exclaimed.

"That's nice," Mary said with a smile.

"That's very nice," Mort said. "We don't serve tongue at the diner. We can't get enough of it, and not enough people would order it if we did."

"Well, here it is," Mary told him. "Sit down, make yourself at home, and it'll be ready in a minute." The way things turned out, making himself at home kept him from sitting down for a while, because Alec tried to tackle him. Any football referee would have thrown a penalty flag. Mort only laughed.

"And Mommy fixed something up in the kitchen," Alec said, trying to tell Mort about the day.

"I know she did, sport," his father answered. "And now we're going to have it for supper."

"No, something else. Something this morning," Alec insisted. Mary wondered if Mort would ask more questions. He didn't. Instead, he got Alec in a half nelson and tickled him with his free hand. Alec squealed and wiggled and kicked. Mary hoped he wouldn't have an accident. That sort of treatment was asking for trouble.

But Alec didn't. He was growing up. He'd start school pretty soon. Part of Mary reacted to that with surprise and horror, and not just because school would teach what the Yanks wanted taught. Where had the time gone? But part of her looked forward to getting him out of the apartment during the day. He really was starting to notice too much of what went on around him.

"Yum," Mort said when he dug into dinner. Mary liked it, too, although she would have preferred the tender meat without cloves. To her, they distracted from the flavor; they didn't improve it. And Alec made supper exciting when he bit into one and yelled that it was burning his tongue off. A swig of milk helped put out the fire.

The next morning, the sun shone brilliantly. The mercury shot all the way up into the twenties. Mary wrapped the box she'd been working on in brown paper and binder twine. "Come on," she told Alec. "Let's get you dressed up nice and warm. We have to take this to the post office."

"What is it?"

"Something for your cousins, over in Ontario."

Getting to the post office took a while, even if it was only three blocks away. Alec threw snowballs and made snow angels and generally had more fun than should have been legal. He had snow all over his front when they went in. It promptly started to melt, because Wilf Rokeby always kept his potbellied stove well fed with coal. The smell of his hair oil was part of the smell of the post office. He wore his hair parted right down the middle, the way he had when Mary was a little girl. It had been dark then. It was white now.

"What have we got here?" he asked when Mary set the box on the counter.

"Present for my cousins," she answered, as she had with Alec.

Like any small-town postmaster, Rokeby knew a lot about what went on in his customers' lives. "You don't have a lot to do with 'em," he remarked, "nor the rest of your family, either. Been years since I sent anything from you folks to Ontario."

"I got a wire from them," Mary said. "Laura had a baby."

His face softened. "A baby. That's nice." He put the package on the scale, then looked at a chart. "Well, you owe me sixty-one cents for this." She gave him three quarters, got her change, and took Alec back out into the snow.

Jonathan Moss got up from the table. He put on his overcoat and hat. "I'm going to head for the office," he said.

Laura nodded. "I thought you would." She gave him a quick, perfunctory kiss. "Do you really have to go in on a Saturday morning, though?"

"I've got to be in court Monday morning, and I'm not ready," Moss answered. "If I don't want to get slaughtered, I'd better know what I'm doing. Say good morning to Dorothy for me when she finally gets up."

"I will." A faint smile crossed Laura's face. "I wonder where she gets it." Their daughter loved to sleep late, a habit neither of them had.

"Don't know. Wherever it comes from, I wish I could catch it. Well, I'm off." Out the door Moss went. As soon as he closed it behind him, he dropped his right hand into the coat pocket where he carried his pistol. He didn't do that where Laura could see him. It made her nervous. But not doing it once he was out in the hallway made him nervous.

No one lay in wait there. No one troubled Jonathan on the stairs. No one bothered him on the way to his Ford, which he didn't park right in front of the apartment building. He examined the auto before getting in. It looked all right. Nothing blew up when he started the engine.

*Maybe this is all so much moonshine,* he thought as he drove to the office. But he couldn't afford to take the chance. What had happened to occupation headquarters in Berlin proved that. He might have laughed off threatening letters. Nobody but an idiot laughed off a bomb.

As usual, he chose a route to the office different from the one he'd used the day before. He didn't park right in front of the building where he worked, either: he used the guarded lot nearby. All the same, the ends of his daily trips to and from work made him nervous. If anyone was gunning for him, those were the places where danger was worst, because he always had to be there. So far, he'd had no trouble. Maybe all his precautions were snapping his fingers to keep the elephants away. Then again, maybe they weren't. The only way to find out was to stop taking them, and even that might not prove anything. He preferred not to run the risk.

Up the steps and into the building. No assassin lurking in the lobby. Up the stairs to his office, wary every time he turned. No crazed Canuck stalking the stairway. He opened the door, flipped on the light switch, and peered inside. Everything was exactly as he'd left it.

He closed and locked the door. Then he took care of the morning housekeeping: he made a pot of coffee and put it on the hot plate. Even though he'd had a cup with breakfast, waiting for it to get ready was a lonely vigil.

Meanwhile, the case ahead. Somebody—under occupation regulations, the military prosecutor didn't have to say who—claimed his client had played an active role in the Canadian uprising in the mid-1920s. Why whoever this was hadn't come forward years earlier was a question Moss intended to raise as loudly as the judge would let him. He'd been trying to find out who had a grudge against Allen Peterhoff. Somebody who stood to gain from Peterhoff's troubles was the likeliest to cause those troubles.

So far, Moss had had no luck finding anyone like that. As far as he could tell, Peterhoff was a pillar of the community. As for what he'd been doing in 1925 and 1926, nobody seemed to have a lot of hard evidence one way or the other. Of course, in cases like this, hard evidence didn't always matter. Hearsay counted for just as much, and often for more.

"Got to be some bastard after his money," Moss muttered to himself. He hadn't seen a case as blatant as this for a long time. It really belonged to the harsh years right after the revolt, not to 1941. But here it was, and the occupying authorities were taking it very seriously indeed. That worried Moss. Why were they flabbling about Peterhoff if they didn't have a case?

Moss had just poured himself his second cup of coffee from the pot when the telephone rang. His hand jerked, but not enough to make him spill the coffee. He set down the cup and picked up the telephone. "Jonathan Moss speaking."

"Hello, Mr. Moss." That cigarette-roughened baritone could only belong to Lou Jamieson. Moss' one-time client was not a pillar of the community, except perhaps for certain disreputable parts of it. He went on, "I think maybe I found what you were looking for."

"Did you, by God?" That perked Moss up better than coffee. "Tell me about it, Mr. Jamieson, if you'd be so kind."

Tell him about it Jamieson did. If the man with dubious connections was telling the truth—always an interesting proposition where he was concerned—then a couple of Peterhoff's business associates stood to make a bundle if he vanished from the scene for ten or twenty years. It wasn't anything showy or obvious, but it was there.

"By God!" Moss said again. His pen raced across a yellow legal pad as he jotted down notes. The more he heard, the happier he got. "Thank you from the bottom of my heart!" he exclaimed when Jamieson finally finished. "You've just saved an innocent man a hell of a lot of trouble. Even a military court will have to sit up and take notice when I use this."

"That's nice, Mr. Moss," Jamieson said affably. "You done me a good turn a while ago with the goddamn Yanks. Figured this was the least I could do for you." He couldn't have cared less whether Allen Peterhoff was guilty or innocent. What mattered was that he owed Moss a favor. If he hadn't, Peterhoff would have been welcome to rot in jail, as far as he was concerned.

His sometime client's amoral cynicism would have bothered Moss much more if Jamieson hadn't proved so valuable. As things were, Moss threw the notes in his briefcase, thanked Jamieson again, and got ready to go home early. *Dorothy will be glad to see me,* he thought, *and I hope Laura will, too.*

He made sure he turned off the hot plate. He didn't want to burn down the building by accident. Then he went out to his auto. His hand stayed in the overcoat pocket with the pistol, but he wasn't very worried. Nobody could reasonably expect him to leave at this hour. He might even be back before the mailman got to the apartment building where he lived.

As usual, he parked around the corner from the building. Even though he didn't expect trouble, it was one of those days where he would almost have welcomed it. He felt as if he were trouble's master. He remembered that for a very long time. The thought filled his mind as he turned the corner. That was when the explosion knocked him off his feet.

"Holy Jesus!" he said. Bright shards of glass glittered in the snow, blown out of nearby windows. He picked himself up and ran toward the sound of the blast. If anyone needed help, he'd do what he could.

He hadn't gone more than a few steps before he realized his building was the one that had suffered. The hole in the front wall gaped from his floor. And . . .

"No," Moss whispered. But that was his apartment. Or rather, that had been his apartment. Not much seemed left of it. Not a whole lot seemed left of the ones to either side, either. Smoke started pouring out of the hole as broken gas lines or wires set things ablaze.

"Call the police!" someone shouted. "Call the fire department!" somebody else yelled. Jonathan Moss heard them as if from very far away. He ran toward the front steps of the building where he'd lived for so long. Try as he would, though, he couldn't go up them, because all the people who'd lived in the apartment building were flooding out. Some of them were bloodied and limping. Others just had panic on their faces.

"Laura!" Moss shouted. "Dorothy!"

He didn't see them anywhere. He hadn't really thought he would. But hope died hard. Hope, sometimes, died harder than people. People, as he knew too well, could be awfully easy to kill.

A man who lived on the same floor as he did pushed him away. "You don't want to try to go in, Mr. Moss," he said. "The whole goddamn building's liable to fall down."

"My wife! My little girl!"

"Wasn't that your place where it happened?" his neighbor asked. Helplessly, he nodded. The other man said, "Then there's nothing you can do for 'em now, and that's the Lord's truth. If they come out, they come out. If they don't . . ." He spread his hands.

More people pushed out of the building. More bricks fell off it. Some landed in the snow. One hit a man in the shoulder. He howled like a wolf. Moss tried again to go into the building. Again, he failed. People took hold of him and dragged him back by main force.

Sirens screamed in the distance, rapidly drawing closer. Screams bubbled in Moss' throat. Why they didn't burst out, he had no idea. Everything he cared about had been in that flat. Now the flat was gone, and twenty-five years of his dreams and hopes with it.

He tried to think, though his stunned wits made it next to impossible. He'd been getting threats for a long time. He hadn't taken them too seriously till the bomb went off in the occupation center. After that, he realized disaster really could happen to him. And now it had.

"Who?" he muttered. Who would have wanted to blow up a woman and a child? For if this was a bomb, as seemed horribly likely, whoever had sent it must have addressed it to Laura or Dorothy. Had it had his name on it, they would have left it alone. He would have opened it. And it would have blown up in his face.

Fire engines howled to a stop. The police came right behind them. And soldiers in green-gray helped clear people away from the building. "Move it!" they shouted. "The whole thing may collapse!"

"Get out of the way!" the firemen shouted. They began playing streams of water on the spreading flames. A lot of the water splashed down onto the people who had lived in the building. That moved them away faster than the soldiers could have.

A major called, "Whose place was it that went up?"

"Mine," Moss said dully.

"You weren't inside there." The officer stated the obvious. "You'd be hamburger if you were."

"Hamburger." *My wife is hamburger. My little girl is hamburger.* Moss managed to shake his head. "No. I was doing some work at the office. I had just got out of my auto when . . . when it happened. Laura . . . Dorothy . . ." He began to weep.

"Christ! You're Jonathan Moss." Recognizing him, the major suddenly put two and two together. "This wasn't a gas leak, or anything like that. This was a bomb, or it probably was a bomb, anyway."

Now Moss' head moved up and down as mechanically as it had gone back and forth. "Yes. I think you're right. Somebody killed them." He could say it. It didn't sound as if it meant anything. He was still deep in shock. But part of him knew it would mean something before long. The major seemed to sense it was too soon for questions. He led Moss down the street. Docile as a child, Moss went with him. Behind them, the building fell in on itself.

# XVIII

"**A**lec!" Mary Pomeroy called. "Don't you dare pull the cat's tail. If he scratches you or bites you, it's your own fault."

Mouser was, on the whole, a patient cat. Little boys, though, were liable to drive even patient cats past the limits of what they'd put up with. Mouser had bitten Alec only a couple of times, but he scratched whenever he thought he had to. Alec was still learning what would annoy him enough to bring out the claws. Sometimes his experiments seemed deliberately hair-raising.

Mary turned on the wireless just ahead of the hour to catch the news. The lead story was a bomb that had blown up a police station in Frankfort, Kentucky. Seventeen policemen were dead, another two dozen wounded. A group called the American Patriots—a group, the newscaster said sarcastically, that no one had ever heard of till they committed this outrage—was claiming responsibility.

And the president of the Confederate States was all but foaming at the mouth. Jake Featherston claimed the bombing proved Kentucky was full of pro-U.S. fanatics who refused to accept the results of the plebiscite. The newscaster poured more scorn on that idea. Mary was willing to believe it, simply because this smooth-voiced stooge for the Yanks didn't.

"In another bombing case," the broadcaster went on, "investigators continue to probe the ruins of a Berlin, Ontario, apartment building, seeking clues to the perpetrator of the atrocity. A mother and child, Laura and Dorothy Moss, are confirmed dead. Several other persons were injured in the blast, and three remain missing. . . ."

A mother and a child. That wasn't how Mary had thought of them. A traitor and her half-American brat was more what she had in mind. That way, she didn't have to remind herself that the woman who'd been born Laura Secord—born with the name of a great Canadian patriot—had been a person as well as a political symbol. She didn't want to think of the late Laura Moss as a person. If she did, she had to think about what she'd done.

She couldn't remember the last time she'd physically hurt anyone, aside from spanking Alec when he needed it. Maybe when she was little, in a fight with her older sister. But Julia had several years on her, so she might not have managed it even then.

Well, she'd managed it now. She'd blown a woman and her little girl to kingdom come, and she'd hurt some other people with them. Not bad for a package she'd mailed from Wilf Rokeby's post office. Not bad? Or not good?

*This is war,* she told herself. *Look what the Americans did to my family. Why should I care what happens to them, or to the people who collaborate with them?*

Had the Americans blown up women and children? Mary nodded defiantly. Of course they had, with their bombs and their artillery. She didn't feel guilty. She paused, too honest to go on with that. The trouble was, she did feel guilty. Unlike the Yanks—or so she insisted to herself— she had a working conscience. At the moment, it was working overtime.

"No one has claimed to be responsible for the murderous attack in Berlin," the newsman continued. "Attention is, however, focusing on several known subversive groups. When the truth is known, severe punishment will be meted out."

Mary laughed at that. The Yanks were liable to grab somebody, say he was guilty, and shoot him just to make themselves look good. She remained certain that was what they'd done with her brother, Alexander, Alec's namesake. Her conscience twinged again. Did she want them to punish someone else, someone who hadn't done anything, for what she'd done?

She wanted them to get out of Canada. Past that, she didn't—or tried not to—care.

"Ironically, the victims' husband and father, barrister Jonathan Moss, though a U.S. aviation ace during the Great War, was well known in Ontario for his work on behalf of Canadians involved in disputes with the occupying authorities," the man on the wireless said. "Only desperate madmen who hate Americans simply because they are Americans would have—"

*Click!* "Why'd you turn it off, Mommy?" Alec asked.

"Because he was spouting a lot of drivel," Mary answered.

Alec laughed. "That's a funny word. What does it mean?"

"Nonsense. Hooey. Rubbish."

"Drivel!" Alec yelled, alarming Mouser. "Hooey!" He liked that one, too. The cat didn't, at least not yelled in its ears. It fled. Alec ran after it, screeching, "Drivel! Hooey! Hooey! Drivel!"

"Enough," Mary said. He didn't listen to her. "Enough!" she said again. Still no luck. *"Enough!"* Now she was yelling, too. Short of clouting Alec with a rock, yelling at him was the only way to get his attention.

She didn't usually turn off the wireless in the middle of the news. She found she missed it, and turned it back on, hoping it would be done talking about what had happened in Berlin. It was. The newscaster said, "King Charles XI of France has declared that the German Empire is using Kaiser Wilhelm's illness as an excuse for delay on consideration of returning Alsace-Lorraine to France. 'If strong measures prove necessary, we are not afraid to take them,' he added. Prime Minister Churchill of Great Britain voiced his support for the French. In a speech before Parliament, he said, 'High time the Germans go.' "

Music blared from the speaker. A chorus of women with squeaky voices praised laundry soap to the skies. When Mary first listened to the wireless, she wanted to go out and buy everything she heard advertised on it. She was vaccinated against that nonsense these days. She did sometimes wonder why a singer with a voice good enough to make money would choose to sing about laundry soap. Because she couldn't make money with her voice any other way? Sometimes that didn't seem reason enough.

*I killed two people, one of them a little girl who never did anybody any harm.* The thought didn't want to go away; even if she hadn't watched them die, they were as dead as if she'd taken them to a chopping block and whacked off their heads with a hatchet, the way she had with so many chickens on her mother's farm. *Laura Secord betrayed her country.* Mary had no doubt of that. *But who appointed you her executioner?* she asked herself.

Her back stiffened. She was damned if she'd let herself feel guilty for long. *Who appointed me her executioner? The Yanks did.* If they hadn't shot Alexander, her father never would have felt the need to go on the war path against them. She was entitled to revenge for that. She was entitled to it, and she'd taken it.

She nodded to herself. Nothing was going to make her feel sorry about ridding the world of Laura Secord. Every so often, though, she couldn't help feeling bad about Dorothy Moss. She wished she'd blown up the girl's father instead. Yes, the newsman went on and on about how he struggled for Canadians' rights, but that overlooked several little details. First and foremost, no Yank should have had any business saying what rights a Canadian had or didn't have. And Jonathan Moss had been one of the Yanks who'd beaten Canada down during the Great War. *And* he was still a combat flier; she remembered the newspaper stories about him. Yes, better the bomb should have got him.

She was cutting up a chicken for stew in the kitchen when two trucks pulled to a stop in front of the diner. They looked like the sort of trucks in which U.S. Army soldiers rode, but they were painted a bluish gray, not the green-gray she'd known and loathed since she was a little girl. The men who piled out of the back of the trucks were in uniforms cut about the same as those U.S. soldiers wore—but, again, of bluish gray and not the familiar color. Mary wondered if the Yanks had decided to change their uniforms after keeping them pretty much the same for so long. Why would they do that?

The soldiers all tramped into the diner. *That will make Mort happy,* Mary thought. Soldiers ate like starving wolves. These days, they also paid their bills. The occupation was more orderly than it had been during the war and just afterwards. That made it very little better, not as far as Mary was concerned.

Forty-five minutes later, the soldiers came out and climbed into the trucks again. The engines started up with twin roars. Away the trucks went, beyond what Mary could see from the window. She reminded herself to ask Mort about the men when he came back to the flat, and hoped she wouldn't forget.

As things turned out, she needn't have worried about that. When her husband got home, he was angrier than she'd ever seen him. "What's the matter?" she asked; he hardly ever lost his temper.

"What's the matter?" he repeated. "Did you see those trucks a couple of hours ago? The trucks, and the soldiers in them?"

Mary nodded. "I wanted to ask you—"

He talked right through her: "Do you know who those soldiers were? Do you? No, of course you don't." He wasn't going to let her get a word in edgewise. "I'll tell you who they were, by God. They were a pack of Frenchies, that's who."

"Frenchies? From Quebec?" The news made Mary no happier than it had Mort. She was damned if she would call their home the Republic of Quebec, though, even if it had been torn away from Canada for twenty-five years now.

"That's right," Mort answered. "And do you know what else? They're going to be part of the garrison here. At least the United States beat us in the war. What did the Frenchies do? Nothing. Not one single thing. They don't even talk English, most of 'em. I swear to God, honey, I'd sooner have a pack of niggers watching over us than those people."

"What's even worse is, they're Canadians, too," Mary said. Her husband gave her a look. "Well, they are." Even to herself, she sounded defensive. "They used to be, anyhow."

"Maybe," Mort said. "They sure don't act like Canadians now, though. They sat there in the diner jabbering back and forth in French like a bunch of monkeys. The only one who spoke enough English to order anything for them was a sergeant who'd been in the Canadian Army once upon a time. And he sounded like the devil, too."

"That's terrible," Mary said, and Mort nodded. She asked him, "Why are there Frenchies here? Did you find out? Would they say?"

"Oh, yes. They aren't shy about talking, even if they don't do it very well," he answered. "Reason they're here is, some of the U.S. soldiers who've been on garrison duty are going back to the States."

"That doesn't explain anything," Mary said. "Why would the Yanks want to do a thing like that after all these years?" The USA had occupied Rosenfeld since she was a little girl. No matter how much she hated that, it was in a way part of the natural order of things by now.

"I don't know for sure. The Frenchies didn't say anything about that," Mort replied. "But I know what my guess would be—that the Yanks are starting to worry about that Featherston fellow down in the Confederate States."

"You think they're moving men to stop him?" Mary asked. Her husband nodded again. Excitement blazed through her. "If you're right, we've got a chance to be free!" *And maybe this has been a war all along, and I don't have to think I'm a murderer. Maybe. Please, God.*


Cincinnatus Driver watched a spectacle he had hoped he would never see, a spectacle he'd gone to Kentucky to keep from seeing: Confederate troops marching into Covington. He was, by then, just starting to get up on crutches and move around. He supposed he was lucky. The auto that hit him could easily have killed him. There were times, when he'd lain in the hospital and then back at his parents' house, that he wished it would have.

His mother took care of him as if he were a little boy. She plainly thought he was. All the years that had gone by since might as well not have happened. She didn't even realize anything was wrong. That, to Cincinnatus, was the cruelest part of her long, slow slide into senility.

And his father took care of both of them, with as much dignity as he could muster and without much hope. Some of the neighbors helped, as they found the chance. His mother wandered off a couple of times, but she didn't get far. People watched her more closely than they had till Cincinnatus got hit. That was funny, in a bitter way.

Getting out of the house for a little while felt good to Cincinnatus. He'd stared at the cracked, water-stained plaster of the ceiling for too long. He was weak as a kitten and he still got dreadful headaches that aspirin did nothing to knock down, but he was alive and he was upright. When a little more strength returned, he would figure out how to get himself and his father and mother back to the USA. Meanwhile . . .

Meanwhile, he stumped along the neglected sidewalks of the colored district of Covington toward the parade route. The whole district seemed even more rundown than it had when he came back to Covington. It also seemed half deserted, and so it was. A lot of Negroes had already fled to the United States.

He glanced over to his father, who walked beside him, ready to steady him if he stumbled. "You sure Ma be all right while we're gone?"

"I ain't sure o' nothin," Seneca Driver answered, "but I reckon so." He walked on for a few paces, then said, "One thing I ain't sure of is how come you wants to see these bastards comin' back."

Cincinnatus wasn't altogether sure of that himself. After a little thought, he said, "I got to remind myself why I want to git back to Iowa so bad, maybe."

"Maybe." His father sounded deeply skeptical.

Seneca had reason to sound that way, too. Only a handful of blacks headed for the parade route. Most of the people who came out to see this underscoring of the return of Confederate sovereignty were white men with Freedom Party pins in their lapels—or, if they didn't wear lapels, as many didn't, on the front of denim jackets or wool sweaters. Cincinnatus hadn't been the target of looks like the ones they gave him for many years. People in Des Moines thought Negroes curious beasts, not dangerous ones.

One of the blacks on the street was a familiar face: Lucullus Wood. He'd visited Cincinnatus at the hospital, and several times at his parents' house. As far as a Negro could be, Lucullus was a man to reckon with in Covington. A generation earlier, his father had been, too.

Seeing Cincinnatus and Seneca, Lucullus came across the street to say hello. "Ain't this a fine day?" he said. A Freedom Party man might have used the same words. A Freedom Party man might even have used the same tone of voice. But the words and the tone would have had a very different meaning in a Freedom Party man's mouth. Lucullus understood irony—blacks who'd been born in the CSA understood irony from the moment they could talk—and no Party stalwart ever would.

"Never thought I'd see it," Cincinnatus agreed.

None of the plump, eager white men in earshot could have taken exception to his words or tone, either. In fact, one of them turned to another and said, "You see? Even the niggers is glad to have the damnyankees gone."

"They know they was well off before," his friend replied.

Cincinnatus didn't look at Lucullus. Neither of them looked at Seneca. He didn't look at them. None of them had any trouble knowing what the other two were thinking. Remarking on it would have been a waste of breath.

Off to the south, Cincinnatus heard a peculiar noise: partly musical, partly a low, mechanical rumble. Both pieces of the noise got louder as it came closer. Before too long, Cincinnatus recognized the music. A marching band was blaring out "Dixie," playing the tune for all it was worth.

"That there song used to be against the law here," Lucullus said. By the way he said it, he thought it was too bad "Dixie" had been illegal. Cincinnatus knew better. A casual listener—a white listener—wouldn't have.

"Wonder what ever happened to that Luther Bliss," Cincinnatus said. "Reckon he ain't never gonna show his face here no more. Don't miss him one damn bit." Since the former head of the Kentucky State Police had thrown him in jail, most of him meant that. The rest, though, couldn't help remembering how hard and how well Bliss had fought Confederate diehards—and anyone else he didn't care for.

"Reckon you's right," Lucullus answered. Cincinnatus sent him a sharp look. A casual listener wouldn't have heard anything wrong with his words there, either. Cincinnatus wondered if he knew more than he was letting on.

Here came the band. The Freedom Party men—and the smaller number of women with them—burst into applause. A lot of them began to sing. Cincinnatus couldn't applaud, not with his hands on the crutches. His father and Lucullus did. He couldn't blame them. Better safe than sorry.

Behind the band marched several companies of Confederate soldiers. Their uniforms didn't look much different from the ones C.S. troops had worn during the Great War, but there were changes. Most of them had to do with comfort and protection. The collars on these tunics were open at the neck. The cut was looser, less restrictive. Their helmets came down farther over the ears and the back of the neck than the Great War models had. They weren't the steel pots U.S. soldiers wore, but they weren't much different from them.

The rifles they carried . . . "Funny-lookin' guns," Cincinnatus said to Lucullus in a low voice.

"Gas-operated. Don't need to work the bolt to chamber a round after the first one in the clip." Lucullus spoke with authority. "They's new. Not everybody's got 'em. They is very bad news, though."

Not even all the parading soldiers carried the new rifles. Some had submachine guns instead. Cincinnatus didn't see any with ordinary, Great War–vintage Tredegars. The Confederate States couldn't arm as many men as the United States. They seemed to want to make sure the men they did have would put a lot of lead in the air.

The barrels that grumbled and clanked up the street were different from the ones Cincinnatus remembered from the Great War, too. They carried their cannon in a turret on top of the hull. They also looked as if they could go a lot faster than the walking pace that had been their top speed a generation earlier.

Trucks towed artillery pieces. Fighters and bombers with the C.S. battle flag on wings and tail roared low overhead. More marching soldiers finished the parade.

"Wonder what they think o' this on the other side of the Ohio," Cincinnatus said. The city that was nearly his namesake lay right across the river from Covington.

"If they's happy, they's crazy," Lucullus said after looking around to make sure no white was paying undue attention. "Jake Featherston, he promised there wouldn't be no Confederate soldiers in Kentucky for twenty-five years. He jump the gun just a little bit, I reckon."

Cincinnatus' father looked around, too. "We done seen the parade," he said. "What I reckon is, we better git back to our own part o' town."

He was bound to be right. Even Negroes who weren't doing anything to anybody were liable to be fair game in Covington. Moving on his crutches made Cincinnatus sweat with effort and pain in spite of the chilly day, but he moved anyhow. Once back inside the colored district, he said, "We got to get out of here. Ain't easy no more, now that this here is a Confederate state, but we got to."

"Best thing you kin do is jus' walk right across the bridge to Cincinnati," Lucullus said. "Ain't quite legal like it was, but the U.S. soldiers don't bother niggers much."

Since neither Cincinnatus nor his mother was up to much in the way of walking, he and his parents took a taxi to the nearest bridge two days later. His mother stared out the window as if she'd never been in an auto in her life. As far as she could remember, she hadn't.

They didn't get across. No one got across. To protest the Confederates' military occupation of Kentucky, the USA had sealed the border between the two countries. Cincinnatus thought of getting a boat and crossing the Ohio any way he could. He thought of it, but not for long. He remembered too many stories about Negroes trying to cross into the USA getting turned back at gunpoint or sometimes just shot. He couldn't take the chance, especially since his mother, with her wits wandering, was liable to give them away.

When U.S. forces pulled out of Kentucky, a consulate had opened in Covington. Hoping the official there might help, Cincinnatus visited the place. That turned out to be another wasted trip. A large sign on the window said, CLOSED INDEFINITELY DUE TO ILLEGAL CONFEDERATE ACTION. Frustrated and frightened, Cincinnatus went back to his parents' house.

"Dammit, I'm a citizen of the USA. I live in Iowa," he raged. "How come I can't get home?"

"Be thankful it ain't worse," his father said: the philosophy of a man who'd spent the early years of his life as a piece of property. No matter how bad things were, he could easily imagine them worse.

Not so Cincinnatus. "Bein' stuck here in Covington is as bad as it gits," he said.

But Seneca was right. A few days later, the *Covington Courier* ran what it called, A NOTIFICATION TO THE COLORED RESIDENTS OF THE CON-FEDERATE STATE OF KENTUCKY. It told them they had to be photographed for passbooks, "as is the accepted and required practice for Negroes throughout the Confederate States of America."

Seneca took the order in stride. "Had to do this afore the war, I recollects," he said.

That was so. Cincinnatus remembered his own passbook. But he said, "I done without one o' them things the last twenty-five years. Don't you recollect what it's like to be free?"

"I recollects the trouble you finds if you don't got one," his father answered.

"I ain't no Confederate nigger. I ain't gonna be no Confederate nigger, neither," Cincinnatus said. "I'm a citizen of the United States. What the hell I need a passbook for?"

"You don't want to get in trouble with them Freedom Party fellas, you better have one," his father answered.

That was all too likely to be true. Cincinnatus raged against it anyhow. Raging against it did him exactly no good. For the time being, he was stuck here in Kentucky. Sooner or later, he expected things to get back to normal and the border between the CSA and the USA to open up again. He also expected to get the cast off his leg and to learn to walk without crutches once more. And he expected to take his father and mother back to Des Moines with him. He always had been an optimist.

For a long time, Dr. Leonard O'Doull had been satisfied—no, more than satisfied, happy—to live in a place like Rivière-du-Loup. *The world forgetting, by the world forgot.* He couldn't remember where he'd seen that line of poetry, but it suited the town very well. And it had suited him, too.

But, however much he sometimes wanted to, he couldn't quite forget that he was an American, that he came from a wider world than the one in which he chose to live. Reading about the gathering storm far to the south—even reading about it in French, which made it seem all the farther away—brought that home to him. In an odd way, so did the passing of his father-in-law.

To Leonard O'Doull, Lucien Galtier had stood for everything he admired about Quebec: a curious mix of adaptability and a deeper stubbornness. Now that the older man was gone, O'Doull felt as if he'd lost an anchor that had been mooring him to *la belle République*.

His wife, of course, had other feelings about the way her father had died: one part shock, O'Doull judged, to about three parts mortification. "Did it have to be *there*?" she would say, over and over again. "Did he have to be doing *that*?"

"Coronary thrombosis comes when it comes," O'Doull would reply, as patiently and sympathetically as he could. "The exertion, the excitement—they could, without a doubt, help bring it on."

Patience and sympathy took him only so far. About then, Nicole would usually explode: "But people will never let us live it down!"

Knowing how places like Rivière-du-Loup and the surrounding farms worked, O'Doull suspected she was right. Even so, he said, "You worry too much. Many of the people I've talked to say they're jealous of such an end."

"Men!" Nicole snarled. "*Tabernac!* What do you know?" That was unfair to half the human race, not that she cared. Then she went on, "And what of poor Éloise Granche? Is she jealous of such an end?"

That, unfortunately, wasn't unfair, and was very much to the point. Éloise wasn't jealous. She was horror-stricken, and who could blame her? To have to watch someone die at such a moment . . . How would she ever forget that? How could she ever want to get close to another man as long as she lived?

O'Doull said, "Your father didn't leave us . . . unappreciated." He needed to pause there to pick the right word. After another moment, he went on, "Would you rather it had happened while he was mucking out the barn?"

"I'd rather it didn't happen at all," Nicole answered. But that wasn't what he'd asked, and she knew it. Now she hesitated. At last, she said, "Maybe I would. It would have been more, more dignified."

"Death is never dignified." O'Doull spoke with a doctor's certainty. "Never. Dignity in death is something we invent afterwards to make the living feel better."

"I would have felt better if it had happened while Papa was in the barn," Nicole said. "Whether he—" She broke off, not soon enough, and burst into tears. " *'Osti!* Do you see? Even I'm starting to make jokes about it. And if I do, what's everyone else doing?"

"The same thing, probably," O'Doull said. "People are like that."

"It's not right!" Nicole said. "He wouldn't have wanted to be remembered—this way." She cried harder than ever.

Although Leonard held her and patted her and did his best to comfort her, he was far from sure she was right. He'd known his father-in-law for a quarter of a century. Wouldn't Lucien Galtier have taken a certain wry pride in the reputation that grew out of his end? Lucien might even have taken a pride that wasn't so ordinary. Any number of ways to go. To how many, though, was it given to go like a *man*?

Which brought him back to the question Nicole had asked. What about Éloise? She was wounded, no doubt about it, and Lucien wouldn't have wanted that. He'd cared for her, even if he hadn't necessarily loved her. But would things have been any easier for her if he'd dropped dead while they were dancing, not after they'd gone back to her farmhouse? Maybe a little. Maybe a little, yes, but not much.

*One of these days,* O'Doull told himself, *yes, one of these days, I'll have to pour a few drinks into Georges and find out what* he *really thinks about this.* The time wasn't ripe yet. He knew that. But it would come. A lot of things for which the time hadn't been ripe looked to be coming. Most of them were a lot less appetizing than lying down with a nice woman and being unlucky enough not to get up again.

That evening, the newscaster on the wireless gave an account of a speech President Smith had made at Camp Hill, Pennsylvania. "The president of the United States spoke with just anger regarding the Confederate States' violation of their pledge not to send soldiers into Kentucky and the state formerly known as Houston." The French-speaker made heavy going of the place names. He continued, "The president of the United States also reminded the president of the Confederate States that he had pledged himself to ask for no more territorial changes on the continent of North America. If he ignores this solemn undertaking, President Smith said, he cannot seriously expect the United States to return to him the portions of Virginia, Arkansas, and Sonora to which he has referred." He had trouble pronouncing *Arkansas*, too. And why not? Arkansas was a long, long way from the Republic of Quebec.

Al Smith finally seemed to have decided he couldn't trust Jake Featherston. As far as O'Doull could see, the U.S. president had taken longer than he might have to figure that out. He had it down now, though. More than what he'd said, where he'd made the speech spoke volumes. Almost eighty years ago now, Robert E. Lee's Army of Northern Virginia had crushed McClellan's Army of the Potomac at Camp Hill, ensuring that the Confederate States would triumph in the War of Secession. No president of the United States would have anything to do with the place these days unless he wanted to tell his own people, *We're in trouble again.*

Nicole didn't understand any of that. Neither did little Lucien, who was anything but little these days. O'Doull found himself envying his wife and son for being so thoroughly Quebecois. He also found himself reminded that, no matter how long he'd lived here, he was at bottom an American. He'd sometimes wondered about that. He didn't any more.

When he went to his office the next morning, newsboys were hawking papers by shouting about President Smith's speech. Papers in Quebec always seemed to back the USA to the hilt: more royalist than the king, more Catholic than the Pope. Again, why not? The Great War had touched lightly here, which it hadn't anywhere else between Alaska and the Empire of Mexico.

O'Doull's receptionist was already at the office when he got there. She smiled at him and said, *"Bonjour, monsieur. Ça va?"*

*"Pas pire, merci,"* he answered, which made her smile. Nobody who spoke Parisian French would have said, *Not bad, thanks,* like that. O'Doull had put down deep roots here, and he knew it. He went on, "When is the first appointment?"

"Half an hour, Doctor," she said.

"Good. I'll see what I can catch up on till then." He went into his private office to skim through medical journals. He wished he had time to do more than skim. He had never known—had never imagined—such an exciting age in medicine. Back when he was a boy, immunization and sanitation had begun to cut into death rates, which had kept on falling ever since. Now, though, some of the new drugs on the market were doing what quack nostrums had promised since the beginning of time: they really were curing diseases that could easily have been fatal. How many times had he watched someone die of infection after surgery that would have succeeded without it? More than he cared to recall, certainly. Now, with luck, he—and his patients—wouldn't have to go through that particular hell any more.

And here was an article about some new medicine that was said to be even more effective than the sulfonamides, which had been the last word for the past year or two. Drugs that killed germs without poisoning people were, to him, far more exciting than fighters that flew twenty miles an hour faster and five thousand feet higher than previous models.

Not everybody thought so, though, which meant new models of fighters came out more often and got more fanfare than new drugs did. They were liable to be used, too, which worried him.

"Madness," he muttered, and went back to reading about this fungus with what seemed a miraculous ability to murder microbes.

His first patient was a pregnant woman due in about six weeks. He'd always liked working with women who were going to have babies. Their condition was obvious, and usually had a happy outcome. He only wished the rest of what he did were as easy and rewarding.

Then he saw a child with mumps. He couldn't do anything about that despite the new drugs in the medical journal. The little boy was very unhappy, but he would get better in a few days.

A man with a bad back came in next. "I'm sorry, *Monsieur* Papineau," he said, "but aspirins and liniment and rest are the most I have to offer you."

"*Tabernac!*" Papineau said. "Can't you cure it? If you could put me under the knife for it, I would go in a minute. I can't pick up my children or make love to my wife without feeling I'm breaking in two."

Dr. O'Doull considered. Papineau was younger than he was, and might not be shocked at a suggestion. On the other hand, he might. Rivière-du-Loup was a straitlaced place in a lot of ways. Still, worth a try . . . "Since you mention it, *monsieur,* it could be that you might have less pain during intimacy if your wife were to assume the, ah, superior position."

There. That sounded properly medical. Was it too medical for Papineau to understand? Evidently not, for he turned red. "What? You mean her on top? *Calisse!*"

"I didn't mean to offend," O'Doull said hastily. "I offered the suggestion only for reasons of health and comfort. You were the one who mentioned the, ah, difficulty, after all."

"Well, so I did." His patient looked thoughtful. "For reasons of health, maybe. I wonder what Louise would say." Papineau left the office rubbing his chin. O'Doull managed to hold in a snort of laughter till he was gone. Then it came out.

He was still smiling when his next patient, a little old lady with arthritis, came in. "What's funny, Doctor?" she asked suspiciously.

"Nothing to do with you, *Madame* Villehardouin," he assured her. "I was just . . . remembering a joke I heard last night." She gave him a fishy stare, but couldn't prove he was lying. He had only aspirins and liniment to offer her, too. As far as things had come in the past few years, they still had at least as far to go.

A few days later, he ran into Papineau in a grocery. As usual, the man moved in a gingerly way, but he greeted O'Doull with a smile. "That was a wonderful prescription you gave me, Doctor," he said. "Wonderful!"

"Well, I'm glad it did you some good," O'Doull said. Papineau nodded enthusiastically. O'Doull *was* pleased at helping him, and his pleasure diminished only a little when he reflected that Hippocrates could have given the same advice. Yes, medicine still had a long way to go.

The ground unrolled beneath Jonathan Moss. His fighter dove like a falcon—dove, in fact, far faster than any falcon could dream of diving. He was coming out of the sun. The young hotshot calmly tooling along in the other fighter had no idea he was there—till he zoomed past. Had it been a dogfight, his opponent never would have known what hit him.

His wireless set let out a burst of static, and then a startled squawk: "Son of a bitch! How the hell did you do that? Uh, over."

Moss started to make a joke, to say something like, *Clean living.* But the smile and the words died unspoken. He thumbed his own wireless and answered, "Son, I did that because I wanted it more than you." He thought he'd stopped, but his mouth kept going: "I want it more than anybody does." A long, long pause followed before he remembered to add, "Over."

Wasn't all that the Lord's bitter truth? He *did* want it more than anybody else, and what he'd known since the war *was* over. Ever since he got his law degree, he'd done everything he could to make things better, make them more tolerable, for Canadians. He'd married a Canadian patriot. He'd had himself a half-Canadian little girl.

And what thanks had he got? Some other Canadian, someone who no doubt thought of himself as a patriot, had blown up everything in the world that mattered to him. Wherever that other Canadian lived, he was bound to be laughing and cheering these days. He'd settled his score with a Yank, all right. He sure had.

*I wasted twenty years of my life.* The only thing Moss wanted more than sitting in this fighter was to be able to pilot the biggest bomber the United States had. He wanted to fly it at random over some good-sized Canadian town, open the bomb-bay doors, and pour out a couple of tons of death, the way that Canadian had sent Laura and Dorothy death through the mail. He wanted that so badly, he could all but taste it. He could practically feel the bomber jump and get livelier as its heavy load of explosives fell away. Hallucination? Of course. It seemed very real just the same.

Maybe the bombs had been meant for him. Maybe, but he didn't think so. People in his family didn't open mail unless it was addressed to them. Had the bomb had his name on it, his wife and daughter would have left it alone. *And they might still be alive, and I wouldn't.* He'd had that thought the day the bomb went off.

Why would anyone want to kill a woman and a little girl? That ate at Moss. Could somebody have been angry enough at Laura for marrying an American to want to see her dead? Moss knew some of the people who wanted Canada free once more were a fanatical lot, but that fanatical? It seemed excessive, even for them. And most of them were willing to admit he'd done a few useful things in his time there. He'd had some threats, but they'd never amounted to anything—not till now.

What he'd done here didn't matter any more. He'd had his life rearranged for him. The sooner he got out of Canada now, the happier he'd be.

The wireless crackled again. The other fighter pilot said, "I'm going back to the airstrip now, Major. Over."

"I'll follow you," Moss answered. "Over and out." He'd put the uniform back on as soon as he'd buried Laura and Dorothy. He hadn't asked for the promotion from the rank he'd held in the Great War. They'd seemed eager to give it to him, though, and acted afraid he wouldn't come back to flying. The way things were looking along the border with the CSA and out in the Pacific, they were anxious to grab all the warm bodies they could.

He wondered what he would have done had Laura lived. Chucking his practice to fly for the USA might have meant chucking his marriage, too. Well, he didn't have to worry about that now.

There was the airstrip, with the snow bulldozed off it. Some airplanes here landed on skis instead of wheels during the winter, but his didn't have them. He lowered his landing gear and bumped to a stop.

Groundcrew men came up to take charge of the fighter. Wearily, Moss pushed back the canopy and got out. The fur and leather of his flying gear kept him warm on the ground in wintertime. He remembered the way that had worked from the days of the Great War. Ever since he'd lost Laura and Dorothy, those days seemed more real, more vivid, more *present* in his mind than much of what had happened since.

A young lieutenant emerged from one of the buildings flanking the airstrip and struggled through the snow till he got to the cleared runway. Then he could hurry, as young lieutenants were supposed to do. Saluting, he told Moss, "The base commandant's compliments, sir, and he'd like to see you in his office right away."

"Well, then, I'd better get over there, hadn't I?" Moss said.

Ambiguity permeated his relations with Captain Oscar Trotter. He'd got on fine with Major Finley, Trotter's predecessor. They'd both been Great War veterans, and understood each other. The new commandant was a younger man. He'd never seen combat, never drunk himself blind three or four nights in a row so he wouldn't have to think about friends going down in flames three or four dreadful days in a row, never drunk himself blind so he wouldn't have to think about going down in flames himself. And, of course, Trotter was only a captain. Even though he was in charge of the field outside of London, he had trouble giving Moss orders now that Moss had put the uniform back on and wore golden oak leaves on his shoulder straps.

Moss saw no point in making things worse than they were already. "Reporting as ordered," he said when he walked into Trotter's office. That let the commandant know he was willing to take his orders, even if he didn't call him *sir* or salute first.

Trotter nodded. He didn't salute, either. "Have a seat, Major," he said, acknowledging Moss' rank that way so he also didn't have to say *sir*. He waved the older man into the chair in front of his desk. It creaked when Moss sat down in it. It always did.

"What's up?" Moss asked.

Trotter lit a cigarette before he answered. He shoved the pack of Raleighs across the desk so Moss could have one, too. As Moss lit up, the commandant pushed a sheet of paper across the desk after the Raleighs. "Your orders have come through."

Was that relief in his voice? Moss wouldn't have been surprised. Base commandants didn't like ambiguity, and with reason: it weakened their authority. If Trotter got Moss out of his hair, he could go back to being senior officer here in every sense of the term.

The cigarette hanging from the corner of his mouth, Moss reached for the paper. It bore the embossed eagle in front of crossed swords that had symbolized the USA since the revival after the Second Mexican War. He read through the orders, then looked up at Captain Trotter. "You have an atlas of the United States here, sir? Where the hell is Mount Vernon, Illinois?"

"I thought you were from Illinois," Trotter answered, pulling a book off a shelf behind his chair.

"I'm from Chicago," Moss replied with dignity. "Downstate is all the back of beyond, as far as I'm concerned." He might have been talking about darkest Africa.

Captain Trotter opened the atlas, then pointed. "Here it is." He turned the book around so Moss could see, too. "Right in the middle of the pointy end that goes down to where the Ohio and the Mississippi meet."

"Uh-*huh*," Moss said. "Hell of a nice place to fly missions into Kentucky from, looks like to me."

"Or to defend if the Confederates start flying missions out of Kentucky," Trotter agreed.

"I don't want to defend. To hell with defending," Moss said savagely. "If those bastards think they can start a new war, I want to go out and tear 'em a new asshole so they'll goddamn well think twice."

That made Captain Trotter grin. "No wonder you're still a good pilot. You've got the killer instinct, all right."

Moss knew he should have smiled, too. Try as he would, he couldn't. Yes, he had a killer instinct. He'd been thinking about that while he was up in the fighter. But he hadn't thought about it in terms of the Confederates then. He'd thought about Canadians, people he'd been dealing with—hell, people he'd liked, people he'd loved—for more than twenty years.

Trotter might have picked that out of his head. "Maybe getting away from these parts will do you good," he said.

"Will it? I have my doubts," Moss answered. "It won't bring Laura and Dorothy back to life. It won't make me stop wanting to blow Canada to hell and gone."

The commandant shifted uneasily in his swivel chair. He didn't seem to know what to make of that. Moss could hardly blame him. He hadn't known what an explosive mixture grief and rage and hate could be till it overwhelmed him. For a moment, he wondered if the damned Canuck who'd sent Laura the bomb had had that same hot, furious blend blazing in him. Only for a moment. Then Moss shoved the thought aside. To hell with what the damned Canuck had been thinking. *If I knew who it was . . .* Regretfully, Moss shoved that thought aside, too. He didn't know. From what U.S. investigators said, it wasn't likely he ever would.

"Well," Trotter said, "any which way, you will be going back to the States. Your orders say, 'as quickly as practicable.' How soon can you be on a train?"

If Moss hadn't had tragedy strike him, he knew he wouldn't have got that much consideration. The other officer would have said, *Be on the train at seven tomorrow morning,* and off he would have gone. Here, though, even if he didn't think getting away would do much for him, he was far from sorry to put Canada behind him. "I don't have much left to do here," he said. "I've been settling affairs ever since . . . since it happened. After my apartment got blown to hell, it's not like I've got much left to throw in a suitcase. If it wasn't for your kindness, I wouldn't have a suitcase to throw my stuff in, either."

"I'd say we owe you more than a suitcase, Major Moss," Trotter told him. "I've taken the liberty of checking the train schedules. . . ." He paused to see if that would annoy Moss. It didn't; he knew the commandant was only doing his job. When he nodded, Trotter continued, "Next train from Toronto to Chicago gets into London at 4:34 this afternoon."

"That's what the schedule says, anyway," Moss observed dryly. If the train was within half an hour of that, it would be doing all right.

Trotter nodded. "Yeah, that's what it says. And a train from Chicago to Mount Vernon goes out at half past nine tomorrow night. You'll have to kill some time in Chicago, but if you're from there it shouldn't be too bad."

"Maybe," Moss said. He didn't want to see his family. He'd had enough trouble with them at the funeral. But Captain Trotter didn't need to know about his difficulties there. His family had thought he was crazy to marry Laura Secord, and they'd seemed offended when the union didn't fall apart in short order. But he could find ways to spend time in Chicago without having anything to do with them. He could, and he intended to.

"Good luck," Trotter said.

Moss didn't laugh in his face. For the life of him, he couldn't figure out why. If he'd had anything remotely approaching good luck, his wife and daughter would still be alive, and he wouldn't be wearing a U.S. uniform again. But he hadn't, they weren't, and he was. "Thanks, Captain," he said, very much as if he meant it.

When Hipolito Rodriguez walked into Freedom Party headquarters in Baroyeca, the first thing he saw was a new map on the wall. It showed the Confederate States as they were now, with Kentucky and what had been called Houston back in the fold. The lands the United States had seized in the Great War and not yet returned—chunks of Virginia, Arkansas, and Sonora—had a new label: *Unredeemed Territory.* That same label was applied to Sequoyah, even though the plebiscite there had gone against the CSA.

Part of Rodriguez—the part that had hated *los Estados Unidos* ever since their soldiers tried to kill him during the Great War—rejoiced to see that label on Sequoyah. A lingering sense of fairness made him wonder about it, though. Pointing to the map, and to Sequoyah in particular, he asked Robert Quinn, "Is that truly the way it should be?"

"*Sí, Señor* Rodriguez. *Absolutamente,*" the local Freedom Party leader answered. "The election in Sequoyah was a shame and a sham. Since the war, *los Estados Unidos* sent so many settlers into that state that the result of the vote could not possibly be just. Since they had no business occupying the land in the first place, they had no business settling it, either."

"Is this what *Señor* Featherston says?" Rodriguez asked.

Quinn nodded. "It certainly is. And it is something more than that. It is the truth." A priest celebrating the Mass could have sounded no more sure of himself.

Rodriguez eyed the map again. Slowly, he nodded. But he could not help saying, "If *Señor* Featherston tells this to the United States, they will not be happy. They thought the plebiscite settled everything."

"Are you going to lie awake at night flabbling about what the United States think?" Quinn dropped the English slang into the middle of a Spanish sentence, which only strengthened its meaning.

But Hipolito Rodriguez gave back a shrug. "It could be that I am, *señor,*" he said. "Please remember, I have a son who is in the Army. I have two more sons who could easily be conscripted." Since he was only in his mid-forties himself, he was not too old to put the butternut uniform on again, but he said nothing about that. He was not afraid for himself in the same way as he was afraid for his boys.

"How long have you wanted revenge against the United States?" Quinn asked softly.

"A long time," Rodriguez admitted. "Oh, *sí, señor,* a very long time indeed. But now it occurs to me, as it did not before, that some things may be bought at too high a price. And is it not possible that what is true for me may also be true for the whole country?"

"Jake Featherston won't let anything go wrong." Quinn spoke with utmost confidence. "He's been right before. He'll keep on being right. We'll have our place in the sun, and we'll get it without much trouble, too. You wait and see."

Rodriguez let that certainty persuade him, too—certainty, after all, was a big part of what he'd been looking for when he joined the Freedom Party. *"Bueno,"* he said. "I hope very much that you are right."

"Sure I am," Quinn said easily. "Why don't you just sit down and relax, and we'll go ahead with the meeting."

Falling back into that weekly routine did help ease Rodriguez's mind. Robert Quinn went through the usual announcements. There were more of those than there had been in the old days, for the Party had more members in Baroyeca now. Rodriguez and the other veterans of the hard times couldn't help looking down their noses a little at the men who had joined because joining suddenly looked like the way to get ahead. No denying, though, that some of the newcomers had proved useful.

Once the announcements were done, the Party men sang patriotic songs, mostly in Spanish, a few in English. As they always did, they finished with "Dixie." Then Quinn said, "Now there is something I want you men to think about when you go home tonight. It is possible—not likely, mind you, but possible—that *los Estados Unidos* will give us a hard time about our rightful demands against them. If that does happen, we may have to take a very firm line with them. If we do, they'll be sorry. You can bet your bottom dollar on that. And you can bet *los Estados Confederados* won't back down again."

Applause filled the crowded room. Rodriguez joined it, even though that wasn't exactly what Quinn had told him before the formal meeting started. Then he'd sounded as if he didn't think the United States would fight. Of course, he was a politician, and politicians had a habit of telling people what they wanted to hear. But Rodriguez hadn't thought Freedom Party men did that sort of thing.

Then Quinn said, "I'll tell you something else, too, friends. During the last war, the *mallates* stabbed us in the back. We would have licked *los Estados Unidos* then if those black bastards hadn't betrayed us. Well, that isn't going to happen this time, *por Dios*. Jake Featherston will clamp down on them good and hard to make sure it doesn't."

He got another round of applause, a louder one this time. Rodriguez pounded his callused palms together till they hurt. He didn't care what happened to the Confederacy's Negroes, as long as it was nothing good. He'd got his baptism by fire against the black rebels in Georgia in 1916, before his division went to fight the damnyankees in Texas. He'd hardly seen a Negro since he got out of the Army. If he never saw another one, that wouldn't break his heart.

"As long as we stand behind Jake Featherston a hundred percent, nothing can go wrong," Quinn said. "He knows what's what. This country will be great again—great, I tell you! And every one of you, every one of us, will help."

More applause. Again, Hipolito Rodriguez joined it. Why not? Seeing the Confederate States back on their feet was another reason he'd joined the Freedom Party. One more was that Robert Quinn had never treated him like a damn greaser, an English phrase he knew much too well. The Party had nothing against men from Sonora and Chihuahua. It saved all its venom for the *mallates*.

*Why shouldn't it?* Rodriguez thought. *They deserve it. We never tried to hurt the country. We've been loyal.* He scorned the men from the Empire of Mexico who sneaked into the CSA trying to find work, too. If any people deserved to be called greasers, they were the ones.

Robert Quinn held up a hand. "Before we call it a night and go home, I've got one more announcement to make. I've been trying to push this through for a long time, but I haven't had any luck till now. I heard from the state Party chairman the other day. Now it's certain: the silver mine in the hills outside of town is going to open up again next month. And, even though this part isn't so sure, it does look like the railroad will be coming back to Baroyeca." He grinned at the Freedom Party men. "Remember, you heard it here first."

This time, he got something better than applause. He got delighted silence, followed by a low, excited buzz. The mine had been closed ever since the collapse, and the railroad had stopped coming to Baroyeca not much later. Rodriguez wondered what had made the authorities change their minds after so long.

Two men sitting in the next row back answered the question for him. One of them remarked, "Need plenty of *plata* to fight a war."

"*Sí, sí,*" the other agreed. "And where there's a little silver, there's always a lot of lead. Need plenty of lead to fight a war, too."

"Ahh," Rodriguez murmured to himself. He liked seeing how things worked. He always had. Maybe the authorities hadn't decided to reopen the mine from the goodness of their hearts alone. Maybe they'd seen that they would need silver and especially lead.

Well, what if they had? It would still do the town a lot of good. If the railroad came back, prices at Diaz's general store would drop like a rock. Shipping goods in by truck on bad roads naturally made everything cost more. After the train line shut down, the storekeeper had been lucky to stay in business at all. Plenty of other places in town hadn't.

"Three cheers for *Señor* Quinn!" somebody shouted. The cheers rang out. Quinn stood there, looking suitably modest, as if the news hadn't been his doing at all. Maybe it really hadn't, not altogether. But he deserved some credit for it.

When the Party meeting did end, several men headed over to *La Culebra Verde* to celebrate. Rodriguez thought of what Magdalena would say if he came home drunk. Sometimes, after he had that thought, he had another one: *I don't care.* Then he would go off to the Green Snake and see how much *cerveza* or, more rarely, tequila, he could pour down. When he did that, Magdalena had some very pointed things to say the next morning, things a headache often did not improve.

Tonight, he just started out into the countryside beyond Baroyeca. The new line of poles supporting the wires that carried electricity made sure he couldn't get lost even if he were drunk. The sky was black velvet scattered with diamonds. A lot of stars seemed to be out tonight.

One of them, a bright red one, startled him by moving. Then he heard the faint buzz of a motor overhead. "*Un avion,*" he muttered in surprise. He couldn't remember the last time he'd seen an airplane above Baroyeca. It was flying south. He wondered where it was going. Off to scout the border with the Empire of Mexico? That seemed most likely. But wouldn't it do better to scout the border with the USA?

Maybe other airplanes were doing that. Rodriguez hoped so. When he fought up in west Texas, the only airplanes he'd seen had belonged to the United States. The Confederate States, stretched too thin, hadn't been able to deploy many on that distant, less than vital front.

Would things be any different in a new war? Yes, *los Estados Confederados* had Kentucky and Houston back again, so that Texas was whole once more. Maybe they'd even get back the other territory they had lost in the Great War. But that map on the wall of Freedom Party headquarters still said *los Estados Unidos* were bigger, and bigger still meant stronger in a long, drawn-out fight.

Maybe Jake Featherston knew something he didn't. He hoped so. He couldn't see what it might be, though. With one son in the Army, with two more likely to be called up, he also couldn't help worrying.

When he got back to the farmhouse, he smiled at the fine white electric light shining out through the windows. Magdalena had left a lamp burning—no, not burning: she'd left a lamp *on*—for him. She'd waited up for him, too. He didn't say anything about the growing threat of war. Instead, he talked about the silver mine's reopening and the likely return of the railroad to Baroyeca.

His wife smiled. She nodded. And then she said, "This is all very good, but I still hope there will be peace with *los Estados Unidos*."

Rodriguez realized he wasn't the only one worrying.

Chester Martin passed a newsboy on his way to the trolley stop. The kid had a stack of the *Los Angeles Times* in front of him as tall as the bottoms of his knickers. He waved a paper at Chester and shouted out the morning's headline: "Smith says no!"

Usually, Chester walked right past newsboys. That was enough to stop him, though. "Oh, he does, does he? Says no to what, exactly?"

The newsboy couldn't tell him. They'd told the kid what to yell before they turned him loose, and that was it. He yelled it again, louder this time. "Smith says no!" For good measure, he added, "Read all about it!"

"Give me one." Chester parted with a nickel. The newsboy handed him a paper. He carried it to the stop. As soon as he got there, he unfolded it and read the headline and the lead story. Al Smith had said no to Jake Featherston. The Confederates weren't going to get back the pieces of Sonora and Arkansas and Virginia they'd lost in the war—or Sequoyah, either.

Smith was quoted as saying, "The president of the Confederate States personally promised me that he would make no more territorial demands on the North American continent. He has taken less than a year to break his solemn word. No matter what he may feel about his promise, however, I am resolved to hold him to it. These territories will remain under the administration and sovereignty of the United States."

"About time!" Martin said, and turned the paper over to read more.

Just then, though, the trolley came clanging up. Chester threw another nickel in the fare box and found a seat. His was far from the only open copy of the *Times* as the streetcar rattled away.

A man of about Martin's age sitting across the aisle from him folded his newspaper and put it in his lap with an air of finality. "There's going to be trouble," he said gloomily.

The woman sitting behind him said, "There'd be worse trouble if we gave that Featherston so-and-so what he wants. How soon would he be back trying to squeeze something else out of us?"

"Lady, I spent three stinking years in the trenches," the man answered. "There isn't any trouble worse than that." He looked over at Chester for support. "Aren't I right? Were you there?"

"Yeah, I was there," Martin said. "I don't know what to tell you, though. Looks to me like that guy is spoiling for a fight. The longer we keep ducking, the harder he's going to hit us when he finally does."

"Yikes!" The man jerked in surprise. He sent Martin a betrayed look. "Who cares about those lousy little chunks of land?"

"Well, I don't, not much," Chester admitted. "But suppose we give them back to him and *then* he jumps on us anyway? We'd look like a bunch of boobs, and we'd be that much worse off, too."

"Why would he jump on us if he's got everything he wants?" the man demanded.

Before Chester could say anything, the woman who'd been arguing beat him to it: "Because somebody like that *never* has everything he wants. As soon as you give him something, he wants something else. When you see a little kid like that, you spank him so he behaves himself from then on."

"How do you spank somebody who'll shoot back if you try?" the man asked.

"If we don't spank him, he'll shoot first," Chester said. The woman in back of the other man nodded emphatically. They all kept on wrangling about it till first the woman and then the other man got off at their stops.

Chester kept on going down into the South Bay. The area was growing fast; builders wanted to run up lots of new houses. The construction workers' union was doing its best to stop them till they met its terms. This tract in Torrance had been carved from an orange grove. The trees had gone down. The houses weren't going up, or not very fast, anyway.

When Martin walked into the union tent across from the construction

site, the organizer who kept an eye on things during the night, a tough little guy named Pete Mazzini, wore a worried expression. "What's up?"
Chester asked, grabbing the coffee pot that perked lazily over the blue
flame of canned heat.

"I hear they really are gonna sic the goddamn Pinkertons on us
today," Mazzini said.

"Shit," Chester said, and the other man nodded. "Pinkertons are bad
news." Mazzini nodded again. Martin hadn't seen Pinkerton goons since
the steel-mill strikes in Toledo after the Great War. In a way, fighting
them was even worse than fighting cops. A fair number of cops were fun-
damentally decent guys. Anybody who'd sign up to use a club or a black-
jack or a pistol for the Pinkertons had to be a son of a bitch.

"At least I found out." Mazzini jerked a thumb toward the building
site. "Dumb night watchmen over there don't think about how voices
carry once everything quiets down."

"Good." Martin had never got more than three stripes on his sleeve
during the war, but he'd commanded a company for a while. Now he had
to think not like a captain, but like a general. "We've got to let the pickets
know as soon as they start showing up. They'll be ready, because we've
had word the builders might pull this. We've got to bring in as many
weapons as we can. Not just sticks for the signs, either. We'll need knives.
Guns, too, if we can get 'em in a hurry."

"We start shooting, that gives the cops all the excuse they need to
land on us with both feet," Mazzini said.

He wasn't wrong. All the same, Chester answered, "If we let the
goons break us, we're screwed, too. If they break us, we might as well
pack it in. You want that?"

"Hell, no," Mazzini said. "I just wanted to make sure you were thinking about it."

"Oh, I am. Bet your ass I am." Martin scratched his chin. "I'm going
to call somebody from the *Daily Breeze*. Torrance papers aren't down on
unions the way the goddamn *Times* is. We ought to have an honest witness here. I think I'll talk to the Torrance cops, too. The builders don't
have them in their pocket, like in L.A. If they know the Pinkertons are
going to raise hell ahead of time, maybe they can step on 'em."

Pete Mazzini looked as if he would have laughed in anybody else's
face. "Good luck," he said. His shrug declared that he washed his hands
of dealing with all police anywhere. "I don't suppose it can make things
any worse."

Yawning, he agreed to hang around and warn the incoming pickets of
the trouble ahead while Chester went to talk with the man from the *Daily*

*Breeze* and the police and make other arrangements. When Chester got back, he said, "Thanks, Pete. You can go home and get your forty winks now."

Mazzini gave him a look. "Hell, no. If there's gonna be a brawl, I want in on it. Those bastards aren't going to lick us as easy as they think they are." He yawned again, and fixed himself what had to be his millionth cup of coffee.

The reporter from the *Daily Breeze* showed up an hour or so later. He had a photographer with him, which gladdened Chester's heart. Meanwhile, union backers came up to the men on the picket line, slipped them this or that, and then went on their way. Martin and Mazzini exchanged knowing glances. Neither said a word.

At twenty past eleven, half a dozen autos with Torrance cops in them pulled up by the building site. Martin wondered if they'd known what would go on before he told them. When a reporter from the *Times* showed up five minutes later, he stopped wondering. They had.

At twenty to twelve, two buses that had seen a lot of better years pulled up around the corner. "Here we go," Chester said softly. It had been a long, long time—half a lifetime—since he'd shot at anybody, but he knew he could. Nobody who'd been through the Great War was likely to forget what gunplay was all about.

Here came the Pinkerton men. They looked like goons: drunks and toughs and guys down on their luck who'd take anybody's money and do anything because they hadn't had any real work for such a long time. They carried a motley assortment of iron bars and wooden clubs. One guy even had what Martin belatedly recognized as a baseball bat, something far, far from its New England home. Others, grim purpose on their faces, kept one hand out of sight. *Knife men and shooters,* Martin thought, and made sure he could get at his own pistol in a hurry.

"We don't want any trouble, now," said a Torrance policeman with the map of Ireland on his face. He and his pals formed a thin line between the advancing goons and the picketers, who were shaping a line of their own: a skirmish line. Chester warily watched the scabs on the site. If they took his men from behind while the Pinkertons hit them from the front . . . He grimaced. That wouldn't be good at all.

As if reading his mind, Mazzini said, "I told a couple of our guys to start shooting at the scabs if they even take a step towards us. Some bullets go past their heads, I don't think they've got the balls to keep coming."

Chester laid a hand on his shoulder for a moment. "Good. Thanks."

A short, scrawny, ferret-faced man in a loud, snappy suit seemed to be the Pinkertons' commander. "Time to teach these damn Reds a lesson," he said in a voice that carried. Low growls rose from his men, as if from a pack of angry dogs. He pointed. "Go get 'em!"

Instead of growling, the goons roared and charged. Some of the Torrance cops swung their billy clubs. Most of them let the Pinkertons go by. The union men roared, too. They were outnumbered, but not too badly. Some of them ran forward to meet the goons head on. A few others hung back, watching the scabs.

"Here we go!" Chester said, an odd note of exultation in his voice. He snatched up a club and waded into the brawl. He didn't want to start shooting first, but he had nothing at all against breaking a few heads.

He almost got his broken as soon as he started fighting. A goon carrying an iron bar with a chunk of concrete on the end swung it for all he was worth. It hummed past Chester's ear. He clobbered the Pinkerton before the fellow could take another swing at him.

That scrawny guy in the sharp suit didn't mix it up along with the strikebreakers he'd brought. He stayed out of the fight and yelled orders. Martin pointed at the man with his club. "Get him!" he yelled to one of the Torrance cops, who'd managed to whack his way clear and was standing on the sidewalk as if it were the sideline of a football game. The cop paid him no attention.

But when the union men started getting the better of the strikebreakers, their boss was the one who first pulled a pistol out of his pocket. Chester tried to shift his club to his left hand so he could grab his own gun, but a goon had hold of his left arm. In desperation, he threw the club instead. He got lucky. It caught the fellow in the sharp suit right in the bridge of the nose.

He let out a howl that pierced the shouts and curses of the brawling men in front of him, dropped the pistol, and clapped both hands to his face. When he took them away a moment later, he had a mustache made of blood.

He bent for the pistol. But the *Daily Breeze* photographer, not content to stay neutral, dashed up and grabbed it. Screaming, "You fucker!" the Pinkertons' boss jumped on him. They had their own private brawl till the reporter from the local paper weighed in on the photographer's side. Then the little guy with the gaudy clothes took his lumps.

So did his goons. Thanks to Martin and that photographer, nobody started shooting. Chester knew how lucky that was. The union men drove the toughs back to their buses in headlong retreat. A rock smashed the windshield on one of the buses. Both drivers got out of there a lot faster than they'd come.

The next morning, the *Times* called it "a savage labor riot." The *Daily Breeze* knew better. So did Chester. He also knew the union had won a round. They wouldn't see the Pinkertons for a while—but when they did, the other side would be loaded for bear.

# XIX

The *Sweet Sue* jounced west across the rough waters of the Atlantic, back toward Boston harbor. George Enos Jr. stood near the bow of the fishing boat, thinking about things that had changed and things that hadn't. He turned to Carlo Lombardi, who was smoking a cigarette beside him. "Back in 1914," George said, "my old man was coming home from a fishing run. He didn't have a wireless set on his ship. When he got back into port, he found out that goddamn Serb had blown up the Austrian archduke and his wife, and everything was going to hell."

Lombardi paused to take another drag before he answered, "We're lucky. We can find out everything's going to hell before we get into port. Ain't life grand nowadays?"

"Yeah. Grand." George tried to look every which way at once. "Of course, it's liable not to be the wireless that tells us."

"How do you mean?" the other fisherman asked, scratching his head.

"If a war starts, you've got to bet the Confederates'll have their submarines up here ahead of time. Only stands to reason, right?" George said. "If they do, first thing we'll know about it is—*wham!*"

"Fuck," Lombardi said, and pitched his cigarette into the green water. He eyed George sourly. "You bastard. Now you're going to have me looking around for a periscope or a goddamn torpedo all the way till we tie up at T Wharf."

"Yeah, well, I've been doing that ever since we started back from the Grand Bank," George said. "That sneaky Confederate son of a bitch torpedoed my father after the last war was done. It'd be just like one of those bastards to nail me before this one even starts."

"Fuck," Lombardi said again, and gave George an even more jaundiced once-over. "You better not be a goddamn Jonah, that's all I've got to say."

"My old man was the one with the bad luck," George said. The other man thought that over, then slowly nodded. If he didn't believe it, he kept it to himself. George went on, "Maybe there won't be a war this time around. Maybe. I keep on hoping there won't, anyway."

"I hope for free pussy, too, when I go to a whorehouse," Lombardi said, lighting another cigarette. "I hope for it, but that ain't how things work." He sucked in smoke. "Better not be another war. If there is, the tobacco'll all be shitty. My pa used to bitch about that all the goddamn time, how lousy the smokes were 'cause we couldn't get no Confederate tobacco."

George didn't remember whether his father had complained about bad tobacco. He'd been too little when George Enos Senior got killed, and his father had been away at sea too much while alive to leave behind a lot of memories. George did recall one night when his father kept asking if he and Mary Jane were ready to go to bed yet. He hadn't been ready, and his indignation still rankled across a quarter of a century.

All of a sudden, out of a clear blue sky, he started laughing like hell. "What's so goddamn funny?" Lombardi asked.

"Nothing, not really," George answered. The other fisherman gave him a particularly fishy stare. He didn't care. It wasn't the sort of joke he could explain. Just the same, he suddenly understood *why* his father had kept wanting him to go to bed, which he hadn't when he was a little boy. He was liable to use that same impatient tone of voice to find out if his own boys were ready to go to sleep so he could be alone with Connie. As a matter of fact, he knew damn well he'd used that tone of voice with them before.

*And if a new war does start, and if your boat goes to the bottom, is that what you want them to remember you for?* he wondered. Had the same question ever occurred to his father? Probably not. But then, his father hadn't known anything about a big war before he found himself in the middle of the biggest one of all time. People living in the USA nowadays didn't have that excuse.

Neither did people living in the CSA. The Great War had hurt them even worse. They, or at least Jake Featherston, seemed ready—hell, seemed eager—for another round. George wondered why.

He found an answer, too, the same way as he'd found an answer when he thought about his old man. *The Confederates lost. That means they want revenge.* The USA had lost two wars in a row to the CSA. That had made people here twice as serious about getting their own back. Now, after a win, people here thought everything was square. South of the border, they didn't.

*Will there ever be an end? Will both sides ever be satisfied at the same time?* He thought that one over, too. Unlike the other questions, it didn't have an answer that leaped into sight.

No Confederate submersible or commerce raider challenged the *Sweet Sue*. No dive bomber dropped explosives on her from the sky. She sailed back into Boston harbor as if pulling fish from the sea were the hardest, most dangerous thing to do men had ever invented. In peacetime, it came close. Peacetime, though, felt like summertime. Even as you enjoyed it, you knew it wouldn't last.

When the *Sweet Sue* tied up at T Wharf, the first officer made the best deal he could with the buyers. Normally, George would have stuck around to find out how good the deal was. His own share of the pie depended on how big a pie he was looking at. Today, though, he drew fifty dollars against whatever the total would be and headed for the apartment where he spent rather less time than he did at sea.

He had to get past all the harborside attractions that tried to separate fishermen from their money and make them forget about their wives. Football games and raucous music blared from wireless sets in saloons. A drunk reeled out of a tavern. He almost ran into George. "Easy, pal," George said, and dodged.

Music with more of a thump and pound to it, music played by real live musicians, poured out of strip joints. Hearing that kind of music made you think about the girls who'd dance to it, and about what they would—or wouldn't—be wearing. You could get drinks in those joints, too, but they'd cost twice as much.

If you didn't want to drink, if you didn't want to watch, if you wanted to get down to business ... A swarthy, tired-looking woman about George's age leaned out of a second-story window and beckoned to him. She wasn't wearing anything from the waist up. Her breasts drooped. They seemed tired, too. She tried to sound alluring when she called, "How about it, big boy?"

George kept walking. The whore swore at him. Even her curses sounded tired.

His block of flats stood only a couple of streets farther on. He hurried to it. Unlike the one where he'd lived with his mother, it had an elevator. Most of the time, he took that as proof he'd come up in the world. When he stepped into the lobby now, though, the cage was empty. The car was on some upper floor. He didn't have the patience to wait for it. He went up four flights of stairs, taking them two at a time till his knees got tired.

The key to his apartment was brass. A good thing, too; with all the time he spent out on the ocean, an iron key would have rusted on the chain. He put the key in the lock and turned it.

Connie's startled voice came from the kitchen: "Who's there?" And then, realizing only one person besides her had a key, she went on, "Is that you, George?"

"Well, it's not the tooth fairy and it's not the Easter Bunny and it's not Santa Claus," he answered.

She came rocketing out of the kitchen and into his arms. He squeezed her till she squeaked. She felt wonderful. He didn't stop to think that he'd been at sea so long, the Wicked Witch of the North would have felt good to him. He kissed her. Things might have—no, things would have—gone straight on from there if Bill and Pat hadn't charged him and tried tackling him in ways that would have got flags thrown on any gridiron in the country. Fortunately, they weren't big enough to do any serious damage.

"Daddy! Daddy! Daddy!" they squealed. If they went on after that, it was in voices only dogs could hear.

He let go of Connie and hugged the boys. They were also good to come home to, in a different way. His wife asked, "How long will you be here this time?"

"Don't know. Didn't hang around to find out," he said. "I just drew part of my pay and headed on over here. When they want me again, they'll come after me."

"Well, at least they won't have to scour the saloons to find you," Connie said. "Some of those people . . ."

George didn't say anything to that. He just tried to look virtuous. He didn't know how good a job he did. For one thing, he intended to take a drink or three while he had the chance. For another, Connie's father had seen the inside of a tavern and the bottom of a glass more than a few times in his day.

But George didn't want to think about that right this minute, either. He asked, "How are things here?"

"Pretty good," Connie answered. "They've been good boys. They haven't tried to pull the ears off the cat or flush the Sears, Roebuck catalogue down the toilet." They had committed the felony with the catalogue, one crumpled page and then more than one crumpled page at a time, till a flood and two spankings resulted. They hadn't messed with the cat's ears, at least not where their parents could catch them. But then Whiskers, unlike the hapless catalogue, could take care of himself.

The cat strolled up to see what the commotion was about. He gave George a leisurely glance, then yawned, showing needle teeth. *Oh, it's you,* he might have said. He remembered George between trips just well enough to tolerate being petted. And, of course, George smelled of fish, which made him interesting.

"How was the run?" Connie did her best not to sound anxious. Her best could have been better. If the run wasn't good, things got tight. She had to make ends meet on whatever George brought home.

"Pretty good. We brought back a lot of tuna," he answered. "Only question now is how much it'll bring."

"News hasn't been good," Connie said, and he nodded. She went on, "That might drive prices up."

"Maybe. I can hope." He sniffed. "What smells good?"

"I was stewing a chicken," she told him. "We were going to have it for two nights, maybe three, but who cares? I've got to show you I'm a better cook than the Cookie, don't I?"

"You're a lot cuter than Davey, anyhow," he said, which made her squawk. He went on, "I just hope Bill and Pat get sleepy pretty soon." Both boys let out indignant howls. If he'd listened to them, he would have believed they would never fall asleep again. Fortunately, he knew better.

Connie turned red. "My father used to say things like that when he came home from a fishing run."

"So did mine," George said. "I never understood why till not very long ago. I don't remember much about my pa, but that sticks in my mind."

"How come, Daddy?" Bill asked.

"I don't know. It just does," George answered. "It's the sort of thing a fisherman would say, that's for sure." Bill asked why again. George didn't say, not in words. He kissed Connie again instead. As far as he was concerned, that was the best answer he could give.


Jefferson Pinkard looked around at his kingdom and found it . . . not so good. He turned to Mercer Scott, the guard chief at Camp Dependable. "For Chrissake, Mercer," he said, "what the hell are we gonna do when those goddamn sons of bitches in Richmond send us another shipment of niggers? This camp'll go boom, on account of there just ain't no room for any more spooks in here. Do they care? Do they give a shit? Don't make me laugh."

Scott shifted a chaw of Red Man from his left cheek to his right. He spat a stream of tobacco juice onto the ground. "You sure as hell ain't wrong," he said. "We got us coons hangin' from their heels like they was bats. Dunno where else we can put 'em. On the roofs, maybe?" He laughed to show that was a joke.

Jeff laughed, too, though it was anything but funny. If he could have put bunks on the roofs of the prisoner barracks, he would have done it. He didn't know where else to put them, that was for sure. "Bastards don't send us enough in the way of rations, neither. We got pellagra, we got hookworm, we got plain old-fashioned starvation. Wouldn't take a whole lot more food to make all that stuff a hell of a lot better."

"Damned if I can see why you're gettin' your ass in an uproar about *that*," Scott said. "They're only niggers. No, they ain't *only* niggers. They're a bunch of goddamn Reds, too. So who gives a shit if they die? Ain't nobody gonna miss 'em."

"It's not . . ." Pinkard frowned, looking for the word that summed up how he felt about it. "It's not *orderly*, dammit. If they give me so many prisoners, they're supposed to give me enough food for that many, too. That's just the way things work."

As a matter of fact, that wasn't the way things worked. They'd worked that way in the prisoner camps down in the Empire of Mexico, not least because Jeff had made sure they did. And they'd worked that way in the Birmingham jail, because it was longstanding policy that they work so. There was no longstanding policy for camps housing political prisoners and Negroes taken in rebellion. Every day that passed saw such policy made.

Scott seemed to understand instinctively the root of that policy. It was, *Who gives a shit if they die?* Pinkard could see that for himself. A hell of a lot of prisoners left Camp Dependable feet first. He didn't like it. He scavenged across the countryside for more rations than he was officially issued. No doubt that did some good. Against the kind of overcrowding he was facing, it didn't do much.

A guard trotted up to him, heavy belly bouncing above his belt. "Telephone call for you, boss," the man said. He hadn't missed any meals. None of the guards had. Neither had Pinkard himself.

"Thanks, Eddie," he said, though he didn't know why he was thanking the guard. Telephone calls weren't likely to be good news. He tramped back to the office and picked up the phone. "Pinkard speaking."

"Hello, Pinkard." The clicks and pops on the line said it was a long-distance call. "This is Ferdinand Koenig, calling from Richmond."

"Yes, sir!" The attorney general was Jake Featherston's right-hand man. "Freedom!"

"Freedom! I've heard you aren't happy because you haven't been getting enough advance notice of prisoner shipments," Koenig said, as if he'd just finished listening to Jeff bitching to Mercer Scott.

"Uh, yes, sir. That's true," Jeff said. Meanwhile, he was thinking, *Goddammit, some son of a bitch here is telling stories about me back in Richmond. Have to find out who the bastard is.* He didn't suppose he should have been surprised that Koenig—as attorney general or as Freedom Party big wig?—had spies in Camp Dependable. All the same, he wanted to be rid of them.

The attorney general didn't sound too angry as he said, "Don't suppose I can blame you for that. Here's your news then: you've got about fifteen hundred niggers—maybe two thousand—heading your way. They ought to be there in three, four days."

"Jesus Christ!" It wasn't a scream, but it came close. Pinkard went on, "Sir, no way in hell this camp will hold that many more people. We're overflowing already."

"That's why I'm telling you now." Koenig spoke with what sounded like exaggerated patience. "You have the time to get ready for those black bastards."

"I don't suppose we'll get the rations we need to feed 'em," Jeff said. Only silence answered him. He hadn't really expected anything else. Reproachfully, he continued, "Sir, you know I'm a good Party man. I don't mean any disrespect or anything like that. But what the hell am I supposed to do to get my camp ready for a shipment that big?"

"Whatever you have to do." Ferdinand Koenig paused. Pinkard didn't think he would say anything more, but he did, repeating, "Whatever you have to do. Is that plain enough, or do I have to draw you a picture? I'd better not have to draw you a picture. I heard you were a pretty smart fellow."

Maybe he had just drawn a picture. "Jesus Christ!" Jeff said again, not much liking what he thought he saw. "You mean—?"

Koenig cut him off. "Whatever you have to do," he said for the third time. "You can take care of it, or I'll find somebody else who will. Your choice, Pinkard. Which would you rather?"

Jeff thought it over. It didn't take long. He *was* a good Party man. The Party mattered more to him than anything else. The ruins of his marriage proved that. And, where Emily had screwed around, the Party had always been faithful. Without it, God only knew what he would have done when he lost his job at the Sloss Works. Didn't loyalty demand loyalty in return? "I'll take care of it, Mr. Attorney General. Don't you worry about a thing."

"I wasn't worried," Koenig said. "Like I told you, if you didn't, somebody else would. But I'm glad it's you. I know you've put in a lot of time for us. And I know you'll do a good job here, too. You won't screw it up and leave a bunch of loose ends or anything like that." *You'd better not,* was what he meant.

"Hell, no," Jeff said quickly. "When I do somethin', I do it right and proper."

"Good," Koenig said, and the line went dead.

Pinkard stared at the telephone for close to half a minute. "Fuck," he muttered, and finally hung it up. He trudged out of the office.

"What's up?" Mercer Scott called to him.

*Are you the spy? I wouldn't be surprised. I've run my mouth around you. Well, no more, goddammit.* But Scott had to know about this. Jeff said, "In three or four days, we're getting another fifteen hundred, two thousand niggers."

Scott stared. "Holy shit!" he said. "They can't do that! This place won't hold 'em."

"Oh, yes, it will," Pinkard said.

"How?" Scott demanded. "You were just now telling me it wouldn't hold the niggers we've got, and you were right. You know damn well you were right."

"I'll tell you how." And Pinkard did.

"Holy shit," Scott said again, this time in an altogether different tone of voice. "You sure you know what you're talking about? You sure you know what you're doing?" Under other circumstances, the questions would have infuriated Jeff. Not now.

He nodded uneasily. "I know, all right. Get the guards we need—you'll know the ones we can count on. Then pull out the niggers."

"All at once?" Scott asked.

After a moment, Jeff shook his head. "No. That'd be asking for trouble. Take out a couple hundred. Less chance of anything going wrong."

"Yeah." The guard chief eyed him. "How come I'm the lucky one? What are you gonna be doing? Sittin' in your office pouring down a cold beer?"

Had things been different, that would have infuriated Jeff, too. The way things were, Mercer Scott had the right to ask. Pinkard shook his head. "You stay here and get the next bunch ready. I'm going out with the first ones, and I won't come back till the job's done."

"All right." Scott nodded. "That's fair. I can't tell you it ain't." He stuck out his hand. Pinkard shook it. He was grateful for any sort of reassurance he could get.

Along with fifteen guards, he led two hundred Negroes away from Camp Dependable. The black men came willingly enough. As far as they knew, it was just another work detail. When they'd gone two or three miles from the camp, he ordered them to dig a long, deep trench. "This here ain't nothing but a waste o' time," one of them said. But he was only complaining, the way people did when they had to do work they didn't care for.

Pinkard didn't argue with him. When the ditch was dug, he ordered the Negroes to lie down in it. That drew more complaints. "You gots to put us on top of each other?" a man said. "We ain't no goddamn fairies."

The guards stepped up onto a parapet made from the dirt the Negroes had dug out. Even when they aimed their submachine guns at the men in the trench, the blacks didn't seem to believe what was happening. *This is my camp,* Jeff thought miserably. *I'm responsible for what goes on here.* He nodded to the guards. The order was his to give, and he gave it: "Fire!"

They did. As soon as they started shooting, it was as if the ground convulsed. The submachine guns roared and stuttered and spat flame. The guards slapped in magazine after magazine. Pinkard was appalled at how much ammunition his men needed to kill the prisoners. The stenches of blood and shit filled the humid air. At last, the screaming stopped. Only the groans of the dying were left.

More than one guard vomited into the trench. Jeff felt like heaving up his guts, too, but sternly refrained. "Scrape dirt over 'em," he told the guards. "We've got more work to do." The guards grumbled, but not too much. They seemed too stunned to do a whole lot in the way of grumbling.

And it got harder after that. The Negroes at the camp had to have understood what was going on when the guards came back and the men they'd been guarding didn't. But Mercer Scott was no fool. The first gang of blacks had gone off willingly enough, yes. He made sure the next bunch were shackled. That way, nobody tried to run off into the woods and swamp.

Over the course of the next three days, Pinkard reduced the population of Camp Dependable by two thousand men. That was how he referred to it in his reports. That was how he tried to think about it, too. If he thought about reducing population, he didn't have to dwell on shooting helpless prisoners.

A few of the guards were exhilarated after the job was done. They were the ones who thought Negroes had it coming to them. Most of the men were very subdued, though. They didn't mind jailing blacks or starving them. Shooting them in cold blood seemed to be something else again.

One shot rang out in the middle of the night: a guard blowing his brains out. He got buried, too, with almost as little fuss as if he were one of the blacks so casually disposed of.

When the promised—the threatened—new shipment of Negro prisoners arrived, Camp Dependable was able to take them. Pinkard wondered if he would get a congratulatory call from Ferd Koenig. He didn't. Maybe that made sense, too. After all, he'd only done what the attorney general needed him to do.

\* \* \*

Scipio wished to God he could get out of Augusta. But it wasn't so easy as it would have been a few years before. Things had tightened up. Everywhere a black man went, it was, "Show me your passbook, boy." If he started working in, say, Atlanta, he would have to produce the document that proved he was himself—or proved he was Xerxes, which amounted to the same thing. And if he did that, he would be vulnerable to either Anne Colleton or Jerry Dover.

He didn't think his boss at the Huntsman's Lodge had anything in particular against him. He knew damned well his former boss at the former Marshlands plantation did. But he didn't like the idea of being vulnerable to Dover much better than he liked being vulnerable to Miss Anne. Being vulnerable to anybody white terrified him.

At the restaurant, the rich white men who ate there talked more and more of war. So did the newspapers. Jake Featherston was thumping his chest and foaming at the mouth because Al Smith wouldn't give him what he'd promised not to ask for the year before. Scipio remembered too well what a catastrophe the last war had been for the Confederate States. Under other circumstances, the prospect of a new one would have appalled him.

Under other circumstances ... As things were, he more than half hoped the CSA did start fighting the USA again. All eyes, all thoughts, would turn toward the front. They would turn away from a town in the middle of nowhere like Augusta. And he had heard some of the things bombing airplanes could do nowadays. That made him all the gladder Augusta was a long, long way from the border.

What made life harder was that whites weren't all he had to worry about in Augusta. The Terry was full of sharecroppers displaced from the land by the tractors and harvesters and combines that had revolutionized farming in the CSA since the Freedom Party came to power. The Terry, in fact, held far more people than it held jobs. A man who wasn't careful could easily get knocked over the head for half a dollar—especially a man who wasn't young and who had to wear a penguin suit to and from work, so he looked as if he had money.

Scipio made a point of being careful.

Coming home was worse than going up to the Huntsman's Lodge. Going to work, he had to face harassment from whites who fancied themselves wits. Most of them overestimated by a factor of two. He had to give soft answers. He'd been doing that all his life. He managed.

He came home in the middle of the night. Darkness gave predators cover—and the Augusta police rarely wasted their time looking into crimes blacks committed against each other. Every street corner on the way to his apartment building was an adventure.

Most of the time, of course, the corners were adventures only in his own imagination. He could—and did—imagine horrors whether they were there or not. Every once in a while, they were. He walked as quietly as he could. He always paused in the blackest shadows he could find before exposing himself by crossing a street. Nobody had worried about street lights in the Terry even before the rise of the Freedom Party. These days, the idea of anyone worrying about anything that had to do with blacks was a painful joke.

Voices from a side street made Scipio decide he would do better to stay where he was for a little while. One black man said, "Ain't seen Nero for a while."

"You won't, neither," another answered. "Goddamn ofays cotched him with a pistol in his pocket."

"Do Jesus!" the first man exclaimed. "Nero always the unluckiest son of a bitch you ever seen. What they do with him?"

"Ship him out West, one o' them camps," his friend said.

"Do Jesus!" the first man said again. "You go into one o' them places, you don't come out no more."

"Oh, mebbe you do," the other man said. "Mebbe you do—but it don't help you none."

"Huh!" the first man said—a noise half grunt, half the most cynical laugh Scipio had ever heard. "You got dat right. They throws you in a hole in the ground, or else they throws you in the river fo' the gators and the snappers to finish off."

"I hear the same thing," his friend agreed. "Gator sausage mighty tasty. I ain't gonna eat it no mo'. Never can tell who dat gator knowed." He laughed, too. The black men walked on. They had no idea Scipio had been listening.

He waited till their footsteps faded before he went on to his apartment. The Huntsman's Lodge served a fair amount of wild game: venison, raccoon, bear every once in a while, and alligator. Scipio had been fond of garlicky alligator sausage himself. He didn't think he would ever touch it again.

Three days later, he was walking to work when police and Freedom Party stalwarts with submachine guns swept into the Terry. They weren't trying to solve any specific crime. Instead, they were checking passbooks. Anybody whose papers didn't measure up or who didn't have papers, they seized.

"Let me have a look at that there passbook, boy," a cop growled at Scipio.

"Yes, suh." Scipio was old enough to be the policeman's father, but to most whites in the CSA he would always be a boy. He didn't argue. He just handed over the document. Arguing with a bad-tempered man with a submachine gun was apt to be hazardous to your life expectancy.

The cop took a brief look at his papers, then gave them back. "Hell, I know who you are," he said. "You been paradin' around in them fancy duds for years. Go on, get your black ass outa here."

"Yes, suh. Thank you kindly, suh." Scipio had taken a lot of abuse from whites for going to work in a tuxedo. Here, for once, it looked to have paid off. He got out of there in a hurry. That was unheroic. He knew it. It gnawed at him. But what could he do against dozens of trigger-happy whites? Not one damned thing, and he knew that, too.

He'd gone only a few blocks when gunfire rang out behind him: first a single shot, then a regular fusillade. He didn't know what had happened, and he wasn't crazy or suicidal enough to go back and find out, but he thought he could make a pretty good guess. Somebody must have figured his chances shooting it out were better than they would have been if he'd gone wherever the cops and the stalwarts were taking people they grabbed.

The fellow who'd started shooting was probably—almost certainly—dead now. Even so, who could say for sure he was wrong? He'd died quickly, and hadn't suffered much. Scipio thought of alligators, and wished he hadn't.

One of the waiters, a skinny young man named Nestor, didn't show up at the Huntsman's Lodge. Jerry Dover muttered and fumed. Scipio told him about the dragnet in the Terry. The manager eyed him. "You reckon they picked up Nestor for something or other?"

"Dunno, Mistuh Dover," Scipio said. "Reckon mebbe they could've, though."

"What do you suppose he did?" Dover asked. "He's never given anybody any trouble here."

"Dunno," Scipio said again. "Dunno if he done anything. Them *po*lice, I don't reckon they was fussy." They were standing right outside the kitchen, in a nice, warm corridor. He wanted to shiver even so. Nestor would have been wearing a tuxedo, too. Fat lot of good it had done him.

Jerry Dover rubbed his chin. "He's a pretty fair worker. Let me make a call or two, see what I can find out."

What would he have done if Nestor were a lazy good-for-nothing? Washed his hands like Pilate? Scipio wouldn't have been surprised. He didn't dwell on it. With the crew shorthanded because Nestor wasn't there, he stayed hopping.

And Nestor didn't show up, either. Dover wore a tight-lipped expression, one that discouraged questions. Scipio and the rest of the crew got through the evening. When he went back the next day, the missing waiter still wasn't there. That nerved him to go up to the manager and ask, "Nestor, he come back?"

"Doubt it." Dover sounded as if he had to pay for every word that passed his lips. "Time for a new hire. He won't know his ass from Richmond, either."

"Nestor, what he do?" Scipio persisted. "You find out?"

"He got himself arrested, that's what." Jerry Dover sounded angry at Scipio—or possibly angry at the world. "He picked the wrong goddamn time to do it, too."

"What you mean?" Scipio asked. "Ain't no right time to git arrested."

Dover nodded. "Well, that's so. There's no right time. But there's sure as hell a wrong time. What the cops told me yesterday was, the city jail's full. So those niggers they caught in the Terry—you know about that?"

"Oh, yes, suh," Scipio said softly. "I tol' you, remember? They almost 'rests me, too."

"That's right, you did. Well, I'm damn glad they didn't, because I'd be down two waiters if they had." If the restaurant manager was glad for any other reason that they hadn't arrested Scipio, he didn't show it. He went on, "Jail's full up, like I said. So they went and shipped these here niggers off to one of those camps they've started."

"Lord he'p Nestor, then," Scipio said. "Somebody go into one of them places, I hear tell he don't come out no mo', not breathin', anyways." He'd heard it as gossip between two men he'd never seen, but that didn't mean he didn't believe it. It had the horrid feel of truth.

Jerry Dover shifted uncomfortably from foot to foot. What had *he* heard? Back in the days when Scipio worked at Marshlands, he'd been convinced the Colletons couldn't keep a secret for more than a few minutes before the blacks on the plantation also knew it. Here at the Huntsman's Lodge, the colored cooks and waiters and cleaners quickly found out whatever their white bosses knew. Or did they? Just as blacks kept secrets from whites out of necessity, so whites might also find it wise to keep certain things from blacks.

But if Dover had *that* kind of knowledge, it didn't show on his face. Scipio thought it would. Dover did what he had to do to get along in the world in which he found himself. Who didn't, except crazy people and saints? But the manager was pretty honest, pretty decent. He was no "Freedom!"-yelling stalwart without two brain cells to rub against each other.

He said, "You want to watch yourself on the street, then, don't you?

You know I've got some pull. But it doesn't look like I can do anything about one of those places."

"I watches myself real good, suh," Scipio answered. "You say de city jail full up?" Jerry Dover nodded. Scipio asked him, "They 'rest white folks now, de white folks go to dese camps, too?"

His boss looked at him as if he'd asked whether the stork brought mothers their babies. "Don't be stupid," Dover said.

That was good advice, too. It always was. What worried Scipio was, it might not be enough. He'd escaped the last dragnet as much by luck as by anything else. You could tell a man not to be stupid, and maybe—if he wasn't stupid to begin with—he'd listen. But how the devil could you tell a man not to be unlucky?

Five-thirty in the morning. Reveille blared. Armstrong Grimes groaned. He had time for that one involuntary protest before he rolled out of his cot and his feet hit the floor of the barracks hall at Fort Custer outside of Columbus, Ohio. Then he started functioning, at least well enough. He threw on his green-gray uniform, made up the cot, and dashed outside to his place in the roll call—all in the space of five minutes.

What happened to men who were late had long since convinced him being late was a bad idea. Back home, his mother had made the bed for him most of the time. He'd been sloppy at it when he first got here. Now a dime bounced off his blanket, and bounced high. The drill sergeant didn't have cause to complain about him or even notice him—the two often being synonymous.

He stood there trying not to shiver in the chilly dawn. When the time came, he sang out to announce his presence. Other than that, he kept quiet. Everybody else did the same. For once, the drill sergeants seemed in a merciful mood. They let the assembled soldiers march off to breakfast after only a minimum of growling and cursing.

Everybody marched everywhere at Fort Custer. Armstrong had begun to think *Thou shalt march* was in the Bible somewhere right below *Thou shalt not kill* and *Thou shalt not take the name of the Lord in vain*—two commandments he was learning more about violating every day.

He took a tray and a plate and a mug and silverware, then advanced on the food. A cook's helper loaded the plate with scrambled eggs and hash browns and greasy, overdone bacon. Another one poured the mug full of coffee almost strong enough to eat through the bottom. Armstrong grabbed a seat at a long, long table. He put enough cream and sugar in the coffee to tame it a little, threw salt on the eggs and potatoes and pepper on the eggs, and then started shoveling in chow.

Nobody talked much at breakfast. Nobody had time. The drill here was simple: feed your face as fast as you could. Armstrong had never much cared for manners. He didn't have to worry about them here. Compared to the way some of the guys ate, he might have come from the upper crust. Every once in a while, he thought that was pretty funny. More often than not, he didn't have time to worry about it one way or the other.

As soon as he finished, he shoved his tray and dirty dishes at the poor slobs who'd drawn KP duty. Then he hustled out to the exercise yard. He wasn't the first one there, but he was a long way from the last. Bad things happened to the guys who brought up the rear.

Of course, bad things happened to everybody right after breakfast. Violent calisthenics and a three-mile run weren't the way Armstrong would have used to settle his stomach. The drill sergeants didn't care about his opinion. They had their own goals. His conscription class, like any other, had had some fat guys, some weak guys. He remembered who they'd been. But the fat guys weren't fat any more, and the weak guys weren't weak any more. Oh, a few had washed out, simply unable to stand the strain. People said one fellow had died trying, but Armstrong didn't know if he believed that. Most of the recruits, no matter what kind of shape they'd been in to start with, had toughened up since.

After the run, the conscripts "relaxed" with close-order drill. "Left . . . ! Left . . . ! Left, right, left!" the drill sergeant bawled. "To the rear . . . *haarch!*" He screamed at somebody who couldn't keep the rhythm if his life depended on it. Armstrong's company had a couple of those unfortunates, who drew more than their fair share of abuse. He'd never figured out why the Army still needed close-order drill. Doing it where the enemy could see you was a recipe for getting massacred. But he didn't have any trouble telling one foot from the other, or turning right and not left when he heard, "To the right flank . . . *haarch!*"

Lunch that day was creamed chipped beef on toast, otherwise creamed chipped beast or, more often, shit on a shingle. Armstrong didn't care what people called it. He didn't care what he got, either, as long as there was plenty of it. He would have eaten a horse and chased the driver—and, considering how fast he could pound out the three miles, he probably would have caught him.

After lunch came dirty fighting and rifle practice. Like any reasonably tough kid who got out of high school, Armstrong had thought he knew something about dirty fighting. The drill sergeant who'd mercilessly thumped him in the first day's lesson taught him otherwise. He'd been amazed to discover what all you could do with elbows, knees, feet, and bent fingers. If you happened to have a knife . . .

"Any civilian who fucks with me better have his funeral paid for," he said.

The drill sergeant shook his head. "He may have been through the mill, too. Or he may have a gun. You can't kick a gun in the nuts. Remember that, or you'll end up dead."

That struck Armstrong as good advice. A lot of what the drill sergeants said struck him as good advice. Whether he would take it was another question. He was no more interested than any other male his age in getting answers from someone else. He thought he had everything figured out for himself.

After the fighting drill, he and his company marched off to the rifle range. That did help reinforce what the sergeant had said. If you had a Springfield in your hand, you could put a hole in a man—or a man-shaped target—from a hell of a lot farther away than a man could put a boot in your belly. And Armstrong was a good shot.

"A lot of you guys think you're hot stuff," another drill sergeant said. This one had a fine collection of Sharpshooter and Expert medals jingling on his chest. "Listen to me, though. There's one big difference between doing it on the range here and doing it in the field. In the field, the other son of a bitch shoots back. And if you think that doesn't matter, you're dreaming."

Armstrong only grunted. He was sure it didn't matter. He could do it here. As far as he was concerned, that meant he could do it, period.

The drill sergeant said, "Some of you think I'm kidding. Some of you think I'm talking with my head up my ass. Well, you'll find out. It's different in the field. A hell of a lot of guys get out there and they don't shoot at all. There's plenty of others who don't aim first. They just point their piece somewhere—in the air, probably—and start banging away."

"What a bunch of fools," Armstrong whispered to the recruit next to him. He wanted to laugh out loud, but he didn't. That would have drawn the drill sergeant's eye to him, which he didn't want at all.

As things were, the sergeant sent a scowl in his general direction, but it didn't light on him personally. The veteran noncom went on, "There's just one thing you're lucky about. The other side will have as many fuck-ups as we do. That may keep some of you alive longer than you deserve. On the other hand, it may not, too. A machine gun isn't awful goddamn choosy about who it picks out." His face clouded. "I ought to know." He wore the ribbon for a Purple Heart, too.

"Question, Sergeant?" somebody called.

"Yeah, go ahead."

"Is it true the Confederates are giving their soldiers lots and lots of submachine guns?" the youngster asked.

"Yeah, that's supposed to be true," the sergeant said. "I don't think all that much of the idea myself. Submachine gun only fires a pistol round. It doesn't have a lot of stopping power, and the effective range is pretty short." He stopped and rubbed his chin. It was blue with stubble, though he'd surely scraped it smooth that morning. "Of course, submachine guns do put a hell of a lot of lead in the air. And the goddamn Confederates can hold their breath till they turn blue, but they're never gonna have as many men as we do. I expect that's why they're trying it."

Another recruit piped up: "Why hasn't somebody made an automatic rifle, if a submachine gun isn't good enough?"

"The Confederates are supposed to be trying that, too, but there are problems," the sergeant said. "Recoil, wear on the mechanism, overheating, having the weapon pull up when you fire it on full automatic, keeping it clean in the field—those are some of the things you've got to worry about. I wouldn't fall over dead with surprise if we start using something like that, too, one of these days, but don't hold *your* breath, either. And the Springfield is a goddamn good weapon. We won a war with it. We can win another one if we have to."

He waited. Sure enough, that drew another question: "Are we going to fight another war with the Confederate States?"

"Beats me," the drill sergeant answered. "I've done my share of fighting, and I am plumb satisfied. But if that Featherston son of a bitch isn't . . . You need two for peace, but one can start a war. If he does start it, it's up to us—it'll be up to *you*—to finish it."

Armstrong Grimes had no complaints. If he had to be in the Army, he wanted to be there while it was in action. What point to it otherwise? He didn't think about getting hurt. He especially didn't think about getting killed. That kind of stuff happened to other people. It couldn't possibly happen to him. He was going to live forever.

The sergeant said, "And if he does start another war, you *will* finish it, right? You'll kick the CSA's mangy ass around the block, right?"

"Yes, Sergeant!" the young men shouted. They were all as convinced of their own immortality as Armstrong Grimes.

"I can't hear you." The sergeant cupped a hand behind one ear.

*"Yes, Sergeant!"* The recruits might have been at a football game. Armstrong yelled as loud as anybody else.

"That's better," the drill sergeant allowed. "Not good, but better." Hardly anything anybody did in basic training was good. You might be perfect, but you still weren't good enough. They wanted you to try till you keeled over. People did, too.

Supper was fried chicken and canned corn and spinach, with apple pie à la mode for dessert. It wasn't great fried chicken, but you could eat as much as you wanted, which made up for a lot. Armstrong used food to pay his body back for the sleep it wasn't getting.

After supper, he had a couple of hours to himself—the only time during the day when he wasn't either unconscious or being run ragged. He could write home—which he didn't do often enough to suit his mother— or read a book or get into a poker game or shoot the breeze with other recruits winding down from an exhausting day or do what he usually did: lie on his cot smoking cigarette after cigarette. People said they were bad for your wind. He didn't care. He got through his three miles without any trouble, and the smokes helped him relax.

"You think there's going to be a war?" somebody asked. The question had been coming up more and more often lately.

"If there is, the goddamn Confederates'll be sorry," somebody else answered.

"Damn right," Armstrong said in the midst of a general rumble of agreement.

"We can lick 'em," someone said, and then added what might have been the young man's creed: "If our fathers did it, hell, we can do it easy."

"Damn right," Armstrong said again. Two hours after he sacked out, they had a simulated night attack. He bounced out of bed to repel imaginary enemies. He didn't miss the sleep. Why would he? He was already too far behind for a little more to matter.


Colonel Clarence Potter imagined a man he had never seen. He didn't know if the man lived in Dallas or Mobile or Nashville or Charleston or Richmond. Wherever he lived, he fit right in. He sounded like the people around him. He looked like them, too, and acted like them. When the time came to shout, "Freedom!" he yelled as loud as anybody. When he had a few beers in a saloon, he grumbled about what the damnyankee innovation of the forward pass had done to the great game of football.

And when he was by himself, this man Potter had never seen would write innocent-looking letters or send innocent-sounding wires up to the United States. He would be doing business with or for some firm or other based north of the Mason-Dixon line. And some of his messages really would be innocent, and some of them would go straight to the U.S. War Department in Philadelphia.

The man Potter had never met—would never meet—was the mirror image of the spies he ran in the USA. He'd had the idea. He had to assume his opposite number up in the United States had had it, too. He didn't like that, but he had to believe it. He kept wondering how much damage that imaginary U.S. spy could do.

Trouble was, the bastard almost certainly wasn't imaginary. A German had trouble sounding like a Frenchman, and vice versa. But a Yankee and a Confederate were too close to begin with. Differences in accent were small things. If you came from the USA, you had to remember to say things like note or banknote instead of bill. People would follow you if you used your own word, but they'd know you were a foreigner. But if you were careful, you could get by.

Something else worried Clarence Potter. He ran spies. The probable counterpart of one of the fellows he ran would also be a spy. If you had people in place as spies, though, wouldn't you also have them in place as provocateurs? As saboteurs?

He didn't know whether the Confederates had provocateurs and saboteurs lurking in the USA. He didn't know because it was none of his business. What he didn't know, he couldn't tell. In philosophy up at Yale, though, he'd learned about what Plato called true opinions. He was pretty damn sure he had one of those about this question. He also had some strong opinions about where he'd put provocateurs and saboteurs.

He sat down in front of his typewriter to bang out a memorandum. In it he said not a word about spies, provocateurs, and saboteurs in the United States. He did mention the possibility that their U.S. equivalents were operating in the Confederate States. *It would be unfortunate,* he wrote, *if the USA were able to take advantage of similarities between the two countries in language, custom, and dress, and it is to be hoped that steps to prevent such dangerous developments are currently being taken.*

When he reread the sentence, the corners of his mouth turned down in distaste. He didn't like writing that way; it set his teeth on edge. He would rather have come straight to the point. But he knew the officers who would see the memorandum. They wrote gobbledygook. They expected to read it, too. Active verbs would only scare them. They were none too active themselves.

As soon as he fired the memorandum up the chain of command, he stopped worrying about it. He judged he probably wouldn't get an answer. If the Army or the Freedom Party or somebody was watching out for suspicious characters, he wouldn't. Nobody would bother patting a busybody colonel on the hand and saying, "There, there. No need to worry, dear."

A few days later, he was writing a note when the telephone on his desk rang. His hand jerked a little—just enough to spoil a word. He scratched it out before picking up the handset. "Clarence Potter." He didn't say he was in Intelligence. Anyone who didn't already know had the wrong number.

"Hello, Potter. You *are* a sneaky son of a bitch, aren't you?"

"Hello, Mr. President," Potter answered cautiously. "Is that a compliment or not? In my line of work, I'm supposed to be."

"Hell, yes, it's a compliment," Jake Featherston answered. "It's also a judgment on us. We've been thinking a lot about what we can do to the damnyankees. We ain't worried near enough about what them bastards can do to us."

When his grammar slipped that far, he was genuinely irate. He'd also told Potter what the call was about. "You've read the memorandum, then?"

"Damn right I've read it. Those two whistle-ass peckerheads above you kicked it up to me. They were going, 'What do you want to do about this here?' "

Clarence Potter had a hard time swallowing a snort. Featherston might be president of the CSA, but he still talked like a foul-mouthed sergeant, especially when he took aim at officers. Potter asked, "What *do* you want to do about it, Mr. President?"

"You asked the questions. I want somebody to get me some answers. I sure as shit don't have enough of 'em right now. How would you like to do it? I'll make you a brigadier general on the spot."

Only two promotions really mattered: the one up from buck private and the one to general's rank. All the same, Potter said, "Sir, if I have a choice, I'd rather work on our assets there than their assets here. I want to *hit* those people when the time comes."

"Even if it costs you the promotion?" Featherston could only mean, *How serious are you?*

"Even if it does," Potter said firmly. "I didn't expect to come back into the Army anyway. I didn't do it for a wreath around my stars. I did it for the country." *And to keep from giving you an excuse for getting rid of me.* He didn't say that. Why remind Featherston?

"All right, then. You've got it—and the promotion," the president said. "That's your baby now, General Potter."

It *did* feel good. It felt damn good, as a matter of fact. And it felt all the better because Potter hadn't expected he would ever get it. When he said, "Thank you, Mr. President!" he sounded much more sincere than he'd thought he would while talking to Jake Featherston.

"I reckon you've earned it," Featherston answered. "I reckon you'll do a good job with it, too. You wait half an hour, and then you go right on into Brigadier General McGillivray's office and get to work. From here on out, it's yours."

"Yes, sir," Potter said, but he was talking to a dead line. He wondered briefly why the president wanted him to wait, but only briefly. He'd known Jake Featherston more than twenty-five years. He could guess what Jake would be doing with that half hour.

And his guess proved good. When he walked into his superior's—no, his former superior's—office, Brigadier General Stanley McGillivray was white and trembling. "I gather you are to replace me?" he choked out when he saw Potter.

"I gather I am." Potter had ripped into a good many incompetent officers in his time, but he didn't have the heart to say anything snide to McGillivray. The other Intelligence officer was a broken man if ever he'd seen one. He was so terribly broken, in fact, that Potter, for once, was moved more to sympathy than to sarcasm. "I hope the president wasn't too hard on you?"

"That, Colonel Potter—excuse me: *General* Potter—is what they call a forlorn hope," McGillivray answered bitterly. "I think you will find everything in order here. I think you will find it in better condition than I have been given credit for. Good day. Good luck." By the way he stumbled out of the office, he might almost have been a blind man.

"Poor bastard," Potter muttered. Anyone who ran into the cutting torch of Jake Featherston's fury was going to get charred. He'd seen that for himself, more often than he cared to remember.

And then he put Stanley McGillivray out of his mind. He was familiar with only about a third of the work that this desk did. He had to learn the rest of it . . . and he had the strong feeling he had to learn it in a tearing hurry. Featherston sure as hell wouldn't wait for him. Featherston had never been in the habit of waiting for anybody.

Potter went through the manila folders on the desk one by one. Some of them held things he'd expected to find. A few held surprises. He'd hoped they would. If he'd been able to figure out everything McGillivray was doing, wouldn't the damnyankees have done the same thing?

Some of the surprises were surprises indeed. The Confederates had been running people in Philadelphia since before the Great War. They'd recruited young men who needed this or that—and some who needed to make sure this or that never became public. Not all those young men had lasted. Some had died in the war. Some hadn't had the careers they'd hoped they would, and so proved useless as sources. But a handful of them, by now, were in position to know some very interesting things, and to pass them on.

The assets farther west were interesting, too. Most of Potter's notions of where they were proved right. Again, he got some surprises about who they were. That didn't matter so much. As long as he could use them . . .

He also checked the procedures Brigadier General McGillivray had in place for staying in touch with his people in the USA in case normal communications channels broke down—in plain English, in case there was a war. They weren't bad. He hoped he could find a way to make them better. The real problem he saw was how slow they were. He understood why that was so, but he didn't like it. "There's got to be a better way," he muttered, not sure if he was right.

Late that afternoon, the telephone in the new office rang. When he picked it up, Anne Colleton was on the other end of the line. "Congratulations, General Potter," she purred in his ear.

"Jesus Christ!" Potter sat bolt upright in his new swivel chair. It was a different make from the one he'd used before; he wasn't used to it yet. Its squeak sounded funny, too. "How did you know that?"

"I had to talk with the president about something," she answered. "He told me he'd promoted you."

"Oh." Potter's alarm evaporated. If she'd heard it from Jake Featherston, it was hardly a security breach. "All right."

"He told me some of why he promoted you, too," Anne said. "Do you really think the damnyankees are going to raise hell here if we go to war?"

"Well, I can't know, not for sure. But I would, if I were in their shoes. I do know they gave our niggers guns during the last war. If there's another one, they'd be fools not to do it again. They're bastards. They aren't fools. We thought they were in 1914. We've been paying for it ever since."

"Can we track down the people they've got here?" Anne asked.

"Of course we can," Potter answered, thinking, *No way in hell.* More truthfully, he went on, "The harder we go after them, the more careful they'll have to be, too."

"Uh-*huh*," Anne said in thoughtful tones.

She was, dammit, plenty smart enough to see the contradictions between the two things he'd said. He changed the subject: "What were you talking about with the president?"

"The timing of a propaganda campaign here in South Carolina," she said. Potter wondered just what that meant. He didn't want to go into details with her. God only knew how secure this line was. But the likeliest explanation he could come up with on his own was, *We were talking about when the war will start.*


**A**bner Dowling raised field glasses to his eyes and looked across the Ohio River into Kentucky. The mere act of observing Kentucky from afar made him so angry, he wanted to swell up like a bullfrog. As far as he was concerned, he shouldn't have been looking into a foreign country when he eyed Kentucky. He should have been in the state, getting ready to defend it against the Confederates. If they wanted to take it away from him, they would have been welcome to try. He could have promised them a warm reception.

Now . . . Now he had to figure out how to defend Ohio instead. The General Staff had generously sent him some plans prepared before the Great War. They would have been just what he needed, except that they ignored airplanes and barrels and barely acknowledged the existence of trucks. Things had changed since 1914. Dowling knew that. He hoped to God the General Staff did, too.

Some of what the old plans suggested was still sound. All the bridges across the Ohio had demolition charges in place. Artillery covered the bridges and other possible crossing points. Antiaircraft guns poked their noses up among the camouflaged cannons. If the Confederates were going to try to bomb his guns to silence, they wouldn't have an easy time of it.

He kept his main force farther back in Ohio than the old plans recommended. Again, the airplane was the main reason why. He also wanted to get some notion of what the Confederates were doing before he committed his men.

*Custer would have charged right at them, wherever they first showed themselves,* he thought. The way he rolled his eyes showed his opinion of that. Custer would have charged, sure as the devil. Maybe he would have smashed everything in his way. Maybe he would have blundered straight into an ambush. But he could no more keep from charging than a bull could when a matador waved his cape. *Sword? What sword?* Custer would have thought, bullishly.

For better or worse—for better *and* worse—Dowling was more cautious. If the Confederate Army crossed into the USA, he wanted to slow it down. The way he looked at things, if the Confederates didn't win quick victories, they'd be in trouble. In a long, drawn-out grapple, the USA had the edge. Dowling didn't think that had changed since the Great War.

He raised the field glasses again. Kentucky seemed to leap toward him. Jake Featherston had lied about keeping soldiers out of the state. He'd lied about not asking for more land. How was anybody in the United States supposed to trust him now? You couldn't. It was as simple as that.

Even Al Smith had seen the light. The president of the USA had said he would fight back if the CSA tried to take land by force. Dowling was all for that. But so much more could have been done. It could have, but it hadn't. Everybody'd known the Confederates were rearming. If the USA had been serious about showing Featherston who was boss, the country could have done it quickly and easily in 1935. Nothing would be quick or easy now.

And the United States weren't so ready as they should have been.

Dowling thought about all the time wasted in the 1920s. The Confederates had been on the ropes then, either on the ropes or smiling and saying how friendly they were. Why build better barrels when you'd never have to use them? As happened too often in politics, *never* turned out not to be so very long after all.

"Sir?" said an aide at Dowling's elbow. "Sir?"

Dowling had been lost in his own gloom. He wondered how long the younger man had been trying to draw his notice. However long it was, he'd finally succeeded. "Yes, Major Chandler? What is it?"

"Sir, Captain Litvinoff from the Special Weapons Section in Philadelphia has come down from Columbus to confer with you," Chandler answered.

"Has he?" Dowling was damned if he wanted to confer with anybody from what was euphemistically called the Special Weapons Section. Regardless of what he wanted, he had little choice. "All right. Let's get it over with." He might have been talking about a trip to the dentist.

"Max Litvinoff, sir," the captain said, saluting.

Dowling returned the salute. "Pleased to meet you," he lied. Litvinoff looked even more like a brain than he'd expected. The captain with the cobalt blue and golden yellow arm-of-service piping on his collar couldn't have been more than thirty. He was about five feet four, skinny, and homely, with thick steel-rimmed glasses and a thin, dark mustache that looked as if he'd drawn it on with a burnt match for an amateur theatrical.

However he looked, he was all business. "This will be good terrain for the application of our special agents," he said briskly.

He might have been talking about spies. He might have been, but he wasn't. Dowling knew too well what he *was* talking about. Dowling also had a pretty good idea why Litvinoff didn't come right out and say what he meant. People who ended up in the Special Weapons Section often didn't. It was magic of a sort: if they didn't say the real name, they didn't have to think about what they were doing.

"You're talking about poison gas." Dowling had no such inhibitions.

Max Litvinoff coughed. His sallow cheeks turned red. "Well . . . yes, sir," he mumbled. He was only a captain. He couldn't reprove a man with a star on each shoulder. Every line of his body, though, shouted out that he wanted to.

*Too bad,* Dowling thought. He'd been up at the front with General Custer the first time the USA turned chlorine loose on the Confederates in 1915. "Gas is a filthy business," he said, and Captain Litvinoff's cheeks got redder yet. "We use it, the Confederates use it, some soldiers on both sides end up dead, and nobody's much better off. What's the point?"

"The point, sir, is very simple," Litvinoff answered stiffly. "If the enemy uses the special agent"—he still wouldn't say *gas*—"and we don't, then our men end up dead and his don't. Therefore . . ."

What Dowling wanted to do was yell, *Fuck you!* and kick the captain in the ass. Unfortunately, he couldn't. Litvinoff was right. Handing the CSA an edge like that would be stupid, maybe suicidal. "Go on," Dowling growled.

"Yes, sir. You will be familiar with the agents utilized in the last war?" Captain Litvinoff sounded as if he didn't believe it. When Dowling nodded, Litvinoff shrugged. He went on, "You may perhaps be less familiar with those developed at the close of hostilities and subsequently."

*So I am,* Dowling thought. *And thank God for small favors.* But he couldn't say that to Litvinoff. He was, heaven help him, going to have to work with the man. What he did say was, "I'm all ears."

"Good." Captain Litvinoff looked pleased. He liked talking about his toys, showing them off, explaining—in bloodless-seeming terms—what they could do. If that wasn't a measure of his damnation, Dowling couldn't imagine what would be. Litvinoff continued, "First, there's nitrogen mustard. We did use some of this in 1917. It's a vesicant."

"A what?" Dowling asked. The Special Weapons Section man might have his vocabulary of euphemisms, but that didn't even sound like a proper English word.

Reluctantly, Litvinoff translated: "A blistering agent. Mucus membranes and skin. It does not have to be inhaled to be effective, though it will produce more and more severe casualties if the lungs are involved. And it is a persistent agent. In the absence of strong direct sunlight or rain, it can remain in place and active for months. An excellent way to deny access to an area to the enemy."

"And to us," Dowling said.

Captain Litvinoff looked wounded. "By no means, sir. Troops with proper protective gear and an awareness the agent is in the area can function quite well."

"All right," Dowling said, though it was anything but. "What other little toys have you got?"

"Walk with me, sir, if you'd be so kind," Litvinoff said, and led him away from the officers and men in his entourage. When the young captain was sure they were out of earshot, he went on, "We also have what we are terming nerve agents. They are a step up in lethality from other agents we have been utilizing."

Dowling needed a second or two to figure out what lethality meant. When he did, he wished he hadn't. "Nerve agents?" he echoed queasily.

"That's right." Litvinoff nodded. "Again, these are effective both by inhalation and through cutaneous contact. They prevent nerve impulses from initiating muscular activity." That didn't sound like anything much. But his next sentence told what it meant: "Lethality occurs through cardiopulmonary failure. Onset is quite rapid, and the amount of agent required to induce it is astonishingly small."

"How nice," Dowling said. Captain Litvinoff beamed. Dowling muttered, "I wonder why we bother with bullets any more."

"So do I, sir. So do I." Litvinoff was dead serious—under the circumstances, the exact right phrase. But then, as grudging as a spinster talking about the facts of life, he admitted, "These nerve agents do have an antidote. But it must be administered by injection, and if it is administered in error, it is in itself toxic."

"This is all wonderful news," Dowling said—another thumping lie. He had been looking forward to lunch. He usually did. Now, though, his appetite had vanished. And a new and important question occurred to him: "Good to know we have these things available. But tell me, Captain, what are the Confederates likely to throw at us if the war starts?"

Max Litvinoff blinked behind his spectacles. "I am more familiar with our own program. . . ."

"Dammit, Captain, I'm not just going to shoot these things at the enemy. I'll be on the receiving end, too. What am I going to receive? What can I do about it?"

"Respirators are current issue. Protective clothing is rather less widely available, and does tend to restrict mobility in warm, humid climates," Litvinoff said. Dowling tried to imagine running around in a rubberized suit in Ohio or Kentucky in July. The thought did not bring reassurance with it. The Special Weapons Section officer went on, "The Confederate States are likely to be familiar with nitrogen mustard. Whether they know of nerve agents, and of which sorts, I am less prepared to state."

"Does somebody in the War Department have any idea? Can you tell me who would?" Dowling asked. "It might be important, you know."

"Well, yes, I can see how it might," Litvinoff said. "Unfortunately, however, defenses against these agents are not my area of expertise."

"Yes, I gathered that. I'm trying to find out from you whose area of expertise they are."

"Knowing that does not fall within my area of expertise, either."

Dowling looked at him. "Captain, why the hell did you come out here in the first place?"

"Why, to give you information, sir."

He meant it. Dowling could see as much. Seeing as much didn't make him very happy—or give him much information, either.

Flora Blackford had been to a lot of Remembrance Day parades, in New York and in Philadelphia. This year's parade in New York City took her back to the days before the Great War, when the holiday had truly been a day of national mourning. People had commemorated the loss of the War of Secession and of the Second Mexican War, and had pledged not to fail again. Flags had flown upside down on Remembrance Day, symbolizing the country's distress.

Since the Great War, Remembrance Day had faded some in the nation's consciousness. People had a triumph to remember now, not just a pair of scalding defeats. The custom of flying flags upside down had fallen into disuse. Teddy Roosevelt had been the first to abandon it, in the Philadelphia parade in 1918, the year after the war ended.

This year, the custom was back. Anyone who cared to look could see war clouds looming up from the south, bigger and blacker with each passing day. If that wasn't cause for distress, Flora didn't know what would be.

In the limousine just ahead of hers rode Hjalmar Horace Greeley Schacht, the ambassador from the German Empire, and his Austro-Hungarian opposite number, whose name Flora never could recall. Schacht was a much more memorable character. He spoke fluent English, as well he might, given his two middle names. He was a financial wizard, even in hard times. Nobody knew how much money he had, or exactly how he'd got it.

In 1915, riots had marred the Remembrance Day parade here. Even now, no one knew if Socialists or Mormons had started the fighting. Then, Flora had been in the crowd lining Fifth Avenue. She remembered the then ambassadors from Germany and Austria-Hungary going past.

She'd never imagined that she might be taking part in the parade herself one day.

Socialists wouldn't protest or disrupt the parade this year, not with Al Smith in Powel House. What heckling there was came from Democrats. Flora heard shouts like, "We should have cleaned house a long time ago!" and, "*Now* you Red bastards say you're patriots!" That infuriated her and stung at the same time, for she knew it held a little truth. In politics as in life, the best slams often held a little truth.

There might have been more rude shouts than she heard. Her open car rolled along in front of a marching band that blared out martial music. The conductor wasn't John Philip Sousa, whom she'd seen in 1915, but he thought he was.

Behind the band rolled another limousine. This one carried two ancient veterans of the War of Secession. More limousines carried survivors from the Second Mexican War. A handful of veterans from that war were still spry enough to march down the street on their own, too.

After them came what seemed like an endless stream of Great War veterans, organized by the year of their conscription class. They were the solid, middle-aged men who shaped opinion and ran the country these days. The way they marched said they knew it, too.

More limousines followed them. They carried Great War veterans who wanted to parade but had been too badly wounded to march. Her brother rode in one of them. David Hamburger hadn't asked Flora to keep him out of the Army. He'd come out of the war with only one leg. He'd never asked Flora to pull strings for him since . . . till this Remembrance Day parade. She'd done it, and gladly. If he was a stubborn Democrat— so what? The Democrats turned out to have been closer to right about Jake Featherston than the Socialists had. Flora didn't admit that in public, but she knew it was true.

Few cheers came from the crowds that lined the streets. Remembrance Day wasn't a holiday for cheers. But the crowds were thicker than on any Remembrance Day that Flora remembered since the euphoric one after the end of the Great War.

The parade rolled along Fifth Avenue: limousines, marching bands, veterans, clanking military hardware, and all. More people filled Central Park, where it ended. Spring made the air taste sweet and green. Wherever people weren't standing, robins and starlings hopped on the grass, digging up worms.

Strangely, the cheery birds made Flora sad. *There are liable to be plenty of fat worms soon,* she thought, *because the bodies of our young men will feed them.*

A temporary speaker's platform stood in the middle of a meadow now packed with people. Policemen—one tough Irish mug after another—kept a lane clear for the limousines. They pulled up behind the platform. Dignitaries got out and ascended. Flora took her place with the rest. The other women on the platform were there because they were wives. Flora had her place because of what she did, and she was proud of it.

Governor LaGuardia, a peppery little Socialist in an outsized fedora, called the German ambassador to the microphone. Hjalmar Horace Greeley Schacht spoke better, more elegant English than the governor. "We have been rivals, your country and mine, because we are both strong," he said. "The strong notice each other. They also draw the jealousy of the weak. Like you, we have neighbors who would like to bite our ankles." That patrician scorn drew a laugh. Schacht went on, "So long as we stand together, though, nothing can overcome us both." He got another big hand, and sat down.

The Austro-Hungarian envoy—his name was Schussnigg, Governor LaGuardia said—delivered a thickly accented speech that sounded ferocious but didn't make much sense. When he stepped away from the microphone, the applause he got seemed more relieved than anything else.

LaGuardia himself made a speech that called down fire and brimstone on the Democratic Party and the Confederate States in equal measure. Then he introduced the mayor of New York City, who was just as Italian as he was, and who ripped the Socialists and the Confederate States up one side and down the other. The two men glared at each other. Flora couldn't help laughing.

More speeches followed, some very partisan, others less so. Then Governor LaGuardia said, "And now, the former First Lady of the United States, New York City's favorite daughter, Congresswoman Flora Blackford!"

Flora stood up and strode to the microphone. A few cries of, "Blackfordburghs!" floated out of the crowd, but only a few. She hadn't expected not to hear them. If anything, she got less heckling than she'd looked for.

"I don't want to talk about political parties today," she said, and enough applause erupted to drown out the jeers. "I want to talk about what's facing the United States. It will be trouble. I don't see how it can be anything but trouble. The government now ruling the Confederate States does not respect the rights of its own people. That being so, how can we hope it will respect the rights of its neighbors?"

That got a big hand. She went on, "Many of you came to the United States or had parents who came to the United States to escape pogroms in Europe. And now we see pogroms in North America. Is a man any less a man because he has a dark skin? Jake Featherston thinks so. Is he right?"

This time, the applause was sparser, less comfortable. Again, Flora had thought it would be. She'd seen again and again that the plight of Negroes in the Confederate States did not get people in the United States hot and bothered. When people in the USA thought about Negroes, it was generally with relief that the vast majority of them were the CSA's worry.

That wasn't right. Flora drove the point home: "A lot of you have ancestors who came here because someone was persecuting them in Europe. Someone is persecuting the Negroes in the Confederate States right now, and we won't let them in. We turn them back. We shoot them if we have to. But we keep them out. And don't you see? That's wrong."

Now she got almost no applause. She would have been more disappointed if she were more surprised. "A lot of you don't care," she said. "You think, *They're only niggers,* and you go on about your business. And do you know what? That sound you hear from Richmond is Jake Featherston, laughing. If you don't care about a wrong to people in his country, he thinks you won't care about a wrong to people in your country, either. Is that so?"

"No!" She got the answer she wanted, but from perhaps a third of the throats that should have shouted it.

"I'm going to say one more thing, and then I'm through," she told the crowd. "If you say that oppression of anybody anywhere is all right, you say that oppression of everybody everywhere is all right. I don't think that's what the United States are all about. Do you?"

*"No!"* This time, the shout was louder. A lot of people clapped and cheered as she went back to her seat.

Governor LaGuardia introduced another member of Congress. The man, a Democrat, harangued the crowd about how good they were and how wicked the Confederates were. He said not a word about the Negroes in the Confederate States. To him, the Confederates were wicked for no other reason than that they presumed to challenge the people of the United States of America.

He told the people in Central Park what they wanted to hear. They ate it up. The park rang with cheers. Flora had done her best to tell the people the truth. They hadn't liked that nearly so well.

The dignitary sitting next to her leaned over and said, "I see why they call you the conscience of the Congress."

"Thank you," she whispered. Someone, at least, had understood.

Then he went on, "But really! To get excited about a bunch of niggers? Those black bastards—pardon my French, ma'am—aren't worth it. We'd all be better off if they were back in Africa swinging through the trees."

He was, she remembered with something approaching horror, a

judge. "What do you do if one of them comes into your court?" she asked.

"Oh, I try to be fair," he answered. "You have to. But they're usually guilty. That's just how things go."

He didn't see anything wrong with what he said. The only way Flora could have let sense into his head would have been to bash it open with a rock. She knew that. She'd met the type before. If she did it here at a Remembrance Day rally, people would talk. Even telling him off was useless. He'd just get offended. She could talk till Doomsday without persuading him.

Sitting there quietly felt as much like a compromise with evil to her as letting the Confederates do what they wanted to the Negroes in their country. She made herself remember there were degrees of wickedness, as there were with anything else. If you couldn't tell the difference between one and another, how were you supposed to make choices?

You couldn't. She knew that, however distasteful she found it. The Confederates were worse than the judge. *That still doesn't mean he's good,* she thought defiantly. At the microphone, the Democratic Congressman kept on laying into the CSA. The crowd ate up every word.

When Jake Featherston told the people who protected him that he was going to make a speech in Louisville, they started having conniptions. They screamed about black men with guns. They screamed about white men with guns who didn't want to live in the CSA. They screamed about damnyankees with mortars on the other side of the Ohio River. For the USA to try to bump him off would be an act of war, but it wouldn't be a war he got to run if they went ahead and did it.

That last comment worried him, because he didn't think anyone else in the Confederacy had the driving will and energy to do what needed doing when the war started. But he stuck out his chin and told the Freedom Party guards, "I'm going, goddammit. You keep the people in Louisville from shooting me. That's your job. I'll worry about the rest. That's mine."

Even Ferdinand Koenig flabbled about the trip. "You're the one man we can't replace, Jake," he said.

These days, he was almost the one man who could call Jake by his Christian name. Featherston looked across his desk at the attorney general. "It's worth the risk," he said. "The Party guards'll keep me safe from niggers and nigger-loving bastards who wish they were Yankees. And Al Smith is too nice a fellow to turn his artillery loose while we're at peace."

Al Smith was a damned fool, as far as Jake was concerned. Had the

USA had a dangerous leader—say, another Teddy Roosevelt—Jake would have done everything he could to get rid of the man. People like that were worth an army corps of soldiers, likely more.

But Ferd Koenig had another worry. Quietly, he asked, "And who's going to keep you safe from the guards?"

Featherston glared at him. He'd already lived through two assassination tries—three if you counted Clarence Potter, who hadn't come to Richmond to play checkers. The stalwarts who'd backed Willy Knight against him still shook him to the core. But he said, "If I can't trust the Party guards, I can't trust anybody, and I might as well cash in my chips. And if I can't trust them, they can try and do me in right here in Richmond as easy as they can in Louisville."

By the look on Koenig's heavy-featured, jowly face, he might have just bitten down on a lemon. "You're bound and determined to do this, aren't you?"

"You bet I am," Jake answered. "You take over a place, you need to let the people there get a look at you." He'd been reading *The Prince*. He couldn't pronounce Machiavelli's name to save his life, and if he wrote it down he wouldn't have spelled it the same way twice running. All the same, he knew good sense when he ran into it, and that was one hell of a sly dago.

He went to Louisville. He'd decided he would, and his deciding was what made things so. And when he went, he went in style. He didn't just fly in, make a speech, and fly out again. He took a train up from Nashville, and at every whistle stop all the way north across Kentucky he stood on a platform at the back of his Pullman and made a speech.

The Pullman had armor plating and bulletproof glass. Nothing short of a direct hit by an artillery shell would make it say uncle. The lectern on the platform was armored, too. But from the chest up and from the sides, he was vulnerable. The Freedom Party guards told him so, over and over. He went right on ignoring them.

Nobody shot him. Nobody shot at him. People swarmed to the train stations to hear him. They waved Confederate and Freedom Party flags. They shouted, "Freedom!" and, "Feather*ston!*"—sometimes both at once. Women screamed. Men held up little boys so they'd see him and remember for the rest of their lives. The Party had organized some of the crowds, but a lot of the response was genuine and unplanned. That made it all the more gratifying.

He didn't see any black faces in the crowds. He would have been surprised and alarmed if he had. If he never saw any black faces anywhere in the CSA, that wouldn't have broken his heart.

"You folks helped us take back what's ours," he told the crowds at the whistle stops. "We got part of the job done, but the damnyankees won't make the rest of it right. They're nothing but a pack of thieves, and how are you supposed to live with a thief next door?"

People cheered. People howled. People shook their fists toward the north, as if Al Smith could see them. They'd been back in the Confederate States not even a handful of months, but they were ready to fight for them.

Jake tasted their jubilation. It was different from the cold lust for revenge he felt in the rest of the CSA. People here had spent a generation under Yankee rule. They'd had their men conscripted into the U.S. Army. They knew what they'd abandoned, and they were glad to be back where they belonged.

Or most of them were: enough to have voted Kentucky back into the CSA, even with Negroes given the franchise to try to queer the deal. But there were white men—white men!—who looked north with longing, not with hate. If they knew what was good for them, they'd be lying low right now. If they didn't know what was good for them, Confederate officials and Party stalwarts would give them lessons on the subject.

He got into Louisville a little before six in the evening. People waving flags lined the route from the train station to the Galt House, the hotel where he would spend the night. He didn't stop there for long now—just enough time to grab a bite to eat and run a comb through his hair. Then it was on to the Memorial Auditorium a few blocks away for his speech.

The auditorium was a postwar building, of reinforced concrete that could have gone into a fortress. Most of Louisville was new. The city had been destroyed twice in the past sixty years. The USA had tried to take it in the Second Mexican War—tried and got a bloody nose. In the Great War, General Pershing's Second Army had driven the Confederates out, but not till the defenders, fighting from house to house, made the Yankees wreck the city to be rid of them.

Before the Second Mexican War, and to a degree after it, Louisville had been an un-Confederate sort of place. Because it did so much business with the United States, it had looked north as well as south. But once it got taken into the USA, it wasn't a booming border town any more. Even before the collapse of 1929, business was slow here. That made people all the more glad to return to the Confederacy.

A rhythmic cry of, "Feather*ston*! Feather*ston*! Feather*ston*!" greeted Jake as he strode up to the lectern. The bright lights glaring into his face kept him from getting a good look at the blocks of stalwarts who kept the chant strong, but he knew they were there. They weren't the only ones shouting, though—far from it. When he held up his hands for quiet, they fell silent at once. The rest of the crowd, less disciplined, took longer.

When he had enough quiet to suit him, he said, "I *am* Jake Featherston, and I'm here to tell you the truth." That brought him a fresh eruption of cheers. They knew his catch phrase, and had known it for years. Wireless stations from northern Tennessee had beamed his speeches up into Kentucky long before it returned to the Confederate States. He went on, "Here's what the truth is. The truth is, the Yankees don't want peace in North America. Oh, Al Smith says he does, but he's lying through his teeth."

Boos and hisses rose when he named the president of the United States. One loudmouthed fellow yelled, "We didn't vote for him!" That drew a laugh. Jake scowled. Nobody was supposed to get laughs at his speeches but him.

He said, "It's been almost twenty-five years since the United States stole our land from us. They coughed up a couple of pieces, and now they think they ought to get a pat on the head and a dish of ice cream on account of it. Well, folks, they're wrong. No two ways about it. They are *wrong*.

"And they think that might makes right. They aren't *so* wrong about that. But they think it gives 'em the right to hold on to things. They may think it does, but I'm here to tell you it isn't so. We've got the right to take back what's ours, and we'll do it if we have to.

"I want peace. Anybody who's seen a war and wants another one has to have a screw loose somewhere." Jake got a hand when he said that. He'd known he would, which was why he put it in the speech. He didn't believe it, though. He'd never felt more alive than when he was blasting Yankees to hell and gone in the First Richmond Howitzers. By contrast, peacetime was *boring*. He went on, "But if you back away from a war now, a lot of the time that just means you'll have to fight it later, when it costs you more. If the people in the United States reckon we're afraid to fight, they'd better think twice."

He got another hand for that, a bigger one. He'd hoped it would. It meant people were ready. They might not be eager, but they were ready. And ready was all that really counted.

Shaking his fist toward the country across the Ohio, he rolled on: "And if the damnyankees reckon they can get our own niggers to stab us in the back again, they'd better think twice about that, too." A great roar of applause went up then. Louisville had been in U.S. hands when the Negroes in the CSA rebelled in 1915, but the white folks here were just as leery of blacks as if they'd never left the Confederacy. Negroes had never got the right to vote in Kentucky, not till the plebiscite earlier this year. There wouldn't be a next time for them, either. Jake went on, "We've got our niggers under control now, by God. Oh, there's still some trouble from 'em—I won't try to tell you any different—but we're teaching 'em who's boss."

More thunderous applause. Jake hoped that, if he killed enough rebellious blacks, the rest of them *would* learn who held the whip hand. As an overseer's son, he took that literally. And if the Negroes didn't care to learn from their lessons . . . He shrugged. He'd go on teaching. Sooner or later, they would get it.

He knew damn well the United States *were* helping blacks resist the Confederate government. His people had already seized more than one arms shipment right here in Kentucky. His mouth opened in a predatory grin. Two could play at that game.

"Here's the last thing I've got to say to you, folks," he cried. "Kentucky is Confederate again. As God is my witness, Kentucky will always be Confederate from here on out. And I promise you, I won't take off this uniform till we've got everything back that belongs to us. We don't retreat. We go forward!"

He slammed his fist down on the podium. The Memorial Auditorium went wild. He couldn't make out individual cheers amid the din. He might have been in the middle of artillery barrages louder than this, but he wasn't sure. After a while, it all got to be more than the ears could handle.

He looked north toward the United States again. He was ready. Were they? He didn't think so. They'd started rearming a lot more slowly than he had. *They're soft. They're rotten. They're just waiting for somebody to kick the door in.*

"Feather*ston*! Feather*ston*! Feather*ston*!" Little by little, the chant emerged from chaos. Jake waved to the crowd. The cheers redoubled. *The Yanks are waiting for somebody to kick the door in, and I'm the man to do it.*


**A**nne Colleton muttered a mild obscenity when someone knocked on the door to her St. Matthews apartment. She hadn't been home for long, and she'd head out on the road again soon. She wanted to enjoy what time she had here, and her idea of enjoyment didn't include gabbing with the neighbors.

She took a pistol to the door, as she usually did when someone unexpected knocked. The Congaree Socialist Republic was dead, but Negro unrest in these parts had never quite subsided. If a black man wanted to try to do her in, she aimed to shoot first.

But it wasn't a homicidal Red. It was a middle-aged white man in a lieutenant-colonel's uniform, two stars on each collar tab. That was all she saw at first. Then she did a double take. "Tom!" she exclaimed.

"Hello, Sis," her younger brother said. "I came to say good-bye. I've been called up, and I'm on my way out to report to my unit."

"My God," Anne said. "But you're married. You've got a family. What will Bertha do with the kids?"

"The best she can," Tom Colleton answered, which didn't leave much room for argument. "You're right—I didn't have to go. But I couldn't have looked at myself in a mirror if I hadn't. The Yankees have got more men than we do. If we don't use everybody we can get our hands on, we're in a hell of a lot of trouble."

She knew perfectly well that he was right. The USA had always outweighed the CSA two to one. If the United States could bring their full strength to bear, the Confederate States would face the same squeeze as they had a generation earlier. The USA hadn't managed that in the War of Secession, and had failed spectacularly in the Second Mexican War. In the Great War, they'd succeeded, and they'd won. Keeping them from succeeding again would be essential if the Confederacy was to have a chance.

All of which passed through Anne's mind in a space of a second and a half and then blew away. "For God's sake come in and have a drink," she said. "You've got time for that, don't you?"

"The day I don't have time for a drink is the day they bury me," Tom Colleton answered with a trace of the boyish good nature he'd largely submerged over the past few years.

Anne was all for revenge. She was all for teaching the United States a lesson. When it came to putting her only living brother's life on the line, she was much less enthusiastic. She poured him an enormous whiskey, and one just as potent for herself. "Here's to you," she said. Half of hers sizzled down her throat.

Tom drank, too. He stared at the glass, or maybe at the butternut cuff of his sleeve. "Christ, I did a lot of drinking in this uniform," he said. He might have been talking about somebody else. In a way, he was. He'd been in his early twenties, not fifty. He'd been sure the bullet that could hurt him hadn't been made. Men were at that age, which went a long way toward making war possible. By the time you reached middle age—if you did—you knew better. *Ask not for whom the bell tolls, . . .*

"How's Bertha doing?" Anne asked. She'd always thought her brother had married below his station, but she couldn't deny that he and his wife loved each other.

He shook his head now. "She's not very happy. I don't reckon I can blame her for that. But I have to go." He finished the whiskey and held out the glass. "Pour me another one. Then I've got to head for the station and catch the northbound train."

"All right." Anne poured herself another drink, too, even though the first one was already making her head swim. It loosened her tongue, too. Without it, she never would have asked, "What do you think our chances are?"

Tom only shrugged. "Damned if I can tell you. Last time I went off to war, I was sure we'd lick the Yankees in six weeks and be home in time for the cotton harvest. One whole hell of a lot I knew about that, wasn't it? This time, I've got no idea. We'll find out."

"Maybe there won't be a war." Anne knew she was trying to talk herself into believing what she suddenly wanted with all her heart to believe, but she went on, "Maybe the damnyankees will back down and give us what we're asking for."

"Not a chance," Tom said. "I thought they were a pack of cowards last time. I know better now. They're as tough as we are. And even if they did, how much difference would it make?"

"What do you mean?"

"You know what I mean. If the damnyankees back down tomorrow, what'll Jake Featherston do the day after? Ask 'em for something else, that's what. And he'll keep right on doing it till they say no and have to fight. Because whether you want a war or I want a war, Featherston damn well does, and he's got the only vote that counts. You going to tell me I'm wrong?"

Part of Anne—most of Anne—wanted to, but she knew she couldn't. She shook her head. "No, you're not wrong. But the time is ripe, too, and you know it. Things are going to blow up in Europe any day. The old Kaiser can't possibly last much longer, and his son's going to spit in France's eye. What'll happen then?"

"Boom," Tom said solemnly. "I'm surprised the French have waited as long as they have, but *Action Française* doesn't seem to have one clear voice at the top, the way the Freedom Party does."

"No, they don't," Anne agreed. "But if they and the British and the Russians can put Germany in her place and give us even a little help against the USA, we'll do all right. If you don't think so, why are you wearing the uniform again?"

"It's not for the Freedom Party. You can tell that to Jake Featherston's face next time you see him. I don't care," Tom said. "It's for the country. I'd fight for my country no matter who was in charge."

Anne had no intention of telling the president any such thing, regardless of what Tom said. It wouldn't do her brother any good, and might do him a lot of harm. Tom didn't seem to understand how thoroughly politics had twined themselves around everything else in the CSA these days. If you said uncomplimentary things about the Freedom Party, you'd probably be thought disloyal to the Confederate States, too.

Anne wondered if she ought to warn him. The only thing that held her back was the near certainty he wouldn't listen to her. Maybe he'd learn better when he got back on active duty. Or maybe he wouldn't, and he'd run his mouth once too often, and get cashiered and sent home.

He was her kid brother. Having him safe back here in South Carolina wouldn't break her heart. Oh, no, not at all.

"Be careful," was all she did tell him.

He nodded. "You know what they say: old soldiers and bold soldiers, but no old bold soldiers. I'm going out there to do a job, Anne. I'm not going out there looking to get shot. I've got too much to come home to."

"All right, Tom." Was it? Anne wondered. She never liked it when somebody whose life she'd run for a long time slipped away from her control. She'd made more allowances for Tom than she did for most because they were flesh and blood. And now here he was, leaving not only her control but his wife's as well, heading off into the brutal, masculine world of war.

Clarence Potter was going the same way. He actively despised the regime. He was ready to put his life on the line for it just the same, and for the same reason: it was in charge of the country, and the country mattered to him.

"Be careful," she said again, and reminded herself to say the same thing to Clarence as soon as she could.

"You, too," Tom said then.

"Me?" She laughed. "I won't be up at the front, and you probably will." That *probably* was her hope against hope. She knew damn well he would. She took another sip of whiskey. However much she drank, though, the most she could do was blur that knowledge. She couldn't make it leave.

But her brother was serious, even if he'd taken on enough in the way of whiskey to speak with owlish intensity: "How much difference do you think being at the front will make? Bombers have a long reach these days. In this war, everybody's going to catch hell, not just the poor bastards in uniform."

That had an unpleasant feel of truth to it. Anne said, "Bite your tongue."

He took her literally. He stuck it out and clamped his teeth down on it so she could see. She laughed; she'd had enough that things like that were funny. But she couldn't help asking, "You think they'll bomb civilians, then?"

"Look what they did to Richmond last time," he said. "And it's not like our hands are clean. They had more airplanes, that's all."

Anne had been in Richmond for one of the U.S. air raids. She still remembered the helpless terror it had roused in her. "Well, we'd better have more this time, that's all," she said. "Let them find out what they did to us."

"I hope so," Tom said. "I expect so, as a matter of fact. But God help us if it turns out they give us another dose."

He got to his feet. Anne stood up, too. They hugged. "You be careful," she said for a third time.

"I promise," he answered. She didn't believe him for a minute. He would do what he would do. The only reason he hadn't got killed in the last war was dumb luck. She wished him more of that. It might serve where promises didn't.

Tom went out the door and off to the train station. Anne watched him from the window. He wobbled as he walked; she'd poured a lot of whiskey into him. That was all right. He'd sober up before he got to wherever he needed to go. She realized he hadn't said where that was. Military security had fallen between them like a blanket.

She muttered a curse against military security. She muttered another curse against war. That second one was halfhearted, and she knew it. She wanted all the horrors of war to come down on the damnyankees' heads. She just didn't want anything to happen to Tom or to Clarence or to the people of the Confederate States. That wasn't fair, of course. She couldn't have cared less.

Tom turned a corner and was gone. No. Anne shook her head. He wasn't gone. She just couldn't see him any more. There was a difference. "Of course there's a difference," she said aloud, as if someone had told her there wasn't.

Another drink didn't seem likely to let her know what the difference was. She fixed one for herself anyway. She'd thought Tom would have the sense to stay home with his wife and children. She'd thought so, but she'd been wrong. She hated being wrong.

And she even saw how she'd been wrong. Jake Featherston had spent years building up the passion for war in the Confederate States. He'd needed to, to get the revenge on the United States he wanted. Anne also wanted that revenge, and so she'd helped him. What could be more natural, then, than that the passion took someone who otherwise would have stayed home?

What indeed? Anne gulped the new drink in a hurry. Somehow, seeing where she'd been wrong didn't help a bit.


Even in late spring, the North Atlantic pitched and tossed. The USS *Remembrance* was a big ship, but the waves flung her about even so. Sam Carsten thanked heaven for his strong stomach and for the cloudy skies that kept his fair, fair skin from burning. Other than that, he had little for which to be thankful.

To put it mildly, things did not look good. The *Remembrance* and the cruisers and destroyers surrounding her were on full war alert. Everyone seemed sure it was coming. The only questions left were about when and where and how.

Maybe the clouds in the sky didn't matter so much. Sam spent almost all of his time belowdecks, either at his battle station in damage control or in the officers' mess or sacked out in his tiny cabin. On his schedule, a vampire would have had trouble getting a sunburn.

He might as well have been married to Lieutenant Commander Hiram Pottinger. He saw his superior nearly every waking moment. The two of them prowled through the bowels of the ship, looking for trouble they could eliminate before it got the chance to eliminate them. Every once in a while, they would find something and turn their sailors loose on it. Then they would pause and nod and sometimes shake hands. That was what they were supposed to do, and by now they were both damn good at the job.

Sam still remembered that he wanted to get in on the aviation side of things. He remembered, but nostalgically, as if thinking of a long-lost love. Years of doing the duty he was in had shaped him and scraped him till he wasn't a square peg in a round hole any more. By now, he fit the slot in which the Navy had put him. That was how things worked.

He kept right on going up to the wireless shack whenever he found the chance. Maybe that proved he was a mustang; he still had a rating's insatiable appetite for scuttlebutt. The yeomen who kept the *Remembrance* in touch with the wider world grinned whenever he poked his head in. They teased him about it, as much as they could tease a superior officer.

"Going to tell the limeys everything you know, sir?" one of them asked.

"Hell, no." Sam shook his head. "I'm going to save it till we get over to the Pacific. Then I'll tell it to the Japs."

They all laughed. The only thing Sam wanted to tell the Japanese was where to head in. He would gladly have helped guide them on the way, too. They'd shelled a ship he was on once and torpedoed him twice. If they hadn't sunk him, it sure as hell wasn't for lack of effort.

Before any of the yeomen could say something else slyly rude, loud, mournful music started coming out of the wireless set. "Something's up," Sam said. "What station is that?"

"German Imperial Wireless, sir," answered the man who'd been teasing him. The yeomen and Carsten looked at one another. Wilhelm II had been failing for a long time now. If he'd finally gone and failed . . .

A torrent of German poured from the speaker. "You picking that up, Gunther?" another yeoman asked.

"I will if you don't jog my elbow," Gunther answered. He was a big blond kid, not so fair as Sam but fair enough. Another Midwestern farm boy who'd decided to go to sea instead of spending the rest of his life walking behind a couple of horses' asses. (These days, he'd probably ride a tractor. That still wasn't Sam's idea of fun.)

"Is it the Kaiser?" Sam asked.

"Yeah. Uh, yes, sir." Gunther corrected himself. "It's him, all right. Blood clot on the lung, the wireless says. Went into a coma last night, died this morning." More music replaced the announcer's voice. This time, Sam recognized the tune: *Deutschland über Alles*. When the German anthem ended, the announcer came back on the air. "He's hailing the accession of Friedrich Wilhelm—King Friedrich Wilhelm V of Prussia and Kaiser Friedrich I of Germany," Gunther reported.

"Kaiser Bill had a hell of a run: better than fifty years," Sam said. His son and heir wouldn't match that; Friedrich Wilhelm, who'd lived so long in his father's shadow, was already close to sixty.

More German came out of the wireless. This was a different voice. Gunther said, "Uh-oh. This is the new Kaiser's mouthpiece. He says Friedrich Wilhelm's first act is to declare that he can't possibly give up anything his father won."

"Uh-oh is right," Sam said. "That means trouble with France and England and probably Russia, too." He whistled softly. "Big trouble, I think. I wonder what the hell we do now."

"Well, sir, we're already on battle alert," Gunther said practically.

"Yeah," Sam said: not the ideal reply, perhaps, for an officer and a gentleman, but one both accurate and concise.

Gunther got on the telephone to the bridge. Sam ambled out of the wireless shack, whistling tunelessly to himself. For the next little while, he would know something the skipper didn't. Of course, knowing did him no good. He couldn't bring the *Remembrance*, or even the damage-control parties, to a higher state of alert than they were already in.

*British airplane carriers,* he thought unhappily. *British battleships, if they can get in close enough. British and French submersibles. French destroyers, too, I suppose. What a joy.* Would Britain and France declare war on the USA, too, once they went to war with Germany, which they sure looked as if they'd do? The frogs might not. They were taking dead aim at their next-door neighbors.

The limeys? Carsten worried more about them. They owed the USA a kick in the teeth. The United States had booted them out of Canada, Newfoundland, Bermuda, and the Bahamas. Sam couldn't see them mounting an invasion to take back Toronto. The islands out in the Atlantic? They were a different story. And to get to the islands, the British would have to get past the U.S. Navy.

With a spatter of static, the *Remembrance*'s intercom came to life. Sam blinked. The squawkboxes didn't get used very often. "This is the captain speaking." Sam blinked again. When the intercom did come on, Captain Stein hardly ever spoke himself. That was usually the exec's job. But the skipper continued, "Men, you need to know that the German Empire has just announced that Kaiser Wilhelm II has passed away. His son, Crown Prince Friedrich Wilhelm, has just become the new German Kaiser.

"Friedrich Wilhelm has formally rejected the demands France has made for the return of territory lost in the Great War. The international situation will grow more dangerous as a result of this. For the moment, we are not at war with France or Britain or anyone else." That could only mean the CSA. Sam shook his head. No, it could mean Japan and even Russia, too. Captain Stein went on, "However, we must not let ourselves be caught off guard by a sneak attack. Be more alert than ever. If in doubt about anything, let a superior know. You may save your ship. That is all." With another spatter of static, the intercom went dead.

Later, after Sam had gone back on duty, Lieutenant Commander Pottinger said, "The French and the English won't declare war on us, will they, Carsten?"

"Damned if I know, sir," Sam answered. He wondered why the devil Pottinger was asking him. The other officer had two grades on him and wore an Annapolis ring to boot. If anybody knew the answers, Pottinger should have been the man. On the other hand, though, Sam had twenty years on his superior officer. Maybe Pottinger thought that counted for something.

"We'll just have to lick 'em if they do," Pottinger said. He hadn't been old enough to see action in the Great War, but he'd seen his share in the Pacific War against the Japanese. He'd be all right.

Even though the Atlantic was rough, airplanes roared off the *Remembrance*'s flight deck. Having a combat air patrol up could save the ship if the British or French or Confederates decided to declare war by attacking, the way the Japs had.

No doubt the cruisers in the squadron were launching their seaplanes, too. Those would range farther afield. With luck, they would spot the enemy before he got close enough to launch an airborne strike force.

Unlike Pottinger, Carsten wasn't usually the sort who borrowed trouble. Even so, he wished he hadn't decided to contemplate the meaning of the phrase *with luck*. It reminded him too vividly of what could happen without luck.

Day followed day. An oiler came alongside to refuel the *Remembrance*. Sam remembered an oiler refueling the USS *Dakota* just before the USA attacked Pearl Harbor and took the Sandwich Islands away from Britain. Back then, most ships had been coal-fired. Even the Dakota had burned both oil and coal. Things had changed since. He didn't think any front-line ships burned coal any more.

He was in the officers' wardroom fueling up himself—on coffee—when Commander Cressy came in looking thoroughly grim. "Oh, boy," said one of the other officers in there.

"Oh boy is about the size of it," the exec agreed. "France has declared war on Germany and sent soldiers and barrels into Alsace and Lorraine. Britain has joined in the declaration. Her airplanes are bombing several cities in northern Germany. The Tsar has recalled his ambassadors from Berlin and Vienna and Constantinople. It can't be more than a matter of days before Russia joins in."

"Here we go again," somebody said, which summed up exactly what Sam was thinking.

"That wasn't all," Cressy said. "Latest word is that Jake Featherston's declared war on Germany."

Several sharp exclamations rang out. "On Germany?" Sam said. "Not on us?"

"Not yet, anyhow," Commander Cressy replied. "Declaring war on Germany sounds good and doesn't cost him anything. It's almost like the Ottoman Empire declaring war on the CSA. Even if they do it, so what? They can't reach each other."

"We're still formally allied to Germany, and we've got a bunch of the same enemies," Sam said. "If the Confederates declared war on the Kaiser, does that mean we have to declare war on them?"

"You do ask interesting questions, Carsten," the exec said. "I don't think we have to do anything. There was that stretch in the twenties when it looked like we might square off against Kaiser Bill, and the alliance pretty much lapsed. But then the old snakes stuck their heads up again, so we never duked it out with Germany. Anyway, though, my guess is that Al Smith will sprout wings and fly before he goes and declares war on his own hook."

A lot of men with stripes on their sleeves nodded at that. Most officers were Democrats. That made sense: they defended the status quo, which was what the Democratic Party stood for.

Sam supposed he was a Democrat himself. But whether he defended the status quo or not, he feared it was going to get a hell of a kicking around.

Colonel Irving Morrell saluted. "Reporting as ordered, sir," he said, and then, smiling, "Good to see you again, sir, too. It's been too long."

"It has, hasn't it?" Brigadier General Abner Dowling replied.

The last time they'd been together, Morrell had outranked Dowling. He tried not to resent the fat officer's promotions. They weren't Dowling's fault: how could anybody blame him for grabbing with both hands? Instead, they—and Morrell's own long, long freeze in rank—spoke volumes about the War Department's peacetime opinion of barrels.

"We're going to be doing something different here," Dowling remarked. "The other side's got the ball, and they'll try to run with it."

"And we have to tackle them," Morrell said.

"That's about the size of it," Dowling agreed.

Morrell whistled tunelessly between his teeth. "We're not going to be able to keep them from crossing the river," he said.

"Oh, good," the fat brigadier general said. Morrell looked at him in some surprise. Dowling went on, "I'm glad somebody besides me can see that. Officially, my orders are to throw them back into Kentucky right away."

"Sir, you'd bust me down to second lieutenant if I told you what I thought of the War Department," Morrell said.

Abner Dowling surprised him again, this time by laughing till his jowls quivered like the gelatin on a cold ham. "Colonel, I spent more than ten years of my life listening to General George Armstrong Custer. If you think *you* can shock me, go ahead. Take your best shot. And good luck."

That made Morrell laugh, too, but not for long. "If we were fighting the Confederate Army of 1914, we'd kick the crap out of it," he said. "That's a lot of what the big brains in Philadelphia have us ready to do."

The laughter drained out of Dowling's face, too. "Custer would have been louder about it, but I don't know if he could have been much ruder. We've got plenty of men, we've got plenty of artillery; our air forces are about even, I think. Our special weapons—gas, I should say; call a spade a spade—will match theirs atrocity for atrocity. Have you met Captain Litvinoff?"

"Yes, sir." When Morrell thought about Captain Litvinoff, he didn't feel like laughing at all any more. "I get the feeling he's very good at what he does." He could say that and mean it. It was as much praise as he could give the skinny little officer with the hairline mustache.

It was June. It was already warm and muggy. It would only get worse. He didn't like to think about being buttoned up in a barrel. He especially didn't like to think about being buttoned up in a barrel while wearing a gas mask. When he thought about Litvinoff, he couldn't help it.

Thinking about being buttoned up in a barrel made him think about barrels in general, something else he wasn't eager to do. "Sir, if we are going to play defense, we don't just need gas. We need more barrels than we've got."

"I am aware of that, thank you," Dowling replied. "Philadelphia may be in the process of becoming aware of it. On the other hand, Philadelphia may not, too. You never can tell with Philadelphia."

"But if we're going to stop them—" Morrell began.

His superior held up a hand. "If we're going to stop them, we've got to have some notion of what they'll try. We'd better, anyhow. What's your best estimate of that, Colonel?"

"Have you got a map, sir?" Morrell asked. "Always easier to talk with a map."

"Right here." Dowling took one from his breast pocket and unfolded it. It was printed on silk, which could be folded or crumpled any number of times without coming to pieces and which didn't turn to mush if it got wet. Morrell drew a line with his fingers. Dowling's eyebrows leaped. "You think they'll do that?"

"It's what I'd do, if I were Jake Featherston," Morrell answered. "Can you think of a better way to cripple us?"

"The War Department thinks they'll strike in the East, the same as they did in the last war," Dowling said. Morrell said nothing. Dowling studied the line he had drawn. "That could be . . . unpleasant."

"Yes, sir," Morrell said. "I don't know that they have the men and the machines to bring it off. But I don't know that they don't, either."

Dowling traced the same path with his finger. It seemed to exert a horrid fascination. "That could be very unpleasant. I'm going to get on the telephone to the War Department about it. If you're right . . ."

"They won't take you seriously," Morrell predicted. "They'll say, 'All the way out there? Don't be silly.' " He tried to sound like an effete, almost effeminate General Staff officer.

"I have to make the effort," Dowling said. "Otherwise, it's my fault, not theirs."

Morrell could see the logic in that. He changed the subject, asking, "Have we got sabotage under control?"

"I hope so," Dowling said, which wasn't what he wanted to hear. The general went on, "Sabotage and espionage are a nightmare anyway. We aren't like Germans and Russians. We all speak the same language. And downstate Ohio and Indiana were settled by people whose ancestors came up from what are the Confederate States now. Most of 'em—almost all, in fact—are loyal, but they still have some of the accent. That makes spies even harder to spot. My one consolation is, the Confederates have the same worry."

"Happy day," Morrell said.

His superior laughed. So did he, not that it was really funny. Not being sure who was on your side made any war more difficult. Neither the CSA nor the USA had done all they could with that truth in the Great War. Morrell had the feeling both would make up for it if and when they met again.

Abner Dowling asked, seemingly out of the blue, "Did you ever serve in Utah, Colonel?"

"No, sir," Morrell answered. "Can't say I ever had that pleasure. I helped draw up the plan that involved outflanking the rebels there, but I was never stationed there myself."

"You know we still have colored friends down south of what's the border now," Dowling said—he seemed to be all over the conversational map.

"I don't know that for a fact, or I didn't till now, but it doesn't surprise me," Morrell said. "We'd be damned fools if we didn't."

"Hasn't stopped us before," Dowling observed. Morrell blinked. He hadn't thought the older man had that kind of cynicism in him. Of course, he'd known Dowling when the latter served under Custer, whose own personality tended to overwhelm those of the people around him. Custer had even managed to keep Daniel MacArthur in check, which couldn't possibly have been easy. While Morrell contemplated the rampant ego of his recent C.O., Dowling went on, "I don't think the Confederates are damned fools, either. I wish they were; it would make our lives easier. They were sniffing around in Salt Lake City when I commanded there the same way we are with niggers in the CSA. Only edge we've got is that there are more niggers in the Confederate States than Mormons here, thank God."

"Ah." Morrell nodded. Brigadier General Dowling hadn't been talking at random, then. He'd actually been going somewhere, and now Morrell could see where. "So you think the Mormons are going to try and stick a knife in our backs?"

"Colonel, they hate our guts," Dowling said. "They've hated our guts for sixty years now. I won't deny we've given them some reason to hate us."

"Not like they haven't given us reason to sit on them," Morrell said.

"Oh, there's plenty of injustice to go around," Dowling agreed. "And if another war starts, there'll be more. But I wish to high heaven President Smith hadn't lifted military occupation."

"Don't you think he's got people watching the Mormons?" Morrell asked.

"Oh, I'm sure he does," Dowling replied. "But it's not the same. If we see the Mormons gathering arms, say, it's not so easy to send troops back into Utah to take away the rifles or whatever they've got. That might touch off the explosion we're trying to stop."

"The police—" Morrell began.

Dowling's laugh might have burst from the throat of the proverbial jolly fat man—except he didn't look jolly. "The police are Mormons, too, or most of them are. They'll look the other way. Either that or they'll be the ones with the weapons in the first place. *Quis custodiet ipsos custodes?*"

"You *are* cheerful today, sir," Morrell said. "Who *will* watch the watchmen?"

"I suppose Al Smith will, or his people. He means well. I've never said he doesn't. He's doing the best he can. I only wish he weren't quite so trusting. He kept us out of war—till after the election. Me, I'd sooner have trusted a rattlesnake than Jake Featherston."

"You mean there's a difference?" Morrell asked. Dowling shook his head. His chins danced. But there was a difference, and Morrell knew it. Featherston was likely to prove more deadly than any rattler ever hatched.

An orderly poked his nose into Dowling's office. He brightened when he spotted Morrell. "Sir, I'm supposed to tell you a new shipment of barrels just came in at the Columbus train station."

Morrell bounced to his feet. The thigh where he'd been wounded in the opening days of the Great War twinged. It would remind him the rest of his life of what had happened down there in Sonora. No help for it, though, so he ignored it. The leg still worked. What else mattered? He saluted Brigadier General Dowling. "If you'll excuse me, sir . . ."

"Of course," Dowling said. "The sooner the barrels get off their flat-cars and into units, the better off we'll be."

The orderly had a command car. It was no different from the one Morrell had used on the border between Houston and Texas. He didn't mind sitting behind a machine gun at all. If the Confederates didn't have saboteurs and assassins in Columbus, he would have been amazed.

When he got to the station, he discovered how eager the factory in Pontiac had been to ship those barrels. They were all bright metal; they hadn't even been painted. He hoped his own men would have the time to slap green and brown paint on them before the shooting started. If they did, fine. If they didn't . . . Well, if they didn't, the barrels were still here, and not back at the factory in Michigan. He would throw them into the fight. He would lose more of them than if they were harder to see at a distance, but they would take out a good many Confederate barrels, too.

How many barrels did the Confederates have? How many could they afford to lose? Those were both interesting questions—the most interesting questions in the world for the U.S. officer in charge of armored operations along the central Ohio. And Morrell didn't have good answers. The U.S. might have had plenty of saboteurs on the other side of the border. Spies who could count and report back? Evidently not.

Morrell looked south. *I'll find out. Soon, I think.*

The U.S. ambassador to the Confederate States was a bright young Californian named Jerry Voorhis. He was, of course, a Socialist like Al Smith. As far as Jake Featherston was concerned, that made him a custardhead right from the start. He didn't look or sound like a custardhead at the moment, though.

"No," he said. He didn't bother sitting down in the presidential office. He stood across the desk from Featherston, looking dapper and cool in a white linen suit despite the stifling blanket of June heat and humidity.

"No, what?" Jake rasped.

"No to all your demands," Voorhis answered. "President Smith has made his position very clear. He does not intend to change it. The United States will not return any further territory ceded to us by the CSA. You agreed to abide by plebiscites and to make no more demands. You have broken your agreement. The president does not consider you trustworthy enough for more negotiations, and he will yield no more land. That is final."

"Oh, it is, is it?" Jake said.

"Yes, it is." The U.S. ambassador stuck out his chin and gave back a stony glare.

Featherston only shrugged. "Well, he'll be sorry for that. As for you, Ambassador, I'm going to give you your walking papers. As of right now, you are what they call *persona non grata* here. You have twenty-four hours to get the hell out of my country, or I'll throw you out on your ear."

Voorhis started to say something, then checked himself. After a moment's pause for thought, he resumed: "I was going to tell you you couldn't do me a bigger favor than sending me back to the United States. But I'm afraid you're doing no favors to millions of young men in your country and mine who may be shooting at each other very soon."

"That's not my fault," Jake said in a flat, hard voice. "If President Smith was ready to be reasonable about what I want—"

"My ass," Jerry Voorhis said, which was not the usual diplomatic language. Maybe he thought the rules changed for expelled ambassadors. Maybe he was right. His bluntness made Jake blink. And he went on, "If the president gave you everything you say you want, you'd just say you wanted something else. That's how you are." He didn't bother hiding his bitterness.

And he was right. Featherston knew it perfectly well. Knowing it and admitting it were two different beasts. He pointed toward the door. "Get out."

"My pleasure." As Voorhis turned to go, he added, "You can start a war whenever you please. If you think you can end one whenever you please, you're making a big mistake."

Jake thought about saying something like, *We'll see about that.* He didn't. The damnyankee could have the last word here. Who got the last word once the balloon went up—that would be a different story.

An hour later, the telephone rang in his office. "Featherston," he snapped.

"Mr. President, the ambassador to the USA is on the line," his secretary said. "He sounds upset."

"Put him through, Lulu." Jake could guess what the ambassador was calling about.

The Confederate ambassador to the United States was a Georgian named Russell. Jake never remembered his Christian name. All he remembered was that the man was reasonably smart and a solid Freedom Party backer. When he heard Featherston's voice on the line, he blurted, "Mr. President, the damnyankees are throwing me out of the country."

"Don't you worry about it," Jake answered. "Don't you worry about it one little bit, on account of I just heaved Jerry Voorhis out of Richmond."

"Oh." Russell sounded relieved, at least for one word. But then he said, "Holy Jesus, Mr. President, is there gonna be another war?"

"Not if we get what we want," Featherston said. "Get what's ours by rights, I ought to say." As far as he was concerned, there was no difference between the one and the other.

"All right, then, Mr. President. I'll see you back there soon," Russell said. "I sure as hell hope everything goes the way you want it to."

"It will." Jake never had any doubts. *Why should I?* he thought. *Everything's always gone good up till now. It won't change.* He spent a few more minutes calming the ambassador down, then hung up the phone on him.

No sooner had he done that than Lulu poked her head into his office and said, "General Potter is here to see you, sir."

"Is he?" Jake grinned. "Well, send him right on in."

"Good morning, Mr. President," Clarence Potter said, saluting. He carried a manila folder under his left arm. Tossing it onto Featherston's desk, he went on, "Here are some of the latest photographs we've got."

"Out-fucking-standing!" Jake said, which produced an audible sniff from Lulu in the outer office. "These are what I want to see, all right. If you have to, you'll walk me through some of them."

Some of the pictures that Potter brought him were aerial photos. Getting reconnaissance airplanes up over the USA wasn't that hard. Every so often, Featherston wondered how many flying spies the United States had above his own country. Too many, probably. The photographs Potter brought him were neatly labeled, each one showing exactly where and when it had been taken.

"Doesn't look like there's a whole lot of change," Jake remarked. "Everything still seems out in the open."

"Yes, sir," Potter answered.

Something in his tone made Jake's head come up. He might have been a wolf taking a scent. "All right," he said. "What's different in the stuff they don't want us to see?"

He almost laughed at the way Potter looked at him. The Intelligence officer didn't want to respect him, but couldn't help it. *Yeah, sonny boy, I run this country for a reason,* Jake thought. Potter said, "If you'll look at some of these ground shots, Mr. President, you'll see the Yankees are starting to move up into concealed forward positions. They should have done it sooner, but they are starting."

"How did we get these ground photos back here so fast?" Featherston asked. "Some of 'em are from yesterday morning."

"Sir, we're still at peace with the USA," Potter replied. "If a drummer or a tourist crosses back into Kentucky from Illinois or Indiana or Ohio, who's to say what kind of prints are on his Brownie? They're only just now starting to wake up to the idea that we might really mean this." He couldn't resist adding, "It might have been better if we'd left them even more in the dark."

Nobody criticized Jake Featherston to his face and got away with it. "Listen, Potter," he snapped, "the damnyankees'll get more surprises from me than a fellow does from his doctor after he lays a fifty-cent whore." The other man guffawed in surprise. Jake went on, "You don't know all my business, so don't go making like you do."

He waited to see if Potter would get angry or get sniffy. The other man didn't. Instead, he nodded. "All right. That makes sense. Does anybody know all your secrets? Besides you, I mean?"

"Hell, no," Jake answered automatically. "There are things I could brag about—but I won't." If he hadn't checked himself, he might have started boasting about what was going on down in Louisiana, for instance. But the whole point of knowing things other people didn't was to be able to use what you knew against them and to keep them from using what they knew against you.

Clarence Potter, he saw, got that. Well, Potter was in Intelligence. If anybody could see the point of secrets, he was the man. And he nodded now. "When I first got to know you, you would have run your mouth," he said. "There's more to you than there used to be. That's why I'm here, I expect."

"Instead of still being a goddamn stubborn Whig and wanting to blow my head off, you mean?" Featherston asked.

Potter nodded. He smiled a crooked smile. "Yeah. Instead of that." The smile got wider. Now he was waiting—waiting to find out if Jake would send him off to a camp for admitting it.

And Jake wanted to. But Potter, damn him, had made himself too useful to be jugged like a hare. And from now on he'd be too busy to worry about blowing the head off of anybody who wasn't wearing a green-gray uniform. Jake jerked a thumb at the door. "All right. Get the hell out of here, and take all your pictures of naked women with you."

"Yes, sir." Chuckling, Potter scooped up the folder of reconnaissance photos and started out. He paused with his hand on the doorknob. "Good luck," he said. "You've done everything you could to get us ready, but we'll still need it."

"I'll put in a fresh requisition with the Quartermaster Corps," Jake said. Potter nodded and left. Jake shook his head in bemusement. He might have made stupid jokes like that with Ferd Koenig and a couple of other old-time Party buddies, but not with anybody else. So why make them with Potter?

But he didn't need long to find the answer. He'd known Potter longer than he'd known Koenig or any of the other Party men. They'd both hung tough when the Army of Northern Virginia was falling to pieces all around them. If the president of the greatest country in North America—no, in the *world!*—couldn't joke around with the one man who'd known him when he was just a sergeant, with whom could he joke? Nobody. Nobody at all.

If the Confederate States were going to become the greatest country in the world, they had to go through the United States first. *Bastards beat us once, when the niggers stabbed us in the back,* Jake thought. *This time, I'll sit on the niggers but good, right from the start. Let's see those damnyankee fuckers do it again, especially when we're ready—when I'm ready—and they aren't quite.* The photos Potter had shown him proved that.

Lulu made most of his telephone calls. He made this one himself, on a special line that didn't pass through her desk. It went straight from his office to the War Department. Men checked twice a day to make sure the damnyankees didn't tap it. It rang only once before the Chief of the General Staff picked it up. "Forrest speaking."

"Featherston," Jake said, and then, "Blackbeard." He hung up.

There. It was done. The die was cast. Whatever was going to happen would happen . . . starting tomorrow morning, *early* tomorrow morning.

Summer had just come in. Jake worked through the rest of June 21. He ate supper, and then went right on working through the night. Lulu brought him cup after cup of coffee. After a while, yawning, she went home to bed. He worked on, behind blackout curtains that kept light from leaking out of the Gray House and showing where it was from the air.

June 21 passed into June 22. All that coffee made Jake's heart thud and soured his stomach. He gulped a Bromo-Seltzer and went on. At a quarter past three, the drone of airplane engines and the thunder of distant artillery—not distant enough; damn those Yankee robbers!—made him whoop for sheer glee. He'd waited so long. Now his day was here.